The Collected Stories of
Robert Silverberg

VOLUME FIVE

The Palace at Midnight
1980-82

The Collected Stories of
Robert Silverberg

VOLUME FIVE

The Palace at Midnight
1980-82

ROBERT SILVERBERG

SUBTERRANEAN PRESS 2010

SF
SIL

First Edition

978-1-59606-321-1

Subterranean Press
PO Box 190106
Burton, MI 48519

www.subterraneanpress.com

COPYRIGHT ACKNOWLEDGMENTS

TABLE OF CONTENTS

For Robert Sheckley
Ben Bova
Alice Saunders
Harlan Ellison
Alice K. Turner
George Scithers
Kathy Green
Judith Sims
Alan Ryan
T.E.D. Klein
Marta Randall
Jessica Amanda Salmonson
Don Myrus

LEBANON PUBLIC LIBRARY

Welcome to Lebanon Public Library!
You checked out the following items:

1. Coronets and steel
   Barcode: 34330512478786 Due:
   2010-11-22
2. The Collected Stories of Robert
   Silverberg : Volume five : The
   Palace at Midnight, 1980-82
   Barcode: 34330512490468 Due:
   2010-11-22

INTRODUCTION

Since the beginning of my writing career, more than fifty years ago, I've always written both novels and short stories. My first professional sale was a short story and the second was a novel, or perhaps it was the other way around. (It was a long time ago.) The rhythm of my writing life was established right at the beginning: a few short stories, then a novel, then some more short stories, and then another book. I never thought twice, or even once, about whether I was primarily a short-story writer or a novelist. I was a writer, period. I've always written at whatever length seemed appropriate to the story at hand; and, because I have always been a writer by trade rather than one who follows the ebb and flow of inspiration, I've also written according to the needs of the marketplace. When it was novel-writing time, I wrote novels. When editors wanted short stories from me, I wrote short stories.

It isn't that way with all writers. Some are distinctly novelists, and some are not. Ray Bradbury has written a couple of novels, but he's basically a short-story writer. The same is true of Harlan Ellison. On the other hand, John le Carre and John Fowles may have written short stories at some time in their lives, but I haven't seen them. (Fowles wrote a a few novellas, at least.) Robert A. Heinlein did few, if any, short stories after the first dozen years of his career. Hemingway's lifetime output of short stories was enough to fill just one good-sized volume, and he too wrote most of them in his first dozen years. And so on: I could make long lists of writers who are basically one thing or the other, but not both. In science fiction and fantasy such names as Frank Herbert, E.E. Smith, Jack Vance, Stephen Donaldson, and Andre Norton come quickly to mind as writers mainly of novels; outside it, those of Graham Greene, William Golding, John Steinbeck, Norman Mailer. As for other short-story writers whose ventures into longer lengths are just as uncommon, we have Theodore Sturgeon, Clark Ashton Smith, William Tenn, and Damon Knight, and in the mainstream world, Edgar Allan Poe, John Collier, William Trevor, and Mavis Gallant.

Certainly temperament has something to do with this. Some writers feel impossibly cramped within the rigid confines of the short story; they need hundreds of thousands of words to move around in. Others see the novel as a vast and interminable journey that they would rather not undertake, and prefer the quick, incisive thrust of the short story. But then there are those who are masters of both forms and choose in the second half of their careers to work in only one, usually the novel, like Hemingway or Heinlein. Surely the author of "The Snows of Kiliminjaro" and "Capital of the World" still knew how to write short stories after 1940, and the author of "Requiem" and "The Green Hills of Earth" did not mysteriously lose his ability at the short lengths around 1949; but *For Whom the Bell Tolls* and *Stranger in a Strange Land* were matters of higher priority and the short stories ceased. It's harder to cite writers who gave up novels after an early start to concentrate only on the short story: Truman Capote and Paul Bowles, perhaps.

In today's American science-fiction field, where hundreds of novels are published every year and only a handful of short-story markets exist, very few of the well-established writers bother much about short fiction, and even the newcomers tend to move on as quickly as they can to immense trilogies. Writing short stories doesn't make much sense financially. If you write them today you have to want to write them for their own sake. The pay is almost incidental: you do them for love.

Or, in my case, because you really can't stop yourself.

At the beginning of my career, in the 1950s, only the most famous science-fiction writers—the Heinleins, the Asimovs—could get novels published, and most of us, if we earned our livings primarily from writing, concentrated on writing short stories and novelettes for the magazines. That meant coming up with two or three worthwhile story ideas a week—an insane way to live and an almost impossible thing to succeed at; but those of us who chose to live that way and who did actually succeed at it (about five of us) didn't realize it couldn't be done, and so we just went ahead and did it. You had to be very stubborn, very resilient, and very prolific in order to survive.

It helped also if you were young, young enough to stay up all night if necessary to knock out a story to meet some editor's sudden request for help. I was the youngest writer in the business in those days, not much past twenty, full of the sort of vitality and drive that was already beginning to diminish among the old guys in their thirties who were my rivals for those few places on the contents pages of the magazines, guys like Fred Pohl, Ted Sturgeon, Phil Dick, Bob Sheckley. So I earned a decent living and always paid the rent on time, and eventually things got a lot easier for us all. But I never had the luxury of being able to think of myself as a "novelist" or a "short story writer" or any other kind of specialist. I wrote what seemed to make the most sense, economically speaking, to write at the moment.

Today, of course, everything is different. I haven't had to worry about paying next month's rent for a long time, and if I were still an active novelist—it's been a few years now since I last felt like writing one, and I don't know if I'll ever do another—I'd sell my books at prices that would have been beyond all belief when I was starting out. My annual income can't begin to match the earnings of the writers at the top of the best-seller lists, but it's lofty enough to seem startling to someone like me who remembers writing stories at a cent a word as fast as he could type. My financial situation is secure, as such things go for writers. And yet I continue to do one or two short stories a year, and even the occasional novella of 25,000 words or so. Why? Certainly not for the money.

But sometimes, even for the professional, more than just the money is involved.

This discussion so far has concentrated almost entirely on the production side of writing. I haven't said a word about art; I might just as well have been talking about manufacturing bookcases, or raising potatoes, or some other useful and straightforward activity in which the muses aren't generally considered to be involved. I've made it more than clear that writing is my business; that I am in the profession of producing verbal objects which I place on sale to the highest bidder. I chose from the outset to make writing my sole source of income, and so I have always worked hard, produced my verbal objects at a steady pace, and taken care to be paid, and well, for my labor.

But writing fiction is different from manufacturing bookcases or raising potatoes. The muses *are* involved, however much the writer wants to think of himself as nothing more than a hard-nosed businessman. And a lifetime devoted exclusively to maximizing one's income per word seems to me like a pretty stultifying affair. Money's a useful thing and you won't hear me saying a word against it. But a writer who's totally money-oriented—who writes the same thing over and over, for example, or who writes things he despises, or who writes with only a fraction of his skill because he thinks his readers are simple-minded, or who writes about things that don't interest him because that's where the money is—is a writer who over the years will dry out from within, whose spirit will corrode and decay, who will sooner or later find himself embittered and hollow, trapped in an anger he can barely understand.

I've done my share of writing purely for money, when circumstances made that necessary. And I'm not one to write purely for the love of the art—sonnet sequences, let's say, that I stash away in the secret recesses of my desk, have never been part of my creative agenda. I write for publication and pay, not for private pleasure. But I try to guard myself against the death of the soul that comes from making money the be-all and end-all of my days.

Novels are more profitable to write than short stories, and, for me at least, they were easier to do, page for page. Nevertheless, although novel-writing was my main line of work for most of my career and my chief source of income (and a considerable source of pride and pleasure, when things went the right way) I always continued to do short stories, however much sweat and pain they might cost me, because of the challenge they represented. Though you will see again and again that this story or that one in this book was written at the request or suggestion of some editor, rather than out of dire internal compulsion, the dire internal compulsion was there none the less: the compulsion to test myself against the rigorous demands of the shorter forms. It's an exhausting kind of mental exercise that gets harder all the time. Short-story writing, as I have said many times, is hard on the nerves: you have no room to make any real mistakes, by which I mean that every word has to count, every line of dialogue has to serve three or four simultaneous purposes, every scene has to sweep the story inexorably along toward the culminating moment of insight that is the classic short-story payoff. In a novel you can go off course for whole chapters at a time and no one will mind; you may even find yourself being praised for the wonderful breadth of your concept. But a short story with so much as half an irrelevant page is a sad, lame thing, and even the casual and uncritical reader is aware that something is wrong with it.

I did in fact stop writing short stories once, in 1973—the prelude to a total withdrawal from writing, the first and only one of my life, that was to last the next five years. As I noted in the previous volume of this series, my life had taken a troubled turn then and I had grown weary, disheartened, generally sick of everything—especially writing. Putting even more words on paper, concocting still more stories of imaginary and remote times and places, had begun to seem pointless to me. So I gave it up. I thought I was quitting it forever. As things turned out, "forever" lasted until the autumn of 1978, when I began to write the novel *Lord Valentine's Castle,* and by January of 1980 I had begun writing short stories again too. The stories collected in this book were written between 1980 and 1982. I've continued to write short stories ever since. I have two new ones awaiting publication as I write this.

Somehow, for all my outward pretence of cold-eyed professionalism, all my insistence that writing is simply a job like any other, I've discovered to my surprise and chagrin that there's more than that going on around here, that I write as much out of karmic necessity and some inescapable inner need to rededicate my own skills constantly to my— what? My craft? My art? My profession? I wrote these stories because the only way of earning a living I have ever had has been by writing, but mainly, I have to admit, I wrote these stories because I couldn't *not* write them. Well, so be it. They involved me in a lot of hard work, but for me, at least, the results justify the toil. I'm glad I wrote them. Writing them, it turns out, was important for me, and even pleasurable, in a curiously complex after-the-fact kind of way. May they give you pleasure now too.

Robert Silverberg

OUR LADY OF THE SAUROPODS

As I pointed out in the introduction to this volume, I abandoned short-story writing in 1973 after doing "Schwartz Between the Galaxies" and felt only relief, no regret, at giving it up. Short stories were just too much trouble to do. You needed a stunning idea, for one thing—the ideal science-fiction short story, I think, should amaze and delight—and you had to develop it with cunning and craft, working at the edge of your nervous system every moment, polishing and repolishing to hide all those extraneous knees and elbows. Doing a good short story at that level of quality meant a week or two of strenuous work, for which the immediate cash reward in the 1970s was likely to be about $250, and then maybe $100 every year or two thereafter if you had written something good enough to be reprinted in anthologies. Though cash return is not the most important factor in a writer's life (if it were, we'd all be writing the most debased popular commodity possible), it is a consideration, especially when a good short story takes fifty or a hundred working hours, as mine were tending to take by 1973. At $2.50 an hour I often felt I'd prefer some other kind of work.

But then came a magazine called Omni.

It was printed on slick, shiny paper and its publishers understood a great deal about the techniques of promotion, and it started its life with a circulation about six times as great as any science fiction magazine had ever managed to achieve, along with dozens of pages of expensive advertising. It could, therefore, afford to pay a great deal of money for its material.

After some comings and goings in the editorial chair the job of fiction editor for Omni went to my old friend Ben Bova, who began to hint broadly *that it would be a nice idea if I wrote a short story for him. He mentioned a sum of money. It was approximately as much as I had been paid for each of my novels prior to the year 1968. Though cash return, as I've just said, is not the most important factor in a writer's life, the amount of money Ben mentioned was at least capable of causing me to rethink my antipathy to short-story writing.*

By the time I was through rethinking, however, Bova had moved upstairs to become Omni's executive editor. The new fiction editor was another old friend of mine, the veteran science-fiction writer Robert Sheckley, who also thought I ought to be writing stories for Omni. All through 1979 he and Bova sang their siren song to me, and in the first month of the new year I gave in. I phoned Sheckley and somewhat timidly told him I was willing to risk my nervous system on one more short story after all. "He's going to do it," I heard Sheckley call across the office to Bova. It was as though they had just talked Lawrence Olivier into doing one more Hamlet. So much fuss over one short story!

But for me it was a big thing indeed: at that moment short-story writing seemed to me more difficult than writing novels, more difficult than learning Sanskrit, more difficult than winning the Olympic broad-jump. I had promised Bob and Ben that I would write a story, though; and I sat down to try. Though in an earlier phase of my career I had thought nothing of turning out three or four short stories a week, it took me about five working days to get the opening page of this one written satisfactorily, and I assure you that that week was no fun at all. But then, magically, the barriers dissolved, the words began to flow, and in a couple of days toward the end of January, 1980, the rest of the story emerged. "Our Lady of the Sauropods," I called it, and when Omni published it in the September, 1980 issue, the cover announced, "Robert Silverberg Returns!" I imagined the puzzled readers, who surely were unaware that it was seven years since I had deigned to write short stories, turning to each other and saying, "Why, wherever has he been?"

---

21 August. 0750 hours. Ten minutes since the module meltdown. I can't see the wreckage from here, but I can smell it, bitter and sour against the moist tropical air. I've found a cleft in the rocks, a kind of shallow cavern, where I'll be safe from the dinosaurs for a while. It's shielded by thick clumps of cycads, and in any case it's too small for the big predators to enter. But sooner or later I'm going to need food, and then what? I have no weapons. How long can one woman last, stranded and more or less helpless, aboard a habitat unit not quite five hundred meters in diameter that she's sharing with a bunch of active, hungry dinosaurs?

I keep telling myself that none of this is really happening. Only I can't quite convince myself of that.

My escape still has me shaky. I can't get out of my mind the funny little bubbling sound the tiny powerpak made as it began to overheat. In something like fourteen seconds my lovely mobile module became a charred heap of fused-together junk, taking with it my communicator unit, my food supply, my laser gun, and just about everything else. And but for the warning that funny little sound gave me, I'd be so much charred junk now, too. Better off that way, most likely.

When I close my eyes, I imagine I can see Habitat Vronsky floating serenely in orbit a mere 120 kilometers away. What a beautiful sight! The walls gleaming like platinum, the great mirror collecting sunlight and flashing it into the windows, the agricultural satellites wheeling around it like a dozen tiny moons. I could almost reach out and touch it. Tap on the shielding and murmur, "Help me, come for me, rescue me." But I might just as well be out beyond Neptune as sitting here in the adjoining Lagrange slot. No way I can call for help. The moment I move outside this cleft in the rock I'm at the mercy of my saurians and their mercy is not likely to be tender.

Now it's beginning to rain—artificial, like practically everything else on Dino Island. But it gets you just as wet as the natural kind. And clammy. Pfaugh.

Jesus, what am I going to do?

0815 hours. The rain is over for now. It'll come again in six hours. Astonishing how muggy, dank, thick, the air is. Simply breathing is hard work, and I feel as though mildew is forming on my lungs. I miss Vronsky's clear, crisp, everlasting springtime air. On previous trips to Dino Island I never cared about the climate. But, of course, I was snugly englobed in my mobile unit, a world within a world, self-contained, self-sufficient, isolated from all contact with this place and its creatures. Merely a roving eye, traveling as I pleased, invisible, invulnerable.

Can they sniff me in here?

We don't think their sense of smell is very acute. Sharper than a crocodile's, not as good as a cat's. And the stink of the burned wreckage dominates the place at the moment. But I must reek with fear-signals. I feel calm now, but it was different as I went desperately scrambling out of the module during the meltdown. Scattering pheromones all over the place, I bet.

Commotion in the cycads. *Something's coming in here!*

Long neck, small birdlike feet, delicate grasping hands. Not to worry. Struthiomimus, is all—dainty dino, fragile, birdlike critter barely two meters high. Liquid golden eyes staring solemnly at me. It swivels its head from side to side, ostrichlike, click-click, as if trying to make up its mind about coming closer to me. *Scat!* Go peck a stegosaur. Let me alone.

The struthiomimus withdraws, making little clucking sounds.

Closest I've ever been to a live dinosaur. Glad it was one of the little ones.

0900 hours. Getting hungry. What am I going to eat? They say roasted cycad cones aren't too bad. How about raw ones? So many plants are edible when cooked and poisonous otherwise. I never studied such things in detail. Living in our antiseptic little L5 habitats, we're not required to be outdoors-wise, after all. Anyway, there's a fleshy-looking cone on the cycad just in front of the cleft, and it's got an edible look. Might as well try it raw, because there's no other way. Rubbing sticks together will get me nowhere.

Getting the cone off takes some work. Wiggle, twist, snap, tear—*there*. Not as fleshy as it looks. Chewy, in fact. Like munching on rubber. Decent flavor, though. And maybe some useful carbohydrate.

The shuttle isn't due to pick me up for thirty days. Nobody's apt to come looking for me, or even think about me, before then. I'm on my own. Nice irony there: I was desperate to get out of Vronsky and escape from all the bickering and maneuvering, the endless meetings and memoranda, the feinting and counterfeinting, all the ugly political crap that scientists indulge in when they turn into administrators. Thirty days of blessed isolation on Dino Island! An end to that constant dull throbbing in my head from the daily infighting with Director Sarber. Pure research again! And then the meltdown, and here I am cowering in the bushes wondering which comes first, starving or getting gobbled.

0930 hours. Funny thought just now. Could it have been sabotage?

Consider. Sarber and I, feuding for weeks over the issue of opening Dino Island to tourists. Crucial staff vote coming up next month. Sarber says we can raise millions a year for expanded studies with a program of guided tours and perhaps some rental of the island to film companies. I say that's risky both for the dinos and the tourists, destructive of scientific values, a distraction, a sellout. Emotionally the staff's with me, but Sarber waves figures around, showy fancy income-projections, and generally shouts and blusters. Tempers running high, Sarber in lethal fury at being opposed, barely able to hide his loathing for me. Circulating rumors—designed to get back to me—that if I persist in blocking him, he'll abort my career. Which is malarkey, of course. He may outrank me, but he has no real authority over me. And then his politeness yesterday. (*Yesterday?* An aeon ago.) Smiling smarmily, telling me he hopes I'll rethink my position during my observation tour on the island. Wishing me well. Had he gimmicked my powerpak? I guess it isn't hard if you know a little engineering, and Sarber does. Some kind of timer set to withdraw the insulator rods? Wouldn't be any harm to Dino Island itself, just a quick, compact, localized disaster that implodes and melts the unit and its passenger, so sorry, terrible scientific tragedy, what a great loss. And even if by some fluke I got out of the unit in time, my chances of surviving here as a pedestrian for thirty days would be pretty skimpy, right? Right.

It makes me boil to think that someone's willing to murder you over a mere policy disagreement. It's barbaric. Worse than that: it's tacky.

1130 hours. I can't stay crouched in this cleft forever. I'm going to explore the island and see if I can find a better hideout. This one simply isn't adequate for anything more than short-term huddling. Besides, I'm not as spooked as I was right after the meltdown. I realize now that I'm not going to find a tyrannosaur hiding behind every tree. And tyrannosaurs aren't going to be much interested in scrawny stuff like me.

Anyway I'm a quick-witted higher primate. If my humble mammalian ancestors seventy million years ago were able to elude dinosaurs well enough to survive and inherit the earth, I should be able to keep from getting eaten for the next thirty days. And with or without my cozy little mobile module, I want to get out into this place, whatever the risks. Nobody's ever had a chance to interact this closely with the dinos before.

Good thing I kept this pocket recorder when I jumped from the module. Whether I'm a dino's dinner or not, I ought to be able to set down some useful observations.

Here I go.

1830 hours. Twilight is descending now. I am camped near the equator in a lean-to flung together out of tree-fern fronds—a flimsy shelter, but the huge fronds conceal me, and with luck I'll make it through to morning. That cycad cone doesn't seem to have poisoned me yet, and I ate another one just now, along with some tender new fiddleheads uncoiling from the heart of a tree-fern. Spartan fare, but it gives me the illusion of being fed.

In the evening mists I observe a brachiosaur, half-grown but already colossal, munching in the treetops. A gloomy-looking triceratops stands nearby and several of the ostrichlike struthiomimids scamper busily in the underbrush, hunting I know not what. No sign of tyrannosaurs all day. There aren't many of them here, anyway, and I hope they're all sleeping off huge feasts somewhere in the other hemisphere.

What a fantastic place this is!

I don't feel tired. I don't even feel frightened—just a little wary.

I feel exhilarated, as a matter of fact.

Here I sit peering out between fern fronds at a scene out of the dawn of time. All that's missing is a pterosaur or two flapping overhead, but we haven't brought those back yet. The mournful snufflings of the huge brachiosaur carry clearly even in the heavy air. The struthiomimids are making sweet honking sounds. Night is falling swiftly and the great shapes out there take on dreamlike primordial wonder.

What a brilliant idea it was to put all the Olsen-process dinosaur-reconstructs aboard a little L5 habitat of their very own and turn them loose to recreate the Mesozoic! After that unfortunate San Diego event with the tyrannosaur, it became politically unfeasible to keep them anywhere on earth, I know, but even so this is a better scheme. In just a little more than seven years Dino Island has taken on an altogether convincing illusion of reality. Things grow so fast in this lush, steamy, high-CO_2 tropical atmosphere! Of course, we haven't been able to duplicate the real Mesozoic flora, but we've done all right using botanical survivors, cycads and tree ferns and horsetails and palms and ginkgos and auracarias, and thick carpets of mosses and selaginellas and liverworts covering the ground. Everything has blended and merged and run amok: it's hard now to recall the bare and unnatural look of the island when we first laid it out. Now it's a seamless tapestry in green and brown, a dense jungle broken only by streams, lakes and meadows, encapsulated in spherical metal walls some two kilometers in circumference.

And the animals, the wonderful fantastic grotesque animals—

We don't pretend that the real Mesozoic ever held any such mix of fauna as I've seen today, stegosaurs and corythosaurs side by side, a triceratops sourly glaring at a brachiosaur, struthiomimus contemporary with iguanodon, a wild unscientific jumble of Triassic, Jurassic and Cretaceous, a hundred million years of the dinosaur reign scrambled together. We take what we can get. Olsen-process reconstructs require sufficient fossil DNA to permit the computer synthesis, and we've been able to find that in only some twenty species so far. The wonder is that we've accomplished even that much: to replicate the complete DNA molecule from battered and sketchy genetic information millions of years old, to carry out the intricate implants in reptilian host ova, to see the embryos through to self-sustaining levels. The only word that applies is *miraculous*. If our dinos come from eras millions of years apart, so be it: we do our best. If we have no pterosaur and no allosaur and no archaeopteryx, so be it: we may have them yet. What we already have is plenty to work with. Some day there may be separate Triassic, Jurassic and Cretaceous satellite habitats, but none of us will live to see that, I suspect.

Total darkness now. Mysterious screechings and hissings out there. This afternoon, as I moved cautiously, but in delight, from the wreckage site up near the rotation axis to my present equatorial camp, sometimes coming within fifty or a hundred meters of living dinos, I felt a kind of ecstasy. Now my fears are returning, and my anger at this stupid marooning. I imagine clutching claws reaching for me, terrible jaws yawning above me.

I don't think I'll get much sleep tonight.

22 August. 0600 hours. Rosy-fingered dawn comes to Dino Island, and I'm still alive. Not a great night's sleep, but I must have had some, because I can remember fragments of dreams. About dinosaurs, naturally. Sitting in little groups, some playing pinochle and some knitting sweaters. And choral singing, a dinosaur rendition of *The Messiah* or maybe Beethoven's Ninth.

I feel alert, inquisitive, and hungry. Especially hungry. I know we've stocked this place with frogs and turtles and other small-size anachronisms to provide a balanced diet for the big critters. Today I'll have to snare some for myself, grisly though I find the prospect of eating raw frog's legs.

I don't bother getting dressed. With rain showers programmed to fall four times a day, it's better to go naked anyway. Mother Eve of the

Mesozoic, that's me! And without my soggy tunic I find that I don't mind the greenhouse atmosphere half as much.

Out to see what I can find.

The dinosaurs are up and about already, the big herbivores munching away, the carnivores doing their stalking. All of them have such huge appetites that they can't wait for the sun to come up. In the bad old days when the dinos were thought to be reptiles, of course, we'd have expected them to sit there like lumps until daylight got their body temperatures up to functional levels. But one of the great joys of the reconstruct project was the vindication of the notion that dinosaurs were warm-blooded animals, active and quick and pretty damned intelligent. No sluggardly crocodilians these! Would that they were, if only for my survival's sake.

1130 hour. A busy morning. My first encounter with a major predator.

There are nine tyrannosaurs on the island, including three born in the past eighteen months. (That gives us an optimum predator-to-prey ratio. If the tyrannosaurs keep reproducing and don't start eating each other, we'll have to begin thinning them out. One of the problems with a closed ecology—natural checks and balances don't fully apply.) Sooner or later I was bound to encounter one, but I had hoped it would be later.

I was hunting frogs at the edge of Cope Lake. A ticklish business—calls for agility, cunning, quick reflexes. I remember the technique from my girlhood—the cupped hand, the lightning pounce—but somehow it's become a lot harder in the last twenty years. Superior frogs these days, I suppose. There I was, kneeling in the mud, swooping, missing, swooping, missing; some vast sauropod snoozing in the lake, probably our diplodocus; a corythosaur browsing in a stand of gingko trees, quite delicately nipping off the foul-smelling yellow fruits. Swoop. Miss. Swoop. Miss. Such intense concentration on my task that old T. rex could have tiptoed right up behind me, and I'd never have noticed. But then I felt a subtle something, a change in the air, maybe, a barely perceptible shift in dynamics. I glanced up and saw the corythosaur rearing on its hind legs, looking around uneasily, pulling deep sniffs into that fantastically elaborate bony crest that houses its early-warning system. *Carnivore alert!* The corythosaur obviously smelled something wicked this way coming, for it swung around between two big ginkgos and started to go galumphing away. Too late. The treetops parted, giant boughs toppled, and out of the forest came our original tyrannosaur, the pigeon-toed one we call Belshazzar, moving in its heavy, clumsy waddle, ponderous legs working hard, tail absurdly swinging from side to side. I slithered into the lake and scrunched down as deep as I could go in the warm oozing mud. The corythosaur had no place to slither. Unarmed, unarmored, it could only make great bleating sounds, terror mingled with defiance, as the killer bore down on it.

I had to watch. I had never seen a kill.

In a graceless but wondrously effective way, the tyrannosaur dug its hind claws into the ground, pivoted astonishingly, and, using its massive tail as a counterweight, moved in a ninety-degree arc to knock the corythosaur down with a stupendous sidewise swat of its huge head. I hadn't been expecting that. The corythosaur dropped and lay on its side, snorting in pain and feebly waving its limbs. Now came the coup de grace with hind legs, and then the rending and tearing, the jaws and the tiny arms at last coming into play. Burrowing chin-deep in the mud, I watched in awe and weird fascination. There are those among us who argue that the carnivores ought to be segregated into their own island, that it is folly to allow reconstructs created with such effort to be casually butchered this way. Perhaps in the beginning that made sense, but not now, not when natural increase is rapidly filling the island with young dinos. If we are to learn anything about these animals, it will only be by reproducing as closely as possible their original living conditions. Besides, would it not be a cruel mockery to feed our tyrannosaurs on hamburger and herring?

The killer fed for more than an hour. At the end came a scary moment: Belshazzar, blood-smeared and bloated, hauled himself ponderously down to the edge of the lake for a drink. He stood no more than ten meters from me. I did my most convincing imitation of a rotting log; but the tyrannosaur, although it did seem to study me with a beady eye, had no further appetite. For a long while after he departed, I stayed buried in the mud, fearing he might come back for dessert. And eventually there was another crashing and bashing in the forest—not Belshazzar this time, though, but a younger one with a gimpy arm. It uttered a sort of whinnying sound and went to work on the corythosaur carcass. No surprise: we already knew that tyrannosaurs had no prejudices against carrion.

Nor, I found, did I.

When the coast was clear, I crept out and saw that the two tyrannosaurs had left hundreds of kilos of meat. Starvation knoweth no pride and also few qualms. Using a clamshell for my blade, I started chopping away.

Corythosaur meat has a curiously sweet flavor—nutmeg and cloves, dash of cinnamon, The first chunk would not go down. You are a pioneer, I told myself, retching. You are the first human ever to eat dinosaur meat. *Yes, but why does at have to be raw?* No choice about that. Be dispassionate, love. Conquer your gag reflex or die trying. I pretended I was eating oysters. This time the meat went down. It didn't stay down. The alternative, I told myself grimly, is a diet of fern fronds and frogs, and you haven't been much good at catching the frogs. I tried again. Success!

I'd have to call corythosaur meat an acquired taste. But the wilderness is no place for picky eaters.

23 August. 1300 hour. At midday I found myself in the southern hemisphere, along the fringes of Marsh Marsh about a hundred meters below the equator. Observing herd behavior in sauropods—five brachiosaurs, two adult and three young, moving in formation, the small ones in the center. By "small" I mean only some ten meters from nose to tail-tip. Sauropod appetites being what they are, we'll have to thin that herd soon, too, especially if we want to introduce a female diplodocus into the colony. *Two* species of sauropods breeding and eating like that could devastate the island in three years. Nobody ever expected dinosaurs to reproduce like rabbits—another dividend of their being warm-blooded, I suppose. We might have guessed it, though, from the vast quantity of fossils. If that many bones survived the catastrophes of a hundred-odd million years, how enormous the living Mesozoic population must have been! An awesome race in more ways than mere physical mass.

I had a chance to do a little herd-thinning myself just now. Mysterious stirring in the spongy soil right at my feet, and I looked down to see triceratops eggs hatching! Seven brave little critters, already horny and beaky, scrabbling out of a nest, staring around defiantly. No bigger than kittens, but active and sturdy from the moment of birth.

The corythosaur meat has probably spoiled by now. A more pragmatic soul very likely would have augmented her diet with one or two little ceratopsians. I couldn't do it.

They scuttled off in seven different directions. I thought briefly of catching one and making a pet out of it. Silly idea.

25 August. 0700 hours. Start of the fifth day. I've done three complete circumambulations of the island. Slinking around on foot is fifty times as risky as cruising around in a module, and fifty thousand times as rewarding. I make camp in a different place every night. I don't mind the humidity any longer. And despite my skimpy diet, I feel pretty healthy. Raw dinosaur, I know now, is a lot tastier than raw frog. I've become an expert scavenger—the sound of a tyrannosaur in the forest now stimulates my salivary glands instead of my adrenals. Going naked is fun, too. And I appreciate my body much more, since the bulges that civilization puts there have begun to melt away.

Nevertheless, I keep trying to figure out some way of signaling Habitat Vronsky for help. Changing the position of the reflecting mirrors, maybe, so I can beam an SOS? Sounds nice, but I don't even know where the island's controls are located, let alone how to run them. Let's hope my luck holds out another three and a half weeks.

27 August. 1700 hours. The dinosaurs know that I'm here and that I'm some extraordinary kind of animal. Does that sound weird? How can great dumb beasts *know* anything? They have such tiny brains. And my own brain must be softening on this protein-and-cellulose diet. Even so, I'm starting to have peculiar feelings about these animals. I see them *watching* me. An odd knowing look in their eyes, not stupid at all. They stare and I imagine them nodding, smiling, exchanging glances with each other, discussing me. I'm supposed to be observing them, but I think they're observing me, too, somehow.

This is crazy. I'm tempted to erase the entry. But I'll leave it as a record of my changing psychological state if nothing else.

28 August. 1200 hours. More fantasies about the dinosaurs. I've decided that the big brachiosaur—Bertha—plays a key role here. She doesn't move around much, but there are always lesser dinosaurs in orbit around her. Much eye contact. *Eye contact between dinosaurs?* Let it stand. That's my perception of what they're doing. I get a definite sense that there's communication going on here, modulating over some wave that I'm not capable of detecting. And Bertha seems to be a central nexus, a grand totem of some sort, a—a switchboard? What am I talking about? What's happening to me?

30 August. 0945 hours. What a damned fool I am! Serves me right for being a filthy voyeur. Climbed a tree to watch iguanodons mating at the foot of Bakker Falls. At climatic moment the branch broke. I dropped twenty meters. Grabbed a lower limb or I'd be dead now. As it is, pretty badly smashed around. I don't think anything's broken, but my left leg won't support me and my back's in bad shape. Internal injuries too? Not sure. I've crawled into a little rock-shelter near the falls. Exhausted and maybe feverish. Shock, most likely. I suppose I'll starve now. It would have been an honor to be eaten by a tyrannosaur, but to die from falling out of a tree is just plain humiliating.

The mating of iguanodons is a spectacular sight, by the way. But I hurt too much to describe it now.

31 August. 1700 hours. Stiff, sore, hungry, hideously thirsty. Leg still useless and when I try to crawl even a few meters, I feel as if I'm going to crack in half at the waist. High fever.

How long does it take to starve to death?

1 Sep. 0700 hours. Three broken eggs lying near me when I awoke. Embryos still alive—probably stegosaur—but not for long. First food in forty-eight hours. Did the eggs fall out of a nest somewhere overhead? Do stegosaurs make their nests in trees, dummy?

Fever diminishing. Body aches all over. Crawled to the stream and managed to scoop up a little water.

1330 hours. Dozed off. Awakened to find haunch of fresh meat within crawling distance. Struthiomimus drumstick, I think. Nasty sour taste, but it's edible. Nibbled a little, slept again, ate some more. Pair of stegosaurs grazing not far away, tiny eyes fastened on me. Smaller dinosaurs holding a kind of conference by some big cycads. And Bertha Brachiosaur is munching away in Ostrom Meadow, benignly supervising the whole scene.

This is absolutely crazy.

I think the dinosaurs are taking care of me.

2 Sep. 0900 hours. No doubt of it at all. They bring eggs, meat, even cycad cones and tree-fern fronds. At first they delivered things only when I slept, but now they come hopping right up to me and dump things at my feet. The struthiomimids are the bearers—they're the smallest, most agile, quickest hands. They bring their offerings, stare me right in the eye, pause as if waiting for a tip. Other dinosaurs watching from the distance. This is a coordinated effort. I am the center of all activity on the island, it seems. I imagine that even the tyrannosaurs are saving choice cuts for me. Hallucination? Fantasy? Delirium of fever? I feel lucid. The fever is abating. I'm still too stiff and weak to move very far, but I think I'm recovering from the effects of my fall. With a little help from my friends.

1000 hours. Played back the last entry. Thinking it over. I don't *think* I've gone insane. If I'm insane enough to be worried about my sanity, how crazy can I be? Or am I just fooling myself? There's a terrible conflict between what I think I perceive going on here and what I know I ought to be perceiving.

1500 hours. A long, strange dream this afternoon. I saw all the dinosaurs standing in the meadow and they were connected to one another by gleaming threads, like the telephone lines of olden times, and all the threads centered on Bertha. As if she's the switchboard, yes. And telepathic messages were traveling. An extrasensory hookup, powerful pulses moving along the lines. I dreamed that a small dinosaur came to me and offered me a line and, in pantomime, showed me how to hook it up, and a great flood of delight went through me as I made the connection. And when I plugged it in, I could feel the deep and heavy thoughts of the dinosaurs, the slow rapturous philosophical interchanges.

When I woke, the dream seemed bizarrely vivid, strangely real, the dream-ideas lingering as they sometimes do. I saw the animals about me in a new way. As if this is not just a zoological research station, but a community, a settlement, the sole outpost of an alien civilization— an alien civilization native to earth.

Come off it. These animals have minute brains. They spend their days chomping on greenery, except for the ones that chomp on other dinosaurs. Compared with dinosaurs, cows and sheep are downright geniuses.

I can hobble a little now.

8 Sep. 0600 hours. The same dream again last night, the universal telepathic linkage. Sense of warmth and love flowing from dinosaurs to me.

Fresh tyrannosaur eggs for breakfast.

6 Sep. 1100 hours. I'm making a fast recovery. Up and about, still creaky but not much pain left. They still feed me. Though the struthiomimids remain the bearers of food, the bigger dinosaurs now come close, too. A stegosaur nuzzled up to me like some Goliath-sized pony, and I petted its rough scaly flank. The diplodocus stretched out flat and seemed to beg me to stroke its immense neck.

If this is madness, so be it. There's community here, loving and temperate. Even the predatory carnivores are part of it: eaters and eaten are aspects of the whole, yin and yang. Riding around in our sealed modules, we could never have suspected any of this.

They are gradually drawing me into their communion. I feel the pulses that pass between them. My entire soul throbs with that strange new sensation. My skin tingles.

They bring me food of their own bodies, their flesh and their unborn young, and they watch over me and silently urge me back to health. Why? For sweet charity's sake? I don't think so. I think they want something from me. I think they need something from me.

What could they need from me?

6 Sep. 0600 hours. All this night I have moved slowly through the forest in what I can only term an ecstatic state. Vast shapes, humped monstrous forms barely visible by dim glimmer, came and went about me. Hour after hour I walked unharmed, feeling the communion intensify. Until at last, exhausted, I have come to rest here on this mossy carpet, and in the first light of dawn I see the giant form of the great brachiosaur standing like a mountain on the far side of Owen River.

I am drawn to her. I could worship her. Through her vast body surge powerful currents. She is the amplifier. By her are we all connected. The holy mother of us all. From the enormous mass of her body emanate potent healing impulses.

I'll rest a little while. Then I'll cross the river to her.

0900 hours. We stand face to face. Her head is fifteen meters above mine. Her small eyes are unreadable. I trust her and I love her.

Lesser brachiosaurs have gathered behind her on the riverbank. Farther away are dinosaurs of half a dozen other species, immobile, silent.

I am humble in their presence. They are representatives of a dynamic, superior race, which but for a cruel cosmic accident would rule the earth to this day, and I am coming to revere them.

OUR LADY OF THE SAUROPODS

Consider: they endured for a hundred forty million years in ever-renewing vigor. They met all evolutionary challenges, except the one of sudden and catastrophic climate change against which nothing could have protected them. They multiplied and proliferated and adapted, dominating land and sea and air, covering the globe. Our own trifling, contemptible ancestors were nothing next to them. Who knows what these dinosaurs might have achieved if that crashing asteroid had not blotted out their light? What a vast irony: millions of years of supremacy ended in a single generation by a chilling cloud of dust. But until then—the wonder, the grandeur—

Only beasts, you say? How can you be sure? We know just a shred of what the Mesozoic was really like, just a slice, literally the bare bones. The passage of a hundred million years can obliterate all traces of civilization. Suppose they had language, poetry, mythology, philosophy? Love, dreams, aspirations? No, you say, they were beasts, ponderous and stupid, that lived mindless bestial lives. And I reply that we puny hairy ones have no right to impose our own values on them. The only kind of civilization we can understand is the one we have built. We imagine that our own trivial accomplishments are the determining case, that computers and spaceships and broiled sausages are such miracles that they place us at evolution's pinnacle. But now I know otherwise. Humanity has done marvelous things, yes. But we would not have existed at all had this greatest of races been allowed to live to fulfill its destiny.

I feel the intense love radiating from the titan that looms above me. I feel the contact between our souls steadily strengthening and deepening.

The last barriers dissolve.

And I understand at last.

I am the chosen one. I am the vehicle. I am the bringer of rebirth, the beloved one, the necessary one. Our Lady of the Sauropods am I, the holy one, the prophetess, the priestess.

Is this madness? Then it is madness.

Why have we small hairy creatures existed at all? I know now. It is so that through our technology we could make possible the return of the great ones. They perished unfairly. Through us, they are resurrected aboard this tiny glove in space.

I tremble in the force of the need that pours from them.

I will not fail you, I tell the great sauropods before me, and the sauropods send my thoughts reverberating to all the others.

31

20 September. 0600 hours. The thirtieth day. The shuttle comes from Habitat Vronsky today to pick me up and deliver the next researcher.

I wait at the transit lock. Hundreds of dinosaurs wait with me, each close beside the nest, both the lions and the lambs, gathered quietly, their attention focused entirely on me.

Now the shuttle arrives, right on time, gliding in for a perfect docking. The airlocks open. A figure appears. Sarber himself! Coming to make sure I didn't survive the meltdown, or else to finish me off.

He stands blinking in the entry passage, gaping at the throngs of placid dinosaurs arrayed in a huge semicircle around the naked woman who stands beside the wreckage of the mobile module. For a moment he is unable to speak.

"Anne?" he says finally. "What in God's name—"

"You'll never understand," I tell him. I give the signal. Belshazzar rumbles forward. Sarber screams and whirls and sprints for the airlock, but a stegosaur blocks the way.

"No!" Sarber cries, as the tyrannosaur's mighty head swoops down. It is all over in a moment.

Revenge! How sweet!

And this is only the beginning. Habitat Vronsky lies just 120 kilometers away. Elsewhere in the Lagrange belt are hundreds of other habitats ripe for conquest. The earth itself is within easy reach. I have no idea yet how it will be accomplished, but I know it will be done and done successfully, and I will be the instrument by which it is done.

I stretch forth my arms to the mighty creatures that surround me. I feel their strength, their power, their harmony. I am one with them, and they with me.

The Great Race has returned, and I am its priestess. Let the hairy ones tremble!

WAITING FOR THE EARTHQUAKE

I did make one attempt at writing fiction during that fallow period that ran from early in 1975 to late in 1978, and it was a horrifying failure.

Harlan Ellison, one of my oldest friends, was editing an anthology called Medea, *for which a lot of well-known science-fiction writers were supposed to invent the specifications of an imaginary world and then write stories set in the fictional background they had devised. Although I had already retired "forever" from writing in the spring of 1975, and had said so publicly, I agreed to help Harlan in planning* Medea. *But I warned him that I wasn't going to write a story for the book. And so I took part in a spectacular event in Los Angeles in which, before an audience of a thousand or more astonished science-fiction enthusiasts, Frank Herbert, Thomas M. Disch, Theodore Sturgeon, and I, using suggestions laid down by Frederik Pohl and Poul Anderson, created a story framework for the* Medea *anthology.*

Then it was time to write the actual stories. Herbert wrote one; so did Sturgeon; Pohl did; Anderson did; Disch did. So did various other people. But I had said I wasn't going to write a story, and I didn't write one. I can be a very stubborn man.

Harlan Ellison can be stubborn, too. Over the next two years he telephoned me constantly with progress reports on Medea *and urged me to do a story after all. I told him repeatedly that I was sticking to my decision never to write again. He persisted, though, and finally overcame my resistance to the extent that one day in 1977 I actually put a piece of paper in the typewriter—typewriters were what people used for writing fiction back in that era—and started a* Medea *story.*

I got one sentence written, at the very most. Then a powerful wave of nausea came over me—literally—and I pulled the page from the machine and threw it away, and phoned Harlan and told him that I was not only unwilling but, apparently physically and mentally unable to write anything just then, and when he realized I was serious he relented and let me off the hook. That was the one and only attempt I made at writing stories during my long "retirement."

But a year or so later whatever sinister spell had prevented me from writing wore off, and I wrote the first of the Majipoor novels without extraordinary difficulty, and then after a time I wrote "Our Lady of the Sauropods" for Omni. Harlan, upon finding out that I seemed to be capable of writing again, informed me that Medea was still waiting for me. He is a very stubborn man, yes, but he is also one of the least punctual beings on this planet, and the anthology that I thought had been completed two years before had not yet gone to the publisher. Harlan hadn't even written his own story for the book—indeed was having great trouble with it.

Since the anthology was now complete except for my story and Harlan's, and Harlan had already sketched out the one he was planning to write, the difficult job of writing the final piece, the one that summed everything up, fell to me. But I did have the advantage, denied to all of the other contributors, of being able to read the whole manuscript (except for the unwritten Ellison story) before I started. And so "Waiting for the Earthquake," which I wrote with relatively little difficulty in February, 1980, became an unusual technical stunt in which I made at least one reference to a scene or event from each of the other stories, regardless of the inconsistencies that had developed among those stories. I don't know if anyone ever noticed how careful I had been to touch every base.

The contributors to Medea were permitted to publish their stories elsewhere before the appearance of the anthology. I sold mine to Robert Sheckley of Omni. It was used, not in the magazine itself, but in a companion publication called The Best of Omni Science Fiction, in 1981.

Harlan, meanwhile, was continuing to have problems with his Medea story. He had a title for it and most of a plot, but he was as thoroughly unable to write it as I had been with mine, years before. In the end he came up from Los Angeles to my home near San Francisco and I held him prisoner here for several days, not letting him out of his room except for meals, while he wrote and revised his story, "With Virgil Oddums at the East

Pole." After a gestation period of something like nine years, Medea *was at last finished. The book, which is one of the greatest of all science-fiction anthologies, finally appeared in 1985.*

It was eleven weeks and two days and three hours—plus or minus a little—until the earthquake that was going to devastate the planet and suddenly Morrissey found himself doubting that the earthquake was going to happen at all. The strange notion stopped him in his tracks. He was out strolling the shore of the Ring Ocean, half a dozen kilometers from his cabin, when the idea came to him. He turned to his companion, an old fux called Dinoov who was just entering his post-sexual phase, and said in a peculiar tone, "What if the ground doesn't shake, you know?"

"But it will," the aborigine said calmly. "What if the predictions are *wrong?*"

The fux was a small elegant blue-furred creature, sleek and compact, with the cool all accepting demeanor that comes from having passed safely through all the storms and metamorphoses of a fux's reproductive odyssey. It raised itself on its hind legs, the only pair that remained to it now, and said, "You should cover your head when you walk in the sunlight at flare time, friend Morrissey. The brightness damages the soul."

"You think I'm crazy, Dinoov?"

"I think you are under great stress."

Morrissey nodded vaguely. He looked away and stared westward across the shining blood-hued ocean, narrowing his eyes as though trying to see the frosty crystalline shores of Farside beyond the curve of the horizon. Perhaps half a kilometer out to sea he detected glistening patches of bright green on the surface of the water—the spawning bloom of the balloons. High above those dazzling streaks a dozen or so brilliant iridescent gasbag-creatures hovered, going through the early sarabandes of their mating dance. The quake would not matter at all to the balloons. When the surface of Medea heaved and buckled and crumpled, they would be drifting far overhead, dreaming their transcendental dreams and paying no attention.

But maybe there will be no quake, Morrissey told himself.

He played with the thought. He had waited all his life for the vast apocalyptic event that was supposed to put an end to the thousand-year-long human occupation of Medea, and now, very close to earthquake time, he found a savage perverse pleasure in denying the truth of what he knew to be coming. No earthquake! No earthquake! Life will go on and on and on! The thought gave him a chilling prickling feeling. There was an odd sensation in the soles of his feet, as if he were standing with both his feet off the ground.

Morrissey imagined himself sending out a joyful message to all those who had fled the doomed world: *Come back, all is well, it didn't happen! Come live on Medea again!* And he saw the fleet of great gleaming ships swinging around, heading back, moving like mighty dolphins across the void, shimmering like needles in, the purple sky, dropping down by the hundred to unload the vanished settlers at Chong and Enrique and Pellucidar and Port Medea and Madogozar. Swarms of people rushing forth, tears, hugs, raucous laughter, old friends reunited, the cities coming alive again! Morrissey trembled. He closed his eyes and wrapped his arms tight around himself. The fantasy had almost hallucinatory power. It made him giddy, and his skin, bleached and leathery from a lifetime under the ultraviolet flares of the twin suns, grew hot and moist. *Come home, come home, come home! The earthquake's been canceled!*

He savored that. And then he let go of it and allowed the bright glow of it to fade from his mind.

He said to the fux, "There's eleven weeks left. And then everything on Medea is going to be destroyed. Why are you so calm, Dinoov?"

"Why not?"

"Don't you *care*?"

"Do you?"

"I love this place," Morrissey said. "I can't bear to see it all smashed apart."

"Then why didn't you go home to Earth with the others?"

"Home? Home? This is my home. I have Medean genes in my body. My people have lived here for a thousand years. My great-grandparents were born on Medea and so were *their* great-grandparents."

"The others could say the same thing. Yet when earthquake time drew near, they went home. Why have you stayed?"

Morrissey, towering over the slender little being, was silent a moment. Then he laughed harshly and said, "I didn't evacuate for the same reason that you don't give a damn that a killer quake is coming.

We're both done for anyway, right? I don't know anything about Earth. It's not my world. I'm too old to start over there. And you? You're on your last legs, aren't you? Both your wombs are gone, your male itch is gone, you're in that nice quiet burned-out place, eh, Dinoov?" Morrissey chuckled. "We deserve each other. Waiting for the end together, two old hulks."

The fux studied Morrissey with glinting, unfathomable, mischievous eyes. Then he pointed downwind, toward a headland maybe three hundred meters away, a sandy rise thickly furred with bladder-moss and scrubby yellow-leaved anglepod bushes. Right at the tip of the cape, outlined sharply against the glowing sky, were a couple of fuxes. One was female, six-legged, yet to bear her first litter. Behind her, gripping her haunches and readying himself to mount, was a bipedal male, and even at this distance Morrissey could see his frantic, almost desperate movements.

"What are they doing?" Dinoov asked.

Morrissey shrugged. "Mating."

"Yes. And when will she drop her young?"

"In fifteen weeks."

"Are they burned out?" the fux asked. "Are they done for? Why do they make young if destruction is coming?"

"Because they can't help—"

Dinoov silenced Morrissey with an upraised hand. "I meant the question not to be answered. Not yet, not until you understand things better. Yes? Please?"

"I don't—"

"—understand. Exactly." The fux smiled a fuxy smile. "This walk has tired you. Come now: I'll go with you to your cabin."

They scrambled briskly up the path from the long crescent of pale blue sand that was the beach to the top of the bluff, and then walked more slowly down the road, past the abandoned holiday cabins toward Morrissey's place. Once this had been Argoview Dunes, a bustling shoreside community, but that was long ago. Morrissey in these latter days would have preferred to live in some wilder terrain where the hand of man had not weighed so heavily on the natural landscape, but he dared not risk it. Medea, even after ten centuries of colonization, still was a world of sudden perils. The unconquered places had gone uncon-quered for good reason; and, living on alone since the evacuation, he needed to keep close to some settlement, with its stores of food and materiel. He could not afford the luxury of the picturesque.

In any case the wilderness was rapidly reclaiming its own now that most of the intruders had departed. In the early days this steamy low-latitude tropical coast had been infested with all manner of monstrous beasts. Some had been driven off by methodical campaigns of extermi-nation and others, repelled by the effluvia of the human settlements, had simply disappeared. But they were starting to return. A few weeks ago Morrissey had seen a scuttlefish come ashore, a gigantic black-scaled tubular thing, hauling itself onto land by desperate heaves of its awesome curved flippers and actually digging its fangs into the sand, biting the shore to pull itself onward. They were supposed to be extinct. By a fantastic effort the thing had dug itself into the beach, burying all twenty meters of its body in the azure sand, and a couple of hours later hundreds of young ones that had tunnelled out of the mighty carcass began to emerge, slender beasts no longer than Morrissey's arm that went writhing with demonic energy down the dunes and into the rough surf. So this was becoming a sea of monsters again. Morrissey had no objections. Swimming was no longer one of his recreations.

He had lived by himself beside the Ring Ocean for ten years in a little low-roofed cabin of the old Arcan wing-structure design that so beautifully resisted the diabolical Medean winds. In the days of his marriage, when he had been a geophysicist mapping the fault lines, he and Nadia and Paul and Danielle had had a house on the outskirts of Chong on Northcape within view of the High Cascades, and had come here only in winter; but Nadia had gone to sing cosmic harmonies with the serene and noble and incomprehensible balloons, and Danielle had been caught in the Hotlands at doubleflare time and had not returned, and Paul, tough old indestructible Paul, had panicked over the thought that the earthquake was only a decade away, and between Darkday and Dimday of Christmas week had packed up and boarded an Earthbound ship. All that had happened within the space of four months, and afterward Morrissey found he had lost his fondness for the chilly air of Northcape. So he had come down to Argoview Dunes to wait out the final years in the comfort of the humid tropics, and now he was the only one left in the shore-side community. He had brought persona-cubes of Paul and Nadia and Danielle with him, but playing them turned out to be too painful, and it was a long time since he had talked with anyone but Dinoov. For all he knew, he was the only one left on Medea. Except, of course, the fuxes and the balloons. And the scuttlefish and the rock demons and the wingfingers and the not-turtles and all of those.

Morrissey and Dinoov stood silently for a time outside the cabin, watching the sunset begin. Through a darkening sky mottled with the green and yellow folds and streaks of Medea's perpetual aurora, the twin suns Phrixus and Helle—mere orange red daubs of feeble light—drifted toward the horizon. In a few hours they would be gone, off to cast their bleak glow over the dry-ice wastelands of Farside. There could never be real darkness on the inhabited side of Medea, though, for the oppressive great sullen bulk of Argo, the huge red-hot gas giant planet whose moon Medea was, lay just a million kilometers away. Medea, locked in Argo's grip, kept the same face turned toward her enormous primary all the time. From Argo came the warmth that made life possible on Medea, and also a perpetual dull reddish illumination.

The stars were beginning to come out as the twin suns set.

"See there," Dinoov said. "Argo has nearly eaten the white fires."

The fux had chosen deliberately archaic terms, folk-astronomy; but Morrissey understood what he meant. Phrixus and Helle were not the only suns in Medea's sky. The two orange-red dwarf stars, moving as a binary unit, were themselves subject to a pair of magnificent blue-white stars, Castor A and B. Though the blue-white stars were a thousand times as far from Medea as the orange-red ones were, they were plainly visible by day and by night, casting a brilliant icy glare. But now they were moving into eclipse behind great Argo, and soon—eleven weeks, two days, one hour, plus or minus a little—they would disappear entirely.

And how, then, could there not be an earthquake?

Morrissey was angry with himself for the pathetic soft-headedness of his fantasy of an hour ago. No earthquake? A last-minute miracle? The calculations in error? Sure. Sure. If wishes were horses, beggars might ride. The earthquake was inevitable. A day would come when the configuration of the heavens was exactly *thus*, Phrixus and Helle positioned *here*, and Castor A and B *there*, and *there* and *there*, and Argo as ever exerting its inexorable pull above the Hotlands, and when the celestial vectors were properly aligned, the gravitational stresses would send a terrible shudder through the crust of Medea.

This happened every 7,160 years. And the time was at hand.

Centuries ago, when the persistence of certain apocalyptic themes in fux folklore had finally led the astronomers of the Medea colony to run a few belated calculations of these matters, no one had really cared. Hearing that the world will come to an end in five or six hundred years is much like hearing that you yourself are going to die in another fifty or sixty: it makes no practical difference in the conduct of everyday life. Later, of course, as the seismic tickdown moved along, people began to think about it more seriously, and beyond doubt it had been a depressive factor in the Medean economy for the past century or so. Nevertheless, Morrissey's generation was the first that had confronted the dimensions of the impending calamity in any realistic way. And in one manner or another the thousand-year-old colony had melted away in little more than a decade.

"How quiet everything is," Morrissey said. He glanced at the fux. "Do you think I'm the only one left, Dinoov?"

"How would I know?"

"Don't play those games with me. Your people have ways of circulating information that we were only just beginning to suspect. You know."

The fux said gravely, "The world is large. There were many human cities. Probably some others of your kind are still living here, but I have no certain knowledge. You may well be the last one."

"I suppose. Someone had to be."

"Does at give you satisfaction, knowing you are last?"

"Because it means I have more endurance, or because I think it's good that the colony has broken up?"

"Either," said the fux.

"I don't feel a thing," Morrissey said. "Either way. I'm the last, if I'm the last, because I didn't want to leave. That's all. This is my home and here I stay. I don't feel proud or brave or noble for having stayed. I wish there wasn't going to be an earthquake, but I can't do anything about that, and by now I don't think I even care."

"Really?" Dinoov asked. "That's not how it seemed a little while ago."

Morrissey smiled. "Nothing lasts. We pretend we build for the ages, but time moves and everything fades and art becomes artifacts and sand becomes sandstone, and what of it? Once there was a world here and we turned it into a colony. And now the colonists are gone and soon the colony will be gone and this will be a world again as our rubble blows away. And what of it?"

"You sound very old," said the fux.

"I am very old. Older even than you."

"Only in years. Our lives move faster than yours, but in my few years I have been through all the stages of my life, and the end would soon be coming for me even if the ground were not going to shake. But you still have time left."

Morrissey shrugged.

The fux said, "I know that there are starships standing fueled and ready at Port Medea. Ready to go, at the push of a button."

"Are you sure? Ships ready to go?"

"Many of them. They were not needed. The Ahya have seen them and told us."

"The balloons? What were they doing at Port Medea?"

"Who understands the Ahya? They wander where they please. But they have seen the ships, friend Morrissey. You could still save yourself."

"Sure," Morrissey said. "I take a flitter thousands of kilometers across Medea, and I singlehandedly give a starship the checkdown for a voyage of fifty light-years, and then I put myself into coldsleep and I go home all alone and wake up on an alien planet where my remote ancestors happened to have been born. What for?"

"You will die, I think, when the ground shakes."

"I will die, I think, even if it doesn't."

"Sooner or later. But this way, later."

"If I had wanted to leave Medea," Morrissey said, "I would have gone with the others. It's too late now."

"No," said the fux. "There are ships at Port Medea. Go to Port Medea, my friend."

Morrissey was silent. In the dimming light he knelt and tugged at tough little hummocks of stickweed that were beginning to invade his garden. Once he had landscaped this place with exotic shrubs from all over Medea, everything beautiful that was capable of surviving the humidity and the rainfall of the Wetlands, but now as the end drew near, the native plants of the coast were closing in, smothering his lovely whiptrees and dangletwines and flamestripes and the rest, and he no longer was able to hold them back. For minutes he clawed at the sticky stoloniferous killers, baleful orange against the tawny sand, that suddenly were sprouting by his doorway.

Then he said, "I think I will take a trip, Dinoov."

The fux looked startled. "You'll go to Port Medea?"

"There, yes, and other places. It's years since I've left the Dunes. I'm going to make a farewell tour of the whole planet." He was amazed himself at what he was saying. "I'm the last one here, right? And this is almost the last chance, right? And it ought to be done, right? Saying good-bye to Medea. Somebody has to make the rounds, somebody has to turn off the lights. Right? Right. Right. Right. And I'm the one."

"Will you take the starship home?"

"That's not part of my plan. I'll be back here, Dinoov. You can count on that. You'll see me again, just before the end. I promise you that."

"I wish you would go home," said the fux, "and save yourself."

"I will go home," Morrissey answered. "To save myself. In eleven weeks. Plus or minus a little."

Morrissey spent the next day, Darkday, quietly—planning his trip, packing, reading, wandering along the beach front in the red twilight glimmer. There was no sign all day of Dinoov or indeed of any of the local fuxes, although in mid-afternoon a hundred or more balloons drifted by in tight formation, heading out to sea. In the darkness their shimmering colors were muted, but still they were a noble sight, huge taut globes trailing long coiling ropy organs. As they passed overhead Morrissey saluted them and said quietly, "A safe flight to you, cousins." But of course the balloons took no notice of him.

Toward evening he drew from his locker a dinner that he had been saving for some special occasion, Madagozar oysters and filet of vandaleur and newly ripened peeperpods. There were two bottles of golden red Palinurus wine left and he opened one of them. He drank and ate until he started to nod off at the table; then he lurched to his cradle, programmed himself for ten hours' sleep, about twice what he normally needed at his age, and closed his eyes.

When he woke it was well along into Dimday morning, with the double sun not yet visible but already throwing pink light across the crest of the eastern hills. Morrissey, skipping breakfast altogether, went into town and ransacked the commissary. He filled a freezercase with provisions enough to last him for three months, since he had no idea what to expect by way of supplies elsewhere on Medea. At the landing strip where commuters from Enrique and Pellucidar once had parked their flitters after flying in for the weekend, he checked out his own, an '83 model with

sharply raked lines and a sophisticated moire-pattern skin, now somewhat pitted and rusted by neglect. The powerpak still indicated a full
charge-ninety-year half-life; he wasn't surprised—but just to be on the
safe side he borrowed an auxiliary pak from an adjoining flitter and keyed
it in as a reserve. He hadn't flown in years, but that didn't worry him
much: the flitter responded to voice-actuated commands, and Morrissey
doubted that he'd have to do any manual overriding.

Everything was ready by mid-afternoon. He slipped into the pilot's
seat and told the flitter, "Give me a systems checkout for extended
flight."

Lights went on and off on the control panels. It was an impressive
display of technological choreography, although Morrissey had forgotten
what the displays signified. He called for verbal confirmation, and the
flitter told him in a no-nonsense contralto that it was ready for takeoff.

"Your course," Morrissey said, "is due west for fifty kilometers at an
altitude of five hundred meters, then north-northeast as far as Jane's
Town, east to Hawkman Farms, and southwest back to Argoview
Dunes. Then without landing, head due north by the shortest route to
Port Kato. Got it?"

Morrissey waited for takeoff. Nothing happened.

"Well?" he said.

"Awaiting tower clearance," said the flitter.

"Consider all clearance programs revoked."

Still nothing happened. Morrissey wondered how to key in a program override. But the flitter evidently could find no reason to call
Morrissey's bluff, and after a moment takeoff lights glowed all over the
cabin, a low humming came from aft. Smoothly the little vehicle
retracted its wind jacks, gliding into flight position, and spun upward
into the moist, heavy, turbulent air.

He had chosen to begin his journey with a ceremonial circumnavigation of the immediate area—ostensibly to be sure that his flitter still
could fly after all these years, but he suspected also that he wanted to
show himself aloft to the fuxes of the district, to let them know that at
least one human vehicle still traversed the skies. The flitter seemed all
right. Within minutes he was at the beach, flying directly over his own
cabin—it was the only one whose garden had not been overtaken by

jungle scrub—and then out over the dark, tide-driven ocean. Up north then to the big port of Jane's Town, where tourist cruisers lay rusting in the crescent harbor, and inland a little way to a derelict farming settlement where the tops of mighty gattabangus trees, heavily laden with succulent scarlet fruit, were barely visible above swarming strangler vines. And then back, over sandy scrubby hills, to the Dunes. Everything below was desolate and dismal. He saw a good many fuxes, long columns of them in some places, mainly six-leg females and some four-leg ones, with males leading the way. Oddly, they all seemed to be marching inland toward the dry Hotlands, as though some sort of migration were under way. Perhaps so. To a fux the interior was holier than the coast, and the holiest place of all was the great jagged central peak that the colonists called Mount Olympus, directly under Argo, where the air was hot enough to make water boil and only the most specialized of living creatures could survive. Fuxes would die in that blazing terrible highland desert almost as quickly as humans, but maybe, Morrissey thought, they wanted to get as close as possible to the holy mountain as the time of the earthquake approached. The coming round of the earthquake cycle was the central event of fux cosmology, after all—a millennial time, a time of wonders.

He counted fifty separate bands of migrating fuxes. He wondered whether his friend Dinoov was among them. Suddenly he realized how strong was his need to find Dinoov waiting at Argoview Dunes when he returned from his journey around Medea.

The circuit of the district took less than an hour. When the Dunes came in view again, the flitter performed a dainty pirouette over the town and shot off northward along the coast.

The route Morrissey had in mind would take him up the west coast as far as Arca, across the Hotlands to Northcape and down the other coast to tropical Madagozar before crossing back to the Dunes. Thus he would neatly touch base wherever mankind had left an imprint on Medea.

Medea was divided into two huge hemispheres separated by the watery girdle of the Ring Ocean. But Farside was a glaciated wasteland that never left Argo's warmth, and no permanent settlements had ever been founded there, only research camps, and in the last four hundred years very few of those. The original purpose of the Medea colony had been scientific study, the painstaking exploration of a wholly alien environment, but, of course, as time goes along original purposes have a way of being forgotten. Even on the warm continent human occupation had been limited to twin arcs along the coasts from the tropics through the high temperate latitudes, and timid incursions a few hundred kilometers inland. The high desert was uninhabitable, and few humans found the bordering Hotlands hospitable, although the balloons and even some tribes of fuxes seemed to like the climate there. The only other places where humans had planted themselves was the Ring Ocean, where some floating raft-cities had been constructed in the kelp-choked equatorial water. But during the ten centuries of Medea the widely scattered human enclaves had sent out amoeboid extensions until they were nearly continuous for thousands of kilometers.

Now, Morrissey saw, that iron band of urban sprawl was cut again and again by intrusions of dense underbrush. Great patches of orange and yellow foliage already had begun to smother highways, airports, commercial plazas, residential suburbs.

What the jungle had begun, he thought, the earthquake would finish.

On the third day Morrissey saw Hansonia Island ahead of him, a dark orange slash against the breast of the sea, and soon the flitter was making its approach to the airstrip at Port Kato on the big island's eastern shore. Morrissey tried to make radio contact but got only static and silence. He decided to land anyway.

Hansonia had never had much of a human population. It had been set aside from the beginning as an ecological-study laboratory, because its population of strange life-forms had developed in isolation from the mainland for thousands of years, and somehow it had kept its special status even in Medea's boom years.

A few groundcars were parked at the airstrip: Morrissey found one that still held a charge, and ten minutes later he was in Port Kato.

The place stank of red mildew. The buildings, wicker huts with thatched roofs, were falling apart. Angular trees of a species Morrissey did not know sprouted everywhere, in the streets, on rooftops, in the crowns of other trees. A cool hard-edged wind was blowing out of Farside. Two fuxes, four-leg females herding some young six-leggers, wandered out of a tumbledown warehouse and stared at him in what surely was astonishment. Their pelts were so blue they seemed black—the island species, different from mainlanders.

"You come back?" one asked. Local accent, too.

"Just for a visit. Are there any humans here?"

"You," said the other fux. He thought they laughed at him. "Ground shake soon. You know?"

"I know," he said.

They nuzzled their young and wandered away.

For three hours Morrissey explored the town, holding himself aloof from emotion, not letting the rot and decay and corruption get to him. It looked as if the place had been abandoned at least fifty years. More likely only five or six, though.

Late in the day he entered a small house where the town met the forest and found a functioning persona-cube setup.

The cubes were clever things. You could record yourself in an hour or so—facial gestures, motion habits, voice, speech patterns. Scanners identified certain broad patterns of mental response and coded those into the cube, too. What the cube playback provided was a plausible imitation of a human being, the best possible memento of a loved one or friend or mentor, an electronic phantom programmed to absorb data and modify its own program, so that it could engage in conversation, ask questions, pretend to be the person who had been cubed. A soul in a box, a cunning device.

Morrissey jacked the cube into its receptor slot. The screen displayed a thin-lipped man with a high forehead and a lean, agile body. "My name is Leopold Brannum," he said at once. "My specialty is xenogenetics. What year is this?"

"It's '97, autumn," Morrissey said. "Ten weeks and a bit before the earthquake."

"And who are you?"

"Nobody particular. I just happen to be visiting Port Kato and I felt like talking to someone."

"So talk," Brannum said. "What's going on in Port Kato?"

"Nothing. It's pretty damned quiet here. The place is empty."

"The whole town's been evacuated?"

"The whole planet, for all I know. Just me and the fuxes and the balloons still around. When did you leave, Brannum?"

"Summer of '92," said the man in the cube.

"I don't see why everyone ran away so early. There wasn't any chance the earthquake would come before the predicted time."

"I didn't run away," Brannum said coldly. "I left Port Kato to continue my research by other means."

"I don't understand."

"I went to join the balloons," Brannum said.

Morrissey caught his breath. The words touched his soul with wintry bleakness.

"My wife did that," he said after a moment. "Perhaps you know her now. Nadia Dutoit—she was from Chong, originally—"

The face on the screen smiled sourly. "You don't seem to realize," Brannum said, "that I'm only a recording."

"Of course. Of course."

"I don't know where your wife is now. I don't even know where *I* am now. I can only tell you that wherever we are, it's in a place of great peace, of utter harmony."

"Yes. Of course." Morrissey remembered the terrible day when Nadia told him that she could no longer resist the spiritual communion of the aerial creatures, that she was going off to seek entry into the collective mind of the Ahya. All through the history of Medea some colonists had done that. No one had ever seen any of them again. Their souls, people said, were absorbed, and their bodies lay buried somewhere beneath the dry ice of Farside. Toward the end the frequency of such defections had doubled and doubled and doubled again, thousands of colonists every month giving themselves up to whatever mystic engulfment the balloons offered. To Morrissey it was only a form of suicide; to Nadia, to Brannum, to all those other hordes, it had been the path to eternal bliss. Who was to say? Better to undertake the uncertain journey into the great mind of the Ahya, perhaps, than to set out in panicky flight for the alien and unforgiving world that was Earth. "I hope you've found what you were looking for," Morrissey said. "I hope she has."

He unjacked the cube and went quickly away.

✺

He flew northward over the fog-streaked sea. Below him were the floating cities of the tropical waters, that marvelous tapestry of rafts and barges. That must be Port Backside down there, he decided—a sprawling intricate tangle of foliage under which lay the crumbling splendors of one of Medea's greatest cities. Kelp choked the waterways. There was no sign of human life down there and he did not land.

Pellucidar, on the mainland, was empty also. Morrissey spent four days there, visiting the undersea gardens, treating himself to a concert in the famous Hall of Columns, watching the suns set from the top of Crystal Pyramid. That last evening dense drifts of balloons, hundreds of them, flew; oceanward above him. He imagined he heard them calling to him in soft sighing whispers, saying, *I am Nadia. Come to me. There's still time. Give yourself up to us, dear love. I am Nadia.*

Was it only imagination? The Ahya were seductive. They had called to Nadia, and ultimately Nadia had gone to them. Brannum had gone. Thousands had gone. Now he felt the pull himself, and it was real. For an instant it was tempting. Instead of perishing in the quake, life eternal—of a sort. Who knew what the balloons really offered? A merging, a loss of self, a transcendental bliss—or was it only delusion, folly, had the seekers found nothing but a quick death in the icy wastes? *Come to me. Come to me.* Either way, he thought, it meant peace.

I am Nadia. Come to me.

He stared a long while at the bobbing shimmering globes overhead, and the whispers grew to a roar in his mind.

Then he shook his head. Union with the cosmic entity was not for him. He had sought no escape from Medea up till now, and now he would have none. He was himself and nothing but himself, and when he went out of the world he would still be only himself. And then, only then, the balloons could have his soul. If they had any use for it.

It was nine weeks and a day before the earthquake when Morrissey reached sweltering Enrique, right on the equator. Enrique was celebrated for its Hotel Luxe, of legendary opulence. He took possession of its grandest suite, and no one was there to tell him no. The air conditioning still worked, the bar was well stocked, the hotel grounds still were manicured daily by fux gardeners who did not seem to know that their employers had gone away. Obliging servomechanisms provided Morrissey with meals of supreme elegance that would each have cost him a month's earnings in the old days. As he wandered through the silent grounds, he thought how wonderful it would have been to come here with Nadia and Danielle and Paul. But it was meaningless now, to be alone in all this luxury.

Was he alone, though? On his first night, and again the next, he heard laughter in the darkness, borne on the thick dense sweet-scented air. Fuxes did not laugh. The balloons did not laugh.

On the morning of the third day, as he stood on his nineteenth-floor veranda, he saw movements in the shrubbery at the rim of the lawn. Five, seven, a dozen male fuxes, grim two-legged engines of lust, prowling through the bushes. And then a human form! Pale flesh, bare legs, long unkempt hair! She streaked through the underbrush, giggling, pursued by fuxes.

"Hello!" Morrissey called. "Hey! I'm up here!"

He hurried downstairs and spent all day searching the hotel grounds. Occasionally he caught glimpses of frenzied naked figures, leaping and cavorting far away. He cried out to them, but they gave no sign of hearing him.

In the hotel office Morrissey found the manager's cube and turned it on. She was a dark-haired young woman, a little wild-eyed. "Hey, is it earthquake time yet?" she asked.

"Not quite yet."

"I want to be around for that. I want to see this stinking hotel topple into a million pieces."

"Where have you gone?" Morrissey asked.

She snickered. "Where else? Into the bush. Off to hunt fuxes. And to be hunted." Her face was flushed. "The old recombinant genes are still pretty hot, you know? Me for the fuxes and the fuxes for me. Get yourself a little action, why don't you? Whoever you are."

Morrissey supposed he ought to be shocked. But he couldn't summon much indignation. He had heard rumors of things like this already. In the final years before the cataclysm, he knew, several sorts of migration had been going on. Some colonists opted for the exodus to Earth and some for the surrender to the Ahya soul-collective, and others chose the simple reversion to the life of the beast. Why not? Every Medean, by now, was a mongrel. The underlying Earth stock was tinged with alien genes. The colonists looked human enough, but they were in fact mixed with balloon or fux or both. Without the early recombinant manipulations the colony could never have survived, for human life and native Medean organisms were incompatible, and only by genetic splicing had a race been brought forth that could overcome that natural biological enmity. So now, with doom-time coming near, how many colonists had simply kicked off their clothes and slipped away into the jungles to run with their cousins the fuxes? And was that any worse, he wondered, than climbing in panic aboard a ship bound for Earth or giving up your individuality to merge with the balloons? What did it matter which route to escape was chosen? But Morrissey wanted no escape. Least of all into the jungles, off to the fuxes.

He flew on northward. In Catamount he heard the cube of the city's mayor tell him, "They've all cleared out, and I'm going next Dimday. There's nothing left here." In Yellowleaf a cubed biologist spoke of genetic drift, the reversion of the alien genes. In Sandy's Mishigos, Morrissey could find no cubes at all, but eighteen or twenty skeletons lay chaotically on the broad central plaza. Mass immolation? Mass murder, in the final hours of the city's disintegration? He gathered the bones and buried them in the moist, spongy ochre soil. It took him all day. Then he went on, up the coast as far as Arca, through city after city.

Wherever he stopped, it was the same story—no humans left, only balloons and fuxes, most of the balloons heading out to sea and most of the fuxes migrating inland. He jacked in cubes wherever he found them, but the cube-people had little new to tell him. They were clearing out, they said: one way or another they were giving up on Medea. Why stick around to the end? Why wait for the big shudder? Going home, going to the balloons, going to the bush-clearing out, clearing out, clearing out.

So many cities, Morrissey thought. Such an immense outpouring of effort. We smothered this world. We came in, we built our little isolated research stations, we stared in wonder at the coruscating sky and the double suns and the bizarre creatures. And we transformed ourselves into Medeans and transformed Medea into a kind of crazy imitation of Earth. And for a thousand years we spread out along the coasts wherever our kind of life could dig itself in. Eventually we lost sight of our purpose in coming here, which in the beginning was to learn. But we stayed anyway. We just stayed. We muddled along. And then we found out that it was all for nothing, that with one mighty heave of its shoulders this world was going to cast us off, and we got scared and packed up and went away. Sad, he thought. Sad and foolish.

He stayed at Arca a few days and turned inland, across the hot, bleak desert that sloped upward toward Mount Olympus. It was seven weeks and a day until the quake. For the first thousand kilometers or so he still could see encampments of migrating fuxes below him, slowly making their way into the Hotlands. Why, he wondered, had they permitted their world to be taken from them? They could have fought back. In the beginning they could have wiped us out in a month of guerrilla warfare. Instead they let us come in, let us make them into pets and slaves and flunkies while we paved the most fertile zones of their planet, and whatever they thought about us they kept to themselves. We never even knew their own name for Medea, Morrissey thought. That was how little of themselves they shared with us. But they tolerated us here. Why? Why?

The land below him was furnace-hot, a badland streaked with red and yellow and orange, and now there were no foxes in sight. The first jagged foothills of the Olympus scarp knobbed the desert. He saw the mountain itself rising like a black fang toward the heavy low-hanging sky-filling mass of Argo. Morrissey dared not approach that mountain. It was holy and it was deadly. Its terrible thermal updrafts could send his flitter spinning to ground like a swatted fly; and he was not quite ready to die.

He swung northward again and journeyed up the barren and forlorn heart of the continent toward the polar region. The Ring Ocean came into view, coiling like a world-swallowing serpent beyond the polar shores, and he kicked the flitter higher, almost to its maximum safety level, to give himself a peek at Farside, where white rivers of CO_2 flowed through the atmosphere and lakes of cold gas filled the valleys. It seemed like six thousand years ago that he had led a party of geologists into that forbidding land. How earnest they had all been then! Measuring fault lines, seeking to discover the effects the quake would have over there. As if such things mattered when the colony was doomed by its own hand anyway. Why had he bothered? The quest for pure knowledge, yes. How futile that quest seemed to him now. Of course, he had been much younger then. An aeon ago. Almost in another life. Morrissey had planned to fly into Farside on this trip, to bid formal farewell to the scientist he had been, but he changed his mind. There was no need. Some farewells had already been made.

He curved down out of the polar regions as far south as Northcape on the eastern coast, circled the wondrous red-glinting sweep of the

High Cascades, and landed on the airstrip at Chong. It was six weeks and two days to the earthquake. In these high latitudes the twin suns were faint and feeble even though the day was a Sunday. The monster Argo itself, far to the south, appeared shrunken. He had forgotten the look of the northern sky in his ten years in the tropics. And yet, and yet, had he not lived thirty years in Chong? It seemed like only a moment, as all time collapsed into this instant of now.

Morrissey found Chong painful. Too many old associations, too many cues to memory. Yet he kept himself there until he had seen it all, the restaurant where he and Danielle had invited Nadia and Paul to join their marriage, the house on Vladimir Street where they had lived, the Geophysics Lab, the skiing lode just beyond the Cascades. All the footprints of his life.

The city and its environs were utterly deserted. For day after day Morrissey wandered, reliving the time when he was young and Medea still lived. How exciting it had all been then! The quake was coming someday—everybody knew the day, down to the hour—and nobody cared except cranks and neurotics, for the others were too busy living. And then suddenly everyone cared, and everything changed.

Morrissey played no cubes in Chong. The city itself, gleaming, a vast palisade of silver thermal roofs, was one great cube for him, crying out the tale of his years.

When he could take it no longer, he started his southward curve around the east coat. There were four weeks and a day to go.

His first stop was Meditation Island, the jumping-off point for those who went to visit Virgil Oddums's fantastic and ever-evolving ice sculptures out on Farside. Four newlyweds had come here, a billion years ago, and had gone, laughing and embracing, off in icecrawlers to see the one miracle of art Medea had produced. Morrissey found the cabin where they all had stayed. It had faded and its roof was askew. He had thought of spending the night on Meditation Island, but he left after an hour.

Now the land grew rich and lush again as he passed into the upper tropics. Again he saw balloons by the score letting themselves be wafted toward the ocean, and again there were bands of fuxes slowly journeying inland, driven by he knew not what sense of ritual obligation as the quake came near.

Three weeks two days five hours. Plus or minus.

He flew low over the fuxes. Some were mating. That astounded him—that persistence in the face of calamity. Was it merely the irresistible biological drive that kept the fuxes coupling? What chance did the newly engendered young have to survive? Would their mothers not be better off with empty wombs when the quake came? They all knew what was going to happen, and yet they mated. And yet they mated. It made no sense to Morrissey.

And then he thought he understood. The sight of those coupling fuxes gave him an insight into the Medean natives that explained it all, for the first time. Their patience, their calmness, their tolerance of all that had befallen them since their world had become Medea. Of course they would mate as the catastrophe drew near! They had been waiting for the earthquake all along, and for them it was no catastrophe. It was a holy moment, a purification—so he realized. He wished he could discuss this with Dinoov. It was a temptation to return at once to Argoview Dunes and seek out the old fux and test on him the theory that just had sprung to life in him. But not yet. Port Medea, first.

The east coast had been settled before the other, and the density of development here was intense. The first two colonies—Touchdown City and Medeatown—had long ago coalesced into the urban smear that radiated outward from the third town, Port Medea. When he was still far to the north, Morrissey could see the gigantic peninsula on which Port Medea and its suburbs sprawled: the tropic heat rose in visible waves from it, buffeting his little flitter as he made his way toward that awesome, hideous concrete expanse.

Dinoov had been right. There were starships waiting at Port Medea—four of them, a waste of money beyond imagination. Why had they not been used in the exodus? Had they been set aside for emigrants who had decided instead to run with the rutting fuxes or give their souls to the balloons? He would never know. He entered one of the ships and said, "Operations directory."

"At your service," a bodiless voice replied.

"Give me a report on ship status. Are you prepared for a voyage to Earth?"

"Fueled and ready."

"Everything operational."

Morrissey weighed his moves. So easy, he thought, to lie down and go to sleep and let the ship take him to Earth. So easy, so automatic, so useless.

After a moment he said, "How long do you need to reach departure level?"

"One hundred sixty minutes from moment of command."

"Good. The command is given. Get yourself ticking and take off. Your destination is Earth and the message I give you is this: *Medea says good-bye. I thought you might have some use for this ship. Sincerely, Daniel F. Morrissey. Dated Earthquake Minus two weeks one day seven hours.*"

"Acknowledged. Departure-level procedures initiated."

"Have a nice flight," Morrissey told the ship.

He entered the second ship and gave it the same command. He did the same in the third. He paused before entering the last one, wondering if there were other colonists who even now were desperately racing toward Port Medea to get aboard one of these ships before the end came. To hell with them, Morrissey thought. They should have made up their minds sooner. He told the fourth ship to go home to Earth.

On his way back from the port to the city, he saw the four bright spears of light rise skyward, a few minutes apart. Each hovered a moment, outlined against Argo's colossal bulk, and shot swiftly into the aurora-dappled heavens. In sixty-one years they would descend onto a baffled Earth with their cargo of no one. Another great mystery of space to delight the tale tellers, he thought. The Voyage of the Empty Ships.

With a curious sense of accomplishment he left Port Medea and headed down the coast to the sleek resort of Madagozar, where the elite of Medea had amused themselves in tropic luxury. Morrissey had always thought the place absurd. But it was still intact, still purring with automatic precision. He treated himself to a lavish holiday there. He raided the wine cellers of the best hotels. He breakfasted on tubs of chilled spikelegs caviar. He dozed in the warm sun. He bathed in the juice of gilliwog flowers. And he thought about absolutely nothing at all.

The day before the earthquake he flew back to Argoview Dunes.

"So you chose not to go home after all," Dinoov said. Morrissey shook his head. "Earth was never my home. Medea was my home. I went home to Medea. And then I came back to this place because it was my last home. It pleases me that you're still here, Dinoov."

"Where would I have gone?" the fux asked.

"The rest of your people are migrating inland. I think it's to be nearer the holy mountain when the end comes. Is that right?"

"That is right."

"Why have you stayed, then?"

"This is my home, too. I have so little time left that it matters not very much to me where I am when the ground shakes. But tell me, friend Morrissey: was your journey worth the taking?"

"It was."

"What did you see? What did you learn?"

"I saw Medea, all of it," Morrissey said. "I never realized how much of your world we took. By the end we covered all the land that was worth covering, didn't we? And you people never said a word. You stood by and let it happen."

The fux was silent.

Morrissey said, "I understand now. You were waiting for the earthquake all along, weren't you? You knew it was coming long before we bothered to figure it out. How many times has it happened since fuxes first evolved on Medea? Every 7160 years the fuxes move to high ground and the balloons drift to Farside and the ground shakes and everything falls apart. And then the survivors reappear with new life already in the wombs and build again. How many times has it happened in fux history? So you knew when we came here, when we built our towns everywhere and turned them into cities, when we rounded you up and made you work for us, when we mixed our genes with yours and changed the microbes in the air so we'd be more comfortable here, that what we were doing wouldn't last forever, right? That was your secret knowledge, your hidden consolation, that this, too, would pass. Eh, Dinoov? And now it has passed. We're gone and the happy young fuxes are mating. I'm the only one of my kind left except for a few naked crazies in the bush."

There was a glint in the fux's eyes. Amusement? Contempt? Compassion? Who could read a fux's eyes?

"All along," Morrissey said, "you were all just waiting for the earthquake. Right? The earthquake that would make everything whole again. Well, now its almost upon us. And I'm going to stand here alongside you and wait for the earthquake, too. It's my contribution to inter- species harmony. I'll be the human sacrifice. I'll be the one who atones for all that we did here. How does that sound, Dinoov? Is that all right with you?"

"I wish," the fux said slowly, "that you had boarded one of those ships and gone back to Earth. Your death will give me no pleasure."

Morrissey nodded. "I'll be back in a few minutes," he said, and went into his cabin.

The cubes of Nadia and Paul and Danielle sat beside the screen. Not for years had he played them, but he jacked them into the slots now, and on the screen appeared the three people he had most loved in all the universe. They smiled at him, and Danielle offered a soft greeting, and Paul winked, and Nadia blew a kiss. Morrissey said, "It's almost over now. Today's earthquake day. I just wanted to say good-bye, that's all. I just wanted to tell you that I love you and I'll be with you soon."

"Dan—" Nadia said.

"No. You don't have to say anything. I know you aren't really there, anyway. I just wanted to see you all again. I'm very happy right now."

He took the cubes from their slots. The screen went dark. Gathering up the cubes, he carried them outside and carefully buried them in the soft moist soil of his garden. The fux watched him incuriously.

"Dinoov?" Morrissey called. "One last question."

"Yes, my friend?"

"All the years we lived on Medea, we were never able to learn the name by which you people called your own world. We kept trying to find out, but all we were told was that it was taboo, and even when we coaxed a fux into telling us the name, the next fux would tell us an entirely different name, so we never knew. I ask you a special favor now, here at the end. Tell me what you call your world. Please. I need to know."

The old fux said, "We call it Sanoon."

"Sanoon? Truly?"

"Truly," said the fux.

"What does it mean?"

"Why, it means the World," said Dinoov. "What else?"

"Sanoon," Morrissey said. "It's a beautiful name."

The earthquake was thirty minutes away—plus or minus a little. Sometime in the past hour the white suns had disappeared behind Argo. Morrissey had not noticed that. But now he heard a low rumbling roar, and then he felt a strange trembling in the ground, as though something mighty were stirring beneath his feet and would burst shortly into wakefulness. Not far offshore terrible waves rose and crashed.

Calmly Morrissey said, "This is it, I think."

Overhead a dozen gleaming balloons soared and bobbed in a dance that looked much like a dance of triumph.

There was thunder in the air and a writhing in the heart of the world. In another moment the full force of the quake would be upon them and the crust of the planet would quiver and the first awful tremors would rip the land apart and the sea would rise up and cover the coast. Morrissey began to weep, and not out of fear. He managed a smile. "The cycle's complete, Dinoov. Out of Medea's ruins Sanoon will rise. The place is yours again at last."

THE REGULARS

In the spring of 1980 George Scithers, the founding editor of Isaac Asimov's Science Fiction Magazine, *phoned me to say that he was putting together an anthology of science fiction stories that took place in bars, saloons, and taverns—a remarkably common sub-species of science fiction, which reached its apotheosis in the first of the* Star Wars *movies with the Mos Eisley cantina scene. Scithers assumed that there must surely be a story of that kind among the hundreds and hundreds of stories I had written over the years.*

Probably there was. But I couldn't remember one off hand, and, since I suddenly had begun writing stories again, I made Scithers an offer. "Suppose I write a new one for you? You can publish it in Asimov's *and then reprint it in your anthology."*

He thought that was a fine idea. So I sat down one June morning and wrote "The Regulars," a story firmly set in the classic barroom-science-fiction tradition of Henry Kuttner's "Don't Look Now" and the Gavagan's Bar series of Fletcher Pratt and L. Sprague de Camp. Scithers published it a few months later in the issue of Asimov's *that bore the date of May 11, 1981, and eventually included it in his anthology,* Tales From The Spaceport Bar.

Very likely I did write two or three stories of that sort in my early days, but I still haven't been able to locate them. No matter now: I had some fun writing this one.

It was the proverbial night not fit for man nor beast, black and grim and howling, with the rain coming on in sidewise sheets. But in Charley Sullivan's place everything was as cozy as an old boot, the lights dim, the heat turned up, the neon beer-signs sputtering pleasantly, Charley behind the bar, filling them beyond the Plimsoll line, and all the regulars in their regular places. What a comfort a tavern like Charley Sullivan's can be on a night that's black and grim and howling!

"It was a night like this," said the Pope to Karl Marx, "that you changed your mind about blowing up the stock exchange, as I recall. Eh?"

Karl Marx nodded moodily. "It was the beginning of the end for me as a true revolutionary, it was." He isn't Irish, but in Charley Sullivan's everybody picks up the rhythm of it soon enough. "When you get too fond of your comforts to be willing to go out into a foul gale to attack the enemies of the proletariat, it's the end of your vocation, sure enough." He sighed and peered into his glass. It held nothing but suds, and he sighed again.

"Can I buy you another?" asked the Pope. "In memory of your vocation."

"You may indeed," said Karl Marx.

The Pope looked around. "And who else is needy? My turn to set them up!"

The Leading Man tapped the rim of his glass. So did Ms. Bewley and Mors Longa. I smiled and shook my head, and the Ingenue passed also, but Toulouse-Lautrec, down at the end of the bar, looked away from the television set long enough to give the signal. Charley efficiently handed out the refills—beer for the apostle of the class struggle, Jack Daniels for Mors Longa, Valpolicella for the Pope, scotch and water for the Leading Man, white wine for Ms. Bewley, Perrier with slice of lemon for Toulouse-Lautrec, since he had had the cognac the last time and claimed to be tapering off. And for me, Myers on the rocks. Charley never needs to ask. Of course, he knows us all very well.

"Cheers," said the Leading Man, and we drank up, and then an angel passed by, and the long silence ended only when a nasty rumble of thunder went through the place at about 6.3 on the Richter scale.

"Nasty night," the Ingenue said. "Imagine trying to elope in a downpour like this! I can see it now, Harry and myself at the boathouse, and the car—"

"Harry and *I*," said Mors Longa. "'Myself' is reflexive. As you well know, sweet."

The Ingenue blinked sweetly. "I always forget. Anyway, there was Harry and I at the boathouse, and the car was waiting, my cousin's old Pierce-Arrow with the—"

—bar in the back seat that was always stocked with the best imported liquors, I went on silently, just a fraction of a second ahead of her clear high voice, *and all we had to do was drive ninety miles across the state line to the place where the justice of the peace was waiting—*

I worked on my rum. The Leading Man, moving a little closer to the Ingenue, tenderly took her hand as the nasty parts of the story began to unfold. The Pope wheezed sympathetically into his wine, and Karl Marx scowled and pounded one fist against the other, and even Ms. Bewley, who had very little tolerance for the Ingenue's silliness, managed a bright smile in the name of sisterhood.

"—the rain, you see, had done something awful to the car's wiring, and there we were, Harry on his knees in the mud trying to fix it, and me half-crazy with excitement and impatience, and the night getting worse and worse, when we heard dogs barking and—"

—my guardian and two of his men appeared out of the night—

We had heard it all fifty times before. She tells it every horrid rainy night. From no one else do we tolerate any such repetition—we have our sensibilities, and it would be cruel and unusual to be forced to listen to the same fol-de-rol over and over and over—but the Ingenue is a dear sweet young thing, and her special foible it is to repeat herself, and she and she alone gets away with it among the regulars at Charley Sullivan's. We followed along, nodding and sighing and shaking our heads at all the appropriate places, the way you do when you're hearing Beethoven's Fifth or Schubert's *Unfinished,* and she was just getting around to the tempestuous climax, her fiancé and her guardian in a fight to the death illuminated by baleful flashes of lightning, when there was a crack of real lightning outside, followed almost instantly by a blast of thunder that made the last one seem like the sniffle of a mosquito. The vibrations shook three glasses off the bar and stood Charley Sullivan's frame photos of President Kennedy and Pope John XXIII on their corners.

The next thing that happened was the door opened and a new customer walked in. And you can imagine that we all sat to attention at that, because you would expect only the regulars to be populating Charley's place in such weather, and it was a genuine novelty to have a stranger materialize. Well timed, too, because without him we'd have had fifteen minutes more of the tale of the Ingenue's bungled elopement.

He was maybe thirty-two or a little less, roughly dressed in heavy-duty Levis, a thick black cardigan, and a ragged pea jacket. His dark unruly hair was soaked and matted. On no particular evidence I decided he was a merchant sailor who had just jumped ship. For a moment he stood a little way within the door, eyeing us all with that cautious look a bar-going man has when he comes to a new place where everyone else is obviously a long-time regular; and then he smiled, a little shyly at first, more warmly as he saw some of us smiling back. He took off his jacket, hung it on the rack above the jukebox, shook himself like a drenched dog, and seated himself at the bar between the Pope and Mors Longa. "Jesus," he said, "what a stinking night! I can't tell you how glad I was to see a light burning at the end of the block."

"You'll like it here, brother," said the Pope. "Charley, let me buy this young man his first."

"You took the last round," Mors Longa pointed out. "May I, Your Holiness?"

The Pope shrugged. "Why not?"

"My pleasure," said Mors Longa to the newcomer. "What will it be?"

"Do they have Old Bushmill here?"

"They have everything here," said Mors Longa. "*Charley* has everything. Our host. Bushmill for the lad, Charley, and a double, I think. And is anyone else ready?"

"A sweetener here," said the Leading Man. Toulouse-Lautrec opted for his next cognac. The Ingenue, who seemed to have forgotten that she hadn't finished telling her story, waved for her customary rye and ginger. The rest of us stood pat.

"What's your ship?" I asked.

The stranger gave me a startled look. "*Pequod Maru,* Liberian flag. How'd you know?"

"Good guess. Where bound? D'ye mind?"

He took a long pull of his whiskey. "Maracaibo, they said. Not a tanker. Coffee and cacao. But I'm not going. I—ah—resigned my commission. This afternoon, very suddenly. Jesus, this tastes good. What a fine warm place this is!"

"And glad we are to see you," said Charley Sullivan. "We'll call you Ishmael, eh?"

"Ishmael?"

"We all need names here," said Mors Longa. "This gentleman we call Karl Marx, for example. He's socially conscious. That's Toulouse-Lautrec down there by the tube. And you can think of me as Mors Longa."

Ishmael frowned. "Is that an Italian name?"

"Latin, actually. Not a name, a sort of a phrase. *Mors longa, vita brevis.* My motto. And that's the Ingenue, who needs a lot of love and protection, and this is Ms. Bewley, who can look after herself, and—"

He went all around the room. Ishmael appeared to be working hard at remembering the names. He repeated them until he had them straight, but he still looked a little puzzled. "Bars I've been in," he said, "it isn't the custom to make introductions like this. Makes it seem more like a private party than a bar."

"A family gathering, more like," said Ms. Bewley.

Karl Marx said, "We constitute a society here. It is not the consciousness of men that determines their existence, but on the contrary their social existence determines their consciousness. We look after one another in this place."

"You'll like it here," said the Pope.

"I do. I'm amazed how much I like it." The sailor grinned. "This may be the bar I've been looking for all my life."

"No doubt but that it is," said Charley Sullivan. "And a Bushmill's on me, lad?"

Shyly Ishmael pushed his glass forward, and Charley topped it off.

"So friendly here," Ishmael said. "Almost like—home."

"Like one's club, perhaps," said the Leading Man.

"A club, a home, yes," said Mors Longa, signaling Charley for another bourbon. "Karl Marx tells it truly: we care for each other here. We are friends, and we strive constantly to amuse one another and protect one another, which are the two chief duties of friends. We buy each other drinks, we talk, we tell stories to while away the darkness."

"Do you come here every night?"

"We never miss a one," Mors Longa said.

"You must know each other very well by this time."

"Very well. Very, very well."

"The kind of place I've always dreamed of," Ishmael said wonderingly. "The kind of place I'd never want to leave." He let his eyes pan in a slow arc around the whole room, past the jukebox, the pool table, the dart board, the television screen, the tattered 1934 calendar that had never been changed, the fireplace, the piano. He was glowing, and not just from the whiskey. "Why would anyone ever want to leave a place like this?"

"It is a very good place," said Karl Marx.

Mors Longa said, "And when you find a very good place, it's the place where you want to remain. Of course. It becomes your club, as our friend says. Your home away from home. But that reminds me of a story, young man. Have you ever heard about the bar that nobody actually ever does leave? The bar where everyone stays forever, because they couldn't leave even if they wanted to? Do you know that one?"

"Never heard it," said Ishmael.

But the rest of us had. In Charley Sullivan's place we try never to tell the same story twice, in order to spare each other's sensibilities, for boredom is the deadliest of afflictions here. Only the Ingenue is exempt from that rule because it is her nature to tell her stories again and again, and we love her all the same. Nevertheless, it sometimes happens that one of us must tell an old and familiar story to a newcomer; but though at other times we give each other full attention, it is not required at a time such as that. So the Leading Man and the Ingenue wandered off for a tête-à-tête by the fireplace, and Karl Marx challenged the Pope to a round of darts, and the others drifted off to this corner or that until only Mors Longa and the sailor and I were still at the bar, I drowsing over my rum and Mors Longa getting that faraway look and Ishmael, leaning intently forward, saying, "A bar where nobody can ever leave? What a strange sort of place!"

"Yes," said Mors Longa.

"Where is there such a place?"

"In no particular part of the universe. By which I mean it lies somewhere outside of space and time as we understand those concepts, everywhere and nowhere at once, although it looks not at all alien or strange, apart from its timelessness and its spacelessness. In fact, it looks, I'm told, like every bar you've even been in in your life, only more so. The proprietor's a big man with black Irish in him, a lot like Charley Sullivan here, and he doesn't mind setting one up for the regulars now and then on the house, and he always gives good measure and keeps the heat turned up nicely. And the wood is dark and mellow and well polished, and the railing is the familiar brass, and there are the usual two hanging ferns and the usual aspidistra in the corner next to the spittoon, and there's a dart board and a pool table and all those other things that you find in bars of the kind that this one is. You understand me? This is *a perfectly standard sort of bar,* but it doesn't happen to be in New York City or San Francisco or Hamburg or Rangoon or in any other city you're likely to have visited, though the moment you walk into this place you feel right at home in it."

"Just like here."

"Very much like here," said Mors Longa.

"But people never leave?" Ishmael's brows furrowed.

"Never?"

"Well, actually, some of them do," Mors Longa said. "But let me talk about the other ones first, all right? The regulars, the ones who are there *all the time.* You know, there are certain people who absolutely never go into bars, the ones who prefer to do their drinking at home or in restaurants before dinner or not at all. But then there are the bar-going sorts. Some of them are folks who just like to drink, you know, and find a bar a convenient place to get their whistles wetted when they're en route from somewhere to somewhere else. And there are some who think drinking's a social act, eh? But you also find people in bars, a lot of them, who go to the place because there's an emptiness in them that needs to be filled, a dark, cold, hollow space, to be filled not just with good warm bourbon, you understand, but a mystic and invisible substance that emanates from others who are in the same way, people who somehow have had a bit of their souls leak away from them by accident and need the comfort of being among their own kind. Say, a priest who's lost his calling or a writer who's forgotten the joy of putting stories down on paper or a painter to whom all colors have become shades of gray or a surgeon whose scalpel-hand has picked up a bit of a tremor or a photographer whose eyes don't quite focus right any more. You know the sort, don't you? You find a lot of that sort in bars. Something in their eyes tells you what they are. But in this particular bar that I'm talking about, you find *only* that sort, good people, decent people, but people with that empty zone inside them. Which makes it even more like all the other bars there are, in fact the Platonic ideal of a bar, if you follow me, a kind of three-dimensional stereotype populated by flesh-and-blood clichés, a sort of perpetual stage-set, do you see? Hearing about a place like that where everybody's a little tragic, everybody's a bit on the broken side, everyone is a perfect bar-type, you'd laugh; you'd say it's unreal; it's too much like everybody's idea of what such a place ought to be like to be convincing. Eh? But all stereotypes are rooted firmly in reality, you know. That's what makes them stereotypes, because they're exactly like reality, only more so. And to the people who do their drinking in the bar I'm talking about, it isn't any stereotype and they aren't clichés. It's the only reality they have, the realest reality there is, for them, and it's no good sneering at it, because it's their own little world, the world of the archetypical saloon, the world of the bar regulars."

"Who never leave the place," said Ishmael.

"How can they? Where would they go? What would they do on a day off? They have no identity except inside the bar. The bar is their life. The bar is their universe. They have no business going elsewhere. They simply stay where they are. They tell each other stories and they work hard to keep each other happy, *and for them there is no world outside.* That's what it means to be a regular, to be a Platonic ideal. Every night the bar and everything in it vanishes into a kind of inchoate gray mist at closing time, and every morning when it's legal to open the bar comes back, and meanwhile the regulars don't go anywhere except into the mist, because that's all there is, mist and then bar, bar and then mist. Platonic ideals don't have daytime jobs and they don't go to Atlantic City on the weekend and they don't decide to go bowling one night instead of to their bar. Do you follow me? They stay there the way the dummies in a store window stay in the store window. Only they can walk and talk and feel and drink and do everything else that window dummies can't do. And that's their whole life, night after night, month after month, year after year, century after century—maybe till the end of time."

"Spooky place," said Ishmael with a little shudder.

"The people who are in that bar are happier than they could possibly be anywhere else."

"But they never leave it. Except you said some of them do, and you'd be telling me about those people later."

Mors Longa finished his bourbon, and, unbidden, Charley Sullivan gave him one more and set another rum in front of me and an Irish for the sailor. For a long while Mors Longa studied his drink. Then he said, "I can't really tell you much about the ones who leave, because I don't know much about them. I intuit their existence logically, is all. You see, from time to time there's a newcomer in this bar that's outside of space and time. Somebody comes wandering in out of the night, the way you did here tonight, and sits down and joins the regular crowd and, bit by bit, fits right in. Now, obviously, if every once in a while somebody new drops in, and nobody ever leaves, then it wouldn't take more than a little for the whole place to get terribly crowded, like Grand Central at commuter time, and what kind of a happy scene would that make? So I conclude that sooner or later each of the regulars very quietly must disappear, must just vanish without anybody's knowing it, maybe go into the john and never come out, something like that. And not only does no one ever notice that someone's missing, but *no one remembers that that person was ever there*. Do you follow? That way the place never gets too full."

"But where do they go, once they disappear from the bar that nobody ever leaves, the bar that's outside of space and time?"

"I don't know," said Mors Longa quietly. "I don't have the foggiest idea." After a moment he added, "There's a theory, though. Mind you, only a theory. It's that the people in the bar are really doing time in a kind of halfway house, a sort of purgatory, you understand, between one world and another. And they stay there a long, long time, however long a time it is until their time is up, and then they leave, but they can only leave when their replacement arrives. And immediately they're forgotten. The fabric of the place closes around them, and nobody among the regulars remembers that once there used to be a doctor with the d.t.'s here, say, or a politician who got caught on the take, or a little guy who sat in front of the piano for hours and never played a note. But everybody has a hunch that that's how the system works. And so it's a big thing when somebody new comes in. Every regular starts secretly wondering, Is it me who's going to go? And wondering too, Where am I going to go, if I'm the one?"

Ishmael worked on his drink in a meditative way. "Are they afraid to go, or afraid that they won't?"

"What do you think?"

"I'm not sure. But I guess most of them would be afraid to go. The bar's such a warm and cozy and comforting place. It's their whole world and has been for a million years. And now maybe they're going to go somewhere horrible—who knows?—but for certain they're going to go somewhere *different*. I'd be afraid of that. Of course, maybe if I'd been stuck in the same place for a million years, no matter how cozy, I'd be ready to move along when the chance came. Which would you want?"

"I don't have the foggiest," said Mors Longa. "But that's the story of the bar where nobody leaves."

"Spooky," said Ishmael.

He finished his drink, pushed the glass away, shook his head to Charley Sullivan, and sat in silence. We all sat in silence. The rain drummed miserably against the side of the building. I looked over at the Leading Man and the Ingenue. He was holding her hand and staring meaningfully into her eyes. The Pope, hefting a dart, was toeing the line and licking his lips to sharpen his aim. Ms. Bewley and Toulouse-Lautrec were playing chess. It was the quiet part of the evening, suddenly.

Slowly the sailor rose and took his jacket from the hook. He turned, smiled uncertainly, and said, "Getting late. I better be going." He nodded to the three of us at the bar and said, "Thanks for the drinks. I needed those. And thanks for the story, Mr. Longa. That was one strange story, you know?"

We said nothing. The sailor opened the door, wincing as cold sheets of rain lashed at him. He pulled his jacket tight around him and, shivering a little, stepped out in the darkness. But he was gone only a moment. Hardly had the door closed behind him but it opened again and he stumbled back in, drenched.

"Jesus," he said, "it's raining worse than ever. What a stinking night! I'm not going out into that!"

"No," I said. "Not fit for man nor beast."

"You don't mind if I stay here until it slackens off some, then?"

"Mind? Mind?" I laughed. "This is a public house, my friend. You've got as much right as anyone. Here. Sit down. Make yourself to home."

"Plenty of Bushmill's left in the bottle, lad," said Charley Sullivan.

"I'm a little low on cash," Ishmael muttered.

Mors Longa said, "That's all right. Money's not the only coin of the realm around here. We can use some stories we haven't heard before. Let's hear the strangest story you can tell us, for openers, and I'll undertake to keep you in Irish while you talk. Eh?"

"Fair enough," said Ishmael. He thought a moment. "All right. I have a good one for you. I have a really good one if you don't mind them weird. It's about my uncle Timothy and his tiny twin brother, that he carried around under his arm all his life. Does that interest you?"

"Most assuredly it does," I said.

"Seconded," said Mors Longa. He grinned with a warmth I had not seen on his face for a long time. "Set them up," he said to Charley Sullivan. "On me. For the house."

THE FAR SIDE
OF THE BELL-SHAPED CURVE

Now that I was functioning smoothly as a short-story writer again, I began to respond enthusiastically to editorial requests. Bob Sheckley of Omni, *who had coaxed my first post-retirement story out of me, suggested I try another one for him. It just happened that an idea for a fairly complex time-travel story had wandered into my head, and, since time travel is one of my favorite science-fiction themes, I set about immediately sketching it out.*

It turned out to be the most ambitious story I had done in ten years or so, involving not only a very tricky plot but also a lot of historical and geographical research. (Sarajevo, where the story opens, would be all over the front pages of the newspapers a decade later, but this was 1980, remember, and the only thing anyone knew about Sarajevo then was that it was the place where the Austrian archduke Franz Ferdinand was assassinated in 1914, touching off the First World War.)

So I worked hard and long, with much revising along the way (a big deal, in those pre-computer days), and on August 16, 1980 I mailed it to Sheckley with a note that said, "Somehow I finished the story despite such distractions as the death of my cat and a visit from my mother and a lot of other headaches, some of which I'll tell you about as we sit sobbing into our drinks at the Boston convention and some of which I hope to have forgotten by then."

Though I was now writing regularly again—this was my fourth short story in eight months—I had not yet returned to full creative confidence, and, though I thought "Bell-Shaped Curve" was a fine story, I wasn't completely sure that Sheckley would agree. When we met two weeks later in

Boston, though, he told me at once that he was going to publish it. But he hoped I'd take a second look at it and clean up some logical flaws.

"Sure," I said. "Just give me a list of them."

But Bob Sheckley, sweet man that he was, was not that sort of editor. He didn't have any list of the story's logical flaws—he simply felt sure there must be some. I was on my own. So after the Boston trip I went back to the story, giving it a very rigorous reading indeed, and, sure enough, there were places where the time-travel logic didn't make sense. That came as no surprise to me, because time-travel logic never does make sense, but I did see some ways of concealing, if not removing, the illogicalities. I revised the story and sent it back to him on September 23, telling him this in my accompanying letter:

"I have reworked 'Bell-Shaped Curve' to handle most of the obvious problems, without pretending that I have made time travel into anything as plausible as the internal combustion engine. Aside from a bunch of tiny cosmetic changes, the main revision has been to eliminate the discussion between Reichenbach and Ilsabet about being wary of duplication; they now speak in much more general terms of paradox problems. But in fact they don't understand any more about time travel than I do about what's under the hood of my car....

"And remember that a story that may contain logical flaws is a story that will give the readers something to exercise their wits about. That will be pleasing to them. If they can come away from the issue feeling mentally superior to Robert Silverberg and the entire editorial staff of Omni, haven't they thereby had their two dollars' worth of gratification?"

Omni published the story in its March, 1982 issue. It's been reprinted in a lot of anthologies since then. And you all know what eventually happened to Sarajevo.

Sarajevo was lovely on that early summer day. The air sparkled, the breeze off the mountains was strong and pungent, the whitewashed villas glittered in the morning sunlight. Reichenbach, enchanted by the beauty of the place and spurred by a sense of impending excitement, stepped buoyantly out of a dark cobbled alley and made his way in quick virile strides toward the river's right embankment. It was nearly 10:30.

A crowd of silent, sullen Bosnian burghers lined the embankment. The black-and-gold Hapsburg banners fluttered from every lamppost and balcony. In a little while the archduke Franz Ferdinand, the emperor's nephew and heir, would come this way with his duchess in their open-topped car. Venturing into dangerous territory, they were, into a province of disaffected and reluctant citizens.

The townsfolk stirred faintly. The townsfolk muttered. Like puddings, Reichenbach thought, they awaited in a dull, dutiful way their future monarch. But he knew they must be seething with revolutionary fervor inside.

Reichenbach looked about him for dark taut youths with the peculiar bright-eyed look of assassins. No one nearby seemed to fit the pattern. He let his gaze wander up the hills to the dense cypress groves, the ancient wooden houses, the old Turkish mosques topped by slender, splendid minarets and back down toward the river to the crowd again. And—

Who is she?

He noticed her for the first time, no more than a dozen meters to his left, in front of the Bank of Austria-Hungary building: a tall auburn-haired woman of striking presence and aura, who in this mob of coarse, rough folk radiated such supreme alertness and force that Reichenbach knew at once she must be of his sort. Yes! He had come here alone, certain he would find an appropriate companion, and that confidence now was affirmed.

He began to move toward her.

His eyes met hers and she nodded and smiled in recognition and acknowledgment.

"Have you just arrived?" Reichenbach asked in German.

She answered in Serbian. "Three days ago."

Smoothly he shifted languages. "How did I fail to see you?"

"You were looking everywhere else. I saw you at once. You came this morning?"

"Fifteen minutes ago."

"Does it please you so far?"

"Very much," he said. "Such a picturesque place. Like a medieval fantasy. Time stands still here."

Her eyes were mischievous. "Time stands still everywhere," she said, moving on into English.

Reichenbach smiled. Again he matched her change of language. "I take your meaning. And I think you take mine. This charming architecture, the little river, the ethnic costumes—it's hard to believe, that a vast and hideous war is going to spring from so quaint a place."

"A nice irony, yes. And it's for ironies that we make these journeys, *n'est ce pas?*"

"*Vraiment.*"

They were standing quite close now. He felt a current flowing between them, a pulsating, almost tangible force.

"Join me later for a drink?" he said.

"Certainly. I am Ilsabet."

"Reichenbach."

He longed to ask her when she had come from. But of course that was taboo.

"Look," she said. "The archduke and duchess."

The royal car, inching forward, had reached them. Franz Ferdinand, red-faced and tense in preposterous comic-opera uniform, waved half-heartedly to the bleakly staring crowd. Drab, plump Sophie beside him, absurdly overdressed, forced a smile. They were meaty-looking, florid people, rigid and nervous, all but clinging to each other in their nervousness.

"Now it starts," he said.

"Yes. The foreplay." She slipped her arm through his.

Not far away a tall, young, sallow-faced man appeared as if he had sprung from the pavement—wild hyperthyroid eyes, bobbing Adam's-apple, a sure desperado—and hurled something. It landed just behind the royal car. An odd popping sound—the detonator—and then Reichenbach heard a loud bang. There was a blurt of black smoke and the car behind the archduke's lurched and crumpled, dumping aides-de-camp into the street. The cortege halted abruptly. The imperial couple, unharmed, sat weirdly upright as if their survival depended on keeping their spines straight. A functionary riding with them said in a clear voice, "A bomb has gone off, your highness." And Franz Ferdinand, calm, disgusted: "I rather expected something like that. Look after the injured, will you?"

Ilsabet's hand tightened on Reichenbach's forearm as the bizarre comedy unfolded: the cars motionless, archduke and duchess still in plain view, the assassin wildly vaulting a parapet and plunging into the shallow river, police pursuing, pouncing, beating him with the flats of their swords, the crowd milling in confusion. At last the damaged car was pushed to the side of the road and the remaining vehicles rapidly drove off.

"End of act one," Ilsabet said, laughing.

"And forty minutes until act two. That drink, now?"

"I know a sidewalk café near here."

Under a broad turquoise umbrella Reichenbach had a slivovitz, Ilsabet a mug of dark beer. The stolid citizens at the surrounding tables talked more of hunting and fishing than of the bungled assassination. Reichenbach, pretending to be casual, studied Ilsabet hungrily. A cool, keen intelligence gleamed in her penetrating green eyes. Everything about her was sleek, self-possessed, sure. She was so much like him that he almost feared her, and that was a new feeling for him. What he feared most of all was that he would blunder here at the outset and lose her; but he knew, deep beneath all doubts, that he would not. They were meant for each other. He liked to believe that she came from his moment, and that there would be a chance to continue in realtime, when they had returned from displacement, whatever they began on this jaunt. Of course, one did not speak of such things.

Instead he said, "Where do you go next?"

"The burning of Rome. And you?"

"A drink with Shakespeare at the Mermaid Tavern."

"How splendid. I never thought of doing that."

He drew a deep breath and said, "We could do it together," and hesitated, watching her expression. She did not look displeased. "After we've heard Nero play his concerto. Eh?"

She seemed amused. "I like that idea."

He raised his glass. *"Prosit."*

"Zdravlje."

They snaked wrists, clinked glasses.

For a few minutes more they talked—lightly, playfully. He studied her gestures, her sentence structure, her use of idiom, seeking in the subtlest turns of her style some clue that might tell him that they were co-temporals, but she gave him nothing: a shrewd game player, this one. At length he said, "It's nearly time for the rest of the show."

Ilsabet nodded. He scattered some coins on the table and they returned to the embankment, walked up to the Latin Bridge, turned right into Franz Joseph Street. Shortly the royal motorcade, returning from a city-hall reception, came rolling along. There appeared to be some disagreement over the route: chauffeurs and aides-de-camp engaged in a noisy dispute and suddenly the royal car stopped. The chauffeur seemed to be trying to put the car into reverse. There was a clashing of gears. A gaunt boy emerged from a coffeehouse not three meters from the car, less than ten from Reichenbach and Ilsabet. He

looked dazed, like a sleepwalker, as if astounded to find himself so close
to the imperial heir. This is Gavrilo Princip, Reichenbach thought, the
second and true assassin; but he felt little interest in what was about to
happen. The gun was out, the boy was taking aim. But Reichenbach
watched Ilsabet, more concerned with the quality of her reactions than
with the deaths of two trivial people in fancy costumes. Thus he missed
seeing the fatal shot through Franz Ferdinand's pouter-pigeon chest,
though he observed Ilsabet's quick, frosty smile of satisfaction. When
he glanced back at the royal car he saw the archduke sitting upright,
stunned, tunic and lips stained with red, and the boy firing at the
duchess. There was consternation among the aides-de-camp. The car
sped away. It was 11:15.

"So," said Ilsabet. "Now the war begins, the dynasties topple, a civilization crumbles. Did you enjoy it?"

"Not as much as I enjoyed the way you smiled when the archduke
was shot."

"Silly."

"The slaughter of a pair of overstuffed simpletons is ultimately less
important to me than your smile."

It was risky: too strong too soon, maybe? But it got through to her
the right way, producing a faint quirking of her lip that told him she
was pleased.

"Come," she said, and took him by the hand.

Her hotel was an old gray stone building on the other side of the
river. She had an elegant balconied room on the third floor, river view,
ornate gas chandeliers, heavy damask draperies, capacious canopied bed.
This era's style was certainly admirable, Reichenbach thought—lavish,
slow, rich; even in a little provincial town like this, everything was
deluxe. He shed his tight and heavy clothing with relief. She wore her
timer high, a pale taut band just beneath her breasts. Her eyes glittered as
she reached for him and drew him down beneath the canopy. At this
moment at the other end of town, Franz Ferdinand and Sophie were
dying. Soon there would be exchanges of stiff diplomatic notes, declara-
tions of war by Austria-Hungary against Serbia, Germany against Russia
and France, Europe engulfed in flames, the battle of the Marne, Ypres,
Verdun, the Somme, the flight of the kaiser, the armistice, the transformation of the monarchies—he had studied it all with such keen intensity,
and now, having seen the celebrated assassinations that triggered everything, he was unmoved. Ilsabet had eclipsed the Great War for him.

No matter. There would be other epochal events to savor. They had all history to wander.

"To Rome, now," he said huskily.

They rose, bathed, embraced, winked conspiratorially. They were off to a good start. Hastily they gathered their 1914 gear, waistcoats and petticoats and boots and all that, within the prescribed two-meter radius. They synchronized their timers and embraced again, naked, laughing, bodies pressed tight together, and went soaring across the centuries.

At the halfway house outside imperial Rome, they underwent their preparations, receiving their Roman hairstyles and clothing, their hypnocourses in Latin, their purses of denarii and sestertii, their plague inoculations, their new temporary names. He was Quintus Junius Veranius, she was Flavia Julia Lepida.

Nero's Rome was smaller and far less grand than he expected—the Colosseum was still in the future, there was no Arch of Titus, even the Forum seemed sparsely built. But the city was scarcely mean. The first day, they strolled vast gardens and dense, crowded markets, stared in awe at crazy Caligula's bridge from the Palatine to the Capitoline, went to the baths, gorged themselves at their inn on capon and truffled boar. On the next, they attended the gladiatorial games and afterward made love with frantic energy in a chamber they had hired near the Campus Martius. There was a wonderful frenzy about the city that Reichenbach found intoxicating, and Ilsabet, he knew, shared his fervor: her eyes were aglow, her face gleamed. They could hardly bear to sleep, but explored the narrow winding streets from dark to dawn.

They knew, of course, that the fire would break out in the Circus Maximus where it adjoined the Palatine and Caelian hills, and took care to situate themselves safely atop the Aventine, where they had a fine view. There they watched the fierce blaze sweeping through the Circus, climbing the hills, dipping to ravage the lower ground. No one seemed to be fighting the fire; indeed, Reichenbach thought he could detect subsidiary fires flaring up in the outlying districts, as though arson were the sport of the hour, and soon those fires joined with the main one. They sky rained black soot; the stifling summer air was thick and almost impossible to breathe. For the first two days the destruction had a kind of fascinating beauty, as temples and mansions and arcades melted away, the Rome of centuries being unbuilt before their eyes. But then the discomfort, the danger, the monotony, began to pall on him. "Shall we go?" he said.

"Wait," Ilsabet replied. The conflagration seemed to have an almost sexual impact on her: she glistened with sweat, she trembled with some strange joy as the flames leaped from district to district. She could not get enough. And she clung to him in tight feverish embrace. "Not yet," she murmured, "not so soon. I want to see the emperor."

Yes. And here was Nero now, returning to town from holiday. In grand procession he crossed the charred city, descending from his litter now and then to inspect some ruined shrine or palace. They caught a glimpse of him as he entered the Gardens of Maecenas—thick-necked, paunchy, spindle-shanked, foul of complexion. "Oh, look," Ilsabet whispered. "He's *beautiful!* But where's the fiddle?" The emperor carried no fiddle, but he was grotesquely garbed in some kind of theatrical costume and his cheeks were daubed with paint. He waved and flung coins to the crowd and ascended the garden tower. For a better view, no doubt. Ilsabet pressed herself close to Reichenbach. "My throat is on fire," she said. "My lungs are choked with ashes. Take me to London. Show me Shakespeare."

There was smoke in the dark Cheapside alehouse too, thick sweet smoke curling up from sputtering logs on a dank February day. They sat in a cobwebbed corner playing word games while waiting for the actors to arrive. She was quick and clever, just as clever as he. Reichenbach took joy in that. He loved her for her agility and strength of soul. "Not many could be carrying off this tour," he told her. "Only special ones like us."

She grinned. "We who occupy the far side of the bell-shaped curve."

"Yes. Yes. It's horrible of us to have such good opinions of ourselves, isn't it?"

"Probably. But they're well earned, my dear."

He covered her hand with his, and squeezed, and she squeezed back. Reichenbach had never known anyone like her. Deeper and deeper was she drawing him, and his delight was tempered only by the knowledge that when they returned to realtime, to that iron world beyond the terminator where all paradoxes canceled out and the delicious freedoms of the jaunter did not apply, he must of necessity lose her. But there was no hurry about returning.

Voices, now: laughter, shouts, a company of men entering the tavern, actors, poets perhaps, Burbage, maybe, Heminges, Allen, Condell, Kemp, Ben Jonson possibly, and who was that, slender, high forehead, those eyes like lamps in the dark? Who else could it be? Plainly Shagspere, Chaxper, Shackspire, however they spelled it, surely Sweet Will here among these men calling for sack and malmsey, and behind that broad forehead Hamlet and Mercutio must be teeming, Othello, Hotspur, Prospero, Macbeth. The sight of him excited Reichenbach as Nero had Ilsabet. He inclined his head, hoping to hear scraps of dazzling table-talk, some bit of newborn verse, some talk of a play taking form; but at this distance everything blurred. "I have to go to him," Reichenbach muttered.

"The regulations?"

"*Je m'en fous* the regulations. I'll be quick. People of our kind don't need to worry about the regulations. I promise you, I'll be quick."

She winked and blew him a kiss. She looked gorgeously sluttish in her low-fronted gown.

Reichenbach felt a strange quivering in his calves as he crossed the straw-strewn floor to the far-off crowded table.

"Master Shakespeare!" he cried.

Heads turned. Cold eyes glared out of silent faces. Reichenbach forced himself to be bold. From his purse he took two slender, crude shilling-pieces and put them in front of Shakespeare. "I would stand you a flagon or two of the best sack," he said loudly, "in the name of good Sir John."

"Sir John?" said Shakespeare, blank-faced. He frowned and shook his head. "Sir John Woodcocke, d'ye mean? Sir John Holcombe? I know not your Sir John, fellow."

Reichenbach's cheeks blazed. He felt like a fool.

A burly man beside Shakespeare said, with a rough nudge, "Methinks he speaks of Falstaff, Will. Eh? You recall your Falstaff?"

"Yes," Reichenbach said. "In truth I mean no other."

"Falstaff," Shakespeare said in a distant way. He looked displeased, uncomfortable. "I recall the name, yes. Friend, I thank you, but take back your shillings. It is bad custom for me to drink of strangers' sack."

Reichenbach protested, but only fitfully, and quickly he withdrew lest the moment grow ugly: plainly these folk had no use for his wine or for him, and to be wounded in a tavern brawl here in A.D. 1604 would bring monstrous consequences in realtime. He made a courtly bow and retreated. Ilsabet, watching, wore a cat-grin. He went slinking back to her, upset, bitterly aware he had bungled his cherished meeting with Shakespeare and, worse, had looked bumptious in front of her.

"We should go," he said. "We're unwelcome here."

"Poor dear one. You look so miserable."

"The contempt in his eyes—"

"No," she said. "The man is probably bothered by strangers all the time. And he was, you know, with his friends in the sanctuary of his own tavern. He meant no personal rebuke."

"I expected him to be different—to be one of *us*, to reach out toward me and draw me to him, to—to—"

"No," said Ilsabet gently. "He has his life, his wife, his pains, his problems. Don't confuse him with your fantasy of him. Come, now. You look so glum, my dear. Find yourself again!"

"Somewhen else."

"Yes. Somewhen else."

Under her deft consolations the sting of his oafishness at the Mermaid Tavern eased, and his mood brightened as they went onward. Few words passed between them: a look, a smile, the merest of contacts, and they communicated. Attending the trial of Socrates, they touched fingertips lightly, secretly, and it was the deepest of communions. Afterward they made love under the clear, bright winter sky of Athens on a gray-green hillside rich with lavender and myrtle, and emerged from shivering ecstasies to find themselves with an audience of mournful scruffy goats—a perfect leap of context and metaphor, and for days thereafter they made one another laugh with only the most delicate pantomimed reminder of the scene. Onward they went to see grim, limping, austere old Magellan sail off around the world with his five little ships from the mouth of the Guadalquivir, and at a whim they leaped to India, staining their skins and playing at Hindus as they viewed the expedition of Vasco da Gama come sailing into harbor at Calicut, and then it seemed proper to go on to Spain in dry, hot summer to drink sour white wine and watch ruddy freckled-faced Columbus get his pitiful little fleet out to sea.

Of course, they took other lovers from time to time. That was part of the game, too tasty a treat to forswear. In Byzantium, on the eve of the Frankish conquest, he passed a night with a dark-eyed voluptuous Greek who oiled her breasts with musky mysterious unguents, and Ilsabet with a towering garlicky Swede of the imperial guard, and when they found each other the next day, just as the Venetian armada burst into the Bosporus, they described to one another in the most flamboyant of detail the strangenesses of their night's sport—the tireless Norseman's toneless bellowing of sagas in his hottest moments: the Byzantine's startling, convulsive, climactic fit, almost epileptic in style, and, as she had admitted playfully at dawn, mostly a counterfeit. In Cleopatra's Egypt, while waiting for glimpses of the queen and Antony, they diverted themselves with a dark-eyed Coptic pair, brother and sister, no more than children and blithely interchangeable in bed. At the crowning of Charlemagne she found herself a Frankish merchant who offered her an estate along the Rhine, and he a mysteriously elliptical dusky woman who claimed to be a Catalonian Moor, but who—Reichenbach suddenly realized a few days later—must almost certainly have been a jaunter like himself, playing elegant games with him.

All this lent spice to their love and did no harm. These separate but shared adventures only enhanced the intensity of the relationship they were welding. He prayed the jaunt would never end, for Ilsabet was the perfect companion, his utter match, and so long as they sprinted together through the aeons, she was his, though he knew that would end when realtime reclaimed him. Nevertheless, that sad moment still was far away, and he hoped before then to find some way around the inexorable rules, some scheme for locating her and continuing with her in his own true time. Small chance of that, he knew. In the world beyond the terminator there was no time-jaunting; jaunting could be done only in the fluid realm of "history," and history was arbitrarily defined as everything that had happened before the terminator year of 2187. The rest was realtime, rigid and immutable, and what if her realtime were fifty years ahead of his, or fifty behind? There was no bridging that by jaunting. He did not know her realtime locus, and he did not dare ask. Deep as the love between them had come to be, Reichenbach still feared offending her through some unpardonable breach of their special etiquette.

With all the world to choose from, they sometimes took brief solo jaunts. That was Ilsabet's idea, holidays within their holiday, so that they would not grow stale with one another. It made sense to him. Thereupon he vaulted to the Paris of the 1920s to sip Pernod on the Boulevard Saint-Germain and peer at Picasso and Hemingway and Joyce, she in epicanthic mask of old Cathay to see Kublai Khan ride in triumph through the Great Wall, he to Cape Kennedy to watch the great Apollo rocket roaring moonward, she to London for King Charles's beheading. But these were brief adventures, and they reunited quickly, gladly, and went on hand in hand to their next together, to the fall of Troy and the diamond jubilee of Queen Victoria and the assassination of Lincoln and the sack of Carthage. Always when they returned from separate exploits, they regaled each other with extensive narratives of what had befallen them, the sights, the tastes, the ironies and perceptions, and, of course, the amorous interludes. By now Reichenbach and Ilsabet had accumulated an elaborate fabric of shared experience, a richness of joint history that gave them virtually a private language of evocative recollection, so that the slightest of cues—a goat on a hill, the taste of burned toast, the sight of a lop-eared beggar—sprang them into an intimate realm that no one else could ever penetrate: their unique place, furnished with their own things, the artifacts of love, the treasures of memory. And even that which they did separately became interwoven in that fabric, as the telling of events as they lay in each other's arms had transformed those events into communal possessions.

Yet gradually Reichenbach realized that something was beginning to go wrong.

From a solo jaunt to Paris in 1794, where she toured the Reign of Terror, Ilsabet returned strangely evasive. She spoke in brilliant detail of the death of Robespierre and the sad despoliation of Notre Dame, but what she reported was mere journalism, with no inner meaning. He had to fish for information. Where had she lodged? Had she feared for her safety? Had she had interesting conversations with the Parisians? Shrugs, deflections. Had she taken a lover? Yes, yes, a fleeting liaison, nothing worth talking about; and then it was back to an account of the mobs, the tumbrels, the sound of the guillotine. At first Reichenbach accepted that without demur, though her vaguenesses violated their custom. But she remained moody and oblique while they were visiting the Crucifixion, and as they were about to depart for the Black Death she begged off, saying she needed another day to herself, and would go to Prague for the premiere of *Don Giovanni*. That too failed to trouble him—he was not musical—and he spent the day observing Waterloo from the hills behind Wellington's troops. When Ilsabet rejoined him in the late spring of 1349 for the Black Death in London, though, she seemed even more preoccupied and remote, and told him little of her night at the opera. He began to feel dismay, for they had been marvelously close and now she was obviously voyaging on some other plane. The plague-smitten city seemed to bore her. Her only flicker of animation came toward evening, in a Southwark hostelry, when as they dined on gristly lamb a stranger entered, a tall, gaunt, sharp-bearded man with the obvious aura of a jaunter. Reichenbach did not fail to notice the rebirth of light in Ilsabet's eyes, and the barely perceptible inclining-forward of her body as the stranger approached their table was amply perceptible to him. The newcomer knew them for what they were, naturally, and invited himself to join them. His name was Stavanger; he had been on his jaunt just a few days; he meant to see everything, *everything*, before his time was up. Not for many years had Reichenbach felt such jealousy. He was wise in these things, and it was not difficult to detect the current flowing from Ilsabet to Stavanger even as he sat there between them. Now he understood why she had no casual amours to report of her jaunts to Paris and Prague. This one was far from casual and would bear no retelling.

In the morning she said, "I still feel operatic. I'll go to Bayreuth tonight—the premiere of *Götterdämmerung*."

Despising himself, he said, "A capital idea. I'll accompany you."

She looked disconcerted. "But music bores you!"

"A flaw in my character. Time I began to remedy it."

The fitful panic in Ilsabet's eyes gave way to cool and chilling calmness. "Another time, dear love. I prize my solitude. I'll make this little trip without you."

It was all plain to him. Gone now the open sharing; now there were secret rendezvous and an unwanted third player of their game. He could not bear it. In anguish he made his own arrangements and jaunted to Bayreuth in thick red wig and curling beard, and there she was, seated beside Stavanger in the Festspielhaus as the subterranean orchestra launched into the first notes. Reichenbach did not remain for the performance.

Stavanger now crossed their path openly and with great frequency. They met him at the siege of Constantinople, at the San Francisco earthquake, and at a fete at Versailles. This was more than coincidence, and Reichenbach said so to Ilsabet. "I suggested he follow some of our itinerary," she admitted. "He's a lonely man, jaunting alone. And quite charming. But of course if you dislike him, we can simply vanish without telling him where we're going, and he'll never find us again."

A disarming tactic, Reichenbach thought. It was impossible for her to admit to him that she and Stavanger were lovers, for there was too much substance to their affair; so instead she pretended he was a pitiful forlorn wanderer in need of company. Reichenbach was outraged. Fidelity was not part of his unspoken compact with her, and she was free to slip off to any era she chose for a tryst with Stavanger. But that she chose to conceal what was going on was deplorable, and that she was finding pretexts to drag Stavanger along on their travels, puncturing the privacy of their own rapport for the sake of a few smug stolen glances, was impermissible. Reichenbach was convinced now that Ilsabet and Stavanger were co-temporals, though he knew he had no rational basis for that idea; it simply seemed right to him, a final torment, the two of them now laying the groundwork for a realtime relationship that excluded him. Whether or not that was true, it was unbearable. Reichenbach was astounded by the intensity of his jealous fury. Yet it was a true emotion and one he would not attempt to repress. The joy he had known with Ilsabet had been unique, and Stavanger had tainted it.

He found himself searching for ways to dispose of his rival.

Merely whirling Ilsabet off elsewhen would achieve nothing. She would find ways of catching up with her paramour somewhen along the line. And if Ilsabet and Stavanger were co-temporal, and she and Reichenbach were not—no, no, Stavanger had to be expunged. Reichenbach, a stable and temperate man, had never imagined himself capable of such criminality; a bit of elitist regulation-bending was all he had ever allowed himself. But he had never been faced with the loss of an Ilsabet before, either.

In Borgia, Italy, Reichenbach hired a Florentine prisoner to do Stavanger in with a dram of nightshade. But the villain pocketed Reichenbach's down payment and disappeared without a care for the ducats due him on completion of the job. In the chaotic aftermath of the Ides of March, Reichenbach attempted to finger Stavanger as one of

Caesar's murderers, but no one paid attention. Nor did he have luck denouncing him to the Inquisition one afternoon in 1485 in Torquemada's Castile, though even the most perfunctory questioning would have given sufficient proof of Stavanger's alliance with diabolical powers. Perhaps it would be necessary, Reichenbach concluded morosely, to deal with Stavanger with his own hands, repellent though that alternative was.

Not only was it repellent, it could be dangerous. He was without experience at serious crime, and Stavanger, cold-eyed and suave, promised to be a formidable adversary: Reichenbach needed an ally, an adviser, a collaborator. But who? While he and Ilsabet were making the circuit of the Seven Wonders, he puzzled over it, from Ephesus to Halicarnassus, to Gizeh, and as they stood in the shadow of the Colossus of Rhodes, the answer came to him. There was only one person he could trust sufficiently, and that person was himself.

To Ilsabet he said, "Do you know where I want to go next?"

"We still have the Hanging Gardens of Babylon, the Lighthouse of Alexandria, the Statue of Zeus at—"

"No, I'm not talking about the Seven Wonders tour. I want to go back to Sarajevo, Ilsabet."

"Sarajevo? Whatever for?"

"A sentimental pilgrimage, love, to the place of our first meeting."

"But Sarajevo was a bore. And—"

"We could make it exciting. Consider: our earlier selves would already be there. We would watch them meet, find each other well matched, become lovers. Here for months we've been touring the great events of history, when we're neglecting a chance to witness our own personal greatest event." He smiled wickedly. "And there are other possibilities. We could introduce ourselves to them. Hint at the joys that lie ahead of them. Perhaps even seduce them, eh? A nice kinky quirky business that would be. And—"

"No," she said. "I don't like it."

"You find the idea improper? Morally offensive?"

"Don't be an idiot. I find it dangerous."

"How so?"

"We aren't supposed to reenter a time-span where we're already present. There must be some good reason for that. The rules—"

"The rules," he said, "are made by timid old sods who've never moved beyond the terminator in their lives. The rules are meant to guide us, not to control us. The rules are meant to be broken by those who are smart enough to avoid the consequences."

She stared somberly at him a long while. "And are you?"

"I think I am."

"Yes. A shrewd man, a superior man, a member of the elite corps that lives on the far side of society's bell-shaped curve. Eh? Doing as you please throughout life. Holding yourself above all restraints. Rich enough and lucky enough to be able to jaunt anywhen you like and behave like a little god."

"You live the same way, I believe."

"In general, yes. But I still won't go with you to Sarajevo."

"Why not?"

"Because I don't know what will happen to me if I do. Kinky and quirky it may be to pile into bed with our other selves, but something about the idea troubles me, and I dislike needless risk. Do you believe you understand paradox theory fully?"

"Does anybody?"

"Exactly. It isn't smart to—"

"Paradoxes are much overrated, don't you think? We're in the fluid zone, Ilsabet. Anything goes, this side of the terminator. If I were you I wouldn't worry about—"

"*I* am me. I worry. If I were you, I'd worry more. Take your Sarajevo trip without me."

He saw she was adamant, and dropped the issue. Indeed, he saw it would be much simpler to make the journey alone. They went on from Rhodes to the Babylon of Nebuchadnezzar, where they spent four happy days untroubled by the shadow of Stavanger; it was the finest time they had had together since Carthage. Then Ilsabet announced she felt the need for another brief solo musicological jaunt—to Mantua in 1607 for Monteverdi's *Orfeo*. Reichenbach offered no objection. The instant she was gone, he set his timer for the twenty-eighth of June, 1914, Sarajevo in Bosnia, 10:27 A.M.

In his Babylonian costume he knew he looked ridiculous or even insane, but it was too chancy to have gone to the halfway house for proper preparation, and he planned to stay here only a few minutes. Moments after he materialized in the narrow cobble-paved alleyway, his younger self appeared, decked out elegantly in natty Edwardian finery. He registered only the most brief quiver of amazement at the sight of another Reichenbach already there.

Reichenbach said, "I have to speak quickly. You will go out there and near the Bank of Austria-Hungary you'll meet the most wonderful woman you've ever known, and you'll share with her the greatest joy you've ever tasted. And just as your love for her reaches its deepest strength, you'll lose her to a rival—unless you cooperate with me to rid us of him before they can ever meet."

The eyes of the other Reichenbach narrowed. "Murder?"

"Removal. We'll put him in the way of harm, and harm will come to him."

"Is the woman such a marvel that the risks are worth it?"

"I swear it. I tell you, you'll suffer pain beyond belief if he isn't eliminated. Trust me. My welfare is your welfare, is this not so?"

"Of course." But the other Reichenbach looked unconvinced. "Still, why must there be two of us in this? It's not yet my affair, after all."

"It will be. He's too slippery to tackle without help. I need you. And ultimately you'll be grateful to me for this. Take it on faith."

"And what if this is some elaborate game, and I the victim?"

"Damn it, *this is no game!* Our happiness is at stake—Yours, mine. We're both in this together. We're closer than any twins could ever be, don't you realize? You and me, different phases of the same person's time-line, following the same path? Our destinies are linked. Help me now or live forever with the torment of the consequences. Please help. *Please.*"

The other was wavering. "You ask a great deal."

"I offer a great deal," Reichenbach said. "Look, there's no more time for talking now. You have to get out there and meet Ilsabet before the archduke's assassination. Meet me in Paris, noon on the twenty-fifth of June, 1794, in the rue de Rivoli outside the Hôtel de Ville." He grasped the other's arm and stared at him with all the intensity and conviction at his command. "Agreed?"

A last moment of hesitation.

"Agreed."

Reichenbach touched his timer and disappeared.

In Babylon again he gathered his possessions and jaunted to the halfway house for the French Revolution. Momentarily he dreaded running into his other self there, a malfeasance that would be hard to justify, but the place was too big for that; the Revolution and Terror spanned five years and an immense service facility was needed to handle the tourist demand. Outfitted in the simple countryfolk clothes appropriate to the revolutionary period, equipped with freshly implanted linguistic skills and proper revolutionary rhetoric, altogether disguised to blend with the citizenry, Reichenbach descended into the terrible heat of that bloody Parisian summer and quickly effected his rendezvous with himself.

The face he beheld was clearly his, and yet unfamiliar, for he was accustomed to his mirror image; but a mirror image is a reversed one, and now he saw himself as others saw him and nothing looked quite right. This is what it must be like to have a twin, he thought. In a low, hoarse voice he said, "She's coming tomorrow to hear Robespierre's final speech and then to see his execution. Our enemy is in Paris already, with rooms at the Hôtel Brittanique in the rue Guénégaud. I'll track him down while your make contact with the Committee of Public Safety. I'll bring him here; you arrange the trap and the denunciation; with any luck he'll be hauled away in the same tumbrel that takes Robespierre to the guillotine. *D'accord?*"

"*D'accord.*" A radiance came into the other's eyes. Softly he said, "You were right about Ilsabet. For such a woman even this is justifiable."

Reichenbach felt an unexpected pang. But to be jealous of himself was an absurdity. "Where have you been with her?"

"After Sarajevo, Nero's Rome. She's asleep there now, our third night: I intend to be gone only an instant. We go next to Shakespeare's time, and then—"

"Yes, I know. Socrates, Magellan, Vasco da Gama. All the best still lies ahead for you. But first there's work to do."

Without great difficulty he found his way to the Hôtel Brittanique, a modest place not far from the Pont Neuf. The concierge, a palsied woman with a thin-lipped mouth fixed in an unchanging scowl, offered little aid until Reichenbach spoke of the committee, the Law of Suspects, the dangers of refusing to cooperate with the revolutionary tribunal; then she was quick enough to admit that a dark man of great height with a beard of just the sort that M'sieu described was living on the fifth floor, a certain M. Stavanger. Reichenbach rented the adjoining room. He waited there an hour, until he heard the footsteps in the hallway, sounds next door.

He went out and knocked.

Stavanger peered blankly at him. "Yes?"

He has not yet met her, Reichenbach thought. He has not yet spoken with her, he has not yet touched her body, they have not yet gone to their damned operas together. And never will.

He said, "This is a wonderful place for a jaunt, isn't it."

"Who are you?"

"Reichenbach is my name. My friend and I saw you in the street and she sent me up to speak with you." He made a little self-deprecating gesture. "I often act as her—ah—go-between. She wishes to know if you'll meet her this afternoon and perhaps enjoy a day or two of French history with her. Her name is Ilsabet, and I can testify that you'll find her charming. Her particular interests are assassinations, architecture, and the first performances of great operas."

Stavanger showed sudden alertness. "Opera is a great passion of mine," he said. "Ordinarily I keep to myself when jaunting, but in this case—the possibilities—is she downstairs? Can you bring her to me?"

"Ah, no. She's waiting in front of the Hôtel de Ville."

"And wants me to come to her?"

Reichenbach nodded. "Certain protocols are important to her."

Stavanger, after a moment's consideration, said, "Take me to your Ilsabet, then. But I make no promises. Is that understood?"

"Of course," said Reichenbach.

The streets were almost empty at this hour. The miasma of the atmosphere in this heavy heat must be a factor in that, Reichenbach thought, and also that it was midday and the Parisians were at their *déjeuner*; but beyond that it seemed that the city was suffering a desolation of the spirit, a paralysis of energy under the impact of the monstrous bloodletting of recent months.

He walked quickly, struggling to keep up with Stavanger's long strides. As they approached the Hôtel de Ville, Reichenbach caught sight of his other self, and with him two or three men in revolutionary costume. Good. Good. The other Reichenbach nodded. Everything was arranged. The challenge now was to keep Stavanger from going for his timer the moment he sensed he was in jeopardy.

"Where as she?" Stavanger asked.

"I left her speaking with that group of men," said Reichenbach. The other Reichenbach stood with his face turned aside—a wise move. Now, though they had not rehearsed it, they moved as if parts of a single organism, the other Reichenbach pivoting, pointing, crying out, "I accuse that man of crimes against liberty," while in the same instant Reichenbach stepped behind Stavanger, thrust his arms up past those of the taller man, reached into Stavanger's loose tunic to wrench his timer into ruin with one quick twist, and held him firmly. Stavanger bellowed and tried to break free, but in a moment the street was full of men who seized and overpowered him and dragged him away. Reichenbach, panting, sweating, looked in triumph toward his other self.

"That one, too," said the other Reichenbach.

Reichenbach blinked. "What?"

Too late. They had his arms; the other Reichenbach was groping for his timer, seizing, tearing. Reichenbach fought ferociously, but they bore him to the ground and knelt on his chest.

Through a haze of fear and pain he heard the other saying, "This man is the proscribed aristocrat Charles Evremonde, called Darnay, enemy of the Republic, member of a family of tyrants. I denounce him for having used his privileges in the oppression of the people."

"He will face the tribunal tonight," said the one kneeling on Reichenbach.

Reichenbach said in a shocked voice, "What are you doing?"

The other crouched close to him and replied in English. "We have been duplicated, you see. Why do you think there are rules against entering a time where one is already present? There's room for only one of us back in realtime, is that not so? So, then, how can we both return?"

Reichenbach said, with a gasp, "But that isn't true!"

"Isn't it? Are you sure? Do you really comprehend all the paradoxes?"

"Do *you*? How can you do this to me, when I—when I'm—"

"You disappoint me, not seeing these intricacies. I would have expected more from one of us. But you must have been too muddled by jealousy to think straight. Do you imagine I dare run the risk of letting you jaunt around on the loose? Which of us is to have Ilsabet, after all?"

Already Reichenbach felt the blade hurtling toward his neck.

"Wait—wait—" he cried. "Look at him! His face is mine! We are brothers, twins! If I'm an aristocrat, what is he? I denounce him too! Seize him and try him with me!"

"There is indeed a strange resemblance between you two," said one of those holding Reichenbach.

The other smiled. "We have often been taken for brothers. But there is no kinship between us. He is the aristocrat Evrémonde, citizens. And I, I am only poor Sydney Carton, a person of no consequence or significance whatever, happy to have been of service to the people." He bowed and walked away, and in a moment was gone.

Safe beside Ilsabet in Nero's Rome, Reichenbach thought bitterly.

"Come. Up with him and bring him to trial," someone called. "The tribunal has no time to waste these days."

A THOUSAND PACES
ALONG THE VIA DOLOROSA

I am a reasonably honest man who tries not to tell lies except when it would be impolite to speak the truth; and so I am going to point out right here that this story is not science fiction, and really isn't fantasy, either, though it seems to be from time to time. If the only kind of fiction you read is science fiction and fantasy, you may want to skip it—although I think it's quite a good story, which is why I've included it in this book.

I wrote it in October, 1980, during the period of renewed creative vitality that followed my long dry spell of the mid-1970s. I had returned to writing still thinking of myself primarily as a science-fiction writer, but there are more things for a writer to write about than robots and time machines and spaceships, and once in a while I like to venture into fiction that fits into no particular category. As was the case with this one: I wanted to set it in Jerusalem, one of the most fascinating places I have ever visited, and I wanted to deal in fictional form with the mysteries of psychedelic drugs, with which I had also had a little first-hand experience. Also I wanted finally to have a story published in Playboy, a magazine I had been reading since its first issue back in 1953. What people think of first when Playboy is mentioned is, of course, the photographs of naked ladies; but it has also published some extraordinarily distinguished short stories, stories by such writers as Vladimir Nabokov, Gabriel Garcia Marquez, John Updike, Ray Bradbury. Well, why not Robert Silverberg as well?

So I had my agent send this one to Playboy's fiction editor, Alice K. Turner, who turned it down with one of the most fascinating rejection letters I've ever had. I didn't agree with her reasoning, of course, but I had to admit that she had looked at the story very carefully and her objections to it were not arbitrary or trivial ones. We exchanged a few letters about a revision of the story; she gave me no guarantees, but was willing to see what I might do; in the end, she still didn't want to publish the story, and I sold it to Twilight Zone, a magazine of that era that published horror stories of the Stephen King variety, something I have never written, but also was open to this kind of somewhat surreal psychologically-oriented fiction. It appeared in the July, 1981 issue.

In the course of my correspondence with Alice Turner over a story she didn't buy, however, she mentioned that she would be coming to California in the spring of 1981, and suggested that we get together to discuss not only the art of the short story in general but the likelihood of my writing some for Playboy. *And with that began one of the most interesting editor-writer relationships of my life.*

Hornkastle said to the dapper young Israeli, "When they eat the mushroom, do they think they see God?"

"Far more than that. The mushroom is their god. When they eat it, they become one with Him: they become Him. It is the pure *agapé*," Ben-Horin said, "the true Christian feast."

Ben-Horin's voice, light but firm, crisp and clipped, had a dizzying musical quality. A pounding began in Hornkastle's forehead. Being with the Israeli made Hornkastle—a big man, some years older, nearly forty—feel thick and clumsy and slow. And what Ben-Horin was telling him about these Arab tribal rites stirred in him some mysterious hunger, some incomprehensible longing, that baffled and astounded him. He felt woozy. He suspected he might have had too much to drink. He looked up and across, out the big window of the hotel cocktail lounge. Off there to the west Jerusalem was awesome in the late afternoon sunlight. The domes of the two great mosques, one gold and one silver, glittered like globules of molten metal. Hornkastle closed his eyes and put his drink to his lips and said, "Take me to these people."

"Gently, gently. What they do is very illegal in Israel. And they are Arabs, besides—Christian Arabs, who live between worlds here, who are very cautious people at all times."

"I want to go to them."

"And eat their mushroom? And become one with their god?"

Hornkastle said hoarsely, "To study them. To understand them. You know this is my field."

"You want to eat the mushroom," said Ben-Horin.

Hornkastle shrugged. "Maybe." To swallow God, to be possessed by Him, to entangle one's identity with Him—why not? Why not? "How long before I can go to them?" he asked.

"Who knows? A week? Two? Everything here is conditional. The politics, the inflation rate, the weather, even—one takes everything into account. I promise you you'll see them. Until Easter everything is crazy here—pilgrims, tourists, wandering ecstatics—it gets a little like Benares, almost. After Easter, all right? Can you stay that long?"

Hornkastle considered. He was on sabbatical. He had virtually fled Los Angeles, escaping from the wreckage of his life there. It didn't matter when he went back, or if he ever did. But he was gripped with impatience. He said, "I'll stay as long as possible. But please—soon—"

"We must wait for the right moment," said Ben-Horin firmly. "Come, now. My wife is eager to meet you."

They went out into the surprisingly chilly April air. With a lurch and a roar Ben-Horin's tiny orange Datsun took off, down the hill, around the compact medieval splendor of the walled Old City and through New Jerusalem. Ben-Horin was an outrageous driver, screeching through the streets like a racer in the Grand Prix, honking ferociously at his fellow motorists as if they were all retired Nazis. The Israelis must be the most belligerent drivers in the world, Hornkastle thought. Even a cool cosmopolitan type like Ben-Horin, professor of botany, connoisseur of rare fungi, turned into a lunatic behind the wheel. But that was all right. Life had been a roller-coaster ride for Hornkastle for a couple of years now. One more round of loop-the-loop wasn't going to bother him much. Not after three stiff jobs of arrack on the rocks. Not here. Not now.

Ben-Horin lived in a gray-and-blue high-rise, spectacularly situated on a hilltop near the university. It looked stunning from a distance, but once inside Hornkastle noticed that the stucco was cracking, the lobby tiles were starting to fall out, the elevator made disturbing groaning sounds. The Israeli ushered him into a tiny immaculate apartment. "My wife, Geula," said Ben-Horin with a brusque little wave. "Thomas Hornkastle of the University of California, Los Angeles."

She was a surprise—a big woman, inch or two taller than Ben-Horin, probably twenty pounds heavier, with a ripe, if not overripe, look to her. It was hard to imagine these two as man and wife, for Ben-Horin was dry and precise and contained and she was full of vitality, young and pretty, in a way, and overflowing with life. Her eyes were dark and glossy and it seemed to Hornkastle that she was looking at him with outright interest. Probably a figment of the arrack, he decided.

He needed no more drinks, but he had never been good at refusing them, and soon she had a martini-like thing in his hand, something made with Dutch gin and too much vermouth. The conversation was quick, animated, impersonal. Perhaps that was the style here. Ben-Horin and his wife were both well informed about world affairs, though everything seemed to circle back to analyses of the impact of this event or that on Israel's own situation. Possibly, Hornkastle thought, if you live in a very small country that has been surrounded by fanatical enemies for its entire life, you get fixated on local issues. He had been startled, at the international symposium where he had met Ben-Horin last December, to hear an Israeli historian expounding on the Vietnam war in terms of Israel and Syria. "If your government tells you to defend an outpost," he had said, "you go and defend it. You don't argue with your government about the morality of the thing!" With that sort of outlook even the rainfall in Uganda could become a significant domestic political issue.

Somehow he finished his martini and one after that, and then there was wine with dinner, a dry white wine from the Galilee. Hornkastle always drank a little too heavily, especially when he was traveling, but in the last few turbulent years it had started to be a problem, and the way the Ben-Horins kept him topped off could get troublesome. He knew he was on the edge of becoming sloppy and worked hard at staying together. After a time he was just nodding and smiling while they talked, but suddenly—it was late, and now everyone was drinking a corrosive Israeli brandy—she wanted to know about his field of study. He did his best, but his voice sounded slurred even to him. Professor of experimental psychology, he said, here to investigate rumors of archaic cultist practices among the Arabs just south of Jerusalem. "Oh, the mushroom," she said. "You have tried it in California, perhaps?"

"In a minor way. In the course of my research."

"Everyone in California takes drugs all the time. Yes?"

Hornkastle smiled blearily. "Not these days. Not as much as is commonly believed."

"The mushroom here, the *Amanita muscaria*," she said, "is very strong, maybe because it is holy and this is the Holy Land. Stronger than what is in California, I believe. No wonder they call it a god. You want to try it?"

Hazily he imagined she was offering him some right now, and he looked at her in horror and amazement. But Ben-Horin laughed and said, "He is not sure. I will take him to Kidron and he can conduct his own investigation."

"It is very strong," she said again. "You must be careful."

"I will be careful," Hornkastle said solemnly, although the promise sounded hollow to him, for he had been careful so long, careful to a fault, pathologically careful, and now in Israel he felt strangely reckless and terrified of his own potential recklessness. "My interest is scholarly," he said, but it came out *skhollally,* and as he struggled desperately and unsuccessfully to get the word right, Ben-Horin tactfully rescued him with an apology for having an early class the next day. When they said good night Geula Ben-Horin took his hand and, Hornkastle was certain, held it just a moment too long.

In the morning he felt surprisingly fine, almost jaunty, and at midday he set out for the Old City on foot. Entering it, he looked about in wonder. Before him lay the Via Dolorosa, Christ's route to the Crucifixion, and to all sides spread a tangle of alleys, arcades, stairs, tunnels, passageways and bazaars. Hornkastle had been in plenty of ancient cities, but there was something about this one that put it beyond all others. He could touch a paving stone and think, King David walked here or the Emperor Titus or Saladin, and this was where Jesus had staggered to Golgotha under the weight of his own cross.

So, then: up one winding street and down another, getting himself joyously lost—Monastery of the Flagellation, Western Wall, Dome of the Rock, Street of the Chain, a random walk, poking his nose into the *souks* where old hawk-faced men sold sheepskin rugs, pungent spices out of burlap bags, prayer-beads, shawls, hideous blue ceramic things, camel statuettes, unplucked chickens, sides of lamb, brass pots, hookahs, religious artifacts of every sort and, for all Hornkastle knew, merchandise far more sinister than any of that. In a noisy fly-specked market he bought some falafel and a carbonated beverage, and a little farther on, still hungry, he stopped at a place selling charcoal-grilled kebabs. The fascination of the place was like a drug. These timeless faces, men in worn serge suits who wore flowing Bedouin head-dresses, young women darting from doorway to doorway, grubby children, dogs blithely licking at spilled God-knows-what in the gutters, old peasant women with refrigerators or television sets strapped to their backs, cries and odors, the periodic amplified songs of the muezzins calling the faithful to the mosques, picturesque squalor everywhere, why, it was like a movie, like time-travel even, except that it was actually happening to him: he was here and now in Old Jerusalem, capital of the world. It was exhilarating and a little intoxicating. And there was that extra little thrill, that *frisson,* of knowing—if he could believe Ben-Horin's story—that the ancient religion still flourished somewhat hereabouts, that there still were those who ate of the sacred mushroom that had been the forbidden fruit of the Tree of Good and Evil, the manna of the Israelites, the hallucinogenic phallic fungus that made one like unto a god. Perhaps that boy with glittering eyes in the dark doorway, that old man leaning against the cobbled wall, that powerful fellow in the tinsmiths' stall—secret mystics, devouring God in rites as old as Sumer, undergoing joyous metamorphoses of the spirit, ecstasies. From the Greek *ekstasis,* the flight of the soul from the body. "You must come to Israel," Ben-Horin had told him last winter at that meeting in Monaco after Hornkastle had read his paper on Siberian mushroom intoxication. "The most surprising things still exist among us, a dozen kilometers from the tourist hotels, and scarcely anyone knows about them, and those that do pretend that nothing is going on."

At 2:00 p.m. Hornkastle emerged from the maze of the Old City at the Damascus Gate. Ben-Horin was already there. "A punctual man," the Israeli said, turning a quick grin on and off. "You feel all right today? Good. Come with me." He led Hornkastle back into the heart of the city. Near the Via Dolorosa he said, "Walk slowly and glance to your left. See the man at the falafel stand? He is one. A user of *tigla'.*"

"Tigla'?"

"The word is Aramaic. The mushroom. A reference to its phallic shape. Are you hungry?"

They approached the falafel stand. The man behind the counter, presiding over basins of bubbling oil, was an Arab, about thirty, with a lean triangular face, wide jutting cheekbones tapering down toward a sharp narrow chin. Hornkastle stared at him flagrantly, peering as though he were a shaman, an oracle, a holy man. Questions boiled and raged in his mind, and he felt once again that urgent hunger, that need to surrender himself and be engulfed by a larger force.

Ben-Florin said something curt and harsh in Arabic, and the falafel seller scooped several of the golden chick-pea balls out of the hot oil, stuffing them into envelopes of pita bread. As he handed one across to Hornkastle, his eyes—dark, faintly hyperthyroid, bloodshot—met the American's and locked on them for a long moment, and Hornkastle flinched and looked down as he took the sandwich. Ben-Horin paid. When they walked away, Hornkastle said, "Does he know you?"

"Of course. But I could hardly speak to him here."

"Because he's an Arab and you're a Jew?"

"Don't be absurd. We're both Israeli citizens. It is because I am a professor at Hebrew University and he's a falafel seller and this is the Old City, where I am an intruder. There are class lines here that neither he nor I should cross. Don't believe all you hear about what an egalitarian country this is."

"Why did you take me to him?"

"To show you," said Ben-Horin, "that there are *tigla'* folk right in the midst of the city. And to show him that you have my sponsorship, for they trust me, after a fashion, and now they are likely to trust you. This must all be done very, very slowly. Come now, my car is near the bus station."

With his usual terrifying intensity Ben-Horin circled the northeast corner of the Old City and headed south out Jericho Road toward the Kidron Valley. Quickly they left the urban area behind and entered a rough, scrubby terrain, rocky and parched. Like a tour guide Ben-Horin offered a rapid commentary. "Over there, Mount Zion, Tomb of David. There, Valley of Hinnom, where in ancient times were the high places where Baal and Moloch were worshipped. Still are, perhaps, but if it's going on, they keep very quiet about it. And here—" dry ravines, stony fields—" Kidron. You follow the valley to its end and you are in the Dead Sea." Hornkastle saw shepherds, a camel or two, stone huts. Ben-Horin turned off on an easterly road, poorly maintained. It was amazing how quickly the land became desert once you were a short way down from cool, hilly Jerusalem. The Israeli pointed ahead toward a scruffy village—a few dozen crude buildings clumped around a couple of tin-roofed stores, one emblazoned with a giant red COCA-COLA sign. "This is the place. We will not stop today, but I will drive slowly through."

The town was dusty, ramshackle, drab. Outside COCA-COLA sat a few old men in jeans, battered pea-jackets and Arab headdresses. A couple of sullen boys glowered at the car. Hornkastle heard a radio playing—was that an old Presley number wailing across the wasteland? He said, "How in God's name did you ever get them to open up to you?"

"A long, slow process."

"What was your secret?"

Ben-Horin smiled smugly. "Science. The Arabs had begun to exhaust their traditional fungus sources. I told them other places to look. My price was entree into their rites. I pledge you, it took a long time."

"You've had the mushroom yourself?"

"Several times. To show my good faith. I didn't enjoy it."

"Too heavy for you?"

"Heavy? Heavy?" Ben-Horin seemed puzzled by the idiom. Then he said, "The physiological effects were fascinating—the intensifying of colors and textures, the sense of the earth as a breathing organism, the effect of having music turn into flavors and shapes, all the synesthesias, the familiar psychedelic circus. But also very, very powerful, more than I had experienced elsewhere. I began to feel that there truly was a God and He was touching my consciousness. I am willing to perceive the sound of a flute as something with mottled wings, but I am not willing at the age of thirty-one to begin generating a belief in supernatural deities. And when I began to lose sight of the boundaries between God and Ben-Horin, when I began to think of myself as perhaps partaking of the nature of Jesus—" Ben-Horin shook his head. "For me this is no pastime to pursue. Let those who want to be gods, saviors, divine martyrs, whatever, eat their fill of the mushroom. I am content to study its worshipers."

They were well past the village, now, three or four miles into the empty desert. Hornkastle said, "Do you think this cult has simply survived since ancient times, or is it a deliberate modern revival?"

"I have no idea."

"But what do you think?"

"I said I have no idea. Do you?"

Hornkastle shrugged. "Since the whole Near East once was honey-combed with mushroom cultists, I suppose it's possible that one group has hung on. Especially here. I'm familiar with Allegro's notion that Jesus himself never existed, that *Jesus* is just a code word for the sacred mushroom that rises from the ground, the phallic-looking son of God that is eaten and shows the way to the Godhead. And this is Jesus' own turf, after all. But presumably these cults were all suppressed thousands of years ago."

"Presumably."

"It's exciting to think that the belief simply went underground instead. I want to find out."

"With luck you will, my friend."

"Take me into the village?"

"Eventually."

"Why not now? While we're actually here."

"Your impatience will be your ruin, dear Hornkastle. We must move very slowly."

"If you understood how eager I—"

"I do understand. That is why there must be no haste."

They rounded a bend in the road. An Israeli soldier was standing beside an overturned motorbike, signaling for help. Ben-Horin halted and there was a brief colloquy in Hebrew. Then the soldier clambered into the car, apologizing in mild, inexact English as he jammed himself next to Hornkastle and made room for his machine-gun. "We will give him a lift back to Jerusalem," Ben-Horin explained. That put an end to any talk of sacred mushrooms.

As they passed through the village again, Hornkastle noticed that a younger man had emerged from COCA-COLA and stood outside it, arms folded. For an eerie moment Hornkastle thought he was the falafel seller—the same face, wide cheekbones, pointed chin, bulging, brooding eyes—but of course that was unlikely; this must be a cousin, a brother. In these villages everyone has the same genes.

"I will drop you at your hotel," said Ben-Horin.

Itchy, irritating frustration assailed Hornkastle. He wanted much more than this, and he did not want to wait, and if impatience would be his ruin, so be it: he was impatient. He felt irritable, volatile, explosive. With an effort he calmed himself. Ben-Horin was right: only by moving slowly would anything be accomplished. The trouble was he had moved so slowly so long, all through his tame disciplined academic life. Now those disciplines seemed to be breaking down, and he stood on the brink of strangeness, awaiting the dive.

He said, "When will we meet again?"

"In a few days," Ben-Horin replied. "I must deliver a lecture in Haifa tomorrow, and then there are other responsibilities. I will call you."

The bartender at the hotel recognized Hornkastle and asked him if he wanted arrack again. Hornkastle nodded gloomily and studied the liquor, watching the ice-cubes turn the clear fluid cloudy. Shadows were starting to lengthen over the domes and parapets of the Old City. He was working on his third drink when two tourists came in, obviously mother and daughter, say fifty-five and thirty, good-looking long-legged golden-haired women with delicate slender faces, fragile sharp noses. British, he guessed, from the severe cut of their clothes and from their imperfect, somewhat bucked teeth. Before long he managed to draw them into conversation. British, yes, Claudia and Helena, cool and elegant and self-contained, friendly. Helena, the daughter, asked what he was drinking. "Arrack," he said. "Anise liqueur, like the Greek ouzo, you know? The Turkish raki. Same stuff from Indonesia to Yugoslavia." The daughter ordered one; the mother tried it and called for sherry instead.

Before long the women were on their second drinks and he was ready for his fourth and everyone was a little flushed. There was a pleasant sexual undercurrent to the conversation now, nothing obvious, nothing forced, just there, mature and not unattractive man sitting with two mature women in strange land. Anything might happen. He was fairly certain of the glow in Helena's eyes—that same you-need-but-ask shine that he had imagined he had seen in Geula Ben-Horin's, but this did not seem like imagination. And even the older one had a spark of it. He allowed himself quick foolish fantasies. The mother tactfully excusing herself at the right moment; he and the daughter going off somewhere for dinner, dancing, night of exotic delights, breakfast on the veranda. Or maybe the *daughter* pleading a headache and disappearing, and he and Claudia—why not? She wasn't that much older than he was. Or perhaps both of them at once, something agreeably kinky, one of those nights to treasure forever. They were widows, he learned, their husbands killed in a freak hunting accident in Scotland the previous autumn. Helena spoke matter-of-factly about it, as if being widowed at thirty was no great event. "And now," she said, "mother and I are pilgrims in Jerusalem! We look forward so much to the Easter celebrations. Since the mishap we've felt the presence of God by our sides constantly, and Jesus as a living force." Hornkastle's dreams of a wild threesome upstairs began to fade. They had been Church of England, said Claudia, very high church indeed, but after the mishap they had turned to the Roman faith for solace, and now, in the Holy Land, they would march with other pilgrims along the Via Dolorosa, bearing the cross—

Eventually they asked Hornkastle about himself, and he sketched it all quickly, UCLA, experimental psychology, divorce, sabbatical, hint of severe inner storms, crisis, need to get away from it all. He intended to say nothing about sacred mushrooms, but somehow that slipped out—secret cult, hallucinogens, mysterious village in the desert. His cheeks reddened. "How *fascinating!*" Helena cried. "Will you take us there?" He imagined what Ben-Horin would say about that. He responded vaguely, and she swept onward, bright-eyed, enthusiastic, chattering about drugs, California, mysticism. He began to think he might be able to get somewhere with her after all, and started to angle the conversation back toward dinner, but no, no, they had a prior engagement, dinner at the rectory, was that it? "We must talk again soon," said Claudia, and off they went, and he was alone again.

A suspended time began. He wandered by himself. One night he went down to the Old City—dark, a mysterious and threatening warren of knotted streets and sinister-looking people. He ate at a little Arab place, grilled fish and mashed chick-peas for a few shekels. Afterward he got lost in a deserted area of blank-walled houses. He thought he was being followed—footsteps in the distance, rustling sounds, whispers—but whenever he glanced back, he saw nothing but woebegone lop-eared cats. Somehow he found his way to Jaffa Gate and picked up a taxi.

He rented a car and did standard tourist things, museums and monuments. Jerusalem, he decided, looked a little like Southern California. Not the inner city, God, no, but the environs, the dry tawny rocky hills, the vast open sky, the clusters of flat-faced condominiums and whatnot sprawling over every ridge and crest—he could almost blink and imagine himself somewhere out by Yorba Linda or Riverside. Except that in the middle of it all was the city of David and Solomon and Herod and Pilate, and the place of the cross. Had any of that really happened, he wondered? A slender bearded man lurching up the Via Dolorosa under the weight of the two massive wooden beams? What is it like to carry the cross? What is it like to hang high above the ground in the cool clear springtime air of Jerusalem, waiting for your Father to summon your spirit?

Hornkastle prowled the Old City constantly, getting to know his way around in the maze. His path often took him past the falafel stand. When he bought sandwiches from the Arab, his hand trembled, as if the falafel-seller who had so many times devoured his own god held some awesome numinous power that instilled fear. What wonders had that man seen, what strange heights had he ascended? Hornkastle felt brutally excluded from that arcane knowledge, half as old as time, that the Arab must possess. Looking into his bloodshot eyes, Hornkastle was tempted to blurt out his questions in a rush of *tell me tell me,* but he did not dare, for the Arab would pretend not to speak English and Ben-Horin, when he found out, would simply disown him, and that would be the end of the quest.

From Ben-Horin he continued to hear nothing. At last, unable to contain his impatience, Hornkastle telephoned him at home but got no answer. A call to Ben-Horin's office involved him in a maddening sequence of university switchboard operators; half an hour of persistence got him through at last to someone in Ben-Horin's department who said he had gone to Athens to deliver a lecture.

"Athens? I thought Haifa!"

"No, Athens. He will be back soon."

"Please tell him that Thomas Hornkastle would—" But Hornkastle was holding a dead phone. Break in service or just a hangup? He reminded himself that he was in Asia, that however shiny and modern Israel might look, the mentality here was not necessarily always Western. The idea of trying to call back, of going through all those intermediaries again, was appalling. It would be quicker to drive out there and leave a message on Ben-Horin's desk. Shortly he was on his way, navigating grimly in his flimsy Fiat among the squadrons of Israeli kamikaze drivers. With minor confusions he reached the glossy campus and managed to find a secretary, a trim little Sabra who took his quickly scrawled note and promised to give it to Dr. Ben-Horin tomorrow when he returned from his trip to Geneva. Some communications failures here, Hornkastle thought. He felt like inviting the secretary to lunch. It was absurd; the frustrations of his mushroom chase were translating themselves into random sexual twitches. He got out of there fast, went over to the university library, and used up the afternoon with the five volumes of Farnell's *Cults of the Greek States,* looking for veiled *Amanita* references.

Back at the hotel he ran into Helena and Claudia. They were friendly, even warm, but that moment of unmistakable mutual attraction in the cocktail lounge seemed impossible to recapture, and when he again suggested dining with him, they once more blandly and smoothly refused. To fill their place he found an Episcopalian deacon from Ohio, who suggested an allegedly worthwhile restaurant in East Jerusalem. The Ohio man had come here for Easter services five years in a row. "Overwhelming," he said, nodding forcefully. "When they surge up the Via Dolorosa under those heavy crosses. The pathos, the passion! And then on Holy Saturday, when the Greek patriarch declares the Resurrection, and the cry goes up: *Christos anesti!* Christ is risen! You can't imagine the power of the scene. Bells ringing, people shouting and dancing, everybody going crazy, candles, torches—you'll still be here for it, won't you? You shouldn't miss it!"

Yes, Hornkastle thought bleakly, I will still be here for it and probably for Christmas, too. Restlessness gnawed at him. This night, perhaps, the Arabs were celebrating the eucharist of the magic mushroom, gathered in some cobblestone-walled hut to turn themselves into gods, and he was here in this mediocre restaurant, trapped in the prison of himself, picking at gristly mutton and listening to the raptures of a wide-eyed Midwesterner. He hungered for escape, for the dive into the abyss of the divine, for the whips of oblivion. The Ohioan chattered on and on. Hornkastle, hardly even pretending to listen, wondered about his ex-wife, his ex-house, his ex-life in his far-off ex-city, and asked himself how it had come to pass that in the middle of his journey he had ended up here, scourged by inner demons he barely comprehended. He had no answers.

The next day he phoned the university again, this time getting through quickly to Ben-Horin's department. Yes, yes, Dr. Ben-Horin had returned, he was leaving for Tel-Aviv tomorrow, perhaps you can reach him at home now.

The home number did not answer.

To Hornkastle it was like being released from a vow. In a sudden access of overwhelming anger, he drove out toward the Kidron Valley, toward the village of the *tigla'* users, eyes throbbing, hands tight to the knobby wheel. In the village all was as it had been: the old men outside the shop with the COCA-COLA sign, two or three boys playing dice in the dust, a radio blaring sleazy music. No one paid any attention as Hornkastle stepped from his car and went into the shop. A dark place, cramped—canned goods, piles of sheets and blankets, a rack of used clothes, and, yes, a squat red Coca-Cola cooler that emitted dull clunking humming sounds. Behind the counter was the Arab who looked just like the falafel-seller. They are brothers, Hornkastle thought: this is Mustafa; the other is Hassan. Abdul and Ibrahim and Ismail are out tending the flocks, and they all look exactly alike. The bulging bloodshot eyes regarded him coldly. Hornkastle said, in a tentative, faltering way, "Do you speak English?"

"Yes. What do you want?"

Probably it was meant as a shopkeeper's *What can I do for you?* but it came out a lot more hostile than that. Hornkastle moistened his lips. "I want—I am here for—I am trying to learn about—" He halted in confusion and chagrin. This was impossibly stupid. Blurt it out, ask blunt questions about an illegal secret cult? How many months had it taken Ben-Horin to establish contact with these people? I'm ruining everything, Hornkastle thought. He trembled and said, astonishing himself, "Do you sell liquor here?"

A flicker of the dark menacing eyes. "You must go to Jerusalem for that."

"Wine? Beer?"

"Not here. You are in the wrong place."

Hornkastle leaned closer. "I am a friend of Professor Ben-Horin. I study the red plant. You understand?" He pantomimed, trying to draw *Amanita muscaria*'s phallic shape in the air with his hand, and realized that it looked exactly like pantomiming masturbation. The Arab's expression did not change. Hornkastle was shaking. "The mushroom. You understand me?" he said in a thick throaty voice.

"You are mistaken. This is not the place."

"I know it is. Have no fear: I'm no policeman. An American, a friend of Ben-Horin's. I want the mushroom. The closeness to God, do you understand? To taste God, to know the feeling of being divine, of being something greater than myself, of—"

"You are sick. I call doctor."

"No. Please. Trust me. In the name of the compassionate Jesus, help me!"

The Arab stared. Some changes seemed to be going on at last behind the swarthy facade. Hornkastle, sweating, swaying, gripped the counter to keep from falling.

"You are American. You want only fun."

"I swear it, no—"

"The mushroom is not for fun."

"The mushroom is holy. I understand that. *It* is holy, *God* is holy, I— I am not holy. I want to be made holy. To be made whole, do you see?" Hornkastle laughed, a little too wildly. I am babbling, he thought. But he seemed to be getting through. He whispered urgently, "I want to be part of something, finally, does that make sense? To enter a world where I feel I belong. And the mushroom will open the gate. I swear to my need. By the compassionate Jesus, by the eyes of Mary, by the Holy Spirit itself—"

"You are crazy," said the Arab.

"Perhaps I am. I don't think so. But do you have to be sane to want to enter into God? I've been on the outside all my life—looking in, looking for the way, trying to pass that gate and never letting myself do it, never willing to take the last chance. You know, I've had mushrooms, in California. But I always took an underdose, I guess, or the mushroom was too mild, because I only got a hint of the experience, the shadow of it, a little light shining through the door to where I stood—" He faltered. "Please," he said, in a small voice.

From the Arab came an enormous unending silence, broken after an eternity by a few quick gruff words: "Come with me."

Hornkastle nodded. They left the store through a side door, and he followed the Arab on and on, out of the little village, toward the rocky hill to the east. There were a few stone huts up there. The elders of the tribe are convened there, Hornkastle decided, and that is the place of the mushrooms, and I will be presented to them and allowed to plead my case, and then—and then—

Sudden intense panic surged through him. He felt a buzzing in his kneecaps and fierce pressure in his bladder and stabbing pain at the back of his skull. He had a vision of himself being called into judgment in one of those huts, the prying, snooping, ignorant American arraigned for poking his nose where it did not belong, and found guilty and taken out behind the hill, two quick thrusts of the dagger and over the edge into the dry ravine. *This is how we deal with meddlers, Frankish dog.* It was absurd. These people might *look* sinister, but it was all in his over-heated imagination; they were harmless peasants, simple shepherds and farmers, much closer to God than he would ever be and hardly likely to do evil to a stranger. Yet fear possessed him. Halfway up the hill he turned and ran back toward the village, feeling feverish, dizzy, more than half-crazed. The Arab yelled after him but did not pursue. Somehow Hornkastle managed to start his car, and in chaos, tears streaming from his eyes as they had not done since he was a child, he drove wildly back to the city, past his hotel, out toward the university area. Angry drivers honked and shook fists at him. Near the Knesset building he saw a public telephone and called Ben-Horin's home, expecting nothing. Geula Ben-Horin answered. "Hornkastle," he blurted. "I must come over at once."

"Of course. Are you all right"

"Tell me how to get to your place."

It was only five minutes away. He rang her bell and she peered out. A whiff of musky perfume enveloped him; she was wearing a sheer dressing-gown and nothing else, and he was unprepared for that, the absurd, comical, preposterous seductiveness of her, heavy breasts visibly swaying, all that voluptuous Mediterranean flesh. He said, "Your husband—"

"In Tel-Aviv. Come in. What's wrong with you?"

She put a drink in his hand—the foul Israeli brandy—and he gulped it like medicine, and then a second one. She was warm, sympathetic, trying to find out what was the matter; he was barely coherent. Finally, as the brandy settled him a little, he managed to say, "I've just been to the mushroom village."

"Ah." She looked grave.

"Begging them to give me some. I couldn't wait for your husband to get back from wherever the hell he's been. I stood the waiting as long as I could and then I went out there. I talked the ear off some Arab, I reeled off a whole lot of hysterical drivel about wanting to be one with God, you know, the whole transcendental thing—" His voice trailed off in shame.

She said, "And they gave you some, and now it is beginning to upset your mind, is that it? It will be all right. There will be some hours of great delirium and then ecstasy and then gradually you will—"

"No, They didn't give me any."

"No?"

"The Arab told me to follow him and started to lead me toward some huts on the hillside. And I panicked. I thought it was a trap, that they were going to kill me for asking too many questions, and I ran back to my car, I drove, I—I—I fled here. To the only people I know in Jerusalem."

Her eyes were warm with sorrow and pity and a sort of love, it seemed to him, and yet her mouth was quirked in what looked very much like contempt. "I think you are wrong," she said calmly. "What you were afraid of was not that they would do harm to you, but that they really would give you the mushroom."

He blinked. "How can you say that?"

"I think that is so. Often we turn in fear from that which we desire the most. You were in no danger from them, and you knew that. You were in danger from yourself, from your own troubled and tormented soul, and what you feared was—"

"Please. Stop."

"—not what they would do to you but what you would see when the mushroom allowed you to look within."

"No. Please."

He was shaking again. He could not meet her gaze. She came close to him—she was nearly as tall as he was—and held him, comforting him, murmuring that she was sorry to have upset him when he was already in such a vulnerable state. He pressed himself against her and felt the tension draining from him. He felt like a child, a big foolish child. She was the great soothing mother herself, Isis, Astarte, Ishtar, and the power that she had over him frightened and attracted him all at once; if he could not let himself surrender to the god who was the mushroom, he would at least be capable of losing himself in the goddess who was His mother and consort.

"Come," she said, taking his hand.

Easily she led him to the bedroom and with dreamy willingness he vanished into her warm billowing body, no longer caring, no longer resisting anything. He had no strength left. It was all very quick, too quick, and he collapsed abruptly into deep sleep from which he woke, equally abruptly, finding himself lying in her arms and for a moment not knowing who, how, where.

He stared at her, aghast.

Before he could speak she put her finger to his lips and said softly, "You are feeling better?"

"We shouldn't have—your husband—"

"Life is very risky here. Any day the end might come. We live as though there are no second chances." She winked. "Our little secret, eh?" Helping him up, finding his scattered clothes. "When he gets home I will tell him you called. He has been so busy, running everywhere, lectures, meetings—he has so little time. I am glad you came. About the mushroom village and what happened to you there: fear nothing. They will not harm you."

"Will you tell him I went there?"

"No. He can find that out from you much better."

"What am I going to do, though? I've bungled everything!"

"You are a Christian?" She smiled and touched her lips lightly to his. "Live in the hope of glorious redemption. Even bunglers are forgiven if there is a God. Forgive yourself and He will forgive you too, eh? Eh?" She drew him to her for a brief warm embrace. "Go, now," she whispered. "It will be all right."

For ten minutes Hornkastle sat behind the wheel of his parked car, groggy, stunned, before he could muster enough will to drive. All the manic energy in him was spent; he felt bleak, drained, desolate. All was lost. The sensible thing was to pack up and go to the airport and take the next plane out, but he was too numb even to do that. At the hotel he went to the bar for a few drinks and, in a stupor of guilt and bewilderment, dropped into bed.

He was still sleeping soundly when his telephone rang the next morning. Ben-Horin.

"Is it too early for you?" the Israeli asked.

Sunlight flooded the room. "No, no, I'm up." The hand holding the receiver shook. "Good to hear from you again."

"Will you meet me at eleven by Saint Stephen's Gate?" Ben-Horin said brusquely, icily.

The day was bright and warm. Crowds of tourists swarmed about the Old City: the climax of the Easter season was at hand. From a distance of twenty yards Hornkastle could feel the anger radiating from Ben-Horin, and it was all he could manage to force himself to approach the little Israeli.

Ben-Horin said, "How could you have done it?"

"Sheer idiotic spinelessness. She gave me a couple of drinks, and I was already overwrought, I guess, and—"

In amazement Ben-Horin said, "What in the name of Mohammed are you talking about?"

"I—she—" He could not say it.

Ben-Horin shook his head furiously. "You lunatic, how could you *possibly* have gone to the village after all my warnings about moving cautiously? You have done me harm that is perhaps irreparable. This morning I went to see Yasin, the falafel-peddler—he pretended not to know me. As if I am police. I could hardly believe it when Geula said you had been to the village. Now they want nothing more to do with either of us. My relationship with them is severed and possibly cannot be rebuilt. How could you? The discourtesy, Hornkastle, the absolute stupidity—"

"I couldn't reach you for four days. I thought you were avoiding me, God knows why. Finally the frustration built up and built up and I *had* to talk to those people, *had* to, so I—"

"How very stupid that was."

"Yes. I know. Even as I was doing it, I knew it was a mistake, but I simply went through with it anyway, like a dumb schoolboy, I suppose, and even worse, when they were about to *give* me the damned mushroom—I'm sure that's what they were going to do—I panicked, I bolted—" Hornkastle rubbed his aching forehead. "Can you forgive me?"

"Forgiveness is not the issue. I want nothing more to do with you. You may have crippled my own research."

"All right."

"I advise you not to try to return to the village."

"I'm planning to leave Israel as soon as I can."

"Probably there will be no flights available until after the Easter holiday. But while you are still here, keep away from those people."

"Yes," Hornkastle said meekly.

"I take no responsibility for what will happen to you if you approach them again."

"There's no chance of that."

"I wish I had never invited you here. I want never to hear your name again."

Ben-Horin turned with military precision and strode away.

Hornkastle felt shame and weariness and a deep sense of loss. It was ended now, the quest, the timid tentative adventure. Out there in the judaean desert are people acting out the ancient love-feast, communing with a god older than Rome, and he would never know a thing of it now. Slowly, defeatedly, he made his way back to the hotel. I'll call El Al tomorrow, he thought—they'll be open on Good Friday, won't they?—and get the hell out of here, back to the real world, back to all that I wanted to flee.

But there was still tonight and he could not bear to be alone. Recklessly he phoned the room of the Englishwomen—what did he have to lose?—and Claudia answered. Would they join him for dinner? He had asked twice before; maybe he was making a pest of himself and they would tell him to get lost. But no. A lovely idea, she said. Did he have a place in mind? Hornkastle said, "How about right here? At half past seven?"

They both looked beautiful—fine clothes, pale skins, fluffy blonde hair. He loved the British sound of their serene voices. Helena's gauzy blouse revealed fine collarbones, a delicate bosom. Had she been with a man, he wondered, since the unfortunate hunting mishap? Mother and daughter were heavy drinkers, and Hornkastle matched them two for one, so that things rapidly grew blurred, and he was only dimly aware of his food; he hoped he was being brilliant, suspected he was merely being boorish, and hardly cared. They were tolerating him.

"And your mushroom research?" the mother asked. "How has that been going?"

Painful recollection nearly sobered him. "I've botched it," he said, and as they leaned toward him, eagerly, sympathetically, he poured out his miserable shabby tale of the illicit visit, the conversation with the Arab, the pathetic, inglorious retreat. "I see now that what I was looking for here," he said, "was not just a nice little bit of folk-anthropophar-macology to write up for the *Journal,* but an actual mystic experience, a real communion, and as often happens when you want something too badly, you handle things clumsily, you reach too soon, you blunder—" He paused. "And now it will never happen."

"No," said Claudia. "You will have what you seek."

He half expected her to pull a glowing red *Amanita* mushroom from her tiny purse.

"Impossible now," he said mournfully.

"No. This is the city of divine grace, of redemption. You will have a second chance at whatever you hope to attain. I am quite sure of that."

He thought of Geula Ben-Horin saying, *We live as though there are no second chances.* But maybe for Israelis, living in a state of constant

110

war, things were different. Geula had also said, *Live in the hope of glorious redemption,* and now Claudia had said the same thing. Perhaps. Perhaps. He gave the British woman a bland hopeful smile. But he was without hope.

It was well past eleven by the time the last brandies were gone, and then, without any subtlety at all, Hornkastle asked Helena to spend the night with him, and she, smiling beatifically at her mother as though the barbaric American had just done the most wonderfully characteristic thing, as if he had performed one of his tribal dances for her, thanked him for the offer and pleasantly refused—no second chances there, not even a first one—and they left him to deal with the check.

He sat in the restaurant until they told him it was closing. Somehow he managed to persuade his waiter to sell him a whole bottle of arrack from the bar stock and he took it to his room and through the night he methodically emptied it.

By taxi the next morning he descended to the Old City, where a vast horde of pilgrims had gathered to reenact the Savior's final thousand paces along the Via Dolorosa from the place of condemnation to the place of His interment. It looked like the crowd outside a college football game on Saturday afternoon. There were souvenir-sellers, mischievous boys, peddlers of snacks, police and soldiers, television cameramen—and also brown-robed friars, nuns of a dozen orders, priests, people costumed as Roman legionaries carrying spears, a queue of Japanese in clerical clothes with three cameras apiece.

Hornkastle walked in a lurching, shambling way that evidently had an effect on people, for the mob parted before him wherever he went, and soon he was deep in the city's tangled streets. Occasionally hands passed lightly over his body—pickpockets, no doubt, but that was unimportant. He saw Arabs with wide tapering faces everywhere, bloodshot hyperthyroid eyes.

A small boy tapped his knee and took him by the hand. Hornkastle allowed himself to be led, and found himself shortly at Yasin's falafel stand. Hornkastle felt like cringing before the Arab, who surely knew—they all knew everything—of his numbskull journey to the village, of his half-crazed pleadings and bizarre flight. But there was no condemnation on Yasin's face. He was grinning broadly, bowing, making

Hornkastle welcome to the Holy Land, to Jerusalem, to the Via Dolorosa; to his own humble falafel stand on the morning of Christ's Passion. Yasin handed Hornkastle a bulging sandwich .

"I have no money, " Hornkastle muttered.

The Arab beamed and shook his head. "My gift! Christ will rise!"

His eyes found Hornkastle's and lingered there a long while in what was almost a kind of communion itself. Hornkastle had no idea of what was being communicated, but it left him with a sense of warmth, of trust, of faith. Perhaps Claudia was right, that this is the city of divine grace, of second chances. He thanked Yasin and gobbled the sandwich as if he had not eaten in weeks.

Let it begin soon, he prayed. At last: let it begin.

The boy was still at his side. He had the village face, too, triangular, but his eyes were gentler. Hornkastle realized that the boy had appointed himself his guide. All right. They ploughed together through the hordes and eventually carne to the courtyard of the Omarieh School, where a sign proclaimed the First Station of the Cross. Pilate had sentenced Jesus here. The crowd was flowing up the Via Dolorosa here, slowly, ecstatically, praying in many languages, singing, chanting. Wherever Hornkastle looked, he saw pilgrims tottering under immense wooden crosses, gasping and struggling and staggering. His head throbbed. He felt light-headed, giddy, weightless. He let himself be swept along, to the place where Jesus first had fallen—marked by a broken column—and then up the narrow, killingly steep Via Dolorosa through an Arab bazaar. Claudia and Helena, or two women just like them, were nearby, reading out of a guidebook. You were right, he said to them, not bothering to use words. This *is* the city of second chances. "The Fourth Station," said the younger. "Where Jesus met his fainting Mother. This church is Our Lady of the Spasm. The Fifth: Simon of Cyrene carried the cross here. The Sixth, where Veronica wiped the face of Jesus." It was a hard climb now. Hornkastle felt rivulets of sweat on his body.

He was amazed how intense colors were becoming, how bright everything looked, how strange. The walls of the ancient houses seemed furry and were undulating slightly. The voices of those about him dwindled and swelled, dwindled and swelled, as though some amplifier were being turned up and down. Marching beside him was Ben-Horin, implausibly wearing a friar's cassock. He leaned close and in his crisp, cutting way whispered into Hornkastle's ear, "So you study the ceremony after all. Perhaps at last you learn a thing or two." Out of a doorway came Geula Ben-Horin with some sort of Halloween costume on, stripes and splotches of green and scarlet and brilliant yellow. A succubus, perhaps. She winked at Hornkastle and shimmied her hips. "Put this in your thesis," she murmured, throaty voiced, a kosher Mae West. The two Israelis danced around him, melted and flowed, and were gone. Hornkastle pawed at his eyes. He would have fallen, for his legs were growing swollen and rubbery, but the press of the crowd was too tight. "This is the Seventh Station, where Jesus fell the second time," said the cool clear voice behind him, and the tones echoed and reverberated until they were tolling like gongs. Just ahead a dozen Arabs in dark blue suits were singing some ominous hymn as they hauled their cross along; he perceived the words of the song as individual gleaming blades that severed each instant from the next. "And here," said the woman, "Jesus spoke to the compassionate daughters of Jerusalem. This is where He fell the third time. We are nearly at the end of the Via Dolorosa. The last five stations are within the Church of the Holy Sepulchre."

Hornkastle felt the ancient paving stones squirming and sliding beneath his feet. He stumbled and would have pitched headlong but the blue-suited Arabs caught him, laughing and cheering now, and passed him from hand to hand, tossed him about like a sack of old clothes, moved him uphill. He saw a woman in an upper window making the sign of the cross at him and throwing kisses. The hymn was unbearably loud.

His back was pressed up against the Arabs' enormous wooden cross. He saw clearly, as though he were at a movie, how a dozen men with the same triangular face and fierce swollen eyes were holding him in place and driving in the nails. It was not the nails that bothered him but the sound of the hammer blows, which rang in his head with clamorous frenzy. Hornkastle went limp and let it happen to him. A voice as mighty as that of Zeus cried, "Help him, he's having a fit!" But Hornkastle simply smiled and shook his head. All was well. Push me, kick me, do whatever you want to me. I am yours. God is in me, he thought. God is everywhere, but especially He is within me. He could taste the fiery presence of the Godhead on his lips, his tongue, deep in his belly. They had the cross upright now. "Make room! Get him out of here before he's trampled!" No. No. There are still five more Stations of the Cross, are there not? We have not reached the end of the Via Dolorosa. Hornkastle felt utterly tranquil. This is the true *ekstasis,* the parting of the soul from the body. He closed his eyes.

When he returned to consciousness, he found himself lying in a hospital bed with a placid sweet-faced nun watching him. His arms were rigidly outstretched, his fingers were tightly coiled, the palms of his hands seemed to be on fire, and wave upon wave of nausea swept across his middle. From far away came the sound of wild bells ringing and the roar of mad voices crying a rhythmic slogan over and over.

To the nun he said faintly, "What are they shouting? I can't make it out." She touched his blazing forehead lightly and replied, *"Christos, anesti, Christos anesti,* Christ is risen!"

HOW THEY PASS THE TIME
IN PELPEL

Writing "A Thousand Paces on the Via Dolorosa" had been a pleasing experience, even if I didn't succeed in getting it published in the magazine for which I had intended it. The story had a certain fantastic quality about it, and yet it was set right in our here-and-now twentieth-century reality, not on some remote planet or in some distant era. And, since Ted Klein, the editor of Twilight Zone, had received "Dolorosa" so enthusiastically, I set out soon afterward to write another one in the same vein for him.

The idea behind it was given to me by the famous botanist and horticulturalist Paul Hutchison, who ran a wonderful nursery full of exotic plants in Southern California that I frequently visited. (My garden in California is full of the sort of weird science-fictional plants that Paul's nursery specialized in.) Paul had also been a science-fiction reader for many decades, and we struck up a close friendship based on our two great shared interests. He had made a number of botanical expeditions to the particularly arid and forbidding coast of Chile, and on one of my visits he told me an anecdote—not a story—about something he had observed in a small town down there while on one of his cactus-collecting journeys.

"You ought to make a story out of it," he said.

"I will," I told him.

And I did, in November of 1980, using his situation but adding characters, plot, and a resolution to the central anecdote he had provided, and making Paul himself the narrator. I was pleased with the result; so was Paul, who was fascinated by the way a professional writer had gone about

115

manufacturing a complete story out of a slender anecdote; and Ted Klein of the Twilight Zone *magazine sent me a nice check for it and ran it in his May, 1981 issue.*

"**Y**ou know," Dan Britton said, pointing to a particularly sinister-looking ash-gray cactus on the nursery bench, "all these plants have stories, and some of them are damned strange stories. I don't mean botanical stories. I mean that all these peculiar plants that we grow here in California and that we take pretty much for granted had to be discovered by someone in some nasty corner of the world and collected and brought back and propagated and distributed. And in the process of all that, odd things have occasionally happened to the people who went out and found those plants." He picked up the ash-gray cactus. It was strange even as cacti go, not only because of its deathly color but because of the glossy black spines, heavy and menacing, running in rigidly aligned vertical rows down its sides. "*Copiapoa cinerea,*" said Britton, "from the Atacama Desert in northern Chile. This one and most of the others you'll see are descended from the parent plants that I collected thirty years ago in the Atacama, between Pelpel and Sabroso. I ought to tell you that story some time."

Britton is a compact, weather-beaten-looking man who for the last dozen years or so has run a little nursery in Santa Barbara. That's a quiet town, and he leads a quiet life, selling fuchsias and pelargoniums and chrysanthemums to the local gardeners. But his own enthusiasms run to stranger stuff—proteas and tree aloes and cycads and such—and you can find those things on sale there, too. Now and then he sells one, for in Santa Barbara's gentle climate you can grow almost anything, and a few people thereabouts like to experiment with horticultural strangenesses. Britton never pushes that sort of merchandise, though. He knows that the people who want exotic plants will find them themselves, and the other kind will only mistreat them anyway. He lets the customers do as they please. I don't think running a nursery really interests him. Being around plants, yes: that's what he's done ever since he was a boy. When he was younger, he had a considerable reputation as a field botanist, venturing into remote and unappetizing places, mainly in South America, and coming back with enough unknown cacti and succulents and bromeliads and whatnot to give himself a distinct, if minor, niche in the history of botanical exploration. That's all behind him now, of course. He seems content to be keeping the locals supplied with the standard pretty merchandise that they like, and goes his own way in most things.

Business was slow that winter day, and he closed the nursery about half past four. I was staying overnight. We drove in silence past Mission Santa Barbara and into the foothills where he has his small house, modest adobe surrounded by awesome specimens of botanical rarities. On the way in I saw in his cactus garden a giant clump of the ash-gray *Copiapoa cinerea* that somehow I had never noticed before. Britton nodded. "From the Quebrada Pelpel, east of the town. One of my original specimens, in fact. The Greek told me where to look for them."

"The Greek?"

"It's a long story," Britton said.

He opened a bottle of chilled chenin blanc and we settled on his patio to watch twilight descend on Santa Barbara. An odd winter light made the red-tiled rooftops look almost pink, and fog was beginning to encroach on the harbor. But the air was mild, and the garden surrounding us was lush with blooming things, two enormous aloes sending up giant red spikes and a row of nine-foot-high proteas ablaze with implausibly intricate blossoms and a rare Mexican yucca unfolding a torrent of white flowers. We were halfway through the wine before either of us spoke. Then Britton said, "The Atacama Desert—it must be the driest place in the world. Three, four, five years at a time without any rain, and then maybe an inch, and then dry for two or three more years. But yet there are plants there. They live on the winter fog, the *camanchaca,* and nothing else." He looked straight at me, and his eyes are intense and piercing, but he seemed to be seeing through me into a sere and horrid realm of dryness almost beyond my comprehension. "This happened in January or February of 1952, when I was collecting along the South American coast for the university, trying to make some sense out of the genus *Copiapoa,* which as you may know was at that time very poorly understood and in desperate need of revision—"

❂

My headquarters down there was in Pelpel, a parched little fishing village on the coast a couple of hundred kilometers south of Antofagasta. These days, for all I know, it's a magnificent resort with a high-rise Hilton and a racetrack and six casinos, but I doubt it very much. Back then it was utterly dismal—a thousand people or so living mainly in tin-roofed shacks. Dust blowing everywhere. The water supply was piped in for a few hours every other day. If you went inland a little way, up on the ridges back of town where there's a little fog condensation, you found some cactus growing, but in the town itself nothing at all could grow. You can't imagine how dreary and drab it was. The center of social life was a bleak scruffy plaza that was bordered by a squalid old hotel; and across the way from that a beer parlor and pool hall that was run by a Greek named Panagiotis. The Greek's place had a loudspeaker that blared music into the plaza every evening, and the big event was the grand promenade: single women going around the plaza in one direction, single men in the other, and eventually some couples would form and go off together for the night, and the next night it would all start over.

I was the only guest in the hotel, and from the way people stared at me when I arrived, I suspect that I was the first guest in seven or eight years. The place was clean enough—an old German woman ran it, and she spent hours every day dusting and sweeping—but the beams were dry and shrunken, the plaster was cracking, the roof was a sounding-board that rattled miserably every time the wind blew. My room was upstairs, and I was delighted to find a shower next door—a shower of sorts, anyway, with an overhead bag and a pull-chain. But when I tried to use it, nothing came out but a trickle of sand. Obviously it hadn't held water in a long time. Pelpel was strictly basin-and-sponge-bath territory.

But I didn't mind. I was young and not very concerned with comfort, and I was glad enough to have a roof over my head at all. What really mattered to me were the *Copiapoas* in the hinterlands, not the luxuries available in Pelpel. And I wasn't in Pelpel long before I found out where the *Copiapoas* were.

The Greek helped me. He was the only person in town who showed the slightest warmth toward me. The others simply gave me cold blank stares and tight-lipped scowls, behind which lay an apparent instant hostility that I suppose was the natural response of these hardbitten people—forlorn dwellers in a desolate land—to an intruder, and outsider, a fortunate *Norteamericano* who had come to them out of the cozy world of hot and cold running water, air-conditioning and Technicolor movies. The fact that I spoke only the most basic Spanish at that time, and spoke it with a California/Mexican accent that must have seemed ludicrous, barbarous, and close to unintelligible to these Chileans, did not make it easier for me to win friends in Pelpel.

At least there was Panagiotis. I thought at first that his friendliness was just a professional trait, the standard good-fellowship that any tavern keeper tends to develop, or else that it was only his irrepressible Greek exuberance that led him to greet me with a big toothy smile, whereas I got nothing but sullen frosty scowls from the rest of them. Probably those factors did figure into it to some degree. But also I think he genuinely took a liking to me—that he saw me not as overprivileged and condescending ambassador from a civilization of unimaginable and unattainable marvels, but rather as I really was, a young and rather shy botanist who was voluntarily making a long uncomfortable journey into their disagreeable environment for the sake of bringing back scientific information. I suppose Panagiotis was clever enough to see that what the others must have interpreted as haughtiness and arrogance was actually just the product of my shyness and my difficulties with their language.

I went out into the high county east of the town the first day and came back almost empty-handed. Obviously I am not a person who finds deserts depressing, but this one weighed on my spirits as no other had ever done. It was stark and drab, just bare rock and sand in dull tones of brown and yellow, and dry beyond belief. The desiccated ground was virtually lifeless, no shrubs, no cacti, not even the tiny ground-hugging plants you find in nearly any desert—nothing. Nothing. I could have been on the moon. I wandered for hours in emptiness, growing more discouraged as the day waned. Even though the desert gained in beauty in late afternoon when the sun no longer bleached all color from it and the bare ravines turned dark and mysteriously rich, I sank into a somber, self-pitying mood. It was a mistake to come here, I told myself. I should be up by Iquique, perhaps, or inland on the slopes of the Andes where plant life is more abundant. But of course the whole point of this expedition was to explore this barren and virtually unknown coastal strip, which had not been properly studied by botanists since the pioneering work of Philippi almost a hundred years before.

The afternoon winds stirred up great black clouds of dust, which had the merit of providing me with a spectacular sunset as I trudged back to Pelpel. The rays of the late sun, filtering through the murk and haze, turned from brilliant yellow to a pale violet, and then through a stunningly complex series of ever deeper purples until, suddenly, there was gray and then black. Just before it became dark, I stumbled over what I thought was a rock, and for some reason looked back to discover that I had tripped on an isolated specimen of *Copiapoa cinerea,* a single unbranched plant with short sparse spines, growing, God alone knew why, just a couple of kilometers from town. It was the only plant of interest I had seen in the past six or seven hours. I collected it and went hurrying on into Pelpel as night fell.

Dinner was waiting for me at the hotel—everything out of cans, a watery vegetable soup and some kind of meat stew, washed down by thin, bitter red wine. I ate by myself, served in silence by the Indian woman who seemed to be the hotel's only employee. From across the plaza came the raucous sound of music out of the Greek's loudspeaker. When I was done eating, I walked outside and stood in front of the hotel a long while, watching the townsfolk promenade. Mostly they ignored me. Those that did stare at me stared without amiability and essentially without curiosity. I shrugged and went to my room, but that made things even worse—the bare walls, the fissure in the plaster, the single dim light-bulb, the sound of the dry ugly wind. The idea of trying to work or study or even to relax in such a room until it was time to sleep was a dismal one. And so, although I'm not what anyone would call a drinking man, I found myself going across the plaza to the beer-parlor, simply to have some sort of human contact and a bit of cheer on this cheerless evening in this cheerless town.

Some two dozen men were in the place, mostly gathered around the pool-table, a few slouched at the warped and discolored bar. The look I got from them as I appeared in the doorway was so frigid that I nearly turned and fled. But then Panagiotis boomed out, "Hello, *Norteamericano!* You come in! You have drink with us!" It was impossible to refuse.

The Greek was a big thickset man of about fifty, with gleaming buck teeth and a broad conspicuous nose. His black hair was all but gone, combed across his skull in sparse strands between which a freckled and deeply tanned scalp showed through. He spoke a little English and understood my Spanish, and we were able to communicate. First he tapped the bottles around him on the bar—Peruvian *pisco* and various local brandies and rums and some kind of Scotch that was labeled *Hecho in Mexico,* but I shook them off, not wanting anything so strong after having had wine with dinner, and said, *"Hay cerveza?"* Panagiotis laughed and groped under the bar and came up with a dusty bottle of tepid beer. Getting it down was a challenge, and after that I drank *pisco*.

He introduced me to the other men at the bar. The very tall, almost skeletal one with the sunken burning eyes and the knifelike cheekbones was his brother-in-law, Ramon Sotomayor. The fat one beyond him was Aguirre, the lawyer, and the one with faded red hair was Nuñez de Prado, the doctor, and that was Mendoza, the pharmacist, and so on. Each, when his name was mentioned, gave me a glum, surly glare and a brief reluctant nod of salutation, and that was all.

And then Panagiotis—who, like everyone else, knew from the moment of my arrival that I was here to collect plants—asked me what I was looking for. Cactus, I said, curving my fingers to pantomime their shapes. I had been out all day, I told him, but I had had *mala suerte,* bad luck, I had found *nada.* Panagiotis listened sympathetically. He conferred with Mendoza and Aguirre in Spanish that was too fast and idiomatic for me to understand, and then began drawing crude maps on bar napkins, accompanying his diagrams with a running commentary in broken English and a kind of pidgin Spanish. The maps were impossible to understand. I smiled and held up a hand and ran back to the hotel—a little tipsily—and got my own set of charts, and we spread them out on the bar. The others muttered and grumbled as though Panagiotis were giving me the location of secret gold mines, but he paid no attention to them and marked for me the places where I thought I would find what I was after. Then he slapped me on the back and filled my glass for the third or fourth time. He would take no payment. Eventually I got back to my room, head spinning, and not even the strident sounds of the loudspeaker music kept me awake for long.

The next day I started at dawn, going as far as I could in my battered jeep, covering the last few kilometers on foot. The Greek had guided me toward the rough ravines of the Quebrada Pelpel, ten kilometers east of town, where I already knew Philippi had collected in 1854. Sure enough, I found dense stands of *Copiapoa cinerea* there, several different populations including some plants with bizarre crested stems—the only such deformities ever observed in this species. That night I thanked Panagiotis warmly, and he filled me full of *pisco* until I begged him to stop and turned my glass bottomside up.

And over the days that followed I went south across that silent, ghostly desert into the Sierra Esmeralda, and north along the coastal road to Sabroso, the next town up, and inland along the low plateaus, and I found *cinerea* in a wide range of forms, some with brown spines, some with yellowish ones, some so old they were almost spineless. In the hills above Sabroso I discovered the practically unknown *Copiapoa humilis,* a small plant with roots like turnips, last seen by Philippi in 1860. It's a difficult plant to find, because its dark color is much like that of the surrounding soil, and in times when even the fogs fail it protects itself against desiccation by pulling itself down into the earth until it almost vanishes. After looking in vain for it for hours, I discovered that I had sat right down on one clump of it—fortunately the spines are not very threatening—and thereafter I found plenty of them.

In this time I grew no closer to the people of Pelpel. The only one who as much as spoke to me was Panagiotis, and our conversations were limited by language barriers to the simplest themes. To the others I remained a total alien, unwanted, intrusive, resented. Their blank-eyed disdain was harder for me to take than solitude itself. I felt more comfortable by myself in the midst of a desert all but devoid of life than I did in that town. There was no reason for the locals to love me—they are a strange people, confined by the nature of their country to a narrow and rigid existence in their little oasis—but there wasn't any need for them to treat me as if I had come to steal from them or spy on them. Unless, possibly, they suspected me of secretly being an anthropologist trying to pry into their private ways, for I knew that in these coastal towns some odd customs had evolved out of the mixing of Indian and Spanish blood, a religion in which primitive native rites had been somehow hybridized into the Christian worship, and no doubt they wanted no investigation of that. But I think I never gave them cause to suspect I was anything other than what I said I was.

One afternoon I returned to town after a particularly trying and exhausting field trip, and, barely touching the pathetic dinner the Indian woman set out for me, I went to my room and fell into a deep sleep. A few hours later—it was still early evening—I was awakened by the sound of the Greek's loudspeaker. Booming through the plaza, blurred and distorted by echoes and feedback and the crudity of the equipment, was a man's voice, speaking excitedly and rapidly, delivering what sounded like a news broadcast or, more likely, the commentary on some big sporting event.

Puzzled, I peered out my window. A grand commotion was going on in the plaza. Half the population of Pelpel seemed to be out there, not just those who made the spooky, silent nightly promenades around the plaza's edge. Hundreds of people were gathered, in groups of ten or a dozen or so, listening intently to the broadcast, occasionally cheering, shaking their heads, pointing at the loudspeaker as if arguing with it. I saw money changing hands, too—men taking crumpled wads of hundred-peso notes from their shirts and giving them to others. Every few minutes some loud outcry from the radio voice brought new cheers and groans from the crowd, and more bills went fluttering back and forth.

I went outside, hoping to find out what was going on. Usually when I appeared all activity halted and the townsfolk gave me looks of dark glowering anger as though I were death at the feast. I was a little hesitant to leave the hotel now, not wanting to sour their festivity. But to my surprise they seemed, for the first time, glad to see me. Some of them waved, some of them grinned, some of them tossed their hats in the air. "Norteamericano!" they cried. "Hola, Norteamericano! Viva! Viva!" What was all *that* about? They surrounded me, coming up close, peering right into my face and winking, slapping me on the back like old friends. The change of attitude was absolute and dramatic And also a little frightening. I've studied some anthropology. I began to wonder whether I had been chosen for the starring role in some grim municipal ritual that was to be the peak of this mystifying event. I glanced around for the Greek, looking for explanations, but he was nowhere in sight, and the crowd was too thick for me to get across the plaza to his cantina.

Amid all the chaos I stood still and listened, desperately trying to make sense out of the broadcast. And gradually I began to understand a little of it. The announcer was naming local towns—Santa Catalina, Casabindo, San Antonio, Placilla—which I recognized as dusty little way-stations along the inland roads. And he was calling off names— Godoy, de la Gasca, Lezaeta, Alejandro. I gathered that some sort of automobile race was going on out there. In the harsh and forbidding wastelands of the Atacama Desert, under a black moonless sky, men were roaring across the pitted and parched terrain in motorcars, and here in Pelpel frantic wagering was going on over the ultimate outcome and, so it seemed, over the separate stages of the race.

As I listened with growing comprehension I realized that one of the drivers was an American. *El Nortecamericano,* the announcer kept saying, was doing very well. *El Norteamericano* was showing great skill. *El Norteamericano* was demonstrating true virtuosity on the dangerous track. And every time the announcer mentioned this unknown countryman of mine, the townspeople around me grinned and cheered and waved at me, and made V-for-victory signs, as if they were rooting for him as a way of making amends for their coldness toward me. They pointed and shouted something at me again and again that at first I was unable to understand, until I picked up the verb *vencer* drifting to me like a word out of a vivid dream, and realized that they were telling me, "You will win!" *Me?*

So frenzied and feverish was the scene that only slowly did I start to consider the baffling, inexplicable, downright impossible aspects of what I was hearing.

The road they were racing on was the same one that I had driven so many times in the past ten or twelve days—a miserable, hopeless washboard track that ran along the coast from Pelpel to Sabroso, then curved inland, practically disappearing into the dust and rocky subsoil, and hooked up briefly with the Pan-American Highway. That road was a killer even for jeeps. What kind of supernatural shocks and springs did the racing cars have? How could the drivers possibly be moving at the speeds the announcer was talking about? just to get from Placilla to San Antonio was a harrowing half-day project, with pebbles clanging against your oil pan every foot of the way. It was absurd to think of that narrow scratchy dirt-on-dirt track as a racecourse.

Another little mystery was how the announcer was getting his information. In rapid-fire narrative he was giving continuous reports on at least a dozen drivers spread out between Sabroso and Pelpel. I suppose that could have been done by posting him in a helicopter above the scene, but this was thirty years ago, remember, when helicopters were still rare, especially in out-of-the-way corners of Chile. Perhaps observers stationed along the course were phoning in a steady flow of news that the announcer was deftly weaving together to create his running account, but there weren't even any telephones in the town, let alone out there in the open wastelands. Radio communication? Perhaps. Smoke signals, for all I knew, or a semaphore relay? One guess was as good as another. The whole thing didn't make sense.

It was just as hard to figure out where the broadcast was coming from. Radio stations simply didn't exist in these parts. The music that Panagiotis played through his loudspeaker every night came from ancient phonograph records. There were radio stations in the south down by Valparaiso and Santiago, hundreds of miles away, but their signals didn't get up here. The nearest northern station was probably even further, in Lima, but the curve of the continent put the wall of the Andes between us and it. Short wave, then? Well, maybe. Or maybe some fluky transmission out of the Valparaiso station, although it was hard to see why they would want to devote hours of valuable air-time to an obscure automobile race in a sleepy pocket of the desert.

When I looked toward the northern side of the plaza where the road from Placilla came in, I saw the biggest puzzle of all. A length of sturdy twine, gaudily bedecked with red and green and yellow streamers, had been strung across the road to mark what was obviously the finish line. Boys were stationed on either side of the street with Chilean flags atop long poles, no doubt to wave in the victor's face as he came thundering down the home stretch. How, though, could they expect to conclude the long race right in the middle of Pelpel? A mere fifty or sixty feet behind the finish line was the high brick wall of the church. Did anyone seriously think that a car speeding through the line was going to be able to brake in time to avoid hitting that wall? I thought I must be mistaken, that this was no finish line but merely some kind of ceremonial halting point to which the winner would coast after passing the true finish line somewhere outside of town. But no, this certainly was decked out the way the terminus of a motor race ought to be decked out, and the townspeople were carefully keeping the road in front of it clear, as if they expected cars to go zooming into the plaza at any instant. And some of them were staring expectantly into the blackness of the night beyond the floodlit plaza, trying to make out the headlights of the finishers as they approached the end of the race.

Mystery on mystery. Bewildering, dreamlike, almost hallucinatory—I could make no sense out of any of it. This alien ritual left me feeling more thoroughly alone and out of place in Pelpel than ever before.

And yet, in the giddy and tense carnival atmosphere of the moment, nearly everyone was cheerful and friendly. They clustered around me, offering me drinks, cigarettes, rough *macho* handshakes, splay-toothed grins, winks, nudges. Through the air came the cracking boom of the loudspeaker, the voice furry and distorted, calling out the twists and surprises of the race. It was all but impossible for me to comprehend. Was that Alejandro in the lead, now? Or the *Norteamericano*? Was he saying that Lezaeta's car had gone spinning off the track passing the quebrada? And had someone else overturned just outside Sabroso? It was dreamlike, yes, eerie, confusing—little blips and fragments of information, alternating with static, cheering, shouting, and torrents of the bewildering local dialect. The crowd was wholly caught up in it, following each event of the race with wild excitement. They seemed to be making bets constantly—not just on the ultimate winner, so far as I could tell, but on who would be in the lead at certain key points along the course, and even on who would get through the race without a spin-out or a stall—and the hundred-peso notes were going swiftly from hand to hand. Whenever the *Norteamericano* racer was mentioned, the cheering grew more intense and the people surrounding me laughed and clapped as if to tell me that they liked me more and more because my valiant countryman was performing so well. I wondered who this American racer might be and what he was doing in these parts and whether he would make it safely to Pelpel that evening. It had been too many weeks since I had had a coherent conversation with someone whose language I understood.

The race appeared to be reaching its climax now.

Sotomayor, the Greek's brother-in-law, came swaggering up out of the chaos. He loomed ominously over me, at least a foot taller than I am, though I doubt he weighed a hundred forty pounds—a knifeblade of a man, matador-thin, cold, unfathomable. He glowered at me and said icily, "You will not win."

I had no idea what to say.

"You will lose," he said, as though he felt he needed to clarify his first statement.

I shrugged. He was drunk and wobbling, and I was so captivated by the sudden and unexpected friendliness of everyone else around me that I resented having Sotomayor spoil the mood of cordiality. Something possessed me and I tugged my wallet our of my pocket. In a reckless way—on this expedition I had no funds to waste—I pulled out five hundred-peso notes. The Chilean peso was then worth something like three cents, so a hundred pesos was no great fortune, but I could hardly stand to lose even the fifteen dollars that the five bills represented. Nevertheless I glared up at Sotomayor and said, "On the *Norteamericano* to win. *Cinco cientos.*"

"You bet with me?"

"I bet, yes."

Sotomayor laughed. With a vast flamboyant gesture of his great spidery arms he drew forth a purse from a money belt and counted out *ten* hundred-peso notes, holding each one up so that I could count along with him. His eyes gleamed mockingly in the glaring light of the plaza lamps. He was giving me odds of two to one, unasked—a gesture of contempt, of humiliation. He swept my bills from my hand, folded them into the ten he was holding, wrapped them all in a wad and handed them to fat Aguirre, the lawyer, who stood nearby and somehow had been appointed keeper of the stakes in that moment.

The crowd was screaming. It was all but impossible to make out the announcer's words now.

I said to Aguirre, "Do you know where the racers are at this minute?"

He pointed past the finish line and vaguely up the dark highway. "Two kilometers from Pelpel."

Even on that dreadful road it wouldn't take long to cover two kilometers. The race was almost over. The screaming was frantic. Along with everyone else I looked toward the finish line. I still was unable to understand how the race could possibly end in Pelpel; I imagined the leading drivers barreling down the narrow road, passing between the tin-roofed shacks, roaring across the finish line into the plaza, smashing willy-nilly into the church wall, piling up in a great flaming mound of wreckage, car upon car upon car—

Sudden silence. The voice of the announcer, cracking with the strain:

"Alejandro…Godoy…*Norteamericano*…Alejandro…*Norteamericano*…*Norteamericano*…*Norteamericano primero*…"

Silence.

Everyone frozen, peering out into the night.

"*Norteamericano* wins! Alejandro second! Godoy third!"

Wins? How? Where?

At the far side of the plaza they were tearing down the finish line, pulling off the streamers, fluttering them like banners, and the two flag-bearers were capering about, waving the flags. A mad celebration was beginning, a wild crazy leaping and prancing. But where were the cars?

The road was empty. The race was over and no one had arrived in Pelpel.

I began to understand, but I could not believe that I understood what I thought I understood. I had to find Panagiotis. In the madness of the plaza, with everyone going berserk and hundred-peso notes flapping about like confetti, it was not easy to get to the far side, but I pushed and elbowed my way across and finally entered the cantina. The Greek sat wearily slouched behind the bar, face shiny with sweat, eyes glossy, a drink in one hand and a microphone in the other. He smiled and nodded when he saw me.

"You drove well," he said.

"I?"

"Very well. We are proud of you."

I sat down facing him. "The race was imaginary?" I asked.

No le entiendo.

"Imaginary. You made it up. You invented it. You sat here all evening with that microphone, pretending that a race was going on out in the desert, right?"

"Yes."

"And the *Norteamericano* who was racing—he was me?"

"Yes."

"And the people believe all this? They think there really was a race?"

Panagiotis grinned. "In Pelpel life is very quiet. This is the most real race we have. This is how we pass the time in Pelpel. The people of Pelpel understand what is real and what is not real, better than you think."

"How—often do you have a race?"

"Whenever we need it. Perhaps every two, three months. Sometimes more often. We did this now, in your honor."

"And let me win?"

"Because you would be more popular in Pelpel," said Panagiotis. "You did not have many friends here. Now everyone is your friend in Pelpel."

"Except Sotomayor," I said.

And just then, as if on cue, Sotomayor and his cronies entered the tavern. There was a black gleam in Sotomayor's eyes that I hope never to see again anywhere. He looked at me with loathing and at his brother-in-law with absolute rage, and said something quick and curt in Spanish that I could not understand but which made a sound like the spitting out of teeth. He pointed to me, to Panagiotis, to the microphone. It was very quiet in the cantina. The pharmacist, Mendoza, laughed nervously, but it did not break the tension.

"You have made me a fool," said Sotomayor to Panagiotis.

The Greek replied, "Only a fool can make a fool. But here, Ramon. Let us drink together and make amends."

He swung around and picked up the bottle of *pisco*. When he turned back to face the rest of us, a small shiny snub-nosed pistol had appeared in Sotomayor's hand, and Panagiotis' mouth made a silent little O of amazement, and Sotomayor shot him once, drilling a small startling hole in the center of the Greek's broad, sloping freckled forehead.

Aguirre put a thick wad of hundred-peso notes into my hand. I had won my bet with Sotomayor, after all. Then he and Mendoza and Nuñez de Prado and Ramon Sotomayor turned and walked out of the bar, leaving me alone with the dead Panagiotis.

Britton paused and poured the last of the chenin blanc into my glass and his. Night had fallen over Santa Barbara and the lights of boats sparkled in the marina and I heard distant foghorns. After a moment Britton said, "The next morning I packed up my *Copiapoas* and left town. The Plaza was absolutely deserted, and the only traces of the events of the night before were the shreds and tatters of the colored streamers. I never found out what happened to Sotomayor. And now, I suppose, they have some other way of passing the time in Pelpel."

THE PALACE AT MIDNIGHT

I live just across the bay from San Francisco, which is probably the most beautiful city in the United States, and which also has a well-deserved reputation for eccentricity going back to its earliest Gold Rush days. Much of what goes on in San Francisco strikes me as amusing, though some of it seems downright silly, and a lot of it (the endless political demonstrations, for example) causes real inconvenience for its residents. But since I don't actually live in the city, just nearby, and can enjoy its beauty, its restaurants, and its cultural advantages without having to get entangled very often in its politics, the wilder antics of the San Franciscans rarely have much direct impact on my life and I can afford to look upon the place with some degree of affection and tolerance, however exasperating the behavior of its citizens may be. I think that attitude shows through in "The Palace at Midnight," which was yet another of the stories I wrote during my productive autumn of 1980 and sold to Robert Sheckley in the final months of his tenure as fiction editor of Omni, *where it was published in the issue of July, 1981.*

The foreign minister of the Empire of San Francisco was trying to sleep late. Last night had been a long one, a wild if not particularly gratifying party at the baths, too much to drink, too much to smoke, and he had seen the dawn come up like thunder out of Oakland 'crost the bay. Now the telephone was ringing. He integrated the first couple of rings nicely into his dream, but the next one began to undermine his slumber, and the one after that woke him up. He groped for the receiver and, eyes still closed, managed to croak, "Christensen here."

"Tom, are you awake? You don't sound awake. It's Morty."

The undersecretary for external affairs. Christensen sat up, rubbed his eyes, ran his tongue around his lips. Daylight was streaming into the room. His cats were glaring at him from the doorway. The little Siamese pawed daintily at her empty bowl and looked up expectantly.

"Tom?"

"I'm up, I'm up! What is it, Morty?"

"I didn't mean to wake you. How was I supposed to know, one in the afternoon—"

"What is it, Morty?"

"We got a call from Monterey. There's an ambassador on the way up and you've got to meet with her."

The foreign minister worked hard at clearing the fog from his brain. He was thirty-nine years old and all-night parties took more out of him than they once had.

"You do it, Morty."

"You know I would, Tom. But I can't. You've got to handle this one yourself. It's prime."

"Prime? What kind of prime? Like a great dope deal? Or are they declaring war on us?"

"How would I know the details? The call came in and they said it was prime, Ms. Sawyer must confer with Mr. Christensen. It wouldn't involve dope, Tom. And it can't be war, either. Shit, why would Monterey want to make war on us? They've only got but ten soldiers, I bet, unless they're drafting the Chicanos out of the Salinas *calabozo,* and—"

"All right." Christensen's head was buzzing. "Go easy on the chatter, okay? Where am I supposed to meet her?"

"Berkeley."

"You're kidding."

"She won't come into the city. She thinks it's too dangerous over here."

"What do we do, kill ambassadors and barbecue them? She'll be safe here and she knows it."

"I talked to her. She thinks the city's too crazy. She'll go as far as Berkeley, but that's it."

"Tell her to go to hell."

"Tom, Tom—"

Christensen sighed. "Where in Berkeley will she be?"

"The Claremont, at half past four."

"Jesus," Christensen said. "How did you get me into this? All the way across to the East Bay to meet a lousy ambassador from Monterey! Let her come to San Francisco. This is the Empire, isn't it? They're only a stinking republic. Am I supposed to swim over to Oakland every time an envoy shows up and wiggles a finger? Some bozo from Fresno says boo and I have to haul my ass out to the valley, eh? Where does it stop? What kind of clout do I have, anyway?"

"Tom—"

"I'm sorry, Morty. I don't feel like a goddamned diplomat this morning."

"It isn't morning any more, Tom. But I'd do it for you if I could."

"All right. All right. I didn't mean to yell at you. You make the ferry arrangements?"

"Ferry leaves at three-thirty. Chauffeur will pick you up at your place at three, okay?"

"Okay." Christensen said. "See if you can find out any more about all this and have somebody call me back in an hour with a briefing, will you?"

He fed the cats, showered, shaved, took a couple of pills, brewed some coffee. At half past two the ministry called. Nobody had any idea what the ambassador might want. Relations between San Francisco and the Republic of Monterey were cordial just now. Ms. Sawyer lived in Pacific Grove and was a member of the Monterey Senate and that was all that was known about her. Some briefing, Christensen thought. He went downstairs to wait for his chauffeur. It was a late autumn day, bright and clear and cool. The rains hadn't begun yet and the streets looked dusty. The foreign minister lived on Frederick Street just off Cole, in an old white Victorian with a small front porch. He settled in on the steps, feeling wide awake but surly, and a few minutes before three his car came putt-putting up, a venerable gray Chevrolet with the arms of imperial San Francisco on its doors. The driver was Vietnamese or maybe Thai. Christensen got in without a word, and off they went at an imperial velocity through the practically empty streets, down to Haight, eastward for a while, then onto Oak, up Van Ness past the palace, where at this moment the Emperor Norton VII was probably taking his imperial nap, and along Geary through downtown to the ferry slip. The stump of the Bay Bridge glittered magically against the sharp blue sky. A small power

133

cruiser was waiting for him. Christensen was silent during the slow dull voyage. A chill wind cut through the Golden Gate and made him huddle into himself. He stared broodingly at the low rounded East Bay hills, dry and brown from a long summer of drought, and thought about the permutations of fate that had transformed an adequate architect into the barely competent foreign minister of this barely competent little nation. The Empire of San Francisco, one of the early emperors had said, is the only country in history that was decadent from the day it was founded.

At the Berkeley marina Christensen told the ferry skipper, "I don't know what time I'll be coming back, so no sense waiting. I'll phone in when I'm ready to go."

Another imperial car took him up the hillside to the sprawling nineteenth-century splendor of the Hotel Claremont, that vast antiquated survivor of all the cataclysms. It was seedy now, the grounds a jungle, ivy almost to the tops of the palm trees, and yet it still looked fit to be a palace, hundreds of rooms, magnificent banquet halls. Christensen wondered how often it had guests. There wasn't much tourism these days.

In the parking plaza outside the entrance was a single car, a black-and-white California Highway Patrol job, that had been decorated with the insignia of the Republic of Monterey, a contorted cypress tree and a sea otter. A uniformed driver lounged against it. "I'm Christensen," he told the man.

"You the foreign minister?"

"I'm not the Emperor Norton."

"Come on. She's waiting in the bar."

Ms. Sawyer stood up as he entered—a slender dark-haired woman of about thirty, with cool green eyes—and he flashed her a quick, professionally cordial smile, which she returned just as professionally. He did not feel at all cordial.

"Senator Sawyer," he said. "I'm Tom Christensen."

"Glad to know you." She pivoted and gestured toward the huge picture window that ran the length of the bar. "I just got here. I've been admiring the view. It's been years since I've been in the Bay Area."

He nodded. From the cocktail lounge one could see the slopes of Berkeley, the bay, the ruined bridges, the still imposing San Francisco skyline. Very nice. They took seats by the window and he beckoned to a waiter, who brought them drinks.

"How was your drive up?" Christensen asked.

"No problems. We got stopped for speeding in San Jose, but I got out of it. They could see it was an official car and they stopped us anyway."

"The bastards. They love to look important."

"Things haven't been good between Monterey and San Jose all year. They're spoiling for trouble."

"I hadn't heard," Christensen said.

"We think they want to annex Santa Cruz. Naturally we can't put up with that. Santa Cruz is our buffer."

He said sharply, "Is that what you came here for, to ask our help against San Jose?"

She stared at him in surprise. "Are you in a hurry, Mr. Christensen?"

"Not particularly."

"You sound awfully impatient. We're still making preliminary conversation, having a drink, two diplomats playing the diplomatic game. Isn't that so?"

"Well?"

"I was telling you what happened to me on the way north. In response to your question. Then I was filling you in on current political developments. I didn't expect you to snap at me like that."

"Did I snap?"

"It sounded like snapping to me," she said.

Christensen took a deep pull of his bourbon and water and gave her a long steady look. She met his gaze imperturbably. She looked annoyed, amused and very very tough. After a time, when some of the red haze of irrational anger and fatigue had cleared from his mind, he said quietly, "I had about four hours sleep last night and I wasn't expecting an envoy from Monterey today. I'm tired and edgy, and if I sounded impatient or harsh or snappish, I'm sorry."

"It's all right. I understand."

"Another bourbon or two and I'll be properly unwound." He held his empty glass toward the hovering waiter. "A refill for you, too?" he asked her.

"Yes. Please." In a formal tone she said, "Is the Emperor in good health?"

"Not bad. He hasn't really been well for a couple of years, but he's holding his own. And President Morgan?"

"Fine," she said. "Hunting wild boar in Big Sur this week."

"A nice life it must be, President of Monterey. I've always liked Monterey. So much quieter and cleaner and more sensible down there than in San Francisco."

"Too quiet sometimes. I envy you the excitement here."

"Yes. The rapes, the muggings, the arson, the mass meetings, the race wars, the—"

"Please," she said gently.

He realized he had begun to rant. There was a throbbing behind his eyes. He worked to gain control of himself.

"Did my voice get too loud?"

"You must be terribly tired. Look, we can confer in the morning if you'd prefer. It isn't *that* urgent. Suppose we have dinner and not talk politics at all and get rooms here, and tomorrow after breakfast we can—"

"No," Christensen said. "My nerves are a little ragged, that's all. But I'll try to be more civil. And I'd rather not wait until tomorrow to find out what this is all about. Suppose you give me a précis of it now, and if it sounds too complicated, I'll sleep on it and we can discuss it in detail tomorrow. Yes?"

"All right." She put her drink down and sat quite still, as if arranging her thoughts. At length she said, "The Republic of Monterey maintains close ties with the Free State of Mendocino. I understand that Mendocino and the Empire broke off relations a little while back."

"A fishing dispute; nothing major."

"But you have no direct contact with them right now. Therefore this should come as news to you. The Mendocino people have learned, and have communicated to our representative there, that an invasion of San Francisco is imminent."

Christensen blinked twice. "By whom?"

"The Realm of Wicca," she said.

"Flying down from Oregon on their broomsticks?"

"Please. I'm being serious."

"Unless things have changed up there," Christensen said, "the Realm of Wicca is nonviolent, like all the neopagan states. As I understand it, they tend their farms and practice their little pagan rituals and do a lot of dancing around the maypole and chanting and screwing, and that's it. You expect me to believe that a bunch of gentle goofy witches is going to make war on the Empire?"

She said, "Not war. But definitely an invasion."

"Explain."

"One of their high priests has proclaimed San Francisco a holy place and has instructed them to come down here and build a Stonehenge in Golden Gate Park in time for proper celebration of the winter solstice. There are at least a quarter of a million neopagans in the Willamette Valley and more than half of them are expected to take part. According to our Mendocino man, the migration has already begun, and thousands of Wiccans are spread out between Mount Shasta and Ukiah right now. The solstice is only seven weeks away. The Wiccans may be gentle, but you're going to have a hundred fifty thousand of them in San Francisco by the end of the month, pitching tents all over town."

"Holy Jesus," Christensen muttered, and closed his eyes.

"Can you feed that many strangers? Can you find room for them? Are the people of San Francisco going to meet them with open arms? Is it going to be a festival of love?"

"It'll be a fucking massacre," Christensen said tonelessly.

"Yes. And the witches may be nonviolent but they know how to practice self-defense. Once they're attacked, there'll be rivers of blood in the city, and it won't all be Wiccan blood."

Christensen's head was pounding again. She was absolutely right—chaos, strife, bloodshed. And a merry Christmas to all. He rubbed his aching forehead, turned away from her and stared out at the deepening twilight and the sparkling lights of the city on the other side of the bay. A bleak bitter depression was taking hold of his spirit. He signaled for another round of drinks. Then he said slowly, "They can't be allowed to enter the city. We'll need to close the imperial frontier and turn them back before they get as far as Santa Rosa. Let them build their god-damned Stonehenge in Sacramento if they like." His eyes flickered. He started to assemble ideas. "The Empire might just have enough troops to contain the Wiccans by itself, but I think this is best handled as a regional problem. We'll call in forces from our allies as far out as Petaluma and Napa and Palo Alto. I don't imagine we can expect much help from the Free State or from San Jose. And of course Monterey isn't much of a military power, but still—"

"We are willing to help you," Ms. Sawyer said.

"To what extent?"

"We aren't set up for much actual warfare, no, but we have access to our own alliances from Salinas down to Paso Robles, and we could call up, say, five thousand troops all told."

"That would be very helpful," said Christensen.

"It shouldn't be necessary for there to be any combat. With the imperial border sealed and troops posted along the line from Guerneville to Sacramento, the Wiccans won't force the issue. They'll revise their revelation and celebrate the solstice somewhere else."

"Yes," he said. "I think you're right." He leaned toward her and said, "Why is Monterey willing to help us?"

"We have problems of our own brewing—with San Jose. If we are seen making a conspicuous gesture of solidarity with the Empire, it might discourage San Jose from proceeding with its notion of annexing Santa Cruz, don't you think? That amounts to an act of war against us. Surely San Jose isn't interested in making any moves that will bring the Empire down on its back."

"I see," said Christensen. She wasn't subtle, but she was effective. Quid pro quo, we help you keep the witches out, you help us keep San Jose in line, and all remains well without a shot being fired. These goddamned little nations, he thought, these absurd jerkwater sovereignties, with their wars and alliances and shifting confederations—it was like a game, it was like playground politics. Except that it was real. What had fallen apart was not going to be put back together, not for a long while, and this miniaturized *weltpolitik* was the realest reality there was just now. At least things were saner in Northern California than they were down south where Los Angeles was gobbling everything, but there were rumors that Pasadena had the bomb. Nobody had to contend with that up here. Christensen said, "I'll have to propose all this to the defense ministry, of course. And get the Emperor's approval. But basically I'm in agreement with your thinking."

"I'm so pleased."

"And I'm very glad that you took the trouble to travel up from Monterey to make these matters clear to us."

"Enlightened self-interest," Ms. Sawyer said.

"Mmm. Yes." He found himself studying the sharp planes of her cheekbones, the delicate arch of her eyebrows. Not only was she cool and competent, Christensen thought, but now that the business part of their meeting was over, he was coming to notice that she was a very attractive woman and that he was not as tired as he had thought he was. Did international politics allow room for a little recreational hanky-panky? Metternich hadn't jumped into bed with Talleyrand, nor Kissinger with Indira Gandhi, but times had changed, after all, and—

no. *No.* He choked off that entire line of thought. In these shabby days they might all be children playing at being grownups, but nevertheless, international politics still had its code, and this was a meeting of diplomats, not a blind date or a singles-bar pickup. You will sleep in your own bed tonight, he told himself, and you will sleep alone.

All the same he said, "It's past six o'clock. Shall we have dinner together before I go back to the city?"

"I'd love to."

"I don't know much about Berkeley restaurants. We're probably better off eating right here."

"I think that's best," she said.

They were the only ones in the hotel's enormous dining room. A staff of three waited on them as though they were the most important people who had ever dined there. And dinner turned out to be quite decent, he thought—seafood, calamari and abalone and sand dabs and grilled thresher shark, washed down by a dazzling bottle of Napa chardonnay. Even though the world had ended, it remained possible to eat very well in the Bay Area, and the breakdown of society not only had reduced maritime pollution but also had made local seafood much more readily available for local consumption. There wasn't much of an export trade possible with eleven national boundaries and eleven sets of customs barriers between San Francisco and Los Angeles.

Dinner conversation was light, relaxed—diplomatic chitchat, gossip about events in remote territories, reports about the Voodoo principality expanding out of New Orleans and the Sioux conquests in Wyoming and the Prohibition War now going on in what used to be Kentucky. There was a bison herd again on the Great Plains, she said, close to a million head. He told her what he had heard about the Suicide People who ruled between San Diego and Tijuana and about King Barnum & Bailey III who governed in northern Florida with the aid of a court of circus freaks. She smiled and said, "How can they tell the freaks from the ordinary people? The whole world's a circus now, isn't it?" He shook his head and replied, "No, a zoo," and beckoned the waiter for more wine. He did not ask her about internal matters in Monterey, and she tactfully stayed away from the domestic problems of the Empire of San Francisco. He was feeling easy, buoyant, a little drunk, more than a little drunk; to have to answer questions now about the little rebellion that had been suppressed in Sausalito or the secessionist thing in Walnut Creek would only be a bringdown, and bad for the digestion besides.

About half past eight he said, "You aren't going back to Monterey tonight, are you?"

"God, no! It's a five-hour drive, assuming no more troubles with the San Jose highway patrol. And the road's so bad below Watsonville that only a lunatic would drive it at night. I'll stay at the Claremont."

"Good. Let me put it on the imperial account."

"That isn't necessary. We—"

"The hotel is always glad to oblige the government. Please accept their hospitality."

Ms. Sawyer shrugged. "Very well. Which we'll reciprocate when you come to Monterey."

"Fine."

And then her manner suddenly changed. She shifted in her seat and fidgeted and played with her silverware, looking awkward and ill at ease. Some new and big topic was obviously about to be introduced, and Christensen guessed that she was going to ask him to spend the night with her. In a fraction of a second he ran through all the possible merits and demerits of that and came out on the plus side, and had his answer ready when she said, "Tom, can I ask a big favor?"

Which threw him completely off balance. Whatever was coming, it certainly wasn't what he was expecting.

"I'll do my best."

"I'd like an audience with the Emperor."

"What?"

"Not on official business. I know the Emperor talks business only with his ministers and privy councillors. But I want to see him, that's all." Color came to her cheeks. "Doesn't it sound silly? But it's something I've always dreamed of, a kind of adolescent fantasy. To be in San Francisco, to be shown into the imperial throne-room, to kiss his ring, all that pomp and circumstance—I want it, Tom. Just to *be* there, to *see* him—do you think you could manage that?"

He was astounded. The facade of cool, tough competence had dropped away from her, revealing unanticipated absurdity. He did not know what to answer.

She said, "Monterey's such a poky little place. It's just a *town*. We call ourselves a republic, but we aren't much of anything. And I call myself a senator and a diplomat, but I've never really been anywhere— San Francisco two or three times when I was a girl, San Jose a few times. My mother was in Los Angeles once, but I haven't been anywhere. And to go home saying that I had seen the Emperor—" Her eyes sparkled. "You're really taken aback, aren't you? You thought I was all ice and microprocessors, and instead I'm only a hick, right? But you're being very nice. You aren't even laughing at me. Will you get me an audience with the Emperor for tomorrow or the day after?"

"I thought you were afraid to go into San Francisco."

She looked abashed. "That was just a ploy. To make you come over here, to get you to take me seriously and put yourself out a little. The diplomatic wiles. I'm sorry about that. The word was that you were snotty, that you had to be met with strength or you'd be impossible to deal with. But you aren't like that at all. Tom, I want to see the Emperor. He does give audiences, doesn't he?"

"In a manner of speaking. I suppose it could be done."

"Oh, would you! Tomorrow?"

"Why wait for tomorrow? Why not tonight?"

"Are you being sarcastic?"

"Not at all," Christensen said. "This is San Francisco. The Emperor keeps weird hours just like the rest of us. I'll phone over there and see if we can be received." He hesitated. "It won't be what you're expecting."

"In what way?"

"The pomp, the circumstance—you're going to be disappointed. You may be better off not meeting him, actually. Stick to your fantasy of imperial majesty. Seriously. I'll get you an audience if you insist, but I don't think it's a great idea."

"Can you be more specific?"

"No."

"I still want to see him. Regardless."

"Let me make some phone calls, then."

He left the dining room and, with misgivings, began arranging things. The telephone system was working sluggishly that evening and it took him fifteen minutes to set the whole thing up, but there were no serious obstacles. He returned to her and said, "The ferry will pick us up at the marina in about an hour. There'll be a car waiting on the San Francisco side. The Emperor will be available for viewing around midnight. I tell you that you're not going to enjoy this. The Emperor is old and he's been sick and he—he isn't a very interesting person to meet."

"All the same," she said. "The one thing I wanted, when I volunteered to be the envoy, was an imperial audience. Please don't discourage me."

"As you wish. Shall we have another drink?"

"How about these instead?" She produced an enameled cigarette case. "Humboldt County's finest. Gift of the Free State."

He smiled and nodded and took the joint from her. It was elegantly manufactured, fine cockleshell paper, gold monogram, igniter cap, even a filter. Everything else has come apart, he thought, but the technology of marijuana is at its highest point in history. He flicked the cap, took a deep drag, passed it to her. The effect was instantaneous, a new high cutting through the wooze of bourbon and wine and brandy already in his brain, clearing it, expanding his limp and sagging soul. When they were finished with it, they floated out of the hotel. His driver and hers were still waiting in the parking lot. Christensen dismissed his, and they took the Republic of Monterey car down the slopes of Berkeley to the marina. The boat from San Francisco was late. They stood around shivering at the ferry slip for twenty minutes, peering bleakly across at the glittering lights of the far-off city. Neither of them was dressed for the nighttime chill, and he was tempted to pull her close and hold her in his arms, but he did not do it. There was a boundary he was not yet willing to cross. Hell, he thought, I don't even know her first name.

It was nearly eleven by the time they reached San Francisco.

An official car was parked at the pier. The driver hopped out, saluting, bustling about—one of those preposterous little civil-service types, doubtless keenly honored to be taxiing bigwigs around late at night. He wore the red-and-gold uniform of the imperial dragoons, a little frayed at one elbow. The car coughed and sputtered and reluctantly lurched into life, up Market Street to Van Ness and then north to the palace. Ms. Sawyer's eyes were wide and she stared at the ancient high-rises along Market as though they were cathedrals. When they came to the Civic Center area she gasped, obviously overwhelmed by the majesty of everything, the shattered hulk of Symphony Hall, the Museum of Modern Art, the great domed enormity of the City Hall, the Hall of Justice and the Imperial Palace itself, awesome, imposing, a splendid many-columned building that long ago had been the War Memorial Opera House. A bunch of imperial cars were parked outside. With the envoy from the Republic of Monterey at his elbow, Christensen marched up the steps of the palace and through the center doors into the lobby, where a great many of the ranking ministers and plenipotentiaries of the Empire were assembled. "How absolutely marvelous," Ms. Sawyer murmured. Smiling graciously, bowing, nodding, Christensen pointed out the notables, the defense minister, the minister of finance, the minister of suburban affairs, the chief justice, the minister of transportation, and all the rest. At midnight precisely there was a grand flourish of trumpets and the door to the throne room opened. Christensen offered Ms. Sawyer his arm; together they made the long journey down the center aisle and up the ramp to the stage, where the imperial throne, a resplendent thing of rhinestones and foil, glittered brilliantly under the spotlights. Ms. Sawyer was wonderstruck. She pointed toward the six gigantic portraits suspended high over the stage and whispered a question, and Christensen replied, "The first six emperors. And here comes the seventh one."

"Oh," she gasped—but was it awe, surprise, or disgust?

He was in his full regalia, the scarlet robe, the bright green tunic with ermine trim, the gold chains. But he was wobbly and tottering, a clumsy staggering figure, gray-faced and feeble, supported on one side by Mike Schiff, the imperial chamberlain, and on the other by the grand sergeant-at-arms, Terry Coleman. He was not so much leaning on them as being dragged by them. Bringing up the rear of the procession were two sleek, pretty boys, one black and one Chinese, carrying the orb, the scepter and the massive crown. Ms. Sawyer's fingers tightened on Christensen's forearm and he heard her catch her breath as the Emperor, in the process of being lowered into his throne, went boneless and nearly spilled to the floor. Somehow the imperial chamberlain and the grand sergeant-at-arms settled him properly in place, balanced the crown on his head, stuffed the orb and scepter into his trembling hands. "His Imperial Majesty, Norton the Seventh of San Francisco!" cried Mike Schiff in a magnificent voice that went booming up into the highest balcony. The Emperor giggled.

"Come on," Christensen whispered, and led her forward.

The old man was really in terrible shape. It was weeks since Christensen last had seen him, and by now he looked like something dragged from the crypt, slack-jawed, drooling, vacant-eyed, utterly burned out. The envoy from Monterey seemed to draw back, tense and rigid, repelled, unable or unwilling to go closer, but Christensen persisted, urging her onward until she was no more than a dozen feet from the throne. A sickly-sweet odor emanated from the old man.

"What do I do?" she asked in a panicky voice.

"When I introduce you, go forward, curtsy if you know how, touch the orb. Then step back. That's all."

She nodded.

Christensen said, "Your Majesty, the ambassador from the Republic of Monterey, Senator Sawyer, to pay her respects."

Trembling, she went to him, curtseyed, touched the orb. As she backed away, she nearly fell, but Christensen came smoothly forward and steadied her. The Emperor giggled again, a shrill horrific cackle. Slowly, carefully, Christensen guided the shaken and numbed Ms. Sawyer from the stage.

"How long has he been like that?" she asked.

"Two years, three, maybe more. Completely insane. Not even housebroken any more. You could probably tell. I'm sorry. I told you you'd be better off skipping this. I'm enormously sorry, Ms.—Ms.—what's your first name, anyway?"

"Elaine."

"Elaine. Let's get out of here, Elaine. Yes?"

"Yes. Please."

She was shivering. He walked her up the side aisle. A few of the other courtiers were clambering up onto the stage now, one with a guitar, one with a juggler's clubs. The imperial giggle pierced the air again and again, becoming shrill and rasping and wild. The royal levee would probably go on half the night. Emperor Norton VII was one of San Francisco's most popular amusements.

"Now you know," Christensen said.

"How does the Empire function, if the Emperor is crazy?"

"We manage. We do our best without him. The Romans managed it with Caligula. Norton's not half as bad as Caligula. Not a tenth. Will you tell everyone in Monterey?"

"I think not. We believe in the power of the Empire and in the grandeur of the Emperor. Best not to disturb that faith."

"Quite right," said Christensen.

They emerged into the dark clear cold night.

Christensen said, "I'll ride back to the ferry slip with you, before I go home."

"Where do you live?"

"The other way. Out near Golden Gate Park."

She looked up at him and moistened her lips. "I don't want to ride across the bay in the dark alone at this hour of the night. Is it all right if I come home with you?"

"Sure," he said.

She managed a jaunty smile. "You're straight, aren't you?"

"Sure. Most of the time, anyway."

"I thought you were. Good."

They got into the car. "Frederick Street," he told the driver, "between Belvedere and Cole."

The trip took twenty minutes. Neither of them spoke. He knew what she was thinking about—the crazy Emperor, dribbling and babbling under the bright spotlights. The mighty Norton VII, ruler of everything from San Rafael to San Mateo, from Half Moon Bay to Walnut Creek. Such is pomp and circumstance in imperial San Francisco in these latter days of Western civilization. Christensen sent the driver away and they went upstairs. The cats were hungry again.

"It's a lovely apartment," she told him.

"Three rooms, bath, hot and cold running water. Not bad for a mere foreign minister. Some of the boys have suites at the palace, but I like it better here." He opened the door to the deck and stepped outside. Somehow, now that he was home, the night was not so cold. He thought about the Realm of Wicca, far off up there in green, happy Oregon sending a hundred fifty thousand kindly Goddess-worshiping neopagans down here to celebrate the rebirth of the sun. A nuisance, a mess, a headache. Tomorrow he'd have to call a meeting of the cabinet, when everybody had sobered up, and start the wheels turning, and probably he'd have to make trips to places like Petaluma and Palo Alto to get the alliance flanged together. Damn. Damn. But it was his job, wasn't it? Someone had to carry the load.

He slipped his arm around the slender woman from Monterey.

"The poor Emperor," she said softly.

"Yes. The poor Emperor. Poor everybody."

He looked toward the east. In a few hours the sun would be coming up over that hill, out of the place that used to be the United States of America and now was a thousand thousand crazy fractured fragmented entities. Christensen shook his head. The Grand Duchy of Chicago, he thought. The Holy Carolina Confederation. The Three Kingdoms of New York. The Empire of San Francisco. No use getting upset—much too late for getting upset. You played the hand that was dealt you and you did your best and you carved little islands of safety out of the night. Turning to her he said, "I'm glad you came home with me tonight." He brushed his lips lightly against hers. "Come. Let's go inside."

THE MAN WHO FLOATED IN TIME

It was an era of odd-concept science-fiction anthologies, and one of the oddest concepts of all was the book called Speculations, *which a writer named Laura Haywood (who wrote and edited under the pseudonym of Alice Laurance) was doing in collaboration with Isaac Asimov. The idea was to commission short stories from a group of well-known science-fiction writers and identify them only in code, so that their names were nowhere visible on the outside of the book and a complex decoding process was necessary in order to figure out who had written what. This didn't strike me as a particularly fruitful way to present a science-fiction anthology, since readers often like to know whose work is contained in the book before they buy it, but I went along with the project anyway. So did Jack Williamson, Gene Wolfe, R.A. Lafferty, Alan Dean Foster, and a bunch of others, including Asimov himself.*

To make it easy for those who didn't want to bother solving the puzzle, I chose a theme that I have been identified with throughout much of my career—time travel—and wrote the story, in January, 1981, in as Silverbergian-sounding style as I could manage. It was published the following year in the Laurance-Asimov anthology under a code name 35 digits long, beginning with "411332lllll323". In retrospect, I see that I played the game the wrong way: I should have written something that no one could possibly have recognized as my work by its style and content alone. If anyone ever asks me to write for such an anthology again, that's what I'll do. But I doubt that the opportunity is going to arise.

here was something shady and sly about him. For one thing he was small and slightly built, and I have an instinctive mistrust of men who stand less than five feet five: they seem too agile and unpredictable, shifty little Napoleons who are apt to come at you from three directions at once. Then, too, his narrow glittery gray eyes, though they did actually make contact with mine, never seemed to be aimed directly at me but rather, somehow, sent a beam of vision hooking around a sharply banked curve even when his face looked at me right square on. I didn't like that. He was about sixty, sixty-five, lean and trim, not well dressed, his gray hair cropped very short and gone at the crown.

"What I do," he said, "is travel in time. I float freely back to other eras."

"Really," I said. "Never forward?"

"Oh, no, never. That's quite impossible. The future doesn't exist. The past is there, solid and real, a *place*, you know, like Des Moines or Wichita. One can go to Wichita if one makes the proper connection. But one can't go to a city that's never been built. It isn't conceivable. Well, perhaps it's conceivable, but it isn't *doable*, do you follow me? I go to the past, though. I've seen Attila the Hun. I've seen Julius Caesar. I wish I could say I went to bed with Catherine the Great, but I didn't, although I had a few vodkas with someone who did. She smelled of garlic, he said, and she took forever to come. You don't believe any of what I'm saying, do you?"

"You're asking me to swallow quite a lot," I said mildly.

He leaned forward in a conspiratorial way. "You're not the kind of man who's easily convinced of the unusual. I can tell. No ancient astronaut stuff for you, no UFO contact stories, no psychic spoon-bendings. That's good. I don't want an easy believer. I want a skeptic to hear me out and test my words and arrive at his own acceptance of the truth his own way. That's all I ask of you, that you don't scoff, that you don't write me off instantly as a crackpot. All right?"

"I'll try."

"Now: what do you feel when I tell you I've traveled in time?"

"Instinctive resistance. An immediate sense that I've got myself mixed up with a crackpot or at best a charming liar."

"Fine. I wouldn't have come to you if I thought you'd react any other way."

"What do you want from me, then?"

"That you listen to me and suspend your disbelief at least now and then and ask me a question or two, probe me, test me, give me the benefit of the doubt long enough to let me get through to you. And then that you help me get my experiences down on paper. I'm old and I'm sick and I'm not going to be here much longer, and I want to leave a memoir, a record, do you see? And I need someone like you to help me."

"Why not write it yourself?" I asked.

"Easy enough to say. But I'm no writer. I don't have the gift. I can't even do letters without freezing up."

"Doing a memoir doesn't require a gift. You simply put down your story on paper, just as though you were telling it to me. Writing's not as hard as nonwriters like to think it is."

"Writing is easy for you," he said, "and time-traveling is easy for me. And I'm about as capable of writing as you are of traveling in time. Do you see?" He put his hand on my wrist, a gesture of premature inti- macy that sent a quick, and quickly suppressed, quiver through my entire arm. "Help me to get my story down, will you? You think I'm a crazy old drunk, and you wish you had never given me minute one of your time, but I ask you to put those feelings aside and accept just for the moment the possibility that this isn't just a mess of lies and fan- tasies. Can you do that?"

"Go on," I said. "Tell me about yourself."

He said his time-traveling had begun when he was a boy. The tech- nique by which he claimed to be able to unhitch himself from the bonds of the continuum and drift back along the time-line was apparently one that he developed spontaneously, a sort of applied meditation that amounted to artfully channeled fantasizing. Through this process, which he refined and perfected between the ages of eight and eleven, he achieved what I suppose must be called out-of-the-body experiences, in which his psyche, his consciousness, his walking intelligence, vanished into the past while his body remained here, ostensibly asleep.

On his first voyage he found himself in an American city of the colonial era. He had no idea where he was when he was older, working from his searingly vivid memories of the journey, he was able to iden- tify it as Charleston, South Carolina—but he knew at once, from his third-grade studies, that the powdered wigs and three-cornered hats must mean the eighteenth century. He was there for three days, fasci- nated at first, then frightened and confused and terribly hungry—

"Hungry?" I said. "A wandering psyche with an appetite?"

"You don't perceive yourself as disembodied," he replied, looking pleased that I had raised an objection. "You feel that you have been quite literally transplanted to the other era. You need to eat, to sleep, to perform bodily functions. I was a small boy lost in a prerevolutionary city. The first night I slept in a forest. In the morning I returned to the city where some people found me, dirty and lost, and took me to a mansion where I was bathed and fed—"

"And given clothes? You must have been in your pajamas."

"No, you are always clothed in the clothing of the era when you arrive," he said. "And equipped with the language of the region and a certain amount of local currency."

"How very convenient. What providential force takes care of those little details?"

He smiled. "Those are part of the illusion. Plainly I have no real coins with me, and of course I haven't magically learned new languages. But the aspect of me that makes the journey has the capacity to lead others to feel that they are receiving true coinage from me; and as my soul makes contact with theirs, they imagine that it is their own language I speak. What I do is not actual bodily travel, you understand. It is astral projection, to use a phrase that I know will arouse hostility in you. My real body, in its pajamas, remained snug in my bed; but the questing *anima,* the roving spirit, arrived fully equipped. Of course the money is dream-money and melts away the moment I go farther from it than a certain range. In my travels I have left angry innkeepers and cheated peddlers and even a few swindled harlots all over the world, I'm afraid. But for the moment what I give them passes as honest coin."

"Yet the astral body must be fed with real food?"

"Indeed. And I think that if the astral body is injured, the sleeping real body feels the pain."

"How can you be sure of that?"

"Because," he said, "I have fallen headlong down temple steps in the Babylon of Hammurabi and awakened to find bruises on my thigh and shoulder. I have slashed myself on vines in the jungles of ancient Cambodia and awakened to see the cuts. I have stood in the snows of Pleistocene Europe shivering with the Neanderthals and awakened with frostbite in July."

There is an Italian saying: *Se non è vero, è ben trovato.* "If it is not true, it is well invented." There was in his eyes and on his thin gray-stubbled face at that moment a look of such passionate conviction, such absolute sincerity, that I began to tremble, hearing him talk of feeling the bite of Pleistocene winds, and for the first time I began to allow myself the possibility of thinking that this man could be something other than a boozy old scamp with a vivid imagination. But I was far from converted.

I said, "Then if through some mischance you were killed when traveling, your real body would perish also?"

"I have every reason to think so," he replied quietly.

He traveled through vast reaches of space and time when he was still a child. Most of the places he visited were bewilderingly alien to him, and he had little idea of where or when he was, but he learned to observe keenly, to note salient details, to bring back with him data that sooner or later would help him to determine what he had experienced. He was a bookish child anyway, and so it caused no amazement when he burrowed feverishly through the *National Geographic* or the *Britannica* or dusty volumes of history. As he grew older and his education deepened, it became easier for him to learn the identity of his destinations; and when he was still older, fully grown, it was not at all difficult for him simply to ask those about him, What is the name of this city? Who is the king here? What is the event of the day? exactly as though he were a traveler newly arrived from a far-off land. For although he had journeyed in the form of a boy at first, his astral self always mirrored his true self, and as he aged, the projection that he sent to the past kept pace with him.

So, then, he visited while still a child the London of the Tudors, where rivers of muck ran in the streets, and he stood at the gates of Peking to watch the triumphal entry of the Great Khan Kublai, and he crept cautiously through the forests of the Dordogne to spy on the encampments of Neolithic huntsmen, and he tiptoed along the brutal brick battlements of a terrifying city of windowless buildings that proved to be Mohenjo-daro on the Indus, and he slipped with awe through the boulevards and plazas of majestic Tenochtitlan of the Aztecs, his pale skin growing sunburned under the heat of the pre-Columbian sun. And when he was older he stood in the frenzied crowd before the bloody guillotine of the Terror, and saw virgins hurled into the sacred well of Chichen Itza, and wandered through the smoldering ruins of Atlanta a week after General Sherman had put it to the torch, and drank thick red wine in a lovely town on the slopes of Vesuvius that may have been Pompeii. The stories rolled from him in wondrous profusion, and I listened to the charming old crank hour after hour, telling me sly tales of a history not to be found in books. Julius Caesar, he said, was a mincing dandy who reeked of vile perfume, and Cleopatra was squat and thicklipped, and the Israelites of King David's time were brawling, conniving primitives no holier than the desert folk the next tribe over, and the Great Wall of China had been mostly a slovenly rampart of mud, decaying as fast as it was slapped together, and Socrates had never lived at all but was only a convenient pedagogical invention of Plato's, and Plato had charged an enormous fee even for mere conversation. As for the Crusaders, they were more feared by Christians than Saracens, for they raped and stole and sacked mercilessly as they trekked across Europe to the Holy Land; and Alexander the Great had rarely been sober enough to stand upright after the age of twenty-three; and the orchestras of Mozart's time played mostly out of tune on feeble, screechy instruments. All this poured from him in long disjointed monologues, which I interrupted less and less frequently for clarifications and amplifications. He spoke with utter conviction and with total disregard for my disbelief: I was invited to accept his tales as whatever I pleased, gospel revelations or amusing fraud, so long as I listened.

At our fifth or sixth meeting, after he had told me about his adventures among the bare-breasted wenches of Minoan Crete—the maze, he said, was nothing much, just some alleyways and gutters—and in the Constantinople of Justinian and in the vast unpeopled bisonherd lands of ancient North America, I said to him, "Is there any time or place you haven't visited?"

"Atlantis," he said. "I kept hoping to identify the unmistakable Atlantis, but never, never once—"

"Everywhere else, and every era?"

"Hardly. I've had only one lifetime."

"I wondered. I haven't been keeping a tally, but it seems to me it must have taken you eighty or ninety years to see all that you've seen. A week here, a month there—it adds up, doesn't it?"

"Yes."

"And while you're gone, you remain asleep here for weeks or months at a time?"

"Oh, no," he said. "You've misunderstood. Time spent *there* has no relation to elapsed time *here*. I can be gone for many days, and no more than an instant will have passed here. At most, an hour or two.

Why, I've taken off on journeys even while I was sitting here talking with you!"

"What?"

"Yesterday, as we spoke of the San Francisco earthquake—between one eye-blink and the next, I spent eighteen hours in some German principality of the fourteenth century."

"And never said a word about it when you returned?"

He shrugged. "You were prickly and unreceptive yesterday, and I was having trouble keeping your sympathies. I felt it would be too stagy to tell you, Oh, by way, I've just been in Augsburg or Reutlingen or Ulm or whichever it was. Besides, it was a boring trip. I found it so dreary I didn't even trouble to ask the name of the place."

"Then why did you stay for so long?"

"Why, I have no control over that," he said.

"No control?"

"None. I drift away and I stay away however long I must and then I come back. It's been like that from the start. I can't choose my destination, either. I can best compare it to getting into a plane and being spirited off for a vacation of unknown length in an unknown land and not having a word to say about any of it. There have been times when I thought I wouldn't ever come back."

"Did that frighten you?"

"Only when I didn't like where I happened to be," he said. "The idea of spending the rest of my life in some mudhole in the middle of Mongolia or in an igloo in Greenland or—well, you get the idea." He pursed his lips. "Another thing—it happens automatically to me."

"I thought there was a ritual, a meditative process—"

"When I was a child, yes. But in time I internalized it so well that it happens of its own accord. Which is terrifying, because it can come over me anywhere, anytime, like a fit. Did you think there were no drawbacks to this? Did you think it was a lifelong picnic, roving space and time? I've had two or three uncontrolled departures a year since I was twenty. It's been my, luck that I haven't fallen down unconscious in the street, or anything like that. Though there have been some great embarrassments."

"How have your explained them?"

"With lies," he said. "You are the first to whom I've told the truth about myself."

"Should I believe that?"

"You are the first," he said with intense conviction. "And that because my time is almost over and I need at last to share my story with someone. Eh? Is that plausible? Do you still think I've fabricated it all?"

Indeed, I had no idea. To treat his story as lies or fantasy was easy enough to do; but for all his shiftiness of expression, there was an odd ring of truth even to his most enormous whoppers. And the wealth of information, the outpouring of circumstantial detail—I suppose a solitary life spent over history books could have explained that, but nevertheless, nevertheless—

And if it was true? What good had it all been? He had written nothing, no anecdotes of his adventures, no revisionist historical essays, no setting down of the philosophical insights that must have grown out of his exploration of thirty thousand years of human history. He had lived a strange and fitful and fragmentary life, flickering in and out of what we call the reality of the everyday world as though he were going to the movies, and bizarre movies they were, a week in Byzantium and a month in old Sumer and an hour among the Pharaohs. A life spent alone, a loveless life by the sound of it, a weird zigzagging chaos of a life such as has been granted no other human being—

If it was true.

And if not? *Se non è vero, è ben trovato.* I listened enraptured. I continued to probe for details of the mechanics of it. His journeys took him anywhere on earth? Anywhere, he said. Once he had arrived in a wasteland of glaciers that he believed from the strangeness of the constellations to have been Antarctica, though it might have been any icy land at a time when the stars were in other places in the sky. Happily that voyage had lasted less than an hour or he would have perished. But there seemed no limits—he might turn up on any continent, he said, and at any time. Or *almost* any time, for I queried him about dinosaurs and the era of the trilobites and the chance that he might find himself some day plunged into the primordial planetary soup of creation, but no, he had never gone back further than the Pleistocene, so far as he could tell, and he did not know why. I wondered also how he had seen so many of the great figures of history, Caesar and Cleopatra and Lincoln and Dante and the rest, when we who live only in today rarely encounter presidents and kings and movie stars in the course of our comings and goings, but he had an answer to that, too, saying that the world had been much smaller in earlier times, cities being deemed great if they had fifty or a hundred thousand people, and the mighty were far more accessible, going out into the marketplace and letting themselves be seen; besides, he had made it his business to seek them out, for what is the point of finding oneself miraculously transported to imperial Rome and coming away without at least a squint at Augustus or Caligula?

So I listened to it all and was caught up in it, and though I will not say that I ever came to believe the literal truth of his claims, I also did not quite disbelieve, and through his rambling discourses I felt the past return to life in an astonishing way. I made time for his visits, cleared all other priorities out of the way when he called to tell me he was coming and, beyond doubt, grew almost dependent on his tales, as though they were a drug, some potent hallucinogen that carried me off into gaudy realms of antiquity.

And in what proved to be his last conversation with me he said, "I could show you how it's done."

The simple words hung between us in the air like dancing swords.

I gaped at him and made no reply.

He said, "It would take perhaps three months of training. For me it was easy, natural, no challenge, but of course I was a child and I had no barriers to overcome. You, with your skepticism, your sophistication, your aloofness—it would be hard for you to master the technique, but I could show you and train you, and eventually you would succeed. Would you like that?"

I thought of watching Caesar's chariot rolling down the Via Flaminia. I thought of clinking canisters with Chaucer in some tavern just outside Canterbury. I thought of penetrating the caves of Lascaux to stare at the freshly painted bulls.

And then I thought of my quiet, orderly life, and how it would be to fall into a narcoleptic trance at unpredictable moments and swing off into the darkness of space and time, and land perhaps in the middle of some hideous massacre or in a season of plague or in a desolate land where no human foot had ever walked. I thought of pain and discomfort and risk, and possible sudden death, and the disruption of patterns of habit, and I looked into his eyes and saw the strangeness there, a strangeness that I did not want to share, and in simple cowardice I said, "I think I would rather not."

A flicker of something like disappointment passed across his features. But then he smiled and stood up and said, "I'm not surprised. But thank you for hearing me out. You were more open-minded than I expected."

He took my hand briefly in his. Then he was gone, and I never saw him again. A few weeks later, I learned of his death, and I heard his soft voice saying "I could show you how it's done," and a great sadness came over me, for although I knew he was a fraud, I knew also that there was a chance that he was not, and if so, I had foreclosed the possibility of infinite wonders for myself. How sad to have refused, I told myself, how pale and gray a thing to have done, how contemptible, really. Yes, contemptible to have refused him out of hand, without even attempting it, without offering him that final bit of credence. For several days I was deeply depressed; and then I went on to other things, as one does, and put him from my mind.

A few weeks after his death one of the big midtown banks called me. They mentioned his name and said they were executors of his estate and told me that he had left something for me, an envelope to be opened only after his death. If I could satisfactorily identify myself, the envelope would be shipped to my bank. So I went through the routine, sending a letter to my bank, which authenticated the signature and forwarded it to *his* bank, and in time my bank informed me that a parcel had come, and I went down to claim it. It was a fairly bulky manila envelope. I had the sudden wild notion that it contained some irrefutable proof of his voyages in time, something like a photograph of Jesus on the cross or a personal letter to my friend from William the Conqueror, but of course that was impossible; he had made it clear that nothing traveled in time except his intangible essence, no possessions, no artifacts. Yet my hand shook as I opened the envelope.

It contained a thick manuscript and a covering note that explained that he had decided, after all, to share with me the secrets of his technique. Without his guidance it might take me much longer to learn the knack, a year or more of diligent application, perhaps, but if I persevered, if I genuinely sought to achieve—

A wondrous dizziness came over me, as though I hung over an infinite abyss by the frailest of fraying threads and was being asked to choose between drab safety and the splendor of the unknown plunge. I felt the temptation.

And for the second time I refused the cup.

I did not read the manuscript. I was too timid for that. Nor did I destroy it, though the idea crossed my mind; but I was too cowardly even for that, I must admit, for I had no wish to bear the responsibility for having cast into oblivion so potent a secret, if potent it really was. I put the sheaf of papers—over which he must have labored with intense dedication, writing being so painfully difficult a thing for him—back into their envelope and sealed it again and put it in my vault, deep down below the bankbooks and the insurance policies and the stock certificates and the other symbols of the barricades I have thrown about myself to make my life secure.

Perhaps the manuscript, like everything else he told me, is mere fantastic nonsense. Perhaps not.

Some day, when life grows too drab for me, when the pleasures of the predictable and safe begin to pall, I will take that envelope from the vault and study its lessons, and if nothing then happens, so be it. But if I feel the power beginning to come to life in me, if I find myself once again swaying above that abyss with the choices within my reach, I hope I will find the courage to sever the thread, to loose all ties and restraints, to say farewell to order and routine, and to send myself soaring into that great uncharted infinite gulf of time.

GIANNI

In the introduction to "A Thousand Paces on the Via Dolorosa" I told how my first attempt to sell a short story to Playboy had resulted not in a sale but in a fascinating correspondence with Alice K. Turner, Playboy's fiction editor. Since she had suggested we meet for dinner while she was visiting the San Francisco area in the spring of 1981, I wanted to offer a new story to her before she arrived. So I wrote "Gianni" that February, and a few weeks later came a three-page letter from Alice, which began by telling me that we were booked for dinner at the famous Chez Panisse restaurant, and went on to an extensive discussion of the revisions she wanted on "Gianni," which she was going to publish. She simply wanted a few small revisions, and she was so confident that I'd do them to her satisfaction that she enclosed a check in payment for the story—quite a large check.

Her letter raised a number of interesting points. Some I agreed with, some I didn't; and I made notations in the margin indicating my reaction to the various changes she wanted. "Yes," I said to one, and "maybe" to another, and "no" to several. But there was one request that seemed absolutely impossible for me to comply with. "Gianni" was a first-person story, narrated by Dave Leavis, the scientist in charge of the time-travel experiment. Alice wanted me to switch the story around so that a different character—Sam Hoaglund, the publicity agent—would be the narrator. I didn't see how that was possible. How could I rewrite a first-person story so that it now would be told by a different narrator, short of completely recon-structing the whole story? I had envisioned it all along as Leavis's story to tell. I couldn't imagine rethinking it so that it would be told by Hoaglund.

159

But it appeared from her letter that Alice would insist on the change. If she did, it would kill the sale. So when I met her for dinner that night at Chez Panisse, I had Playboy's nice, big check in my coat pocket, ready to hand back to her at the end of our discussion.

Eventually the conversation came around to "Gianni." I mentioned that I had a little problem with changing the narrator. And then Alice produced one of the biggest editorial surprises I have ever experienced in my long writing career.

She had anticipated my resistance to that particular change. So she had brought a copy of the story with her that she had marked in pencil to show me how easy it would be to do. She handed it to me now, and I leafed through it in amazement. She had done the impossible. With a few small strokes she had transferred the narrative center from Leavis to Hoagland— a technical stunt that astonished me, and I have been a close and careful student of the technical side of writing fiction for many decades.

So I said nothing about the check in my coat pocket, and I agreed to do the revisions, and I went home and started making them. On April 7, 1981, I sent it back to her, having made the viewpoint switch and having also accepted some (not all) of her other suggestions for changing the story. Playboy published it in the February, 1982 issue.

That was the start of a long and wonderful editor-author relationship that would see me write fifteen or twenty more stories for Playboy and become embroiled in some marvelous arguments with Alice about most of those stories before she was satisfied with them. Many years later, when we were looking back at the "Gianni" event, I told her that I had come to dinner that night prepared to give her back the check if she had insisted on having her way about the viewpoint switch—but hadn't done it, because she had been able to convince me that the switch was possible.

"What would you have done," I asked, "if I had returned the check?"

"I would have published the story the way you wrote it, with Leavis as the narrator," she replied, and we both had a good laugh.

Since then, whenever I have had an opportunity to bring "Gianni" back into print in some anthology or a collection of my own short stories, I have used the Leavis-narrator version. When Alice reprinted the story herself in The Playboy Book of Science Fiction, she used the version published in the magazine, with Hoaglund as the narrator. Which version of the story is the more effective one? I have no idea.

"**B**ut why not Mozart?" Hoaglund said, shaking his head. "Schubert, even? Or you could have brought back Bix Beiderbecke, for Christ's sake, if you wanted to resurrect a great musician."

"Beiderbecke was jazz," I said. "I'm not interested in jazz. Nobody's interested in jazz except you."

"And people are still interested in Pergolesi in the year 2008?"

"*I* am."

"Mozart would have been better publicity. You'll need more funding sooner or later. You tell the world you've got Mozart sitting in the back room cranking out a new opera, you can write your own ticket. But what good is Pergolesi? Pergolesi's totally forgotten."

"Only by the proletariat, Sam. Besides, why give Mozart a second chance? Maybe he died young, but it wasn't all *that* young, and he did his work, a ton of work. Gianni died at twenty-six, you know. He might have been greater than Mozart if he'd had another dozen years."

"Johnny?"

"Gianni. Giovanni Battista. Pergolesi. He calls himself Gianni. Come meet him."

"Mozart, Dave. You should have done Mozart."

"Stop being an idiot," I said. "When you've met him, you'll know I did the right thing. Mozart would have been a pain in the neck, anyway. The stories I've heard about Mozart's private life would uncurl your wig. Come on with me."

I led him down the long hallway from the office past the hardware room and the timescoop cage to the airlock separating us from the semidetached motel unit out back where Gianni had been living since we scooped him. We halted in the airlock to be sprayed. Sam frowned and I explained, "Infectious microorganisms have mutated a lot since the eighteenth century. Until we've got his resistance levels higher, we're keeping him in a pretty sterile environment. When we first brought him back, he was vulnerable to anything—a case of the sniffles would have killed him, most likely. Plus he was a dying man when we got him, one lung lousy with TB and the other one going."

"Hey," Hoaglund said.

I laughed. "You won't catch anything from him. It's in remission now, Sam. We didn't bring him back at colossal expense just to watch him die."

The lock opened and we stepped into the monitoring vestibule, glittering like a movie set with bank upon bank of telemetering instruments. The day nurse, Claudia, was checking diagnostic readouts. "He's expecting you, Dr. Leavis," she said. "He's very frisky this morning."

"Frisky?"

"Playful. You know."

Yes. Tacked to the door of Gianni's room was a card that hadn't been there yesterday, flamboyantly lettered in gaudy, free-flowing baroque script:

GIOVANNI BATTISTA PERGOLESI

Jesi, January 3 1710—Pozzuoli, March 17 1736
Los Angeles, Dec. 20 2007—.
Genuis At Work!!!!
Per Piacere, Knock Before You enter!

"He speaks English?" Hoaglund asked.

"Now he does," I said. "We gave him tapesleep the first week. He picks things up fast, anyway." I grinned. "Genius at work, eh? Or *genuis*. That's the sort of sign I would have expected Mozart to put up."

"They're all alike, these talents," Hoaglund said.

I knocked.

"Chi va là?" Gianni called.

"Dave Leavis."

"Avanti, dottore illustrissimo!"

"I thought you said he speaks English," Hoaglund murmured.

"He's frisky today, Claudia said, remember?"

We went in. As usual he had the blinds tightly drawn, shutting out the brilliant January sunlight, the yellow blaze of acacia blossoms just outside the window, the enormous scarlet bougainvillea, the sweeping hilltop vista of the valley and the mountains beyond. Maybe scenery didn't interest him—or, more likely, he preferred to keep his room a tightly sealed little cell, an island out of time. He had had to absorb a lot of psychic trauma in the past few weeks: it must give you a hell of a case of jet-lag to jump 271 years into the future.

But he looked lively, almost impish—a small man, graceful, delicate, with sharp, busy eyes, quick, elegant gestures, a brisk, confident manner. How much he had changed in just a few weeks! When we fished him out of the eighteenth century, he was a woeful sight, face lined and haggard, hair already gray at twenty-six, body gaunt, bowed, quivering. He looked like what he was, a shattered consumptive a couple of weeks from the grave. His hair was still gray, but he had gained ten pounds; the veils were gone from his eyes; there was color in his cheeks.

I said, "Gianni, I want you to meet Sam Hoaglund. He's going to handle publicity and promotion for our project. *Capisce?* He will make you known to the world and give you a new audience for your music."

He flashed a brilliant smile. "*Bene.* Listen to this."

The room was an electronic jungle, festooned with gadgetry: a synthesizer, a telescreen, a megabuck audio library, five sorts of data terminals and all manner of other things perfectly suited to your basic eighteenth-century Italian drawing room. Gianni loved it all and was mastering the equipment with astonishing, even frightening, ease. He swung around to the synthesizer, jacked it into harpsichord mode and touched the keyboard. From the cloud of floating minispeakers came the opening theme of a sonata, lovely, lyrical, to my ear unmistakably Pergolesian in its melodiousness, and yet somehow weird. For all its beauty there was a strained, awkward, *suspended* aspect to it, like a ballet performed by dancers in galoshes. The longer he played, the more uncomfortable I felt. Finally he turned to us and said, "You like it?"

"What is it? Something of yours?"

"Mine, yes. My new style. I am under the influence of Beethoven today. Haydn yesterday, tomorrow Chopin. I try everything, no? By Easter I get to the ugly composers. Mahler, Berg, Debussy—those men were *crazy,* do you know? Crazy music, so ugly. But I will learn."

"Debussy ugly?" Hoaglund said quietly to me.

"Bach is modern music to him," I said. "Haydn is the voice of the future."

Gianni said, "I will be very famous."

"Yes. Sam will make you the most famous man in the world."

"I was very famous after I—died." He tapped one of the terminals. "I have read about me. I was so famous that everybody forged my music, and it was published as Pergolesi, do you know that? I have played it, too, this 'Pergolesi.' *Merda,* most of it. Not all. The *concerti armonici,* not bad—not mine, but not bad. Most of the rest, trash." He winked. "But you will make me famous while I live, eh? Good. Very good." He came closer to us and in a lower voice said, "Will you tell Claudia that the gonorrhea, it is all cured?"

"What?"

"She would not believe me. I said, The doctor swears it, but she said, "No, it is not safe; you must keep your hands off me; you must keep everything else off me."

"Gianni, have you been molesting your nurse?"

"I am becoming a healthy man, *dottore*. I am no monk. They sent me to live with the *cappuccini* in the monastery at Pozzuoli, yes, but it was only so the good air there could heal my consumption, not to make me a monk. I am no monk now and I am no longer sick. Could you go without a woman for three hundred years?" He put his face close to Hoaglund's, gave him a bright-eyed stare, leered outrageously. "You will make me very famous. And then there will be women again, yes? And you must tell them that the gonorrhea, it is entirely cured. This age of miracles!"

Afterward Hoaglund said to me, "And you thought Mozart was going to be too much trouble?"

When we first got him, there was no snappy talk out of him of women or fame or marvelous new compositions. Then he was a wreck, a dazed wraith, hollow, burned out. He wasn't sure whether he had awakened in heaven or in hell, but whichever it was left him alternately stunned and depressed. He was barely clinging to life, and we began to wonder if we had waited too long to get him. Perhaps it might be wiser, some of us thought, to toss him back and pick him up from an earlier point, maybe summer of 1735, when he wasn't so close to the grave. But we had no budget for making a second scoop, and also we were bound by our own rigid self-imposed rules. We had the power to yank anybody we liked out of the past—Napoleon, Genghis Khan, Jesus, Henry the Eighth—but we had no way of knowing what effects it might have on the course of history if we scooped up Lenin while he was still in exile in Switzerland, say, or collected Hitler while he was still a paperhanger. So we decided *a priori* to scoop only someone whose life and accomplishments were entirely behind him, and who was so close to the time of his natural death that his disappearance would not be likely to unsettle the fabric of the universe. For months I lobbied to scoop Pergolesi, and I got my way, and we took him out of the monastery eighteen days before his official date of death. Once we had him, it was no great trick to substitute a synthetic cadaver, who was duly discovered and buried, and so far as we have been able to tell, no calamities have resulted to history because one consumptive Italian was put in his grave two weeks earlier than the encyclopedia used to say he had been.

Yet it was touch and go at first, keeping him alive. Those were the worst days of my life, the first few after the scooping. To have planned for years, to have expended so many gigabucks on the project, and then to have our first human scoopee die on us anyway—

He didn't, though. The same vitality that had pulled sixteen operas and a dozen cantatas and uncountable symphonies and concerti and masses and sonatas out of him in a twenty-six-year lifespan pulled him back from the edge of the grave now, once the resources of modern medicine were put to work rebuilding his lungs and curing his assorted venereal diseases. From hour to hour we could see him gaining strength. Within days he was wholly transformed. It was almost magical, even to us. And it showed us vividly how many lives were needlessly lost in those archaic days for want of the things that are routine to us antibiotics, transplant technology, micro-surgery, regeneration therapy.

For me those were wondrous days The pallid, feeble young man struggling for his life in the back unit was surrounded by a radiant aura of accumulated fame and legend built up over centuries: he was *Pergolesi*, the miraculous boy, the fountain of melody, the composer of the awesome *Stabat Mater* and the rollicking *Serva Padrona*, who in the decades after his early death was ranked with Bach, with Mozart, with Haydn, and whose most trivial works inspired the whole genre of light opera. But his own view of himself was different: he was a weary, sick, dying young man, poor pathetic Gianni, the failure, the washout, unknown beyond Rome and Naples and poorly treated there, his serious operas neglected cruelly, his masses and cantatas praised but rarely performed, only the comic operas that he dashed off so carelessly winning him any acclaim at all—poor Gianni, burned out at twenty-five, destroyed as much by disappointment as by tuberculosis and venereal disease, creeping off to the Capuchin monastery to die in miserable poverty. How could he have known he was to be famous? But we showed him. We played him recordings of his music, both the true works and those that had been constructed in his name by the unscrupulous to cash in on his posthumous glory. We let him read the biographies and critical studies and even the novels that had been published about him. Indeed, for him it must have been precisely like dying and going to heaven, and from day to day he gained strength and poise, he waxed and flourished, he came to glow with vigor and passion and confidence. He knew now that no magic had been worked on him, that he had been snatched into the unimaginable future and restored to health by ordinary human beings, and he accepted that and quickly ceased to question it. All that concerned him now was music. In the second and third weeks we gave him a crash course in post-Baroque musical history. Bach first, then the shift away from polyphony—"*Naturalmente,*" he said, "it was inevitable, I would have achieved it myself if I had lived"—and he spent hours with Mozart and Haydn and Johann Christian Bach, soaking up their complete works and entering a kind of ecstatic state. His nimble, agile mind swiftly began plotting its own directions. One morning I found him red-eyed with weeping. He had been up all night listening to *Don Giovanni* and *Marriage of Figaro.* "This Mozart," he said. "You bring him back, too?"

"Maybe someday we will," I said.

"I kill him! You bring him back, I strangle him, I trample him!" His eyes blazed. He laughed wildly. "He is wonder! He is angel! He is too good! Send me to his time, I kill him then! No one should compose like that! Except Pergolesi. He would have done it."

"I believe that."

"Yes! This *Figaro*—1786—I could have done it twenty years earlier! Thirty! If only I get the chance. Why this Mozart so lucky? I die, he live—why? Why, *dottore?*"

His love-hate relationship with Mozart lasted six or seven days. Then he moved on to Beethoven, who I think was a little too much for him, overwhelming, massive, crushing, and then the romantics, who amused him—"Berlioz, Tchaikovsky, Wagner, all lunatics, *dementi, pazzi,* but they are wonderful. I think I see what they are trying to do. Madmen! Marvelous madmen!"and quickly on to the twentieth century, Mahler, Schoenberg, Stravinsky, Bartok, not spending much time with any of them, finding them all either ugly or terrifying or simply incomprehensibly bizarre. More recent composers, Webern and the serialists, Penderecki, Stockhausen, Xenakis, Ligeti, the various electronicists and all that came after, he dismissed with a quick shrug, as though he barely recognized what they were doing as music. Their fundamental assumptions were too alien to him. Genius though he was, he could not assimilate their ideas, any more than Brillat-Savarin or Escoffier could have found much pleasure in the cuisine of another planet. After completing his frenzied survey of everything that had happened in music after his time, he returned to Bach and Mozart and gave them his full attention.

I mean *full* attention. Gianni was utterly incurious about the world outside his bedroom window. We told him he was in America, in California, and showed him a map. He nodded casually. We turned on the telescreen and let him look at the landscape of the early twenty-first century. His eyes glazed. We spoke of automobiles, planes, flights to Mars. Yes, he said, *meraviglioso, miracoloso,* and went back to the Brandenburg concerti. I realize now that the lack of interest he showed in the modern world was a sign neither of fear nor of shallowness, but rather only a mark of priorities. What Mozart had accomplished was stranger and more interesting to him than the entire technological revolution. Technology was only a means to an end, for Gianni—push a button, you get a symphony orchestra in your bedroom: *miracoloso!*— and he took it entirely for granted. That the *basso continuo* had become obsolete thirty years after his death, that the diatonic scales would be demoted from sacred constants to inconvenient anachronisms a century or so later, was more significant to him than the fusion reactor, the interplanetary spaceship, or even the machine that had yanked him from his deathbed into this brave new world.

In the fourth week he said he wanted to compose again. He asked for a harpsichord. Instead we gave him a synthesizer. He loved it.

In the sixth week he began asking questions about the outside world, and I realized that the tricky part of our experiment was about to begin.

Hoaglund said, "Pretty soon we have to reveal him. It's incredible we've been able to keep it quiet this long."

He had an elaborate plan. The problem was twofold: letting Gianni experience the world, and letting the world perceive that time-travel as a practical matter involving real human beings—no more frogs and kittens hoisted from last month to this—had finally arrived. There was going to be a whole business of press conferences, media tours of our lab, interviews with Gianni, a festival of Pergolesi music at the Hollywood Bowl with the premiere of a symphony in the mode of Beethoven that he said would be ready by April, et cetera, et cetera, et cetera. But at the same time we would be taking Gianni on private tours of the L.A. area, gradually exposing him to the society into which he had been so unilaterally hauled. The medics said it was safe to let him encounter twenty-first-century microorganisms now. But would it be safe to let him encounter twenty-first-century civilization? He, with his windows sealed and his blinds drawn, his eighteenth-century mind wholly engrossed in the revelations that Bach and Mozart and Beethoven were pouring into it—what would he make of the world of spaceways and slice-houses and overload bands and freebase teams when he could no longer hide from it?

"Leave it all to me," said Hoaglund. "That's what you're paying me for, right?"

On a mild and rainy February afternoon Sam and I and the main physician, Nella Brandon, took him on his first drive through his new reality. Down the hill the back way, along Ventura Boulevard a few miles, onto the freeway, out to Topanga, back around through the landslide zone to what had been Santa Monica, and then straight up Wilshire across the entire heart of Los Angeles—a good stiff jolt of modernity. Dr. Brandon carried her full armamentarium of sedatives and tranks ready in case Gianni freaked out. But he didn't freak out.

He loved it—swinging round and round in the bubbletop car, gaping at everything. I tried to view L.A. through the eyes of someone whose entire life had been spent amid the splendors of Renaissance and Baroque architecture, and it came up hideous on all counts. But not to Gianni. "Beautiful," he sighed. "Wondrous! Miraculous! Marvelous!" The traffic, the freeways themselves, the fast-food joints, the peeling plastic facades, the great fire scar in Topanga, the houses hanging by spider-cables from the hillsides, the occasional superjet floating overhead on its way into LAX—everything lit him up. It was wonderland to him. None of those dull old cathedrals and *palazzi* and marble fountains here—no, everything here was brighter and larger and glitzier than life, and he loved it. The only part he couldn't handle was the beach at Topanga. By the time we got there the sun was out and so were the sunbathers, and the sight of eight thousand naked bodies cavorting on the damp sand almost gave him a stroke."What is this?" he demanded. "The market for slaves? The pleasure house of the king?"

"Blood pressure rising fast," Nella Brandon said softly, eyeing her wrist-monitors. "Adrenalin levels going up. Shall I cool him out?"

I shook my head.

"Slavery is unlawful," I told him. "There is no king. These are ordinary citizens amusing themselves."

"Nudo! Assolutamente nudo!"

"We long ago outgrew feeling ashamed of our bodies," I said. "The laws allow us to go nude in places like this."

"Straordinario! Incredibile!" He gaped in total astonishment. Then he erupted with questions, a torrent of Italian first, his English returning only with an effort. Did husbands allow their wives to come here? Did fathers permit daughters? Were there rapes on the beach? Duels? If the body had lost its mystery, how did sexual desire survive? If a man somehow did become excited, was it shameful to let it show? And on and on and on, until I had to signal Nella to give him a mild needle. Calmer now, Gianni digested the notion of mass public nudity in a more reflective way; but it had amazed him more than Beethoven, that was plain.

We let him stare for another ten minutes. As we started to return to the car, Gianni pointed to a lush brunette trudging along by the tidepools and said, "I want her. Get her."

"Gianni, we can't do that!"

"You think I am eunuch? You think I can see these bodies and not remember breasts in my hands, tongue touching tongue?" He caught my wrist. "Get her for me."

"Not yet. You aren't well enough yet. And we can't just get her for you. Things aren't done that way here."

"She goes naked. She belongs to anyone."

"No," I said. "You still don't really understand, do you?" I nodded to Nella Brandon. She gave him another needle. We drove on, and he subsided. Soon we came to the barrier marking where the coast road had fallen into the sea, and we swung inland through the place where Santa Monica had been. I explained about the earthquake and the landslide. Gianni grinned.

"Ah, *il terremoto,* you have it here too? A few years ago there was great earthquake in Napoli. You have understood? And then they ask me to write a Mass of Thanksgiving afterward because not everything is destroyed. It is very famous mass for a time. You know it? No? You must hear it." He turned and seized my wrist. With an intensity greater than the brunette had aroused in him, he said, "I will compose a new famous mass, yes? I will be very famous again. And I will be rich. Yes? I was famous and then I was forgotten and then I died and now I live again and now I will be famous again. And rich. Yes? Yes?"

Sam Hoaglund looked over at him and said, "In another couple of weeks, Gianni, you're going to be the most famous man in the world."

Casually Sam poked the button turning on the radio. The car was well equipped for overload and out of the many speakers came the familiar pulsing tingling sounds of Wilkes Booth John doing *Membrane*. The subsonics were terrific. Gianni sat up straight as the music hit him. "What is that?" he demanded.

"Overload," Sam said. "Wilkes Booth John."

"Overload? This means nothing to me. It is a music? Of when?"

"The music of right now," said Nella Brandon.

As we zoomed along Wilshire Sam keyed in the colors and lights too, and the whole interior of the car began to throb and flash and sizzle. Wonderland for Gianni again. He blinked, he pressed his hands to his cheeks, he shook his head. "It is like the music of dreams," he said. "The composer? Who is?"

"Not a composer," said Sam. "A group. Wilkes Booth John, it calls itself. This isn't classical music, it's pop. Popular. Pop doesn't have a composer."

"It makes itself, this music?"

"No," I said. "The whole group composes it. And plays it."

"The orchestra. It is pop and the orchestra composes." He looked lost, as bewildered as he had been since the moment of his awakening, naked and frail, in the scoop cage. "Pop. Such strange music. So simple. It goes over and over again, the same thing, loud, no shape. Yet I think I like it. Who listens to this music? *Imbecili? Infanti?*"

"Everyone," Sam said.

The first outing in Los Angeles not only told us Gianni could handle exposure to the modern world but also transformed his life among us in several significant ways. For one thing, there was no keeping him chaste any longer after Topanga Beach. He was healthy, he was lusty, he was vigorously heterosexual—an old biography of him I had seen blamed his ill health and early demise on "his notorious profligacy"—and we could hardly go on treating him like a prisoner or a zoo animal. Sam fixed him up with one of his secretaries, Melissa Burke, a willing volunteer.

Then, too, Gianni had been confronted for the first time with the split between classical and popular music, with the whole modernist cleavage between high art and lowbrow entertainment. That was new to him and baffling at first. "This *pop*," he said, "it is the music of the peasants?" But gradually he grasped the idea of simple rhythmic music that everyone listened to, distinguished from "serious" music that belonged only to an elite and was played merely on formal occasions. "But *my* music," he protested, "it had tunes, people could whistle it. It was everybody's music." It fascinated him that composers had abandoned melody and made themselves inaccessible to most of the people. We told him that something like that had happened in all of the arts. "You poor crazy *futuruomini*," he said gently.

Suddenly he began to turn himself into a connoisseur of overload groups. We rigged an imposing unit in his room, and he and Melissa spent hours plugged in, soaking up the waveforms let loose by Scissors and Ultrafoam and Wilkes Booth John and the other top bands. When I asked him how the new symphony was coming along, he gave me a peculiar look.

He began to make other little inroads into modern life. Sam and Melissa took him shopping for clothing on Figueroa Street, and in the *cholo* boutiques he acquired a flashy new wardrobe of the latest Aztec gear to replace the lab clothes he had worn since his awakening. He had his prematurely gray hair dyed red. He acquired jewelry that went flash, clang, zzz, and pop when the mood-actuated sensoria came into play. In a few days he was utterly transformed: he became the perfect young Angeleno, slim, dapper, stylish, complete with the slight foreign accent and exotic grammar.

"Tonight Melissa and I go to The Quonch," Gianni announced.

"The Quonch," I murmured, mystified.

"Overload palace," Hoaglund explained. "In Pomona. All the big groups play there."

"We have Philharmonic tickets tonight," I said feebly.

Gianni's eyes were implacable. "The Quonch," he said.

So we went to The Quonch. Gianni, Melissa, Sam, Sam's slice-junkie livewith, Oreo, and I. Gianni and Melissa had wanted to go alone, but I wasn't having that. I felt a little like an overprotective mother whose little boy wanted to try a bit of freebasing. No chaperones, no Quonch, I said. The Quonch was a gigantic geodesic dome in Pomona Downlevel, far underground. The stage whirled on antigrav gyros, the ceiling was a mist of floating speakers, the seats had pluggie intensifiers, and the audience, median age about fourteen, was sliced out of its mind. The groups performing that night were Thug, Holy Ghosts, Shining Orgasm Revival and Ultrafoam. For this I had spent untold multi-kilogelt to bring the composer of the *Stabat Mater* and *La Serva Padrona* back to life? The kids screamed, the great hall filled with dense, tangible, oppressive sound, colors and lights throbbed and pulsed, minds were blown. In the midst of the madness sat Giovanni Battista Pergolesi (1710—1736), graduate of the Conservatorio dei Poveri, organist of the royal chapel at Naples, *maestro di capella* to the Prince of Stigliano—plugged in, turned on, radiant, ecstatic, transcendent.

Whatever else The Quonch may have been, it didn't seem dangerous, so the next night I let Gianni go there just with Melissa. And the next. It was healthy for both of us to let him move out on his own a little. But I was starting to worry. It wouldn't be long until we broke the news to the public that we had a genuine eighteenth-century genius among us. But where were the new symphonies? Where were the heaven-sent sonatas? He wasn't producing anything visible. He was just doing a lot of overload. I hadn't brought him back here to be a member of the audience, especially *that* audience.

"Relax," Sam Hoaglund said. "He's going through a phase. He's dazzled by the novelty of everything, and also he's having fun for maybe the first time in his life. But sooner or later he'll get back to composing. Nobody steps out of character forever. The real Pergolesi will take control."

Then Gianni disappeared.

Came the frantic call at three in the afternoon on a crazy hot Saturday with Santa Anas blowing and a fire raging in Tujunga. Dr. Brandon had gone to Gianni's room to give him his regular checkup, and no Gianni. I went whistling across town from my house near the beach. Hoaglund, who had come running in from Santa Barbara, was there already. "I phoned Melissa," he said. "He's not with her. But she's got a theory."

"Tell."

"They've been going backstage the last few nights. He's met some of the kids from Ultrafoam and one of the other groups. She figures he's off jamming with them."

"If that's all, then hallelujah. But how do we track him?"

"She's getting addresses. We're making calls. Quit worrying, Dave."

Easy to say. I imagined him held for ransom in some East L.A. dive. I imagined swaggering machos sending me his fingers, one a day, waiting for fifty megabucks' payoff. I paced for half a dreadful hour, grabbing up phones as if they were magic wands, and then came word that they had found him working out with Shining Orgasm Revival in a studio in West Covina. We were there in half the legal time and to hell with the California Highway Patrol.

The place was a miniature Quonch, electronic gear everywhere, the special apparatus of overload rigged up, and Gianni sitting in the midst of six practically naked young uglies whose bodies were draped with readout tape and sonic gadgetry. So was his. He looked blissful and sweaty. "It is so beautiful, this music," he sighed when I collared him. "It is the music of my second birth. I love it beyond everything."

"Bach," I said. "Beethoven. Mozart."

"This is other. This is miracle. The total effect—the surround, the engulf—"

"Gianni, don't ever go off again without telling someone."

"You were afraid?"

"We have a major investment in you. We don't want you getting hurt or into trouble or—"

"Am I a child?"

"There are dangers in this city that you couldn't possibly understand yet. You want to jam with these musicians, jam with them, but don't just disappear. Understood?"

He nodded.

Then he said, "We will not hold the press conference for a while. I am learning this music. I will make my debut next month, maybe. If we can get booking at The Quonch as main attraction."

"This is what you want to be? An overload star?"

"Music is music."

"And you are Giovanni Battista Pergo—" An awful thought struck me. I looked sidewise at Shining Orgasm Revival. "Gianni, you didn't tell them who you—"

"No. I am still secret."

"Thank God." I put my hand on his arm. "Look, if this stuff amuses you, listen to it, play it, do what you want. But the Lord gave you a genius for real music."

"This is real music."

"Complex music. Serious music."

"I starved to death composing that music."

"You were ahead of your time. You wouldn't starve now. You will have a tremendous audience for your music."

"Because I am a freak, yes. And in two months I am forgotten again. *Grazie,* no, Dave. No more sonatas. No more cantatas. Is not the music of this world. I give myself to overload."

"I forbid it, Gianni!"

He glared. I saw something steely behind his delicate and foppish exterior.

"You do not own me, Dr. Leavis."

"I gave you life."

"So did my father and mother. They didn't own me either."

"Please, Gianni. Let's not fight. I'm only begging you not to turn your back on your genius, not to renounce the gift God gave you for—"

"I renounce nothing. I merely transform." He leaned up and put his nose almost against mine. "Let me free. I will not be a court composer for you. I will not give you masses and symphonies. No one wants such things today, not new ones, only a few people who want the old ones. Not good enough. I want to be famous, *capisce?* I want to be rich. Did you think I'd live the rest of my life as a curiosity, a museum piece? Or that I would learn to write the kind of noise they call modern music? Fame is what I want. I died poor and hungry, the books say. *You* die poor and hungry and find out what it is like, and then talk to me about writing cantatas. I will never be poor again." He laughed. "Next year, after I am revealed to the world, I will start my own overload group. We will wear wigs, eighteenth-century clothes, everything. We will call ourselves Pergolesi. All right? All right, Dave?"

He insisted on working out with Shining Orgasm Revival every afternoon. Okay. He went to overload concerts just about every night. Okay. He talked about going on stage next month. Even that was okay. He did no composing, stopped listening to any music but overload. Okay. He is going through a phase, Sam Hoaglund had said. Okay. You do not own me, Gianni had said.

Okay. Okay.

I let him have his way. I asked him who his overload playmates thought he was, why they had let him join the group so readily. "I say I am rich Italian playboy," he replied. "I give them the old charm, you understand? Remember I am accustomed to winning the favors of kings, princes, cardinals. It is how we musicians earned our living. I charm them, they listen to me play, they see right away I am genius. The rest is simple. I will be very rich."

About three weeks into Gianni's overload phase, Nella Brandon came to me and said, "Dave, he's doing slice."

I don't know why I was surprised. I was.

"Are you sure?"

She nodded. "It's showing up in his blood, his urine, his metabolic charts. He probably does it every time he goes to play with that band. He's losing weight, corpuscle formation dropping off, resistance weakening. You've got to talk to him."

I went to him and said, "Gianni, I've stopped giving a damn what kind of music you write, but when it comes to drugs, I draw the line. You're still not completely sound physically. Remember, you were at the edge of *death* just a few months ago, body-time. I don't want you killing yourself."

"You do not own me." Again, sullenly.

"I have some claim on you. I want you to go on living."

"Slice will not kill me."

"It's killed plenty already."

"Not Pergolesi!" he snapped. Then he smiled, took my hand, gave me the full treatment. "Dave, Dave, you listen. I die once. I am not interested in an encore. But the slice, it is essential. Do you know? It divides one moment from the next. You have taken it? No? Then, you cannot understand. It puts spaces in time. It allows me to comprehend the most intricate rhythms, because with slice there is time for everything, the world slows down, the mind accelerates. *Capisce?* I need it for my music."

"You managed to write the *Stabat Mater* without slice."

"Different music. For this, I need it." He patted my hand. "You do not worry, eh? I look after myself."

What could I say? I grumbled, I muttered, I shrugged. I told Nella to keep a very close eye on his readouts. I told Melissa to spend as much time as possible with him and keep him off the drug if she could manage it.

At the end of the month Gianni announced he would make his debut at The Quonch on the following Saturday. A big bill—five overload bands, Shining Orgasm Revival playing fourth, with Wilkes Booth John, no less, as the big group of the night. The kids in the audience would skull out completely if they knew that one of the Orgasms was three hundred years old, but of course they weren't going to find that out, so they'd just figure he was a new side-man and pay no attention. Later on Gianni would declare himself to be Pergolesi. He and Sam were already working on the altered PR program. I felt left out, off on another track. But it was beyond my control. Gianni now was like a force of nature, a hurricane of a man, frail and wan though he might be.

We all went to The Quonch for Gianni's overload debut.

There we sat, a dozen or more alleged adults, in that mob of screaming kids. Fumes, lights, colors, the buzzing of gadgetized clothes and jewels, people passing out, people coupling in the aisles, the whole crazy bit, like Babylon right before the end, and we sat through it. Kids selling slice, dole, coke, you name it, slipped among us. I wasn't buying but I think some of my people were. I closed my eyes and let it all wash over me, the rhythms and subliminals and ultrasonics of one group after another, Toad Star, then Bubblemilk, then Holy Ghosts, though I couldn't tell one from the next, and finally, after many hours, Shining Orgasm Revival was supposed to go on for its set.

A long intermission dragged on and on. And on.

The kids, zonked and crazed, didn't mind at first. But after maybe half an hour they began to boo and throw things and pound on the walls. I looked at Sam, Sam looked at me, Nella Brandon murmured little worried things.

Then Melissa appeared from somewhere, tugged at my arm and whispered, "Dr. Leavis, you'd better come backstage. Mr. Hoaglund. Dr. Brandon."

They say that if you fear the worst, you keep the worst at bay. As we made our way through the bowels of The Quonch to the performers' territory, I imagined Gianni sprawled backstage, wired with full gear, eyes rigid, tongue sticking out—dead of a slice overdose. And all our fabulous project ruined in a crazy moment. So we went backstage and there were the members of Shining Orgasm Revival running in circles, and a cluster of Quonch personnel conferring urgently, and kids in full war-paint peering in the back way and trying to get through the cordon. And there was Gianni, wired with full overload gear, sprawled on the floor, shirtless, skin shiny with sweat, mottled with dull purplish spots, eyes rigid, tongue sticking out. Nella Brandon pushed everyone away and dropped down beside him. One of the Orgasms said to no one in particular, "He was real nervous, man, he kept slicing off more and more, we couldn't stop him, you know—"

Nella looked up at me. Her face was bleak.

"OD?" I said.

She nodded. She had the snout of an ultrahypo against Gianni's limp arm and she was giving him some kind of shot to try to bring him around. But even in A.D. 2008, dead is dead is dead.

✸

It was Melissa who said afterward through tears, "It was his karma to die young, don't you see? If he couldn't die in 1736, he was going to die fast here. He had no choice."

And I thought of the biography that had said of him long ago, "His ill health was probably due to his notorious profligacy." And I heard Sam Hoaglund's voice in my mind saying, "Nobody steps out of character forever. The real Pergolesi will take control." Yes. Gianni had always been on a collision course with death, I saw now; by scooping him from his own era we had only delayed things a few months. Self-destructive is as self-destructive does, and a change of scenery doesn't alter the case.

If that is so—if, as Melissa says, karma governs all—should we bother to try again? Do we reach into yesterday's yesterday for some other young genius dead too soon, Poe or Rimbaud or Caravaggio or Keats, and give him the second chance we had hoped to give Gianni? And watch him recapitulate his destiny, going down a second time? Mozart, as Sam once suggested? Benvenuto Cellini? Our net is wide and deep. All of the past is ours. But if we bring back another, and he will fully and heedlessly sends himself down the same old karmic chute, what have we gained, what have we achieved, what have we done to ourselves and to him? I think of Gianni, looking to be rich and famous at last, lying purpled on that floor. Would Shelley drown again? Would Van Gogh cut off the other ear before our eyes?

Perhaps someone more mature would be safer, eh? El Greco, Cervantes, Shakespeare? But then we might behold Shakespeare signing up in Hollywood, El Greco operating out of some trendy gallery, Cervantes sitting down with his agent to figure tax-shelter angles. Yes? No. I look at the scoop. The scoop looks at me. It is very very late to consider these matters, my friends. Years of our lives consumed, billions of dollars spent, the seals of time ripped open, a young genius's strange odyssey ending on the floor backstage at The Quonch, and for what, for what, for what? We can't simply abandon the project now, can we?

Can we?

I look at the scoop. The scoop looks at me.

THE POPE OF THE CHIMPS

There's not much to say about this story except that it is a personal favorite of mine. I wrote it in June of 1981, quickly, with great passion and conviction, in response to an invitation from the writer Alan Ryan to do a story for an anthology of science-fiction stories on religious themes called Perpetual Light. *The anthology appeared the following year and the story was nominated for a Nebula award. It probably would have won if it had appeared in one of the widely distributed science-fiction magazines instead of an anthology that relatively few of the voters had read. But it has frequently appeared in anthologies ever since. I think I've rarely managed such a depth of characterization—of man and beast—within such a small compass.*

Early last month Vendelmans and I were alone with the chimps in the compound when suddenly he said, "I'm going to faint." It was a sizzling May morning, but Vendelmans had never shown any sign of noticing unusual heat, let alone suffering from it. I was busy talking to Leo and Mimsy and Mimsy's daughter Muffin, and I registered Vendelmans's remark without doing anything about it. When you're intensely into talking by sign language, as we are in the project, you sometimes tend not to pay a lot of attention to spoken words.

But then Leo began to sign the trouble sign at me, and I turned around and saw Vendelmans down on his knees in the grass, white-faced, gasping, covered with sweat. A few of the chimpanzees who aren't as sensitive to humans as Leo is thought it was a game and began to pantomime him, knuckles to the ground and bodies going limp. "Sick—" Vendelmans said. "Feel—terrible—"

I called for help, and Gonzo took his left arm and Kong took his right and somehow, big as he was, we managed to get him out of the compound and up the hill to headquarters. By then he was complaining about sharp pains in his back and under his arms, and I realized that it wasn't just heat prostration. Within a week the diagnosis was in.

Leukemia.

They put him on chemotherapy and hormones, and after ten days he was back with the project, looking cocky. "They've stabilized it," he told everyone. "It's in remission and I might have ten or twenty years left, or even more. I'm going to carry on with my work."

But he was gaunt and pale, with a tremor in his hands, and it was a frightful thing to have him among us. He might have been fooling himself, though I doubted it, but he wasn't fooling any of us: to us he was a memento mori, a walking death's-head-and-crossbones. That laymen think scientists are any more casual about such things than anyone else is something I blame Hollywood for. It is not easy to go about your daily work with a dying man at your side—or a dying man's wife, for Judy Vendelmans showed in her frightened eyes all the grief that Hal Vendelmans himself was repressing. She was going to lose a beloved husband unexpectedly soon and she hadn't had time to adjust to it and her pain was impossible to ignore. Besides, the nature of Vendelmans's dyingness was particularly unsettling because he had been so big and robust and outgoing, a true Rabelaisian figure, and somehow between one moment and the next he was transformed into a wraith. "The finger of God," Dave Yost said. "A quick flick of Zeus's pinkie and Hal shrivels like cellophane in a fireplace." Vendelmans was not yet forty.

The chimps suspected something, too.

Some of them, such as Leo and Ramona, are fifth-generation signers, bred for alpha intelligence, and they pick up subtleties and nuances very well. "Almost human," visitors like to say of them. We dislike that tag, because the important thing about chimpanzees is that they *aren't* human, that they are an alien intelligent species; but yet I know what people mean. The brightest of the chimps saw right away that something was amiss with Vendelmans, and started making odd remarks. "Big one rotten banana," said Ramona to Mimsy while I was nearby. "He getting empty," Leo said to me as Vendelmans stumbled past us. Chimp metaphors never cease to amaze me. And Gonzo asked him outright: "You go away soon?"

"Go away" is not the chimp euphemism for death. So far as our animals know, no human being has ever died. Chimps die. Human beings go away. We have kept things on that basis from the beginning, not intentionally at first, but such arrangements have a way of institutionalizing themselves. The first member of the group to die was Roger Nixon, in an automobile accident in the early years of the project long before my time here, and apparently no one wanted to confuse or disturb the animals by explaining what had happened to him, so no explanations were offered. My second or third year here, Tim Lippinger was killed in a ski-lift failure, and again it seemed easier not to go into details with them. And by the time of Will Bechstein's death in that helicopter crackup four years ago the policy was explicit: we chose not to regard his disappearance from the group as death, but mere going away, as if he had only retired. The chimps do understand death, of course. They may even equate it with going away, as Gonzo's question suggests. But if they do, they surely see human death as something quite different from chimpanzee death—a translation to another state of being, an ascent on a chariot of fire. Yost believes that they have no comprehension of human death at all, that they think we are immortal, that they think we are gods.

Vendelmans now no longer pretends that he isn't dying. The leukemia is plainly acute, and he deteriorates physically from day to day. His original this-isn't-actually-happening attitude has been replaced by a kind of sullen, angry acceptance. It is only the fourth week since the onset of the ailment and soon he'll have to enter the hospital.

And he wants to tell the chimps that he's going to die.

"They don't know that human beings can die," Yost said.

"Then it's time they found out," Vendelmans snapped. "Why perpetuate a load of mythological bullshit about us? Why let them think we're gods? Tell them outright that I'm going to die, the way old Egbert died and Salami and Mortimer."

"But they all died naturally," Jan Morton said.

"And I'm not dying naturally?"

She became terribly flustered. "Of old age, I mean. Their life cycles clearly and understandably came to an end and they died and the chimps understood it. Whereas you—" She faltered.

"—am dying a monstrous and terrible death midway through my life," Vendelmans said, and started to break down and recovered with a fierce effort, and Jan began to cry, and it was generally a bad scene from which Vendelmans saved us by going on, "It should be of philosophical importance to the project to discover how the chimps react to a revaluation of the human metaphysic. We've ducked every chance we've had to help them understand the nature of mortality. Now I propose we use me to teach them that humans are subject to the same laws they are. That we are not gods."

"And that gods exist," said Yost, "who are capricious and unfathomable and to whom we ourselves are as less than chimps."

Vendelmans shrugged. "They don't need to hear all that now. But it's time they understood what we are. Or rather, it's time that we learned how much they already understand. Use my death as a way of finding out. It's the first time they've been in the presence of a human who's actually in the process of dying. The other times one of us has died, it's always been in some sort of accident."

Burt Christensen said, "Hal, have you already told them anything about—"

"No," Vendelmans said. "Of course not. Not a word. But I see them talking to each other. They know."

We discussed it far into the night. The questions needed careful examination because of the far-reaching consequences of any change we might make in the metaphysical givens of our animals. These chimps have lived in a closed environment here for decades, and the culture they have evolved is a product of what we have chosen to teach them, compounded by their own innate chimpness plus whatever we have unknowingly transmitted to them about ourselves or them. Any radical conceptual material we offer them must be weighed thoughtfully, because its effects will be irreversible, and those who succeed us in this community will be unforgiving if we do anything stupidly premature. If the plan is to observe a community of intelligent primates over a period of many human generations, studying the changes in their intellectual capacity as their linguistic skills increase, then we must at all times take care to let them find things out for themselves, rather than skewing our data by giving the chimps more than their current concept-processing abilities may be able to handle.

On the other hand. Vendelmans was dying right now, allowing us a dramatic opportunity to convey the concept of human mortality. We had at best a week or two to make use of that opportunity: then it might be years before the next chance.

"What are you worried about?" Vendelmans demanded.

Yost said, "Do you fear dying, Hal?"

"Dying makes me angry. I don't fear it; but I still have things to do, and I won't be able to do them. Why do you ask?"

"Because so far as we know the chimps see death—chimp death— as simply part of the great cycle of events, like the darkness that comes after the daylight. But human death is going to come as a revelation to them, a shock. And if they pick up from you any sense of fear or even anger over your dying, who knows what impact that will have on their way of thought?"

"Exactly. *Who knows?* I offer you a chance to find out!" By a narrow margin, finally we voted to let Hal Vendelmans share his death with the chimpanzees. Nearly all of us had reservations about that. But plainly Vendelmans was determined to have a useful death, a meaningful death; the only way he could face his fate at all was by contributing it like this to the project. And in the end I think most of us cast our votes his way purely out of our love for him.

We rearranged the schedules to give Vendelmans more contact with the animals. There are ten of us, fifty of them; each of us has a special field of inquiry—number theory, syntactical innovation, metaphysical exploration, semiotics, tool use, and so on—and we work with chimps of our own choice, subject, naturally, to the shifting patterns of sub-tribal bonding within the chimp community. But we agreed that Vendelmans would have to offer his revelations to the alpha intelligences—Leo, Ramona, Grimsky, Alice and Attila—regardless of the current structure of the chimp-human dialogues. Leo, for instance, was involved in an ongoing interchange with Beth Rankin on the notion of the change of seasons. Beth more or less willingly gave up her time with Leo to Vendelmans, for Leo was essential in this. We learned long ago that anything important had to be imparted to the alphas first, and they will impart it to the others. A bright chimp knows more about teaching things to his duller cousins than the brightest human being.

The next morning Hal and Judy Vendelmans took Leo, Ramona and Attila aside and held a long conversation with them. I was busy in a different part of the compound with Gonzo, Mimsy, Muffin, and Chump, but I glanced over occasionally to see what was going on. Hal looked radiant—like Moses just down from the mountain after talking with God. Judy was trying to look radiant too, working at it, but her grief kept breaking through: once I saw her turn away from the chimps and press her knuckles to her teeth to hold it back.

Afterward Leo and Grimsky had a conference out by the oak grove. Yost and Charley Damiano watched it with binoculars, but they couldn't make much sense out of it. The chimps, when they sign to each other, use modified gestures much less precise than the ones they use with us; whether this marks the evolution of a special chimp-to-chimp argot designed not to be understood by us, or is simply a factor of chimp reliance on supplementary nonverbal ways of communicating, is something we still don't know, but the fact remains that we have trouble comprehending the sign language they use with each other, particularly the form the alphas use. Then, too, Leo and Grimsky kept wandering in and out of the trees, as if perhaps they knew we were watching them and didn't want us to eavesdrop. A little later in the day, Ramona and Alice had the same sort of meeting. Now all five of our alphas must have been in on the revelation.

Somehow the news began to filter down to the rest of them.

We weren't able to observe actual concept transmission. We did notice that Vendelmans, the next day, began to get rather more attention than normal. Little troops of chimpanzees formed about him as he moved—slowly, and in obvious difficulty—about the compound. Gonzo and Chump, who had been bickering for months, suddenly were standing side by side staring intently at Vendelmans. Chicory, normally shy, went out of her way to engage him in a conversation—about the ripeness of the apples on the tree, Vendelmans reported. Anna Livia's young twins, Shem and Shaun, climbed up and sat on Vendelmans's shoulders.

"They want to find out what a dying god is really like," Yost said quietly.

"But look there," Jan Morton said.

Judy Vendelmans had an entourage too: Mimsy, Muffin, Claudius, Buster, and Kong. Staring in fascination, eyes wide, lips extended, some of them blowing little bubbles of saliva.

"Do they think she's dying too?" Beth wondered.

Yost shook his head. "Probably not. They can see there's nothing physically wrong with her. But they're picking up the sorrow vibes, the death vibes."

"Is there any reason to think they're aware that Hal is Judy's mate?" Christensen asked.

"It doesn't matter," Yost said. "They can see that she's upset. That interests them, even if they have no way of knowing why Judy would be more upset than any of the rest of us."

"More mysteries out yonder," I said, pointing into the meadow. Grimsky was standing by himself out there, contemplating something. He is the oldest of the chimps, gray-haired, going bald, a deep thinker. He has been here almost from the beginning, more than thirty years, and very little has escaped his attention in that time.

Far off to the left, in the shade of the big beech tree, Leo stood similarly in solitary meditation. He is twenty, the alpha male of the community, the strongest and by far the most intelligent. It was eerie to see the two of them in their individual zones of isolation, like distant sentinels, like Easter Island statues, lost in private reveries.

"Philosophers," Yost murmured.

Yesterday Vendelmans returned to the hospital for good. Before he went, he made his farewells to each of the fifty chimpanzees, even the infants. In the past week he has altered markedly; he is only a shadow of himself, feeble, wasted. Judy says he'll live only another few weeks.

She has gone on leave and probably won't come back until after Hal's death. I wonder what the chimps will make of her "going away," and of her eventual return.

She said that Leo had asked her if she was dying, too.

Perhaps things will get back to normal here now.

Christensen asked me this morning, "Have you noticed the way they seem to drag the notion of death into whatever conversation you're having with them these days?"

I nodded. "Mimsy asked me the other day if the moon dies when the sun comes up and the sun dies when the moon is out. It seemed like such a standard primitive metaphor that I didn't pick up on it at first. But Mimsy's too young for using metaphor that easily and she isn't particularly clever. The older ones must be talking about dying a lot, and it's filtering down."

"Chicory was doing subtraction with me." Christensen said. "She signed, *'You take five, two die, you have three.'* Later she turned it into a verb: *'Three die one equals two.'*"

Others reported similar things. Yet none of the animals were talking about Vendelmans and what was about to happen to him, nor were they asking any overt questions about death or dying. So far as we were able to perceive, they had displaced the whole thing into metaphorical diversions. That in itself indicated a powerful obsession. Like most obsessives, they were trying to hide the thing that most concerned them, and they probably thought they were doing a good job of it. It isn't their fault that we're able to guess what's going on in their minds. They are, after all—and we sometimes have to keep reminding ourselves of this—only chimpanzees.

They are holding meetings on the far side of the oak grove, where the little stream runs. Leo and Grimsky seem to do most of the talking, and the others gather around and sit very quietly as the speeches are made. The groups run from ten to thirty chimps at a time. We are unable to discover what they're discussing, though of course we have an idea. Whenever one on us approaches such a gathering, the chimps very casually drift off into three or four separate groups and look exceedingly innocent—"We just out for some fresh air, boss."

Charley Damiano wants to plant a bug in the grove. But how do you spy on a group that converses only in sign language? Cameras aren't as easily hidden as microphones.

We do our best with binoculars. But what little we've been able to observe has been mystifying. The chimp-to-chimp signs they use at these meetings are even more oblique and confusing than the ones we had seen earlier. It's as if they're holding their meetings in pig-Latin, or double-talk or in some entirely new and private language.

Two technicians will come tomorrow to help us mount cameras in the grove.

❋

Hal Vendelmans died last night. According to Judy, who phoned Dave Yost, it was very peaceful right at the end, an easy release. Yost and I broke the news to the alpha chimps just after breakfast. No euphemisms, just the straight news. Ramona made a few hooting sounds and looked as if she might cry, but she was the only one who seemed emotionally upset. Leo gave me a long deep look of what was almost certainly compassion, and then he hugged me very hard. Grimsky wandered away and seemed to be signing to himself in the new system. Now a meeting seems to be assembling in the oak grove, the first one in more than a week.

The cameras are in place. Even if we can't decipher the new signs, we can at least tape them and subject them to computer analysis until we begin to understand.

❋

Now we've watched the first tapes of a grove meeting, but I can't say we know a lot more than we did before.

For one thing, they disabled two of the cameras right at the outset. Attila spotted them and sent Gonzo and Claudius up into the trees to yank them out. I suppose the remaining cameras went unnoticed; but by accident or deliberate diabolical craftiness, the chimps positioned themselves in such a way that none of the cameras had a clear angle. We did record a few statements from Leo and some give-and-take between Alice and Anna Livia. They spoke in a mixture of standard signs and the new ones, but, without a sense of the context, we've found it impossible to generate any sequence of meanings. Stray signs such as "shirt," "hat," "human," "change" and "banana fly," interspersed with undecipherable stuff, *seem* to be adding up to something, but no one is sure what. We observed no mention of Hal Vendelmans nor any direct references to death. We may be misleading ourselves entirely about the significance of all this.

Or perhaps not. We codified some of the new signs, and this afternoon I asked Ramona what one of them meant. She fidgeted and hooted and looked uncomfortable—and not simply because I was asking her to do a tough abstract thing like giving a definition. She was worried. She looked around for Leo, and when she saw him she made that sign at him. He came bounding over and shoved Ramona away. Then he began to tell me how wise and good and gentle I am. He may be a genius, but even a genius chimp is still a chimp, and I told him I wasn't fooled by all his flattery. Then I asked him what the new sign meant.

"Jump high come again," Leo signed.

A simple chimpy phrase referring to fun and frolic? So I thought at first, and so did many of my colleagues. But Dave Yost said, "Then why was Ramona so evasive about defining it?"

"Defining isn't easy for them," Beth Rankin said.

"Ramona's one of the five brightest. She's capable of it. Especially since the sign can be defined by use of four other established signs, as Leo proceeded to do."

"What are you getting at, Dave?" I asked.

Yost said, 'Jump high come again' might be about a game they like to play, but it could also be an eschatological reference, sacred talk, a concise metaphorical way to speak of death and resurrection, no?"

Mick Falkenburg snorted. "Jesus, Dave, of all the nutty Jesuitical bullshit—"

"Is it?"

"It's possible sometimes to be too subtle in your analysis," Falkenburg said. "You're suggesting that these chimpanzees have a theology?"

"I'm suggesting that they may be in the process of evolving a religion," Yost replied.

Can it be?

Sometimes we lose our perspective with these animals, as Mick indicated, and we overestimate their intelligence; but just as often, I think, we underestimate them.

Jump high come again.

I wonder. Secret sacred talk? A chimpanzee theology? Belief in life after death? A religion?

They know that human beings have a body of ritual and belief that they call religion, though how much they really comprehend about it is hard to tell. Dave Yost, in his metaphysical discussions with Leo and some of the other alphas, introduced the concept long ago. He drew a hierarchy that began with God and ran downward through human beings and chimpanzees to dogs and cats and onward to insects and frogs, by way of giving the chimps some sense of the great chain of life. They had seen bugs and frogs and cats and dogs, but they wanted Dave to show them God, and he was forced to tell them that God is not actually tangible and accessible, but lives high overhead although His essence penetrates all things. I doubt that they grasped much of that. Leo, whose nimble and probing intelligence is a constant illumination to us, wanted Yost to explain how we talked to God and how God talked to us if He wasn't around to make signs, and Yost said that we had a thing called religion, which was a system of communicating with God. And that was where he left it, a long while back.

Now we are on guard for any indications of a developing religious consciousness among our troop. Even the scoffers—Mick Falkenburg, Beth, to some degree, Charley Damiano—are paying close heed. After all, one of the underlying purposes of this project is to reach an understanding of how the first hominids managed to cross the intellectual boundary that we like to think separates the animals from humanity. We can't reconstruct a bunch of Australopithecines and study them; but we *can* watch chimpanzees who have been given the gift of language build a quasi-protohuman society, and it is the closest thing to traveling back in time that we are apt to achieve. Yost thinks, I think, Burt Christensen is beginning to think, that we have inadvertently kindled an awareness of the divine, of the numinous force that must be worshipped, by allowing them to see that their gods—us—can be struck down and slain by an even higher power.

The evidence so far is slim. The attention given Vendelmans and Judy; the solitary meditations of Leo and Grimsky; the large gatherings in the grove; the greatly accelerated use of modified sign language in chimp-to-chimp talk at those gatherings; the potentially eschatological reference we think we see in the sign that Leo translated as "jump high come again." That's it. To those of us who want to interpret that as the foundations of religion, it seems indicative of what we want to see; to the rest, it all looks like coincidence and fantasy. The problem is that we are dealing with nonhuman intelligence and we must take care not to impose our own thought-constructs. We can never be certain if we are operating from a value system anything like that of the chimps. The built-in ambiguities of the sign-language grammar we must use with them complicate the issue. Consider the phrase "banana fly" that Leo used in a speech—a sermon?—in the oak grove, and remember Ramona's reference to the sick Vendelmans as "rotten banana." If we take *fly* to be a verb, "banana fly" might be considered a metaphorical description of Vendelman's ascent to heaven. If we take it to be a noun, Leo might have been talking about the *Drosophila* flies that feed on decaying fruit, a metaphor for the corruption of the flesh after death. On the other hand, he may simply have been making a comment about the current state of our garbage dump.

We have agreed for the moment not to engage the chimpanzees in any direct interrogation about any of this. The Heisenberg principle is eternally our rule here: the observer can too easily perturb the thing observed, so we must make only the most delicate of measurements. Even so, of course, our presence among the chimps is bound to have its impact, but we do what we can to minimize it by avoiding leading questions and watching in silence.

Two unusual things today. Taken each by each, they would be interesting without being significant; but if we use each to illuminate the other, we begin to see things in a strange new light, perhaps.

One thing is an increase in vocalizing, noticed by nearly everyone, among the chimps. We know that chimpanzees in the wild have a kind of rudimentary spoken language—a greeting call, a defiance call, the grunts that mean "I like the taste of this," the male chimp's territorial hoot, and such—nothing very complex, really not qualitatively much beyond the language of birds and dogs. They also have a fairly rich nonverbal language, a vocabulary of gestures and facial expressions. But it was not until the first experiments decades ago in teaching chimpanzees human sign-language that any important linguistic capacity became apparent in them. Here at the research station the chimps communicate almost wholly in signs, as they have been trained to do for generations and as they have taught their young ones to do; they revert to hoots and grunts only in the most elemental situations. We ourselves communicate mainly in signs when we are talking to each other while working with the chimps, and even in our humans-only conferences, we use signs as much as speech, from long habit. But suddenly the chimps are making sounds at each other. Odd sounds, unfamiliar sounds, weird, clumsy imitations, one might say, of human speech. Nothing that we can understand, naturally: the chimpanzee larynx is simply incapable of duplicating the phonemes humans use. But these new grunts, these tortured blurts of sound, seem intended to mimic our speech. It was Damiano who showed us, as we were watching a tape of a grove session, how Attila was twisting his lips with his hands in what appeared unmistakably to be an attempt to make human sounds come out.

Why?

The second thing is that Leo has started wearing a shirt and a hat. There is nothing remarkable about a chimp in clothing; although we have never encouraged such anthropomorphization here, various animals have taken a fancy from time to time to some item of clothing, have begged it from its owner and have worn it for a few days or even weeks. The novelty here is that the shirt and the hat belonged to Hal Vendelmans, and that Leo wears them only when the chimps are gathered in the oak grove, which Dave Yost has lately begun calling the "holy grove." Leo found them in the toolshed beyond the vegetable garden. The shirt is ten sizes too big, Vendelmans having been so brawny, but Leo ties the sleeves across his chest and lets the rest dangle down over his back almost like a cloak.

What shall we make of this?

Jan is the specialist in chimp verbal processes. At the meeting tonight she said, "It sounds to me as if they're trying to duplicate the rhythms of human speech even though they can't reproduce the actual sounds. They're playing at being human."

"Talking the god-talk," said Dave Yost.

"What do you mean?" Jan asked.

"Chimps talk with their hands. Humans do, too, when speaking with chimps, but when humans talk to humans, they use their voices. Humans are gods to chimps, remember. Talking in the way the gods talk is one way of remaking yourself in the image of the gods, of putting on divine attributes."

"But that's nonsense," Jan said. "I can't possibly—"

"Wearing human clothing," I broke in excitedly, "would also be a kind of putting on divine attributes, in the most literal sense of the phrase. Especially if the clothes—"

"—had belonged to Hal Vendelmans," said Christensen.

"The dead god," Yost said.

We looked at each other in amazement.

Charley Damiano said, not in his usual skeptical way, but in a kind of wonder, "Dave, are you hypothesizing that Leo functions as some sort of priest, that those are his sacred garments?"

"More than just a priest," Yost said. "A high priest, I think. A pope. The pope of the chimps."

Grimsky is suddenly looking very feeble. Yesterday we saw him moving slowly through the meadow by himself, making a long circuit of the grounds as far out as the pond and the little waterfall, then solemnly and ponderously staggering back to the meeting place at the far side of the grove. Today he has been sitting quietly by the stream, occasionally rocking slowly back and forth, now and then dipping his feet in. I checked the records: he is forty-three years old, well along for a chimp, although some have been known to live fifty years and more. Mick wanted to take him to the infirmary, but we decided against it; if he is dying, and by all appearances he is, we ought to let him do it with dignity in his own way. Jan went down to the grove to visit him and reported that he shows no apparent signs of disease. His eyes are clear; his face feels cool. Age has withered him and his time is at hand. I feel an enormous sense of loss, for he has a keen intelligence, a long memory, a shrewd and thoughtful nature. He was the alpha male of the troop for many years, but a decade ago, when Leo came of age, Grimsky abdicated in his favor with no sign of a struggle. Behind Grimsky's grizzled forehead there must lie a wealth of subtle and mysterious perceptions, concepts and insights about which we know practically nothing, and very soon all that will be lost. Let us hope he's managed to teach his wisdom to Leo and Attila and Alice and Ramona.

Today's oddity: a ritual distribution of meat.

Meat is not very important in the diet of chimps, but they do like to have some, and as far back as I can remember, Wednesday has been meat-day here, when we give them a side of beef or some slabs of mutton or something of that sort. The procedure for dividing up the meat betrays the chimps' wild heritage, for the alpha males eat their fill first while the others watch, and then the weaker males beg for a share and are allowed to move in to grab, and finally the females and young ones get the scraps. Today was meat-day. Leo, as usual, helped himself first, but what happened after that was astounding. He let Attila feed, and then told Attila to offer some meat to Grimsky, who is even weaker today and brushed it aside. *Then Leo put on Vendelmans's hat* and began to parcel out scraps of meat to the others. One by one they came up to him in the current order of ranking and went through the standard begging maneuver, hand beneath chin, palm upward, and Leo gave each one a strip of meat.

"Like taking communion," Charley Damiano muttered. "With Leo the celebrant at the Mass."

Unless our assumptions are totally off base, there is a real religion going on here, perhaps created by Grimsky and under Leo's governance. And Hal Vendelmans's faded old blue work hat is the tiara of the pope.

Beth Rankin woke me at dawn and said, "Come fast. They're doing something strange with old Grimsky."

I was up and dressed and awake in a hurry. We have a closed circuit system now that pipes the events in the grove back to us, and we paused at the screen so that I could see what was going on. Grimsky sat on his knees at the edge of the stream, eyes closed, barely moving. Leo, wearing the hat, was beside him, elaborately tying Vendelmans's shirt over Grimsky's shoulders. A dozen or more of the other adult chimps were squatting in a semicircle in front of them.

Burt Christensen said, "What's going on? Is Leo making Grimsky the assistant pope?"

"I think Leo is giving Grimsky the last rites," I said.

What else could it have been? Leo wore the sacred headdress. He spoke at length using the new signs—the ecclesiastical language, the chimpanzee equivalent of Latin or Hebrew or Sanskrit—and as his oration went on and on, the congregation replied periodically with outbursts of—I suppose—response and approval, some in signs, some with grunting garbled pseudohuman sounds that Dave Yost thought was their version of godtalk. Throughout it all Grimsky was—silent and remote, though occasionally he nodded or murmured or tapped both his shoulders in a gesture whose meaning was unknown to us. The ceremony went on for more than an hour. Then Grimsky leaned forward, and Kong and Chump took him by the arms and eased him down until he was lying with his cheek against the ground.

For two, three, five minutes all the chimpanzees were still. At last Leo came forward and removed his hat, setting it on the ground beside Grimsky, and with great delicacy he untied the shirt Grimsky wore. Grimsky did not move. Leo draped the shirt over his own shoulders and donned the hat again.

He turned to the watching chimps and signed, using the old signs that were completely intelligible to us, "Grimsky now be human being."

We stared at each other in awe and astonishment. A couple of us were sobbing. No one could speak.

The funeral ceremony seemed to be over. The chimps were dispersing. We saw Leo sauntering away, hat casually dangling from one hand, the shirt in the other, trailing over the ground: Grimsky alone remained by the stream. We waited ten minutes and went down to the grove. Grimsky seemed to be sleeping very peacefully, but he was dead, and we gathered him up—Burt and I carried him; he seemed to weigh almost nothing—and took him back to the lab for the autopsy.

In mid-morning the sky darkened and lightning leaped across the hills to the north. There was a tremendous crack of thunder almost instantly and sudden tempestuous rain. Jan pointed to the meadow. The male chimps were doing a bizarre dance, roaring, swaying, slapping their feet against the ground, hammering their hands against the trunks of the trees, ripping off branches and flailing the earth with them. Grief? Terror? Joy at the translation of Grimsky to a divine state? Who could tell? I had never been frightened by our animals before—I knew them too well, I regarded them as little hairy cousins—but now they were terrifying creatures and this was a scene out of time's dawn, as Gonzo and Kong and Attila and Chump and Buster and Claudius and even Pope Leo himself went thrashing about in that horrendous rain, pounding out the steps of some unfathomable rite.

The lightning ceased and the rain moved southward as quickly as it had come, and the dancers went slinking away, each to his favorite tree. By noon the day was bright and warm and it was as though nothing out of the ordinary had happened.

Two days after Grimsky's death I was awakened again at dawn, this time by Mick Falkenburg. He shook my shoulder and yelled at me to wake up, and as I sat there blinking he said, "Chicory's dead! I was out for an early walk and I found her near the place where Grimsky died."

"Chicory? But she's only—"

"Eleven, twelve, something like that. I know."

I put my clothes on while Mick woke the others, and we went down to the stream. Chicory was sprawled out, but not peacefully—there was a dribble of blood at the corner of her mouth, her eyes were wide and horrified, her hands were curled into frozen talons. All about her in the moist soil of the stream bank were footprints. I searched my memory for an instance of murder in the chimp community and could find nothing remotely like it—quarrels, yes, and lengthy feuds and some ugly ambushes and battles, fairly violent, serious injuries now and then. But this had no precedent.

"Ritual murder," Yost murmured.

"Or a sacrifice, perhaps?" suggested Beth Rankin.

"Whatever it is," I said, "they're learning too fast. Recapitulating the whole evolution of religion, including the worst parts of it. We'll have to talk to Leo."

"Is that wise?" Yost asked.

"Why not?"

"We've kept hands off so far. If we want to see how this thing unfolds—"

"During the night," I said, "the pope and the college of cardinals ganged up on a gentle young female chimp and killed her. Right now they may be off somewhere sending Alice or Ramona or Anna Livia's twins to chimp heaven. I think we have to weigh the value of observing the evolution of chimp religion against the cost of losing irreplaceable members of a unique community. I say we call in Leo and tell him that it's wrong to kill."

"He knows that," said Yost. "He must. Chimps aren't murderous animals."

"Chicory's dead."

"And if they see it as a holy deed?" Yost demanded.

"Then one by one we'll lose our animals, and at the end we'll just have a couple of very saintly survivors. Do you want that?"

We spoke with Leo. Chimps can be sly and they can be manipulative, but even the best of them, and Leo is the Einstein of chimpanzees, does not seem to know how to lie. We asked him where Chicory was and Leo told us that Chicory was now a human being. I felt a chill at that. Grimsky was also a human being, said Leo. We asked him how he knew that they had become human and he said, "They go where Vendelmans go. When human go away, he become god. When chimpanzee go away, he become human. Right?"

"No," we said.

The logic of the ape is not easy to refute. We told him that death comes to all living creatures, that it is natural and holy, but that only God could decide when it was going to happen. God, we said, calls His creatures to Himself one at a time. God had called Hal Vendelmans, God had called Grimsky, God would someday call Leo and all the rest here. But God had not yet called Chicory. Leo wanted to know what was wrong with sending Chicory to Him ahead of time. Did that not improve Chicory's condition? No, we replied. No, it only did harm to Chicory. Chicory would have been much happier living here with us than going to God so soon. Leo did not seem convinced. Chicory, he said, now could talk words with her mouth and wore shoes on her feet. He envied Chicory very much.

We told him that God would be angry if any more chimpanzees died. We told him that *we* would be angry. Killing chimpanzees was wrong, we said. It was not what God wanted Leo to be doing.

"Me talk to God, find out what God wants," Leo said.

We found Buster dead by the edge of the pond this morning, with indications of another ritual murder. Leo coolly stared us down and explained that God had given orders that all chimpanzees were to become human beings as quickly as possible, and this could only be achieved by the means employed on Chicory and Buster.

Leo is confined now in the punishment tank and we have suspended this week's meat distribution. Yost voted against both of those decisions, saying we ran the risk of giving Leo the aura of a religious martyr, which would enhance his already considerable power. But these killings have to stop. Leo knows, of course, that we are upset about them. But if he believes his path is the path of righteousness, nothing we say or do is going to change his mind.

Judy Vendelmans called today. She has put Hal's death fairly well behind her, misses the project, misses the chimps. As gently as I could, I told her what has been going on here. She was silent a very long time—Chicory was one of her favorites, and Judy has had enough grief already to handle for one summer—but finally she said, "I think I know what can be done. I'll be on the noon flight tomorrow."

We found Mimsy dead in the usual way late this afternoon. Leo is still in the punishment tank—the third day. The congregation has found a way to carry out its rites without its leader. Mimsy's death has left me stunned, but we are all deeply affected, virtually unable to proceed with our work. It may be necessary to break up the community entirely to save the animals. Perhaps we can send them to other research centers for a few months, three of them here, five there, until this thing subsides. But what if it doesn't subside? What if the dispersed animals convert others elsewhere to the creed of Leo?"

The first thing Judy said when she arrived was, "Let Leo out. I want to talk with him."

We opened the tank. Leo stepped forth, uneasy, abashed, shading his eyes against the strong light. He glanced at me, at Yost, at Jan, as if wondering which one of us was going to scold him; and then he saw Judy and it was as though he had seen a ghost. He made a hollow rasping sound deep in his throat and backed away. Judy signed hello and stretched out her arms to him. Leo trembled. He was terrified. There was nothing unusual about one of us going on leave and returning after a month or two, but Leo must not have expected Judy ever to return, must in fact have imagined her gone to the same place her husband had gone, and the sight of her shook him. Judy understood all that, obviously, for she quickly made powerful use of it, signing to Leo, "I bring you message from Vendelmans."

"Tell tell tell!"

"Come walk with me," said Judy.

She took him by the hand and led him gently out of the punishment area and into the compound and down the hill toward the meadow. I watched from the top of the hill, the tall, slender woman and the compact, muscular chimpanzee close together, side by side, hand in hand, pausing now to talk, Judy signing and Leo replying in a flurry of gestures, then Judy again for a long time, a brief response from Leo, another cascade of signs from Judy, then Leo squatting, tugging at blades of grass, shaking his head, clapping hand to elbow in his expression of confusion, then to his chin, then taking Judy's hand. They were gone for nearly an hour. The other chimps did not dare approach them. Finally Judy and Leo, hand in hand, came quietly up the hill to headquarters again. Leo's eyes were shining and so were Judy's.

She said, "Everything will be all right now. That's so, isn't it, Leo?"

Leo said, "God is always right."

She made a dismissal sign and Leo went slowly down the hill. The moment he was out of sight, Judy turned away from us and cried a little, just a little; then she asked for a drink; and then she said, "It isn't easy, being God's messenger."

"What did you tell him?" I asked.

"That I had been in heaven visiting Hal. That Hal was looking down all the time and he was very proud of Leo, except for one thing, that Leo was sending too many chimpanzees to God too soon. I told him that God was not yet ready to receive Chicory and Buster and Mimsy, that they would have to be kept in storage cells for a long time until their true time came, and that was not good for them. I told him that Hal wanted Leo to know that God hoped he would stop sending him chimpanzees. Then I gave Leo Hal's old wristwatch to wear when he conducts services, and Leo promised he would obey Hal's wishes. That was all. I suspect I've added a whole new layer of mythology to what's developing here, and I trust you won't be angry with me for doing it. I don't believe any more chimps will be killed. And I think I'd like another drink."

Later in the day we saw the chimps assembled by the stream. Leo held his arm aloft and sunlight blazed from the band of gold on his slim hairy wrist, and a great outcry of grunts in god-talk went up from the congregation and they danced before him, and then he donned the sacred hat and the sacred shirt and moved his arms eloquently in the secret sacred gestures of the holy sign language.

There have been no more killings. I think no more will occur. Perhaps after a time our chimps will lose interest in being religious, and go on to other pastimes. But not yet, not yet. The ceremonies continue, and grow ever more elaborate, and we are compiling volumes of extraordinary observations, and God looks down and is pleased. And Leo proudly wears the emblems of his papacy as he bestows his blessing on the worshipers in the holy grove.

THESME AND THE GHAYROG

The very active year of 1981, though it was a year in which I wrote only short stories, was colored for me in many ways by the publication the year before of the big novel Lord Valentine's Castle, *which had marked my return to writing after the four-year retirement period. The book got a lot of attention, and not simply because it demonstrated that I hadn't really given up writing after all. It flirted for a little while with the best-seller lists; it gained me a Hugo nomination; and, as I looked at it a year or so after having written it, I realized that Majipoor, the giant world that I had created for it, was one of my most fully realized science-fictional inventions, and did not deserve to be abandoned after a single visit.*

So I began to prowl through the 14,000-year history of Majipoor that I had put together for Lord Valentine's Castle, *looking for episodes that deserved stories in their own right. When Underwood-Miller, a small press publisher then doing a great deal of high-quality work, asked me for an original novella, I responded in October of 1980 with a long Majipoor story, "The Desert of Stolen Dreams," set about a thousand years before the novel. A few months later, George Scithers, then the editor of* Isaac Asimov's Science Fiction Magazine, *suggested I do a Majipoor story for him, and I responded with another novella, "A Thief in Ni-Moya." At that point I realized that I had now written about one-third of the material I would need for a collection of new Majipoor tales, and, since the huge planet abounded in potential story material, I set to work in earnest in the spring and summer of 1981 to bring that book into being.*

Story followed story quickly: one in April, one in May, one in June, three in July, one in August, and the tenth and last in September. By then I

had found a new book publisher, Arbor House, run by the dynamic and iras-
cible Don Fine, and I assembled the ten new stories into a sort of
pseudo-novel for him under the title of Majipoor Chronicles, *which would*
appear in 1982, with an actual sequel to Lord Valentine's Castle *called*
Valentine Pontifex *to be written the following year.*

It would be impractical, of course, to include all ten of the Majipoor
Chronicles *stories in this volume of my collected short work. But it does*
seem appropriate to offer at least one example, and the one I have chosen is
one of the three that I wrote in July of 1981: the opening story of the book,
"Thesme and the Ghayrog", which I held back from magazine publication
and allowed to appear only in Chronicles. *It is set in the early years of*
human settlement on Majipoor, long before the events depicted in Lord
Valentine's Castle, *and, I think, provides a vivid glimpse into the relation-*
ships between the various intelligent species that had come from all over the
galaxy to take up residence on that vast, all but infinite planet.

1

For six months now Thesme had lived alone in a hut that she had
built with her own hands, in the dense tropical jungle half a dozen
miles or so east of Narabal, in a place where the sea breezes did not
reach and the heavy humid air clung to everything like a furry shroud.
She had never lived by herself before, and at first she wondered how
good she was going to be at it; but she had never built a hut before
either, and she had done well enough at that, cutting down slender sijaneel saplings, trimming away the golden bark, pushing their slippery
sharpened ends into the soft moist ground, lashing them together with
vines, finally tying on five enormous blue vramma leaves to make a
roof. It was no masterpiece of architecture, but it kept out the rain, and
she had no need to worry about cold. Within a month her sijaneel timbers, trimmed though they were, had all taken root and were sprouting
leathery new leaves along their upper ends, just below the roof; and the
vines that held them were still alive too, sending down fleshy red tendrils that searched for and found the rich fertile soil. So now the house
was a living thing, daily becoming more snug and secure as the vines
tightened and the sijaneels put on girth, and Thesme loved it. In

Narabal nothing stayed dead for long; the air was too warm, the sunlight too bright, the rainfall too copious, and everything quickly transformed itself into something else with the riotous buoyant ease of the tropics.

Solitude was turning out to be easy too. She had needed very much to get away from Narabal, where her life had somehow gone awry: too much confusion, too much inner noise, friends who became strangers, lovers who turned into foes. She was twenty-five years old and needed to stop, to take a long look at everything, to change the rhythm of her days before it shook her to pieces. The jungle was the ideal place for that. She rose early, bathed in a pond that she shared with a sluggish old gromwark and a school of tiny crystalline chichibors, plucked her breakfast from a thokka vine, hiked, read, sang, wrote poems, checked her traps for captured animals, climbed trees and sunbathed in a hammock of vines high overhead, dozed, swam, talked to herself, and went to sleep when the sun went down. In the beginning she thought there would not be enough to do, that she would soon grow bored, but that did not seem to be the case; her days were full and there were always a few projects to save for tomorrow.

At first she expected that she would go into Narabal once a week or so, to buy staple goods, to pick up new books and cubes, to attend an occasional concert or a play, even to visit her family or those of her friends that she still felt like seeing. For a while she actually did go to town fairly often. But it was a sweaty, sticky trek that took half a day, nearly, and as she grew accustomed to her reclusive life she found Narabal ever more jangling, ever more unsettling, with few rewards to compensate for the drawbacks. People there stared at her. She knew they thought she was eccentric, even crazy, always a wild girl and now a peculiar one, living out there by herself and swinging through the treetops. So her visits became more widely spaced. She went only when it was unavoidable. On the day she found the injured Ghayrog she had not been to Narabal for at least five weeks.

She had been roving that morning through a swampy region a few miles northeast of her hut, gathering the sweet yellow fungi known as calimbots. Her sack was almost full and she was thinking of turning back when she spied something strange a few hundred yards away: a creature of some sort with gleaming, metallic-looking gray skin and thick tubular limbs, sprawled awkwardly on the ground below a great sijaneel tree. It reminded her of a predatory reptile her father and brother once had killed in Narabal Channel, a sleek, elongated, slow-moving thing with curved claws and a vast toothy mouth. But as she drew closer she saw that this life-form was vaguely human in construction, with a massive rounded head, long arms, powerful legs. She thought it might be dead, but it stirred faintly when she approached and said, "I am damaged. I have been stupid and now I am paying for it."

"Can you move your arms and legs?" Thesme asked.

"The arms, yes. One leg is broken, and possibly my back. Will you help me?"

She crouched and studied it closely. It did look reptilian, yes, with shining scales and a smooth, hard body. Its eyes were green and chilly and did not blink at all; its hair was a weird mass of thick black coils that moved of their own accord in a slow writhing; its tongue was a serpent-tongue, bright scarlet, forked, flickering constantly back and forth between the narrow fleshless lips.

"What are you?" she asked.

"A Ghayrog. Do you know of my kind?"

"Of course," she said, though she knew very little, really. All sorts of non-human species had been settling on Majipoor in the past hundred years, a whole menagerie of aliens invited here by the Coronal Lord Melikand because there were not enough humans to fill the planet's immensities. Thesme had heard that there were four-armed ones and two-headed ones and tiny ones with tentacles and these scaly snake-tongued snake-haired ones, but none of the alien beings had yet come as far as Narabal, a town on the edge of nowhere, as distant from civilization as one could get. So this was a Ghayrog, then? A strange creature, she thought, almost human in the shape of its body and yet not at all human in any of its details, a monstrosity, really, a nightmare being, though not especially frightening. She pitied the poor Ghayrog, in fact—a wanderer, doubly lost, far from its home world and far from anything that mattered on Majipoor. And badly hurt, too. What was she going to do with it? Wish it well and abandon it to its fate? Hardly. Go all the way into Narabal and organize a rescue mission? That would take at least two days, assuming anyone cared to help. Bring it back to her hut and nurse it to good health? That seemed the most likely thing to do, but what would happen to her solitude, then, her privacy, and how did one take care of a Ghayrog, anyway, and did she really want the responsibility? And the risk, for that matter: this was an alien being and she had no idea what to expect from it.

It said, "I am Vismaan."

Was that its name, its title, or merely a description of its condition? She did not ask. She said, "I am called Thesme. I live in the jungle an hour's walk from here. How can I help you?"

"Let me brace myself on you while I try to get up. Do you think you are strong enough?"

"Probably."

"You are female, am I right?"

She was wearing only sandals. She smiled and touched her hand lightly to her breasts and loins and said, "Female, yes."

"So I thought. I am male and perhaps too heavy for you."

Male? Between his legs he was as smooth and sexless as a machine. She supposed that Ghayrogs carried their sex somewhere else. And if they were reptiles, her breasts would indicate nothing to him about her sex. Strange, all the same, that he should need to ask.

She knelt beside him, wondering how he was going to rise and walk with a broken back. He put his arm over her shoulders. The touch of his skin against hers startled her: it felt cool, dry, rigid, smooth, as though he wore armor. Yet it was not an unpleasant texture, only odd. A strong odor came from him, swampy and bitter with an undertaste of honey. That she had not noticed it before was hard to understand, for it was pervasive and insistent; she decided she must have been distracted by the unexpectedness of coming upon him. There was no ignoring the odor now that she was aware of it, and at first she found it intensely disagreeable, though within moments it ceased to bother her.

He said, "Try to hold steady. I will push myself up."

Thesme crouched, digging her knees and hands into the soil, and to her amazement he succeeded in drawing himself upward with a peculiar coiling motion, pressing down on her, driving his entire weight for a moment between her shoulder blades in a way that made her gasp. Then he was standing, tottering, clinging to a dangling vine. She made ready to catch him if he fell, but he stayed upright.

"This leg is cracked," he told her. "The back is damaged but not, I think, broken."

"Is the pain very bad?"

"Pain? No, we feel little pain. The problem is functional. The leg will not support me. Can you find me a strong stick?"

She scouted about for something he might use as a crutch and spied, after a moment, the stiff aerial root of a vine dangling out of the forest canopy. The glossy black root was thick but brittle, and she bent it backward and forward until she succeeded in snapping off some two yards of it. Vismaan grasped it firmly, draped his other arm around Thesme, and cautiously put his weight on his uninjured leg. With difficulty he took a step, another, another, dragging the broken leg along. It seemed to Thesme that his body odor had changed: sharper, now, more vinegar, less honey. The strain of walking, no doubt. The pain was probably less trivial than he wanted her to think. But he was managing to keep moving, at any rate.

"How did you hurt yourself?" she asked.

"I climbed this tree to survey the territory just ahead. It did not bear my weight."

He nodded toward the slim shining trunk of the tall sijaneel. The lowest branch, which was at least forty feet above her, was broken and hung down by nothing more than shreds of bark. It amazed her that he had survived a fall from such a height; after a moment she found herself wondering how he had been able to get so high on the slick smooth trunk in the first place.

He said, "My plan is to settle in this area and raise crops. Do you have a farm?"

"In the jungle? No, I just live here."

"With a mate?"

"Alone. I grew up in Narabal, but I needed to get away by myself or a while." They reached the sack of calimbots she had dropped when he first noticed him lying on the ground, and she slung it over her shoulder. "You can stay with me until your leg has healed. But it's going to take all afternoon to get back to my hut this way. Are you sure you're able to walk?"

"I am walking now," he pointed out.

"Tell me when you want to rest."

"In time. Not yet."

Indeed it was nearly half an hour of slow and surely painful hobbling before he asked to halt, and even then he remained standing, leaning against a tree, explaining that he thought it unwise to go through the whole difficult process of lifting himself from the ground a second time. He seemed altogether calm and in relatively little discomfort, although it was impossible to read expression into his unchanging face and unblinking eyes: the constant flickering of his forked tongue was the only indicator of apparent emotion she could see, and she had no idea how to interpret those ceaseless darting movements. After a few minutes they resumed the walk. The slow pace was a burden to her, as was his weight against her shoulder, and she felt her own muscles cramping and protesting as they edged through the jungle. They said little. He seemed preoccupied with the need to exert control over his crippled body, and she concentrated on the route, searching for short-cuts, thinking ahead to avoid streams and dense undergrowth and other obstacles he would not be able to cope with. When they were halfway back to her hut a warm rain began to fall, and after that they were enveloped in hot clammy fog the rest of the way. She was nearly exhausted by the time her little cabin came into view.

"Not quite a palace," she said, "but it's all I need. I built it myself. You can lie down here." She helped him to her zanja-down bed. He sank onto it with a soft hissing sound that was surely relief. "Would you like something to eat?" she asked.

"Not now."

"Or to drink? No? I imagine you just want to get some rest. I'll go outside so you can sleep undisturbed."

"This is not my season of sleep," Vismaan said.

"I don't understand."

"We sleep only one part of the year. Usually in winter."

"And you stay awake all the rest of the time?"

"Yes," he said. "I am finished with this year's sleep. I understand it is different with humans."

"Extremely different," she told him. "I'll leave you to rest by your-self, anyway. You must be terribly tired."

"I would not drive you from your home."

"It's all right," Thesme said, and stepped outside. The rain was beginning again, the familiar, almost comforting rain that fell every few hours all day long. She sprawled out on a bank of dark yielding rub-bermoss and let the warm droplets of rain wash the fatigue from her aching back and shoulders.

A houseguest, she thought. And an alien one, no less. Well, why not? The Ghayrog seemed undemanding: cool, aloof, tranquil even in calamity. He was obviously more seriously hurt than he was willing to admit, and even this relatively short journey through the forest had been a struggle for him. There was no way he could walk all the way into Narabal in this condition. Thesme supposed that she could go into town and arrange for someone to come out in a floater to get him, but the idea displeased her. No one knew where she was living and she did not care to lead anyone here, for one thing. And she realized in some confusion that she did not want to give the Ghayrog up, that she wanted to keep him here and nurse him until he had regained his strength. She doubted that anyone else in Narabal would have given shelter to an alien, and that made her feel pleasantly perverse, set apart in still another way from the citizens of her native town. In the past year or two she had heard plenty of muttering about the offworlders who were coming to settle on Majipoor. People feared and disliked the reptilian Ghayrogs and the giant hulking hairy Skandars and the little tricky ones with the many tentacles—Vroons, were they?—and the rest of that bizarre crew, and even though aliens were still unknown in remote Narabal the hostility toward them was already there. Wild and eccentric Thesme, she thought, was just the kind who *would* take in a Ghayrog and pat his fevered brow and give him medicine and soup, or whatever you gave a Ghayrog with a broken leg. She had no real idea of how to care for him, but she did not intend to let that stop her. It occurred to her that she had never taken care of anyone in her life, for somehow there had been neither opportunity nor occasion; she was the youngest in her family and no one had ever allowed her any sort of responsibility, and she had not married or borne children or even kept pets, and during the stormy period of her innumerable turbulent love affairs she had never seen fit to visit any of her lovers while he was ill. Quite likely, she told herself, that was why she was suddenly so determined to keep this Ghayrog at her hut. One of the reasons she had quitted Narabal for the jungle was to live her life in a new way, to break with the uglier traits of the former Thesme.

She decided that in the morning she would go into town, find out if she could what kind of care the Ghayrog needed, and buy such medicines or provisions as seemed appropriate.

2

After a long while she returned to the hut. Vismaan lay as she had left him, flat on his back with arms stiff against his sides, and he did not seem to be moving at all, except for the perpetual serpentine writhing of his hair. Asleep? After all his talk of needing none? She went to him and peered down at the strange massive figure on her bed. His eyes were open, and she saw them tracking her.

"How do you feel?" she asked.

"Not well. Walking through the forest was more difficult than I realized."

She put her hand to his forehead. His hard scaly skin felt cool. But the absurdity of her gesture made her smile. What was a Ghayrog's normal body temperature? Were they susceptible to fever at all, and if so, how could she tell? They were reptiles, weren't they? Did reptiles run high temperatures when they were sick? Suddenly it all seemed preposterous, this notion of nursing a creature of another world.

He said, "Why do you touch my head?"

"It's what we do when a human is sick. To see if you have a fever. I have no medical instruments here. Do you know what I mean by running a fever?"

"Abnormal body temperature. Yes. Mine is high now."

"Are you in pain?"

"Very little. But my systems are disarranged. Can you bring me some water?"

"Of course. And are you hungry? What sort of things do you normally eat?"

"Meat. Cooked. And fruits and vegetables. And a great deal of water."

She fetched a drink for him. He sat up with difficulty—he seemed much weaker than when he had been hobbling through the jungle; most likely he was suffering a delayed reaction to his injuries—and drained the bowl in three greedy gulps. She watched the furious movements of his forked tongue, fascinated. "More," he said, and she poured a second bowl. Her water-jug was nearly empty, and she went outside to fill it at the spring. She plucked a few thokkas from the vine, too, and brought them to him. He held one of the juicy blue-white berries at arm's length, as though that was the only way he could focus his vision properly on it, and rolled it experimentally between two of his fingers. His hands were almost human, Thesme observed, though there were two extra fingers and he had no fingernails, only lateral scaly ridges running along the first two joints.

"What is this fruit called?" he asked.

"Thokka. They grow on a vine all over Narabal. If you like them, I'll bring you as many as you want."

He tasted it cautiously. Then his tongue flickered more rapidly, and he devoured the rest of the berry and held out his hand for another. Now Thesme remembered the reputation of thokkas as aphrodisiacs, but she looked away to hide her grin, and chose not to say anything to him about that. He described himself as male, so the Ghayrogs evidently had sexes, but did they have sex? She had a sudden fanciful image of male Ghayrogs squirting milt from some concealed orifice into tubs into which female Ghayrogs climbed to fertilize themselves. Efficient but not very romantic, she thought, wondering if that was actually how they did it—fertilization at a distant remove, like fishes, like snakes.

She prepared a meal for him of thokkas and fried calimbots and the little many-legged delicate-flavored hiktigans that she netted in the stream. All her wine was gone, but she had lately made a kind of fermented juice from a fat red fruit whose name she did not know, and she gave him some of that. His appetite seemed healthy. Afterward she asked him if she could examine his leg, and he told her she could.

The break was more than midway up, in the widest part of his thigh. Thick though his scaly skin was, it showed some signs of swelling there. Very lightly she put her fingertips to the place and probed. He made a barely audible hiss but otherwise gave no sign that she might be increasing his discomfort. It seemed to her that something was moving inside his thigh. The broken ends of the bone, was it? Did Ghayrogs *have* bones? She knew so little, she thought dismally—about Ghayrogs, about the healing arts, about anything.

"If you were human," she said, "we would use our machines to see the fracture, and we would bring the broken place together and bind it until it knitted. Is it anything like that with your people?"

"The bone will knit of its own," he replied. "I will draw the break together through muscular contraction and hold it until it heals. But I must remain lying down for a few days, so that the leg's own weight does not pull the break apart when I stand. Do you mind if I stay here that long?"

"Stay as long as you like. As long as you need to stay."

"You are very kind."

"I'm going into town tomorrow to pick up supplies. Is there anything you particularly want?"

"Do you have entertainment cubes? Music, books?"

"I have just a few here. I can get more tomorrow."

"Please. The nights will be very long for me as I lie here without sleeping. My people are great consumers of amusement, you know."

"I'll bring whatever I can find," she promised.

She gave him three cubes—a play, a symphony, a color composition—and went about her after-dinner cleaning. Night had fallen, early as always, this close to the equator. She heard a light rainfall beginning again outside. Ordinarily she would read for a while, until it grew too dark, and then lie down to sleep. But tonight everything was different. A mysterious reptilian creature occupied her bed; she would have to put together a new sleeping-place for herself on the floor; and all this conversation, the first she had had in so many weeks, had left her mind buzzing with unaccustomed alertness. Vismaan seemed content with his cubes. She went outside and collected bubblebush leaves, a double armful of them and then another, and strewed them on the floor near the door of her hut. Then, going to the Ghayrog, she asked if she could do anything for him; he answered by a tiny shake of his head, without taking his attention from the cube. She wished him a good night and lay down on her improvised bed. It was comfortable enough, more so than she had expected. But sleep was impossible. She turned this way and that, feeling cramped and stiff, and the presence of the other a few yards away seemed to announce itself by a tangible pulsation in her soul. And there was the Ghayrog's odor, too, pungent and inescapable. Somehow she had ceased noticing it while they ate, but now, with all her nerve-endings tuned to maximum sensitivity as she lay in the dark, she perceived it almost as she would a trumpet-blast unendingly repeated. From time to time she sat up and stared through the darkness at Vismaan, who lay motionless and silent. Then at some point slumber overtook her, for when the sounds of the new morning came to her, the many familiar piping and screeching melodies, and the early light made its way through the door-opening, she awakened into the kind of disorientation that comes often when one has been sleeping soundly in a place that is not one's usual bed. It took her a few moments to collect herself, to remember where she was and why.

He was watching her. "You spent a restless night. My being here disturbs you."

"I'll get used to it. How do you feel?"

"Stiff. Sore. But I am already beginning to mend, I think. I sense the work going on within."

She brought him water and a bowl of fruit. Then she went out into the mild misty dawn and slipped quickly into the pond to bathe. When she returned to the hut the odor hit her with new impact. The contrast between the fresh air of morning and the acrid Ghayrog-flavored atmosphere indoors was severe; yet soon it passed from her awareness once again.

As she dressed she said, "I won't be back from Narabal until nightfall. Will you be all right here by yourself?"

"If you leave food and water within my reach. And something to read."

"There isn't much. I'll bring more back for you. It'll be a quiet day for you, I'm afraid."

"Perhaps there will be a visitor."

"A visitor?" Thesme cried, dismayed. "Who? What sort of visitor? No one comes here! Or do you mean some Ghayrog who was traveling with you and who'll be out looking for you?"

"Oh, no, no. No one was with me. I thought, possibly friends of yours—"

"I have no friends," said Thesme solemnly.

It sounded foolish to her the instant she said it—self-pitying, melodramatic. But the Ghayrog offered no comment, leaving her without a way of retracting it, and to hide her embarrassment she busied herself elaborately in the job of strapping on her pack.

He was silent until she was ready to leave. Then he said, "Is Narabal very beautiful?"

"You haven't seen it?"

"I came down the inland route from Til-omon. In Til-omon they told me how beautiful Narabal is."

"Narabal is nothing," Thesme said. "Shacks. Muddy streets. Vines growing over everything, pulling the buildings apart before they're a year old. They told you that in Til-omon? They were joking with you. The Til-omon people despise Narabal. The towns are rivals, you know—the two main tropical ports. If anyone in Til-omon told you how wonderful Narabal is, he was lying, he was playing games with you."

"But why do that?"

Thesme shrugged. "How would I know? Maybe to get you out of Til-omon faster. Anyway, don't look forward to Narabal. In a thousand years it'll be something, I suppose, but right now it's just a dirty frontier town."

"All the same, I hope to visit it. When my leg is stronger, will you show me Narabal?"

"Of course," she said. "Why not? But you'll be disappointed, I promise you. And now I have to leave. I want to get the walk to town behind me before the hottest part of the day."

3

As she made her way briskly toward Narabal she envisioned herself turning up in town one of these days with a Ghayrog by her side. How they'd love that, in Narabal! Would she and Vismaan be pelted with rocks and clots of mud? Would people point and snicker, and snub her when she tried to greet them? Probably. There's that crazy Thesme, they would say to each other, bringing aliens to town, running around with snaky Ghayrogs, probably doing all sorts of unnatural things with them out in the jungle. Yes. Yes. Thesme smiled. It might be fun to promenade about Narabal with Vismaan. She would try it as soon as he was capable of making the long trek through the jungle.

The path was no more than a crudely slashed track, blaze marks on the trees and an occasional cairn, and it was overgrown in many places. But she had grown skilled at jungle travel and she rarely lost her way for long; by late morning she reached the outlying plantations, and soon Narabal itself was in view, straggling up one hillside and down another in a wobbly arc along the seashore.

Thesme had no idea why anyone had wanted to put a city here—halfway around the world from anywhere, the extreme southwest point of Zimroel. It was some idea of Lord Melikand's, the same Coronal who had invited all the aliens to settle on Majipoor, to encourage development on the western continent. In Lord Melikand's time Zimroel had only two cities, both of them terribly isolated, virtual geographic accidents founded in the earliest days of human settlement on Majipoor, before it became apparent that the other continent was going to be the center of Majipoori life. There was Pidruid up in the northwest, with its wondrous climate and its spectacular natural harbor, and there was Piliplok all the way across on the eastern coast, where the hunters of the migratory sea-dragons had their base. But now also there was a little outpost called Ni-moya on one of the big inland rivers, and Til-omon had sprung up on the western coast at the edge of the tropical belt, and evidently some settlement was being founded in the central mountains, and supposedly the Ghayrogs were building a town a thousand miles or so east of Pidruid, and there was Narabal down here in the steaming rainy south, at the tip of the continent with sea all around. If one stood by the shore of Narabal Channel and looked toward the water one felt the terrible weight of the knowledge that at one's back lay thousands of miles of wilderness, and then thousands of miles of ocean, separating one from the continent of Alhanroel where the real cities were. When she was young Thesme had found it frightening to think that she lived in a place so far from the centers of civilized life that it might as well be on some other planet; and other times Aihanroel and its thriving cities seemed merely mythical to her, and Narabal the true center of the universe. She had never been anywhere else, and had no hope of it. Distances were too great. The only town within reasonable reach was Til-omon, but even that was far away, and those who had been there said it was much like Narabal, anyway, only with less rain and the sun standing constantly in the sky like a great boring inquisitive green eye.

In Narabal she felt inquisitive eyes on her wherever she turned: everyone staring, as though she had come to town naked. They all knew who she was—wild Thesme who had run off to the jungle—and they smiled at her and waved and asked her how everything was going, and behind those trivial pleasantries were the eyes, intent and penetrating and hostile, drilling into her, plumbing her for the hidden truths of her life. *Why do you despise us? Why have you withdrawn from us? Why are you sharing your house with a disgusting snake-man?* And she smiled and waved back, and said, "Nice to see you again," and "Everything's just fine," and replied silently to the probing eyes, *I don't hate anybody, I just needed to get away from myself, I'm helping the Ghayrog because it's time I helped someone and he happened to come along.* But they would never understand.

No one was at home at her mother's house. She went to her old room and stuffed her pack with books and cubes, and ransacked the medicine cabinet for drugs that she thought might do Vismaan some good, one to reduce inflammation, one to promote healing, a specific for high fever, and some others—probably all useless to an alien, but worth trying, she supposed. She wandered through the house, which was becoming strange to her even though she had lived in it nearly all her life. Wooden floors instead of strewn leaves—real transparent windows—doors on hinges—a cleanser, an actual mechanical cleanser with knobs and handles!—all those *civilized* things, the million and one humble little things that humanity had invented so many thousands of years ago on another world, and from which she had blithely walked away to live in her humid little hut with live branches sprouting from its walls—

"Thesme?"

She looked up, taken by surprise. Her sister Mirifaine had come in: her twin, in a manner of speaking, same face, same long thin arms and legs, same straight brown hair, but ten years older, ten years more reconciled to the patterns of her life, a married woman, a mother, a hard worker. Thesme had always found it distressing to look at Mirifaine. It was like looking in a mirror and seeing herself old.

Thesme said, "I needed a few things."

"I was hoping you'd decided to move back home."

"What for?"

Mirifaine began to reply—most likely some standard homily, about resuming normal life, fitting into society and being useful, et cetera, et cetera—but Thesme saw her shift direction while all that was still unspoken, and Mirifaine said finally, "We miss you, love."

"I'm doing what I need to do. It's been good to see you, Mirifaine."

"Won't you at least stay the night? Mother will be back soon—she'd be delighted if you were here for dinner—"

"It's a long walk. I can't spend more time here."

"You look good, you know. Tanned, healthy. I suppose being a hermit agrees with you, Thesme."

"Yes. Very much."

"You don't mind living alone?"

"I adore it," Thesme said. She began to adjust her pack. "How are you, anyway?"

A shrug. "The same. I may go to Til-omon for a while."

"Lucky you."

"I think so. I wouldn't mind getting out of the mildew zone for a little holiday. Holthus has been working up there all month, on some big scheme to build new towns in the mountains—housing for all these aliens that are starting to move in. He wants me to bring the children up, and I think I will."

"Aliens?" Thesme said.

"You don't know about them?"

"Tell me."

"The offworlders that have been living up north are starting to filter this way, now. There's one kind that looks like lizards with human arms and legs that's interested in starting farms in the jungles."

"Ghayrogs."

"Oh, you've heard of them, then? And another kind, all puffy and warty, frog-faced ones with dark gray skins—they do practically all the government jobs now in Pidruid, Holthus says, the customs-inspectors and market clerks and things like that—well, they're being hired down here too, and Holthus and some syndicate of Til-omon people are planning housing for them inland—"

"So that they won't smell up the coastal cities?"

"What? Oh, I suppose that's part of it—nobody knows how they'll fit in here, after all—but really I think it's just that we don't have accommodations for a lot of immigrants in Narabal, and I gather it's the same in Til-omon, and so—"

"Yes, I see," said Thesme. "Well, give everyone my love. I have to begin heading back. I hope you enjoy your holiday in Til-omon."

"Thesme, please—"

"Please what?"

Mirifaine said sadly, "You're so brusque, so distant, so chilly! It's been months since I've seen you, and you barely tolerate my questions, you look at me with such anger—anger for what, Thesme? Have I ever hurt you? Was I ever anything other than loving? Were any of us? You're such a mystery, Thesme."

Thesme knew it was futile to try once more to explain herself. No one understood her, no one ever would, least of all those who said they loved her. Trying to keep her voice gentle, she said, "Call it an overdue adolescent rebellion, Miri. You were all very kind to me. But nothing was working right and I had to run away." She touched her fingertips lightly to her sister's arm. "Maybe I'll be back one of these days."

"I hope so."

"Just don't expect it to happen soon. Say hello to everybody for me," said Thesme, and went out.

She hurried through town, uneasy and tense, afraid of running into her mother or any of her old friends and especially any of her former lovers; and as she carried out her errands she looked about furtively, like a thief, more than once ducking into an alleyway to avoid someone she needed to avoid. The encounter with Mirifaine had been disturbing enough. She had not realized, until Mirifaine had said it, that she had been showing anger; but Miri was right, yes, Thesme could still feel the dull throbbing residue of fury within her. These people, these dreary little people with their little ambitions and their little fears and their little prejudices, going through the little rounds of their meaningless days— they infuriated her. Spilling out over Majipoor like a plague, nibbling at the unmapped forests, staring at the enormous uncrossable ocean, founding ugly muddy towns in the midst of astounding beauty, and never once questioning the purpose of anything—that was the worst of it, their bland unquestioning natures. Did they never once look up at the stars and ask what it all meant, this outward surge of humanity from Old Earth, this replication of the mother world on a thousand conquered planets? Did they care? This could *be* Old Earth for all it mattered, except that that was a tired drab plundered forgotten husk of a world and this, even after centuries and centuries of human occupation, was still beautiful; but long ago Old Earth had no doubt been as beautiful as Majipoor was now; and in five thousand more years Majipoor would be the same way, with hideous cities stretching for hundreds of miles wherever you looked, and traffic everywhere, and filth in the rivers, and the animals wiped out and the poor cheated Shapeshifters penned up in reservations somewhere, all the old mistakes carried out once again on a virgin world. Thesme boiled with an indignation so fierce it amazed her. She had never known that her quarrel with the world was so cosmic. She had thought it was merely a matter of failed love affairs and raw nerves and muddled personal goals, not this irate dissatisfaction with the entire human universe that had so suddenly overwhelmed her. But the rage held its power in her. She wanted to seize Narabal and push it into the ocean. But she could not do that, she could not change a thing, she could not halt the spread of what they called civilization here; all she could do was flee, back to her jungle, back to the interlacing vines and the steamy foggy air and the shy creatures of the marshes, back to her hut, back to her lame Ghayrog, who was himself part of the tide that was overwhelming the planet but for whom she would care, whom she would even cherish, because the others of her kind disliked or even hated him and so she could use him as one of her ways of distinguishing herself from *them*, and because also he needed her just now and no one had ever needed her before.

Her head was aching and the muscles of her face had gone rigid, and she realized she was walking with her shoulders hunched, as if to relax them would be to surrender to the way of life that she had repudiated. As swiftly as she could, she escaped once again from Narabal; but it was not until she had been on the jungle trail for two hours, and the last outskirts of the town were well behind her, that she began to feel the tensions ebbing. She paused at a little lake she knew and stripped and soaked herself in its cool depths to rid herself of the last taint of town, and then, with her going-to-town clothes slung casually over her shoulder, she marched naked through the jungle to her hut.

4

Vismaan lay in bed and did not seem to have moved at all while she was gone. "Are you feeling better?" she asked. "Were you able to manage by yourself?"

"It was a very quiet day. There is somewhat more of a swelling in my leg."

"Let me see."

She probed it cautiously. It *did* seem puffier, and he pulled away slightly as she touched him, which probably meant that there was real trouble in there, if the Ghayrog sense of pain was as weak as he claimed. She debated the merit of getting him into Narabal for treatment. But he seemed unworried, and she doubted that the Narabal doctors knew much about Ghayrog physiology anyway. Besides, she wanted him here. She unpacked the medicines she had brought from town and gave him the ones for fever and inflammation, and then prepared fruits and vegetables for his dinner. Before it grew too dark she checked the traps at the edge of the clearing and found a few small animals in them, a young sigimoin and a couple of mintuns. She wrung their necks with a practiced hand—it had been terribly hard at first, but meat was important to her and no one else was likely to do her killing for her, out here—and dressed them for roasting. Once she had the fire started she went back inside. Vismaan was playing one of the new cubes she had brought him, but he put it aside when she entered.

"You said nothing about your visit to Narabal," he remarked.

"I wasn't there long. Got what I needed, had a little chat with one of my sisters, came away edgy and depressed, felt better as soon as I was in the jungle."

"You have great hatred for that place."

"It's worth hating. Those dismal boring people, those ugly squat little buildings—" She shook her head. "Oh: my sister told me that they're going to found some new towns inland for offworlders, because so many are moving south. Ghayrogs, mainly, but also some other kind with warts and gray skins—"

216

"Hjorts," said Vismaan.

"Whatever. They like to work as customs-inspectors, she told me. They're going to be settled inland because no one wants them in Tilomon or Narabal, is my guess."

"I have never felt unwanted among humans," the Ghayrog said.

"Really? Maybe you haven't noticed. I think there's a great deal of prejudice on Majipoor."

"It has not been evident to me. Of course, I have never been in Narabal, and perhaps it is stronger there than elsewhere. Certainly in the north there is no difficulty. You have never been in the north?"

"No.

"We find ourselves welcome among humans in Pidruid."

"Is that true? I hear that the Ghayrogs are building a city for themselves somewhere east of Pidruid, quite a way east, on the Great Rift. If everything's so wonderful for you in Pidruid, why settle somewhere else?"

Vismaan said calmly, "It is we who are not altogether comfortable living with humans. The rhythms of our lives are so different from yours—our habits of sleep, for instance. We find it difficult living in a city that goes dormant eight hours every night, when we ourselves remain awake. And there are other differences. So we are building Dulorn. I hope you see it some day. It is quite marvelously beautiful, constructed entirely from a white stone that shines with an inner light. We are very proud of it."

"Why don't you live there, then?"

"Is your meat not burning?" he asked.

She reddened and ran outside, barely in time to snatch dinner from the spits. A little sullenly she sliced it and served it, along with some thokkas and a flask of wine she had bought that afternoon in Narabal. Vismaan sat up, with some awkwardness, to eat.

He said after a while, "I lived in Dulorn for several years. But that is very dry country, and I come from a place on my planet that is warm and wet, like Narabal. So I journeyed down here to find fertile lands. My distant ancestors were farmers, and I thought to return to their ways. When I heard that in the tropics of Majipoor one could raise six harvests a year, and that there was land everywhere for the claiming, I set out to explore the territory."

"Alone?"

"Alone, yes. I have no mate, though I intend to obtain one as soon as I am settled."

"And you'll raise crops and market them in Narabal?"

"So I intend. On my home world there is scarcely any wild land any-where, and hardly enough remaining for agriculture. We import most of our food, do you know that? And so Majipoor has a powerful appeal for us, this gigantic planet with its sparse population and its great wilderness awaiting development. I am very happy to be here. And I think that you are not right, about our being unwelcome among your fellow citizens. You Majipoori are kind and gentle folk, civil, law-abiding, orderly."

"Even so; if anyone knew I was living with a Ghayrog, they'd be shocked."

"Shocked? Why?"

"Because you're an alien. Because you're a reptile."

Vismaan made an odd snorting sound. Laughter? "We are not rep-tiles! We are warm-blooded, we nurse our young—"

"Reptilian, then. *Like* reptiles."

"Externally, perhaps. But we are nearly as mammalian as you, I insist."

"Nearly?"

"Only that we are egg-layers. But there are some mammals of that sort, too. You much mistake us if you think—"

"It doesn't really matter. Humans perceive you as reptiles, and we aren't comfortable with reptiles, and there's always going to be awk-wardness between humans and Ghayrogs because of that. It's a tradition that goes back into prehistoric times on Old Earth. Besides—" She caught herself just as she was about to make a reference to the Ghayrog odor. "Beside," she said clumsily, "you look scary."

"More so than a huge shaggy Skandar? More so than a Su-Suheris with two heads?" Vismaan turned toward her and fixed his unsettling lidless eyes on her. "I think you are telling me that *you* are uncomfort-able with Ghayrogs yourself, Thesme."

"No."

"The prejudices of which you speak have never been visible to me. This is the first time I have heard of them. Am I troubling to you, Thesme? Shall I go?"

"No. No. You're completely misunderstanding me. I want you to stay here. I want to help you. I feel no fear of you at all, no dislike, noth-ing negative whatever. I was only trying to tell you—trying to explain about the people in Narabal, how they feel, or how I think they feel, and—" She took a long gulp of her wine. "I don't know how we got into all of this. I'm sorry. I'd like to talk about something else."

"Of course."

But she suspected that she had wounded him, or at least aroused some discomfort in him. In his cool alien way he seemed to have considerable insight, and maybe he was right, maybe it was her own prejudice that was showing, her own uneasiness. She had bungled all of her relationships with humans; quite conceivably she was incapable of getting along with anyone, she thought, human or alien, and had shown Vismaan in a thousand unconscious ways that her hospitality was merely a willed act, artificial and half reluctant, intended to cover an underlying dislike for his presence here. Was that so? She understood less and less of her own motivations, it appeared, as she grew older. But wherever the truth might lie, she did not want him to feel like an intruder here. In the days ahead, she resolved, she would find ways of showing him that her taking him in and caring for him were genuinely founded.

She slept more soundly that night than the one before, although she was still not accustomed to sleeping on the floor in a pile of bubblebush leaves or having someone with her in the hut, and every few hours she awakened. Each time she did, she looked across at the Ghayrog, and saw him each time busy with the entertainment cubes. He took no notice of her. She tried to imagine what it was like to do all of one's sleeping in a single three-month stretch, and to spend the rest of one's time constantly awake; it was, she thought, the most alien thing about him. And to lie there hour after hour, unable to stand, unable to sleep, unable to hide from the discomfort of the injury, making use of whatever diversion was available to consume the time—few torments could be worse. And yet his mood never changed: serene, unruffled, placid, impassive. Were all Ghayrogs like that? Did they never get drunk, lose their tempers, brawl in the streets, bewail their destinies, quarrel with their mates? If Vismaan was a fair sample, they had no human frailties. But, then, she reminded herself, they were not human.

5

In the morning she gave the Ghayrog a bath, sponging him until his scales glistened, and changed his bedding. After she had fed him she went off for the day, in her usual fashion; but she felt guilty wandering the jungle by herself while he remained marooned in the hut, and wondered if she should have stayed with him, telling him stories or drawing him into a conversation to ease his boredom. But she was aware that if she were constantly at his side they would quickly run out of things to talk about, and very likely get on each other's nerves; and he had dozens of entertainment cubes to help him ward off boredom, anyway. Perhaps he preferred to be alone most of the time. In any case she needed solitude herself, more than ever now that she was sharing her hut with him, and she made a long reconnaissance that morning, gathering an assortment of berries and roots for dinner. At midday it rained, and she squatted under a vramma tree whose broad leaves sheltered her nicely. She let her eyes go out of focus and emptied her mind of everything, guilts, doubts, fears memories, the Ghayrog, her family, her former lovers, her unhappiness, her loneliness. The peace that settled over her lasted well into the afternoon.

She grew used to having Vismaan living with her. He continued to be easy and undemanding, amusing himself with his cubes, showing great patience with his immobility. He rarely asked her questions or initiated any sort of talk, but he was friendly enough when she spoke with him, and told her about his home world—shabby and horribly overpopulated, from the sound of things—and about his life there, his dream of settling on Majipoor, his excitement when he first saw the beauty of his adopted planet. Thesme tried to visualize him showing excitement. His snaky hair jumping around, perhaps, instead of just coiling slowly. Or maybe he registered emotion by changes of body odor.

On the fourth day he left the bed for the first time. With her help he hauled himself upward, balancing on his crutch and his good leg and tentatively touching the other one to the ground. She sensed a sudden sharpness of his aroma—a kind of olfactory wince—and decided that her theory must be right, that Ghayrogs did show emotion that way.

"How does it feel?" she asked. "Tender?"

"It will not bear my weight. But the healing is proceeding well. Another few days and I think I will be able to stand. Come, help lift walk a little. My body is rusting from so little activity."

He leaned on her and they went outside, to the pond and back at a slow, wary hobble. He seemed refreshed by the little journey. To her surprise she realized that she was saddened by this first show of progress, because it meant that soon—a week, two weeks?—he would be strong enough to leave, and she did not want him to leave. *She did not want him to leave.* That was so odd a perception that it astonished her. She

220

longed for her old reclusive life, the privilege of sleeping in her own bed and going about her forest pleasures without worrying about whether her guest was being sufficiently well amused, and all of that; in some ways she was finding it more and more irritating to have the Ghayrog around. And yet, and yet, and yet, she felt downcast and disturbed at the thought that he would shortly leave her. How strange, she thought, how peculiar, how very Thesme-like.

Now she took him walking several times a day. He still could not use the broken leg, but he grew more agile without it, and he said that the swelling was abating and the bone appeared to be knitting properly. He began to talk of the farm he would establish, the crops, the ways of clearing the jungle.

One afternoon at the end of the first week Thesme, as she returned from a calimbot-gathering expedition in the meadow where she had first found the Ghayrog, stopped to check her traps. Most were empty or contained the usual small animals; but there was a strange violent thrashing in the underbrush beyond the pond, and when she approached the trap she had placed there she discovered she had caught a bilantoon. It was the biggest creature she had ever snared. Bilantoons were found all over western Zimroel—elegant fast-moving little beasts with sharp hooves, fragile legs, a tiny upturned tufted tail—but the Narabal form was a giant, twice the size of the dainty northern one. It stood as high as a man's waist, and was much prized for its tender and fragrant meat. Thesme's first impulse was to let the pretty thing go: it seemed much too beautiful to kill, and much too big, also. She had taught herself to slaughter little things that she could seize in one hand, but this was another matter entirely, a major animal, intelligent-looking and noble, with a life that it surely valued, hopes and needs and yearnings, a mate probably waiting somewhere nearby. Thesme told herself that she was being foolish. Droles and mintuns and sigimoins also very likely were eager to go on living, certainly as eager as this bilantoon was, and she killed them without hesitation. It was a mistake to romanticize animals, she knew—especially when in her more civilized days she had been willing to eat their flesh quite gladly, if slain by other hands. The bilantoon's bereaved mate had not mattered to her then.

As she drew nearer she saw that the bilantoon in its panic had broken one of its delicate legs, and for an instant she thought of splinting it and keeping the creature as a pet. But that was even more absurd. She could not adopt every cripple the jungle brought her. The bilantoon would never calm down long enough for her to examine its leg; and if by some miracle she did manage to repair it, the animal would probably run away the first chance that it got. Taking a deep breath, she came around behind the struggling creature, caught it by its soft muzzle, and snapped its long graceful neck.

The job of butchering it was bloodier and more difficult than Thesme expected. She hacked away grimly for what seemed like hours, until Vismaan called from within the hut to find out what she was doing.

"Getting dinner ready," she answered. "A surprise. A great treat: roast bilantoon!"

She chuckled quietly. She sounded so wifely, she thought, as she crouched here with blood all over her naked body, sawing away at haunches and ribs, while a reptilian alien creature lay in her bed waiting for his dinner.

But eventually the ugly work was done and she had the meat smouldering over a smoky fire, as one was supposed to do, and she cleansed herself in the pond and set about collecting thokkas and boiling some ghumba-root and opening the remaining flasks of her new Narabal wine. Dinner was ready as darkness came, and Thesme felt immense pride in what she had achieved.

She expected Vismaan to gobble it without comment, in his usual phlegmatic way, but no: for the first time she thought she detected a look of animation on his face—a new sparkle in the eyes, maybe, a different pattern of tongue-flicker. She decided she might be getting better at reading his expressions. He gnawed the roast bilantoon enthusiastically, praised its flavor and texture, and asked again and again for more. For each serving she gave him she took one for herself, forcing the meat down until she was glutted and going onward anyway well past satiation, telling herself that whatever was not consumed now would spoil before morning. "The meat goes so well with the thokkas," she said, popping another of the blue-white berries into her mouth.

"Yes. More, please."

He calmly devoured whatever she set before him. Finally she could eat no more, nor could she even watch him. She put what remained within his reach, took a last gulp of the wine, shuddered a little, laughed as a few drops trickled down her chin and over her breasts. She sprawled out on the bubblebush leaves. Her head was spinning. She lay face down, clutching the floor, listening to the sounds of biting and chewing going on and on and on not far away. Then even the Ghayrog was done feasting, and all was still. Thesme waited for sleep, but sleep would not come. She grew dizzier, until she feared being flung in some terrible centrifugal arc through the side of the hut. Her skin was blazing, her nipples felt hard and sore. I have had much too much to drink, she thought, and I have eaten too many thokkas. Seeds and all, the most potent way, a dozen berries at least, their fiery juice now coursing wildly through her brain.

She did not want to sleep alone, huddled this way on the floor.

With exaggerated care Thesme rose to her knees, steadied herself, and crawled slowly toward the bed. She peered at the Ghayrog, but her eyes were blurred and she could make out only a rough outline of him.

"Are you asleep?" she whispered.

"You know that I would not be sleeping."

"Of course. Of course. Stupid of me."

"Is something wrong, Thesme?"

"Wrong? No, not really. Nothing wrong. Except—it's just that—" She hesitated. "I'm drunk, do you know? Do you understand what being drunk means?"

"Yes."

"I don't like being on the floor. Can I lie beside you?"

"If you wish."

"I have to be very careful. I don't want to bump into your bad leg. Show me which one it is."

"It's almost healed, Thesme. Don't worry. Here: lie down." She felt his hand closing around her wrist and drawing her upward. She let herself float, and drifted easily to his side. She could feel the strange hard shell-like skin of him against her from breast to hip, so cool, so scaly, so smooth. Timidly she rubbed her hand across his body. Like a fine piece of luggage, she thought, digging her fingertips in a little, probing the powerful muscles beneath the rigid surface. His odor changed, becoming spicy, piercing.

"I like the way you smell," she murmured.

She buried her forehead against his chest and held tight to him. She had not been in bed with anyone for months and months, almost a year, and it was good to feel him so close. Even a Ghayrog, she thought. Even a Ghayrog. Just to have the contact, the closeness. It feels so good.

He touched her.

She had not expected that. The entire nature of their relationship was that she cared for him and he passively accepted her services. But suddenly his hand—cool, ridged, scaly, smooth—was passing over her body. Brushing lightly across her breasts, trailing down her belly, pausing at her thighs. What was this? Was Vismaan making *love* to her? She thought of his sexless body, like a machine. He went on stroking her. This is very weird, she thought. Even for Thesme, she told herself, this is an extremely weird thing. He is not human. And I—And I am very lonely—

And I am very drunk—

"Yes, please," she said softly. "Please."

She hoped only that he would continue stroking her. But then he slipped one arm about her shoulders and lifted her easily, gently, rolling her over on top of him and lowering her, and she felt the unmistakable jutting rigidity of maleness against her thigh. What? Did he carry a concealed penis somewhere beneath his scales, that he let slide out when it was needed for use? And was he going to—

Yes.

He seemed to know what to do. Alien he might be, uncertain at their first meeting even whether she was male or female, and nevertheless he plainly understood the theory of human lovemaking. For an instant, as she felt him entering her, she was engulfed by terror and shock and revulsion, wondering if he would hurt her, if he would be painful to receive, and thinking also that this was grotesque and monstrous, this coupling of human and Ghayrog, something that quite likely had never happened before in the history of the universe. She wanted to pull herself free and run out into the night. But she was too dizzy, too drunk, too confused to move; and then she realized that he was not hurting her at all, that he was sliding in and out like some calm clockwork device, and that waves of pleasure were spreading outward from her loins, making her tremble and sob and gasp and press herself against that smooth leathery carapace of his—

She let it happen, and cried out sharply at the best moment, and afterward lay curled up against his chest, shivering, whimpering a little, gradually growing calm. She was sober now. She knew what she had done, and it amazed her, but more than that it amused her. Take *that*, Narabal! The Ghayrog is my lover! And the pleasure had been so intense, so extreme. Had there been any pleasure in it for him? She did not dare ask. How did one tell if a Ghayrog had an orgasm? Did they have them at all? Would the concept mean anything to him? She wondered if he had made love to human women before. She did not dare ask that, either. He had been so capable—not exactly skilled, but definitely very certain about what needed to be done, and he had done it rather more competently than many men she had known, though whether it was because he had had experience with humans or simply because his clear, cool mind could readily calculate the anatomical necessities she did not know, and she doubted that she would ever know.

He said nothing. She clung to him and drifted into the soundest sleep she had had in weeks.

6

In the morning she felt strange but not repentant. They did not talk about what had passed between them that night. He played his cubes; she went out at dawn for a swim to clear her throbbing head, and tidied some of the debris left from their bilantoon feast, and made breakfast for them, and afterward she took a long walk toward the north, to a little mossy cave, where she sat most of the morning, replaying in her mind the texture of his body against her and the touch of his hand on her thighs and the wild shudder of ecstasy that had run through her body. She could not say that she found him in any way attractive. Forked tongue, hair like live snakes, scales all over his body—no, no, what had happened last night had not had anything whatever to do with physical attraction, she decided. Then why had it happened? The wine and the thokkas, she told herself, and her loneliness, and her readiness to rebel against the conventional values of the citizens of Narabal. Giving herself to a Ghayrog was the finest way she knew of showing her defiance for all that those people believed. But of course such an act of defiance was meaningless unless they found out about it. She resolved to take Vismaan to Narabal with her as soon as he was able to make the trip.

After that they shared her bed every night. It seemed absurd to do otherwise. But they did not make love the second night, or the third, or the fourth; they lay side by side without touching, without speaking. Thesme would have been willing to yield herself if he had reached out for her, but he did not. Nor did she choose to approach him. The silence between them became an embarrassment to her, but she was afraid to break it for fear of hearing things that she did not want to hear—that he had disliked their lovemaking, or that he regarded such acts as obscene and unnatural and had done it that once only because she seemed so insistent, or that he was aware that she felt no true desire for him but was merely using him to make a point in her ongoing warfare against convention. At the end of the week, troubled by the accumulated tensions of so many unspoken uncertainties, Thesme risked rolling against him when she got into the bed, taking trouble to make it seem accidental, and he embraced her easily and willingly, gathering her into his arms without hesitation. After that they made love on some nights and did not on others, and it was always a random and unpremeditated thing, casual, almost trivial, something they occasionally did before she went to sleep, with no more mystery or magic about it than that. It brought her great pleasure every time. The alienness of his body soon became invisible to her.

He was walking unaided now and each day he spent more time taking exercise. First with her, then by himself, he explored the jungle trails, moving cautiously at the beginning but soon striding along with only a slight limp. Swimming seemed to further the healing process, and for hours at a time he paddled around Thesme's little pond, annoying the gromwark that lived in a muddy burrow at its edge; the slow-moving old creature crept from its hiding-place and sprawled out at the pond's rim like some bedraggled bristly sack that had been discarded there. It eyed the Ghayrog glumly and would not return to the water until he was done with his swim. Thesme consoled it with tender green shoots that she plucked upstream, far beyond the reach of the gromwark's little sucker-feet.

"When will you take me to Narabal?" Vismaan asked her one rainy evening.

"Why not tomorrow?" she replied.

That night she felt unusual excitement, and pressed herself insistently against him.

They set out at dawn in light rainshowers that soon gave way to brilliant sunshine. Thesme adopted a careful pace, but soon it was apparent that the Ghayrog was fully healed, and before long she was walking swiftly. Vismaan had no difficulty keeping up. She found herself chattering—telling him the names of every plant or animal they encountered, giving him bits of Narabal's history, talking about her brothers and sisters and people she knew in town. She was desperately eager to be seen by them with him—*look, this is my alien lover, this is the Ghayrog I've been sleeping with*—and when they came to the outskirts she began looking around intently, hoping to find someone familiar; but scarcely anyone seemed to be visible on the outer farms, and she did not recognize those who were. "Do you see how they're staring at us?" she whispered to Vismaan, as they passed into a more thickly inhabited district. "They're afraid of you. They think you're the vanguard of some sort of alien invasion. And they're wondering what I'm doing with you, why I'm being so civil to you."

"I see none of that," said Vismaan. "They appear curious about me, yes. But I detect no fear, no hostility. Is it because I am unfamiliar with human facial expressions? I thought I had learned to interpret them quite well."

"Wait and see," Thesme told him. But she had to admit to herself that she might be exaggerating things a little, or even more than a little. They were nearly in the heart of Narabal, now, and some people had glanced at the Ghayrog in surprise and curiosity, yes, but they had quickly softened their stares, while others had merely nodded and smiled as though it were the most ordinary thing in the world to have some kind of offworld creature walking through the streets. Of actual hostility she could find none. That angered her. These mild sweet people, these bland amiable people, were not at all reacting as she had expected. Even when she finally met familiar people—Khanidor, her oldest brother's best friend, and Hennimont Sibroy who ran the little inn near the waterfront, and the woman from the flower-shop—they were nothing other than cordial as Thesme said, "This is Vismaan, who has been living with me lately." Khanidor smiled as though he had always known Thesme to be the sort of person who would set up housekeeping with an alien, and spoke of the new towns for Ghayrogs and Hjorts that Mirifaine's husband was planning to build. The innkeeper reached out jovially to shake Vismaan's hand and invited him down for some wine on the house, and the flower-shop woman said over and over, "How interesting, how interesting! We hope you like our little town!" Thesme felt patronized by their cheerfulness. It was as if they were going out of their way not to let her shock them—as if they had already taken all the wildness from Thesme that they were going to take, and now would accept anything, anything at all from her, without caring, without surprise, without comment. Perhaps they misunderstood the nature of her relationship with the Ghayrog and thought he was merely boarding with her. Would they give her the reaction she wanted if she came right out and said they were lovers, that his body had been inside hers, that they had done that which was unthinkable between human and alien? Probably not. Probably even if she and the Ghayrog lay down and coupled in Pontifex Square it would cause no stir in this town, she thought, scowling.

And did Vismaan like their little town? It was, as always, difficult to detect emotional response in him. They walked up one street and down another, past the haphazardly planned plazas and the flat-faced scruffy shops and the little lopsided houses with their overgrown gardens, and he said very little. She sensed disappointment and disapproval in his silence, and for all her own dislike of Narabal she began to feel defensive about the place. It was, after all, a young settlement, an isolated outpost in an obscure corner of a second-class continent, just a few generations old. "What do you think?" she asked finally. "You aren't very impressed by Narabal, are you?"

"You warned me not to expect much."

"But it's even more dismal than I led you to expect, isn't it?"

"I do find it small and crude," he said. "After one has seen Pidruid, or even—"

"Pidruid's thousands of years old."

"—Dulorn," he went on. "Dulorn is extraordinarily beautiful even now, when it is just being built. But of course the white stone they use there is—"

"Yes," she said. "Narabal ought to be built out of stone too, because this climate is so damp that wooden buildings fall apart, but there hasn't been time yet. Once the population's big enough, we can quarry in the mountains and put together something marvelous here. Fifty years from now, a hundred, when we have a proper labor force. Maybe if we got some of those giant four-armed aliens to work here—"

"Skandars," said Vismaan.

"Skandars, yes. Why doesn't the Coronal send us ten thousand Skandars?"

"Their bodies are covered with thick hair. They will find this climate difficult. But doubtless Skandars will settle here, and Vroons, and Su-Suheris, and many, many wet-country Ghayrogs like me. It is a very bold thing your government is doing, encouraging offworld settlers in such numbers. Other planets are not so generous with their land."

"Other planets are not so large," Thesme said. "I think I've heard that even with all the huge oceans we have, Majipoor's land mass is still three or four times the size of any other settled planet. Or something like that.

We're very lucky, being such a big world, and yet having such gentle gravity, so that humans and humanoids can live comfortably here. Of course, we pay a high price for that, not having anything much in the way of heavy elements, but still—oh. Hello." The tone of her voice changed abruptly, dropping off to a startled blurt. A slim young man, very tall, with pale wavy hair, had nearly collided with her as he emerged from the bank on the corner, and now he stood gaping at her, and she at him. He was Ruskelorn Yulvan, Thesme's lover for the four months just prior to her withdrawal into the jungle, and the person in Narabal she was least eager to see. But if there had to be a confrontation with him, she intended to make the most of it; and, seizing the initiative after her first moment of confusion, she said, "You look well, Ruskelorn."

"And you. Jungle life must agree with you."

"Very much. It's been the happiest seven months of my life. Ruskelorn, this is my friend Vismaan, who's been living with me the past few weeks. He had an accident while scouting for farmland near my place—broke his leg falling out of a tree—and I've been looking after him."

"Very capably, I imagine," Ruskelorn Yulvan said evenly. "He seems to be in excellent condition." To the Ghayrog he said, "Pleased to meet you," in a way that made it seem as though he might actually mean it.

Thesme said, "He comes from a part of his planet where the climate is a lot like Narabal's. He tells me that there'll be plenty of his countrypeople settling down here in the tropics in the next few years."

"So I've heard." Ruskelorn Yulvan grinned and said, "You'll find it amazingly fertile territory. Eat a berry at breakfast time and toss the seed away, you'll have a vine as tall as a house by nightfall. That's what everyone says, so it must be true."

The light and casual manner of his speaking infuriated her. Did he not realize that this scaly alien creature, this offworlder, this Ghayrog, was his replacement in her bed? Was he immune to jealousy, or did he simply not understand the real situation? With a ferocious silent intensity she attempted to convey the truth of things to Ruskelorn Yulvan in the most graphic possible way, thinking fierce images of herself in Vismaan's arms, showing Ruskelorn Yulvan the alien hands of Vismaan caressing her breasts and thighs and flicking his little scarlet two-pronged tongue lightly over her closed eyelids, her nipples, her loins. But it was useless. Ruskelorn was no more of a mind-reader than she. *He is my lover,* she thought, *he enters me, he makes me come again and again, I can't wait to get back to the jungle and tumble into bed with him,* and all the while Ruskelorn Yulvan stood there smiling, chatting politely with the Ghayrog, discussing the potential for raising niyk and glein and stajja in these parts, or perhaps lusavender-seed in the swampier districts, and only after a good deal of that did he turn his glance back toward Thesme and ask, as placidly as though he were asking the day of the week, whether she intended to live in the jungle indefinitely.

She glared. "So far I prefer it to life in town. Why?"

"I wondered if you missed the comforts of our splendid metropolis, that's all."

"Not yet, not for a moment. I've never been happier."

"Good. I'm so pleased for you, Thesme." Another serene smile. "How nice to have run into you. How good to have met you," he said to the Ghayrog, and then he was gone.

Thesme smouldered with rage. He had not cared, he had not cared in the slightest, she could be coupling with Ghayrogs or Skandars or the gromwark in the pond for all it mattered to him! She had wanted him to be wounded or at least shocked, and instead he had simply been polite. Polite! It must be that he, like all the others, failed to comprehend the real state of affairs between her and Vismaan—that it was simply inconceivable to them that a woman of human stock would offer her body to a reptilian offworlder, and so they did not consider—they did not even suspect—

"Have you seen enough of Narabal now?" she asked the Ghayrog.

"Enough to realize that there is little to see."

"How does your leg feel? Are you ready to begin the journey back?"

"Have you no errands to perform in town?"

"Nothing important," she said. "I'd like to go."

"Then let us go," he answered.

His leg did seem to be giving him some trouble—the muscles stiffening, probably; that was a taxing hike even for someone in prime condition, and he had traveled only much shorter distances since his recovery—but in his usual uncomplaining way he followed her toward the jungle road. This was the worst time of day to be making the trip, with the sun almost straight overhead and the air moist and heavy from the first gatherings of what would be this afternoon's rainfall. They walked slowly, pausing often, though never once did he say he was tired; it was Thesme herself who was tiring, and she pretended that she wanted to show him some geological formation here, some unusual plant there, in order to manufacture occasions to rest. She did not want to admit fatigue. She had suffered enough mortification today.

The venture into Narabal had been a disaster for her. Proud, defiant, rebellious, scornful of Narabal's conventional ways, she had hauled her Ghayrog lover to town to flaunt him before the tame city-dwellers, and they had not cared. Were they such puddings that they could not guess at the truth? Or had they seen instantly through her pretensions, and were determined to give her no satisfaction? Either way she felt outraged, humiliated, defeated—and very foolish. And what about the bigotry she imagined she had found earlier among the Narabal folk? Were they not threatened by the influx of these aliens? They had all been so charming to Vismaan, so friendly. Perhaps, Thesme thought gloomily, the prejudice was in her mind alone and she had misinterpreted the remarks of others, and in that case it had been stupid to give herself to the Ghayrog, it had accomplished nothing, flouted no Narabal decorum, served no purpose at all in the private war she had been fighting against those people. It had only been a strange and willful and grotesque event.

Neither she nor the Ghayrog spoke during the long slow uncomfortable return to the jungle. When they reached her hut he went inside and she bustled about ineffectually in the clearing, checking traps, pulling berries from vines, setting things down and forgetting what she had done with them.

After a while she entered the hut and said to Vismaan, "I think you may as well leave."

"Very well. It is time for me to be on my way."

"You can stay here tonight, of course. But in the morning—"

"Why not leave now?"

"It'll be dark soon. You've already walked so many miles today—"

"I have no wish to trouble you. I will go now, I think."

Even now she found it impossible to read his feelings. Was he surprised? Hurt? Angry? He showed her nothing. He offered no gestures of farewell, either, but simply turned and began walking at a steady pace toward the interior of the jungle. Thesme watched him, throat dry, heart pounding, until he disappeared beyond the low-hanging vines. It was all she could do to keep herself from running after him. But then he was gone, and soon the tropical night descended.

She rummaged together a sort of dinner for herself, but she ate very little, thinking, He is out there sitting in the darkness, waiting for the morning to come. They had not even said goodbye. She could have made some little joke, warning him to stay out of sijaneel trees, or he could have thanked her for all she had done on his behalf, but instead there had been nothing, just her dismissal of him and his calm uncomplaining departure. An alien, she thought, and his ways were alien. And yet, when they had been together in bed, and he had touched her and held her and drawn her body down on top of his—

It was a long bleak night for her. She lay huddled in the crudely sewn zanja-down bed that they had so lately shared, listening to the night rain hammering on the vast blue leaves that were her roof, and for the first time since she had entered the jungle she felt the pain of loneliness. Until this moment she had not realized how much she had valued the bizarre parody of domesticity that she and the Ghayrog had enacted here; but now that was over, and she was alone again, somehow more alone than she had been before, and far more cut off from her old life in Narabal than before, also, and he was out there, unsleeping in the darkness, unsheltered from the rain. I am in love with an alien, she told herself in wonderment, I am in love with a scaly *thing* that speaks no words of endearment and asks hardly any questions and leaves without saying thank you or goodbye. She lay awake for hours, crying now and then. Her body felt tense and clenched from the long walk and the day's frustrations; she drew her knees to her breasts and stayed that way a long while, and then put her hands between her legs and stroked herself, and finally there came a moment of release, a gasp and a little soft moan, and sleep after that.

7

In the morning she bathed and checked her traps and assembled a breakfast and wandered over all the familiar trails near her hut. There was no sign of the Ghayrog. By midday her mood seemed to be lifting, and the afternoon was almost cheerful for her; only as nightfall approached, the time of solitary dinner, did she begin to feel the bleakness descending again. But she endured it. She played the cubes she had brought from home for him, and eventually dropped into sleep, and the next day was a better day, and the next, and the one after that.

Gradually Thesme's life returned to normal. She saw nothing of the Ghayrog and he started to slip from her mind. As the solitary weeks went by she rediscovered the joy of solitude, or so it seemed to her, but then at odd moments she speared herself on some sharp and painful memory of him—the sight of a bilantoon in a thicket or the sijaneel tree with the broken branch or the gromwark sitting sullenly at the edge of the pond—and she realized that she still missed him. She roved the jungle in wider and wider circles, not quite knowing why, until at last she admitted to herself that she was looking for him.

It took her three more months to find him. She began seeing indications of settlement off to the southeast—an apparent clearing, visible two or three hilltops away, with what looked like traces of new trails radiating from it—and in time she made her way in that direction and across a considerable river previously unknown to her, to a zone of felled trees, beyond which was a newly established farm. She skulked along its perimeter and caught sight of a Ghayrog—it was Vismaan, she was certain of that—tilling a field of rich black soil. Fear swept her spirit and left her weak and trembling. Could it be some other Ghayrog? No, no, no, she was sure it was he, she even imagined she detected a little limp. She ducked down out of sight, afraid to approach him. What could she say to him? How could she justify having come this far to seek him out, after having so coolly dismissed him from her life? She drew back into the underbrush and came close to turning away altogether. But then she found her courage and called his name.

He stopped short and looked around.

"Vismaan? Over here! It's Thesme!"

Her cheeks were blazing, her heart pounded terrifyingly. For one dismal instant she was convinced that this was a strange Ghayrog, and apologies for her intrusion were already springing to her lips. But as he came toward her she knew that she had not been mistaken.

"I saw the clearing and thought it might be your farm," she said, stepping out of the tangled brush. "How have you been, Vismaan?"

"Quite excellent. And yourself?"

She shrugged. "I get along. You've done wonders here, Vismaan. It's only been a few months, and look at all this!"

"Yes," he said. "We have worked hard."

"We?"

"I have a mate now. Come: let me introduce you to her, and show you what we have accomplished here."

His tranquil words withered her. Perhaps they were meant to do that—instead of showing any sort of resentment or pique over the way she had sent him out of her life, he was taking his revenge in a more diabolical fashion, through utter dispassionate restraint. But more likely, she thought, he felt no resentment and saw no need for revenge. His view of all that had passed between them was probably entirely unlike hers. Never forget that he is an alien, she told herself.

She followed him up a gentle slope and across a drainage ditch and around a small field that was obviously newly planted. At the top of the hill, half hidden by a lush kitchen-garden, was a cottage of sijaneel timbers not very different from her own, but larger and somewhat more angular in design. From up here the whole farm could be seen, occupying three faces of the little hill. Thesme was astounded at how much he had managed to do—it seemed impossible to have cleared all this, to have built a dwelling, to have made ready the soil for planting, even to have begun planting, in just these few months. She remembered that Ghayrogs did not sleep; but had they no need of rest?

"Turnome!" he called. "We have a visitor, Turnome!"

Thesme forced herself to be calm. She understood now that she had come looking for the Ghayrog because she no longer wanted to be alone, and that she had had some half-conscious fantasy of helping him establish his farm, of sharing his life as well as his bed, of building a true relationship with him; she had even, for one flickering instant, seen herself on a holiday in the north with him, visiting wonderful Dulorn, meeting his countrymen. All that was foolish, she knew, but it had had a certain crazy plausibility until the moment when he told her he had a mate. Now she struggled to compose herself, to be cordial and warm, to keep all absurd hints of rivalry from surfacing—

Out of the cottage came a Ghayrog nearly as tall as Vismaan, with the same gleaming pearly armor of scales, the same slowly writhing serpentine hair; there was only one outward difference between them, but it was a strange one indeed, for the Ghayrog woman's chest was festooned with dangling tubular breasts, a dozen or more of them, each tipped with a dark green nipple. Thesme shivered. Vismaan had said Ghayrogs were mammals, and the evidence was impossible to refute, but the reptilian look of the woman was if anything heightened by those eerie breasts, which made her seem not mammalian but weirdly hybrid and incomprehensible. Thesme looked from one to the other of these creatures in deep discomfort.

Vismaan said, "This is the woman I told you about, who found me when I hurt my leg, and nursed me back to health. Thesme: my mate Turnome."

"You are welcome here," said the Ghayrog woman solemnly.

Thesme stammered some further appreciation of the work they had done on the farm. She wanted only to escape, now, but there was no getting away; she had come to call on her jungle neighbors, and they insisted on observing the niceties. Vismaan invited her in. What was next? A cup of tea, a bowl of wine, some thokkas and grilled mintun? There was scarcely anything inside the cottage except a table and a few cushions and, in the far corner, a curious high-walled woven container of large size, standing on a three-legged stool. Thesme glanced toward it and quickly away, thinking without knowing why that it was wrong to display curiosity about it; but Vismaan took her by the elbow and said, "Let us show you. Come: look." She peered in.

It was an incubator. On a nest of moss were eleven or twelve leathery round eggs, bright green with large red speckles.

"Our firstborn will hatch in less than a month," Vismaan said.

Thesme was swept by a wave of dizziness. Somehow this revelation of the true alienness of these beings stunned her as nothing else had, not the chilly stare of Vismaan's unblinking eyes nor the writhing of his hair nor the touch of his skin against her naked body nor the sudden amazing sensation of him moving inside her. Eggs! A litter! And Turnome already puffing up with milk to nurture them! Thesme had a vision of a dozen tiny lizards clinging to the woman's many breasts, and horror transfixed her: she stood motionless, not even breathing, for an endless moment, and then she turned and bolted, running down the hillside, over the drainage ditch, right across, she realized too late, the newly planted field, and off into the steaming humid jungle.

8

She did not know how long it was before Vismaan appeared at her door. Time had gone by in a blurred flow of eating and sleeping and weeping and trembling, and perhaps it was a day, perhaps two, perhaps a week, and then there he was, poking his head and shoulders into the hut and calling her name.

"What do you want?" she asked, not getting up.

"To talk. There were things I had to tell you. Why did you leave so suddenly?"

"Does it matter?"

He crouched beside her. His hand rested lightly on her shoulder.

"Thesme, I owe you apologies."

"For what?"

"When I left here, I failed to thank you for all you had done for me. My mate and I were discussing why you had run away, and she said you were angry with me, and I could not understand why. So she and I explored all the possible reasons, and when I described how you and I had come to part, Turnome asked me if I had told you that I was grateful for your help, and I said no, I had not, I was unaware that such things were done. So I have come to you. Forgive me for my rudeness, Thesme. For my ignorance."

"I forgive you," she said in a muffled voice. "Will you go away, now?"

"Look at me, Thesme."

"I'd rather not."

"Please. Will you?" He tugged at her shoulder.

Sullenly she turned to him.

"Your eyes are swollen," he said.

"Something I ate must have disagreed with me."

"You are still angry. Why? I have asked you to understand that I meant no discourtesy. Ghayrogs do not express gratitude in quite the same way humans do. But let me do it now. You saved my life, I believe. You were very kind. I will always remember what you did for me when I was injured. It was wrong of me not to have told you that before."

"And it was wrong of me to throw you out like that," she said in a low voice. "Don't ask me to explain why I did, though. It's very complicated. I'll forgive you for not thanking me if you'll forgive me for making you leave like that."

"No forgiveness was required. My leg had healed; it was time for me to go, as you pointed out; I went on my way and found the land I needed for my farm."

"It was that simple, then?"

"Yes. Of course."

She got to her feet and stood facing him. "Vismaan, why did you have sex with me?"

"Because you seemed to want it."

"That's all?"

"You were unhappy and did not seem to wish to sleep alone. I hoped it would comfort you. I was trying to do the friendly thing, the compassionate thing."

"Oh. I see."

"I believe it gave you pleasure," he said.

"Yes. Yes. It did give me pleasure. But you didn't desire me, then?"

His tongue flickered in what she thought might be the equivalent of a puzzled frown.

"No," he said. "You are human. How can I feel desire for a human? You are so different from me, Thesme. On Majipoor my kind are called aliens, but to me *you* are the alien, is that not so?"

"I suppose. Yes."

"But I was very fond of you. I wished your happiness. In that sense I had desire for you. Do you understand? And I will always be your friend. I hope you will come to visit us, and share in the bounty of our farm. Will you do that, Thesme?"

"I—yes, yes, I will."

"Good. I will go now. But first—"

Gravely, with immense dignity, he drew her to him and enfolded her in his powerful arms. Once again she felt the strange smooth rigidity of his alien skin; once again the little scarlet tongue fluttered across her eyelids in a forked kiss. He embraced her for a long moment.

When he released her he said, "I am extremely fond of you, Thesme I can never forget you."

"Nor I you."

She stood in the doorway, watching until he disappeared from sight beyond the pond. A sense of ease and peace and warmth had come over her spirit. She doubted that she ever would visit Vismaan and Turnome and their litter of little lizards, but that was all right: Vismaan would understand. Everything was all right. Thesme began to gather her possessions and stuff them into her pack. It was still only mid-morning, time enough to make the journey to Narabal.

She reached the city just after the afternoon showers. It was over a year since she had left it, and a good many months since her last visit; and she was surprised by the changes she saw now. There was a boom-town bustle to the place, new buildings going up everywhere, ships in the Channel, the streets full of traffic. And the town seemed to have been invaded by aliens—hundreds of Ghayrogs, and other kinds too, the warty ones that she supposed were Hjorts, and enormous double-shouldered Skandars, a whole circus of strange beings going about their business and taken absolutely for granted by the human citizens. Thesme found her way with some difficulty to her mother's house. Two of her sisters were there, and her brother Dalkhan. They stared at her in amazement and what seemed like fear.

"I'm back," she said. "I know I look like a wild animal, but I just need my hair trimmed and a new tunic and I'll be human again."

She went to live with Ruskelorn Yulvan a few weeks later, and at the end of the year they were married. For a time she thought of confessing to him that she and her Ghayrog guest had been lovers, but she was afraid to do it, and eventually it seemed unimportant to bring it up at all. She did, finally, ten or twelve years later, when they had dined on roast bilantoon at one of the fine new restaurants in the Ghayrog quarter of town, and she had had much too much of the strong golden wine of the north, and the pressure of old associations was too powerful to resist. When she had finished telling him the story she said, "Did you suspect any of that?" And he said, "I knew it right away, when I saw you with him in the street. But why should it have mattered?"

AT THE CONGLOMEROID
COCKTAIL PARTY

Another easy and pleasant effort. After spending the summer of 1981 writing most of the stories that became my book Majipoor Chronicles, *it seemed like time to try another one for Alice Turner of* Playboy, *and in early October I wrote "At the Conglomeroid Cocktail Party" in a single sitting—the first time in many years that I had written a complete short story in one swift burst. Alice liked it. She did want some minor revisions at the beginning and the end, and in each case she was right, as she usually was when she requested revisions from me. ("Cut the first line," she said, and I did. The final paragraph needed fixing, and I fixed it.) The check came by return mail and* Playboy *published the story in the August, 1982 issue, the second of my many appearances in that magazine.*

I am contemporary. I am conglomeroid. I am post-causal, contra-linear, pepto-modern. To be anything else is to be dead, nezpah? Is to be a fossil. A sense of infinite potential and a stance of infinite readiness: that's the right philosophy for our recombinant era. Alert to all possibilities, holding oneself always in an existentially pliant posture.

So when quasi-cousin Spinifex called and said, "Come to my fetus-party tonight," I accepted unhesitatingly. Spinifex lives in Wongamoola on the slopes of the Dandenongs, looking across into Melbourne. I happened to be in Gondar on my way to Lalibela when his call came.

"Mortissa and I have a new embryo," said Spinifex. "We want everyone to help us engineer it. There'll be a contest for the best design. The whole crowd's coming, and some new people." *Some new people.* Could I resist? It's not such a big deal to go from Ethiopia to Australia for a fetus-party. Two hours, with transfers. I was on the pop-chute in half a flick. Pop to Addis, pop to Delhi, pop to Singapore, pop to Melbourne, pop pop pop pop and I was there. *Some new people.* Irresistible. That was the night I met Domitilla.

Spinifex and Mortissa live in a great golden egg on jeweled stilts, with oscillator windows and three captive rainbows moored overhead. In his current Shaping, Spinifex is aquatic, a big jolly blue dolphinoid with spangled red flukes, and spends most of his time in his moat. Mortissa's latest Shaping is more traditionally conglomeroid, no single identifiable style, a bit of tapir and a bit of giraffe and some very high-precision machine-tooled laminations, altogether elegant. I blew kisses to them both.

About thirty guests had already arrived. I knew most of them. There was Hapshash in his ten-year-old Shaping, the carpeted look, last word in splendor then. Negresca still in her tortoise-cum-chinchilla, and Holy Mary looking sublime in the gilded tubular body that becomes her so well. There is a tendency among the ultra-elite to keep the same Shaping longer and longer, with Hapshash the outstanding example of that. At first I thought it was a sign of the recent economic dreariness, but lately I was coming to understand it as a significant underground trend: out of fashion is height of fashion. That sort of thing requires one to stay really aware. When Melanoleum came slithering up to me, she asked me at once how I liked her new Shaping. She looked exactly as she had the last time, a year ago at the big potlatch in Joburg—tendrils, iridescence, lateral oculars, high-spectrum pulse-nodes. For an instant I was baffled, and I came close to telling her I had already seen this Shaping, and then I caught on, comprehending that she had just had herself Shaped *exactly like her last Shaping*, which carried Hapshash's gambit to the next level of subtlety, and I hugged her with all my arms and said, "It's brilliant, love, it's devastating!"

"I knew you'd pick up," she said. "Have you seen the fetus?"

"I just got here."

"Up there. In the globe."

"Ah. Beautiful!"

They had rigged a crystalline sphere in a gravity-candle's beam, so that it hovered twenty feet above the cocktail altar, and in it the new fetus solemnly swam in a phosphorescent green fluid. It was, I suppose, eleven or twelve weeks old, a little alien-looking fish with a big furrowed forehead, altogether weird but completely normal, a standard human fetus with no genetic reprogramming at all. Prenatal engineering is too terribly tacky for people like Mortissa and Spinifex, naturally. Let the standard folk do that, going to the cheapjack helixers to get their offsprings' clubfeet and sloping chins and bandy legs cleaned up ahead of time, so that they can look just like everybody else when they come squirting out of the womb. That's not our way.

Melanoleum said, "The design contest starts in half an hour. Do you have a good one ready?"

"I expect to. What's the prize?"

"A month with anyone at the party," she said. "Do you know Domitilla?"

I had heard of her, naturally—last season's hot debutante, making the party circuit from San Francisco to the Seychelles. But I had been going the other way last season. Suddenly she was at my elbow, a dazzling child in a blaze of cold blue fire. It was her only garment, and under that chilly radiance I saw a slim furry form, five small breasts, sleek muscular thighs, vertebrae elongated to form the underpinning for a webbed sail down her back—an inspired conglomeroid of wolverine and dinosaur. My hearts thundered and my lymph congealed. She noted instantly the power she had over me, and her fiery cloak flared to double volume, a dazzling nimbus that briefly enfolded me and dizzied me with the scent of ozone. She was no more than nineteen, and I was ninety-three, existentially pliant, ready to be overwhelmed. I congratulated her on her ingenuity.

"My fifth Shaping," she said. "I'll be getting a new one soon, I think."

"Your *fifth?*" I considered Hapshash and Negresca and Holy Mary, trendily clinging to their old bodies. "So quickly? Don't. This one is extraordinary."

"I know," she said. "That's why it's time for a new one. Oh, look, the fetus is trying to get born!"

Indeed the little pseudo-fish that my quasi-cousins had conceived was making violent but futile efforts to escape its gleaming tank. We applauded. The servants took that as their signal to come among us with hors d'oeuvres: five standard humans, big and stupid and docile, bearing glittering food-fabrics on platinum trays. We did our dainty best; the trays were bare in no time and back came the standards with a second round, caviars of at least a dozen creatures and sweetmeats and tiny cocktail-globules to rub on our tongues and all the rest. And then Spinifex heaved himself out of the moat with a great jovial flapping of flippers that splashed everyone, and a beveled screen descended and hovered in midair and it was time for the contest. Domitilla was still at my side.

"I've heard about you," she said in a voice like shaggy wine. "I thought I'd meet you at the moon-party. Why weren't you there?"

"I never go there," I said.

"Oh. Of course. Do you know who's going to win the contest?"

"Is it rigged?"

"Aren't they all?" she asked. "*I* know who." She laughed.

Mortissa was on the podium under merciless spotlights that her new Shaping reflected flawlessly. She explained the contest. We were to draw lots and each in turn seize the control-stick and project on the screen our image of what the new child should look like. Judging would be automatic: the design that elicited the greatest amazement would win, and the winner was entitled to choose as companion for a month any of the rest of us. There were two provisos: Spinifex and Mortissa would not be bound to use the winning design if they deemed it life-threatening in any way, and none of the designs could be used by the contestants for future Shapings of their own. The lots were drawn and we took our turns: Hapshash, Melanoleum, Mandragora, Peachbloom, Hannibal—

The designs ranged from brilliant to merely clever. Hapshash proposed a sort of jeweled amoeba; Peachbloom conjured up a hybrid Spinifex-Mortissa, half dolphin, half machine; Melanoleum's concept was out of the Greek myths, Medusa hair and Poseidon tail; my one-time para-wife Nullamar invented a geometrical shape, rigid and complex, that gave us all headaches; and my own contribution, entirely improvised, involved two slender tapering shells that parted to reveal a delicate and sinuous being, virtually translucent. I was surprised at my own inspiration and felt instant regret for having thrown away something so beautiful that I might well have worn myself someday. It caused a stir and I suspected I would win, and I knew who I would choose as my prize. What, I wondered, did Domitilla have as her entry? I glanced toward her and smiled, and she returned the smile with an airy rippling of her flaming cloak.

The contest went on and on. Hungering for victory, I grew tense, apprehensive, gloomy, despondent. Candelabra's design was spectacular, and Mingimang's was fascinatingly perplexing, and Vishnu's was awesomely cunning. Some, indeed, seemed almost beyond the capacity, of contemporary genetic engineering to accomplish. I saw no hope of winning, and my month with Domitilla seemed in jeopardy. Her own turn came last. She took the podium, grasped the stick, closed her eyes, sent her thought-projection to the screen with an intensity of effort that turned her fiery mantle bright yellow and sent it arching out to expose her blue-black furry nakedness.

On the screen a standard human form appeared.

Not quite standard, for it was hermaphrodite, round rosy-nippled breasts above and male genitals below. Yet it was the old basic body other than that, the traditional pre-Shaping shape, used now only by the unfortunate billions of the serving classes. I gasped, and I was not alone. It's no easy thing to amaze a group so worldly as we, but we were transfixed with amazement, dumbstruck by Domitilla's bizarre notion. Was she mocking us? Was she merely naive? Or was she so far beyond our level of sophistication that we couldn't comprehend her motives? Trays clattered to the ground, drinks were spilled, we coughed and wheezed and muttered. The meters that were judging the contest whirled and flashed. No doubt of the winner: Domitilla had plainly provoked the most intense surprise, and that was the criterion. The party was at the edge of scandal. But Mortissa was equal to the moment.

"The winner, of course, is Domitilla," she said calmly. "We salute her for the audacity of her design. But my husband and I regard it as hazardous to the life of our child to give it the standard form for its first Shaping because of the possibility of misunderstanding by its play-mates, and so we invoke our right to choose another entry, and we select that of our quasi-cousin Sandalphon, so remarkable for its combination of subtlety and strength."

"Well done!" Melanoleum called, and I did not know whether she was cheering Mortissa for her astuteness or Domitilla for her boldness or me for the beauty of my design. "Well done!" cried Vishnu, and Candelabra and Hannibal took it up, and the tensions of the party dissolved into a kind of forced jubilation that swiftly became the real thing.

"The prize!" someone shouted. "Who's the prize?"

Spinifex thumped his huge fins. "The prize! The prize!"

Mortissa beckoned to Domitilla. She stepped forward, small and fragile-looking but not in the least vulnerable, and said in a clear, cool voice, "I choose Sandalphon."

We left the party within the hour and popped to San Francisco, where Domitilla lived alone in a spherical pod of a house suspended by spider-cables a mile above the bay.

I had my wish. And yet she frightened me, and I don't frighten easily.

Her fiery mantle engulfed me. She was nineteen, I was ninety-three, and she ruled me. In that frosty blue radiance I was helpless. Five Shapings, and only nineteen? Her eyes were narrow and cat-yellow, and there were worlds of strangeness in them that made me feel like a mud-flecked peasant. "The famous Sandalphon," she whispered. "Would you have picked me if you had won? Yes, I know you would. It was all over your face. How long have you had this Shaping?"

"Four years."

"Time for a new one."

I started to say that Hapshash and the other leaders of our set were traveling in the other direction, that the fashionable thing was to keep one's old Shaping; but that seemed idiocy to me now as I lay in her arms with her dense harsh fur rubbing my scales. She was the new thing, the terrifying, inexorable voice of the dawning day, and what did our modes matter to her? We made love, my worlds of experience against her tiger-ish youthful vitality, and there, at least, I think I matched her stroke for stroke. Afterward she showed me holograms of her first four Shapings. One by one her earlier selves stepped from the projector and pirouetted before me: the form her parents had given her that she had kept for nine years, and then the second Shaping that one always tends to cling to through puberty, and the two of her adolescence. They were true con-glomeroid Shapes, a blending of images out of all the biological spectrum, a bit of butterfly and a bit of squid, a tinge of reptile and a hint of insect, the usual genetic fantasia that our kind adores, but a common thread bound them all, and her current Shape as well. That was the compactness of her body, the taut narrowness of her slender frame, powerful but minimal, like some agile little carnivore, mink or mongoose or marten. When we redesign ourselves, we can be any size we like, whale-mighty or cat-small, within certain basic limitations imposed by the need to house a human-sized brain in the frame that the gene-splicers build for us; but Domitilla had opted always to construct her fantasies on the splendid little armature with which she had come into the world. That too was ominous. It spoke of a persistence, a self-sufficiency, that is not common.

"Which of them do you like best?" she asked, when I had seen them all.

I stroked her strong smooth thighs, "This one. How tight your fur lies against your skin! How beautiful the sail is on your back! You've brought out your deepest self."

"How would you know my deepest self after two hours?"

"Don't underestimate me." I touched my lips to hers. "Part hunting-cat, part dinosaur—the metaphor's perfect."

"Let's make love again. Then we'll pop to Jerusalem."

"All right."

"And then Tibet."

"Certainly."

"And Baltimore."

"Baltimore?"

"Why not?" she said. "Hold me tighter. Yes. Yes."

"Do I get only a month with you?"

"Thirty days. Those were the terms of the contest."

"Do you always abide by terms?"

"Always," she said.

We popped to Jerusalem at dawn, and then to Tibet, and then, yes, to Baltimore. And many more places in the thirty days. She was trying to exhaust me, thinking that nineteen has some superiority over ninety-three, but there, at least, she had misjudged things; at each Shaping we are renewed, you know. I loved her beyond measure, though she terrified me. What did I fear? What does anyone fear most? That in a vulnerable moment someone will say, "I understand what a fraud you are: I have seen all your facades fall away: I know the truth about you." I would not say such a thing to Melanoleum, nor Nullamar to me, nor any of us to any of us, but yet I felt Domitilla wouldn't hesitate to flay me down to the core beneath the Shapings if that suited her whim, and I lived in dread of that, and I always will.

On the thirtieth day she said goodbye.

"Please," I said. "Another week."

"Those were the terms."

"Even so."

"If we refuse to honor contracts, all society collapses."

"Have I bored you?" Foolish question, inviting destruction.

"Not nearly as much as I thought you would," she replied, and I loved her for it, having expected worse. "But I have other things to do. My new Shaping, Sandalphon."

"You won't. What you are now is too beautiful to discard."

"What I will be next will surpass it."

"I beg you—stay as you are a little longer."

"I undergo engineering tomorrow at dawn," she said, "at the gene-surgery in Katmandu."

Arguing with her was hopeless. We had our last night, a night of miracles, and while I slept she vanished, and the walls of the world fell in on me. I hurried out to my friends, and was houseguest in turn with Nullamar and Mandragora and Melanoleum and Candelabra, and not one of them said the name of Domitilla to me, and at the end of the year I went to Spinifex and Mortissa to admire the new child in the graceful shell of my happy designing, and then, despondent, I popped to Katmandu. All year long a new Domitilla had been emerging from the altered genetic material of the previous one, and now her Shaping was nearly complete. They wouldn't let me see her, but they sent messages in, and she agreed to my request to have dinner with her on the day of her coming-forth. That was still a month away. I could have gone any-where in the world, but I stayed in Katmandu, staring at the mountains, thinking that my month of Domitilla had gone by in a flick and this month of waiting was taking an eternity; and then it was the day.

The inner door opened and nurses came out, standard humans, and an orderly or two and then the surgeon and then Domitilla. I recognized her at once, the same wiry armature as ever. The new body she wore was the one she had designed for the child of Spinifex and Mortissa. A stan-dard human frame, mortifyingly human, the body of a servant, of a hewer of wood and drawer of water, except that it glowed with the inner fire that burned in Domitilla and that no member of the lower orders could conceivably have. And she was different from the standards in another way, for she was naked, and she had used the hermaphrodite design, breasts above, male organs below. I felt as if I had been kicked; I wanted to clutch my gut and double over. Her eyes gleamed.

"Do you like it?" she asked, mocking me.

I was unable to look. I turned and tried to run, but she called after me, "Wait, Sandalphon!"

Trembling, I halted. "What do you want?"

"Tell me if you like it?"

"The terms of the contest bound you not to use any of the designs," I said bitterly. "You claimed always to abide by terms."

"Always. Except when I choose not to." She spread her arms. "What do you think? Tell me you like it and I'm yours for tonight!"

"Never, Domitilla."

She touched her groin. "Because of *this*?"

"Because of you," I said. I shivered. "How could you do it? A standard, Domitilla. A *standard!*"

"You poor old fool," she said.

Again I turned, and this time she let me go. I traveled to Madagascar and Turkey and Greenland and Bulgaria, and her images blazed in my mind, the wolverine-girl I had loved and the grotesque thing she had become. Gradually the pain grew less. I went in for a new Shaping, despite Hapshash and his coterie, and came out simpler, more sleek, less conglomeroid. I felt better, then. I was recovering from her.

A year went by. At a party in Oaxaca I told the story, finally, to Melanoleum, stunning in her new streamlined form. "If I had it all to do over, I would," I said, "One has to remain in an existentially pliant posture, of course. One must keep alert to all possibilities. And so I have no regrets. But yet—but yet—she hurt me so badly, love—"

"Look over there," said Melanoleum.

I followed her glance, past Hapshash and Mandragora and Negresca, to the slender, taut-bodied stranger scooping fish from the pond: beetle-wings, black and yellow, luminescent spots glowing on thighs and forearms, cat-whiskers, needle-sharp fangs. She looked toward me and our eyes met, a contact that seared me, and she laughed and her laughter shriveled me with post-causal mockery, contra-linear scorn. In front of them all she destroyed me. I fled. I am fleeing still. I may flee her forever.

THE TROUBLE WITH SEMPOANGA

This was one of those odd jobs that come a professional writer's way every now and then. A magazine called Beyond *was getting started, published out of Los Angeles, and intended, I think, for distribution entirely on college campuses. They wanted to publish a science-fiction story by a well-known writer in each issue. Harlan Ellison put its editor, Judith Sims, in touch with me in September of 1981; a good price was being offered and I was then in the midst of the rush of creative activity that in recent months had produced the* Majipoor Chronicles *short stories and four or five others; after doing "The Conglomeroid Cocktail Party" for* Playboy *I sat right down and wrote "The Trouble With Sempoanga" for this new magazine. At this late date it may seem to have been inspired by the AIDS epidemic, but in fact AIDS had not yet surfaced as a major problem in 1981 and if there was any kind of real-world inspiration for this little story, it was the epidemic of genital herpes that then was a big topic of conversation in the United States.*

At any rate, I wrote the story and Beyond *published it in its second issue (I think the magazine lasted four issues altogether) and that was that. I haven't given that ephemeral magazine a thought for decades. Even Google seems to know nothing about it and I'm not sure where my file copy is. (I had to ask Harlan for some of the details I've noted here.) But I did get a nice nasty story out of the project.*

When Helmet Schweid decided to go to Sempoanga for his holiday, he knew the risks, but of course he assumed they didn't apply to him. "You'll pick up a dose of *zanjak* and never get out of quarantine," his friends told him. Helmet laughed. He was a careful man, especially with his body. He would avoid getting *zanjak* by avoiding going to bed with women who had *zanjak*: that was simple enough to manage, wasn't it?

By common agreement Sempoanga was the most beautiful planet in the galaxy. See one sunrise on Sempoanga, everyone said, and you won't care if you never see anything else anywhere. The trouble with Sempoanga was the dismal parasite its humanoid natives harbored. There was only one way to transmit that parasite—by making love. Since the natives of Sempoanga are a good deal less attractive to humans than its sunrises, it is not easy to understand how any human could ever have caught it, but somehow someone had, and it had adapted nicely to human bodies, thriving and multiplying and making itself remarkably contagious, and in the past few years a good many human visitors to Sempoanga had passed it around to one another, with horrendous results. Biologists were working on a cure and hoped they might see results in just a few more years. But meanwhile no one went home from Sempoanga without undergoing tests and if you caught *zanjak*, you stayed quarantined there indefinitely, because the parasite's effect on the human reproductive system was so startling that the future of the entire species might be in jeopardy if it were allowed to spread to the other civilized worlds.

For his first few days on Sempoanga Helmut was so busy experiencing the gorgeous planet itself that he was in no danger of catching any kind of venereal disease, neither the old standbys nor the exotic local specialty. His own world, Waldemar, was a frosty place with a planetwide winter for three-quarters of the year, and on Sempoanga he erupted with great gusto into eternal tropical summer. From dawn to midnight he toured the wonders—Hargillin Falls, where the water is the color of red wine, and Stinivong Chute, a flawless mountain of obsidian at the edge of a lake of phosphorescent pink gas, and The Bubbles, where subterranean psychedelic vapors percolate upward through a shield of porous yellow rock with delightful effect. He ran naked through a grove of voluptuous ferns that wrapped him in their fleshy fronds. He swam in crystalline rivers, eye to eye with vast harmless turtles the size of small islands. And each night he staggered back to his hotel, wonderfully weary, to collapse into his solitary sleep-tube for a few hours.

But after those early greedy gulps of natural marvels, his normal social instincts reasserted themselves. On the fourth day he saw a striking-looking radium-blonde from one of the Rigel worlds at the gravity-ball court. She met his tentative grin with a dazzling one of her own and quickly agreed to have dinner with him. Everything was going beautifully until she excused herself for a moment late in the meal, and the waiter who was bringing the brandies paused to whisper to Helmut, "Watch out for that one. *Zanjak.*"

He was stunned. Was she trying to hide it from him, then? No, give her more credit than that: as they strolled through the garden under the light of the five moons she said, "I'd like to spend the night with you. But only if you're already carrying. I am, you know." So that was that. He walked her to her room and kissed her sadly and warmly goodnight, and trembled for a moment as her soft elegant body moved close against his; but he managed to escape without doing anything foolish.

The next night, sitting alone in the hotel cocktail lounge and beginning to feel more than lonely, he noticed another woman noticing him. She was dark-haired and long-legged and perhaps two or three years younger than he was. They exchanged glances and then smiles and he tapped his empty glass and she nodded and they rose and went to the bar and ritualistically bought each other drinks. Her name was Marbella and she had been on holiday here since last month, escaping from a collapsed six-group on the planet of Tlon. "The divorce is going to take *years*," she told him. "It's a universal-option planet, the six of us come from four different worlds and everybody's home-world laws apply, some of the lawyers aren't even *human*—"

"And you plan to hide out on Sempoanga until it's all over?"

"Can you imagine a better place?"

"Except for—"

"Well, yes, there's *that*. But every paradise has its little snake, after all." Quickly she shifted topics. "I saw you this morning at the puff-glider field. You looked like you wanted to try it."

"How is it done?" he asked. Helmut had watched hotel guests clambering into huge fungoid puff-balls, which immediately broke free of their moorings and went drifting out across golden Lake Mangalole in what looked like guided flight.

"Would you like me to teach you? It's a matter of controlling the puffer's hydrogen-synthesis. Stroke it one way and it gets more buoyant, another and it sinks. And you learn how to ride the thermals and all. Where did you say you were from?"

"Waldemar."

"Brr," she said. "Are you free for dinner tonight?"

He liked her forthright, aggressive ways. They arranged to meet for dinner and to try the puff-gliders in the morning. What might happen in between was left undiscussed, but once again Helmut found himself confronting the problem of *zanjak*. She had been here more than long enough to pick up an infection, and, coming out of a turbulent marriage, it was hardly likely that she had been chaste in this sensuous place. On the other hand, if she did carry the parasite, she would certainly tell him about it ahead of time, as the other woman had. There was bound to be an etiquette about such things.

Over dinner they spoke of her complex marriage and his simpler, but ultimately just as disastrous, one, and briefly of his work and hers and of his planet and hers, and then of the splendors of Sempoanga. He liked her very much. And the gleam in her eyes told him he was making the right impression.

When he invited her to his room, though, she turned him down—warmly and graciously and with what seemed like genuine regret, explaining that this was the last night of her five-day contraceptive holiday; she was fertile as a mink just now and feared giving way to temptation. She seemed sincere. "There'll be other nights, you know," she said, and her smile left him with no doubts.

In the morning they met at the puff glider field and she taught him quickly and expertly how to control the great organisms. Within an hour they were off and soaring. They crossed the lake, landed on the slopes of jag-toothed Mount Monolang for a lunch of sun-grilled fish and wineberries and ran laughing toward a glistening stream for a dip. Later, when they lay sunning themselves on shelves of glassy rock, he studied her bare body as surreptitiously as possible for signs of *zanjak*—some swelling around the thighs, perhaps, or maybe little puckered red marks below the navel, anything at all that seemed irregular. Nothing visible, at any rate. The pamphlet on *zanjak* that the hotel had thoughtfully left beside his bed had told him there were no external symptoms, but he was uneasy all the same.

It would have been simple enough to drift into lovemaking on this secluded hillside, but his uncertainties held him back, nor did she try to take the initiative. Eventually they dressed and resumed their glider-journey. They halted again to visit a village of natives—flat-faced warty creatures with furry mothlike antennae, so ugly that Helmut wondered what sort of tourist could have been desperate enough to catch the original parasite from one of *them*—and then in late afternoon, strolling hand in hand in fields of mildly aphrodisiac blossoms, they slipped into one of those low-toned, earnest, intimate conversations that only people who are about to become lovers engage in. "What a lovely day this has been," she told him when they were heading back to the hotel.

That night she asked him to her room. Two themes marched through his mind as they undressed. One was his admiration for her beauty, her warmth and intelligence, her desirability. And the other was *zanjak, zanjak, zanjak.*

What to do? By dimmed light he came to her. He imagined himself saying, "Forgive me, Marbella, but I need to know. That terrible parasite—that monstrous disease—" And he could see her turning bleak and furious as he blurted his tactless questions, demanding icily whether he thought she were the sort of woman who might deliberately hide from him anything so ghastly and shoving him into the hall, slamming the door, screaming curses after him—

He faltered. She smiled. Her eyes were bright with desire and refusing her was absurd. He drew her into his arms.

They were inseparable, night and day, the rest of the week. He had no illusions: this was only a resort-planet romance, and when his time was up he would go back to Waldemar and that would be the end of it. But it was wondrous while it lasted. She was a fine companion, and she appeared to be altogether in love with him, sincerely and a little worrisomely so. He was already rehearsing the speech he was going to have to make after breaking the news to her that business responsibilities would not permit him to extend his Sempoangan holiday beyond the five days that remained.

Then one drowsy morning as they were lying in bed he felt a dismaying internal twitch, as if some tiny supple creature were trying to swim downsteam in his urethra.

He said nothing to her. But after breakfast he invented the need to put a call through to his firm on Waldemar and, in terror, got himself off to the hotel medical office, where a blandly unsympathetic doctor processed him through the diagnostat and told him he had *zanjak*. "You see those little red flecks in your urine? Just a couple of microns in diameter. They're symptomatic. And this blood sample—it's loaded with *zanjak* excreta."

Helmut shivered. "I can't have had it more than a couple of days. Perhaps because we've detected it so soon—"

"Sorry. It doesn't work that way."

"What do I do now?" he asked tonelessly.

The doctor was already tapping data into a terminal. "We put you on the master list, first. That slaps a hold on your passport. You know about the quarantine, don't you? If your home world is covered by the covenant, your government will pay the expenses of transferring your funds and a certain quantity of your possessions to Sempoanga. You can live in the hotel as long as you can afford to, of course. After that, you're entitled to a rent-free room at the Quarantine Center, which is on the southern continent in a very pleasant region where the fishing is said to be superb. You'll be asked to take part in the various test programs for cures, but otherwise you'll be left alone."

"I don't believe this," Helmut muttered.

"These harsh measures are absolutely necessary, of course. You must realize that. The parasite has passed through your genitourinary tract and has taken up residence in your bloodstream, where it's busy filling you with threadlike reproductive bodies known as microfilariae. Whenever you have sexual relations with a woman—or with another man, for that matter, or with any mammalian organism at all—you'll inevitably transmit microfilariae. If the organism you infect is female, the microfilariae will travel in a few weeks to the ovaries, infiltrate unfertilized eggs and impose their own genetic material by a process we call pseudofertilization, causing the eggs to mature into hybrids, part *zanjak* and part host-species. What appears to be a normal pregnancy follows, though the term is only about twelve weeks in human hosts; offspring are born in litters, adapted quite cunningly to penetrate whatever ecosphere they find themselves in."

"All right. Don't tell me any more."

"No need to. You see the picture. These things could take over the universe if they ever got beyond Sempoanga."

"Then Sempoanga should be closed to interplanetary travel!"

"Ah, but this is a major resort area! Besides, the quarantine is one hundred percent effective. If only new tourists were not so careless or unethical as they seem to be, we would isolate all cases in a matter of weeks and after that—"

"I thought I was being careful!"

"Not careful enough, it seems."

"And you? Don't *you* worry about getting it?"

The doctor gave Helmut a scathing look. "When I was a small child, I learned quickly not to put my fingers into electrical sockets. I conduct my sexual activities with the same philosophy. Good morning, Mr. Schweid. I'll have your quarantine documents sent round to your room when they're ready."

Numbed, staggering, Helmut wandered in a lurching dazed way over the hotel's vast grounds, looking for Marbella. He felt unclean and outcast; he could not bear to look at any of the other guests who amiably greeted him as he went by; he yearned to thrust his fouled body into a vat of corrosive acid. Infected! Quarantined! Exiled, maybe forever, from his home! No. No. It went beyond all comprehension. That he, that precise and intelligent and meticulous man, with his insurance policies and his alarm systems and his annual medical checkups, should—should have—

He found her watching a game of body-tennis, caught her by the wrist from behind and whispered savagely, "I've got *zanjak!*"

She looked at him, startled. "Of course you do, love."

"You say it so casually? You let me believe you were clean!"

"Yes. Certainly. I knew you were already infected, even if you didn't. Since you apparently didn't know it yourself then, you'd never have gone to bed with me if I admitted I was carrying. And I wanted you so much, love. I'd have told any kind of harmless little lie then for the sake of—"

"Wait a minute. What do you mean, you knew I was already carrying?"

"That blonde bitch from Rigel, the night before you and I met—I saw the two of you together at dinner. I had my eye on you even then, you know. And I could tell that that unscrupulous little tramp would conceal from you that she was carrying. When I saw you go off to her room with her, I knew you'd be joining the club."

Icily he said, "I didn't sleep with her, Marbella."

"What? But I was sure—"

"You were, were you?" He laughed bitterly. "I walked her home and she told me she was a carrier and I kissed her goodnight and went away. You can't catch it from a kiss, can you? *Can you?*"

"No," she said in a very small voice.

"So you knowingly and shamelessly gave me a hideous incurable disease because you had decided I had been dumb enough to sleep with someone who was carrying it. I guess you were right about that, in a way."

She turned away, looking stricken. "Helmut, please—if you knew how sorry I am—"

"No sorrier than I am. Do you realize I'm quarantined here, and maybe for life?"

She shrugged. "Well, yes. So am I. There are worse places to spend one's life."

"I ought to kill you!"

She began to tremble. "I suppose I'd deserve it. Oh, Helmut—I was so completely fascinated by you—I didn't want to take the slightest risk of losing you. I should have waited until the infection I thought you got from *her* had showed itself. Then it wouldn't have mattered. But I couldn't wait—I tried, I couldn't—and I figured that we'd fall in love and by the time your *zanjak* showed it would be all right for me to admit that I had it, too."

He was silent a long moment. Then he said, "Maybe you figured that even if I *didn't* have it, you'd give it to me, by way of making absolutely sure I'd be stuck here on Sempoanga?"

"No. I swear it." There was shock and horror in her eyes. "You have to believe me, Helmut!"

"I could really kill you now," he said, and for an instant he thought he would. But instead he turned and fled, running in long loping, crazy strides, across the field of octopus palms and down a garden of electric orchids that flashed indignant lights at him and rang their bells, and through a swamp of warm sticky mud filled with little furry snakes, and up the side of Stinivong Chute, thinking he might throw himself over the edge. But halfway up he yielded to exhaustion and fell to the ground and lay there panting and gasping for what seemed like hours. When he returned to his room at dusk, there was a thick packet of documents beside his bed—his responsibilities and rights under the quarantine, how to transfer assets from his home world, pros and cons of applying for Sempoangan citizenship, and much more. He skimmed it quickly and tossed it aside before he was midway through. Thinking about such things was impossible now. He closed his eyes and pressed his face against his pillow, and suddenly scenes from Waldemar burned in his mind: the Great Glacier at Christmas, the ice-yacht races, the warm well-lit tunnels of his city, his snug dome-roofed home, his last night in it with Elissa, his trim little office with the rows of communicator panels—

He would never see any of that again, and it was all so stupid, so impossibly dumb, that he could not believe it.

He could not go to the dining room for dinner that evening. He ordered a meal from room service but left it untouched and nibbled a little of it the next morning after a night of loathsome dreams. That day he wandered at random, alone, getting used to what had happened to him. It was a magnificent day, the sky pink and soft, the flame-trees glowing, but it was all lost on him now. Even though this place might be paradise, he was condemned to dwell in it, and paradise on that basis was not very different from hell.

For two days he haunted the hotel grounds like his own ghost, speaking to no one. He didn't see Marbella again until the third evening after the *zanjak* had emerged in him. To break free of his depression he had gone to the cocktail lounge, and she was there, alone, apparently brooding. She brightened when he appeared, but he glared coldly at her and went past, to the bar. A newcomer was sitting there by herself, an attractive fragile-looking woman with large dark eyes and frosted auburn hair. Deliberately, maliciously, Helmut made a point of picking her up in front of Marbella. Her name was Sinuise; she came from a planet called Donegal; like so many others here, she was trying to forget a bad marriage. When they left the cocktail lounge together, Helmut could feel Marbella's eyes on him and it was like being skewered with hard radiation.

He and Sinuise dined and danced and drifted toward the evening's inevitable conclusion. In the casino he spotted Marbella again, watching them somberly from a distance. "Come," he said to the woman from Donegal. "Let's go for a walk." He slipped his arm over her shoulder. She was delicate and lovely and beyond doubt she was hungry for warmth and closeness, and he knew that he need only ask and she would go to his room with him. But as they strolled down the leafy paths he knew he could not do it. To carry his revenge on Marbella to the point of giving *zanjak* to an unsuspecting woman—no. No.

Under the rustling fronds of a limberwillow tree, he kissed her long and lovingly, and when he released her he said, "It's been a beautiful evening, Sinuise."

"Yes. For me also."

"Perhaps we'll go puff gliding tomorrow."

"I'd like that. But—tonight—I thought—"

"I can't. Not with you, I have *zanjak* , you know. And unless you've already got it also—"

Her face seemed to crumple. The great dark eyes swam with tears. He took her hand lightly, but a convulsive quiver of disappointment and anguish ran through her, and she pulled away and fled from him, sobbing.

"I'm sorry," he called after her. "More than you can imagine!"

Marbella was still in the casino, still alone. She looked astonished that he had returned. He shot her a venomous look and headed for the gravity-dice table, and in fifteen minutes managed to lose half the money he was carrying. He thought of lovely little Sinuise alone in her bed. He thought of Helmut Schweid, infested by bizarre alien organisms. He thought of Marbella, her energy, her passionate little cries, her quick wit and sly humor. Perhaps she was telling the truth, he thought bleakly. Perhaps she genuinely thought I had picked up a dose from the blonde from Rigel.

Besides, what choice do I have now?

Slowly, wearily, he made his way across the huge room. Marbella was playing five-chip cargo in a reckless way. He watched her lose her stake. Then he lightly touched her arm.

"You win," he said.

They stayed together at the hotel another eight days, and then, because his money was gone and he would not take any from her, they moved to the Quarantine Center. It was, he quickly discovered, just as beautiful as the hotel, with glorious natural features every bit as strange and wonderful. They shared a small cabin and spent their days swimming and fishing and their nights making love. Over the next ten weeks Marbella's breasts grew heavy and her belly began to swell; but when her time came she would not go to the Quarantine Center hospital. Instead she bore her Sempoangan young behind the cabin, a litter of sleek little creatures like tiny green otters, ten or fifteen of them that came sliding out of her without effort. Helmut dug a pit and shoveled them all in, and after she had rested for an hour or so they went down to the beach to watch the translucent waves lapping against the azure sand. He thought of the snows of Waldemar, and of his home there, his lovers, his friends, and it all seemed terribly long ago and more than a million light-years far away.

JENNIFER'S LOVER

Now that I was writing short stories with fluency and ease once again, and selling them to high-paying slick magazines like Omni *and* Playboy, *I began to look around for other markets of the same sort, since those two could handle only one or two Silverberg stories a year and at my current rate of production I would quickly exceed that figure. So my attention fastened on* Penthouse, *the chief competitor to* Playboy *in the field of slick-paper male-oriented magazines, which had published a story of mine ("In the Group") in 1973. In what was for me the unusually active month of October, 1981, I wrote to Kathy Green, the fiction editor of* Penthouse, *asking whether she'd be interested in seeing the occasional short story of the sort that I was currently writing for* Playboy *and* Omni. *She was, and the following month yet another time-travel idea occurred to me and I sent her "Jennifer's Lover," which she promptly accepted, and used in her May, 1982 issue. But I never felt comfortable with* Penthouse *as a magazine, and did not make much of an attempt to develop a regular relationship there, as I had done with* Playboy.

Finch had married very young—he had been only twenty-three, and Jennifer even younger—and even so he hoped they would live happily ever after. Marriage had been back in fashion for a few years, then, but all the same it was unusual to do it so early, and friends and

259

relatives warned them of the risks. Get out and live in the adult world for a while, they said. There's plenty of time later for settling down.

But marrying was more than a matter of fashion for Finch. He had since adolescence felt himself to be a basically married person. Like one of the primordial creatures of Plato's *Symposium* is how he saw himself—a twofold being that somehow had been divided and could not be happy until it had been reunited with its missing half. He searched diligently until he found Jennifer, who seemed to be that separated segment of himself; and then he quickly took care to join her securely to him once again. They settled in a sleek and snug Connecticut suburb. He sold portable computer terminals for a dynamic little hi-tech outfit in Bridgeport, and she worked for a publishing company in Greenwich, and before long they had a daughter named Samantha and a son named Jason, after which Jennifer quit her job and began doing some volunteer work at the local museum. Their parents, who had been pretty wild items in their own day, doing dope and marching for peace and trashing campuses, were amazed at the way everything had come around full circle in just one generation.

Finch was on the road a lot, making sales calls in a territory that stretched from Rhode Island to Delaware, and occasionally he wondered if Jennifer might someday amuse herself with a lover. But the idea was really too alien to make sense to him. Even when he was away from home three or four nights in a row, sleeping in drab motels in New Jersey or Pennsylvania, he saw no need to go outside his warm and secure marriage, and he imagined Jennifer felt the same way. He wondered if that was naive and decided it wasn't. As a couple they were complete, a single entity, a unity. Naturally the early raptures were only warm memories now, but the expectable cooling of passion had been followed by deep friendship. They were together even when they were apart; a lover would be a superfluity; Finch told himself that if he learned Jennifer had been unfaithful to him, he would not so much be jealous as merely mystified.

And of course there were the children to bind them always: Samantha was already beautiful at seven, a slim golden creature who was as apt to speak French as English. She awed them both, and they were immensely proud of her precocious elegance. Jason, not quite six, was of a different substance, a stolid and literal person whose toys were made of microprocessors and LEDs. He had his father's love of technology, and Finch saw in him a chance to create what he himself had not managed to be—a genuinely original scientific intellect rather than a peddler of other people's inventions. Whenever he returned from a long trip he brought gifts for everyone, a book or a record for Jennifer, something pretty for Samantha, and invariably a computer game or mechanical puzzle for Jason. They were splendid children, and he and Jennifer often congratulated one another on having produced them.

At a computer showroom in Philadelphia one rainy autumn afternoon, Finch bought a wonderful toy for Jason, a little synthesizer that played lively tunes when you tapped out signals in a binary code. Not only would it develop Jason's musical skills—and that side of the brain needed to be trained too, Finch thought—but it would sharpen his ability to count in binary. It was so expensive that he felt guilty and eased his conscience by getting the new supercassette of *Die Meistersinger* for Jennifer and a sweater of some glittering furry fabric for Samantha; but on the long drive home he thought only of Jason creating buoyant melodies out of skeins of binary digits.

Jason accepted it politely but seemed not very interested. He watched as Finch demonstrated it, and when it was his turn he generated a few fragmentary atonal squawks. Then a call from Jennifer's parents interrupted things, and afterward, Finch noticed, the child wandered off to his room without taking the synthesizer with him. That was disappointing, but Finch reminded himself that six-year-olds had a way of being preoccupied with one thing at a time, and possibly Jason's preoccupation of the moment was so compelling that even a wondrous new device could not gain much of a grip on his attention.

After dinner, feeling a little miffed, Finch took the synthesizer to Jason's room and found him hunched over an odd glowing thing the size of a large marble. When he saw Finch enter, the boy disingenuously pushed it into the clutter on his tabletop and pretended to be busy with his holographic viewer. "You left this in the living room," Finch said, giving him the synthesizer. Jason took it and obligingly hit the keys in his mild, obedient way, but he looked uncomfortable and impatient. Finch said, pointing at the little glowing thing, "What's that?"

"Nothing much."

"It's very pretty. Mind if I see it?"

Jason shrugged. He generated a jagged screeching tune. Finch picked up the sphere. Jason looked even more restless.

"What does it do?" Finch asked.

"You press it in places. It turns colors. You have to get it the same color all over."

"Rubik's Cube," Finch said. "An old idea brought up to date, I guess." He put his fingertips to the sphere and watched in surprise as colors of eerie indefinable hues came and went, blending, shifting. Touch it a certain way and there were stripes; another and there were triangular patterns; another and the surface of the sphere burst into thick, brilliant, throbbing patches of color, almost like a Van Gogh landscape. He had never seen anything like it. "Where'd you get it?" he asked. "Jennifer buy it for you?"

"No."

"Grandpa Finch send it?"

"No."

Finch felt himself growing annoyed. "Then who gave it to you?"

The child looked momentarily troubled, tugging at his lower lip, twisting his head at a peculiar angle. Then he began to contemplate the synthesizer, and the old serene Jason, imperturbable, studious, returned.

"Nort gave it to me," he said.

"Nort?"

"*You* know."

"I don't. Who's Nort?"

Jason was manipulating the synthesizer, quickly getting the hang of it, making something close to a tune emerge. He had dismissed Finch from his awareness as thoroughly as though Finch had been transported to Pluto. Gently Finch said, "You aren't answering me. Who's Nort?"

"He plays with me sometimes."

Finch decided to drop it. Jason would tell him about Nort in his own good time, he supposed. Meanwhile the boy was mastering the synthesizer with gratifying swiftness; no point distracting him from that. Finch picked up the sphere again, stroked it so that it went through a whole new series of color changes, and brought it almost to the single hue that apparently one was meant to achieve. But he did something wrong and kicked it into a geometrical pseudo-Mondrian pattern instead. A clever gadget, he thought, and went off to find Jennifer and to catch up on local gossip. The mysterious Nort quickly slipped from his mind, and he might never have thought of him again at all if Samantha had not remarked, when he was in her room to say good night to her, "I'm glad you're back. I don't like Nort, really. I hope he doesn't come here any more."

Very calmly Finch said, "Oh, he was here again?"

"Two days, this time. Tell him not to come, will you?"

"I don't know if I can do that. You know who Nort is, after all, don't you?"

"Sure. *Maman's* nephew. A nephew is something like a brother, *n'est ce pas?*"

"A little bit," said Finch. He kissed her lightly. "I'll see what I can do about Nort, all right? And if he comes back when I'm gone, you tell me about it, sweet. I don't think I like him either. But let's not say anything about this to *maman,* okay? She's very fond of her nephew, you know, and it would upset her if she knew that you and I didn't like him."

He paused a moment in the hallway, pressing his forehead against the wall, catching his breath. *Maman's nephew* Jennifer had no nephews. Finch was trembling. Visiting lovers usually claimed to be uncles, he thought. A nephew? *Jennifer's lover?* It was craziness, a phantasm, a melodrama of a tired mind. Jennifer had no lovers. Finch could visualize their marriage, that abstraction, as a solid concrete thing, a gleaming polished marble sphere rather like Jason's glowing toy, and in the perfection of that sphere there was neither need nor room for lovers. In his own way he would find out who Nort was, he resolved, but above all else he would stay calm. He poured himself a drink and rejoined Jennifer, studying her covertly as if looking for signs of adultery on her forehead, in her cheeks. She was playing *Meistersinger,* humming along with the jollier choruses. When they went to bed, he turned to her as he always did when he came home from a long trip, but he imagined that something strange had descended between them like a curtain of metal links, and he was unable to embrace her. The unknown Nort lay as a barrier in their bed. Finch ran his hands halfheartedly over her breasts and flanks but did nothing else. "You must be very tired," Jennifer whispered.

"I am. All that rain—the traffic skidding around—"

She kissed the tip of his nose. "Get a good night's rest," she said.

He had trouble sleeping. He felt her presence inches away as a pulsating vibration that made his fingers and toes tingle disagreeably. That she might have a lover frightened him, for it meant he held faulty assumptions about their relationship, that his evaluation of reality was defective. And he had to admit that he was upset on a much simpler level: a stranger was creeping into his bed, and he hated that as a violation of his rights. He found his reaction embarrassing. Mere jealousy, he thought, is ugly and stupid and very much beneath me. Nonetheless, beneath him or not, he felt what he felt, and it hurt him keenly.

Eventually he fell asleep, and when he woke to brilliant October sunlight streaming through the blazing leaves of the red maple outside their bedroom everything seemed normal again. Jason was using the synthesizer, getting it to play something that almost might have been *Three Blind Mice*. Finch was intensely pleased by that. At work that day he thought sometimes about Nort, but not in any very painful way—some neighborhood person, he supposed, an artist Jennifer had met at the museum, maybe, who drops around for a drink and some artistic chitchat, most likely gay, gentle, fond of children, harmless. He was much more interested in that peculiar glowing sphere. That night he went into Jason's room to examine it again. Ingenious, the play of colors, the tantalizing way it *almost* went one-toned as you handled it and then slipped away into patterns. He had no idea how it worked. Sensitive to skin-temperature fluctuations, perhaps, or possibly even pressure-sensitive, though it was solid as a marble. And what generated the changing colors and projected them to the surface? He was tempted to ask Jason to get a second sphere from Nort that he could try to take apart.

The week after next he was up in Boston for three days on his regular monthly trip. The first two went well; but on the evening of the third, as he returned to his motel after an overly winy dinner with a buyer from a Cambridge data-shop chain, the incandescent image of Jennifer getting into bed with Nort suddenly blazed in his soul. The Nort that Finch invented was older than he, perhaps thirty-seven, dark and muscular, with a dancer's supple body and an easy, self-assured manner. Finch bit his lip and tried to force the unwanted vision away, but it grew ever more vivid and ever more graphic, and the pain of it was astonishing. He thought seriously of driving home in the middle of the night. But that would be insane, he realized.

He came home on schedule with the usual gifts, and when he gave Jason his—a little screen on which he could draw with a light-pen—he feared the boy, still enthralled by some phenomenal incomprehensible thing that Nort had just brought him, might snub it. But Jason said nothing about Nort and was instantly fascinated by the screen. Finch felt a surge of relief until Samantha drew him aside, an hour later, to tell him, "He was here again."

"Nort?"

"Oui. Mardi et marcredi."

264

"*Mercredi,*" he corrected automatically. Her French still had some flaws; but she was only seven. He turned away to hide his look of torment. Two nights, again. Tuesday, Wednesday. He had no idea what he was supposed to do. Confront her with his suspicions and demand an explanation? They had never even had a real quarrel. Swallow his agony and count himself grateful that there was someone here protecting his home and family while he was away? Sure. Sure. In a dull voice he said, "What do Nort and *maman* do when he's visiting her?"

"They have dinner after we go to sleep. Then they stay up late and talk. In the morning he asks us questions about school and things and tries to be nice to us."

In the morning. Finch winced.

He forced himself to make love with Jennifer that evening so she would not suspect that he suspected, but he was without desire and barely managed to enter her, which made it all even worse. Guilty herself, she would want to assume the worst in him, and this uncharacteristic failure of virility after three nights away from her probably would lead her to think he had been with women in Boston, which would encourage her to give herself even more flagrantly to her own lover, which—

In the two weeks before his next road-trip he thought constantly of what would take place between Jennifer and Nort while he was away. He was jittery, remote, short-tempered, and morose; Jennifer seemed to be trying to please him, but whatever she did was counterproductive, and he was reduced to pleading business worries and headaches to keep from having to blurt out what was really on his mind. He wanted no confrontations with her. The love he bore her should be great enough to allow scope for a little discreet adultery, and if it did not, well, he would try to work on his attitudes.

But as he drove off toward Hartford under gray November skies, he imagined Nort's car gliding into the garage, Nort entering the house, Nort with his hands on her breasts, Nort leading her toward the bedroom. The absurd intensity of his obsession alarmed and dismayed him. But he could not control his feelings. In Hartford he checked into his motel and drifted like a man in a daze through his first three calls; he must have seemed in terrible shape, because everyone commented on the way he looked; he had two drinks before making his fourth call, which he never did, and then he canceled the call and returned to the motel. There he had another drink, ate a hamburger in the coffee-shop, and stared unseeingly at the television set until midnight, when he abruptly rose, dressed, stumbled outside, and grimly began to drive homeward. He knew that this was absolute madness. He would let himself into the house and catch them in bed together, and then the three of them would sit down and discuss things. And he had no idea what would happen after that.

Just before two in the morning he parked in front of his house and saw, with perverse satisfaction, that a lamp was lit in the bedroom. Strangely calm, Finch peered through the garage window, but saw only Jennifer's station-wagon inside. So Nort *was* a neighborhood person, Finch thought. She phones him and he walks over here and she lets him in.

Noiselessly Finch unlocked the door, punched in his identity code on the burglar-alarm keyboard, slipped off his shoes, and tiptoed upstairs. His heart pounded with such startling force that he began to fear real damage to it. At the top of the stairs he paused, paralyzed with shame and misgivings. Leave them alone, he told himself. This is unquestionably the most stupid and reckless and self-defeating thing you've done in your life. He was quivering. He did not dare go forward.

"Dale?" Jennifer called from the bedroom. "Dale, is that you? It *better* be you!"

"Me," he croaked, and lurched into the room.

She was alone, sitting up in bed, looking frightened and surprised. Finch, ashen and shaking, still had the presence of mind to scan the room for spoor of Nort, an overlooked wristwatch, a stray sock. Nothing. Jennifer was naked. She slept that way with him, but she had once told him that she always wore pajamas when he was away, for warmth. Certainly Nort was still here. Nobody jumps out a second-floor window to escape an angry husband. In the closet? In the bathroom? Under the bed? Finch knew he had created a preposterous farce.

"I felt ill," he mumbled. "Dizzy—hot flashes—I couldn't be alone. I just climbed into the car and headed for home—to be with you—the kids—"

"Dale, what's the matter? What hurts you?" She was as tense and anguished as he was, but she seemed to be recovering her poise. She got out of bed—were those the red imprints of Nort's fingers on her breasts and thighs?—and pulled on her robe and came to him. "If you were so sick, you shouldn't have tried to drive all the way from Hartford. Why didn't you call first? Why didn't you try to have the motel get you a doctor?" He swayed. His legs felt like concrete. He leaned against her, sniffing for the other man's cologne or even the smell of his sweat, and let Jennifer ease him down to the bed. He wanted to ask her where she had hidden Nort. But the words would not come. She helped him undress and brought him aspirins, and turned the thermostat up because he was shivering so violently, and clasped him in her arms. Her body was so warm and yielding and tender against him that he nearly began to cry. He let himself relax in her embrace, and to his amazement his desires rose and he reached for her. She tried to quiet him, telling him she was too exhausted for any such thing, but there was no halting him and he took her quickly and with uncharacteristic force. Jennifer met his thrusts with a vigor he had not encountered in months. It must be because Nort's done all the foreplay for me, he thought bitterly, and came at once, with a sob, and collapsed against her breast. At once he was asleep, and in the morning it all seemed like a dreadful dream, nothing more. Finch insisted on going back to Hartford and making his rounds, and would hear no objection from Jennifer. But first he went into Samantha's room and, cutting short her expression of surprise at seeing her father return from his trip so soon, asked her bluntly whether Nort had come for dinner the night before.

"Yes," she said. "He was here when I got home from school. Is he still upstairs with *maman?*"

Finch asked himself, as he drove shakily back to Hartford, whether to seek the advice of friends, his parents, the local minister, a therapist. He had never done any of that. His life had always been an amiable progression toward deeper happiness. By the time he reached the motel, he knew he would consult no one, would take no action at all, would simply wait and see. He would let Jennifer make the next move.

But she said nothing and he said nothing and after his next trip, a brief one, he found Jason with another strange new toy, an arrangement of gleaming wires that crossed and recrossed and seemed to disappear at one juncture into a baffling uncharted dimension, visible only as a dazzling flicker of green light. Yes, the boy said, Nort had given it to him. Finch felt a surge of frantic anger. He was almost desperate now to bring this thing to some sort of resolution, for it was devouring him. Jennifer remained tender and loving and outwardly unchanged. Finch suffered. He could not push his fears and confusions below the threshold of awareness for more than an hour or two at a time; he was losing weight; everyone commented on his frayed and frazzled appearance. He was drowning in the silent turbulence of his altered life.

A second time he returned prematurely from a sales trip, hoping to catch them together. Again the light was on in the bedroom in the middle of the night. Again he stumbled in to find Jennifer flustered but alone. He explained that he was drunk and bewildered. "I think I'm having some sort of a breakdown," he told her, and this time he called in sick and took a week off, though the Christmas holidays were coming and it looked very bad to do that now. Impulsively he went with Jennifer to Bermuda for four days, leaving the children with his parents, and it was like a second honeymoon for them, the pink sandy shore, the palm trees. But the moment they came home his mind was full of Nort again. A few days before Christmas he had to go to Pittsburgh for a meeting, but when still at the airport he was consumed with the awareness that Nort was in his house, joking amiably with Jason and Samantha. Grimly Finch boarded his plane, sat in a cold funk of silence all the way and, in Pittsburgh, bought a ticket on the next flight back to JFK. A light snowfall had begun, and his car, sitting in the vast lot, looked dainty and virginal in its thin white mantle. He reached home at midnight. The bedroom light was on. Finch let himself in and took the stairs two at a time. Jennifer was sitting up in bed, naked at least to the waist, her bare breasts blazing at him like beacons, and next to her, relaxed, comfortable, his hands clasped behind his head, was a slender, naked young man, perhaps thirty at most, with cool green eyes and dense red hair that clung to his head in a curious caplike way.

Finch felt a kind of relief. "You're Nort?"

"Yes. Is time we finally met, I think, Mr. Dale."

"Mr. *Finch*. Or Dale." Nort had some slight accent. Finch said, "I don't know what the protocol is in a thing like this. I suppose I should be furious and smash things and make threats. But I'm hollow inside by now. I've known about this a long time."

"We know," Jennifer said. "Why else would you have kept coming here trying to catch us in the middle of the night?"

"Twice," said Nort. "This be the third. I thought this time I stay and talk with you."

"You were here the other two times?"

"Certainly. But Jennifer wanted no face-to-face. So when the Dale-detector went off, I did the vanish. You follow?"

Finch stared wearily at his wife. "Jennifer, who is this man and how did he get into our lives?"

"He's my nephew," she said.

"You have no—"

"—eleven generations removed."

"What?"

"A remote descendant in my sister's line. He comes from A.D. 2215. He's here to do research."

Finch thought of the toys Nort had given Jason. His eyes glazed.

Nort said. "I make the field trip, you follow? I do genealogical research, visit the ancestors, family anecdotes. In my era is very important, knowing the history. I have made many journeys over a long span."

"He has my whole family tree," said Jennifer. "I never knew it, but I'm descended from Millard Fillmore and Johann Sebastian Bach and possibly John of Gaunt."

Finch nodded. "That's fascinating."

Nort said, "We do not interfere, you know. We move around like spies, doing our studies and never interacting with the past-folk, out of fear of consequences, of course. But this was an exception. I was captivated by Jennifer instantly."

"Captivated," said Finch bleakly.

"Captivated, yes. We became lovers. It is a kind of incest, I imagine, but is not very serious, outside the direct maternal line, yes? My studies suffer. Now I come only to this year. Jennifer is a wonderful woman. You know?"

"I know, yes." Finch looked toward Jennifer. "I haul my ass over eight states peddling primitive data-processing devices while you amuse yourself with a lover from the twenty-third century. That absolutely captivates me, Jennifer. I can't tell you how—"

"Dale, please. You know I love you. But—but—"

Nort looked troubled. "You are not accepting of this?"

"I am not accepting, no," Finch said.

"But this is the late twentieth century, a decadent time for the marriage custom, and you are sophisticated, educated, elite persons. It is my understanding that toleration of nonmarital sexual interpersonation is widespread in your cohort. You are displeased I love your wife?"

"Very," said Finch in a gray voice. He lowered himself into the chair by the window and said, "You're a hell of a guy for keeping a straight face, Nort. I have to admire that. Throughout this whole routine you've been very convincing. But I'm worn out, and I can't take any futuristic rigmarole any more. Please put your clothes on and go away and don't come back, and leave Jennifer and me to pick up the pieces of our marriage. Okay? Because if I catch you here again, I might do something violent, which is against my nature, and I'll probably have to divorce Jennifer, which is the last thing in the world I want to do even now."

"You doubt I am from a future time?"

"I doubt you are from a future time, yes."

Nort climbed out of the bed. Finch noticed a thin plastic band of some constantly oscillating greenish color around his left thigh. He touched it and disappeared, and when he reappeared, a moment later, he was in a different corner of the room, holding out a folded newspaper to Finch. Finch glanced at it: the New York *Times* for April 16, 2037. The main headline was something about Pope Sixtus performing Easter services on the moon. Finch made a little choking sound and started to scan the other stories, but Nort, with an apologetic smile, took the paper from him, vanished again, and reappeared without it, back in the bed. "I have sorrow," he said softly, "but I am forbidden to let you inspect the newspaper in detail. Shall I do other things? What would convince you I am genuine?"

Finch wanted to sob. He shook his head and said, "Don't bother. I don't need to know. You probably are what you say you are. Will you go away now? Go annoy Millard Fillmore."

"I am loving your wife."

"You *have loved* my wife. That's the correct grammar. It's over. Listen, I'm a ruthless late-twentieth-century man, and you're on dangerous ground. I have weapons. If you're killed while on a field trip, will you stay dead in 2215?"

Jennifer said, "Dale, stop talking that way."

"What do you want me to say? He flashes in here like something out of Buck Rogers, he screws my wife every time I look the other way, he upsets my daughter and alienates my son with his crazy future toys, and now I'm supposed to—"

"You mustn't threaten him, Dale. You're behaving *extremely* prehistorically. Haven't you ever had an affair?"

"Never. Not once."

"Those motels—"

"Not once. I suppose you've had plenty, though."

"Two before this one," she said, reddening a little. "I thought you knew. This isn't 1906, after all. They were both absolutely casual."

Finch thought of that polished perfect sphere that was his metaphor for the flawlessness of his relationship with Jennifer. He thought of the two-bodied male-female entities of Plato's *Symposium*. His face was leaden and his hands shook.

She said, "'This is more serious, Dale. I'm terribly fond of Nort. I love you as much as ever, but he's shown me other aspects of life, things I never dreamed of, and I'm not talking about sex. I mean spiritual concepts, human potentialities, the—"

"All right," said Finch. "I won't try to compete. I won't shoot him and I won't punch him and I won't do anything else uncivilized. Why don't the two of you get the hell off to A.D. 2215 and carry on the rest of your affair there, okay? Go have a flying fuck in the century after next and let me alone. Okay? Okay? The two of you. *Let—me—*"

Nort disappeared. So did Jennifer.

"Alone," Finch finished weakly. "Jennifer? Jennifer? Where are you? Hey, I wasn't serious! Jennifer! Goddamn it, what kind of sadistic stunt is this? Where are you?"

The cruelty of their game astounded him. He waited for them to pop back into the room as Nort had done with the newspaper, but they did not, and as the minutes went by he began to suspect that they were not going to. Numb with disbelief, he prowled the house, searching closets for them. Suddenly horror-struck, he rushed to Jason's room, then to Samantha's, but the children were still there, Jason asleep, Samantha awake and troubled by the shouting she had heard. He picked her up and held her a long moment, and tears came to him. "It's all right," he murmured. "Go back to sleep." He returned to the bedroom and sat there until dawn, waiting for Jennifer.

In the morning he phoned the office to say that severe family problems had forced him to return from Pittsburgh suddenly and that he needed an indefinite leave of absence, with or without pay. His supervisor was wholly understanding, not at all skeptical, as if Finch's voice communicated precisely how stunned and bewildered he was. He managed to deliver the children to school, and then spent the morning by the telephone, hoping to hear from Jennifer. But no word came from her all day. In late afternoon he called his parents to say that Jennifer had gone off somewhere without warning and could they please come early for their holiday visit, because he wasn't sure he could handle all this domestic stuff alone. They arrived the next day and asked blessedly few questions. In their generation, he thought, it must have been the usual thing for marriages to break up without warning.

Jennifer did not come back. He felt like someone who had been given a single wish and had used it stupidly: now she was off in the inconceivable future with Nort. Was that possible? Was this not all some kind of bizarre dream? Apparently not, for on Christmas Eve a note from Jennifer materialized inexplicably on the livingroom table, dated 14 Oct 2215 and wishing him happy holidays and assuring him of her love and telling him not to expect her back. "Sometimes you simply have to follow your destiny," she concluded. "I had only a fraction of a second to make my decision and I made it, and maybe I'll regret it, but I did what I had to do. I miss you, darling. And you know how much I miss Samantha and Jason." Next to the note was a little package, with a tag marked Merry Christmas from Nort. It contained a tiny crystal ball that when held close to his eye showed him what looked like an Antarctic landscape, gales howling and placid penguins wandering around on an ice floe. He put it down, and when he picked it up a second time it displayed the Pyramids, with a long line of tourists milling about. Finch flung it against the wall and it cracked in half and turned cloudy. He wished he had not done that.

Getting through the holidays was even more of an ordeal than usual, but his parents were an immense help, and his friends, once they discovered that Jennifer was gone, came magnificently to his aid. He was scarcely alone the whole week, and he suspected that it would not have been hard for him to find company for the night, either, but of course that was out of the question. The children were perplexed by Jennifer's disappearance, but after some disorientation they appeared to adapt, which Finch found more than a little chilling. He hired a housekeeper early in January and, feeling like a sleepwalker, went back to work. Because of the change in his family circumstances, the company took him off the outlying routes, so that he would not have to spend nights away from home.

Some time in early spring he started genuinely to believe that Jennifer had skipped away into the future with her lover. Notes from her arrived now and then, always friendly, with regards for the children and reminders about oiling the furnace and taking the cars in for tune-ups. She said she was having a wonderful time but missed him terribly. There was never any mention of coming back. From time to time, also, little gifts appeared—gadgets, toys, knicknacks of the future. Perhaps they were meant for Jason, but Finch kept them himself, hoarding them in his closet and examining them at night with awe. He had always loved gadgets—computers, remote-control devices, wrist videos, and such—but these seemed more like miracles than gadgets to him, and he ceased to doubt that Nort was what he said he was. Finch hoped another of the crystal balls would turn up, but it never did. He did get something that appeared to tune in the music of the spheres, and another that could be programmed to give him the dreams he wanted, and one that displayed abstract color-fields of a serene unearthly kind.

When summer came, he drifted with surprising ease into a romance with Estelle, the company's PR consultant, and that carried him into late autumn. Gently she extricated herself from the relationship then, but he had learned how to meet and win women once again, and he ran through a lively bachelorhood in the months that followed. The first anniversary of Jennifer's disappearance passed. The notes from her and the gifts from Nort came less frequently and then not at all. He was quite competent at running a family without a wife by now, but he had never lost that old sense of himself as an innately married man, as half of a couple, and so, admitting that Jennifer was never coming back, he filed for divorce and won an uncontested decree. That was the strangest part thus far, the knowledge that he was no longer married to Jennifer. He looked for a new wife in his diligent, serious-minded way and, within six months, found one. Her name was Sharon and she was warm-hearted and lovely and rather like Jennifer, though her interests ran more to drama and poetry than to music and painting. She had had an unhappy marriage just after college and had a boy of four, Joshua, very bright. Joshua got along wonderfully with Jason and Samantha, they accepted Sharon readily as their new mother— Jennifer was only a hazy memory to them now—and everything seemed to have worked out for the best. Sometimes Finch called Sharon "Jennifer" when they made love, but she was very understanding about that. Sometimes, too, he woke up drenched with sweat, wondering where he had misplaced his one true wife, his sundered half; but whenever that happened, Sharon held him until he regained his grasp on reality. He moved up nicely in the firm, which was expanding at a remarkable rate, and stayed trim and agile all through his forties. Samantha and Jason turned out well, too: Jason went to Cal Tech, joined a West Coast company, and invented an information-encapsulating device that made him a stock-option millionaire by the time he was twenty-two. Samantha grew tall and radiant and even more beautiful, pursued her interest in French, and achieved splendid translations of Rabelais and Ronsard and married the French ambassador. Finch saw less and less of his children once they were grown, of course, but they always came home for a family reunion at Christmas. They were with him that afternoon twenty-three years after Jennifer's disappearance when Jennifer reappeared.

Finch did not know who she was, at first. She quite suddenly was *there* in the living room, a handsome, slender, full-breasted young woman of about thirty, with golden hair in tight waves against her scalp, who wore a clinging garment of metallic mesh. She blinked and looked about and gasped as she saw Finch, who was in his mid-fifties and reasonably youthful-looking for his age.

"Dale?" she said doubtfully.

He let his drink clatter to the floor. "No," he said. "It isn't possible. Christ, what are you doing here?"

"I had to come back. Oh, Dale, it's the wrong year, isn't it? I wanted to see the children again!"

"There they are," he said stonily. "Take a look."

"Where—which—"

Jason was there and Samantha, and also Joshua and some of their friends; and obviously Jennifer did not recognize her own. Finch pointed. The stocky broad-shouldered young man with the earnest myopic gaze was Jason. The long-legged, awesomely beautiful woman was Samantha. Jennifer's glossy poise seemed to shatter. She was trembling and close to tears. "I wanted to see the children," she whispered. "They were so small—he was six, she was seven—oh, Dale, I've set the timer wrong! I've made a mess of it, haven't I?"

Samantha, quick as always, was the only other one who understood. She went toward her mother and stared at her as though Jennifer were an intruder from some other planet. Finch had heard that Samantha often used her beauty as a weapon, but he had never before seen it. Jennifer appeared to shrivel before the sleek, dazzling woman she had helped to create. In a low husky voice Samantha said, "You don't belong here now, you know. This is a happy time for us, and we don't need you and we don't want you. Will you go away?"

"Wait," Finch muttered.

Too late. Jennifer, reddening, dismayed, nodded and said to Samantha, "I'm terribly sorry. I'm sorry for everything." She ran from the room. Finch raced after her, out to the hall, but of course she had disappeared. White-faced, Finch returned to the party. He looked toward Sharon, who was both smiling and frowning. He had never told her or anyone else exactly what had become of his first wife.

"Who was that?" Sharon asked amiably. "Some girlfriend of yours, Dale?" There was nothing like jealousy in her voice. She was only mildly curious.

"No—no, nothing like that—"

"I wonder how she got in here. Like coming out of thin air, almost. Strange. Why did she dash away like that?"

"She didn't belong here," Finch said hoarsely. He poured himself another drink. "She was in the wrong time, the wrong place." He glanced at his daughter, who was flushed with triumph. What power she had, what force! All the same, he was starting to regret that Samantha had driven her off so quickly. With a wobbly hand he raised his glass. "Merry Christmas, everybody! Merry, merry, merry Christmas!"

For a few years after that he found himself wondering, as the holiday season approached, whether Jennifer would make another appearance, like some ghost of marriages past coming round again. Had she tired of Nort and Nort's century? Did she yearn for all she had abandoned? Though there was no longer any room in Finch's life for her, he held no grudge after all this time; he was almost eager to go off and talk with her a little, to find out who she had become, this woman who had once been part of him. But she never again returned. Perhaps she spent her holidays with Millard Fillmore now, he thought. Or singing carols by the blazing Yule log at the fireside of great-great-great-grandpa Johann Sebastian Bach.

NOT OUR BROTHER

In the autumn of 1981 short stories were emanating from me with a swift-
ness that I had not experienced in several decades. No sooner was
"Jennifer's Lover" out of the way than I embarked on "Not Our Brother," a
story that grew out of my fascination with Mexico and Mexican dance
masks, which I had begun to collect. It was not science fiction but horrific
fantasy, and I thought Playboy *might like it; but Alice Turner replied on*
November 25, "I hate to do this, but I'm turning it down. It is very similar
in both structure and content to 'Via Dolorosa,' and I think it had the same
problems. I won't go into detail unless you want it, for I know you will eas-
ily sell the story elsewhere, but what it comes down to is that I don't love
this the way I love 'Gianni' and 'Conglomeroid.' So I'm going to wait for the
next one. The way you're going, I expect to see it in a week or two."

I thought that the resemblances between "Not Our Brother" and "Via
Dolorosa" were fairly superficial ones. Perhaps they ran deeper than that,
though, because when I sent it to Ted Klein of Twilight Zone Magazine,
who had published "Via Dolorosa" and "How They Pass the Time in Pelpel,"
he commented that it seemed "awfully similar to both of them in theme
and other elements." Well, all three were stories about Americans experi-
encing strange events in Third World countries, I suppose. Despite his
qualms Ted accepted the story gladly and Twilight Zone *published it in*
the July, 1982 issue.

Halperin came into San Simón Zuluaga in late October, a couple of days before the fiesta of the local patron saint, when the men of the town would dance in masks. He wanted to see that. This part of Mexico was famous for its masks, grotesque and terrifying ones portraying devils and monsters and fiends. Halperin had been collecting them for three years. But masks on a wall are one thing, and masks on dancers in the town plaza quite another.

San Simón was a mountain town about halfway between Acapulco and Taxco. "Tourists don't go there," Guzmán López had told him. "The road is terrible and the only hotel is a Cucaracha Hilton—five rooms, straw mattresses." Guzmán ran a gallery in Acapulco where Halperin had bought a great many masks. He was a suave, cosmopolitan man from Mexico City, with smooth dark skin and a bald head that gleamed as if it had been polished. "But they still do the Bat Dance there, the Lord of the Animals Dance. It is the only place left that performs it. This is from San Simón Zuluaga," said Guzmán, and pointed to an intricate and astonishing mask in purple and yellow depicting a bat with outspread leathery wings that was at the same time somehow also a human skull and a jaguar. Halperin would have paid ten thousand pesos for it, but Guzmán was not interested in selling. "Go to San Simón," he said. "You'll see others like this."

"For sale?"

Guzman laughed and crossed himself. "Don't suggest it. In Rome, would you make an offer for the Pope's robes? These masks are sacred."

"I want one. How did you get this one?"

"Sometimes favors are done. But not for strangers. Perhaps I'll be able to work something out for you."

"You'll be there, then?"

"I go every year for the Bat Dance," said Guzmán. "It's important to me. To touch the real Mexico, the old Mexico. I am too much a Spaniard, not enough an Aztec; so I go back and drink from the source. Do you understand?"

"I think so," Halperin said. "Yes."

"You want to see the true Mexico?"

"Do they still slice out hearts with an obsidian dagger?"

Guzmán said, chuckling, "If they do, they don't tell me about it. But they know the old gods there. You should go. You would learn much. You might even experience interesting dangers."

"Danger doesn't interest me a whole lot," said Halperin.

"Mexico interests you. If you wish to swallow Mexico, you must swallow some danger with it, like the salt with the tequila. If you want sunlight, you must have a little darkness. You should go to San Simón." Guzmán's eyes sparkled. "No one will harm you. They are very polite there. Stay away from demons and you will be fine. You should go."

Halperin arranged to keep his hotel room in Acapulco and rented a car with four-wheel drive. He invited Guzmán to ride with him, but the dealer was leaving for San Simón that afternoon, with stops en route to pick up artifacts at Chacalapa and Hueycantenango. Halperin could not go that soon. "I will reserve a room for you at the hotel," Guzmán promised, and drew a precise road map for him.

The road was rugged and winding and barely paved, and turned into a chaotic dirt-and-gravel track beyond Chichihualco. The last four kilometers were studded with boulders like the bed of a mountain stream. Halperin drove most of the way in first gear, gripping the wheel desperately, taking every jolt and jounce in his spine and kidneys. To come out of the pink-and-manicured Disneyland of plush Acapulco into this primitive wilderness was to make a journey five hundred years back in time. But the air up here was fresh and cool and clean, and the jungle was lush from recent rains, and now and then Halperin saw a mysterious little town half-buried in the heavy greenery: dogs barked, naked children ran out and waved, leathery old Nahua folk peered gravely at him and called incomprehensible greetings. Once he heard a tremendous thump against his undercarriage and was sure he had ripped out his oil pan on a rock, but when he peered below everything seemed to be intact. Two kilometers later, he veered into a giant rut and thought he had cracked an axle, but he had not. He hunched down over the wheel, aching, tense, and imagined that splendid bat mask, or its twin, spotlighted against a stark white wall in his study. Would Guzmán be able to get him one? Probably. His talk of the difficulties involved was just a way of hyping the price. But even if Halperin came back empty-handed from San Simón, it would be reward enough simply to have witnessed the dance, that bizarre, alien rite of a lost pagan civilization. There was more to collecting Mexican masks, he knew, than simply acquiring objects for the wall.

In late afternoon he entered the town just as he was beginning to think he had misread Guzmán's map. To his surprise it was quite imposing, the largest village he had seen since turning off the main highway—a great bare plaza ringed by stone benches, marketplace on one side, vast heavy-walled old church on the other, giant gnarled trees, chickens, dogs, children about everywhere, and houses of crumbling adobe spreading up the slope of a gray flat-faced mountain to the right and down into the dense darkness of a barranca thick with ferns and elephant-ears to the left. For the last hundred meters into town an impenetrable living palisade of cactus lined the road on both sides, unbranched spiny green columns that had been planted one flush against the next. Bougainvillea in many shades of red and purple and orange cascaded like gaudy draperies over walls and rooftops.

Halperin saw a few old Volkswagens and an ancient ramshackle bus parked on the far side of the plaza and pulled his car up beside them. Everyone stared at him as he got out. Well, why not? He was big news here, maybe the first stranger in six months. But the pressure of those scores of dark amphibian eyes unnerved him. These people were all Indians, Nahuas, untouched in any important way not only by the twentieth century but by the nineteenth, the eighteenth, all the centuries back to Moctezuma. They had nice Christian names like Santiago and Francisco and Jesús, and they went obligingly to the iglesia for mass whenever they thought they should, and they knew about cars and transistor radios and Coca-Cola. But all that was on the surface. They were still Aztecs at heart, Halperin thought. Time-travelers. As alien as Martians.

He shrugged off his discomfort. Here he was the Martian, dropping in from a distant planet for a quick visit. Let them stare: he deserved it. They meant no harm. Halperin walked toward them and said, *"Por favor, donde está el hotel del pueblo?"*

Blank faces. *"El hotel?"* he asked, wandering around the plaza. *"Por favor. Donde?"* No one answered. That irritated him. Sure, Nahuatl was their language, but it was inconceivable that Spanish would be unknown here. Even in the most remote towns someone spoke Spanish. *"Por favor!"* he said, exasperated. They melted back at his approach as though he were ablaze. Halperin peered into dark cluttered shops. *"Habla usted Español?"* he asked again and again, and met only silence. He was at the edge of the marketplace, looking into a chaos of fruit stands, tacos stands, piles of brilliant serapes and flimsy sandals and stacked sombreros, and booths where vendors were selling the toys of next week's Day of the Dead holiday, candy skeletons and green banners emblazoned with grinning red skulls. *"Por favor?"* he said loudly, feeling very foolish.

A woman in jodhpurs and an Eisenhower jacket materialized suddenly in front of him and said in English, "They don't mean to be rude. They're just very shy with strangers."

Halperin was taken aback. He realized that he had begun to think of himself as an intrepid explorer, making his way with difficulty through a mysterious primitive land. In an instant she had snatched all that from him, both the intrepidity and the difficulties.

She was about thirty, with close-cut dark hair and bright, alert eyes, attractive, obviously American. He struggled to hide the sense of let-down her advent had created in him and said, "I've been trying to find the hotel."

"Just off the plaza, three blocks behind the market. Let's go to your car and I'll ride over there with you."

"I'm from San Francisco," he said. "Tom Halperin."

"That's such a pretty city. I love San Francisco."

"And you?"

"Miami," she said. "Ellen Chambers." She seemed to be measuring him with her eyes. He noticed that she was carrying a couple of Day of the Dead trinkets—a crudely carved wooden skeleton with big eye-glasses, and a rubber snake with a gleaming human skull of white plastic, like a cue-ball, for a head. As they reached his car she said, "You came here alone?"

Halperin nodded. "Did you?"

"Yes," she said. "Come down from Taxco. How did you find this place?"

"Antiquities dealer in Acapulco told me about it. Antonio Guzmán López. I collect Mexican masks."

"Ah."

"But I've never actually seen one of the dances."

"They do an unusual one here," she said as he drove down a street of high, ragged, mud-colored walls, patched and plastered, that looked a thousand years old. "Lord of the Animals, it's called. Died out every-where else. Pre-Hispanic shamanistic rite, invoking protective deities, fertility spirits."

"Guzmán told me a little about it. Not much. Are you an anthro-pologist?"

"Strictly amateur. Turn left here." There was a little street, an open wrought-iron gateway, a driveway of large white gravel. Set back a con-siderable distance was a squat, dispiriting hovel of a hotel, one story, roof of chipped red tiles in which weeds were growing. Not even the ubiquitous bougainvillea and the great clay urns overflowing with dazzling geraniums diminished its ugliness. Cucaracha Hilton indeed, Halperin thought dourly. She said, "This is the place. You can park on the side."

The parking lot was empty. "Are you and I the only guests?" he asked. "So it seems."

"Guzmán was supposed to be here. Smooth-looking man, bald shiny head, dresses like a financier."

"I haven't seen him," she said. "Maybe his car broke down."

They got out, and a slouching fourteen-year-old mozo came to get Halperin's luggage. He indicated his single bag and followed Ellen into the hotel. She moved in a sleek, graceful way that kindled in him the idea that she and he might get something going in this forlorn place. But as soon as the notion arose, he felt it fizzling: she was friendly, she was good-looking, but she radiated an offputting vibe, a noli-me-tangere sort of thing, that was unmistakable and made any approach from him inappropriate. Too bad. Halperin liked the company of women and fell easily and uncomplicatedly into liaisons with them wherever he traveled, but this one puzzled him. Was she a lesbian? Usually he could tell, but he had no reading on her except that she meant him to keep his distance. At least for the time being.

The hotel was grim, a string of lopsided rooms arranged around a weedy courtyard that served as a sort of lobby. Some hens and a rooster were marching about, and a startling green iguana, enormous, like a miniature dinosaur, was sleeping on a branch of a huge yellow-flowered hibiscus just to the left of the entrance. Everything was falling apart in the usual haphazard tropical way. Nobody seemed to be in charge. The mozo put Halperin's suitcase down in front of a room on the far side of the courtyard and went away without a word. "You've got the one next to mine," Ellen said. "That's the dining room over there and the cantina next to it. There's a shower out in back and a latrine a little further into the jungle."

"Wonderful."

"The food isn't bad. You know enough to watch out for the water. There are bugs but no mosquitoes."

"How long have you been here?" Halperin asked.

"Centuries," she said. "I'll see you in an hour and we'll have dinner, okay?"

His room was a whitewashed irregular box, smelling faintly of disinfectant, that contained a lumpy narrow bed, a sink, a massive mahogany chest of drawers that could have come over with the Spaniards, and an ornate candlestick. The slatted door did not lock and the tile-rimmed window that gave him an unsettling view of thick jungle close outside was without glass, an open hole to the wall. But there was a breathtaking mask mounted above the bed, an armadillo-faced man with a great gaping mouth, and next to the chest of drawers was a weatherbeaten but extraordinary helmet mask, a long-nosed man with an owl for one ear and a coyote for another, and over the bed was a double mask, owl and pig, that was finer than anything he had seen in any museum. Halperin felt such a rush of possessive zeal that he began to sweat. The sour acrid scent of it filled the room. Could he buy these masks? From whom? The dull-eyed mozo? He had done all his collecting through galleries; he had no idea how to go about acquiring masks from natives. He remembered Guzmán's warning about not trying to buy from them. But these masks must no longer be sacred if they were mere hotel decorations. Suppose, he thought, I just *take* that owl-pig when I check out, and leave three thousand pesos on the sink. That must be a fortune here. Five thousand, maybe. Could they find me? Would there be trouble when I was leaving the country? Probably. He put the idea out of his mind. He was a collector, not a thief. But these masks were gorgeous.

He unpacked and found his way outside to the shower—a cubicle of braided ropes, a creaking pipe, yellowish tepid water—and then he put on clean clothes and knocked at Ellen's door. She was ready for dinner. "How do you like your room?" she asked.

"The masks make up for any little shortcomings. Do they have them in every room?"

"They have them all over," she said.

He peered past her shoulder into her room, which was oddly bare, no luggage or discarded clothes lying around, and saw two masks on the wall, not as fine as his but fine enough. But she did not invite him to take a close look, and closed the door behind her. She led him to the dining room. Night had fallen some time ago, and the jungle was alive with sounds, chirpings and rachetings and low thunking booms and something that sounded the way the laughter of a jaguar might sound. The dining room, oblong and lit by candles, had three tables and more masks on the wall, a devil face with a lizard for a nose, a crudely carved mermaid, and a garish tiger-hunter mask. He wandered around studying them in awe, and said to her, "These aren't local. They've been collected from all over Guerrero."

"Maybe your friend Guzmán sold them to the owner," she suggested. "Do you own many?"

"Dozens. I could bore you with them for hours. Do you know San Francisco at all? I've got a big old three-story Victorian in Noe Valley and there are masks in every room. I've collected all sorts of primitive art, but once I discovered Mexican masks they pushed everything else aside, even the Northwest Indian stuff. You collect too, don't you?"

"Not really. I'm not an acquirer. Of things, at any rate. I travel, I look, I learn, I move on. What do you do when you aren't collecting things?"

"Real estate," he said. "I buy and sell houses. And you?"

"Nothing worth talking about," she said.

The mozo appeared, silently set their table, brought them, unbidden, a bottle of red wine. Then a tureen of albóndigas soup, and afterward tortillas, tacos, a decent turkey molé. Without a word, without a change of expression.

"Is that kid the whole staff?" Halperin asked.

"His sister is the chambermaid. I guess his mother is the cook. The patrón is Filiberto, the father, but he's busy getting the fiesta set up. He's one of the important dancers. You'll meet him. Shall we get more wine?"

"I've had plenty," he said.

"They went for a stroll after dinner, skirting the jungle's edge and wandering through a dilapidated residential area. He heard music and handclapping coming from the plaza but felt too tired to see what was happening there. In the darkness of the tropical night he might easily have reached for Ellen and drawn her against him, but he was too tired for that, too, and she was still managing to be amiable, courteous, but distant. She was a mystery to him. Moneyed, obviously. Divorced, widowed young, gay, what? He did not precisely mistrust her, but nothing about her seemed quite to connect with anything else.

About nine-thirty he went back to his room, toppled down on the ghastly bed, and dropped at once into a deep sleep that carried him well past dawn. When he woke, the hotel was deserted except for the boy. "Cómo se llama?" Halperin asked, and got an odd smouldering look, probably for mocking a mere mozo by employing the formal construction. "Elustesio," the boy muttered. Had Elustesio seen the

Norteamericano señorita? Elustesio hadn't seen anyone. He brought Halperin some fruit and cold tortillas for breakfast and disappeared. Afterward Halperin set out on a slow stroll into town.

Though it was early, the plaza and surrounding marketplace were already crowded. Again Halperin got the visiting-Martian treatment from the townsfolk—fishy stares, surreptitious whispers, the occasional shy and tentative grin. He did not see Ellen. Alone among these people once more, he felt awkward, intrusive, vulnerable; yet he preferred that, he realized, to the curiously unsettling companionship of the Florida woman.

The shops now seemed to be stocking little except Day of the Dead merchandise, charming and playful artifacts that Halperin found irresistible. He had long been attracted to the imagery of brave defiance of death that this Mexican version of Halloween, so powerful in the inner life of the country, called forth. Halperin bought a yellow papier-mâché skull with brilliant flower-eyes and huge teeth, an elegant little guitar-playing skeleton and a bag of grisly, morbid marzipan candies. He stared at the loaves of bread decorated with skulls and saints in a bakery window. He smiled at a row of sugar coffins with nimble skeletons clambering out of them. There was some extraordinary lacquer work on sale too, trays and gourds decorated with gleaming red-and-black patterns. By mid-morning he had bought so much that carrying it was a problem, and he returned to the hotel to drop off his purchases.

A blue Toyota van was parked next to his car and Guzmán, looking just as dapper in khakis as he always did in his charcoal gray suits, was rearranging a mound of bundles in it. "Are you enjoying yourself?" he called to Halperin.

"Very much. I thought I'd find you in town when I got here yesterday."

"I came and went again, to Tlacotepec, and I returned. I have bought good things for the gallery." He nodded toward Halperin's armload of toy skulls and skeletons. "I see you are buying too. Good. Mexico needs your help."

"I'd rather buy one of the masks that's hanging in my room," Halperin said. "Have you seen it? Pig and owl, and carved like—"

"Patience. We will get masks for you. But think of this trip as an experience, not as a collecting expedition, and you will be happier. Acquisitions will happen of their own accord if you don't try to force them, and if you enjoy the favor of *amo tokinwan* while you are here."

Halperin was staring at some straw-wrapped wooden statuettes in the back of the van. *"Amo tokinwan?* Who's that?"

"The Lords of the Animals," said Guzmán. "The protectors of the village. Perhaps protectors is not quite the right word, for protectors are benevolent, and *amo tokinwan* often are not. Quite dangerous sometimes, indeed."

Halperin could not decide how serious Guzmán was. "How so?"

"Sometimes at fiesta time they enter the village and mingle. They look like anyone else and attract no special attention, and they have a way of making the villagers think that they belong here. Can you imagine that, seeing a stranger and believing you have known him all your life? Beyond doubt they are magical."

"And they are what? Guardians of the village?"

"In a sense. They bring the rain; they ward off the lightning; they guard the crops. But sometimes they do harm. No one can predict their whims. And so the dancing, to propitiate them. Beyond doubt they are magical. Beyond doubt they are something very other. *Amo tokinwan.*"

"What does that mean?" Halperin asked.

"In Nahuatl it means, 'Not our brother,' of different substance. Alien. Supernatural. I think I have met them, do you know? You stand in the plaza watching the dancers, and there is a little old woman at your elbow or a boy or a pregnant woman wearing a fine rebozo, and everything seems all right, but you get a little too close and you feel the chill coming from them, as though they are statues of ice. So you back away and try to think good thoughts." Guzmán laughed. "Mexico! You think I am civilized because I have a Rolex on my wrist? Even I am not civilized, my friend. If you are wise you will not be too civilized while you are here, either. They are not our brother, and they do harm. I told you you will see the real Mexico here, eh?"

"I have a hard time believing in spirits," Halperin said. "Good ones and evil ones alike."

"These are both at once. But perhaps they will not bother you." Guzmán slammed shut the door of the van. "In town they are getting ready to unlock the masks and dust them and arrange them for the fiesta. Would you like to be there when that is done? The mayordomo is my friend. He will admit you."

"I'd like that very much. When?"

"After lunch." Guzmán touched his hand lightly to Halperin's wrist. "One word, first. Control your desire to collect. Where we go today is not a gallery."

The masks of San Simón were kept in a locked storeroom of the municipal building. Unlocking them turned out to be a solemn and formal occasion. All the town's officials were there, Guzmán whispered: the alcalde, the five alguaciles, the regidores, and Don Luis Gutierrez, the mayordomo, an immense mustachioed man whose responsibility it was to maintain the masks from year to year, to rehearse the dancers and to stage the fiesta. There was much bowing and embracing. Most of the conversation was in Nahuatl, which Halperin did not understand at all, and he was able to follow very little of the quick, idiosyncratic Spanish they spoke either, though he heard Guzmán introduce him as an important *Norteamericano* scholar and tried thereafter to look important and scholarly. Don Luis produced an enormous old-fashioned key, thrust it with a flourish into the door and led the way down a narrow, musty corridor to a large white-walled storeroom with a ceiling of heavy black beams. Masks were stacked everywhere, on the floor, on shelves, in cupboards. The place was a museum. Halperin, who could claim a certain legitimate scholarly expertise by now in this field, recognized many of the masks as elements in familiar dances of the region, the ghastly faces of the Diablo Macho Dance, the heavy-bearded elongated Dance of the Moors and Christians masks, the ferocious cat-faces of the Tigre Dance. But there were many that were new and astounding to him, the Bat Dance masks, terrifying bat-winged heads that all were minglings of bat characters and other animals, bat-fish, bat-coyote, bat-owl, bat-squirrel, and some that were unidentifiable except for the weird outspread rubbery wings, bats hybridized with creatures of another world, perhaps. Once by one the masks were lifted, blown clean of dust, admired, passed around, though not to Halperin. He trembled with amazement at the power and beauty of these bizarre wooden effigies. Don Luis drew a bottle of mescal from a niche and handed it to the alcalde, who took a swig and passed it on; the bottle came in time to Halperin, and without a thought for the caterpillar coiled in the bottom of the bottle he gulped the fiery liquor. Things were less formal now. The high officials of the town were laughing, shuffling about in clumsy little dance steps, picking up gourd rattles from the shelves and shaking them. They called out in Nahuatl, all of it lost on Halperin, though the words *amo tokinwan* at one point suddenly stood out in an unintelligible sentence, and someone shook rattles with curious vehemence. Halperin stared at the masks but did not dare go close to them or try to touch them. This is not a gallery, he reminded himself. Even when things got so uninhibited that Don Luis and a couple of the others put masks on and began to lurch about the room in a weird lumbering polka, Halperin remained tense and controlled. The mescal bottle came to him again. He drank, and this time his discipline eased; he allowed himself to pick up a wondrous bat mask, phallic and with great staring eyes. The carving was far finer than on the superb one he had seen at Guzmán's gallery. He ran his fingers lovingly over the gleaming wood, the delicately outlined ribbed wings. Guzmán said, "In some villages the Bat Dance was a Christmas dance, the animals paying homage to little Jesus. But here it is a fertility rite, and therefore the bat is phallic. You would like that mask, no?" He grinned broadly. "So would I, my friend. But it will never leave San Simón."

Just as the ceremony appeared to be getting rowdy, it came to an end: the laughter ceased, the mescal bottle went back to its niche, the officials grew solemn again and started to file out. Halperin, in school-boy Spanish, thanked Don Luis for permitting him to attend, thanked the alcalde, thanked the alguaciles and the regidores. He felt flushed and excited as he left the building. The cache of masks mercilessly stirred his acquisitive lust. That they were unattainable made them all the more desirable, of course. It was as though the storeroom were a gallery in which the smallest trifle cost a million dollars.

Halperin caught sight of Ellen Chambers on the far side of the plaza, sitting outside a small café. He waved to her and she acknowledged it with a smile.

Guzmán said, "Your traveling companion?"

"No. She's a tourist down from Taxco. I met her yesterday."

"I did not know any other Americans were here for the fiesta. It surprises me." He was frowning. "Sometimes they come, but very rarely. I thought you would be the only *extranjero* here this year."

"It's all right," said Halperin. "We gringos get lonely for our own sort sometimes. Come on over and I'll introduce you."

Guzmán shook his head. "Another time. I have business to attend to. Commend me to your charming friend and offer my regrets."

He walked away. Halperin shrugged and crossed the plaza to Ellen, who beckoned him to the seat opposite her. He signaled the waiter. "Two margaritas," he said.

She smiled. "Thank you, no."

"All right. One."

"Have you been busy today?" she asked.

"Seeing masks. I salivate for some of the things they have in this town. I find myself actually thinking of stealing some if they won't sell to me. That's shocking. I've never stolen anything in my life. I've always paid my own way."

"This would be a bad place to begin, then."

"I know that. They'd put the curse of the mummy on me, or the black hand, or God knows what. The sign of Moctezuma. I'm not serious about stealing masks. But I do want them. Some of them."

"I can understand that," she said. "But I'm less interested in the masks than in what they represent. The magic character, the transformative power. When they put the masks on, they *become* the otherworldly beings they represent. That fascinates me. That the mask dissolves the boundary between our world and *theirs*."

"*Theirs?*"

"The invisible world. The world the shaman knows, the world of the were-jaguars and were-bats. A carved and painted piece of wood becomes a gateway into that world and brings the benefits of the supernatural. That's why the masks are so marvelous, you know. It isn't just an aesthetic thing."

"You actually believe what you've just said?" Halperin asked.

"Oh, yes. Yes, definitely."

He chose not to press the point. People believed all sorts of things, pyramid power, yoghurt as a cure for cancer, making your plants grow by playing Bach to them. That was all right with him. Just now he found her warmer, more accessible, than she had been before, and he had no wish to offend her. As they strolled back to the hotel, he asked her to have dinner with him, imagining hopefully that that might lead somewhere tonight, but she said she would not be eating at the hotel this evening. That puzzled him—where else around here could she get dinner, and with whom?—but of course he did not probe.

He dined with Guzmán. The distant sound of music could be heard, shrill, alien. "They are rehearsing for the fiesta," Guzmán explained. The hotel cook outdid herself, preparing some local freshwater flatfish in a startlingly delicate sauce that would have produced applause in Paris. Filiberto, the patron, came into the dining room and greeted Guzmán with a bone-crushing *abrazo*. Guzmán introduced Halperin once again as an important *Norteamericano* scholar. Filiberto, tall and very dark-skinned, with cheekbones like blades, showered Halperin with effusive courtesies.

"I have been admiring the masks that decorate the hotel," Halperin said, and waited to be invited to buy whichever one took his fancy, but Filiberto merely offered a dignified bow of thanks. Praising individual ones, the owl-pig, the lizard-nose, also got nowhere. Filiberto presented Guzmán with a chilled bottle of a superb white wine from Michoacan, crisp and deliciously metallic on the tongue; he spoke briefly with Guzmán in Nahuatl; then, saying he was required at the rehearsal, he excused himself. The music grew more intense.

Halperin said, "Is it possible to see the rehearsal after dinner?"

"Better to wait for the actual performance," said Guzmán.

Halperin slept poorly that night. He listened for the sound of Ellen Chambers entering the room next door, but either he was asleep when she came in or she was out all night.

And now finally the fiesta was at hand. Halperin spent the day watching, the preparations: the stringing of colored electric lights around the plaza, the mounting of huge papier-mâché images of monsters and gods and curious spindly-legged clowns, the closing down of the shops and the clearing away of the tables that displayed their merchandise. All day long the town grew more crowded. No doubt people were filtering in from the outlying districts, the isolated jungle farms, the little remote settlements on the crest of the sierra. Through most of the day he saw nothing of Guzmán or Ellen, but that was all right. He was quite accustomed now to being here, and the locals seemed to take him equally for granted. He drank a good deal of mescal at one cantina or another around the plaza and varied it with the occasional bottle of the excellent local beer. As the afternoon waned, the crowds in the plaza grew ever thicker and more boisterous, but nothing particular seemed to be happening, and Halperin wondered whether to go back to the hotel for dinner. He had another mescal instead. Suddenly the fiesta lights were switched on, gaudy, glaring, reds and yellows and greens, turning everything into a psychedelic arena, and then at last Halperin heard music, the skreeing bagpipy sound of bamboo flutes, the thump of drums, the whispery, dry rattle of tambourines, the harsh punctuation of little clay whistles. Into the plaza came ten or fifteen boys, leaping, dancing cartwheels, forming impromptu human pyramids that promptly collapsed, to general laughter. They wore no masks. Halperin, disappointed and puzzled, looked around as though to find an explanation and discovered Guzmán, suave and elegant in charcoal gray, almost at his elbow. "No masks?" he said. "Shouldn't they be masked?"

"This is only the beginning," said Guzmán.

Yes, just the overture. The boys cavorted until they lost all discipline and went pell-mell across the plaza and out of sight. Then a little old man, also unmasked, tugged three prancing white goats caparisoned with elaborate paper decorations into the center of the plaza and made them cavort, too. Two stilt-walkers fought a mock duel. Three trumpeters played a hideous discordant fanfare and got such cheers that they played it again and again. Guzmán was among those who cheered. Halperin, who had not eaten, was suddenly captured by the aroma from a stand across the way where an old woman was grilling tacos on a brazier and a tin griddle. He headed toward her, but paused on the way for a tequila at an improvised cantina someone had set up on the streetcorner, using a big wooden box as the bar. He saw Ellen Chambers in the crowd on the far side of the plaza and waved, but she did not appear to see him, and when he looked again he could not find her.

The music grew wilder and now, at last, the first masked dancers appeared. A chill ran through him at the sight of the nightmare figures marching up the main avenue, bat-faced ones, skull-faced ones, grinning devils, horned creatures, owls, jaguars. Some of the masks were two or three feet high and turned their wearers into malproportioned dwarfs. They advanced slowly, pausing often to backtrack, circling one another, kicking their legs high, madly waving their arms. Halperin, sweating, alert, aroused, realized that the dancers must have been drinking heavily, for their movements were jerky, ragged, convulsive. As they came toward the plaza he saw that they were herding four figures in white robes and pale human-faced masks before them, and were chanting something repetitively in Nahuatl. He caught that phrase again, *amo tokinwan*. Not our brother.

To Guzmán he said, "What are they saying?"

"The prayer against the *amo tokinwan*. To protect the fiesta, in case any of the Lords of the Animals actually are in the plaza tonight."

Those around Halperin had taken up the chant now.

"Tell me what it means," Halperin said.

Guzmán said, chanting the translation in a rhythm that matched the voices around them: *"They eat us! They are—not our brother. They are worms, wild beasts. Yes!"*

Halperin looked at him strangely. "'They eat us?'" he said. "Cannibal gods?"

"Not literally. Devourers of souls."

"And these are the gods of these people?"

"No, not gods. Supernatural beings. They lived here before there were people, and they naturally retain control over everything important here. But not gods as Christians understand gods. Look, here come the bats?"

They eat us, Halperin thought, shivering in the warm humid night. A new phalanx of dancers was arriving now, half a dozen bat-masked ones. He thought he recognized the long legs of Filiberto in their midst. Darkness had come and the dangling lights cast an eerier, more brilliant glow. Halperin decided he wanted another tequila, a mescal, a cold cerveza, whatever he could find quickest. *Not our brother.* He excused himself vaguely to Guzmán and started through the crowd. *They are worms, wild beasts.* They were still chanting it. The words meant nothing to him, except *amo tokinwan,* but from the spacing, the punctuation, he knew what they were saying. *They eat us.* The crowd had become something fluid now, oozing freely from place to place; the distinction between dancers and audience was hard to discern. *Not our brother.* Halperin found one of the little curbside cantinas and asked for mescal. The proprietor splashed some in a paper cup and would not take his pesos. A gulp and Halperin felt warm again. He tried to return to Guzmán but no longer saw him in the surging, frenzied mob. The music was louder. Halperin began to dance—it was easier than walking—and found himself face to face with one of the bat-dancers, a short man whose elegant mask showed a bat upside down, in its resting position, ribbed wings folded like black shrouds. Halperin and the dancer, pushed close together in the press, fell into an inadvertent pas de deux. "I wish I could buy that mask," Halperin said. "What do you want for it? Five thousand pesos? Ten thousand? *Habla usted Español?* No? Come to the hotel with the mask tomorrow. You follow? *Venga mañana.*" There was no reply. Halperin was not even certain he had spoken the words aloud.

He danced his way back across the plaza. Midway he felt a hand catch his wrist. Ellen Chambers. Her khaki blouse was open almost to the waist and she had nothing beneath it. Her skin gleamed with sweat, as if it had been oiled. Her eyes were wide and rigid. She leaned close to him and said, "Dance! Everybody dances! Where's your mask?"

"He wouldn't sell it to me. I offered him ten thousand pesos, but he wouldn't—"

"Wear a different one," she said. "Any mask you like. How do you like mine?"

"Your mask?" He was baffled. She wore no mask.

"Come! Dance!" She moved wildly. Her breasts were practically bare and now and then a nipple flashed. Halperin knew that that was wrong, that the villagers were cautious about nudity and a *gringa* especially should not be exhibiting herself. Drunkenly he reached for her blouse, hoping to button one or two of the buttons, and to his chagrin his hand grazed one of her breasts. She laughed and pushed herself against him. For an instant she was glued to him from knees to chest, with his hand wedged stupidly between their bodies. Then he pulled back, confused. An avenue seemed to have opened around them. He started to walk stumblingly to some quieter part of the plaza, but she caught his wrist again and grinned a tiger-grin, all incisors and tongue. "Come on!" she said harshly.

He let her lead him. Past the tacos stands, past the cantinas, past a little brawl of drunken boys, past the church, on whose steps the dancer in the phallic bat mask was performing, juggling pale green fruits and now and then batting one out into the night with the phallus that jutted from his chin. Then they were on one of the side streets, blind crumbling walls hemming them on both sides and cold moonlight the only illumination. Two blocks, three, his heart pounding, his lungs protesting. Into an ungated courtyard of what looked like an abandoned house, shattered tumbledown heaps of masonry everywhere and a vining night-blooming cactus growing over everything like a tangle of terrible green snakes. The cactus was in bloom and its vast white trumpetlike flowers emitted a sickly sweet perfume, overpoweringly intense. He wanted to gag and throw up, but Ellen gave him no time, for she was embracing him, pressing herself fiercely against him, forcing him back against a pile of shattered adobe bricks. In the strange moonlight her skin glistened and then seemed to become transparent, so that he could see the cage of her ribs, the flat long plate of her breastbone, the throbbing purplish heart behind it. She was all teeth and bones, a Day of the Dead totem come to life. He did not understand and he could not resist. He was without will. Her hands roamed him, so cold they burned his skin, sending up puffs of steam as her icy fingers caressed him. Something was flowing from him to her, his warmth, his essence, his vitality, and that was all right. The mescal and the beer and the tequila and the thick musky fragrance of the night-blooming cereus washed through has soul and left it tranquil. From far away came the raw dissonant music, the flutes and drums, and the laughter, the shouts, the chants. *They eat us.* Her breath was smoke in his face. *They are worms, wild beasts.* As they embraced one another, he imagined that she was insubstantial, a column of mist, and he began to feel misty himself, growing thinner and less solid as his life-force flowed toward her. Now for the first time he was seized by anguish and fright. As he felt himself being pulled from his body, his soul rushing forth and out and out and out, helpless, drawn, his drugged calm gave way to panic. *They are—not our brother.* He struggled, but it was useless. He was going out swiftly, the essence of him quitting his body as though she were reeling it in on a line. Bats fluttered above him, their faces streaked with painted patterns, yellow and green and brilliant ultramarine. The sky was a curtain of fiery bougainvillea. He was losing the struggle. He was too weak to resist or even to care. He could no longer hear himself breathe. He drifted freely, floating in the air, borne on the wings of the bats.

Then there was confusion, turmoil, struggle. Halperin heard voices speaking sharply in Spanish and in Nahuatl, but the words were incomprehensible to him. He rolled over on his side and drew his knees to his chest and lay shivering with his cheek against the warm wet soil. Someone was shaking him. A voice said in English, "Come back. Wake up. She is not here."

Halperin blinked and looked up. Guzmán was crouched above him, pale, stunned-looking, his teeth chattering. His eyes were wide and tensely fixed.

"Yes," Guzmán said. "Come back to us. Here. Sit up, let me help you."

The gallery-owner's arm was around his shoulders. Halperin was weak and trembling, and he realized Guzmán was trembling too. Halperin saw figures in the background—Filiberto from the hotel and his son Elustesio, the mayordomo Don Luis, the alcalde, one of the alguaciles.

"Ellen?" he said uncertainly.

"She is gone. *It* is gone. We have driven it away."

"It?"

"*Amo tokinwan.* Devouring your spirit."

"No," Halperin muttered. He stood up, still shaky, his knees buckling. Don Luis offered him a flask; Halperin shook it away, then changed his mind, reached for it, took a deep pull. Brandy. He walked four or five steps, getting his strength back. The reek of the cactus-flowers was nauseating. He saw the bare ribs again, the pulsating heart, the sharp white teeth. "No," he said. "It wasn't anything like that. I had too much to drink—maybe ate something that disagreed with me—the music, the scent of the flowers—"

"We saw," Guzmán said. His face was bloodless. "We were just in tine. You would have been dead."

"She was from Miami—she said she knew San Francisco—"

"These days they take any form they like. The woman from Miami was here two years ago, for the fiesta. She vanished in the night, Don Luis says. And now she has come back. Perhaps next year there will be one who looks like you and talks like you and sniffs around studying the masks like you, and we will know it is not you, and we will keep watch. Eh? You should come back to the hotel now. You need to rest."

Halperin walked between them down the walled streets. The fiesta was still in full swing, masked figures capering everywhere, but Guzmán and Don Luis and Filiberto guided him around the plaza and toward the hotel. He thought about the woman from Miami, and remembered that she had had no car and there had been no luggage in her room. *They eat us.* Such things are impossible, he told himself. *They are worms, wild beasts.* And next year would there be a diabolical counterfeit Halperin haunting the fiesta? *They are—not our brother.* He did not understand.

Guzmán said, "I promised you you would see the real Mexico. I did not think you would see as much of it as this."

Halperin insisted on inspecting her hotel room. It was empty and looked as if it had not been occupied for months. He stretched out on his bed fully clothed, but he did not particularly want to be left alone in the darkness, and so Guzmán and Filiberto and the others took turns sitting up with him through the night while the sounds of the fiesta filled the air. Dawn brought a dazzling sunrise. Halperin and Guzmán stepped out into the courtyard. The world was still.

"I think I'll leave here now," Halperin said.

"Yes. That would be wise. I will stay another day, I think."

Filiberto appeared, carrying the owl-pig mask from Halperin's room. "This is for you," he said. "Because that you were troubled here, that you will think kindly of us. Please take it as our gift."

Halperin was touched by that. He made a little speech of gratitude and put the mask in his car.

Guzmán said, "Are you well enough to drive?"

"I think so. I'll be all right once I leave here." He shook hands with everyone. His fingers were quivering. At a very careful speed he drove away from the hotel, through the plaza, where sleeping figures lay sprawled like discarded dolls, and mounds of paper streamers and other trash were banked high against the curb. At an even more careful speed he negotiated the cactus-walled road out of town. When he was about a kilometer from San Simón Zuluaga he glanced to his right and saw Ellen Chambers sitting next to him in the car. If he had been traveling faster, he would have lost control of the wheel. But after the first blinding moment of terror came a rush of annoyance and anger. "No," he said. "You don't belong in here. Get the hell out of here. Leave me alone." She laughed lightly. Halperin felt like sobbing. Swiftly and unhesitatingly he seized Filiberto's owl-pig mask, which lay on the seat beside him, and scaled it with a flip of his wrist past her nose and out the open car window. Then he clung tightly to the wheel and stared forward. When he could bring himself to look to the right again, she was gone. He braked to a halt and rolled up the window and locked the car door.

It took him all day to reach Acapulco. He went to bed immediately, without eating, and slept until late the following afternoon. Then he phoned the Aeromexico office.

Two days later he was home in San Francisco. The first thing he did was call a Sacramento Street dealer and arrange for the sale of all his masks. Now he collects Japanese netsuke, Hopi kachina dolls, and Navaho rugs. He buys only through galleries and does not travel much any more.

GATE OF HORN, GATE OF IVORY

An odd concatenation of ironies surrounds this little story.

I was, for ten years beginning in 1969, the editor of an annual anthology of original science fiction stories called New Dimensions. *During that time I published a good many interesting and important stories by such writers as Ursula K. Le Guin, Gardner Dozois, George Alec Effinger, James Tiptree, Jr., Harlan Ellison, Joanna Russ, Philip Jose Farmer, Gregory Benford, Isaac Asimov, and Barry Malzberg. Some of the stories I ran won Hugo and Nebula awards, and a few, like Le Guin's "The Ones Who Walk Away from Omelas" and Joanna Russ's "Nobody's Home," have become much-reprinted classics.*

In all that time, New Dimensions *never published a story by Robert Silverberg. One minor but not insignificant reason for that was that I didn't write any short stories between November, 1973 and January, 1980. Even if I had, though, you wouldn't have seen them in* New Dimensions, *because it isn't much of a challenge for editors to sell stories to themselves, and I would have felt foolish filling* New Dimensions *with my own work.*

By 1979, though, I was beginning to emerge from my five-year mid-1970s retirement from fiction writing, and I wanted to free myself from my editorial tasks in order to have more time and energy for doing stories. So I invited my friend and neighbor Marta Randall, then at the peak of her own science-fiction career, to take over New Dimensions. *We worked out a complicated transitional mode: the eleventh* New Dimensions *would carry the byline, "edited by Robert Silverberg and Marta Randall." Issue twelve would be slugged "edited by Marta Randall and Robert Silverberg." And from the thirteenth issue onward,* New Dimensions *would carry Marta's name alone.*

And so it came to pass: a Silverberg-Randall issue in 1980, a Randall-Silverberg issue in 1981. In November of 1981, as Marta was putting the finishing touches on her first solo issue, she caught me by surprise by saying to me, "Since your name won't be on number thirteen as editor, how about writing a story for me?"

Well, why not? I thought. Nearly every well-known science-fiction writer of the period had been published in New Dimensions *except me. I had already decided to spend the autumn and winter of 1981 writing short stories anyway. And now that I was no longer connected with the anthology in any way, there was no reason to disqualify myself from contributing. A week or two later I delivered "Gate of Horn, Gate of Ivory" to Marta. Now I, too, had sold a story to* New Dimensions.

But it never appeared there. New Dimensions' *publisher underwent a turbulent internal upheaval the following year, and its entire science-fiction line, including* New Dimensions *and a host of other books in progress, was canceled before publication.* New Dimensions 13 *exists today only in galley-proof form.*

*However, a second anthology of original science fiction—*Universe*— was being edited just then by yet another Bay Area resident, Terry Carr. It had begun publication about the same time as* New Dimensions, *had won just about as much acclaim for its material, and indeed had been in direct although friendly—very friendly—competition with* New Dimensions *for stories, all along. I had written a few stories for* Universe *in its early days, and when I resumed writing them in 1980 I had vaguely promised to do another for it, but never had. When Terry heard that* New Dimensions *had been suspended with an entire issue of fiction in inventory, including one of mine, he asked Marta to show him the stories, and a little while later he called to ask if it was all right to use "Gate of Horn." Which is why the story with which I had intended to make my* New Dimensions *debut appeared instead in the 1984 number of its chief competitor,* Universe.

O ften at night on the edge of sleep I cast my mind toward the abyss of time to come, hoping that I will tumble through some glowing barrier and find myself on the shores of a distant tomorrow. I strain at the moorings that hold me to this time and this place, and yearn to break free. Sometimes I feel that I have broken free, that the journey is at last beginning, that I will open my eyes in the inconceivable dazzling future. But it is only an illusion, like that fluent knowledge of French or Sanskrit or calculus that is born in dreams and departs by dawn. I awaken and it is the year 1983 and I am in my own bed with the striped sheets and the blue coverlet, and nothing has changed.

But I try again and again and still again, for the future calls me and the bleak murderous present repels me, and again the illusion that I am cutting myself loose from the time line comes over me, now more vivid and plausible than ever before, and as I soar and hurtle and vanish through the permeable membranes of the eons I wonder if it is finally, in truth, happening. I hover suspended somewhere outside the fabric of time and space and look down upon the earth, and I can see its contours changing as though I watch an accelerated movie: roads sprout and fork and fork once more, villages arise and exfoliate into towns and then into cities and then are overtaken by the forest, rivers change their courses and deliver their waters into great mirror-bright lakes that shrivel and become meadows. And I hover, passive, a dreamer, observing. There are two gates of sleep, says Homer and also Virgil. One is fashioned of horn, and one of ivory. Through the gate of horn pass the visions that are true, but those that emerge from the gate of ivory are deceptive dreams that mean nothing. Do I journey in a dream of the ivory gate? No, no, this is a true sending, this has the solidity and substance of inexorable reality. I have achieved it this time. I have crossed the barrier. Hooded figures surround me; somber eyes study me; I look into faces of a weird sameness, tawny skin, fleshless lips, jutting cheekbones that tug the taut skin above them into drumheads. The room in which I lie is high-vaulted and dark, but glows with a radiance that seems inherent in the material of its walls. Abstract figurings, like the ornamentation of a mosque, dance along those walls in silver inlay; but this is no mosque, nor would the tribe of Allah have loved those strange and godless geometries that restlessly chase one another like lustful squirrels over the wainscoting. I am there; I am surely there.

"I want to see everything," I say.

"See it, then. Nothing prevents you."

One of them presses into my hand a shining silver globe, an orb of command that transports me at the tiniest squeeze of my hand. I fly upward jerkily and in terror, rising so swiftly that the air grows cold and the sky becomes purple, but in a moment I regain control and come to govern my trajectory more usefully. At an altitude of a few dozen yards I pass over a city of serene cubical buildings of rounded corners, glittering with white Mediterranean brilliance in the gentle sunlight. I see small vehicles, pastel-hued, teardrop-tapered, in which citizens with the universal face of the era ride above crystalline roadbeds. I drift over a garden of plants I cannot recognize, perhaps new plants entirely, with pink succulent leaves and great mounding golden inflorescences, or ropy stems like bundles of coaxial cable, or jagged green thorns tipped with tiny blue eyes. I come to a pond of air where serene naked people swim with minimal motions of their fingertips. I observe a staircase of some yielding rubbery substance that vanishes into a glowing nimbus of radiance, and children are climbing that staircase and disappearing into that sparkling place at its top. In the zoological gardens I look down on creatures from a hundred worlds, stranger than any protozoan made lion-sized.

For days I tour this place, inexhaustibly curious, numb with awe. There is no blade of grass out of place. There is no stain nor blemish. The sounds I hear are harmonious sounds, and no other. The air is mild and the winds are soft. Only the people seem stark and austere to me, I suppose because of their sameness of features and the hieratic Egyptian solemnity of their eyes, but after a while I realize that this is only my poor archaic sensibility's misunderstanding, for I feel their love and support about me like a harness as I fly, and I know that these are the happiest, most angelic of all the beings that have walked the earth. I wonder how far in time I have traveled. Fifty thousand years? Half a million? Or perhaps—perhaps, and that possibility shrivels me with pain—perhaps much less than that. Perhaps this is the world of a hundred fifty years from now, eh? The postapocalyptic era, the coming utopia that lies just on the farther shore of our sea of turbulent nightmares. Is it possible that our world can be transformed into this so quickly? Why not? Miracles accelerate in an age of miracles. From the wobbly thing of wood and paper that flew a few seconds at Kitty Hawk to the gleaming majesty of the transcontinental jetliner was only a bit more than fifty years. Why not imagine that a world like this can be assembled in just as little time? But if that is so—

The torment of the thought drives me to the ground. I fall; they are taken by surprise, but ease my drop; I land on the warm moist soil and kneel, clutching it, letting my head slacken until my forehead touches the ground. I feel a gentle hand on my shoulder, just a touch, steadying me, soothing me.

"Let go," I say, virtually snarling. "Take your hand off!"

The hand retreats.

I am alone with my agony. I tremble, I sob, I shiver. I am aware of them surrounding me, but they are baffled, helpless, confused. Possibly they have never seen pain before. Possibly suffering is no part of their vocabulary of spirit.

Finally one of them says softly, "Why do you weep?"

"Out of anger. Out of frustration."

They are mystified. They surround me with shining machinery, screens and coils and lights and glowing panels, that I suspect is going to diagnose my malady. I kick everything over. I trample the intricate mechanisms and shove wildly at those who reach for me, even though I see that they are reaching not to restrain me but to soothe me.

"What is it?" they keep asking. "What troubles you?"

"I want to know what year this is."

They confer. It may be that their numbering system is so different from ours that they are unable to tell me. But there must be a way: diagrams, analogies, astronomical patterns. I am not so primitive that I am beyond understanding such things.

Finally they say, "Your question has no meaning for us."

"No meaning? You speak my language well enough. *I need to know what year this is.*"

"Its name is Eligorda," one of them says.

"Its *name?* Years don't have names. Years have numbers. My year is numbered 1983. Are we so far in my future that you don't remember the years with numbers?" I begin stripping away my clothing. "Here, look at me. This hair on my body—do you have hair like that? These teeth—see, I have thirty-two of them, arranged in an arc." I hold up my hands. "Nails on my fingers! Have fingernails evolved away?" I tap my belly. "In here, an appendix dangling from my gut! Prehistoric, useless, preposterous! How long ago did that disappear? Look at me! See the ape-man, and tell me how ancient I am!"

"Our bodies are just like yours," comes the quiet reply. "Except that we are healthier and stronger, and resistant to disease. But we have hair. We have fingernails. We have the appendix." They are naked before me, and I see that it is true. Their bodies are lean and supple, and there is a weird and disconcerting similarity of physique about them all, but they are not alien in any way; these could be twentieth-century bodies.

301

"I want you to tell me," I say, "how distant in time your world is from mine."

"Not very," someone answers. "But we lack the precise terminology for describing the interval."

"Not very," I say. "Listen, does the earth still go around the sun?"

"Of course."

"The time it takes to make one circuit—has that changed?"

"Not at all. "

"How many times, then, do you think the earth has circled the sun since my era?"

They exchange glances. They make quick rippling gestures—a kind of counting, perhaps. But they seem unable to complete the calculation. They murmur, they smile, they shrug. At last I understand their problem, which is not one of communication but one of tact. They do not want to tell me the truth for the same reason that I yearn to know it. The truth will hurt me. The truth will split me with anguish.

They are people of the epoch that immediately succeeds yours and mine. They are, quite possibly, the great-great-grandchildren of some who live in our world of 1983; or it may be that they are only grandchildren. The future they inhabit is not the extremely distant future. I am positive of that. But time stands still for them, for they do not know death.

Fury and frenzy return to me. I shake with rage; I taste burning bile; I explode with hatred, and launch myself upon them, scratching, punching, kicking, biting, trying in single outpouring of bitter resentment to destroy the entire sleek epoch into which I have fallen.

I harm several of them quite seriously.

Then they recover from their astonishment and subdue me, without great effort, dropping me easily with a few delicate musical tones and holding me captive against the ground. The casualties are taken away.

One of my captors kneels beside me and says, "Why do you show such hostility?"

I glare at him. "Because I am so close to being one of you."

"Ah. I think I can comprehend. But why do you blame us for that?"

The only answer I can give him is more fury; I tug against my invisible bonds and lunge as if to slaughter him with sheer energy of rage; from me pours such a blaze of madness as to sear the air, and so intense is my emotion that it seems to me I am actually breaking free, and seizing him, and clawing at him and smashing him. But I am only clutching at phantoms. My arms move like those of a windmill and I lose my balance and topple and topple and topple and when I regain my balance I am in my own bed once more, striped sheets, blue coverlet, the red eye of the digital clock telling me that it is 4:36 A.M. So they have punished me by casting me from their midst. I suppose that is no more than I deserve. But do they comprehend, do they really comprehend, my torment? Do they understand what it is like to know that those who will come just a little way after us will have learned how to live forever, and to live in paradise, and that one of us, at least, has had a glimpse of it, but that we will all be dead when it comes to pass? Why should we not rage against the generations to come, aware that we are nearly the last ones who will know death? Why not scratch and bite and kick? An awful iron door is closing on us, and *they are on the far side*, safe. Surely they will begin to understand that, when they have given more thought to my visit. Possibly they understood it even while I was there. I suspect they did, finally. And that when they returned me to my own time I was given a gift of grace by those gilded futurians: that their mantle of immortality has been cast over me, that I will be allowed to live on and on until time has come round again and I am once more in their era, but now as one of them. That is their gift to me, and perhaps that is their curse on me as well, that I must survive through all the years of terrible darkness that must befall before that golden dawn, that I will tarry here until they come again.

DANCERS IN THE TIME-FLUX

Long ago, in what almost seems to me now another geological epoch, I wrote a novel called Son of Man. *The year was 1969, when the world was new and strange and psychedelic, and* Son of Man *was my attempt to reproduce in prose form some of the visionary aspects of life in that heady era and pass the result off as a portrait of the world of the far, far future. The results were very strange indeed, but to me, at least, exciting and rewarding; and over the years* Son of Man *has retained a small but passionate audience. It's the sort of book that polarizes readers in an extremely sharp way: some find themselves unable to get past page three, others read it over and over again. (I read it now and then myself, as a matter of fact.)*

Writing Son of Man *had been such an extraordinarily exhilarating experience that when I began writing again in 1980 after my long period of retirement, I found myself tempting to dip into the world of that novel again, possibly for a short story or two, perhaps even for a whole new book. But I gave the idea no serious thought until July of 1981, when the Pacific Northwest writer and editor Jessica Amanda Salmonsen asked me to write a story for an anthology called* Heroic Visions *that she was assembling. (At that time Jessica dated all her letters "9981." I haven't heard from her lately, so I don't know whether she still regards herself as living in the hundredth century.)* Heroic Visions *was intended as an anthology of new stories of "high fantasy and heroic fantasy," according to Jessica's prospectus. High fantasy—Eddison, Dunsany, Charles Williams, William Morris—is something I read occasionally with pleasure, but have never intentionally written. Heroic fantasy—exemplified by such characters as Robert E.*

Howard's Conan, Fritz Leiber's Fafhrd and the Gray Mouser, and Michael Moorcock's Elric—is something that holds less interest for me as a reader, and though I suppose I could fake it as a writer if I saw some reason to do so, I have no true natural aptitude for it. So I really didn't belong in Jessica's book. Nor was the financial aspect of the project especially enticing. But I was just rediscovering writing again that year and was willing to do almost anything just then. I jotted at the bottom of the prospectus, "World of Son of Man. Two figures from the remote past are swept into the time-flux—a woman of 20th century, a man of—where? ancient China? Sumer?" and dropped Jessica a card saying I might possibly send her a story a few months from then, when I had finished the project—the collection known as Majipoor Chronicles that I was working on at the time.

She was surprised and, I suppose, skeptical, justifiably so; I went on to other things and forgot all about Heroic Visions. But on December 19, "9981," she tried again, asking me if there was any hope of getting the story. I replied that I'd do it, provided she could see a Son of Man spinoff as appropriate to her theme. She had read the book and knew it well. Back came her enthusiastic okay, and on January 9, 1982, I sent "Dancers in the Time-Flux" to her.

As you'll see, it departs considerably from the scrawled original note of the previous July. The twentieth-century woman disappears from the plot— I tried without success to return to her later on, in a sequel that I never finished writing—and the man of ancient China or Sumer is transmogrified into the sixteenth-century Dutch circumnavigator Olivier van Noort, an actual historical figure about whom I had written at length years before in a non-fiction book called The Longest Voyage. I do think the story recaptures the tone of Son of Man to a considerable extent, but whether it has the head-long wildness of that book is not so clear to me. It may be that years like 1969 come around only once in a lifetime. Which is, perhaps, a good thing.

Under a warm golden wind from the west, Bhengarn the Traveler moves steadily onward toward distant Crystal Pond, his appointed place of metamorphosis. The season is late. The swollen scarlet sun clings close to the southern hills. Bhengarn's body—a compact silvery tube supported by a dozen pairs of sturdy three-jointed legs—throbs with the need for transformation. And yet the Traveler is unhurried. He has been bound on this journey for many hundreds of years. He has traced across the face of the world a glistening trail that zigzags from zone to zone, from continent to continent, and even now still glimmers behind him with a cold brilliance like a thread of bright metal stitching the planet's haunches. For the past decade he has patiently circled Crystal Pond at the outer end of a radial arm one-tenth the diameter of the Earth in length; now, at the prompting of some interior signal, he has begun to spiral inward upon it.

The path immediately before him is bleak. To his left is a district covered by furry green fog; to his right is a region of pale crimson grass sharp as spikes and sputtering with a sinister hostile hiss; straight ahead a roadbed of black clinkers and ashen crusts leads down a shallow slope to the Plain of Teeth, where menacing porcelaneous outcroppings make the wayfarer's task a taxing one. But such obstacles mean little to Bhengarn. He is a Traveler, after all. His body is superbly designed to carry him through all difficulties. And in his journeys he has been in places far worse than this.

Elegantly he descends the pathway of slag and cinders. His many feet are tough as annealed metal, sensitive as the most alert antennae. He tests each point in the road for stability and support, and scans the thick layer of ashes for concealed enemies. In this way he moves easily and swiftly toward the plain, holding his long abdomen safely above the cutting edges of the cold volcanic matter over which he walks.

As he enters the Plain of Teeth he sees a new annoyance: an Eater commands the gateway to the plain. Of all the forms of human life—and the Traveler has encountered virtually all of them in his wanderings, Eaters, Destroyers, Skimmers, Interceders, and the others—Eaters seem to him the most tiresome, mere noisy monsters. Whatever philosophical underpinnings form the rationale of their bizarre way of life are of no interest to him. He is wearied by their bluster and offended by their gross appetites.

All the same, he must get past this one to reach his destination. The huge creature stands straddling the path with one great meaty leg at each edge and the thick fleshy tail propping it from behind. Its steely claws are exposed, its fangs gleam, driblets of blood from recent victims stain its hard reptilian hide. Its chilly inquisitive eyes, glowing with demonic intelligence, track Bhengarn as the traveler draws near.

The Eater emits a boastful roar and brandishes its many teeth.

"You block my way," Bhengarn declares.

"You state the obvious," the Eater replies.

"I have no desire for an encounter with you. But my destiny draws me toward Crystal Pond, which lies beyond you."

"For you," says the Eater, "nothing lies beyond me. Your destiny has brought you to a termination today. We will collaborate, you and I, in the transformation of your component molecules."

From the spiracles along his sides the Traveler releases a thick blue sigh of boredom. "The only transformation that waits for me is the one I will undertake at Crystal Pond. You and I have no transaction. Stand aside."

The Eater roars again. He rocks slightly on his gigantic claws and swishes his vast saurian tail from side to side. These are the preliminaries to an attack, but in a kind of ponderous courtesy he seems to be offering Bhengarn the opportunity to scuttle back up the ash-strewn slope.

Bhengarn says, "Will you yield place?"

"I am an instrument of destiny"

"You are a disagreeable boastful ignoramus," says Bhengarn calmly, and consumes half a week's energy driving the scimitars of his spirit to the roots of the world. It is not a wasted expense of soul, for the ground trembles, the sky grows dark, the hill behind him creaks and groans, the wind turns purplish and frosty. There is a chill droning sound that the Traveler knows is the song of the time-flux, an unpredictable force that often is liberated at such moments. Despite that, Bhengarn will not relent. Beneath the Eater's splayed claws the fabric of the road ripples. Sour smells rise from sudden crevasses. The enormous beast utters a yipping cry of rage and lashes his tail vehemently against the ground. He sways; he nearly topples; he calls out to Bhengam to cease his onslaught, but the Traveler knows better than to settle for a half-measure. Even more fiercely he presses against the Eater's bulky form.

"This is unfair," the Eater wheezes. "My goal is the same as yours: to serve the forces of necessity."

"Serve them by eating someone else today," answers Bhengarn curtly, and with a final expenditure of force shoves the Eater to an awkward untenable position that causes it to crash down onto its side. The downed beast, moaning, rakes the air with his claws but does not arise, and as Bhengarn moves briskly past the Eater he observes that fine transparent threads, implacable as stone, have shot forth from a patch of swamp beside the road and are rapidly binding the fallen Eater in an unbreakable net. The Eater howls. Glancing back, Bhengarn notices the threads already cutting their way through the Eater's thick scales like tiny streams of acid. "So, then," Bhengarn says, without malice, "the forces of necessity will be gratified today after all, but not by me. The Eater is to be eaten. It seems that this day *I* prove to be the instrument of destiny." And without another backward look he passes quickly onward into the plain. The sky regains its ruddy color, the wind becomes mild once more, the Earth is still. But a release of the time-flux is never without consequences, and as the Traveler trundles forward he perceives some new creature of unfamiliar form staggering through the nests ahead, confused and lost, lurching between the shining lethal formations of the Plain of Teeth in seeming ignorance of the perils they hold. The creature is upright, two-legged, hairy, of archaic appearance. Bhengarn, approaching it, recognizes it finally as a primordial human, swept millions of years past its own true moment.

"Have some care," Bhengarn calls. "Those teeth can bite!"

"Who spoke?" the archaic creature demands, whirling about in alarm.

"I am Bhengarn the Traveler. I suspect I am responsible for your presence here."

"Where are you? I see no one! Are you a devil?"

"I am a Traveler, and I am right in front of your nose."

The ancient human notices Bhengarn, apparently for the first time, and leaps back, gasping. "Serpent!" he cries. "Serpent with legs! Worm! Devil!" Wildly he seizes rocks and hurls them at the Traveler, who deflects them easily enough, turning each into a rhythmic juncture of gold and green that hovers, twanging softly, along an arc between the other and himself. The archaic one lifts an immense boulder, but as he hoists it to drop it on Bhengarn he overbalances and his arm flies backward, grazing one of the sleek teeth behind him. At once the tooth releases a turquoise flare and the man's arm vanishes to the elbow. He sinks to his knees, whimpering, staring bewilderedly at the stump and at the Traveler before him.

Bhengarn says, "You are in the Plain of Teeth, and any contact with these mineral formations is likely to be unfortunate, as I attempted to warn you." He slides himself into the other's soul for an instant, pushing his way past thick encrusted stalagmites and stalactites of anger, fear, outraged pride, pain, disorientation, and arrogance, and discovers himself to be in the presence of one Olivier van Noort of Utrecht, former tavernkeeper at Rotterdam, commander of the voyage of circumnavigation that set forth from Holland on the second day of July

1598 and traveled the entire belly of the world, a man of exceedingly strong stomach and bold temperament, who has experienced much, having gorged on the meat of penguins at Cape Virgines and the isle called Pantagoms, having hunted beasts not unlike stags and buffaloes and ostriches in the cold lands by Magellan's Strait, having encountered whales and parrots and trees whose bark had the bite of pepper, having had strife with the noisome Portugals in Guinea and Brazil, having entered into the South Sea on a day of diverse storms, thunders, and lightnings, having taken ships of the Spaniards in Valparaiso and slain many Indians, having voyaged thence to the Isles of Ladrones or Thieves, where the natives bartered bananas, coconuts, and roots for old pieces of iron, overturning their canoes in their greed for metal, having suffered a bloody flux in Manila of eating palms, having captured vessels of China laden with rice and lead, having traded with folk on a ship of the Japans, whose men make themselves bald except a tuft left in the hinder part of the head, and wield swords that would, with one stroke cut through three men, having traded also with the bare-breasted women of Borneo, bold and impudent and shrewd, who carry iron-pointed javelins and sharp darts, and having after great privation and the loss of three of his four ships and all but forty-five of his 248 men, many of them executed by him or marooned on remote islands for their mutinies but a good number murdered by the treacheries of savage enemies, come again to Rotterdam on the twenty-sixth of August in 1601, bearing little in the way of salable goods to show for his hardships and calamities. None of this has any meaning to Bhengarn the Traveler except in the broadest, which is to say that he recognizes in Olivier van Noort a stubborn and difficult man who has conceived and executed a journey of mingled heroism and foolishness that spanned vast distances, and so they are brothers, of a sort, however millions of years apart. As a fraternal gesture Bhengarn restores the newcomer's arm. That appears to be as bewildering to the other as was its sudden loss. He squeezes it, moves it cautiously back and forth, scoops up a handful of pebbles with it. "This is Hell, then," he mutters, "and you are a demon of Satan."

"I am Bhengarn the Traveler, bound toward Crystal Pond, and I think that I conjured you by accident out of your proper place in time while seeking to thwart that monster." Bhengarn indicates the fallen Eater, now half dissolved. The other, who evidently had not looked that way before, makes a harsh choking sound at the sight of the giant creature, which

310

still struggles sluggishly. Bhengarn says, "The time-flux has seized you and taken you far from home, and there will be no going back for you. I offer regrets."

"You offer regrets? A worm with legs offers regrets! Do I dream this, or am I truly dead and gone to Hell?"

"Neither one."

"In all my sailing round the world I never saw a place so strange as this, or the likes of you, or of that creature over yonder. Am I to be tortured, demon?"

"You are not where you think you are."

"Is this not Hell?"

"This is the world of reality."

"How far are we, then, from Holland?"

"I am unable to calculate it," Bhengarn answers. 'A long way, that's certain. Will you accompany me toward Crystal Pond, or shall we part here?"

Noort is silent a moment. Then he says, "Better the company of demons than none at all, in such a place. Tell me straight, demon: am I to be punished here? I see hellfire on the horizon. I will find the rivers of fire, snow, toads, and black water, will I not? And the place where sinners are pronged on hooks jutting from blazing wheels? The ladders of red-hot iron, eh? The wicked broiling on coals? And the Arch-Traitor himself, sunk in ice to his chest—he must be near, is he not?" Noort shivers. "The fountains of poison. The wild boars of Lucifer. The aloes biting bare flesh, the dry winds of the abyss—when will I see them?"

"Look here," says Bhengarn. Beyond the Plain of Teeth a column of black flame rises into the heavens, and in it dance creatures of a hundred sorts, melting, swirling, coupling, fading. A chain of staring lidless eyes spans the sky. Looping whorls of green light writhe on the mountaintops. "Is that what you expect? You will find whatever you expect here."

"And yet you say this is not Hell?"

"I tell you again, it is the true world, the same into which you were born long ago."

"And is this Brazil, or the Indies, or some part of Africa?"

"Those names mean little to me."

"Then we are in the Terra Australis," says Noort. "It must be. A land where worms have legs and speak good Dutch, and rocks can bite, and arms once lost can sprout anew—yes, it must surely be the Terra

Australis, or else the land of Prester John. Eh? Is Prester John your king?" Noort laughs. He seems to be emerging from his bewilderment. "Tell me the name of this land, creature, so I may claim it for the United Provinces, if ever I see Holland again."

"It has no name."

"No name! No name! What foolishness! I never found a place whose folk had no name for it, not even in the endless South Sea. But l will name it, then. Let this province be called New Utrecht, eh? And all this land, from here to the shores of the South Sea, I annex hereby to the United Provinces in the name of the States-General. You be my witness, creature. Later I will draw up documents. You say I am not dead?"

"Not dead, not dead at all. But far from home. Come, walk beside me, and touch nothing. This is troublesome territory."

"This is strange and ghostly territory," says Noort. "I would paint it, if I could, and then let Mynheer Brueghel look to his fame, and old Bosch as well. Such sights! Were you a prince before you were transformed?"

"I have not yet been transformed," says Bhengarn. "That awaits me at Crystal Pond." The road through the plain now trends slightly uphill; they are advancing into the farther side of the basin. A pale-yellow tint comes into the sky. The path here is prickly with little many-faceted insects whose hard sharp bodies assail the Dutchman's bare tender feet. Cursing, he hops in wild leaps, bringing him dangerously close to outcroppings of teeth, and Bhengarn, in sympathy, fashions stout gray boots for him. Noort grins. He gestures toward his bare middle, and Bhengarn clothes him in a shapeless gray robe.

"Like a monk, is how I look!" Noort cries. "Well, well, a monk in Hell! But you say this is not Hell. And what kind of creature are you, creature?"

"A human being," says Bhengarn, "of the Traveler sort."

"A human being!" Noort booms. He leaps across a brook of sparkling bubbling violet-hued water and waits on the far side as Bhengarn trudges through it. "A human under an enchantment, I would venture."

"This is my natural form. Humankind has not worn your guise since long before the falling of the Moon. The Eater you saw was human. Do you see, on yonder eastern hill, a company of Destroyers turning the forest to rubble? They are human."

"The wolves on two legs up there?"

"Those, yes. And there are others you will see. Awaiters, Breathers, Skimmers—"

"These are mere noises to me, creature. What is human? A Dutchman is human! A Portugal is human! Even a Chinese, a black, a Japonder with a shaven head. But those beasts on yon hill? Or a creature with more legs than I have whiskers. No, Traveler, no! You flatter yourself. Do you happen to know, Traveler, how it is that I am here? I was in Amsterdam, to speak before the Lords Seventeen and the Company in general, to ask for ships to bring pepper from the Moluccas, but they said they would choose Joris van Spilbergen in my place—do you know Spilbergen? I think him much overpraised—and then all went dizzy, as though I had taken too much beer with my gin—and then—then—ah, this is a dream, is it not, Traveler? At this moment I sleep in Amsterdam. I am too old for such drinking. Yet never have I had a dream so real as this, and so strange. Tell me: when you walk, do you move the legs on the right side first, or the left?" Noort does not wait for a reply. "If you are human, Traveler, are you also a Christian, then?"

Bhengarn searches in Noort's mind for the meaning of that, finds something approximate, and says, "I make no such claim."

"Good. Good. There are limits to my credulity. How far is this Crystal Pond?"

"We have covered most of the distance. If I proceed at a steady pace I will come shortly to the land of smoking holes, and not far beyond that is the approach to the Wall of Ice, which will demand a difficult but not impossible ascent, and just on the far side of that I will find the vale that contains Crystal Pond, where the beginning of the next phase of my life will occur." They are walking now through a zone of sparkling rubbery cones of a bright vermilion color, from which small green Stangarones emerge in quick succession to chant their one-note melodies. The flavor of a heavy musk hangs in the air. Night is beginning to fall. Bhengarn says, "Are you tired?"

"Just a little."

"It is not my custom to travel by night. Does this campsite suit you?" Bhengarn indicates a broad circular depression bordered by tiny volcanic fumaroles. The ground here is warm and spongy, moist, bare of vegetation. Bhengarn extends an excavator claw and pulls free a strip of it, which he hands to Noort, indicating that he should eat. Noort tentatively nibbles. Bhengarn helps himself to some also. Noort, kneeling, presses his knuckles against the ground, makes it yield, mutters to himself, shakes his head, rips off another strip and chews it in wonder. Bhengarn says, "You find the world much changed, do you not?"

"Beyond all understanding, in fact."

"Our finest artists have worked on it since time immemorial, making it more lively, more diverting. We think it is a great success. Do you agree?"

Noort does not answer. He is staring bleakly at the sky, suddenly dark and jeweled with blazing stars. Bhengarn realizes that he is searching for patterns, navigators' signs. Noort frowns, turns round and round to take in the full circuit of the heavens, bites his lip, finally lets out a low groaning sigh and says, "I recognize nothing. Nothing. This is not the northern sky, this is not the southern sky, this is not any sky I can understand." Quietly he begins to weep. After a time he says somberly, "I was not the most adept of navigators, but I knew something, at least. And I look at this sky and I feel like a helpless babe. All the stars have changed places. Now I see how lost I am, how far from anything I ever knew, and once it gave me great pleasure to sail under strange skies, but not now, not here, because these skies frighten me and this land of demons offers me no peace. I have never wept, do you know that, creature, never, not once in my life! But Holland—my house, my tavern, my church, my sons, my pipe—where is Holland? Where is everything I knew? The skies above Magellan's Strait were not the thousandth part so strange as this." A harsh heavy sob escapes him, and he turns away, huddling into himself.

Compassion floods Bhengarn for this miserable wanderer. To ease Noort's pain he summons fantasies for him, dredging images from the reservoirs of the ancient man's spirit and hurling them against the sky, building a cathedral of fire in the heavens, and a royal palace, and a great armada of ships with bellying sails and the Dutch flag fluttering, and the watery boulevards of busy Amsterdam and the quiet streets of little Haarlem, and more. He paints for Noort the stars in their former courses, the Centaur, the Swan, the Bear, the Twins. He restores the fallen Moon to its place and by its cold light creates a landscape of time lost and gone, with avenues of heavy-boughed oaks and maples, and drifts of brilliant red and yellow tulips blaring beneath them, and golden roses arching in great bowers over the thick, newly mowed lawn. He creates fields of ripe wheat, and haystacks high as barns, and harvesters toiling in the hot sultry afternoon. He gives Noort the aroma of the Sunday feast and the scent of good Dutch gin and the sweet dense fumes of his long clay pipe. Noort nods and murmurs and clasps his hands, and gradually his sorrow ebbs and his weeping ceases, and he drifts off into a deep and easy slumber. The images fade. Bhengarn, who rarely sleeps, keeps watch until first light comes and a flock of finger-winged birds passes overhead, shouting shrilly, jesting and swooping.

Noort is calm and quiet in the morning. He feeds again on the spongy soil and drinks from a clear emerald rivulet and they move onward toward Crystal Pond. Bhengarn is pleased to have his company. There is something crude and coarse about the Dutchman, perhaps even more so than another of his era might be, but Bhengarn finds that unimportant. He has always preferred companions of any sort to the solitary march, in his centuries of going to and fro upon the Earth. He has traveled with Skimmers and Destroyers, and once a ponderous Ruminant, and even on several occasions visitors from other worlds who have come to sample the wonders of Earth. At least twice Bhengarn has had as his traveling companion a castaway of the time-flux from some prehistoric era, though not so prehistoric as Noort's. And now it has befallen him that he will go to the end of his journey with this rough hairy being from the dawn of humanity's day. So be it. So be it.

Noort says, breaking a long silence as they cross a plateau of quivering gelatinous stuff, "Were you a man or a woman before the sorcery gave you this present shape?"

"I have always had this form."

"No. Impossible. You say you are human, you speak my language—"

"Actually, you speak *my* language," says Bhengarn.

"As you wish. If you are human you must once have looked like me. Can it be otherwise? Were you born a thing of silvery scales and many legs? I will not believe that."

"Born?" says Bhengarn, puzzled.

"Is this word unknown to you?"

"Born," the Traveler repeats. "I think I see the concept. To *begin*, to *enter*, to *acquire one's shape*—"

"Born," says Noort in exasperation. "To come from the womb. To hatch, to out, to drop. Everything alive has to be born!"

"No," Bhengarn says mildly. "Not any longer."

"You talk nonsense," Noort snaps, and scours his throat angrily and spits. His spittle strikes a node of assonance and blossoms into a dazzling mound of green and scarlet jewels. "Rubies," he murmurs. "Emeralds. I could puke pearls, I suppose." He kicks at the pile of gems and scatters them; they dissolve into spurts of moist pink air. The

Dutchman gives himself over to a sullen brooding. Bhengarn does not transgress on the other's taciturnity; he is content to march forward in his steady plodding way, saying nothing.

Three Skimmers appear, prancing, leaping. They are heading to the south. The slender golden-green creatures salute the wayfarers with pulsations of their great red eyes. Noort, halting, glares at them and says hoarsely to Bhengarn, "These are human beings, too?"

"Indeed."

"Natives of this realm?"

"Natives of this era," says Bhengarn. "The latest form, the newest thing, graceful, supple, purposeless." The Skimmers laugh and transform themselves into shining streaks of light and soar aloft like a trio of auroral rays. Bhengarn says, "Do they seem beautiful to you?"

"They seem like minions of Satan," says the Dutchman sourly. He scowls. "When I awaken I pray I remember none of this. For if I do, I will tell the tale to Willem and Jan and Piet, and they will think I have lost my senses, and mock me. Tell me I dream, creature. Tell me I lie drunk in an inn in Amsterdam."

"It is not so," Bhengarn says gently.

"Very well. Very well. I have come to a land where every living thing is a demon or a monster. That is no worse, I suppose, than a land where everyone speaks Japanese and worships stones. It is a world of wonders, and I have seen more than my share. Tell me, creature, do you have cities in this land?"

"Not for millions of years."

"Then where do the people live?"

"Why, they live where they find themselves! Last night we lived where the ground was food. Tonight we will settle by the Wall of Ice. And tomorrow—"

"Tomorrow," Noort says, "we will have dinner with the Grand Diabolus and dance in the Witches' Sabbath. I am prepared, just as I was prepared to sup with the penguin-eating folk of the Cape, that stood six cubits high. I will be surprised by nothing." He laughs. "I am hungry, creature. Shall I tear up the earth again and stuff it down?"

"Not here. Try those fruits."

Luminous spheres dangle from a tree of golden limbs. Noort plucks one, tries it unhesitatingly, claps his hands, takes three more. Then he pulls a whole cluster free, and offers one to Bhengarn, who refuses.

"Not hungry?" the Dutchman asks.

"I take my food in other ways."

"Yes, you breathe it in from flowers as you crawl along, eh? Tell me, Traveler: to what end is your journey? To discover new lands? To fulfill some pledge? To confound your enemies? I doubt it is any of these."

"I travel out of simple necessity, because it is what my kind does, and for no special purpose."

"A humble wanderer, then, like the mendicant monks who serve the Lord by taking to the highways?"

"Something like that."

"Do you ever cease your wanderings?"

"Never yet. But cessation is coming. At Crystal Pond I will become my utter opposite, and enter the Awaiter tribe, and be made immobile and contemplative. I will root myself like a vegetable, after my metamorphosis."

Noort offers no comment on that. After a time he says, "I knew a man of your kind once. Jan Huyghen van Linschoten of Haarlem, who roamed the world because the world was there to roam, and spent his years in the India of the Portugals and wrote it all down in a great vast book, and when he had done that went off to Novaya Zemlya with Barents to find the chilly way to the Indies, and I think would have sailed to the Moon if he could find the pilot to guide him. I spoke with him once. My own travels took me farther than Linschoten, do you know? I saw Borneo and Java and the world's hinder side, and the thick Sargasso Sea. But I went with a purpose other than my own amusement or the gathering of strange lore, which was to buy pepper and cloves, and gather Spanish gold, and win my fame and comfort. Was that so wrong, Traveler? Was I so unworthy?" Noort chuckles. "Perhaps I was, for I brought home neither spices nor gold nor most of my men, but only the fame of having sailed around the world. I think I understand you, Traveler. The spices go into a cask of meat and are eaten and gone; the gold is only yellow metal; but so long as there are Dutchmen, no one will forget that Olivier van Noort, the tavernkeeper of Rotterdam, strung a line around the middle of the world. So long as there are Dutchmen." He laughs. "It is folly to travel for profit. I will travel for wisdom from now on. What do you say, Traveler? Do you applaud me?"

"I think you are already on the proper path," says Bhengarn. "But look, look there: the Wall of Ice."

Noort gasps. They have come around a low headland and are confronted abruptly by a barrier of pure white light, as radiant as a mirror at noon, that spans the horizon from east to west and rises skyward like an enormous palisade filling half the heavens. Bhengarn studies it with respect and admiration. He has known for hundreds of years that he must ascend this wall if he is to reach Crystal Pond, and that the wall is formidable; but he has seen no need before now to contemplate the actualities of the problem, and now he sees that they are significant.

"Are we to ascend that?" Noort asks.

"I must. But here, I think, we shall have to part company."

"The throne of Lucifer must lie beyond that icy rampart."

"I know nothing of that," says Bhengarn, "but certainly Crystal Pond is on the farther side, and there is no other way to reach it but to climb the wall. We will camp tonight at its base, and in the morning I will begin my climb."

"Is such a climb possible?"

"It will have to be," Bhengarn replies.

"Ah. You will turn yourself to a puff of light like those others we met, and shoot over the top like some meteor. Eh?"

"I must climb," says Bhengarn, "using one limb after another, and taking care not to lose my grip. There is no magical way of making this ascent." He sweeps aside fallen branches of a glowing blue-limbed shrub to make a campsite for them. To Noort he says, "Before I begin the ascent tomorrow I will instruct you in the perils of the world, for your protection on your future wanderings. I hold myself responsible for your presence here, and I would not have you harmed once you have left my side."

Noort says, "I am not yet planning to leave your side. I mean to climb that wall alongside you, Traveler."

"It will not be possible for you."

"I will make it possible. That wall excites my spirit. I will conquer it as I conquered the storms of the Strait and the fevers of the Sargasso. I feel I should go with you to Crystal Pond, and pay my farewells to you there, for it will bring me luck to mark the beginning of my solitary journey by witnessing the end of yours. What do you say?"

"I say wait until the morning," Bhengarn answers, "and see the wall at close range, before you commit yourself to such mighty resolutions."

During the night a silent lightstorm plays overhead; twisting turbulent spears of blue and green and violet radiance clash in the throbbing sky, and an undulation of the atmosphere sends alternating waves of hot and cool air racing down from the Wall of Ice. The time-flux blows, and frantic figures out of forgotten eras are swept by now far aloft, limbs churning desperately, eyes rigid with astonishment. Noort sleeps through it all, though from time to time he stirs and mutters and clenches his fists. Bhengarn ponders his obligations to the Dutchman, and by the coming of the sharp blood-hued dawn he has arrived at an idea. Together they advance to the edge of the Wall; together they stare upward at that vast vertical field of shining whiteness, smooth as stone. Hesitantly Noort touches it with his fingertip, and hisses at the coldness of it. He turns his back to it, paces, folds and unfolds his arms.

He says finally, "No man or woman born could achieve the summit of that wall. But is there not some magic you could work, Traveler, that would enable me to make the ascent?"

"There is one. But I think you would not like it."

"Speak."

"I could transform you—for a short time, only a short time, no longer than the time it takes to climb the wall—into a being of the Traveler form. Thus we could ascend together."

Noort's eyes travel quickly over Bhengarn's body—the long tubular serpentine thorax, the tapering tail, the multitude of powerful little legs—and a look of shock and dismay and loathing comes over his face for an instant, but just an instant. He frowns. He tugs at his heavy lower lip.

Bhengarn says, "I will take no offense if you refuse."

"Do it."

"You may be displeased."

"Do it! The morning is growing old. We have much climbing to do. Change me, Traveler. Change me quickly." A shadow of doubt crosses Noort's features. "You will change me back, once we reach the top?"

"It will happen of its own accord. I have no power to make a permanent transformation."

"Then do what you can, and do it now!"

"Very well," says Bhengarn, and the Traveler, summoning his fullest force, drains metamorphic energies from the planets and the stars and a passing comet, and focuses them and hurls them at the Dutchman, and there is a buzzing and a droning and a shimmering and when it is done a second Traveler stands at the foot of the Wall of Ice.

Noort seems thunderstruck. He says nothing; he does not move; only after a long time does he carefully lift his frontmost left limb and swing it forward a short way and put it down. Then the one opposite it; then several of the middle limbs; then, growing more adept, he manages to move his entire body, adopting a curious wriggling style, and in another moment he appears to be in control. "This is passing strange," he remarks at length. "And yet it is almost like being in my own body, except that everything has been changed. You are a mighty wizard, Traveler. Can you show me now how to make the ascent?"

"Are you ready so soon?"

"I am ready," Noort says.

So Bhengarn demonstrates, approaching the wall, bringing his penetrator claws into play, driving them like pitons into the ice, hauling himself up a short distance, extending his claws, driving them in, pulling upward. He has never climbed ice before, though he has faced all other difficulties the world has to offer, but the climb, though strenuous, seems manageable enough. He halts after a few minutes and watches as Noort, clumsy but determined in his altered body, imitates him, scratching and scraping at the ice as he pulls himself up the face until they are side by side. "It is easy," Noort says.

And so it is, for a time, and then it is less easy, for now they hang high above the valley and the midday sun has melted the surface of the wall just enough to make it slick and slippery, and a terrible cold from within the mass of ice seeps outward into the climbers, and even though a Traveler's body is a wondrous machine fit to endure anything, this is close to the limit. Once Bhengarn loses his purchase, but Noort deftly claps a claw to the middle of his spine to hold him firmly until he has dug in again; and not much later the same happens to Noort, and Bhengarn grasps him. As the day wanes they are so far above the ground that they can barely make out the treetops below, and yet the top of the wall is too high to see. Together they excavate a ledge, burrowing inward to rest in a chilly nook, and at dawn they begin again, Bhengarn's sinuous body winding upward over the rim of their little cave and Noort following with less agility. Upward and upward they climb, never pausing and saying little, through a day of warmth and soft perfumed breezes and through a night of storms and falling stars, and then through a day of turquoise rain, and through another day and a night and a day and then they are at the top, looking out across the broad unending field of ferns and bright blossoms that covers the summit's flat surface, and as they move inward from the rim Noort lets out a cry and stumbles forward, for he has resumed his ancient form. He drops to his knees and sits there panting, stunned, looking in confusion at his fingernails, at his knuckles, at the hair on the backs of his hands, as though he has never seen such things before. "Passing strange," he says softly.

"You are a born Traveler," Bhengarn tells him.

They rest a time, feeding on the sparkling four-winged fruits that sprout in that garden above the ice. Bhengarn feels an immense calmness now that the climax of his peregrination is upon him. Never had he questioned the purpose of being a Traveler, nor has he had regret that destiny gave him that form, but now he is quite willing to yield it up.

"How far to Crystal Pond?" Noort asks.

"It is just over there," says Bhengarn.

"Shall we go to it now?"

"Approach it with great care," the Traveler warns. "It is a place of extraordinary power."

They go forward; a path opens for them in the swaying grasses and low fleshy-leaved plants; within minutes they stand at the edge of a perfectly circular body of water of unfathomable depth and of a clarity so complete that the reflections of the sun can plainly be seen on the white sands of its infinitely distant bed. Bhengarn moves to the edge and peers in, and is pervaded by a sense of fulfillment and finality.

Noort says, "What will become of you here?"

"Observe," says Bhengarn.

He enters Crystal Pond and swims serenely toward the farther shore, an enterprise quickly enough accomplished. But before he has reached the midpoint of the pond a tolling sound is heard in the air, as of bells of the most pure quality, striking notes without harmonic overtones. Sudden ecstasy engulfs him as he becomes aware of the beginning of his transformation: his body flows and streams in the flux of life, his limbs fuse, his soul expands. By the time he comes forth on the edge of the pond he has become something else, a great cone of passive flesh, which is able to drag itself no more than five or six times its own length from the water, and then sinks down on the sandy surface of the ground and begins the process of digging itself in. Here the Awaiter Bhengarn will settle, and here he will live for centuries of centuries, motionless, all but timeless, considering the primary truths of being. Already he is gliding into the Earth.

Noort gapes at him from the other side of the pond.

"Is this what you sought?" the Dutchman asks.

"Yes. Absolutely."

"I wish you farewell and Godspeed, then!" Noort cries.

"And you—what will become of you?"

Noort laughs. "Have no fears for me! I see my destiny unfolding!"

Bhengarn, nestled now deep in the ground, enwombed by the earth, immobile, established already in his new life, watches as Noort strides boldly to the water's edge. Only slowly, for an Awaiter's mind is less agile than a Traveler's, does Bhengarn comprehend what is to happen.

Noort says, "I've found my vocation again. But if I'm to travel, I must be equipped for traveling!"

He enters the pond, swimming in broad awkward splashing strokes, and once again the pure tolling sound is evoked, a delicate carillon of crystalline transparent tone, and there is sudden brilliance in the pond as Noort sprouts the shining scales of a Traveler, and the jointed limbs, and the strong thick tail. He scuttles out on the far side wholly transformed.

"Farewell!" Noort cries joyously.

"Farewell," murmurs Bhengarn the Awaiter, peering out from the place of his long repose as Olivier van Noort, all his legs ablaze with new energy, strides away vigorously to begin his second circumnavigation of the of the globe.

NEEDLE IN A TIMESTACK

And of course Alice Turner was right that I would be back to her almost immediately with another story. I had heard Bill Rotsler, a friend of mine, say to a young man who was bothering him at a science-fiction convention, "Go away, kid, or I'll change your future." At which I said, "No, tell him that you'll change his past," and suddenly I realized that I had handed myself a nice story idea. I wrote it in January, 1982—its intricate time-travel plot unfolded for me with marvelous clarity as I worked—and Alice bought it immediately for Playboy's *July, 1983 issue.*

Some years later a major American movie company bought it also. They gave me quite a lot of money, which was very pleasant, but so far they haven't done anything about actually making the movie. I hope they do, sooner or later. It's one science-fiction movie I'd actually like to see.

Between one moment and the next the taste of cotton came into his mouth, and Mikkelsen knew that Tommy Hambleton had been tinkering with his past again. The cotton-in-the-mouth sensation was the standard tip-off for Mikkelsen. For other people it might be a ringing in the ears, a tremor of the little finger, a tightness in the shoulders. Whatever the symptom, it always meant the same thing: your time-track has been meddled with, your life has been retroactively transformed. It happened all the time. One of the little annoyances of

323

modern life, everyone always said. Generally, the changes didn't amount to much.

But Tommy Hambleton was out to destroy Mikkelsen's marriage, or, more accurately, he was determined to unhappen it altogether, and that went beyond Mikkelsen's limits of tolerance. In something close to panic he phoned home to find out if he still had Janine.

Her lovely features blossomed on the screen-glossy dark hair, elegant cheekbones, cool sardonic eyes. She looked tense and strained, and Mikkelsen knew she had felt the backlash of this latest attempt too.

"Nick?" she said. "Is it a phasing?"

"I think so. Tommy's taken another whack at us, and Christ only knows how much chaos he's caused this time."

"Let's run through everything."

"All right," Mikkelsen said. "What's your name?"

"Janine."

"And mine?"

"Nick. Nicholas Perry Mikkelsen. You see? Nothing important has changed."

"Are you married?"

"Yes, of course, darling. To you."

"Keep going. What's our address?"

"11 Lantana Crescent."

"Do we have children?"

"Dana and Elise. Dana's five, Elise is three. Our cat's name is Minibelle, and—"

"Okay," Mikkelsen said, relieved. "That much checks out. But I tasted the cotton, Janine. Where has he done it to us this time? What's been changed?"

"It can't be anything major, love. We'll find it if we keep checking. Just stay calm."

"Calm. Yes." He closed his eyes. He took a deep breath. The little annoyances of modern life, he thought. In the old days, when time was just a linear flow from *then* to *now*, did anyone get bored with all that stability? For better or for worse it was different now. You go to bed a Dartmouth man and wake up Columbia, never the wiser. You board a plane that blows up over Cyprus, but then your insurance agent goes back and gets you to miss the flight. In the new fluid way of life there was always a second chance, a third, a fourth, now that the past was open to anyone with the price of a ticket. But what good is any of that,

Mikkelsen wondered, if Tommy Hambleton can use it to disappear me and marry Janine again himself?

They punched for readouts and checked all their vital data against what they remembered. When your past is altered through time-phasing, all records of your life are automatically altered too, of course, but there's a period of two or three hours when memories of your previous existence still linger in your brain, like the phantom twitches of an amputated limb. They checked the date of Mikkelsen's birth, parents' names, his nine genetic coordinates, his educational record. Everything seemed right. But when they got to their wedding date the readout said 8 Feb 2017, and Mikkelsen heard warning chimes in his mind. "I remember a summer wedding," he said. "Outdoors in Dan Levy's garden, the hills all dry and brown, the 24th of August."

"So do I, Nick. The hills wouldn't have been brown in February. But I can see it—that hot dusty day—"

"Then five months of our marriage are gone, Janine. He couldn't unmarry us altogether, but he managed to hold us up from summer to winter." Rage made his head spin, and he had to ask his desk for a quick buzz of tranks. Etiquette called for one to be cool about a phasing. But he couldn't be cool when the phasing was a deliberate and malevolent blow at the center of his life. He wanted to shout, to break things, to kick Tommy Hambleton's ass. He wanted his marriage left alone. He said, "You know what I'm going to do one of these days? I'm going to go back about fifty years and eradicate Tommy completely. Just arrange things so his parents never get to meet, and—"

"No, Nick. You mustn't."

"I know. But I'd love to." He knew he couldn't, and not just because it would be murder. It was essential that Tommy Hambleton be born and grow up and meet Janine and marry her, so that when the marriage came apart she would meet and marry Mikkelsen. If he changed Hambleton's past, he would change hers too, and if he changed hers, he would change his own, and anything might happen. Anything. But all the same he was furious. "Five months of our past, Janine—"

"We don't need them, love. Keeping the present and the future safe is the main priority. By tomorrow we'll always think we were married in February of 2017, and it won't matter. Promise me you won't try to phase him."

"I hate the idea that he can simply—"

"So do I. But I want you to promise you'll leave things as they are."

"Well—"

"Promise."

"All right," he said. "I promise."

Little phasings happened all the time. Someone in Illinois makes a trip to eleventh-century Arizona and sets up tiny ripple currents in time that have a tangential and peripheral effect on a lot of lives, and someone in California finds himself driving a silver BMW instead of a gray Toyota. No one minded trifling changes like that. But this was the third time in the last twelve months, so far as Mikkelsen was able to tell, that Tommy Hambleton had committed a deliberate phasing intended to break the chain of events that had brought about Mikkelsen's marriage to Janine.

The first phasing happened on a splendid spring day—coming home from work, sudden taste of cotton in mouth, sense of mysterious disorientation. Mikkelsen walked down the steps looking for his old ginger tomcat, Gus, who always ran out to greet him as though he thought he was a dog. No Gus. Instead a calico female, very pregnant, sitting placidly in the front hall.

"Where's Gus?" Mikkelsen asked Janine.

"Gus? Gus who?"

"Our cat."

"You mean Max?"

"Gus," he said. "Sort of orange, crooked tail—"

"That's right. But Max is his name. I'm sure it's Max. He must be around somewhere. Look, here's Minibelle." Janine knelt and stroked the fat calico. "Minibelle, where's Max?"

"Gus," Mikkelsen said. "Not Max. And who's this Minibelle?"

"She's our cat, Nick," Janine said, sounding surprised. They stared at each other.

"Something's happened, Nick."

"I think we've been time-phased," he said.

Sensation as of dropping through trapdoor—shock, confusion, terror. Followed by hasty and scary inventory of basic life-data to see what had changed. Everything appeared in order except for the switch of cats. He didn't remember having a female calico. Neither did Janine, although she had accepted the presence of the cat without surprise. As for Gus—Max—he was getting foggier about his name, and Janine couldn't even remember what he looked like. But she did recall that he had been a wedding gift from some close friend, and Mikkelsen remembered that the friend was Gus Stark, for whom they had named him, and Janine was then able to dredge up the dimming fact that Gus was a close friend of Mikkelsen's and also of Hambleton and Janine in the days when they were married, and that Gus had introduced Janine to Mikkelsen ten years ago when they were all on holiday in Hawaii.

Mikkelsen accessed the household callmaster and found no Gus Stark listed. So the phasing had erased him from their roster of friends. The general phone directory turned up a Gus Stark in Costa Mesa. Mikkelsen called him and got a freckle-faced man with fading red hair, who looked more or less familiar. But he didn't know Mikkelsen at all, and only after some puzzling around in his memory did he decide that they had been distantly acquainted way back when, but had had some kind of trifling quarrel and had lost touch with each other years ago.

"That's not how I think I remember it," Mikkelsen said. "I remember us as friends for years, really close. You and Donna and Janine and I were out to dinner only last week, is what I remember, over in Newport Beach."

"Donna?"

"Your wife."

"My wife's name is Karen. Jesus, this has been one hell of a phasing, hasn't it?" He didn't sound upset.

"I'll say. Blew away your marriage, our friendship, and who knows what-all else."

"Well, these things happen. Listen, if I can help you any way, fella, just call. But right now Karen and I were on our way out, and—"

"Yeah. Sure. Sorry to have bothered you," Mikkelsen told him.

He blanked the screen.

Donna. Karen. Gus. Max. He looked at Janine.

"Tommy did it," she said.

She had it all figured out. Tommy, she said, had never forgiven Mikkelsen for marrying her. He wanted her back. He still sent her birthday cards, coy little gifts, postcards from exotic ports.

"You never mentioned them," Mikkelsen said.

She shrugged. "I thought you'd only get annoyed. You've always disliked Tommy."

"No," Mikkelsen said, "I think he's interesting in his oddball way, flamboyant, unusual. What I dislike is his unwillingness to accept the notion that you stopped being his wife a dozen years ago."

"You'd dislike him more if you knew how hard he's been trying to get me back."

"Oh?"

"When we broke up," she said, "he phased me four times. This was before I met you. He kept jaunting back to our final quarrel, trying to patch it up so that the separation wouldn't have happened. I began feeling the phasings and I knew what must be going on, and I told him to quit it or I'd report him and get his jaunt-license revoked. That scared him, I guess, because he's been pretty well behaved ever since, except for all the little hints and innuendoes and invitations to leave you and marry him again."

"Christ," Mikkelsen said. "How long were you and he married? Six months?"

"Seven. But he's an obsessive personality. He never lets go."

"And now he's started phasing again?"

"That's my guess. He's probably decided that you're the obstacle, that I really do still love you, that I want to spend the rest of my life with you. So he needs to make us unmeet. He's taken his first shot by somehow engineering a breach between you and your friend Gus a dozen years back, a breach so severe that you never really became friends and Gus never fixed you up with me. Only it didn't work out the way Tommy hoped. We went to that party at Dave Cushman's place and I got pushed into the pool on top of you and you introduced yourself and one thing led to another and here we still are."

"Not all of us are," Mikkelsen said. "My friend Gus is married to somebody else now."

"That didn't seem to trouble him much."

"Maybe not. But he isn't my friend any more, either, and that troubles *me*. My whole past is at Tommy Hambleton's mercy, Janine! And Gus the cat is gone too. Gus was a damned good cat. I miss him."

"Five minutes ago you weren't sure whether his name was Gus or Max. Two hours from now you won't know you ever had any such cat, and it won't matter at all."

"But suppose the same thing had happened to you and me as happened to Gus and Donna?"

"It didn't, though."

"It might the next time," Mikkelsen said.

❋

But it didn't. The next time, which was about six months later, they came out of it still married to each other. What they lost was their collection of twentieth-century artifacts—the black-and-white television set and the funny old dial telephone and the transistor radio and the little computer with the typewriter keyboard. All those treasures vanished between one instant and the next, leaving Mikkelsen with the telltale cottony taste in his mouth, Janine with a short-lived tic below her left eye, and both of them with the nagging awareness that a phasing had occurred.

At once they did what they could to see where the alteration had been made. For the moment they both remembered the artifacts they once had owned, and how eagerly they had collected them in '21 and '22, when the craze for such things was just beginning. But there were no sales receipts in their files and already their memories of what they had bought were becoming blurry and contradictory. There was a grouping of glittery sonic sculptures to the corner, now, where the artifacts had been. What change had been effected in the pattern of their past to put those things in the place of the others?

They never really were sure—there was no certain way of knowing—but Mikkelsen had a theory. The big expense he remembered for 2021 was the time jaunt that he and Janine had taken to Aztec Mexico, just before she got pregnant with Dana. Things had been a little wobbly between the Mikkelsens back then, and the time jaunt was supposed to be a second honeymoon. But their guide on the jaunt had been a hot little item named Elena Schmidt, who had made a very determined play for Mikkelsen and who had had him considering, for at least half an hour of lively fantasy, leaving Janine for her.

"Suppose," he said, "that on our original time-track we never went back to the Aztecs at all, but put the money into the artifact collection. But then Tommy went back and maneuvered things to get us interested in time jaunting, and at the same time persuaded that Schmidt cookie to show an interest in me. We couldn't afford both the antiques and the trip; we opted for the trip, Elena did her little number on me, it didn't cause the split that Tommy was hoping for, and now we have some gaudy memories of Moctezuma's empire and no collection of early electronic devices. What do you think?"

"Makes sense," Janine said.

"Will you report him, or should I?"

"But we have no proof, Nick!"

He frowned. Proving a charge of time-crime, he knew, was almost impossible, and risky besides. The very act of investigating the alleged crime could cause an even worse phase-shift and scramble their pasts beyond repair. To enter the past is like poking a baseball bat into a spiderweb: it can't be done subtly or delicately.

"Do we just sit and wait for Tommy to figure out a way to get rid of me that really works?" Mikkelsen asked.

"We can't just confront him with suspicions, Nick."

"You did it once."

"Long ago. The risks are greater now. We have more past to lose. What if he's not responsible? What if he gets scared of being blamed for something that's just coincidence, and *really* sets out to phase us? He's so damned volatile, so unstable—if he feels threatened, he's likely to do anything. He could wreck our lives entirely."

"If *he* feels threatened? What about—"

"Please, Nick. I've got a hunch Tommy won't try it again. He's had two shots and they've both failed. He'll quit it now. I'm sure he will."

Grudgingly Mikkelsen yielded, and after a time he stopped worrying about a third phasing. Over the next few weeks, other effects of the second phasing kept turning up, the way losses gradually make themselves known after a burglary. The same thing had happened after the first one. A serious attempt at altering the past could never have just one consequence; there was always a host of trivial—or not so trivial—secondary shifts, a ramifying web of transformations reaching out into any number of other lives. New chains of associations were formed in the Mikkelsens' lives as a result of the erasure of their plan to collect electronic artifacts and the substitution of a trip to pre-Columbian Mexico. People they had met on that trip now were good friends, with whom they exchanged gifts, spent other holidays, shared the burdens and joys of parenthood. A certain hollowness at first marked all those newly ingrafted old friendships, making them seem curiously insubstantial and marked by odd inconsistencies. But after a time everything felt real again, everything appeared to fit.

Then the third phasing happened, the one that pushed the beginning of their marriage from August to the following February, and did six or seven other troublesome little things, as they shortly discovered, to the contours of their existence.

330

"I'm going to talk to him," Mikkelsen said.

"Nick, don't do anything foolish."

"I don't intend to. But he's got to be made to see that this can't go on."

"Remember that he can be dangerous if he's forced into a corner," Janine said. "Don't threaten him. Don't push him."

"I'll tickle him," Mikkelsen said.

He met Hambleton for drinks at the Top of the Marina, Hambleton's favorite pub, swiveling at the end of a jointed stalk a thousand feet long rising from the harbor at Balboa Lagoon. Hambleton was there when Mikkelsen came in—a small sleek man, six inches shorter than Mikkelsen, with a slick confident manner. He was the richest man Mikkelsen knew, gliding through life on one of the big microprocessor fortunes of two generations back, and that in itself made him faintly menacing, as though he might try simply to buy back, one of these days, the wife he had loved and lost a dozen years ago when all of them had been so very young.

Hambleton's overriding passion, Mikkelsen knew, was time-travel. He was an inveterate jaunter—a compulsive jaunter, in fact, with that faintly hyperthyroid goggle-eyed look that frequent travelers get. He was always either just back from a jaunt or getting his affairs in order for his next one. It was as though the only use he had for the humdrum real-time event horizon was to serve as his springboard into the past. That was odd. What was odder still was where he jaunted. Mikkelsen could understand people who went zooming off to watch the battle of Waterloo, or shot a bundle on a first-hand view of the sack of Rome. If he had anything like Hambleton's money, that was what he would do. But according to Janine, Hambleton was forever going back seven weeks in time, or maybe to last Christmas, or occasionally to his eleventh birthday party. Time-travel as tourism held no interest for him. Let others roam the ferny glades of the Mesozoic: he spent fortunes doubling back along his own time-track, and never went anywhen other. The purpose of Tommy Hambleton's time-travel, it seemed, was to edit his past to make his life more perfect. He went back to eliminate every little contretemps and faux pas, to recover fumbles, to take advantage of the new opportunities that hindsight provides—to retouch, to correct, to emend. To Mikkelsen that was crazy, but also somehow charming. Hambleton was nothing if not charming. And Mikkelsen admired anyone who could invent his own new species of obsessive behavior, instead of going in for the standard hand-washing routines, or stamp-collecting or sitting with your back to the wall in restaurants.

The moment Mikkelsen arrived, Hambleton punched the autobar for cocktails and said, "Splendid to see you, Mikkelsen. How's the elegant Janine?"

"Elegant."

"What a lucky man you are. The one great mistake of my life was letting that woman slip through my grasp."

"For which I remain forever grateful, Tommy. I've been working hard lately to hang on to her, too."

Hambleton's eyes widened. "Yes? Are you two having problems?"

"Not with each other. Time-track troubles. You know, we were caught in a couple of phasings last year. Pretty serious ones. Now there's been another one. We lost five months of our marriage."

"Ah, the little annoyances of—"

"—modern life," Mikkelsen said. "Yes. A very familiar phrase. But these are what I'd call frightening annoyances. I don't need to tell you, of all people, what a splendid woman Janine is, how terrifying it is to me to think of losing her in some random twitch of the time-track."

"Of course. I quite understand."

"I wish I understood these phasings. They're driving us crazy. And that's what I wanted to talk to you about."

He studied Hambleton closely, searching for some trace of guilt or at least uneasiness. But Hambleton remained serene.

"How can I be of help?"

Mikkelsen said, "I thought that perhaps you, with all your vast experience in the theory and practice of time-jaunting, could give me some clue to what's causing them, so that I can head the next one off."

Hambleton shrugged elaborately. "My dear Nick, it could be anything! There's no reliable way of tracing phasing effects back to their cause. All our lives are interconnected in ways we never suspect. You say this last phasing delayed your marriage by a few months? Well, then, suppose that as a result of the phasing you decided to take a last bachelor fling and went off for a weekend in Banff, say, and met some lovely person with whom you spent three absolutely casual and non-significant but delightful days, thereby preventing her from meeting someone else that weekend with whom in the original time-track she had fallen in love and married. You then went home and married

Janine, a little later than originally scheduled, and lived happily ever after; but the Banff woman's life was totally switched around, all as a consequence of the phasing that delayed your wedding. Do you see? There's never any telling how a shift in one chain of events can cause interlocking upheavals in the lives of utter strangers."

"So I realize. But why should we be hit with three phasings in a year, each one jeopardizing the whole structure of our marriage?"

"I'm sure I don't know," said Hambleton. "I suppose it's just bad luck, and bad luck always changes, don't you think? Probably you've been at the edge of some nexus of negative phases that has just about run its course." He smiled dazzlingly. "Let's hope so, anyway. Would you care for another filtered rum?"

He was smooth, Mikkelsen thought. And impervious. There was no way to slip past his defenses, and even a direct attack—an outright accusation that he was the one causing the phasings—would most likely bring into play a whole new line of defense. Mikkelsen did not intend to risk that. A man who used time jaunting so ruthlessly to tidy up his past was too slippery to confront. Pressed, Hambleton would simply deny everything and hasten backward to clear away any traces of his crime that might remain. In any case, making an accusation of time-crime stick was exceedingly difficult, because the crime by definition had to have taken place on a track that no longer existed. Mikkelsen chose to retreat. He accepted another drink from Hambleton; they talked in a desultory way for a while about phasing theory, the weather, the stock market, the excellences of the woman they both had married, and the good old days of 2014 or so when they all used to hang out down in dear old La Jolla, living golden lives of wondrous irresponsibility. Then he extricated himself from the conversation and headed for home in a dark and brooding mood. He had no doubt that Hambleton would strike again, perhaps quite soon. How could he be held at bay? Some sort of preemptive strike, Mikkelsen wondered? Some bold leap into the past that would neutralize the menace of Tommy Hambleton forever? Chancy, Mikkelsen thought. You could lose as much as you gained, sometimes, in that sort of maneuver. But perhaps it was the only hope.

He spent the next few days trying to work out a strategy. Something that would get rid of Hambleton without disrupting the frail chain of circumstance that bound his own life to that of Janine—was it possible? Mikkelsen sketched out ideas, rejected them, tried again. He began to think he saw a way.

Then came a new phasing on a warm and brilliantly sunny morning that struck him like a thunderbolt and left him dazed and numbed. When he finally shook away the grogginess, he found himself in a bachelor flat ninety stories above Mission Bay, a thick taste of cotton in his mouth, and bewildering memories already growing thin of a lovely wife and two kids and a cat and a sweet home in mellow old Corona del Mar.

Janine? Dana? Elise? Minibelle?

Gone. All gone. He knew that he had been living in this condo since '22, after the breakup with Yvonne, and that Melanie was supposed to be dropping in about six. That much was reality. And yet another reality still lingered in his mind, fading vanishing.

So it had happened. Hambleton had really done it, this time.

There was no time for panic or even for pain. He spent the first half hour desperately scribbling down notes, every detail of his lost life that he still remembered, phone numbers, addresses, names, descriptions. He set down whatever he could recall of his life with Janine and of the series of phasings that had led up to this one. Just as he was running dry the telephone rang. Janine, he prayed.

But it was Gus Stark. "Listen," he began, "Donna and I got to cancel for tonight, on account of she's got a bad headache, but I hope you and Melanie aren't too disappointed, and—" He paused. "Hey, guy, are you okay?"

"There's been a bad phasing," Mikkelsen said.

"Uh-oh."

"I've got to find Janine."

"Janine?"

"Janine—Carter," Mikkelsen said. "Slender, high cheekbones, dark hair—you know."

"Janine," said Stark. "Do I know a Janine? Hey, you and Melanie on the outs? I thought—"

"This had nothing to do with Melanie," said Mikkelsen.

"Janine Carter." Gus grinned. "You mean Tommy Hambleton's girl? The little rich guy who was part of the La Jolla crowd ten-twelve years back when—"

"That's the one. Where do you think I'd find her now?"

"Married Hambleton, I think. Moved to the Riviera, unless I'm mistaken. Look, about tonight, Nick—"

"Screw tonight," Mikkelsen said. "Get off the phone. I'll talk to you later."

He broke the circuit and put the phone into search mode, all directories worldwide, Thomas and Janine Hambleton. While he waited, the shock and anguish of loss began at last to get to him, and he started to sweat, his hands shook, his heart raced in double time. I won't find her, he thought. He's got her hidden behind seven layers of privacy networks and it's crazy to think the phone number is listed, for Christ's sake, and—

The telephone. He hit the button. Janine calling, this time.

She looked stunned and disoriented, as though she were working hard to keep her eyes in focus. "Nick?" she said faintly. "Oh, God, Nick, it's you, isn't it?"

"Where are you?"

"A villa outside Nice. In Cap d'Antibes, actually. Oh, Nick—the kids—they're gone, aren't they? Dana. Elise. They never were born, isn't that so?"

"I'm afraid it is. He really nailed us, this time."

"I can still remember just as though they were real—as though we spent ten years together—oh, Nick—"

"Tell me how to find you. I'll be on the next plane out of San Diego."

She was silent a moment.

"No. No, Nick. What's the use? We aren't the same people we were when we were married. An hour or two more and we'll forget we ever were together."

"Janine—"

"We've got no past left, Nick. And no future."

"Let me come to you!"

"I'm Tommy's wife. My past's with him. Oh, Nick, I'm so sorry, so awfully sorry—I can still remember, a little, how it was with us, the fun, the running along the beach, the kids, the little fat calico cat—but it's all gone, isn't it? I've got my life here, you've got yours. I just wanted to tell you—"

"We can try to put it back together. You don't love Tommy. You and I belong with each other. We—"

"He's a lot different, Nick. He's not the man you remember from the La Jolla days. Kinder, more considerate, more of a human being, you know? It's been ten years, after all."

Mikkelsen closed his eyes and gripped the edge of the couch to keep from falling. "It's been two hours," he said. "Tommy phased us. He just tore up our life, and we can't ever have that part of it back, but still we can salvage something, Janine, we can rebuild, if you'll just get the hell out of that villa and—"

"I'm sorry, Nick." Her voice was tender, throaty, distant, almost unfamiliar. "Oh, God, Nick, it's such a mess. I loved you so. I'm sorry, Nick. I'm so sorry."

The screen went blank.

Mikkelsen had not time-jaunted in years, not since the Aztec trip, and he was amazed at what it cost now. But he was carrying the usual credit cards and evidently his credit lines were okay, because they approved his application in five minutes. He told them where he wanted to go and how he wanted to look, and for another few hundred the makeup man worked him over, taking that dusting of early gray out of his hair and smoothing the lines from his face and spraying him with the good old Southern California tan that you tend to lose when you're in your late thirties and spending more time in your office than on the beach. He looked at least eight years younger, close enough to pass. As long as he took care to keep from running into his own younger self while he was back there, there should be no problems.

He stepped into the cubicle and sweet-scented fog enshrouded him and when he stepped out again it was a mild December day in the year 2012, with a faint hint of rain in the northern sky. Only fourteen years back, and yet the world looked prehistoric to him, the clothing and the haircuts and the cars all wrong, the buildings heavy and clumsy, the advertisements floating overhead offering archaic and absurd products in blaring gaudy colors. Odd that the world of 2012 had not looked so crude to him the first time he had lived through it; but then the present never looks crude, he thought, except through the eyes of the future. He enjoyed the strangeness of it: it told him that he had really gone backward in time. It was like walking into an old movie. He felt very calm. All the pain was behind him now; he remembered nothing of the life that he had lost, only that it was important for him to take certain countermeasures against the man who had stolen something precious from him. He rented a car and drove quickly up to La Jolla. As he expected, everybody was at the beach club except for young Nick Mikkelsen, who was back in Palm

Beach with his parents. Mikkelsen had put this jaunt together quickly but not without careful planning.

They were all amazed to see him—Gus, Dan, Leo, Christie, Sal, the whole crowd. How young they looked! Kids, just kids, barely into their twenties, all that hair, all that baby fat. He had never before realized how young you were when you were *young*. "Hey," Gus said, "I thought you were in Florida!" Someone handed him a popper. Someone slipped a capsule to his ear and raucous overload music began to pound against his cheekbone. He made the rounds, grinning hugging, explaining that Palm Beach had been a bore, that he had come back early to be with the gang. "Where's Yvonne?" he asked.

"She'll be here in a little while," Christie said.

Tommy Hambleton walked in five minutes after Mikkelsen. For one jarring instant Mikkelsen thought that the man he saw was the Hambleton of his own time, thirty-five years old, but no: there were little signs, and certain lack of tension in this man's face, a certain callowness about the lips, that marked him as younger. The truth, Mikkelsen realized, is that Hambleton had *never* looked really young, that he was ageless, timeless, sleek and plump and unchanging. It would have been very satisfying to Mikkelsen to plunge a knife into that impeccably shaven throat, but murder was not his style, nor was it an ideal solution to his problem. Instead, he called Hambleton aside, bought him a drink and said quietly, "I just thought you'd like to know that Yvonne and I are breaking up."

"Really, Nick? Oh, that's so sad! I thought you two were the most solid couple here!"

"We were. We were. But it's all over, man. I'll be with someone else New Year's Eve. Don't know who, but it won't be Yvonne."

Hambleton looked solemn. "That's so sad, Nick."

"No. Not for me and not for you." Mikkelsen smiled and nudged Hambleton amiably. "Look, Tommy, it's no secret to me that you've had your eye on Yvonne for months. She knows it too. I just wanted to let you know that I'm stepping out of the picture, I'm very gracefully withdrawing, no hard feelings at all. And if she asks my advice, I'll tell her that you're absolutely the best man she could find. I mean it, Tommy."

"That's very decent of you, old fellow. That's extraordinary!"

"I want her to be happy," Mikkelsen said.

Yvonne showed up just as night was falling. Mikkelsen had not seen her for years, and he was startled at how uninteresting she seemed, how bland, how unformed, almost adolescent. Of course, she was very pretty, close-cropped blonde hair, merry greenish-blue eyes, pert little nose, but she seemed girlish and alien to him, and he wondered how he could ever have become so involved with her. But of course all that was before Janine. Mikkelsen's unscheduled return from Palm Beach surprised her, but not very much, and when he took her down to the beach to tell her that he had come to realize that she was really in love with Hambleton and he was not going to make a fuss about it, she blinked and said sweetly, "In love with Tommy? Well, I suppose I *could* be— though I never actually saw it like that. But I could give it a try, couldn't I? That is, if you truly are tired of me, Nick." She didn't seem offended. She didn't seem heartbroken. She didn't seem to care much at all.

He left the club soon afterward and got an express-fax message off to his younger self in Palm Beach: *Yvonne has fallen for Tommy Hambleton. However upset you are, for God's sake get over it fast, and if you happen to meet a young woman named Janine Carter, give her a close look. You won't regret it, believe me. I'm in a position to know.*

He signed it *A Friend*, but added a little squiggle in the corner that had always been his own special signature-glyph. He didn't dare go further than that. He hoped young Nick would be smart enough to figure out the score.

Not a bad hour's work, he decided. He drove back to the jaunt-shop in downtown San Diego and hopped back to his proper point in time.

There was the taste of cotton in his mouth when he emerged. So it feels that way even when you phase *yourself*, he thought. He wondered what changes he had brought about by his jaunt. As he remembered it, he had made the hop in order to phase himself back into a marriage with a woman named Janine, who apparently he had loved quite considerably until she had been snatched away from him in a phasing. Evidently the unphasing had not happened, because he knew he was still unmarried, with three or four regular companions—Cindy, Melanie, Elena and someone else—and none of them was named Janine. Paula, yes, that was the other one. Yet he was carrying a note, already starting to fade, that said: *You won't remember any of this, but you were married in 2016 or 17 to the former Janine Carter, Tommy Hambleton's ex-wife, and however much you may like your present life, you*

were a lot better off when you were with her. Maybe so, Mikkelsen thought. God knows he was getting weary of the bachelor life, and now that Gus and Donna were making it legal, he was the only singleton left in the whole crowd. That was a little awkward. But he hadn't ever met anyone he genuinely wanted to spend the rest of his life with, or even as much as a year with. So he had been married, had he, before the phasing? Janine? How strange, how unlike him.

He was home before dark. Showered, shaved, dressed, headed over to the Top of the Marina. Tommy Hambleton and Yvonne were in town, and he had agreed to meet them for drinks. Hadn't seen them for years, not since Tommy had taken over his brother's villa on the Riviera. Good old Tommy, Mikkelsen thought. Great to see him again. And Yvonne. He recalled her clearly, little snub-nosed blonde, good game of tennis, trim compact body. He'd been pretty hot for her himself, eleven or twelve years ago, back before Adrienne, before Charlene, before Georgiana, before Nedra, before Cindy, Melanie, Elena, Paula. Good to see them both again. He stepped into the skylift and went shooting blithely up the long swivel-stalk to the gilded little cupola high above the lagoon. Hambleton and Yvonne were already there.

Tommy hadn't changed much—same old smooth slickly dressed little guy—but Mikkelsen was astonished at how time and money had altered Yvonne. She was poised, chic, sinuous, all that baby-fat burned away, and when she spoke there was the smallest hint of a French accent in her voice. Mikkelsen embraced them both and let himself be swept off to the bar.

"So glad I was able to find you," Hambleton said. "It's been years! Years, Nick!"

"Practically forever."

"Still going great with the women, are you?"

"More or less," Mikkelsen said. "And you? Still running back in time to wipe your nose three days ago, Tommy?"

Hambleton chuckled. "Oh, I don't do much of that any more. Yvonne and I were to the Fall of Troy last winter, but the short-hop stuff doesn't interest me these days. I—oh. How amazing?"

"What is it?" Mikkelsen asked, seeing Hambleton's gaze go past him into the darker corners of the room.

"An old friend," Hambleton said. "I'm sure it's she! Someone I once knew—briefly, glancingly—" He looked toward Yvonne and said, "I met her a few months after you and I began seeing each other, love. Of course, there was nothing to it, but there could have been—there could have been—" A distant wistful look swiftly crossed Hambleton's features and was gone. His smile returned. He said, "You should meet her, Nick. If it's really she, I know she'll be just your type. How amazing! After all these years! Come with me, man!"

He seized Mikkelsen by the wrist and drew him, astounded, across the room.

"Janine?" Hambleton cried. "Janine Carter?"

She was a dark-haired woman, elegant, perhaps a year or two younger than Mikkelsen, with cool perceptive eyes. She looked up, surprised. "Tommy? Is that you?"

"Of course, of course. That's my wife, Yvonne, over there. And this—this is one of my oldest and dearest friends, Nick Mikkelsen. Nick—Janine—"

She stared up at him. "This sounds absurd," she said, "but don't I know you from somewhere?"

Mikkelsen felt a warm flood of mysterious energy surging through him as their eyes met. "It's a long story," he said. "Let's have a drink and I'll tell you all about it."

AMANDA AND THE ALIEN

Some stories seem almost to write themselves. This was one of them. I wish they were all that easy, or that the results were always that pleasing.

"Amanda" was a product of the rainy winter of 1981-2, when I was having a particularly fertile run of short-story writing. (Here I need to pause for a digression on California weather and my writing habits. California is one of five places in the world that have the so-called "Mediterranean" climate—the others are Chile, Western Australia, the western part of South Africa, and the Mediterranean region itself—in which the winters are mild and rainy and the summers are dry. Where I live, in the San Francisco region, the heaviest rains fall between November and March. Then they taper off, and from mid-April to early November there's normally no rain at all. Rain in summertime here has been known to happen occasionally, but so rarely that it's a front-page news item. My working pattern follows the weather: in the days when I was writing novels—it's been a while since I last wrote one—I tended to write them during the period of maximum rainfall, tapering off to short stories as the season's rains began to diminish in the spring, and doing as little work as my conscience would allow during the dry season. By fall, just as the rains were getting ready to return, I would warm up the machinery with a short story or two and then embark on the new season's novel. But 1981 was an unusual year: instead of a novel, my book for the year was Majipoor Chronicles, which is actually a collection of short stories disguised as a novel, and I wrote it in the spring and summer instead of winter. When autumn came, I was out of sequence with my regular writing rhythm, and

I decided to keep on doing short stories and get things straightened out later on.)

And so "Amanda." It wasn't the story I had intended to do just then. I had promised one to Ellen Datlow, the new fiction editor of Omni, and what I had in mind was a sequel to "Dancers in the Time-Flux"—another tale of Olivier van Noort in the far future, this time encountering a Parisian woman from the year 1980 who was, like himself, a creature of antiquity, but nevertheless something out of his own future. My long-range plan was to assemble another story cycle along the lines of Majipoor Chronicles, set in the Son of Man world. But something went wrong and the story died on me after about eight pages. I don't know why. Unfinished stories are as rare around here as heavy rainfall in July. So far as I can recall, that's the only story I've left unfinished in the past fifty years. I have those eight pages around here somewhere, I think, and maybe I'll write the rest of the piece some day. Or maybe not: maybe it would be a mistake to try to return to the world of Son of Man, a closed chapter in my past.

"The thing seems terribly slow and ponderous and wrong," I told Ellen in a letter of February 20, 1982, "and after a few days of work I called a halt to find out what the trouble was. The trouble was, apparently, that I wanted to do a different sort of story for you, something bouncier and zippier and more contemporary. And before I really knew what was happening, the enclosed lighthearted chiller came galloping out of the typewriter." Ellen bought it by return mail, and Terry Carr chose it for the 1983 volume of his annual Best SF of the Year anthology series.

Instead of setting my story in the remote future world of "Dancers in the Time-Flux," I had put it right here, in the San Francisco Bay Area of just a few years hence. And, though I wrote it in cool rainy February, I picked warm sunny September as the time in which it took place. Perhaps that was why I wrote it with such ease. It had been pouring outside for days, but in my mind our long golden summer had already come. And, with it, the utterly unscrupulous Amanda, an all too familiar California life-form.

Ellen Datlow published it in the May, 1983 issue of Omni. Some years later the talented young director Jon Kroll made a very funny television movie out of it, and careful observers will note that in it I made my film debut in a role (non-speaking) that had me on camera for approximately seventeen seconds.

---

manda spotted the alien late Friday afternoon outside the Video Center on South Main. It was trying to look cool and laid-back, but it simply came across as bewildered and uneasy. The alien was disguised as a seventeen-year-old girl, maybe a Chicana, with olive-toned skin and hair so black it seemed almost blue, but Amanda, who was seventeen herself, knew a phony when she saw one. She studied the alien for some moments from the other side of the street to make absolutely certain. Then she walked across.

"You're doing it wrong," Amanda said. "Anybody with half a brain could tell what you really are."

"Bug off," the alien said.

"No. Listen to me. You want to stay out of the detention center or don't you?"

The alien stared coldly at Amanda and said, "I don't know what the crap you're talking about."

"Sure you do. No sense trying to bluff me. Look, I want to help you," Amanda said. "I think you're getting a raw deal. You know what that means, a raw deal? Hey, look, come home with me and I'll teach you a few things about passing for human. I've got the whole friggin' weekend now with nothing else to do anyway."

A flicker of interest came into the other girl's dark chilly eyes. But it went quickly away and she said, "You some kind of lunatic?"

"Suit yourself, O thing from beyond the stars. *Let* them lock you up again. *Let* them stick electrodes up your ass. I tried to help. That's all I can do, is try," Amanda said, shrugging. She began to saunter away. She didn't look back. Three steps, four, five, hands in pockets, slowly heading for her car. Had she been wrong, she wondered? No. No. She could be wrong about some things, like Charley Taylor's interest in spending the weekend with her, maybe. But not this. That crinkly-haired chick was the missing alien for sure. The whole county was buzzing about it—deadly nonhuman life-form has escaped from the detention center out by Tracy, might be anywhere, Walnut Creek, Livermore, even San Francisco, dangerous monster, capable of mimicking human forms, will engulf and digest you and disguise itself in your shape, and there it was, Amanda knew, standing outside the Video Center. Amanda kept walking.

"Wait," the alien said finally

Amanda took another easy step or two. Then she looked back over her shoulder.

"Yeah?"

"How can you tell?"

Amanda grinned. "Easy. You've got a rain slicker on and it's only September. Rainy season doesn't start around here for another month or two. Your pants are the old spandex kind. People like you don't wear that stuff any more. Your face paint is San Jose colors, but you've got the cheek chevrons put on in the Berkeley pattern. That's just the first three things I noticed. I could find plenty more. Nothing about you fits together with anything else. It's like you did a survey to see how you ought to appear, and tried a little of everything. The closer I study you, the more I see. Look, you're wearing your headphones and the battery light is on, but there's no cassette in the slot. What are you listening to, the music of the spheres? That model doesn't have any FM tuner, you know. You see? You may think you're perfectly camouflaged, but you aren't."

"I could destroy yon," the alien said.

"What? Oh, sure. Sure you could. Engulf me right here on the street, all over in thirty seconds, little trail of slime by the door and a new Amanda walks away. But what then? What good's that going to do you? You still won't know which end is up. So there's no logic in destroying me, unless you're a total dummy. I'm on your side. I'm not going to turn you in."

"Why should I trust you?"

"Because I've been talking to you for five minutes and I haven't yelled for the cops yet. Don't you know that half of California is out searching for you? Hey, can you read? Come over here a minute. Here." Amanda tugged the alien toward the newspaper vending box at the curb. The headline on the afternoon *Examiner* was:

BAY AREA ALIEN TERROR

MARINES TO JOIN NINE-COUNTY HUNT
MAYOR, GOVERNOR CAUTION AGAINST PANIC

"You understand that?" Amanda asked. "That's you they're talking about. They're out there with flame guns, tranquilizer darts, web snares, and God knows what else. There's been real hysteria for a day and a half. And you standing around here with the wrong chevrons on! Christ. Christ! What's your plan, anyway? Where are you trying to go?"

"Home," the alien said. "But first I have to rendezvous at the pickup point."

"Where's that?"

"You think I'm stupid?"

"Shit," Amanda said. "If I meant to turn you in, I'd have done it five minutes ago. But okay. I don't give a damn where your rendezvous point is. I tell you, though, you wouldn't make it as far as San Francisco rigged up the way you are. It's a miracle you've avoided getting caught until now."

"And you'll help me?"

"I've been trying to. Come on. Let's get the hell out of here. I'll take you home and fix you up a little. My car's in the lot on the corner."

"Okay."

"Whew!"Amanda shook her head slowly. "Christ, some people are awfully hard to help."

As she drove out of the center of town, Amanda glanced occasionally at the alien sitting tensely to her right. Basically the disguise was very convincing, Amanda thought. Maybe all the small details were wrong, the outer stuff, the anthropological stuff, but the alien *looked* human, it *sounded* human, it even *smelled* human. Possibly it could fool ninety-nine people out of a hundred, or maybe more than that. But Amanda had always had a good eye for detail. And the particular moment she had spotted the alien on South Main she had been unusually alert, sensitive, all raw nerves, every antenna up. Of course, it wasn't aliens she was hunting for, but just a diversion, a little excitement, something to fill the great gaping emptiness that Charley Taylor had left in her weekend.

Amanda had been planning the weekend with Charley all month. Her parents were going to go off to Lake Tahoe for three days, her kid sister had wangled permission to accompany them, and Amanda was going to have the house to herself, just her and Macavity the cat. And Charley. He was going to move in on Friday afternoon and they'd cook dinner together and get blasted on her stash of choice powder and watch five or six of her parents' X-rated cassettes, and Saturday they'd drive over to the city and cruise some of the kinky districts and go to that bathhouse on Folsom where everybody got naked and climbed into the giant Jacuzzi, and then on Sunday—Well, none of that was going to happen. Charley had called on Thursday to cancel. "Something big came up," he said, and Amanda had a pretty good idea what that was, which his hot little cousin from New Orleans who sometimes came flying out here on no notice at all; but the inconsiderate bastard seemed to be entirely unaware of how much Amanda had been looking forward to this weekend, how much it meant to her, how painful it was to be dumped like this. She had run through the planned events of the weekend in her mind so many times that she almost felt as though she had experienced them: it was that real to her. But overnight it had become unreal. Three whole days on her own, the house to herself, and so early in the semester that there was no homework to think about, and Charley had stood her up! What was she supposed to do now, call desperately around town to scrounge up some old lover as a playmate? Or pick up some stranger downtown? Amanda hated to fool around with strangers. She was half tempted to go over to the city and just let things happen, but they were all weirdos and creeps over there, anyway, and she knew what she could expect. What a waste, not having Charley! She could kill him for robbing her of the weekend.

Now there was the alien, though. A dozen of these star people had come to Earth last year, not in a flying saucer as everybody had expected, but in little capsules that floated like milkweed seeds, and they had landed in a wide arc between San Diego and Salt Lake City. Their natural form, so far as anyone could tell for sure, was something like a huge jellyfish with a row of staring purple eyes down one wavy margin, but their usual tactic was to borrow any local body they found, digesting it and turning themselves into an accurate imitation of it. One of them had made the mistake of turning itself into a brown mountain bear and another into a bobcat—maybe they thought that those were the dominant life-forms on Earth—but the others had taken on human bodies, at the cost of at least ten lives. Then they went looking to make contact with government leaders, and naturally they were rounded up very swiftly and interned, some in mental hospitals and some in county jails, but eventually—as soon as the truth of what they really were sank in—they were all put in a special detention camp in Northern California. Of course, a tremendous fuss was made over them, endless stuff in the papers and on the tube, speculation by this heavy thinker and that about the significance of their mission, the nature of their biochemistry, a little wild talk about the possibility that more of their kind might be waiting undetected out there and plotting to do God knows what, and all sorts of that stuff, and then came a government clamp on the entire subject, no official announcements except that "discussions" with the visitors were continuing; and after a while the whole thing degenerated into dumb alien jokes ("Why did the alien cross the road?") and Halloween invader masks, and then it moved into the background of everyone's attention and was forgotten. And remained forgotten until the announcement that one of the creatures had slipped out of the camp somehow and was loose within a hundred-mile zone around San Francisco. Preoccupied as she was with her anguish over Charley's heartlessness, even Amanda had managed to pick up *that* news item. And now the alien was in her very car. So there'd be some weekend amusement for her after all. Amanda was entirely unafraid of the alleged deadliness of the star being: whatever else the alien might be, it was surely no dope, not if it had been picked to come halfway across the galaxy on a mission like this, and Amanda knew that the alien could see that harming her was not going to be in its own best interests. The alien had need of her, and the alien realized that. And Amanda, in some way that she was only just beginning to work out, had need of the alien.

She pulled up outside her house, a compact split-level at the western end of town. "This is the place," she said. Heat shimmers danced in the air, and the hills back of the house, parched in the long dry summer, were the color of lions. Macavity, Amanda's old tabby, sprawled in the shade of the bottlebrush tree on the ragged front lawn. As Amanda and the alien approached, the cat sat up warily, flattened his ears, hissed. The alien immediately moved into a defensive posture, sniffing the air.

"Just a household pet," Amanda said. "You know what that is? He isn't dangerous. He's always a little suspicious of strangers."

Which was untrue. An earthquake couldn't have brought Macavity out of his nap, and a cotillion of mice dancing minuets on his tail wouldn't have drawn a reaction from him. Amanda calmed him with some fur-ruffling, but he wanted nothing to do with the alien, and went slinking sullenly into the underbrush. The alien watched him with care until he was out of sight.

"You have anything like cats on your planet?" Amanda asked as they went inside.

"We had small wild animals once. They were unnecessary."

"Oh," Amanda said. The house had a stuffy, stagnant air. She switched on air-conditioning. "Where is your planet, anyway?"

The alien ignored the question. It padded around the living room, very much like a prowling cat itself, studying the stereo, the television, the couches, the vase of dried flowers.

"Is this a typical Earthian home?"

"More or less," said Amanda. "Typical for around here, at least. This is what we call a suburb. It's half an hour by freeway from here to San Francisco. That's a city. A lot of people living all close together. I'll take you over there tonight or tomorrow for a look, if you're interested." She got some music going, high volume. The alien didn't seem to mind, so she notched the volume up more. "I'm going to take a shower. You could use one, too, actually."

"Shower? You mean rain?"

"I mean body-cleaning activities. We Earthlings like to wash a lot, to get rid of sweat and dirt and stuff. It's considered bad form to stink. Come on, I'll show you how to do it. You've got to do what I do if you want to keep from getting caught, you know." She led the alien to the bathroom. "Take your clothes off first."

The alien stripped. Underneath its rain slicker it wore a stained T-shirt that said "Fisherman's Wharf" with a picture of the San Francisco skyline, and a pair of unzipped jeans. Under that it was wearing a black brassiere, unfastened and with the cups over its shoulder blades, and a pair of black shiny panty briefs with a red heart on the left buttock. The alien's body was that of a lean, tough-looking girl with a scar running down the inside of one arm.

"Whose body is that?" Amanda asked. "Do you know?"

"She worked at the detention center. In the kitchen."

"You know her name?"

"Flores Concepion."

"The other way around, probably. Concepion Flores. I'll call you Connie, unless you want to give me your real name."

"Connie will do."

"All right, Connie. Pay attention. You turn the water on here, and you adjust the mix of hot and cold until you like it. Then you pull this knob and get underneath the spout here and wet your body, and rub soap over it and wash the soap off. Afterward you dry yourself and put fresh clothes on. You have to clean your clothes from time to time, too, because otherwise they start to smell and it upsets people. Watch me shower, and then you do it."

Amanda washed quickly, while plans hummed in her head. The alien wasn't going to last long out there wearing the body of Concepion Flores. Sooner or later someone was going to notice that one of the kitchen girls was missing, and they'd get an all-points alarm out for her. Amanda wondered whether the alien had figured that out yet. The alien, Amanda thought, needs a different body in a hurry.

But not mine, she told herself. For sure, not mine.

"Your turn," she said, shutting the water off.

The alien, fumbling a little, turned the water back on and got under the spray. Clouds of steam rose and its skin began to look boiled, but it didn't appear troubled. No sense of pain? "Hold it," Amanda said. "Step back." She adjusted the water. "You've got it too hot. You'll damage that body that way. Look, if you can't tell the difference between hot and cold, just take cold showers, okay? It's less dangerous. This is cold, on this side." She left the alien under the shower and went to find some clean clothes. When she came back, the alien was still showering, under icy water. "Enough," Amanda said. "Here. Put these on."

"I had more clothes than this before."

"A T-shirt and jeans are all you need in hot weather like this. With your kind of build you can skip the bra, and anyway I don't think you'll be able to fasten it the right way."

"Do we put the face paint on now?"

"We can skip it while we're home. It's just stupid kid stuff anyway, all that tribal crap. If we go out we'll do it, and we'll give you Walnut Creek colors, I think. Concepcion wore San Jose, but we want to throw people off the track. How about some dope?"

"What?"

"Grass. Marijuana. A drug widely used by local Earthians of our age."

"I don't need no drug."

"I don't either. But I'd *like* some. You ought to learn how, just in case you find yourself in a social situation." Amanda reached for her pack of Filter Golds and pulled out a joint. Expertly she tweaked its lighter tip and took a deep hit. "Here," she said, passing it. "Hold it like I did. Put it to your mouth, breathe in, suck the smoke deep." The alien dragged the joint and began to cough. "Not so deep, maybe," Amanda said.

"Take just a little. Hold it. Let it out. There, much better. Now give me back the joint. You've got to keep passing it back and forth. That part's important. You feel anything from it?"

"No."

"It can be subtle. Don't worry about it. Are you hungry?"

"Not yet," the alien said.

"I am. Come into the kitchen." As she assembled a sandwich—peanut butter and avocado on whole wheat, with tomato and onion—she asked, "What sort of things do you eat?"

"Life."

"Life?"

"We never eat dead things. Only things with life."

Amanda fought back a shudder. "I see. *Anything* with life?"

"We prefer animal life. We can absorb plants if necessary."

"Ah. Yes. And when are you going to be hungry again?"

"Maybe tonight," the alien said. "Or tomorrow. The hunger comes very suddenly, when it comes."

"There's not much around here that you could eat live. But I'll work on it.'

"The small furry animal?"

"No. My cat is not available for dinner. Get that idea right out of your head. Likewise me. I'm your protector and guide. It wouldn't be sensible of you to eat me. You follow what I'm trying to tell you?"

"I said that I'm not hungry yet."

"Well, you let me know when you start feeling the pangs. I'll find you a meal." Amanda began to construct a second sandwich. The alien prowled the kitchen, examining the appliances. Perhaps making mental records, Amanda thought, of sink and oven design, to copy on its home world. Amanda said, "Why did you people come here in the first place?"

"It was our mission."

"Yes. Sure. But for what purpose? What are you after? You want to take over the world? You want to steal our scientific secrets?" The alien, making no reply, began taking spices out of the spice rack. Delicately it licked its finger, touched it to the oregano, tasted it, tried the cumin. Amanda said, "Or is it that you want to keep us from going into space? That you think we're a dangerous species, so you're going to quarantine us on our own planet? Come on, you can tell me. I'm not a government spy." The alien sampled the tarragon, the basil, the sage. When it reached for the curry powder, its hand suddenly shook so violently that it knocked the open jars of oregano and tarragon over, making a mess. "Hey, are you all right?" Amanda asked.

The alien said, "I think I'm getting hungry. Are these things drugs, too?"

"Spices," Amanda said. "We put them in our foods to make them taste better." The alien was looking very strange, glassy-eyed, flushed, sweaty. "Are you feeling sick?"

"I feel excited. These powders—"

"They're turning you on? Which one?"

"This, I think." It pointed to the oregano. "It was either the first one or the second."

"Yeah," Amanda said. "Oregano. It can really make you fly." She wondered whether the alien might get violent when zonked. Or whether the oregano would stimulate its appetite. She had to watch out for its appetite. There are certain risks, Amanda reflected, in doing what I'm doing. Deftly she cleaned up the spilled oregano and tarragon and put the caps on the spice jars. "You ought to be careful," she said. "Your metabolism isn't used to this stuff. A little can go a long way."

"Give me some more."

"Later," Amanda said. "You don't want to overdo it."

"More!"

"Calm down. I know this planet better than you, and I don't want to see you get in trouble. Trust me: I'll let you have more oregano when it's the right time. Look at the way you're shaking. And you're sweating like crazy." Pocketing the oregano jar, she led the alien back into the living room. "Sit down. Relax."

"More? Please?"

"I appreciate your politeness. But we have important things to talk about, and then I'll give you some. Okay?" Amanda opaqued the window, through which the hot late-afternoon sun was coming. Six o'clock on Friday, and if everything had gone the right way Charley would have been showing up just about now. Well, she'd found a different diversion. The weekend stretched before her like an open road leading to mysteryland. The alien offered all sorts of possibilities, and she might yet have some fun over the next few days, if she used her head. Amanda turned to the alien and said, "You calmer now? Yes. Good. Okay: first of all, you've got to get yourself another body."

"Why is that?"

"Two reasons. One is that the authorities probably are searching for the girl you absorbed. How you got as far as you did without anybody but me spotting you is hard to understand. Number two, a teenage girl traveling by herself is going to get hassled too much, and you don't know how to handle yourself in a tight situation. You know what I'm saying? You're going to want to hitchhike out to Nevada, Wyoming, Utah, wherever the hell your rendezvous place is, and all along the way people are going to be coming on to you. You don't need any of that. Besides, it's very tricky trying to pass for a girl. You've got to know how to put your face paint on, how to understand challenge codes, and what the way you wear your clothing says, and like that. Boys have a much simpler subculture. You get yourself a male body, a big hunk of a body, and nobody'll bother you much on the way to where you're going. You just keep to yourself, don't make eye contact, don't smile, and everyone will leave you alone."

"Makes sense," said the alien. "All right. The hunger is becoming very bad now. Where do I get a male body?"

"San Francisco. It's full of men. We'll go over there tonight and find a nice brawny one for you. With any luck we might even find one who's not gay, and then we can have a little fun with him first. And then you take his body over—which incidentally solves your food problem for a while, doesn't it?—and we can have some more fun, a whole weekend of fun." Amanda winked. "Okay, Connie?"

"Okay." The alien winked, a clumsy imitation, first one eye, then the other. "You give me more oregano now?"

"Later. And when you wink, just wink *one* eye. Like this. Except I don't think you ought to do a lot of winking at people. It's a very intimate gesture that could get you in trouble. Understand?"

"There's so much to understand."

"You're on a strange planet, kid. Did you expect it to be just like home? Okay, to continue. The next thing I ought to point out is that when you leave here on Sunday you'll have to—"

The telephone rang.

"What's that sound?" the alien asked.

"Communications device. I'll be right back." Amanda went to the hall extension, imagining the worst: her parents, say, calling to announce that they were on their way back from Tahoe tonight, some mixup in the reservations or something. But the voice that greeted her was Charley's. She could hardly believe it, after the casual way he had shafted her this weekend. She could hardly believe what he wanted, either. He had left half a dozen of his best cassettes at her place last week, Golden Age rock, Abbey Road and the Hendrix one and a Joplin and such, and now he was heading off to Monterey for the festival and he wanted to have them for the drive. Did she mind if he stopped off in half an hour to pick them up?

The bastard, she thought. The absolute trashiness of him! First to torpedo her weekend without even an apology, and then to let her know that he and what's-her-name were scooting down to Monterey for some fun, and could he bother her for his cassettes? Didn't he think she had any feelings? She looked at the telephone in her hand as though it was emitting toads and scorpions. It was tempting to hang up on him.

She resisted the temptation. "As it happens," she said, "I'm just on my way out for the weekend myself. But I've got a friend who's here cat-sitting for me. I'll leave the cassettes with her, okay? Her name's Connie."

"Fine," Charley said. "I really appreciate that, Amanda."

"It's nothing," she said.

The alien was back in the kitchen, nosing around the spice rack. But Amanda had the oregano. She said, "I've arranged for delivery of your next body."

"You did?"

"A large healthy adolescent male. Exactly what you're looking for. He's going to be here in a little while. I'm going to go out for a drive, and you take care of him before I get back. How long does it take for you to—engulf—somebody?"

"It's very fast."

"Good." Amanda found Charley's cassettes and stacked them on the living-room table. "He's coming over here to get these six little boxes, which are music-storage devices. When the doorbell rings, you let him in and introduce yourself as Connie and tell him his things are on this table. After that you're on your own. You think you can handle it?"

"Sure," the alien said.

"Tuck in your T-shirt better. When it's tight it makes your boobs stick out, and that'll distract him. Maybe he'll even make a pass at you. What happens to the Connie body after you engulf him?"

"It won't be here. What happens is I merge with him and dissolve all the Connie characteristics and take on the new ones."

"Ah. Very nifty. You're a real nightmare thing, you know? You're a walking horror show. Here, have a little hit of oregano before I go." She put a tiny pinch of spice in the alien's hand. "Just to warm up your engine a little. I'll give you more later, when you've done the job. See you in an hour, okay?"

She left the house. Macavity was sitting on the porch, scowling, whipping his tail from side to side. Amanda knelt beside him and scratched him behind the ears. The cat made a low rough purring sound, not much like his usual purr.

Amanda said, "You aren't happy, are you, fella? Well, don't worry. I've told the alien to leave you alone, and I guarantee you'll be okay. This is Amanda's fun tonight. You don't mind if Amanda has a little fun, do you?" Macavity made a glum snuffling sound. "Listen, maybe I can get the alien to create a nice little calico cutie for you, okay? Just going into heat and ready to howl. Would you like that, guy? Would you? I'll see what I call do when I get back. But I have to clear out of here now, before Charley shows up."

She got into her car and headed for the westbound freeway ramp. Half past six, Friday night, the sun still hanging high above the Bay. Traffic was thick in the eastbound lanes, the late commuters slogging toward home, and it was beginning to build up westbound, too, as people set out for dinner in San Francisco. Amanda drove through the tunnel and turned north into Berkeley to cruise city streets. Ten minutes to seven now. Charley must have arrived. She imagined Connie in her tight T-shirt, all stoned and sweaty on oregano, and Charley giving her the eye, getting ideas, thinking about grabbing a bonus quickie before taking off with his cassettes. And Connie leading him on, Charley making his moves, and then suddenly that electric moment of surprise as the alien struck and Charley found himself turning into dinner. It could be happening right this minute, Amanda thought placidly No more than the bastard deserves, isn't it? She had felt for a long time that Charley was a big mistake in her life, and after what he had pulled yesterday she was sure of it. No more than he deserves. But, she wondered, what if Charley had brought his weekend date along? The thought chilled her. She hadn't considered that possibility at all. It could ruin everything. Connie wasn't able to engulf two at once, was she? And suppose they recognized her as the missing alien and ran out screaming to call the cops?

No, she thought. Not even Charley would be so tacky as to bring his date over to Amanda's house tonight. And Charley never watched the news or read a paper. He wouldn't have a clue as to what Connie really was until it was too late for him to run.

Seven o'clock. Time to head for home.

The sun was sinking behind her as she turned onto the freeway. By quarter past she was approaching her house. Charley's old red Honda was parked outside. Amanda left hers across the street and cautiously let herself in, pausing just inside the front door to listen.

Silence.

"Connie?"

"In here," said Charley's voice.

Amanda entered the living room. Charley was sprawled out comfortably on the couch. There was no sign of Connie.

"Well?" Amanda said. "How did it go?"

"Easiest thing in the world," the alien said. "He was sliding his hands under my T-shirt when I let him have the nullifier jolt."

"Ah. The nullifier jolt."

"And then I completed the engulfment and cleaned up the carpet. God, it feels good not to be hungry again. You can't imagine how tough it was to resist engulfing you, Amanda. For the past hour I kept thinking of food, food, food—"

"Very thoughtful of you to resist."

"I knew you were out to help me. It's logical not to engulf one's allies."

"That goes without saying. So you feel well fed, now? He was good stuff?"

"Robust, healthy, nourishing—yes."

"I'm glad Charley turned out to be good for something. How long before you get hungry again?"

The alien shrugged. "A day or two. Maybe three, on account of he was so big. Give me more oregano, Amanda?"

"Sure," she said. "Sure." She felt a little let down. Not that she was remorseful about Charley, exactly, but it all seemed so casual, so offhanded—there was something anticlimactic about it, in a way. She suspected she should have stayed and watched while it was happening. Too late for that now, though.

She took the oregano from her purse and dangled the jar teasingly. "Here it is, babe. But you've got to earn it first."

"What do you mean?"

"I mean that I was looking forward to a big weekend with Charley, and the weekend is here, and Charley's here too, more or less, and I'm ready for fun. Come show me some fun, big boy."

She slipped Charley's Hendrix cassette into the deck and turned the volume way up.

The alien looked puzzled. Amanda began to peel off her clothes.

"You too," Amanda said. "Come on. You won't have to dig deep into Charley's mind to figure out what to do. You're going to be my Charley for me this weekend, you follow? You and I are going to do all the things that he and I were going to do. Okay? Come on. Come on." She beckoned. The alien shrugged again and slipped out of Charley's clothes, fumbling with the unfamiliarities of his zipper and buttons. Amanda, grinning, drew the alien close against her and down to the living-room floor. She took its hands and put them where she wanted them to be. She whispered instructions. The alien, docile, obedient, did what she wanted.

It felt like Charley. It smelled like Charley. It even moved pretty much the way Charley moved.

But it wasn't Charley, it wasn't Charley at all, and after the first few seconds Amanda knew that she had goofed things up very badly. You couldn't just ring in an imitation like this. Making love with this alien was like making love with a very clever machine, or with her own mirror image. It was empty and meaningless and dumb.

Grimly she went on to the finish. They rolled apart, panting, sweating.

"Well?" the alien said. "Did the earth move for you?"

"Yeah. Yeah. It was wonderful—Charley."

"Oregano?"

"Sure," Amanda said. She handed the spice jar across. "I always keep my promises, babe. Go to it. Have yourself a blast. Just remember that that's strong stuff for guys from your planet, okay? If you pass out, I'm going to leave you right there on the floor."

"Don't worry about me."

"Okay. You have your fun. I'm going to clean up, and then maybe we'll go over to San Francisco for the nightlife. Does that interest you?"

"You bet, Amanda." The alien winked—one eye, then the other—and gulped a huge pinch of oregano. "That sounds terrific."

Amanda gathered up her clothes, went upstairs for a quick shower, and dressed. When she came down the alien was more than half blown away on the oregano, goggle-eyed, loll-headed, propped up against the

356

couch and crooning to itself in a weird atonal way. Fine, Amanda thought. You just get yourself all spiced up, love. She took the portable phone from the kitchen, carried it with her into the bathroom, locked the door, dialed the police emergency number.

She was bored with the alien. The game had worn thin very quickly. And it was crazy, she thought, to spend the whole weekend cooped up with a dangerous extraterrestrial creature when there wasn't going to be any fun in it for her. She knew now that there couldn't be any fun at all. And in a day or two the alien was going to get hungry again.

"I've got your alien," she said. "Sitting in my living room, stoned out of its head on oregano. Yes, I'm absolutely certain. It was disguised as a Chicana girl first, Concepcion Flores, but then it attacked my boyfriend Charley Taylor, and—yes, yes, I'm safe. I'm locked in the john. Just get somebody over here fast—okay, I'll stay on the line—what happened was, I spotted it downtown, it insisted on coming home with me—"

The actual capture took only a few minutes. But there was no peace for hours after the police tactical squad hauled the alien away, because the media was in on the act right away, first a team from Channel 2 in Oakland, and then some of the network guys, and then the *Chronicle,* and finally a whole army of reporters from as far away as Sacramento, and phone calls from Los Angeles and San Diego and—about three that morning—New York. Amanda told the story again and again until she was sick of it, and just as dawn was breaking she threw the last of them out and barred the door.

She wasn't sleepy at all. She felt wired up, speedy, and depressed all at once. The alien was gone, Charley was gone, and she was all alone. She was going to be famous for the next couple of days, but that wouldn't help. She'd still be alone. For a time she wandered around the house, looking at it the way an alien might, as though she had never seen a stereo cassette before, or a television set, or a rack of spices. The smell of oregano was everywhere. There were little trails of it on the floor.

Amanda switched on the radio and there she was on the six a.m. news. "—the emergency is over, thanks to the courageous Walnut Creek high school girl who trapped and outsmarted the most danger-ous life-form in the known universe—"

She shook her head. "You think that's true?" she asked the cat. "Most dangerous life-form in the universe? I don't think so, Macavity. I think I know of at least one that's a lot deadlier. Eh, kid?" She winked. "If they only knew, eh? If they only knew." She scooped the cat up and hugged it, and it began to purr. Maybe trying to get a little sleep would be a good idea around this time, she told herself. And then she had to figure out what she was going to do about the rest of the weekend.

SNAKE AND OCEAN, OCEAN AND SNAKE

We are still in the busy winter of 1982—still in rainy February, in fact. I have just finished "Amanda and the Alien," and the creative urge is still buzzing in me. In my revived career as a short-story writer, Omni and Playboy have become my two primary markets. Neither one can handle more than one or two stories a year from me; "Amanda" has just found a home at Omni, so it's time for me to begin thinking about something for Playboy.

As it turned out, the fiction editor of Playboy had the same thought in mind. I mean the redoubtable Alice K. Turner, of course, with whom I had struck up an instant editorial rapport of the most remarkable kind while we were butting heads over revisions to my first Playboy story, "Gianni," early in 1981. Now, a year later, Alice found herself with two illustrations on hand and no stories to go with them. She phoned me: Would I consider looking at the paintings in the hope one of them would inspire a story? I laughed. In the bad old days of penny-a-word pulp magazines, many editors had routinely bought cover paintings first and then asked writers to concoct stories to go with them. I had done my share of those arsy-versy projects back then, but it was close to twenty years since I had last written a story around an illustration. I told Alice it would be fun to try again, both for nostalgia's sake and for the challenge it represented.

She sent me photostats of two paintings. One showed a naked lady—a very satisfactory one, as I recall, but she wasn't engaged in doing anything that sparked a story idea. The other, a lovely work by Brad Holland, depicted a man of about 35 releasing a snake at least fifteen feet long from a beautiful ceramic jug against a sleek featureless background of hills and *meadows. I liked it very much. But why was that suburban-looking guy pouring a snake out of a jug?*

The old craftsman's rule about writing stories around illustrations is that only a dolt tries to use the picture in any literal way. The idea always is to take it as metaphor, as analogy, as something other than what it purports to be. With the usual inexplicable swiftness of the old pro I saw that snake-as-telepathic-image was more likely to generate an interesting science-fiction story than snake-as-snake, and off I went. By the end of the month I had my story.

Alice was no easy editor to deal with. She came back at me a couple of weeks later with requests for cuts in the middle of the story, some retuning of the dialog, and a restructuring of my pattern of snake/ocean symbolism. As usual, I put up a fight over some things (mainly the dialog changes), made some of the cuts she wanted, and beefed up one erotic passage, not because Playboy necessarily insisted that its stories contain a lot of sexy stuff but because she thought the story lacked vigor just where it needed it most and I agreed. She yielded where I could defend my choices and I yielded where her criticisms seemed apt, which was most of the time. Her ideas about the symbolic substructure, for example, were right on target and I rearranged things slightly and sent her an insert to use midway through the story. Thus "Snake and Ocean" went through what by now had become the familiar knock-down-drag-out dialectic process by which Alice and I got most of my stories for her into final shape, and it duly appeared in the June 1984 issue of Playboy.

Alice had one last revision up her sleeve. When she printed the story she changed the title to "The Affair." She was a terrific editor, but she wasn't infallible. Whenever I've used the story in a collection of mine, I've kept all the textual changes she proposed, but I've reverted to my original title. You be the judge.

He found her by accident, the way it usually happens, after he had more or less given up searching. For years he had been sending out impulses like messages in bottles, random waves of telepathic energy, *Hello, hello, hello,* one forlorn SOS after another from the desert isle of the soul on which he was a castaway. Occasionally messages came back, but all they amounted to was lunacy, strident nonsense, static, spiritual noise, gabble up and down the mind band. There were, he knew, a good many like him out there—a boy in Topeka, an old woman in Buenos Aires, another one in Fort Lauderdale, someone of indeterminate sex in Manitoba, and plenty of others, each alone, each lonely. He fell into short-lived contact with them, because they were, after all, people of his special kind. But they tended to be cranky, warped, weird, often simply crazy, all of them deformed by their bizarre gift, and they could not give him what he wanted, which was communion, harmony, the marriage of true minds. Then one Thursday afternoon when he was absentmind-edly broadcasting his identity wave, not in any way purposefully trolling the seas of perception but only humming, so to speak, he felt a sudden startling click, as of perfectly machined parts locking into place. Out of the grayness in his mind an unmistakably warm, eager image blossomed, a dazzling giant yellow flower unfolding on the limb of a gnarled spiny cactus, and the image translated itself instantly into *Hi there. Where've you been all my life?*

He hesitated to send an answering signal, because he knew that he had found what he was looking for and he was aware how much of a threat that was to the fabric of the life he had constructed for himself. He was thirty-seven years old, stable, settled. He had a wife who tried her best to be wonderful for him, never knowing quite what it was that she lacked but seeking to compensate for it anyway, and two small pleasing children who had not inherited his abnormality, and a com-fortable house in the hills east of San Francisco, and a comfortable job as an analyst for one of the big brokerage houses. It was not the life he had imagined in his old romantic fantasies, but it was not a bad life, either, and it was *his* life, familiar and in its way rewarding; and he knew he was about to rip an irreparable hole in it. So he hesitated. And then he transmitted an image as vivid as the one he had received: a soli-tary white gull soaring in enormous sweeps over the broad blue breast of the Pacific.

The reply came at once: the same gull, joined by a second one that swooped out of a cloudless sky and flew tirelessly at its side. He knew that if he responded to that, there could be no turning back, but that was all right. With uncharacteristic recklessness he switched to the verbal mode.

—Okay. Who are you?

—Laurel Hammett. I'm in Phoenix. I read you clearly. This is better than telephone.

—Cheaper, too. Chris Maitland. San Francisco.

—That's far enough away, I guess.

He didn't understand, then, what she meant by that. But he let the point pass.

—You're the first one I've found who sends images, Laurel.

—I found one once, eight years ago, in Boston. But he was crazy. Most of us are crazy, Chris.

—I'm not crazy.

—Oh, I know! Oh, God, I know!

So that was the beginning. He got very little work done that afternoon. He was supposed to be preparing a report on oil royalty trusts, and after fifteen minutes of zinging interchanges with her he actually did beg off; she broke contact with a dazzling series of visuals, many of them cryptic, snowflakes and geometrical diagrams and fields of blazing red poppies. Depletion percentages and windfall-profits tax recapture were impossible to deal with while those brilliant pictures burned in his mind. Although he had promised not to reach toward her again until tomorrow—judicious self-denial, she observed, is the fuel of love—he finally did send out a flicker of abashed energy, and drew from her a mingling of irritation and delight. For five minutes they told each other it was best to go slow, to let it develop gradually, and again they vowed to keep mental silence until the next day. But when he was crossing the Bay Bridge a couple of hours later, heading for home, she tickled him suddenly with a quick flash of her presence and gave him a wondrous view of the Arizona sunset, harsh chocolate-brown hills under a purple-and-gold sky. That evening he felt shamefully and transparently adulterous, as if he had come home flushed and rumpled, with lipstick on his shirt. He pretended to be edgy and wearied by some fictitious episode of office politics, and helped himself to two drinks before dinner, and was more than usually curious about the details of his wife's day, the little suburban crises, the small challenges, the tiny triumphs. Jan was playful, amiable, almost kittenish. That told him she had not seen through him to the betrayal within, however blatant it seemed to him. She was no actress; there was nothing devious about her.

The transformation of their marriage that had taken place that afternoon saddened him, and yet not deeply, because it was an inevitable one. He and Jan were not really of the same species. He had loved her as well and honestly as was possible for him, but what he had really wanted was someone of his kind, with whom he could join mind and soul as well as body, and it was only because he had not been able to find her that he had settled for Jan. And now he had found her. Where that would lead, and what it meant for Jan and him, he had no idea yet. Possibly he would be able to go on sharing with her the part of his life that they were able to share, while secretly he got from the other woman those things that Jan had never been able to give him: possibly. When they went to bed he turned to her with abrupt passionate ferocity, as he had not for a long time, but even so he could not help wondering what Laurel was doing now, in her bed a thousand miles to the east, and with whom.

During the morning commute Laurel came to him with stunning images of desert landscapes, eroded geological strata, mysterious dark mesas, distant flame-colored sandstone walls. He sent her Pacific surf, cypresses bending to the wind, tidepools swarming with anemones and red starfish. Then, timidly, he sent her a kiss, and had one from her in return, and then, as he was crossing the toll plaza of the bridge, she shifted to words.

—What do you do?

—Securities analyst. I read reports and make forecasts.

—Sounds terribly dull. Is it?

—If it is, I don't let myself notice. It's okay work. What about you?

—I'm a potter. I'm a very good one. You'd like my stuff.

—Where can I see it?

—There's a gallery in Santa Fe. And one in Tucson. And of course Phoenix. But you mustn't come to Phoenix.

—Are you married?

There was a pause.

—Yes. But that isn't why you mustn't come here.

—I'm married, too.

—I thought you were. You feel like a married sort of man.

—Oh? I do?

—That isn't an insult. You have a very stable vibe, do you know what I mean?

—I think so. Do you have children?

—No. Do you?

—Two. Little girls. How long have you been married, Laurel?

—Six years.

—Nine.

—We must be about the same age.

—I'm thirty-seven.

—I'm thirty-four.

—Close enough. Do you want to know my sign?

—Not really.

She laughed and sent him a complex, awesome image: the entire wheel of the Zodiac, which flowered into the shape of the Aztec calendar stone, which became the glowing rose window of a Gothic cathedral. An undercurrent of warmth and love and amusement rode with it. Then she was gone, leaving him on the bridge in a silence so sharp it rang like iron.

He did not reach toward her, but drove on into the city in a mellow haze, wondering what she looked like. Her mental "voice" sounded to him like that of a tall, clear-eyed, straight-backed woman with long, brown hair, but he knew better than to put much faith in that; he had played the same game with people's telephone voices and he had always been wrong. For all he knew, Laurel was squat and greasy. He doubted that; he saw no way that she could be ugly. But why, then, was she so determined not to have him come to Phoenix? Perhaps she was an invalid; perhaps she was painfully shy; perhaps she feared the intrusion of any sort of reality into their long-distance romance.

At lunchtime he tuned himself to her wavelength and sent her an image of the first page of the report he had written last week on Exxon. She replied with a glimpse of a tall olive-hued porcelain jar, of a form both elegant and sturdy at once. Her work in exchange for his: he liked that. It meant they had the same sense of humor. Everything was going to be perfect.

A week later he went out to Salt Lake City for a couple of days to do some field research on a mining company headquartered there. He took an early-morning flight, had lunch with three earnest young Mormon executives overflowing with joy at the bounty of God as manifested by the mineral wealth of the Overthrust Belt in Wyoming, spent the afternoon leafing through geologists' survey sheets, and had dinner alone at his hotel. Afterward he put in his obligatory call to Jan, worked up his notes of the day's conferences, and watched TV for an hour, hoping it would make him drowsy. Maitland didn't mind these business trips, but he slept badly when he slept alone, and any sort of time-zone change, even a trifling one like this, disrupted his internal clock. He was still wide awake when he got into bed about eleven.

He thought of Laurel. He felt very near to her, out here in this spacious mountain-ringed city with the wide bland streets. Probably Salt Lake City was not significantly closer to Phoenix than San Francisco was, but he regarded Utah and Arizona both as the true Wild West, while his own suburban and manicured part of California, paradoxically, did not seem western to him at all. Somewhere due south of here, just on the far side of all these cliffs and canyons, was the unknown woman he loved.

As though on cue, she was in his mind:

—Lonely?

—You bet.

—I've been thinking of you all day. Poor Chris: sitting around with those businessmen, talking all that depletion gibberish.

—I'm a businessman, too.

—You're different, love. You're a businessman outside and a freak inside.

—Don't say that.

—It's what we are, Chris. Face it. Flukes, anomalies, sports, changelings—

—Please stop, Laurel. Please.

—I'm sorry.

A silence. He thought she was gone, taking flight at his rebuke. But then:

—Are you *very* lonely?

—Very. Dull empty city, dull empty bed.

—*You're* in it.

—But you aren't.

—Is that what you want? Right now?

—I wish we could, Laurel.

—Let's try this.

He felt a sudden astounding intensifying of her mental signal, as if she had leaped the hundreds of miles and lay curled against him here. There was a sense of physical proximity, of warmth, even the light perfume of her skin, and into his mind swept an image so acutely clear that it eclipsed for him the drab realities of his room: the shore of a tropical ocean, fine pink sand, gentle pale-green water, a dense line of heavy-crowned palms.

—Go on, Chris. Into the water.

He waded into the calm wavelets until the delicate sandy bottom was far below his dangling feet and he floated effortlessly in an all-encompassing warmth, in an amniotic bath of placid soothing fluid. Placid but not motionless, for he felt, as he drifted, tiny convulsive quivers about him, an electric oceanic caress, pulsations of the water against his bare skin, intimate, tender, searching. He began to tingle. As he moved farther out from shore, so far now that the land was gone and the world was all warm water to the horizon, the pressure of those rhythmic pulsations became more forceful, deeply pleasurable: the ocean was a giant hand lightly squeezing him. He trembled and made soft sighing sounds that grew steadily more vehement, and closed his eyes, and let ecstasy overwhelm him in the ocean's benignly insistent grip. Then he grunted and his heart thumped and his body went rigid and then lax, and moments later he sat up, blinking, astonished, eerily tranquil.

—I didn't think anything like that was possible.

—For us anything's possible. Even sex across seven hundred miles. I wasn't sure it would work, but I guess it did, didn't it? Did you like it?

—Do you need an answer, Laurel?

—I feel so happy.

—How did you do it? What was the trick?

—No trick. Just the usual trick, Chris, a little more intense than usual. And a lot of love. I hated the idea that you were all alone, horny, unable to sleep.

—It was absolutely marvelous.

—And now we're lovers. Even though we've never met.

—No. Not altogether lovers, not yet. Let me try to do it to you, Laurel. It's only fair.

—Later, okay? Not now.

—I want to.

—It takes a lot of energy. You ought to get some sleep, and I can wait. Just lie there and glow and don't worry about me. You can try it with me another time.

—An hour? Two hours?

—Whenever you want. But not now. Rest, now. Enjoy. Good night, love.

—Good night, Laurel.

He was alone. He lay staring up into the darkness, stunned. He had been unfaithful to Jan three times before, not bad for nine years, and always the same innocuous pattern: a business trip far from home, a couple of solitary nights, then an official dinner with some woman executive, too many drinks, the usual half-serious banter turning serious, a blurry one-night stand, remorse in the morning, and never any follow-up. Meaningless, fragmentary stuff. But this—this long-distance event with a woman he had never even seen—this seemed infinitely more explosive. For he had the power and Jan did not and Laurel did; and Jan's mind was closed to his and his to hers, and they could only stagger around blindly trying to find one another, while he and Laurel could unite at will in a communion whose richness was unknown to ordinary humans. He wondered if he could go on living with Jan at all now. He felt no less love for her than before, and powerful ties of affection and sharing held him to her; but yet—even so—

In guilt and confusion Maitland drifted off into sleep. It was still dark when he woke—3:13 a.m., said the clock on the dresser—and he felt different guilt, different confusion, for it was of Laurel now that he thought. He had taken pleasure from her and then he had collapsed into postorgasmic stupor. Never mind that she had told him to do just that. He felt, and always had, a peculiarly puritanical obligation to give pleasure for pleasure, and unpaid debts were troublesome to him. Taking a deep breath, he sent strands of consciousness through the night toward the south, over the fire-hued mountains of central Utah, over the silent splendor of the Grand Canyon, down past the palm trees into torrid Phoenix, and touched Laurel's warm sleepy mind.

—Hnhh.

—It's me. I want to, now.

—All right. Yes.

The image she had chosen was a warm sea, the great mother, the all-encompassing womb. He, reaching unhesitatingly for a male equivalent, sent her a vision of himself coming forth on a hot dry summer day into a quiet landscape of grassy hills round as tawny breasts. Cradled in his arms he held the gleaming porcelain jar that she had showed him last week, and he bent, tipping it, pouring forth from it an enormous snake, long and powerful but not in any way frightening, that flowed like a dark rivulet across the land, seeking her, finding, gliding up across her thighs, her belly. Too obvious? Too coarsely phallic? He wavered for a moment, but only a moment, for he heard her moan and whimper, and she reached with her mind for the serpent as it seemed he was withdrawing it; he drove back his qualms and gave her all the energy at his command, seizing the initiative as he sensed her complete surrender. Her signal shivered and lost focus. Her breathing grew ragged and hoarse, and then into his mind came a quick surprising sound, a strange low growling, that terminated in a swift sharp gasp.

—Oh, love. Oh. Oh. Thank you.

—It wasn't scary?

—Scare me like that as often as you want, Chris.

He smiled across the darkness of the miles. All was well. A fair exchange: symbol for symbol, metaphor for metaphor, delight for delight.

—Sleep well, Laurel.

—You too, love. Mmm.

This time Jan knew that something had happened while he was away. He saw it on her face, which meant that she saw it on his; but she voiced no suspicions, and when they made love the first night of his return it was as good as ever. Was it possible, he wondered, to be bigamous like this, to take part with Laurel in a literally superhuman oneness while remaining Jan's devoted husband and companion? He would, at any rate, try. Laurel had shared his soul as no one ever had and Jan never could, but yet she was a phantom, faceless, remote, scarcely real; and Jan, cut off from him as most humans are from all others, nevertheless was his wife, his partner, his bedmate, the mother of his children. He would try.

So he brought the office gossip home to her as always and went out with her twice a week to the restaurants they loved and sat beside her at night watching cassettes of operas and movies and Shakespeare, and on weekends they did their weekend things, boating on the bay and tennis and picnics in the park and dinner with their friends, and everything was fine. Everything was very fine. And yet he managed to do the other thing, too, as often as he could: snake and ocean, ocean and snake. Just as he had successfully hidden from Jan the enigmatic secret mechanism within his mind that he did not dare reveal to anyone not of his sort, so, too, now did he hide the second marriage, rich and strange; that that mechanism had brought him.

His lovemaking with Laurel had to be furtive, of course, a thing of stolen moments. She could hardly draw him into that warm voluptuous ocean while he lay beside Jan. But there were the business trips—he was careful not to increase their frequency, which would have been suspicious, but she came to him every night while he was away—and there was the occasional Saturday afternoon when he lay drowsing in the sun of the garden and found that whispering transparent surf beckoning to him, and once she enlivened a lunchtime for him on a working day. He roused the snake within his soul as often as he dared and nearly always she accepted it, though there were times when she told him no, not now, the moment was wrong. They had elaborate signals to indicate a clear coast. And for the ordinary conversation of the day there were no limits; they popped into each other's consciousness a thousand times a day, quick flickering interchanges, a joke, a bit of news, a job triumphantly accomplished, an image of beauty too potent to withhold. Crossing the bridge, entering his office, reaching for the telephone, unfolding a napkin—suddenly, there she was, often for the briefest flare of contact, a tag touch and gone. He loved that. He loved her. It was a marriage.

He snooped in Mountain Bell directories at the library and found her telephone number, which he hardly needed, and her address, which at least confirmed that she really did exist in tangible actual Phoenix. He manufactured a trip to Albuquerque to appraise the earnings prospects of a small electronics company and slipped off up the freeway to Santa Fe to visit the gallery that showed her pottery: eight or ten superb pieces, sleek, wondrously skilled. He bought one of the smaller ones. "You don't have any information about the artist, do you?" he asked the proprietor, trying to be casual, heart pounding, hoping to be shown a photograph. The proprietor thought there might be a press release in the files, and rummaged for it. "She lives down Phoenix way," she said. "Comes up here once or twice a year with her new work. I think it's museum quality, don't you?" But she could not find the press release. When Laurel flashed into his mind that night back in Albuquerque, he did not tell her he owned one of her vases or that he had been researching her. But he wondered desperately what she looked like. He played with the idea of visiting Phoenix and somehow getting to meet her without telling her who he was. So long as he kept his mind sheathed she would never know, he thought. But it seemed sneaky and treacherous; and it might be dangerous, too. She had told him often enough not to come to her city.

In the fourth month of their relationship he could no longer control his curiosity. She sent him a view of her studio. amazingly neat, the clay, the wheels, the kiln, the little bowls of pigment and glaze all fastidiously in their proper places.

—You left one thing out, Laurel.

—What's that?

—The potter herself. You didn't show me her.

—Oh, Chris.

—What's the matter? Aren't you ever curious about what I look like? We've been all over each other's minds and bodies for months, and I still don't have any idea what you look like. That's absurd.

—It's so much more abstract and pure this way.

—Wonderful. Abstract love! Save that for Swinburne. I want to see you.

—I have to confess. I want to see you, too.

—Here, then. Now.

He sent her, before she could demur, a mental snapshot of his face, trying not to retouch and enhance it. The nose a trifle too long, the cleft chin absurdly Hollywood, the dark hair thinning a bit at the part line. Not a perfect face, but good enough, pleasant, honest, nothing to apologize for, he thought. It brought silence.

—Well? Am I remotely what you expected?

—Exactly, Chris. Steady-looking, strong, decent—no surprise at all. I like your face. I'm very pleased.

—Your turn.

—You'll promise not to be disappointed?

—Stop being silly.

—All right.

She flared in his mind, not just her face but all of her, long-legged, broad-shouldered, a woman of physical presence and strength, with straightforward open features, wide-set brown eyes, a good smile, blunt nose, conspicuous cheekbones. She was not far from the woman he had imagined, and one aspect, the dark thick straight hair falling past her shoulders, was amazingly as he had thought.

—You're beautiful.

—No, not really. But I'm okay.

—Are you an Indian?

—I must have sent you a good picture, then. I'm half. My mother was Navaho.

—You learned your pottery from her?

—No, dopy. Navahos make rugs. Pueblos make pottery. I learned mine in New York, Greenwich Village. I studied with Hideki Shinoda.

—Doesn't sound Pueblo.

—Isn't. Little Japanese man with marvelous hands.

—I'm glad we did this, Laurel.

—So am I.

But seeing her in the eye of his mind, while gratifying one curiosity, had only intensified another. He wanted to meet her. He wanted to touch her. He wanted to hold her.

Snake. Ocean. They were practiced lovers now, a year of constant mental communion behind them. The novelty was gone, but not the excitement. Again and again he carried the porcelain bowl out to the sun-baked hills and poured the serpent into the grass and sent it gliding toward her eager body. Again and again she surrounded him with buoyant warm sea. Their skill at pleasuring one another struck them both as extraordinary. Of course, they soon began varying the imageries of delight, so that no monotony would taint their embraces. She came to him as a starfish, thousands of tiny suction-cup feet and a startling devouring mouth, and at another time as a moist voluptuous mass of warm smooth white clay, and as a whirlpool, and as a great coy lighthearted amoeba; and he manifested himself to her as a flash flood roaring down a red-rock canyon, and as a glistening vine coiling through a tropic night, and as a spaceship plunging in eternal free-fall between worlds. All of these were effective, for they needed only to touch one another with their minds to bring pleasure; and each new access of ingenuity brought an abstract pleasure of its own. But even so they tended often to revert to the original modes, snake and ocean, ocean and snake, the way one might return to a familiar and modest hotel where one spent a joyous weekend at the beginning of an affair, and somehow it was always best that way. They liked to tell each other that the kind of lovemaking they had invented and of which they were perhaps the sole practitioners in the history of humanity was infinitely superior to the old-fashioned type, which was so blatant, so obvious, so coarse, so messy. Even so, even as he said things like that, he knew he was lying. He wanted her skin against his skin, her breath on his breath.

She was no longer so coy about her life outside their relationship. Maitland knew now that her husband was an artist from Chicago, not very successful, a little envious of her career. She showed him some of his work, unremarkable abstract-expressionist stuff. Maitland was jealous of the fact that this man—Tim, his name was—shared her bed and enjoyed her proximity, but he realized that he had no jealousy of the marriage itself. It was all right that she was married. Maitland had no wish to live with her. He wanted to go on living with Jan, to play tennis with her and go to restaurants with her and even to make love with her; what he wanted from Laurel was just what he was getting from her, that cool amused intelligent voice in his mind, and now and then the strange ecstasy that her playful spirit was able to kindle in his loins across such great distances. That much was true. Yet also he wanted to be her lover in the old blatant obvious coarse messy way, at least once, once at least. Because he knew it was a perilous subject, he stayed away from it as long as he could, but at last it broke into the open one night in Seattle, late, after the snake had returned to its jar and the lapping waves had retreated and he lay sweaty and alone in his hotel-room bed.

—When are we finally going to meet?

—Please, Chris.

—I think it's time to discuss it. You told me a couple of times, early on, that I must never come to Phoenix. Okay. But couldn't we get together somewhere else? Tucson, San Diego, the Grand Canyon?

—It isn't the place that matters.

—What is it, then?

—Being close. Being too close.

—I don't understand. We're so close already!

—I mean physically close, Not emotionally, not even sexually. I just mean that if we came within close range of each other we'd do bad things to each other.

—That's crazy, Laurel.

—Have you ever been close to another telepath? As close as ten feet, say?

—I don't think so.

—You'd know it if you had. When you and I talk, long distance, it's just talking on the phone, right, plus pictures? We tell each other only what we it to tell each other, and nothing else gets through. It's not like that close up.

—Oh?

—There's a kind of radiation, an aura. We broadcast all sorts of stuff automatically. All that foul stinking nasty cesspool stuff that's at the bottom of everybody's mind, the crazy prehistoric garbage that's in us. It comes swarming out like a shriek.

—How do you know that?

—I've experienced it.

—Oh. Boston, years ago?

—Yes. Yes. I told you, I did this once before.

—But he was crazy, you said.

—In a way. But the craziness isn't what brought the other stuff up. I felt it another time, too, and *she* wasn't crazy. Its unavoidable.

—I want to see you.

—Don't you think I want to see you, too, Chris? You think I think snake and ocean's really good enough? But we can't risk it. Suppose we met, and the garbage got out, and we hated each other ever afterward?

—We could control it.

—Maybe. Maybe not.

—Or else we could make allowances for it. Bring ourselves to understand that this stuff, whatever it is that you say is there, is normal, just the gunk of the mind, nothing personal, nothing that we ought to take seriously.

—I'm scared. Let's not try.

He let the issue drop. When it came up again, four months later, it was Laurel who revived it. She had been thinking about his idea of controlling the sinister emanation, throttling it back, shielding one another. Possibly it could be done. The temptation to meet him in the flesh, she said, was overwhelming. Perhaps they could get together and suppress all telepathic contact, meet just like ordinary humans having a little illicit rendezvous, keep their minds rigidly walled off, and that way at last consummate the intimacy that had joined their to souls for a year and a half.

—I'd love to, Laurel.

—But promise me this. Swear it to me. When we do get together, if we can't hold back the bad stuff, if we feel it coming out, that we go away from each other instantly. That we don't negotiate, we don't try to work it out, we don't look for angles—we just split, fast, if either of us says we have to. Swear?

—I swear.

❁

He flew to Denver and spent a fidgety hour and a half having cocktails in the lounge at the Brown Palace. Her flight from Phoenix was supposed to have landed only half an hour after his, and he wondered if she had backed out at the last minute. He got up to call the airport when he saw her come in, unmistakably her, taller than he expected, a big handsome woman in black jeans and a sheepskin wrap. There were flecks of melting snow in her hair.

He sensed an aura.

It wasn't loathsome, it wasn't hideous, but it was there, a kind of dull whining grinding thing as of improperly oiled machinery in use three blocks away. Even as he detected it, he felt it diminish until it was barely perceptible. He struggled to rein in whatever output he might be giving off himself.

She saw him and came straight toward him, smiling nervously, cheeks rigid, eyes worried.

"Chris."

He took her hand in his. "You're cold, Laurel."

"It's snowing. That's why I'm late. I haven't seen snow in years."

"Can I get you a drink?"

"No. Yes. Yes, please. Scotch on the rocks."

"Are you picking up anything bad?"

"No," she said. "Not really. There was just a little twinge, when I walked in—a kind of squeak in my mind."

"I felt it, too. But then it faded."

"I'm fighting to keep it damped down. I want this to work."

"So do I. We mustn't use the power at all today."

"We don't need to. The old snake can have the day off. Are you scared?"

"A little."

"Me, too." She gulped her drink. "Oh, Chris."

"Is it hard work, keeping the power damped down?"

"Yes. It really is."

"For me, too. But we have to."

"Yes," she said. "Do you have a room yet?"

He nodded.

"Let's go upstairs, then."

Like any unfaithful husband having his first rendezvous with a new lover he walked stiffly and somberly through the lobby, convinced that everyone was staring at them. That was ridiculous, he knew. They were more truly married, in their way, than anybody else in Denver. But yet—but yet—

They were silent in the elevator. As they approached their floor the aura of her burst forth again, briefly, a fast sour vibration in his bones, and then it was gone altogether, shut off as though by a switch. He worked at holding his down, too. She smiled at him. He winked. "To the left," he said. They went into the room. Heavy snowflakes splashed against the window; the wide bed was turned down. She was trembling. "Come on," he said. "I love you. You know that. Everything's all right."

They kissed and undressed. Her body was lean, athletic, with small high breasts, a flat belly, a dark appendectomy scar. He drew her toward the bed. It seemed strange, almost perverse, to be doing things in this antiquated fleshly way, no snake, no ocean, no meeting of minds. He was afraid for a moment that in the excitement of their coupling they would lose control of their mental barriers and let their inner selves come flooding out, fierce, intense, a contact too powerful to handle at such short range. But there was no loss of control. He kept the power locked behind the walls of his skull; she did the same; there were only the tiniest leakages of current. But there was no excitement, either, in their lovemaking.

He ran his hands over her breasts and trapped her nipples between his fingers, and gently parted her thighs with his knee, and pressed himself against her as though he had not been with a woman in a year, but the excitement seemed to be all in his head, not in his nerve endings. Even when she ran her lips down his chest and belly and teased him for a moment and then took him fiercely and suddenly in her mouth, it was the *idea* that they were finally doing this, rather than what they were actually doing, that resonated with him. They sighed a little and moaned a little and finally he slipped into her, admiring the tightness of her and the rhythms of her hips and all that, but nevertheless it was as though this had happened between them a thousand times before: he moved, she moved, they did all the standard things and traveled along to the standard result. Not enough was real between them, that was the trouble. He knew her better than he had ever known anyone, and yet in some ways he knew her not at all, and that was what had spoiled things. That, and holding so much in check. He wished he could look into her mind now. But that was forbidden, and probably unwise, too; he guessed that she was annoyed with him for having insisted on this foolish and foredoomed meeting, that she held him responsible for having spoiled things between them, and he did not want to see those thoughts in her mind.

When it was over they whispered to each other and stroked each other and gave each other little nibbling kisses, and he pretended it had been marvelous, but his real impulse was to pull away and light a cigarette and stare out the window at the snow, and he wasn't even a smoker. It was simply the way he felt. It bad been only a mechanical thing, only a hotel-room screw, not remotely anything like snake and ocean: a joining of flesh of the sort that a pair of rabbits might have accomplished, or a pair of apes, without content, without fire, without joy. He and she knew an ever so much better way of doing it.

He took care to hide his disappointment.

"I'm so glad I came here, Chris," she said, smiling, kissing him, taking care to hide her disappointment, too, he guessed. He knew that if he entered her mind he would find it bleak and ashen. But of course he could not do that. "I wish I could stay the night," she said. "My plane's at nine. We could have dinner downstairs, though."

"Is it a terrible strain, keeping the power back?"

"It isn't easy."

"No. It isn't."

"I'm so glad we did this, Chris."

"Are you?"

"Yes. Yes. Of course."

They had an early dinner. The snow had stopped by the time he saw her to her cab. So: you fly up to Denver for a couple of hours of lust and steak, you fly back home, and that's that. He had a brandy is the lounge and went to his room. For a long while he lay staring at the ceiling, sure that she would come to him with the ocean, and make amends for the unsatisfactory thing they had done that afternoon. She did not. He wondered if he ought to send her the snake as she dozed on her plane, and did not want to. He felt timid about any sort of contact with her now. It had all been a terrible mistake, he knew. Not because of that emanation from the dirty depths of the psyche that she had so feared, but only because it had been so anticlimactic, so meaningless. He waited for a sending from her, some bright little flash out of Arizona. She must surely be home now. Nothing came. He went on waiting, not daring to reach toward her, and finally he fell asleep.

Jan said nothing to him about the Denver trip. He was moody and strange, but she let him be. When the silence out of Phoenix continued into the next day and the next he grew even more grim, and skulked about wrapped in black isolation. Gradually it occurred to him that he was not going to hear from Laurel again, that they had broken something in that hotel room in Denver and that it was irreparable, and, oddly, the knowledge of that gave him some ease: if he did not expect to hear from her, he did not have to lament her silence. A week, two, three, and nothing. So it was over. That hollow little grunting hour had ruined it.

Somehow he picked up the rhythms of his life: work, home, wife, kids, friends, tennis, dinner. He did an extensive analysis of southwestern electric utilities that brought him a commendation from on high, and he felt only a mild twinge of anguish while doing his discussion of the prospects for Arizona Public Service as reflected in the municipal growth of the city of Phoenix. He missed the little tickle in his mind immensely, but he was encapsulating it, containing it, and after a fashion he was healing.

One day a month and a half later he found himself idly scanning the mindnoise band again, as he had not done for a long while, just to see who else was out there. He picked up the loony babble out of Fort Lauderdale and the epicene static from Manitoba, and then he encountered someone new, a bright dear signal as intense as Laurel's, and for a dazzled instant a sudden fantasy of a new relationship blossomed in him, but then he heard the nonsense syllables, the slow, firm, strong-willed stream of gibberish. There were no replacements for Laurel.

In Chicago, where he had been sent to do a survey of natural-gas companies, he began talking to a youngish woman at the Art Institute, and by easy stages some chatter about Monet and Sisley turned into a dinner invitation and a night in his hotel room. That was all right. Certainly it was simpler and easier and less depressing than Denver. But it was a bore, it was empty and foolish, and he regretted it deeply by breakfast time, even while he was taking down her number and promising to call the next time he was in the Midwest. Maitland saw the post- Laurel pattern of his life closing about him now: the Christmas bonus, the trip to Hawaii with Jan, braces for the kids, the new house five years from now, the occasional quickie romance in far-off hotel rooms. That was all right. That was the original bargain he had made, long ago, entering adult life: not much ecstasy, not much grief.

On the long flight home that day he thought without rancor or distress about his year and a half with Laurel, and told himself that the important thing was not that it had ended but that it had happened at all. He felt peaceful and accepting, and was almost tempted to reach out toward Laurel and thank her for her love, and wish her well. But he was afraid—afraid that if he touched her mind in any way she would pull away, timid, fearful of contact in the wake of that inexplicably sundering day in Denver. She was close by now, he knew, for the captain had just told them that they were passing over the Grand Canyon. Maitland did not lean to the window, as everyone else was doing, to look down. He sat back, eyes closed, tired, calm.

And felt warmth, heard the lapping of surf, saw in the center of his mind the vast ocean in which Laurel had so many times engulfed him. Really? Was it happening? He let himself slide into it. A little flustered, he hid himself behind a facade of newspapers, the *Tribune,* the *Wall Street Journal.* His face grew flushed. His breathing became rougher. Ah. Ah. It was happening, yes, she had reached to him, she had made the gesture at last. Tears of gratitude and relief came to him, and he let her sweep him off to a sharp and pounding fulfillment five miles above Arizona.

—Hello, Chris.

—Laurel.

—Did you mind? I felt you near me, and I couldn't hold back any more. I know you don't want to hear from me, but—

—What gave you that idea?

—I thought—it seemed to me—

—No. I thought you were the one who wanted to break it up.

—I? I missed you so much, Chris. But I was sure you'd pull away.

—So was I, about you.

—Silly.

—Laurel. Laurel. I'm so glad you took the chance, then.

—So am I.

—Let me have the snake, Chris.

—Yes. Yes,

He stepped out into the tawny sun-baked hills with the heavy porcelain jar and tipped it, and let the snake glide toward her. It was all right after all. They had made mistakes, but they were the mistakes of too much love, and they had survived them. It was going to be all right: snake and ocean, ocean and snake, now and always.

THE CHANGELING

Mysterious Mexico, again. It is a country I have visited many times: its mixture of tropical sunlight and eerie pre-Columbian darkness is endlessly fascinating to me. I went there in March of 1982 to wander around amidst the ancient stone monuments of Tenochtitlan and Oaxaca and to revel in the multitude of weird succulent plants. Soon after my return, George Scithers of Amazing Stories *asked me for a new short story, and when I told him what such slick magazines as* Playboy *and* Omni *were currently paying me, he unhesitatingly offered me a price matching theirs. (It was a heady time for some of us, then!) A few days later the great science fiction writer Philip K. Dick, whom I had known very well, died. With my head full of the strangeness of Mexico, I sat down and wrote a story which, while not at all done in the Philip K. Dick style, played with reality somewhat in the fashion that Dick had made his specialty, and I dedicated it to him. Scithers ran it in his November, 1982 issue.*

In Memoriam: PKD

Just as the startling facade of the Temple of Quetzalcoatl came into view on the far side of the small pyramid, Hilgard felt a sudden touch of vertigo and swayed for a moment, as though a little earthquake had

379

rippled through the Teotihuacan archeological zone. He leaned against a railing until the worst of the queasiness and confusion had passed. The heat? The altitude? Last night's fiery dinner exacting its price? Down here in Mexico a tourist learned to expect that some kind of internal upset could strike at any time.

But the discomfort vanished as quickly as it had come, and Hilgard looked up in awe, at the great stone staircase of the temple. The jutting heads of the feathered serpents burst like the snouts of dinosaurs from the massive blocks. Traces of the original frescoes, perhaps fifteen hundred years old, glinted here and there. Hilgard took eight or nine photos. But he was too hot and dusty and weary to explore the wondrous building with any real vigor, and he still felt a little shaky from that dizzy spell a moment ago. The pressure of time was on him also: he had promised to meet his driver at two o'clock at the main parking lot for the return trip to Mexico City. It was nearly two now, and the parking area was at least a mile to the north, along the searing, shadeless thoroughfare known as the Avenue of the Dead. He wished now that he had started his tour here at the awesome Quetzalcoatl Temple instead of consuming his morning's energy scrambling around on the two huge pyramids at the other end.

Too late to do anything about that. Hilgard trudged quickly toward the parking lot, pausing only to buy a tepid beer from a vendor midway along the path. By quarter past two he was in the lot, sweaty and puffing. There was no sign of his driver and the battered black cab. Still at lunch, probably, Hilgard thought, relieved at not having to feel guilty about his own tardiness but annoyed by yet another example of Mexican punctuality. Well, now he had time to get a few more shots of the Pyramid of the Sun while he waited, and maybe—

"Señor? Señor!"

Hilgard turned. A driver—not his—had emerged from a shiny little Volkswagen cab and was waving to him.

"Your wife, señor, she will be here in two more minutes. She is taking more pictures on the top of the big pyramid, and she says to please wait, she will not be long."

"I think you want someone else," Hilgard said.

The driver looked baffled. "But you are her husband, señor."

"Sorry. I am not anybody's husband."

"Is a joke? I am not understanding." The driver grinned uncertainly. "A blonde woman, dark glasses. I pick you and she up in front of the

Hotel Century, Zona Rosa, ten o'clock this morning, you remember? She said to me, ten minutes ago, tell my husband wait a little, I go take more pyramid pictures, just a few minutes. And—"

"I'm staying at the Hotel Presidente," Hilgard said. "I'm not married. I drove out here this morning in a black Ford cab. The driver's name was Chucho."

The Mexican's grin, earnest and ingratiating, stayed on his face, but it grew ragged, and something hostile came into his eyes, as though he was beginning to think he was being made the butt of some incomprehensible gringo prank. Slowly he said, "I know Chucho, yes. He took some American people down to Xochimilco this morning. Maybe he was your driver yesterday."

"He met me outside the Presidente. We arranged it last night. The fare was seventeen hundred pesos." Hilgard glanced around, wishing the man would show up before things got even more muddled. "You must be mistaking me for a different American. I'm traveling alone. I wouldn't mind meeting an interesting blonde, I guess, but I don't happen to be married to one, and I really am certain that you're not the driver I was with this morning. I'm very sorry if—"

"There is your wife, señor," said the Mexican coolly.

Hilgard turned. A trim, attractive woman in her late thirties, with short golden hair and an alert, open face, was making her way through the clutter of souvenir stands at the entrance to the parking area. "Ted!" she called. "Here I am!"

He stared blankly. He had never seen her before. As she drew closer he forced a smile and held it in a fixed and rigid way. But what was he supposed to say to her? He didn't even know her name. *Excuse me, ma'am, I'm not actually your husband.* Eh? Was there a television program, he wondered, that went to elaborate lengths to stage complicated hoaxes with hapless, unsuspecting victims, and was he at the center of it? Would they shower him with home appliances and cruise tickets once they were done bewildering him? *Pardon me, ma'am, but I'm not really Ted Hilgard. I'm just someone else of the same name and face.* Yes? No.

She came up to him and said, "You should have climbed it with me. You know what they've been doing up there for the past half hour? They're celebrating the spring equinox with some kind of Aztec rite. Incense, chanting, green boughs, two white doves in a cage that they just liberated. Fascinating stuff, and I got pictures of the whole thing. Hold this for me for a minute, will you?" she said casually, slipping her heavy camera bag from her shoulder and pushing it into his hands. "God, it's hot today! Did you have fun at the other temple? I just didn't feel like hiking all the way down there, but I hope I didn't miss—"

The driver, standing to one side, now said mildly, "It is getting late, Missus. We go back to the city now?"

"Yes. Of course." She tucked a stray shirttail back into her slacks, took the camera bag from Hilgard and followed the driver toward the Volkswagen cab. Hilgard, mystified, stayed where he was, scanning the parking lot hopelessly for Chucho and the old black Ford and trying to construct some plausible course of action. After a moment the blonde woman looked back, frowning, and said, "Ted? What's the matter?"

He made an inarticulate sound and fluttered his hands in confusion. Possibly, he told himself, he was having some sort of psychotic episode of fugue. Or perhaps that moment of dizziness at the Temple of Quetzalcoatl had in fact been a light stroke that had scrambled his memory. Could she really be his wife? He felt quite certain that he had been single all his life, except for those eight months a dozen years ago with Beverly. He could clearly envision his bachelor flat on Third Avenue, the three neat rooms, the paintings, the little cabinet of pre-Columbian statuettes. He saw himself at his favorite restaurants with his several lovers, Judith or Janet or Denise. This brisk, jaunty blonde woman fit nowhere into those images. But yet—yet—

He had no idea what to do. His fingers began to tremble and his feet felt like blocks of frozen mud, and he started to walk in a numbed, dazed way toward the Volkswagen. The driver, holding the door open for him, gave him the sort of venomous look of contempt that Hilgard imagined was generally given to gringos who were so drunk at midday that they were unable to remember they were married. But Hilgard was not drunk.

The woman chattered pleasantly as they zipped back toward Mexico City. Evidently they were planning to visit the Museum of Anthropology in Chapultepec Park that afternoon, and tomorrow morning they would move on either to Cuernavaca or Guadalajara, depending on which one of them won a low-keyed disagreement that had evidently been going on for several days. Hilgard faked his way through the conversation answering vaguely and remotely and eventually withdrawing from it altogether by pleading fatigue, a touch of the sun. Before long, gray tendrils of smog were drifting toward them: they were at the outskirts of Mexico City. In the relatively light Sunday traffic, the driver roared flamboyantly down the broad Paseo de la Reforma and cut sharply into the Zona Rosa district to deposit there in front of the slender black-and-white tower of the Hotel Century. "Give him a nice tip, darling," the woman said to Hilgard. "We've kept him out longer than we were supposed to."

Hilgard offered the glowering driver a pair of thousand-peso notes, waved away the change, and they went into the hotel. In the small lobby she said, "Get the key, will you? I'll ring for the elevator." Hilgard approached the desk and looked imploringly at the clerk, who said in fluent English, "Good afternoon, Mr. Hilgard. Did you find the pyramids interesting?" and handed him, without being asked, the key to room 177.

This is not happening. Hilgard told himself, thinking of his comfortable room on the seventh floor of the glossy Hotel Presidente. This is a dream. This is a hallucination. He joined the blonde woman in the elevator; she pressed 17 and it began to ascend slowly, pausing dismayingly for a fraction of a second between the tenth and eleventh floors as the power sagged. Room 177 was compact, efficient, with a semicircular double bed and a little bar unit stocked with miniature bottles of liquor, mixers, and such. The woman took a brandy from it and said to him, "Shall I get you a rum, Ted?"

"No. Thank you." He wandered the room. Feminine things all over the bathroom sink, makeup and lotions and whatnot. Matching his-and-hers luggage in the closet. A man's jacket and shirts hanging neatly—not his, but the sort of things he might have owned—a book on the night-table, the new Updike novel. He had read it a few months ago, but in some other edition, apparently, for this had a red jacket and he remembered it as blue.

"I'm going to grab a shower," she said. "Then we go out to get lunch and head over to the museum, okay?"

He looked up. She padded past him to the bathroom, naked; he had a sudden surprising glimpse of small round breasts and dimpled buttocks, and then the door closed. Hilgard waited until he heard the water running, and took her wallet from her open purse. In it he saw the usual credit cards, some travelers' checks, a thick wad of well-worn Mexican banknotes. And a driver's license: Celia Hilgard, thirty-six years old, five feet five, blond hair, blue eyes, 124 pounds, married. *Married.* An address on East 85th Street. A card in the front of the wallet declared that in case of emergency Theodore Hilgard was to be notified, either at the East 85th Street address or at the offices of Hilgard

& Hilgard on West 57th Street. Hilgard studied the card as though it were written in Sanskrit. His apartment was on East 62nd Street, his gallery two blocks south of it. He was sure of that. He could see himself quite sharply as he walked down Third every morning, glancing toward Bloomingdale's, turning east on 60th—

Two Ted Hilgards? With the same face?

"What are you looking for?" Celia asked, stepping from the bathroom and toweling herself dry.

Hilgard's cheeks reddened. Guiltily he tucked her wallet back in her purse. "Ah—just checking to see how many pesos you have left. I thought we might want to cash some travelers' checks when the banks open tomorrow."

"I cashed some on Friday. Don't you remember?"

"Slipped my mind, I guess."

"Do you want some of my pesos?"

"I've got enough for now," he said.

They had lunch at the hotel. For Hilgard it was like sitting across the table from a keg of dynamite. He was not yet ready to admit that he had gone insane, but very little that he could say to her was likely to make any sense, and eventually she was bound to challenge him. He felt like someone who had come into a movie in the middle and was trying to figure out what was going on, but this was worse, much worse, because he was not merely watching the movie, he was starring in it. And found himself lunching with a total stranger to whom he had been married, it seemed, for years. But people who have been married for years have little new to say to one another at lunch, usually. He was grateful for the long silences. When she did speak, he answered cautiously and briefly. Once he allowed himself the luxury of calling her by name, just to show that he knew her name; but his "Celia" provoked a quick frown in her that puzzled him. Was he supposed to have used some pet name instead? Or was there a name other than Celia by which everybody called her—Cee, perhaps, or Cele, or Charley? He was altogether lost. Lingering over his coffee, he thought again of that dizzying moment at the Temple of Quetzalcoatl, when everything had swayed and swirled in his head. Was there such a thing as a stroke that affected one's memory without causing any sort of paralysis of the body? Well, maybe. But he wasn't suffering merely from amnesia; he had a complete and unblurred set of memories of a life without Celia, as a contented single man running a successful art gallery, living a fulfilling existence, friends, lovers, travel. Arriving in Mexico City three days ago, looking forward to a week of cheerful solitude, warm weather, spicy food, perhaps some interesting new pieces for his collection. How could a stroke build all that into his mind? With such detail, too: the black Ford cab, Chucho the amiable driver, the seventh-floor room at the Hotel Presidente—

"I've left something upstairs," he told Celia. "I'll just run up for it, and then we can go."

From the room he dialed the Presidente. "Mr. Hilgard, please."

"One moment." A long pause. Then: "Please repeat the name."

"Hilgard. Theodore Hilgard. I think he's in room 770." A longer pause.

"I'm sorry, sir. We have no one by that name."

"I see," Hilgard said, not seeing at all, and put the phone down. He stared at himself in the mirror, searching for signs of a stroke, the drooping eyelid, the sagging cheek. Nothing. Nothing. But his face was gray. He looked a thousand years old.

They hailed a cab outside the hotel and went to the Museum of Anthropology. He had been there several times, most recently yesterday afternoon. But from what Celia said it was apparent she had never seen it, which was a new awkwardness for him: he had to pretend he had no familiarity with that very familiar place. As they wandered through it he did his best to feign fresh responses to objects he had known for years, the great Olmec stone heads, the terrifying statue of the goddess Coatlicue, the jade-encrusted masks. Sometimes it was not necessary to feign it. In the Aztec room there was an immense marble stela just to the left of the calendar stone that he could not recall from yesterday's visit, and there was a case of amazing little Olmec figurines of polished jade absolutely new to him, and the Mayan room seemed arranged in an entirely different way. Hilgard found all that impossible to comprehend. Even the huge umbrella-shaped fountain in the museum courtyard was subtly different, with golden spokes now sprouting from it. The cumulative effect of the day's little strangenesses was making him feel giddy, almost feverish: Celia several times asked if he was getting ill.

They had dinner that night at an outdoor café a few blocks from their hotel, and strolled for a long time afterward, returning to their room a little before midnight. As they undressed Hilgard felt new dismay. Was she expecting him to make love? The thought horrified him. Not that she was unattractive, far from it. But he had never been able to go to bed with strangers. A prolonged courtship, a feeling of ease with the other person, of closeness, of real love—that was what he preferred, indeed what he required. Aside from all that, how could he pretend with any success to be this woman's husband? No two men make love quite the same way; in two minutes she'd realize that he was an impostor, or else she'd wonder what he thought he was up to. All the little sexual rituals and adjustments that a couple evolves and permanently establishes were unknown to him. She would be confused or annoyed or possibly frightened if he betrayed complete ignorance of her body's mechanisms.

And until he understood what had happened to him, he was terrified of revealing his sense of displacement from what he still regarded as his real life. Luckily she seemed not to be in an amorous mood. She gave him a quick kiss, a light friendly embrace, and rolled over, pressing her rump against him. He lay awake a long time, listening to her soft breathing and feeling weirdly adulterous in this bed with another man's wife. Even though she was Mrs. Ted Hilgard, all the same—all the same—

He ruled out the stroke theory. It left too much unexplained. Sudden insanity? But he didn't *feel* crazy. The events around him were crazy; but inside his skull he still seemed calm, orderly, precise. Surely true madness was something wilder and more chaotic. If he had not suffered any disruption of his brain or some all-engulfing delusional upheaval, though, what was going on? It was as though some gateway between worlds had opened for him at Teotihuacan, he thought, and in that instant of dizziness he had stepped through into the other Ted Hilgard's universe, and that other Hilgard had stumbled past him into his own world. That sounded preposterous. But what he was experiencing was preposterous, too.

In the morning Celia said, "I've got a solution to the argument over Cuernavaca versus Guadalajara. Let's go to Oaxaca instead."

"Wonderful!" Hilgard cried. "I *love* Oaxaca. We ought to phone the Presidente Convento to see if they've got a room—that's such a splendid hotel, with those old courtyards and—"

She was staring strangely at him. "When were you in Oaxaca, Ted?"

Hesitantly he said, "Why—I suppose—long ago, before we were married—"

"I thought this was the first time you'd ever been in Mexico."

"Did I say that?" His cheeks were reddening. "I don't know what I could have been thinking of. I must have meant this was *our* first trip to Mexico. I mean, I barely remember the Oaxaca trip, years and years and years ago, but I did go there, just for a weekend once—"

It sounded terribly lame. A trip that was only a vague memory, though the mere mention of Oaxaca had made him glow with recollections of a lovely hotel? Celia had registered the inconsistency, but she chose not to probe it. He was grateful for that. But he knew she must be adding up all the little contradictions and false notes in the things he was saying, and sooner or later she was apt to demand an explanation.

Within an hour they had everything arranged, and that afternoon they flew down to Oaxaca. As they checked in at the hotel, Hilgard had a sudden horrified fear that the clerk, remembering him from two years ago, would greet him by name, but that did not happen. Sitting by poolside before dinner, Hilgard and Celia leafed through their guidebooks, planning their Oaxaca excursions—a drive to the ruins at Monte Albán, a trip out to the Mitla site, a visit to the famous Saturday morning market—and once again he found it necessary to pretend little knowledge of a place he knew quite well. He wondered how convincing he was. They had dinner that night at a splendid Basque restaurant on a balcony overlooking the main plaza, and afterward they strolled back slowly to their hotel. The night air was soft and fragrant, and music floated toward them from the plaza bandstand. When they were halfway back, Celia reached for his hand. He forced himself not to pull away, though even that innocent little contact between them made him feel monstrously fraudulent. At the hotel he suggested stopping in the bar for a nightcap, but she shook her head and smiled. "It's late," she said softly. "Let's just go upstairs." At dinner they had had a carafe of sangria and then a bottle of red Mexican wine, and he felt loose-jointed and tranquil, but not so tranquil that he did not fear the confrontation that lay just ahead. He halted a moment on the landing, looking toward the glittering pool. By moonlight the heavy purple clusters of bougainvillea climbing the ancient stone walls of the courtyard seemed almost black. Huge hibiscus blossoms were strewn everywhere on the lawn and strange spiky flowers rose from a border of large bizarre succulents. Celia touched his elbow. "Come," she said. He nodded. They went into their room. She turned on a lamp and began to undress. Hilgard's eyes met hers and he saw a host of expressions cross her face in an instant— affection, desire, apprehension, perplexity. She knew something was wrong. Give it a try, Hilgard told himself fiercely. Fake it. Fake it. He ran his hand timidly along her hips, her thighs. No.

"Ted?" she said. "Ted, what's going on?"

"I can't explain. I think I'm losing my mind."

"You've been so strange. Since yesterday."

He took a deep breath. "Yesterday is the first time I ever laid eyes on you in my life."

"*Ted?*"

"It's true. I'm not married. I run a gallery at 60th near Second. I came to Mexico alone last Thursday and I was staying at the Presidente."

"What are you saying, Ted?"

"Yesterday at Teotihuacan I started to walk past the Temple of Quetzalcoatl and I felt a peculiar sensation in my forehead and since then I seem to be somebody else of the same name. I'm sorry, Celia. Do I sound incoherent? I don't think I do. But I know I'm not making any real sense."

"We've been married nine years. We're partners in a marketing research firm, Hilgard & Hilgard, on 57th and Sixth."

"Marketing research. How strange. Do we have children?"

"No. We live in a co-op on 85th, and in the summers we—oh, Ted! *Ted?*"

"I'm so sorry, Celia."

Her eyes in the moonlit darkness were fixed, bright, terrified. There was the acrid smell of fear-sweat in the room, hers, his. She said huskily, "You don't remember any of our life together? Not a thing? In January we went to San Francisco. We stayed at the Stanford Court and it rained all the time and you bought three ivory carvings at a little place across the street from Ghirardelli Square. Last month we got the contract for the Bryce account and you said, 'Fine, let's celebrate by going to Mexico. We've always wanted to go to Mexico and there's no better time than this.' In April we have a big presentation to do in Atlanta, and in May—Ted? Nothing. Ted?"

"Nothing. It's all a blank."

"How scary that is. Hold me, Ted."

"I'm so sorry."

"You don't remember us in bed either?"

"The first time I saw you was two o'clock yesterday afternoon."

"We'll have to fly home tomorrow. There's got to be some kind of therapy—a drug treatment, or maybe even shock—we'll talk to Judith Rose first thing—"

Hilgard felt a shiver of surprise. "Who?"

"You don't remember her either?"

"That's just it. I do. I know a Judith Rose. Tall handsome olive-skinned woman with curly black hair, professor of neurobiology at Rockefeller University—"

"At New York Medical," Celia said. "All the rest is right. You see? You haven't forgotten everything! You still remember Judith!"

"She's at Rockefeller," said Hilgard. "I've known her four or five years. She and I were supposed to take this trip to Mexico together, but at the last moment she had to cancel because she got tied up on a grant proposal, and it looked like she'd be busy with that for weeks and weeks, so we decided that I would come down here by myself, and—"

"What are you saying?" Celia asked, amazed.

"Why, Judith and I are lovers, Celia."

She began to laugh. "Oh, no! No, that's too much. You and Judith—"

"We both see other people. But Judith has the priority. Neither one of us is the marrying sort, but we have an excellent relationship of its kind, and—"

"Stop it, Ted."

"I'm not trying to hurt you. I'm just telling you how it is between me and Judith."

"If you want to tell me you've had affairs, I can handle it. I wouldn't even be immensely surprised. But not with Judith. That's too absurd. Nothing's ever certain in this world, but one thing I'm positive of is that Judith doesn't have any lovers. She and Ron are still like honeymooners. She must be the most faithful woman in the world."

"Ron?"

"Ron Wolff," Celia said. "Judith's husband."

He turned away and stared through the window. Hollowly he said, "In the world I live in, Judith is single and so am I, and she's at Rockefeller University, and I don't know any Ron Wolffs. Or any Celias. And I don't do marketing research. I don't know anything about marketing research. I'm forty-two years old and I went to Harvard and I majored in art history, and I was married to someone named Beverly once for a little while and it was a very bad mistake that I didn't intend to make twice, and I feel sorry as hell for spoiling your vacation and screwing up your life but I simply don't know who you are or where you came from. Do you believe any of that?"

"I believe that you need a great deal of help. And I'll do whatever I have to do to see that you get it, Ted. Whatever has happened to you can be cured, I'm sure, with love and patience and time and money."

"I don't think I'm crazy, Celia."

"I didn't use that word. You're the one who talked of losing your mind. You've had some kind of grotesque mental accident, you've undergone a disturbance of—"

"No," Hilgard said. "I don't think it's anything mental at all. I have another theory now. Suppose that in front of the Temple of Quetzalcoatl there's a mystery place, a—a whirlpool in the structure of the universe, let's say—a gateway, a vortex, whatever you want to call it. Thousands of people walk through at and nothing ever happens to them. But I was the victim of a one-in-a-trillion shot. I went to Mexico in my world and the Ted Hilgard of your world went there at the same time, and we were both at Teotihuacan at the same time, and some immense coincidence brought us both to the whirlpool place simultaneously, and we both went through the gateway and changed places. It could only have happened because our two worlds were touching and he and I were identical enough to be interchangeable."

"That does sound crazy, Ted."

"Does it? Not as crazy as any other theory: Things are different in this world. You, Judith, Ron. The Updike book has a red jacket here. I'm in marketing research instead of art. The museum has a different kind of fountain. Maybe it costs twenty cents to mail a letter instead of eighteen. Everything's *almost* the same, but not quite, and the longer I look, the more differences I see. I have a complete and vivid picture in my mind of the world on the other side of the gateway, down to the littlest details. That can't be just a mental aberration. No aberration is that detailed. How much does it cost to mail a letter?"

"Twenty cents."

"In my world it's eighteen. You see? You see?"

"I don't see anything," Celia said tiredly. "If you can delude yourself into thinking you're entirely different from who you are, you can also very sincerely believe that the postage rate is eighteen cents. They keep changing it all the time anyway. What does that prove? Listen, Ted, we'll go back to New York. We'll try to get you help for this. I want to repair you. I love you. I want you back, Ted. Do you understand that? We've had a wonderful marriage. I don't want it vanishing like a dream."

"I'm so damn sorry, Celia."

"We'll work something out."

"Maybe. Maybe."

"Let's get some sleep now. We're both exhausted."

"That's a fine idea," he said. He touched his hand lightly to her forearm and she stiffened, as though anticipating his caress to be an initiation of lovemaking. But all he was doing was clutching at her as at a rescue line at sea. He squeezed her arm briefly, let go, rolled to the far side of the bed. Tired as he was, he found it hard to fall asleep, and he lay alert a long time. Once he heard her quietly sobbing. When sleep came to him, it was deep and nearly dreamless.

Hilgard would have liked to roam Oaxaca for a few days, enjoying its clear air, lovely old streets, and easy, unhurried pace, but Celia was insistent that they start at once on the task of restoring his memory. They flew back to Mexico City on the 11:00 A.M. flight. At the airport Celia learned that there was a flight to New York in mid-afternoon, but Hilgard shook his head. "We'll stay over in Mexico City tonight and take the first plane out in the morning," he said.

"Why?"

"I want to go back to Teotihuacan."

She gasped. "For Christ's sake, Ted!"

"Humor me. I won't leave Mexico without making certain."

"You think you're just going to walk back into another world?"

"I don't know what I think. I just want to check it out."

"And you expect the other Ted Hilgard to come strolling out from behind a pyramid as you vanish?"

She was starting to sound distraught. Calmly he said, "I don't expect anything. It's just an investigation."

"What if you do? What if you vanish into that whirlpool of yours, and he *doesn't* come out, and I'm left without either of you? Answer me that, Ted."

"I think you're beginning to believe my theory—"

"Oh, no, Ted, no. But—"

"Look," he said, "if the theory's crazy, then nothing will happen. If it isn't, maybe I'll go back where I belong and the right me will return to this world. Nobody knows. But I can't go to New York until I've checked. Grant me that much. I want you to humor me, Celia. Will you do that?"

In the end she had to yield, of course, and they checked their baggage at the airport and booked a hotel room for the night and a flight for the morning, and then they hired a cab to take them to Teotihuacan. The driver spoke little English and it was hard to make him understand that they did not intend to spend all afternoon at the pyramids, but only

half an hour or less. That seemed unthinkable to him: why would anyone, even two rich gringos, bother driving an hour and a half each way
for a half-hour visit? But finally he accepted the idea. He parked at the
southernmost parking lot, near the museum, and Celia and Hilgard
waked quickly across the road to the Temple of Quetzalcoatl. His throat
was dry and his heart was pounding, and she looked equally tense and
drawn. He tried to retrace his steps exactly. "I came through this way,"
he said, "and just around this corner, as I got my first glimpse of the
facade—"

"Ted, please don't. Please."

"Do you want to try? Maybe you'll go through it after him."

"Please. Let's not."

"I have to," he said. Frowning, he made his way along the paved
walkway, paused as the facade and its fierce serpent-snouts emerged in
sight, caught his breath, plunged onward, waiting for the moment of
vertigo, that sensation as of a highly localized earthquake. Nothing. He
looked back. Celia, pale, grim, arms folded, was staring at him. Hilgard
returned and tried it again. "Maybe I was just six inches off that time.
A little to the left—" Nothing. Nothing the third time, or the fourth. A
few other tourists passed by, staring oddly at him. Back and forth he
went, covering every inch. The pathway was narrow; there were only a
few possible routes. He felt no vertigo. No gateway in space opened for
him. He did not tumble trough into his rightful world.

"Please, Ted. Enough."

"Once more."

"This is embarrassing. You look so damned obsessive."

"I want to go where I belong," Hilgard said.

Back and forth. Back and forth. He was beginning to feel embar-
rassed too. Perhaps she was right: this was mere madness that had
possessed his soul. There are no gateways. He could not walk back and
forth in front of those horrendous stone faces all afternoon. "Once
more," he said, and nothing happened and he turned away. "It doesn't
work," he told her. "Or else it works only when one's counterpart is
passing through it at the same instant. And that would be impossible to
arrange. If I could send him a message—tie it to a rock, toss it through
the gateway, tell him to be here tomorrow at nine sharp—"

"Let's go," Celia said.

"All right. Yes." Defeated, dejected, he let her lead him across the
dry hot temple courtyard to the waiting taxi. They returned to Mexico

City in the full madness of the evening rush hour, saying little to each other. Their hotel room turned out to have two single beds instead of a double. Just as well, Hilgard thought. He felt an immense airless distance between himself and this woman who believed she was his wife. They had a bleak dinner at a Zona Rosa restaurant and went to sleep early, and before daybreak they were up and out and on their way to the airport.

"Maybe when you're in your own home," she said, "you'll begin to get pieces of your memory back."

"Maybe," he said.

But the co-op on East 85th meant nothing to him. It was a handsome apartment, thirty stories up, obviously worth a fortune, and it was furnished beautifully, but it was someone else's house, with someone else's books and clothes and treasures in it. The books included a good many that he also owned, and the clothes fit him, and some of the paintings and primitive artifacts were quite in accordance with his own taste. It was like being in one's twin brother's home, perhaps. But he wandered helplessly and in growing panic from room to room, wondering where his files were, his little hoard of boyhood things, his first editions, his Peruvian pottery collection. Delusions? Phantom memories of a nonexistent life? He was cut off from everything that he thought to be real, and it terrified him. The Manhattan phone book listed no Theodore Hilgard on Third Avenue, and no Hilgard Galleries, either. The universe had swallowed that Ted Hilgard.

"I phoned Judith," Celia said, "and told her something of what happened. She wants to see you first thing tomorrow."

He had been to Judith's Rockefeller University office often enough, just a few blocks east of his gallery. But this was a different Judith and her office was at New York Medical, uptown at the edge of Spanish Harlem. Hilgard walked over to Fifth and caught a bus, wondering if he had to pay his fare with some sort of token in this world, wondering if the Metropolitan Museum was where he remembered it, wondering about Judith. He negotiated the bus problem without difficulty. The gray bulk of the museum still crouched on the flank of Central Park. Upper Fifth Avenue looked more or less untransformed, the Frick Collection building just as dignified as ever, the Guggenheim spiral as peculiar as ever. And Judith was untransformed also: elegant, beautiful, warm, with the light of that wonderful intelligence gleaming in her eyes. The only thing missing was that certain mischievous sparkle, that subliminal aura of shared intimacies, that acknowledged that they had long been lovers. She greeted him as a friend and nothing more than a friend.

"What in God's name has been going on with you?" she asked at once.

He smiled ruefully. "Between one moment and the next I seem to have had a total identity transplant. I used to be a bachelor with an art gallery down the block from Bloomingdale's. Now I'm a married man with a marketing research company on 57th Street. And so on. A burst of dizziness at the ruins of Teotihuacan and everything in my life got switched around."

"You don't remember Celia?"

"It isn't just amnesia, if that's where you're heading. I don't remember Celia or anything else having to do with my life here. But I *do* remember a million other things that don't seem to exist any more, a complete reality substructure: phone numbers, addresses, biographical details. You, for instance. The Judith I know is with Rockefeller University. She's single and lives at 382 East 61st Street and her phone number is—you see what I mean? As a matter of fact, you may be the only link between my old life and this one. Somehow I got to know you in both identities. Figure the odds against that."

Judith looked at him with intense, somber concern. "We'll arrange a full battery of neurological tests right away. This sounds like the damnedest mental short circuit I've ever heard of, though I suspect I'll turn up some similar cases in the literature. People who experienced sudden drastic dissociative reactions leading to complete disruption of personality patterns."

"Some sort of schizoid break, is that what you're saying?"

"We don't use terms like schizophrenia or paranoia much any more, Ted. They've been corrupted by popular misconceptions, and they're too imprecise anyway. We know now that the brain is an enormously complex instrument that has capabilities far beyond our rational understanding—I mean freakish stuff like being able to multiply ten-digit numbers in your head—and it's entirely possible that given the right stimulus it can manufacture a perfectly consistent surrogate identity, which—"

"In layman's terms, I'm crazy."

"If you want to use layman's terms," Judith said, "you're suffering from delusions of an extraordinarily vivid kind."

Hilgard nodded. "Among those delusions, you should know, is that you and I were lovers for the past four years."

394

She smiled. "I'm not at all surprised. You've been carrying on a lovely little flirtation with me from the moment we met."

"Have we ever been to bed together?"

"Of course not, Ted."

"Have I ever seen you naked?"

"Not unless you've been spying on me."

He wondered how much this Judith differed from his. Risking it, he said, "Then how do I know you have a small surgical scar on your left breast?"

Shrugging, she said, "I had a little benign tumor removed years ago. Celia might have mentioned that to you."

"And I'd know which breast?"

"You might."

"I can tell you six or seven other things about your body that only somebody who's plenty familiar with it would know. I can tell you what your favorite lovemaking position is, and why. I can imitate the sound you make at your climax."

"Oh? Can you?"

"Listen," he said, and did his best to duplicate that strange whining passionate cry he had heard so many times. Judith's playful, challenging smile disappeared. Her lips grew taut and her eyes narrowed and splotches of color came to her cheeks. She glanced away from him.

Hilgard said, "I didn't have a tape recorder under your bed. I haven't been discussing your sexual idiosyncrasies with Ron. I wouldn't even know Ron if I tripped over him in the street. And I'm not reading your mind. How do I know all these things, then?"

She was silent. She moved papers about randomly on her desk. Her hands appeared to be shaking.

"Maybe you're the one with dissociative reactions," he said. "You've forgotten all about our affair."

"You know that's nonsense."

"You're right. Because the Judith Rose I've been to bed with is at Rockefeller University. But I've been to bed with a Judith Rose who's very much like you. Do you doubt that now?"

She made no reply. She was staring at him in an astounded way, and there seemed to be something else in her look, a volatility, an excitement, that led him to think he had somehow reached across the barrier of his lost world to touch her, *this* Judith, to arouse her and kindle in her some simulacrum of the love and passion that he knew they had had in another existence. A sudden wild fantasy erupted in him—getting free of Celia, getting Judith free of Ron, and reconstructing in this unfamiliar world the relationship that had been taken from him. But the idea faded as quickly as it had come. It was foolishness; it was nonsense; it was an impossibility.

She said finally, "Describe what you think happened to you?"

He told her in all the detail he could muster—the vertigo, the feeling of passing through a gateway, the gradual discovery of the wrongness of everything. "I want to believe this is all just a mental illness and that six lithium pills will make everything be right again. But I don't think that's how it is. I think what happened to me may be a lot wilder than a mere schizoid break. But I don't want to believe that. I want to think it's just a dissociative reaction."

"Yes. I'm sure you do."

"What do you think it is, Judith?"

"My opinion doesn't matter, does it? What matters is proof."

"Proof?"

She said, "What were you carrying on you when you experienced your moment of vertigo?"

"My camera." He thought. "And my wallet."

"Which had credit cards, driver's license, all that stuff?"

"Yes," he said, beginning to understand. He felt a stab of fear, cold, intense. Pulling his wallet out, he said, "Here—here—" He drew forth his driver's license. It had the Third Avenue address. He took out his Diner's Club card. Judith laid her own next to it. The cards were of different designs. He produced a twenty-dollar bill. She peered at the signatures on it and shook her head. Hilgard closed his eyes an instant and had a flashing vision of the Temple of Quetzalcoatl, the great heavy snouts of the serpents, the massive stone steps. Judith's face was dark and grim, and Hilgard knew she had forced him to confront the final proof, and he had a sense of a mighty gate swinging shut forever behind him. He was not the victim of any psychosis. He had actually made the crossing, and it was irrevocable. His other life was gone—it was dead. Bitterly he said, "I forged all this stuff, right? While I was down in Mexico City I had it all printed up, counterfeit money, a fake driver's license, to make the hoax look really convincing. Right? Right?" He remembered something else and went burrowing for it in his wallet and found it after a frantic search—Judith's own business card, with Department of Neurobiology,

Rockefeller University on it in shining engraved letters. The card was old and worn and creased. She looked at it as though he had put a basilisk in her hand. When she stared at him again, it was with a sad and tender look of pity.

At length she said, "Ted, I'll give you all the help I can."

"What kind of help?"

"Making the adaptation. Learning your role here. Celia and I, between us, ought to be able to fill you in on who you're supposed to be. It's the only thing I can imagine doing now. You're right that lithium won't fix anything."

"No," Hilgard said. "Don't involve Celia."

"We have to."

"No," he said. "She thinks I'm her husband and that I'm suffering from an unfortunate dissociative reaction, or whatever you call it. If she comes to realize I'm the complete stranger I've been insisting I am, I'm lost. She'll throw me out and try to find ways of getting him back. And I have no way to function in this world except in the identity of Theodore Hilgard."

"You *are* Theodore Hilgard."

"Yes, and I intend to go on being him. Doing marketing research and living with Celia and signing my name to checks. You'll help me adapt, yes. You'll have a couple of sessions of therapy with me every week, and you'll tell me where I went to college and what the names of my friends are and who the presidents have been in this world, if they have presidents here. So far as everyone else will know, you're helping me recover from a mysterious mental fog. You won't tell a soul that I don't belong here. And sooner or later I *will* belong here. All right, Judith? You see, I've got no choice. There's no way for me to get back across the barrier. I've managed to prove to one other human being that I'm not crazy, and now I've got to put that behind me and start living the life I've been handed. Will you help me?"

"One condition," she said.

"Which is?"

"You're in love with me. I see that, and I don't blame you because I know you can't help thinking I'm *your* Judith. I'm not. I'm Ron's. Go on flirting with me, go on having fantasies about me, but don't give me any moves, ever. All right? Because you might open up in me something that I don't want opened, do you understand? We remain *friends*. Co-conspirators, even. That's all. Is that agreed?"

Hilgard looked at her unhappily. It was a long while before he could bring himself to say it.

"Agreed," he told her at last.

Celia said, "Judith phoned while you were on the way back. She talked to me for twenty minutes. Oh, Ted—my poor Ted—"

"I'm going to be okay. It'll take time."

"She says these amnesias, these detailed delusions, are extraordinarily rare. You're going to be a textbook case."

"Wonderful. I'm going to need a lot of help from you, Celia."

"Whatever I can do."

"I'm a blank. I don't know who our friends are, I don't know how to practice my profession, I don't even know who *you* are. Everything's wiped out. I'll have to rebuild it all. Judith will do as much as she can, but the real burden, day by day, hour by hour, is going to fall on you."

"I'm prepared for that."

"Then we'll start all over—from scratch. We'll make a go of it. Tonight we'll eat at one of our special restaurants—you'll have to tell me which our special restaurants are—and we'll have the best wine in the house, or maybe a bottle or two of champagne, and then we'll come back here—we'll be like newlyweds, Celia, it'll be like a wedding night. All right?"

"Of course," she said softly.

"And then tomorrow the hard work begins. Fitting me back into the real world."

"Everything will come back, Ted. Don't worry. And I'll give you all the help you need. I love you, Ted. No matter what's happened to you, that hasn't changed. I love you."

He nodded. He took her hands in his. Falteringly, guiltily, with a thick tongue and a numbed heart, he forced himself to get the words out, the words that were his only salvation now, the words that gave him his one foothold on the shores of an unknown continent. "And I love you, Celia," he told the absolute stranger who was his wife.

BASILEUS

Writing instructors often tell novice writers that they'll do their best work when they're writing about subjects they know very well, or when they're expressing some strongly held conviction. It's not bad advice, but it doesn't necessarily hold true for experienced professionals. Here's a case in point.

"Basileus" is about a computer nerd who can call up real angels on his computer. It's full of convincing-sounding stuff about hardware, software, programming, and such. It brims with incidental detail about the special qualities of particular angels.

I don't believe in the existence of angels.

And I had never used a computer at the time, back in October of 1982, when I wrote the story.

You see what tricky characters professional writers of fiction are? Someone—was it L. Sprague de Camp?—once referred to us as people who earn their livings by telling lies. Exactly so. In my personal life I happen to be—trust me—more than usually scrupulous about telling the truth. But when I sit down to write a story, I'm willing to tell you any damn thing at all, and I'm capable of making you believe it, because for the time that I'm writing the story I believe it myself. Trust me. The best liars are those who speak out of the absolute conviction that what they're saying is so.

In the case of "Basileus" I needed a story idea and I had, for the moment, run absolutely dry. It was September, 1982, a warm and golden month, and I was exhausted after having spent the previous six months writing an immense historical novel, Lord of Darkness. In those days I did my writing on a typewriter—a manual typewriter, none of those exotic electric jobs for me—and

Lord of Darkness *was something like 800 pages long in manuscript. I had typed the entire thing twice over, plus perhaps 400 pages of incidental revisions along the way, which came out to more than two thousand pages of typing, blam blam blam all summer long. Now the job was done and I just wanted to sit back about something other than writing stories, or perhaps not think of anything whatever.*

But Don Myrus, one of the editors of Omni *magazine, had conceived the idea of doing a special Robert Silverberg issue. Harlan Ellison would write an article about me, two of my earlier stories would be reprinted, and I would contribute a brand-new piece to top everything off. It was too flattering an offer to refuse. But where was I going to get that brand-new story? I was wiped out. I had reached that point, so dreadfully familiar to any author who has just finished a major project, where I felt convinced that I'd never have a story idea again.*

But Don Myrus wasn't going to believe that. I had to come up with something for him. And it had to be done right away.

One tactic that I've sometimes used when stuck for an idea is to grab two unrelated concepts at random, jam them together, and see if they strike any sparks. I tried it. I picked up the day's newspaper and glanced quickly at two different pages.

The most interesting words that rose to my eye were "computers" and "angels."

All right. I had my story then and there. Geek uses his computer to talk to angels.

Corny? No. Nothing's corny if handled the right way. Trust me.

The antidote for corniness is verisimilitude. I had to write about angels as though I had spent my whole life conversing with them and knew them all by their first names. But I stockpile oddball reference books for just such moments, and among them was a copy of Gustav Davidson's Dictionary of Angels. *(Due credit is given in the story.) I began to leaf through it. Very quickly I read on past Gabriel and Michael and Raphael into the more esoteric ones like Israfel, who will blow the trumpet to get the Day of Judgment under way, and Anaphaxeton, who will summon the entire universe before the court. Once I had found them, I knew that I had the dramatic situation around which to build my plot. The Day of Judgment! Of course, I saw right away that I'd have to invent a few angels of my own to make things work out, but that was no problem; inventing things like angels is what I'm paid to do, and I'm probably at least as good at it as some of the people who had invented the ones who fill the pages of Gustav Davidson's immense dictionary.*

What about the computer stuff, though? Me, with my manual typewriter?

Well, writing the thousands of pages of Lord of Darkness *had finally cured me of the folly of using a typewriter. I had decided, that exhausted September, that my next book would be written on a computer. No more grim typing out of enormous final drafts would I do. From now on, just push the button and let the electrons do the work. So I had a few conversations with that all-knowing computer expert Jerry Pournelle, and he not only explained the whole business to me but sent me a twenty-page letter, telling me what to look for when I went computer-shopping. I studied that with great diligence, and then began wandering into showrooms. Almost at once I found myself deep in the arcana of the trade as it existed in 1982: CPUs, Winchester disks, data basis, algorithms, bytes. Overnight I became capable of creating a sentence like "He has dedicated one of his function keys to its text, so that a single keystroke suffices to load it." I still didn't really know how to operate a computer—you pick that up only by sitting down in front of one and turning it on—but I quickly had all the jargon down pat, and even some sense of what it meant.*

You see how the trick is done? A knack for instant expertise is what you need.

And so I wrote "Basileus." Tired as I was, I managed the job in four or five days. I was happy with the result, and so was Don Myrus. When he phoned to accept it he expressed his awe, as a computer layman, for my obvious familiarity with such high-tech devices. "Well," I said casually, "living so close to Silicon Valley, it's hard not to pick up the lingo." What I didn't tell him was that I knew hardly any more about computers than he did, and I was going to use Omni's check for the story to pay for the printer for my very first computer system, which I had just purchased the day before. "Basileus" was, in fact, the last work of fiction I would ever write on a typewriter. A few weeks later, as you will find out when you get to the story after this one, I was a full-fledged computer user at last, embroiled in the intricacies of my giant-lobster story, "Homefaring," and praying each hour that the damned machine would do what I wanted it to do.

You know to whom I was praying, of course. Israfel. Anaphaxeton. Basileus.

In the shimmering lemon-yellow October light Cunningham touches the keys of his terminal and summons angels. An instant to load the program, an instant to bring the file up, and there they are, ready to spout from the screen at his command: Apollyon, Anauel, Uriel, and all the rest. Uriel is the angel of thunder and terror; Apollyon is the Destroyer, the angel of the bottomless pit; Anauel is the Angel of bankers and commission brokers. Cunningham is fascinated by the multifarious duties and tasks, both exalted and humble, that are assigned to the angels. "Every visible thing in the world is put under the charge of an angel," said St. Augustine in *The Eight Questions.*

Cunningham has 1,114 angels in his computer now. He adds a few more each night, though he knows that he has a long way to go before he has them all. In the fourteenth century the number of angels was reckoned by the Kabbalists, with some precision, at 301,655,722. Albertus Magnus had earlier calculated that each choir of angels held 6,666 legions, and each legion 6,666 angels; even without knowing the number of choirs, one can see that that produces rather a higher total. And in the Talmud, Rabbi Jochanan proposed that new angels are born "with every utterance that goes forth from the mouth of the Holy One, blessed be He."

If Rabbi Jochanan is correct, the number of angels is infinite. Cunningham's personal computer, though it has extraordinary add-on memory capacity and is capable, if he chooses, of tapping into the huge mainframe machines of the Defense Department, has no very practical way of handling an infinity. But he is doing his best. To have 1,114 angels on line already, only eight months of part-time programming, is no small achievement.

One of his favorites of the moment is Harahel, the angel of archives, libraries, and rare cabinets. Cunningham has designated Harahel also the angel of computers: it seems appropriate. He invokes Harahel often, to discuss the evolving niceties of data processing with him. But he has many other favorites, and his tastes run somewhat to the sinister: Azrael, the angel of death, for example, and Arioch, the angel of vengeance, and Zebuleon, one of the nine angels who will govern at the end of the world. It is Cunningham's job, from eight to four every working day, to devise programs for the interception of incoming Soviet nuclear warheads, and that, perhaps, has inclined him toward the more apocalyptic members of the angelic host.

He invokes Harahel now. He has bad news for him. The invocation that he uses is a standard one that he found in Arthur Edward Waite's *The Lemegeton,* or *The Lesser Key of Solomon,* and he has dedicated one of his function keys to its text, so that a single keystroke suffices to load it. "I do invoke, conjure, and command thee, O thou Spirit N, to appear and to show thyself visibly unto me before this Circle in fair and comely shape," is the way it begins, and it proceeds to utilize various secret and potent names of God in the summoning of Spirit N—such names as Zabaoth and Elion and, of course, Adonai—and it concludes, "I do potently exorcise thee that thou appearest here to fulfill my will in all things which seem good to me. Wherefore, come thou, visibly, peaceably, and affably, now, without delay, to manifest that which I desire, speaking with a clear and perfect voice, intelligibly, and to mine understanding." All that takes but a micro-second, and another moment to enter in the name of Harahel as Spirit N, and there the angel is on the screen.

"I am here at your summons," he announces.

Cunningham works with his angels from five to seven every evening. Then he has dinner. He lives alone, in a neat little flat a few blocks west of the Bayshore Freeway, and does not spend much of his time socializing. He thinks of himself as a pleasant man, a sociable man, and he may very well be right about that; but the pattern of his life has been a solitary one. He is thirty-seven years old, five feet eleven, with red hair, pale-blue eyes, and a light dusting of freckles on his cheeks. He did his undergraduate work at Cal Tech, his postgraduate studies at Stanford, and for the last nine years he has been involved in ultrasensitive military-computer projects in Northern California. He has never married. Sometimes he works with his angels again after dinner, from eight to ten, but hardly ever any later than that. At ten he always goes to bed. He is a very methodical person.

He has given Harahel the physical form of his own first computer, a little Radio Shack TRS-80, with wings flanking the screen. He had thought originally to make the appearance of his angels more abstract— showing Harahel as a sheaf of kilobytes, for example—but like many of Cunningham's best and most austere ideas it had turned out impractical in the execution, since abstract concepts did not translate well into graphics for him.

"I want to notify you," Cunningham says, "of a shift in jurisdiction." He speaks English with his angels. He has it on good, though apocryphal, authority that the primary language of the angels is Hebrew, but his computer's audio algorithms have no Hebrew capacity, nor does Cunningham. But they speak English readily enough with him: They have no choice. "From now on," Cunningham tells Harahel, "your domain is limited to hardware only."

Ugly green lines rapidly cross and recross Harahel's screen. "By whose authority do you—"

"It isn't a question of authority," Cunningham replies smoothly. "It's a question of precision. I've just read Vretil into the database, and I have to code his functions. He's the recording angel, after all. So to some degree he overlaps your territory."

"Ah," says Harahel, sounding melancholy. "I was hoping you wouldn't bother about him."

"How can I overlook such an important angel? 'Scribe of the knowledge of the Most High,' according to the Book of Enoch. 'Keeper of the Heavenly books and records.' 'Quicker in wisdom than the other archangels.'"

"If he's so quick," says Harahel sullenly, "give *him* the hardware. That's what governs the response time, you know."

"I understand. But he maintains the lists. That's data base."

"And where does the data base live? The hardware!"

"Listen, this isn't easy for me," Cunningham says. "But I have to be fair. I know you'll agree that some division of responsibilities is in order. And I'm giving him all data bases and related software. You keep the rest."

"Screens. Terminals. CPUs. Big deal."

"But without you, he's nothing, Harahel. Anyway, you've always been in charge of cabinets, haven't you?"

"And archives and libraries," the angel says. "Don't forget that."

"I'm not. But what's a library? Is it the books and shelves and stacks, or the words on the pages? We have to distinguish the container from the thing contained."

"A grammarian." Harahel sighs. "A hair-splitter. A casuist."

"Look, Vretil wants the hardware, too. But he's willing to compromise. Are you?"

"You start to sound less and less like our programmer and more and more like the Almighty every day," says Harahel.

"Don't blaspheme," Cunningham tells him. "Please. Is it agreed? Hardware only?"

"You win," says the angel. "But you always do, naturally."

Naturally. Cunningham is the one with his hands on the keyboard, controlling things. The angels, though they are eloquent enough and have distinct and passionate personalities, are mere magnetic impulses deep within. In any contest with Cunningham they don't stand a chance. Cunningham, though he tries always to play the game by the rules, knows that, and so do they.

It makes him uncomfortable to think about it, but the role he plays is definitely godlike in all essential ways. He puts the angels into the computer; he gives them their tasks, their personalities, and their physical appearances; he summons them or leaves them uncalled, as he wishes.

A godlike role, yes. But Cunningham resists confronting that notion. He does not believe he is trying to be God; he does not even want to think about God. His family had been on comfortable terms with God—Uncle Tim was a priest, there was an archbishop somewhere back a few generations, his parents and sisters moved cozily within the divine presence as within a warm bath—but he himself, unable to quantify the Godhead, preferred to sidestep any thought of it. There were other, more immediate matters to engage his concern. His mother had wanted him to go into the priesthood, of all things, but Cunningham had averted that by demonstrating so visible and virtuosic a skill at mathematics that even she could see he was destined for science. Then she had prayed for a Nobel Prize in physics for him; but he had preferred computer technology. "Well," she said, "a Nobel in computers. I ask the Virgin daily."

"There's no Nobel in computers, Mom," he told her. But he suspects she still offers novenas for it.

The angel project had begun as a lark, but had escalated swiftly into an obsession. He was reading Gustav Davidson's old *Dictionary of Angels,* and when he came upon the description of the angel Adramelech, who had rebelled with Satan and had been cast from heaven, Cunningham thought it might be amusing to build his computer simulation and talk with it. Davidson said that Adramelech was sometimes shown as a winged and bearded lion, and sometimes as a mule with feathers, and sometimes as a peacock, and that one poet had described him as "the enemy of God, greater in malice, guile, ambition, and mischief than Satan, a fiend more curst, a deeper hypocrite." That was appealing. Well, why not build him? The graphics were easy—Cunningham chose the winged-lion form—but getting the personality constructed involved a month of intense labor and some consultations with the artificial-intelligence people over at Kestrel Institute. But finally Adramelech was on line, suave and diabolical, talking amiably of his days as an Assyrian god and his conversations with Beelzebub, who had named him Chancellor of the Order of the Fly (Grand Cross).

Next, Cunningham did Asmodeus, another fallen angel, said to be the inventor of dancing, gambling, music, drama, French fashions, and other frivolities. Cunningham made him look like a very dashing Beverly Hills Iranian, with a pair of tiny wings at his collar. It was Asmodeus who suggested that Cunningham continue the project; so he brought Gabriel and Raphael on line to provide some balance between good and evil, and then Forcas, the angel who renders people invisible, restores lost property, and teaches logic and rhetoric in Hell; and by that time Cunningham was hooked.

He surrounded himself with arcane lore: M.R. James's editions of the Apocrypha, Waite's *Book of Ceremonial Magic* and *Holy Kabbalah*, the *Mystical Theology and Celestial Hierarchies* of Dionysius the Areopagite, and dozens of related works that he called up from the Stanford data base in a kind of manic fervor. As he codified his systems, he became able to put in five, eight, a dozen angels a night; one June evening, staying up well past his usual time, he managed thirty-seven. As the population grew, it took on weight and substance, for one angel cross-filed another, and they behaved now as though they held long conversations with one another even when Cunningham was occupied elsewhere.

The question of actual *belief* in angels, like that of belief in God Himself, never arose in him. His project was purely a technical challenge, not a theological exploration. Once, at lunch, he told a co-worker what he was doing, and got a chilly blank stare. "Angels? *Angels?* Flying around with big flapping wings, passing miracles? You aren't seriously telling me that you believe in angels, are you, Dan?"

To which Cunningham replied, "You don't have to believe in angels to make use of them. I'm not always sure I believe in electrons and protons. I know I've never seen any. But I make use of them."

"And what use do you make of angels?"

But Cunningham had lost interest in the discussion.

BASILEUS

✸

He divides his evenings between calling up his angels for conversations and programming additional ones into his pantheon. That requires continuous intensive research, for the literature of angels is extraordinarily large, and he is thorough in everything he does. The research is time-consuming, for he wants his angels to meet every scholarly test of authenticity. He pores constantly over such works as Ginzberg's seven-volume *Legends of the Jews,* Clement of Alexandria's *Prophetic Eclogues,* Blavatsky's *The Secret Doctrine.*

It is the early part of the evening. He brings up Hagith, ruler of the planet Venus and commander of 4,000 legions of spirits, and asks him details of the transmutation of metals, which is Hagith's specialty. He summons Hadraniel, who in Kabbalistic lore is a porter at the second gate of Heaven, and whose voice, when he proclaims the will of the Lord, penetrates through 200,000 universes; he questions the angel about his meeting with Moses, who uttered the Supreme Name at him and made him tremble. And then Cunningham sends for Israfel the four-winged, whose feet are under the seventh earth, and whose head reaches to the pillars of the divine throne. It will be Israfel's task to blow the trumpet that announces the arrival of the Day of Judgment. Cunningham asks him to take a few trial riffs now—"just for practice," he says, but Israfel declines, saying he cannot touch his instrument until he receives the signal, and the command sequence for that, says the angel, is nowhere to be found in the software Cunningham has thus far constructed.

When he wearies of talking with the angels, Cunningham begins the evening's programming. By now the algorithms are second nature and he can enter angels into the computer in a matter of minutes, once he has done the research. This evening he inserts nine more. Then he opens a beer, sits back, lets the day wind to its close.

He thinks he understands why he has become so intensely involved with this enterprise. It is because he must contend each day in his daily work with matters of terrifying apocalyptic import: nothing less, indeed, than the impending destruction of the world. Cunningham works routinely with megadeath simulation. For six hours a day he sets up hypothetical situations in which Country A goes into alert mode, expecting an attack from Country B, which thereupon begins to suspect a preemptive strike and commences a defensive response, which leads Country A to escalate its own readiness, and so on until the bombs are in the air. He is aware, as are many thoughtful people both in Country A and Country B, that the possibility of computer-generated misinformation leading to a nuclear holocaust increases each year, as the time window for correcting a malfunction diminishes. Cunningham also knows something that very few others do, or perhaps no one else at all: that it is now possible to send a signal to the giant computers—to Theirs or Ours, it makes no difference—that will be indistinguishable from the impulses that an actual flight of airborne warhead-bearing missiles would generate. If such a signal is permitted to enter the system, a minimum of eleven minutes, at the present time, will be needed to carry out fail-safe determination of its authenticity. That, at the present time, is too long to wait to decide whether the incoming missiles are real: a much swifter response is required.

Cunningham, when he designed his missile-simulating signal, thought at once of erasing his work. But he could not bring himself to do that: the program was too elegant, too perfect. On the other hand, he was afraid to tell anyone about it, for fear that it would be taken beyond his level of classification at once, and sealed away from him. He does not want that, for he dreams of finding an antidote for it, some sort of resonating inquiry mode that will distinguish all true alarms from false. When he has it, if he ever does, he will present both modes, in a single package, to Defense. Meanwhile, he bears the burden of suppressing a concept of overwhelming strategic importance. He has never done anything like that before. And he does not delude himself into thinking his mind is unique: if he could devise something like this, someone else probably could do it also, perhaps someone on the other side. True, it is a useless, suicidal program. But it would not be the first suicidal program to be devised in the interests of military security.

He knows he must take his simulator to his superiors before much more times goes by. And under the strain of that knowledge, he is beginning to show distinct signs of erosion. He mingles less and less with other people; he has unpleasant dreams and occasional periods of insomnia; he has lost his appetite and looks gaunt and haggard. The angel project is his only useful diversion, his chief distraction, his one avenue of escape.

BASILEUS

For all his scrupulous scholarship, Cunningham has not hesitated to invent a few angels of his own. Uraniel is one of his: the angel of radioactive decay, with a face of whirling electron shells. And he has coined Dimitrion too: the angel of Russian literature, whose wings are sleighs and whose head is a snow-covered samovar. Cunningham feels no guilt over such whimsies. It is his computer, after all, and his program. And he knows he is not the first to concoct angels. Blake engendered platoons of them in his poems: Urizen and Orc and Enitharmon and more. Milton, he suspects, populated *Paradise Lost* with dozens of sprites of his own invention. Gurdjieff and Alastair Crowley and even Pope Gregory the Great had their turns at amplifying the angelic roster: why, then, not also Dan Cunningham of Palo Alto, California? So from time to time he works one up on his own. His most recent is the dread high lord Basileus, to whom Cunningham has given the title of Emperor of the Angels. Basileus is still incomplete: Cunningham has not arrived at his physical appearance, nor his specific functions, other than to make him the chief administrator of the angelic horde. But there is something unsatisfactory about imagining a new archangel, when Gabriel, Raphael, and Michael already constitute the high command. Basileus needs more work. Cunningham puts him aside, and begins to key in Duma, the angel of silence and of the stillness of death, thousand-eyed, armed with a fiery rod. His style in angels is getting darker and darker.

On a misty, rainy night in late October, a woman from San Francisco whom he knows in a distant, occasional way phones to invite him to a party. Her name is Joanna; she is in her mid-thirties, a biologist working for one of the little gene-splicing outfits in Berkeley; Cunningham had had a brief and vague affair with her five or six years back, when she was at Stanford, and since then they have kept fitfully in touch, with long intervals elapsing between meetings. He has not seen her or heard from her in over a year. "It's going to be an interesting bunch," she tells him. "A futurologist from New York, Thomson the sociobiology man, a couple of video poets, and someone from the chimpanzee language outfit, and I forget the rest, but they all sounded first-rate."

Cunningham hates parties. They bore and jangle him. No matter how first-rate the people are, he thinks, real interchange of ideas is impossible in a large random group, and the best one can hope for is some pleasant low-level chatter. He would rather be alone with his angels than waste an evening that way.

On the other hand, it has been so long since he has done anything of a social nature that he has trouble remembering what the last gathering was. As he had been telling himself all his life, he needs to get out more often. He likes Joanna and it's about time they got together, he thinks, and he fears that if he turns her down she may not call again for years. And the gentle patter of the rain, coming on this mild evening after the long dry months of summer, has left him feeling uncharacteristically relaxed, open, accessible.

"All right," he says. "I'll be glad to go."

The party is in San Mateo, on Saturday night. He takes down the address. They arrange to meet there. Perhaps she'll come home with him afterward, he thinks: San Mateo is only fifteen minutes from his house, and she'll have a much longer drive back up to San Francisco. The thought surprises him. He had supposed he had lost all interest in her that way; he had supposed he had lost all interest in anyone that way, as a matter of fact.

Three days before the party, he decides to call Joanna and cancel. The idea of milling about in a roomful of strangers appalls him. He can't imagine, now, why he ever agreed to go. Better to stay home alone and pass a long rainy night designing angels and conversing with Uriel, Ithuriel, Raphael, Gabriel.

But as he goes toward the telephone, that renewed hunger for solitude vanishes as swiftly as it came. He *does* want to go to the party. He *does* want to see Joanna: very much, indeed. It startles him to realize that he positively yearns for some change in his rigid routine, some escape from his little apartment, its elaborate computer hookup, even its angels.

Cunningham imagines himself at the party, in some brightly lit room in a handsome redwood-and-glass house perched in the hills above San Mateo. He stands with his back to the vast sparkling wrap-around window, a drink in his hand, and he is holding forth, dominating the conversation, sharing his rich stock of angel lore with a fascinated audience.

"Yes, three hundred million of them," he is saying, "and each with his fixed function. Angels don't have free will, you know. It's Church doctrine that they're created with it, but at the moment of their birth they're given the choice of opting for God or against Him, and the choice is irrevocable. Once they've made it they're unalterably fixed, for good or for evil. Oh, and angels are born circumcised, too. At least the Angels of Sanctification and the Angels of Glory are, and probably the seventy Angels of the Presence."

"Does that mean that all angels are male?" asks a slender dark-haired woman.

"Strictly speaking, they're bodiless and therefore without sex," Cunningham tells her. "But in fact the religions that believe in angels are mainly patriarchical ones, and when the angels are visualized they tend to be portrayed as men. Although some of them, apparently, can change sex at will. Milton tells us that in *Paradise Lost*: 'Spirits when they please can either sex assume, or both; so soft and uncompounded is their essence pure.' And some angels seem to be envisioned as female in the first place. There's the Shekinah, for instance, 'the bride of God,' the manifestation of His glory indwelling in human beings. There's Sophia, the angel of wisdom. And Lilith, Adam's first wife, the demon of lust—"

"Are demons considered angels, then?" a tall professorial-looking man wants to know.

"Of course. They're the angels who opted away from God. But they're angels nevertheless, even if we mortals perceive their aspects as demonic or diabolical."

He goes on and on. They all listen as though he is God's own messenger. He speaks of the hierarchies of angels—the seraphim, cherubim, thrones, dominations, principalities, powers, virtues, archangels, and angels—and he tells them of the various lists of the seven great angels, which differ so greatly once one gets beyond Michael, Gabriel, and Raphael, and he speaks of the 90,000 angels of destruction and the 300 angels of light, he conjures up the seven angels with seven trumpets from the Book of Revelation, he tells them which angels rule the seven days of the week and which the hours of the days and night, he pours forth the wondrous angelic names, Zadkiel, Hashmal, Orphaniel, Jehudiel, Phaleg, Zagzagel. There is no end to it. He is in his glory. He is a fount of arcana. Then the manic mood passes. He is alone in his room; there is no eager audience. Once again he thinks he will skip the party. No. No. He will go. He wants to see Joanna.

He goes to his terminal and calls up two final angels before bedtime: Leviathan and Behemoth. Behemoth is the great hippopotamus-angel, the vast beast of darkness, the angel of chaos. Leviathan is his mate, the mighty she-whale, the splendid sea serpent. They dance for him on the screen: Behemoth's huge mouth yawns wide. Leviathan gapes even more awesomely. "We are getting hungry," they tell him. "When is feeding time?" In rabbinical lore, these two will swallow all the damned souls at the end of days. Cunningham tosses them some electronic sardines and sends them away. As he closes his eyes he invokes Poteh, the angel of oblivion, and falls into a black dreamless sleep.

At his desk the next morning he is at work on a standard item, a glitch-clearing program for the third-quadrant surveillance satellites, when he finds himself unaccountably trembling. That has never happened to him before. His fingernails look almost white, his wrists are rigid, his hands are quivering. He feels chilled. It is as though he has not slept for days. In the washroom he clings to the sink and stares at his pallid, sweaty face. Someone comes up behind him and says, "You all right, Dan?"

"Yeah. Just a little attack of the queasies."

"All that wild living in the middle of the week wears a man down," the other says, and moves along. The social necessities have been observed: a question, a noncommittal answer, a quip, good-bye. He could have been having a stroke here and they would have played it the same way. Cunningham has no close friends at the office. He knows that they regard him as eccentric—eccentric in the wrong way, not lively and quirky but just a peculiar kind of hermit—and getting worse all the time. I could destroy the world, he thinks. I could go into the Big Room and type for fifteen seconds, and we'd be on all-out alert a minute later and the bombs would be coming down from orbit six minutes later. I could give that signal. I could really do it. I could do it right now.

Waves of nausea sweep him and he grips the edge of the sink until the last racking spasm is over. Then he cleans his face and, calmer now, returns to his desk to stare at the little green symbols on the screen.

That evening, still trying to find a function for Basileus, Cunningham discovers himself thinking of demons, and of one demon not in the classical demonology—Maxwell's Demon, the one that the physicist James Clerk Maxwell postulated to send fast-moving molecules in one direction and slow ones in another, thereby providing an ultraefficient method for heating and refrigeration. Perhaps some sort of filtering role could be devised for Basileus. Last week a few of the loftier angels had been complaining about the proximity to them of certain fallen angels within the computer. "There's a smell of brimstone on this disk that I don't like," Gabriel had said. Cunningham wonders if he could make Basileus a kind of traffic manager within the program: let him sit in there and ship the celestial angels into one sector of a disk, the fallen ones to another.

The idea appeals to him for about thirty seconds. Then he sees how fundamentally trivial it is. He doesn't need an angel for a job like that; a little simple software could do it. Cunningham's corollary to Kant's categorical imperative: *Never use an angel as mere software.* He smiles, possibly for the first time all week. Why, he doesn't even need software. He can handle it himself, simply by assigning princes of Heaven to one file and demons to a different one. It hadn't seemed necessary to segregate his angels that way, or he would have done it from the start. But if they were complaining—

He begins to flange up a sorting program to separate the files. It should have taken him a few minutes, but he finds himself working in a rambling, muddled way, doing an untypically sloppy job. With it quick swipe he erases what he has done. Gabriel would have to put up with the reek of brimstone a little longer, he thinks.

There is a dull throbbing pain just behind his eyes. His throat is dry, his lips feel parched. Basileus would have to wait a little longer, too. Cunningham keys up another angel, allowing his fingers to choose for him, and finds himself looking at a blank-faced angel with a gleaming metal skin. One of the early ones, Cunningham realizes. "I don't remember your name," he says. "Who are you?"

"I am Anaphaxeton."

"And your function?"

"When my name is pronounced aloud, I will cause the angels to summon the entire universe before the bar of justice on Judgment Day."

"Oh, Jesus," Cunningham says. "I don't want you tonight."

He sends Anaphaxeton away and finds himself with the dark angel Apollyon, fish scales, dragon wings, bear feet, breathing fire and smoke, holding the key to the Abyss. "No," Cunningham says, and brings up Michael, standing with drawn sword over Jerusalem, and sends him away only to find on the screen an angel with 70,000 feet and 4,000 wings, who is Azrael, the angel of death. "No," says Cunningham again. "Not you. Oh, Christ!" A vengeful army crowds his computer. On his screen there passes a flurrying regiment of wings and eyes and beaks. He shivers and shuts the system down for the night. Jesus, he thinks. Jesus, Jesus, Jesus. All night long suns explode in his brain.

On Friday his supervisor, Ned Harris, saunters to his desk in an unusually folksy way and asks him if he's going to be doing anything interesting this weekend. Cunningham shrugs. "A party Saturday night, that's about all. Why?"

"Thought you might be going off on a fishing trip or something. Look like the last nice weekend before the rainy season sets in, wouldn't you say?"

"I'm not a fisherman, Ned."

"Take some kind of trip. Drive down to Monterey, maybe. Or up into the wine country."

"What are you getting at?" Cunningham asks.

'You look like you could use a little change of pace," Harris says amiably. "A couple of days off. You've been crunching numbers so hard they're starting to crunch you, is my guess."

"It's that obvious?"

Harris nods. "You're tired, Dan. It shows. We're a little like air traffic controllers around here, you know, working so hard we start to dream about blips on the screen. That's no good. Get the hell out of town, fellow. The Defense Department can operate without you for a while. Okay? Take Monday off. Tuesday, even. I can't afford to have a fine mind like yours going goofy from fatigue, Dan."

"All right, Ned. Sure. Thanks."

His hands are shaking again. His fingernails are colorless.

"And get a good early start on the weekend, too. No need for you to hang around here today until four."

"If that's okay—"

"Go on. Shoo!"

Cunningham closes down his desk and makes his way uncertainly out of the building. The security guards wave at him. Everyone seems to know he's being sent home early. Is this what it's like to crack up on the job? He wanders about the parking lot for a little while, not sure where he has left his car. At last he finds it, and drives home at thirty miles an hour, with horns honking at him all the way as he wanders up the freeway.

He settles wearily in front of his computer and brings the system on line, calling for Harahel. Surely the angel of computers will not plague him with apocalyptic matters.

Harahel says, "Well, we've worked out your Basileus problem for you."

"You have?"

"Uriel had the basic idea, building on your Maxwell's Demon notion. Israfel and Azrael developed it some. What's needed is an angel embodying God's justice and God's mercy. A kind of evaluator, a filtering angel. He weighs deeds in the balance, and arrives at a verdict."

"What's new about that?" Cunningham asks. "Something like that's built into every mythology from Sumer and Egypt on. There's always a mechanism for evaluating the souls of the dead—this one goes to Paradise, this one goes to Hell—"

"Wait," Harahel says. "I wasn't finished. I'm not talking about the evaluation of individual souls."

"What, then?"

"Worlds," the angel replies. "Basileus will be the judge of worlds. He holds an entire planet up to scrutiny and decides whether it's time to call for the last trump."

"Part of the machinery of Judgment, you mean?"

"Exactly. He's the one who presents the evidence to God and helps Him make his decision. And then he's the one who tells Israfel to blow the trumpet, and he's the one who calls out the name of Anaphaxeton to bring everyone before the bar. He's the prime apocalyptic angel, the destroyer of worlds. And we thought you might make him look like—"

"Ah," Cunningham says. "Not now. Let's talk about that some other time."

He shuts the system down, pours himself a drink, sits staring out the window at the big eucalyptus tree in the front yard. After a while it begins to rain. Not such a good weekend for a drive into the country after all, he thinks. He does not turn the computer on again that evening.

Despite everything, Cunningham goes to the party. Joanna is not there. She has phoned to cancel, late Saturday afternoon, pleading a bad cold. He detects no sound of a cold in her voice, but perhaps she is telling the truth. Or possibly she has found something better to do on Saturday night. But he is already geared for party-going, and he is so tired, so eroded, that it is more effort to change his internal program than it is to follow through on the original schedule. So about eight that evening he drives up to San Mateo, through a light drizzle.

The party turns out not to be in the glamorous hills west of town, but in a small cramped condominium close to the heart of the city, furnished with what looks like somebody's college-era chairs and couches and bookshelves. A cheap stereo is playing the pop music of a dozen years ago, and a sputtering screen provides a crude computer-generated light show. The host is some sort of marketing exec for a large video-games company in San Jose, and most of the guests look vaguely corporate too. The futurologist from New York has sent his regrets; the famous sociobiologist has also somehow failed to arrive; the video poets are two San Francisco gays who will talk only to each other, and stray not very far from the bar; the expert on teaching chimpanzees to speak is in the red-faced-and-sweaty stage of being drunk, and is working hard at seducing a plump woman festooned with astrological jewelry. Cunningham, numb, drifts through the party as though he is made of ectoplasm. He speaks to no one, no one speaks to him. Some jugs of red wine are open on a table by the window, and he pours himself a glassful. There he stands, immobile, imprisoned by inertia. He imagines himself suddenly making a speech about angels, telling everyone how Ithuriel touched Satan with his spear in the Garden of Eden as the Fiend crouched next to Eve, and how the hierarch Ataphiel keeps Heaven aloft by balancing it on three fingers. But he says nothing. After a time he finds himself approached by a lean, leathery-looking woman with glittering eyes, who says, "And what do you do?"

"I'm a programmer," Cunningham says. "Mainly I talk to angels. But I also do national security stuff."

"Angels?" she says, and laughs in a brittle, tinkling way. "You talk to angels? I've never heard anyone say that before." She purrs herself a drink and moves quickly elsewhere.

"Angels?" says the astrological woman. "Did someone say angels?"

Cunningham smiles and shrugs and looks out the window. It is raining harder. I should go home, he thinks. There is absolutely no point in being here. He fills his glass again. The chimpanzee man is still working on the astrologer, but she seems to be trying to get free of him and come over to Cunningham. To discuss angels with him? She is heavy-breasted, a little wall-eyed, sloppy-looking. He does not want to discuss angels with her. He does not want to discuss angels with any-one. He holds his place at the window until it definitely does appear that the astrologer is heading his way; then he drifts toward the door. She says, "I heard you say you were interested in angels. Angels are a special field of mine, you know. I've studied with—"

"Angles," Cunningham says. "I play the angles. That's what I said. I'm a professional gambler."

"Wait," she says, but he moves past her and out into the night. It takes him a long while to find his key and get his car unlocked, and the rain soaks him to the skin, but that does not bother him. He is home a little before midnight.

He brings Raphael on line. The great archangel radiates a beautiful golden glow.

"You will be Basileus," Raphael tells him. "We've decided it by a vote, hierarchy by hierarchy. Everyone agrees."

"I can't be an angel. I'm human," Cunningham replies.

"There's ample precedent. Enoch was carried off to Heaven and became an angel. So was Elijah. St. John the Baptist was actually an angel. You will become Basileus. We've already done the program for you. It's on the disk: just call him up and you'll see. Your own face, looking out at you."

"No," Cunningham says.

"How can you refuse?"

"Are you really Raphael? You sound like someone from the other side. A tempter. Asmodeus. Astaroth. Belphegor."

"I am Raphael. And you are Basileus."

Cunningham considers it. He is so very tired that he can barely think.

An angel. Why not? A rainy Saturday night, a lousy party, a split-ting headache: come home and find out you've been made an angel, and given a high place in the hierarchy. Why not? Why the hell not?

"All right," he says. "I'm Basileus."

He puts his hands on the keys and taps out a simple formulation that goes straight down the pipe into the Defense Department's big Northern California system. With an alteration of two keystrokes he sends the same message to the Soviets. Why not? Redundancy is the soul of security. The world now has about six minutes left.

Cunningham has always been good with computers. He knows their secret language as few people before him have.

Then he brings Raphael on the screen again.

"You should see yourself as Basileus while there's still time," the archangel says.

"Yes. Of course. What's the access key?"

Raphael tells him. Cunningham begins to set it up.

Come now, Basileus! We are one!

Cunningham stares at the screen with growing wonder and delight, while the clock continues to tick.

HOMEFARING

I had always had a sneaking desire to write the definitive giant-lobster story. Earlier science-fiction writers had preempted most of the other appealing monstrosities—including giant aunts (sic!), dealt with by Isaac Asimov in his classic story "Dreamworld," which I have just ruined forever for you by giving away its punchline. But giant lobsters remained fair game. And when George Scithers, the new editor of the venerable science-fiction magazine Amazing Stories, asked me in the autumn of 1982 to do a lengthy story for him, I decided that it was time at last for me to give lobsters their due.

The obvious giant-lobster story, in which horrendous pincer-wielding monsters twenty feet long come ashore at Malibu and set about the conquest of Los Angeles by terrorizing the surfers, might work well enough in a cheap Hollywood sci-fi epic, but it wouldn't have stood much chance of delighting a sophisticated science-fiction reader like Scithers. Nor did it have a lot of appeal for me as a writer. Therefore, following the advice of the brilliant, cantankerous editor Horace Gold, one of my early mentors, I searched for my story idea by turning the obvious upside down. Lobsters are pretty nasty things, after all. They're tough, surly, dangerous, and ugly— surely the ugliest food objects ever to be prized by mankind. A creature so disagreeable in so many ways must have some redeeming feature. (Other than the flavor of its meat, that is.) And so, instead of depicting them as the savage and hideous-looking critters they really are, what about putting them through a few hundred million years of evolution and turning them into wise and thoughtful civilized beings—the dominant life-form, in fact, of a vastly altered Earth?

A challenging task, yes. And made even more challenging for me, back there in the otherwise sunny and pleasant November of 1982, by the fact that I had just made the great leap from computer to typewriter, as I've described in the introduction to the story immediately preceding this one. "Homefaring" marked my initiation into the world of floppy disks and soft hyphens, of backup copies and automatic pagination. It's all second nature to me now, of course, but in 1982 I found myself timidly stumbling around in a brave and very strange new world. Each day's work was an adventure in terror for me. My words appeared in white letters on a black screen, frighteningly impermanent: one electronic sneeze, I thought, and a whole day's brilliant prose could vanish like a time traveler who has just defenestrated his own grandfather. The mere making of backups didn't lull my fears: how could I be sure that the act of backing up itself wouldn't erase what I had just written? Pushing the button marked "Save"—did that really save anything? Switching the computer off at the end of my working day was like a leap into the abyss. Would the story be there the next morning when I turned the machine on again? Warily, I printed out each day's work when it was done, before backing up, saving, or otherwise jiggling with it electronically. I wanted to see it safely onto paper first.

Sometimes when I put a particularly difficult scene together—for example, the three-page scene at the midpoint of the story, beginning with the line, "The lobsters were singing as they marched"—I would stop right then and there and print it out before proceeding, aware that if the computer somehow were to destroy it I would never be able to reconstruct it at that level of accomplishment. (It's an axiom among writers that material written to replace inadvertently destroyed copy can't possibly equal the lost passage—which gets better and better in one's memory all the time.)

Somehow, in fear and trembling, I tiptoed my way through the entire 88-page manuscript of "Homefaring" without any major disasters. The computer made it marvelously easy to revise the story as I went along; instead of typing out an 88-page first draft, then covering it with handwritten alterations and grimly typing the whole thing out again to make it fit to show an editor, I brought every paragraph up to final-draft status with painless little maneuvers of the cursor. When I realized that I had chosen a confusing name for a minor character, I ordered the computer to correct my error, and sat back in wonder as "Eitel" became "Bleier" throughout the story without my having to do a thing. And then at the end came the wondrous moment when I pushed the button marked "Print"— computers had such buttons, in those pre-Microsoft days—and page after page of immaculate typed copy began to come forth while I occupied myself with other and less dreary tasks.

The story appeared in the November, 1983 issue of Amazing Stories, though its actual first publication was as a slender limited-edition volume published in July of that year by Phantasia Press. The readers liked it and it was a finalist in that year's Nebula Award voting—perhaps might even have won, if it had been published in a magazine less obscure than dear old Amazing, which at that stage of its long existence had only a handful of readers. That same year the veteran connoisseur of science fiction, Donald A. Wollheim, chose it for his annual World's Best SF anthology, an honor that particularly pleased me. I had deliberately intended "Homefaring" as a sleek and modern version of the sort of imagination-stirring tale of wonder that Wollheim had cherished in the s-f magazines of the 1930s, and his choice of the story for his book confirmed my feeling of working within a great tradition.

McCulloch was beginning to molt. The sensation, inescapable and unarguable, horrified him—it felt exactly as though his body was going to split apart, which it was—and yet it was also completely familiar, expected, welcome. Wave after wave of keen and dizzying pain swept through him. Burrowing down deep in the sandy bed, he waved his great claws about, lashed his flat tail against the pure white sand, scratched frantically with quick worried gestures of his eight walking-legs.

He was frightened. He was calm. He had no idea what was about to happen to him. He had done this a hundred times before.

The molting prodrome had overwhelming power. It blotted from his mind all questions, and, after a moment, all fear. A white line of heat ran down his back—no, down the top of his carapace—from a point just back of his head to the first flaring segments of his tail-fan. He imagined that all the sun's force, concentrated through some giant glass lens, was being inscribed in a single track along his shell. And his soft inner body was straining, squirming, expanding, filling the carapace to overflowing. But still that rigid shell contained him, refusing to yield to the pressure. To McCulloch it was much like being inside a wet suit that was suddenly five times too small.

—What is the sun? What is glass? What is a lens? What is a wet suit?

The questions swarmed suddenly upward in his mind like little busy many-legged creatures springing out of the sand. But he had no time for providing answers. The molting prodrome was developing with astounding swiftness, carrying him along. The strain was becoming intolerable. In another moment he would surely burst. He was writhing in short angular convulsions. Within his claws, his tissues now were shrinking, shriveling, drawing back within the ferocious shell-hulls, but the rest of him was continuing inexorably to grow larger.

He had to escape from this shell, or it would kill him. He had to expel himself somehow from this impossibly constricting container. Digging his front claws and most of his legs into the sand, he heaved, twisted, stretched, pushed. He thought of himself as being pregnant with himself, struggling fiercely to deliver himself of himself.

Ah. The carapace suddenly began to split.

The crack was only a small one, high up near his shoulders—*shoulders?*—but the imprisoned substance of him surged swiftly toward it, widening and lengthening it, and in another moment the hard horny covering was cracked from end to end. *Ah. Ah.* That felt so good, that release from constraint! Yet McCulloch still had to free himself. Delicately he drew himself backward, withdrawing leg after leg from its covering in a precise, almost fussy way, as though he were pulling his arms from the sleeves of some incredibly ancient and frail garment.

Until he had his huge main claws free, though, he knew he could not extricate himself from the sundered shell. And freeing the claws took extreme care. The front limbs still were shrinking, and the limy joints of the shell seemed to be dissolving and softening, but nevertheless he had to pull each claw through a passage much narrower than itself. It was easy to see how a hasty move might break a limb off altogether.

He centered his attention on the task. It was a little like telling his wrists to make themselves small, so he could slide them out of handcuffs.

—Wrists? Handcuffs? What are those?

McCulloch paid no attention to that baffling inner voice. Easy, easy, there—ah—yes, there, like that! One claw was free. Then the other, slowly, carefully. Done. Both of them retracted. The rest was simple: some shrugging and wiggling, exhausting but not really challenging, and he succeeded in extending the breach in the carapace until he could crawl backward out of it. Then he lay on the sand beside it, weary, drained, naked, soft, terribly vulnerable. He wanted only to return to the sleep out of which he had emerged into this nightmare of shell-splitting.

But some force within him would not let him slacken off. A moment to rest, only a moment. He looked to his left, toward the discarded shell. Vision was difficult—there were peculiar, incomprehensible refraction effects that broke every image into thousands of tiny fragments—but despite that, and despite the dimness of the light, he was able to see that the shell, golden-hued with broad arrow shaped red markings, was something like a lobster's, yet even more intricate, even more bizarre. McCulloch did not understand why he had been inhabiting a lobster's shell. Obviously because he was a lobster; but he was not a lobster. That was so, was it not? Yet he was under water. He lay on fine white sand, at a depth so great he could not make out any hint of sunlight overhead. The water was warm, gentle, rich with tiny tasty creatures and with a swirling welter of sensory data that swept across his receptors in bewildering abundance.

He sought to learn more. But there was no further time for resting and thinking now. He was unprotected. Any passing enemy could destroy him while he was like this. Up, up, seek a hiding place: that was the requirement of the moment.

First, though, he paused to devour his old shell. That, too, seemed to be the requirement of the moment; so he fell upon it with determination, seizing it with his clumsy-looking but curiously versatile front claws, drawing it toward his busy, efficient mandibles. When that was accomplished—no doubt to recycle the lime it contained, which he needed for the growth of his new shell—he forced himself up and began a slow scuttle, somehow knowing that the direction he had taken was the right one.

Soon came the vibrations of something large and solid against his sensors—a wall, a stone mass rising before him—and then, as he continued, he made out with his foggy vision the sloping flank of a dark broad cliff rising vertically from the ocean floor. Festoons of thick, swaying red and yellow water plants clung to it, and a dense stippling of rubbery-looking finger-shaped sponges, and a crawling, gaping, slithering host of crabs and mollusks and worms, which vastly stirred McCulloch's appetite. But this was not a time to pause to eat, lest he be eaten. Two enormous green anemones yawned nearby, ruffling their voluptuous membranes seductively, hopefully. A dark shape passed overhead, huge, tubular, tentacular, menacing. Ignoring the thronging populations of the rock, McCulloch picked his way over and around them until he came to the small cave, the McCulloch-sized cave, that was his goal.

Gingerly he backed through its narrow mouth, knowing there would be no room for turning around once he was inside. He filled the opening nicely, with a little space left over. Taking up a position just within the entrance, he blocked the cave mouth with his claws. No enemy could enter now. Naked though he was, he would be safe during his vulnerable period.

For the first time since his agonizing awakening, McCulloch had a chance to halt: rest, regroup, consider.

It seemed a wise idea to be monitoring the waters just outside the cave even while he was resting, though. He extended his antennae a short distance into the swarming waters, and felt at once the impact, again, of a myriad sensory inputs, all the astounding complexity of the reef world. Most of the creatures that moved slowly about on the face of the reef were simple ones, but McCulloch could feel, also, the sharp pulsations of intelligence coming from several points not far away: the anemones, so it seemed, and that enormous squidlike thing hovering overhead. Not intelligence of a kind that he understood, but that did not trouble him: for the moment, understanding could wait, while he dealt with the task of recovery from the exhausting struggles of his molting. Keeping the antennae moving steadily in slow sweeping circles of surveillance, he began systematically to shut down the rest of his nervous system, until he had attained the rest state that he knew—how?—was optimum for the rebuilding of his shell. Already his soft new carapace was beginning to grow rigid as it absorbed water, swelled, filtered out and utilized the lime. But he would have to sit quietly a long while before he was fully armored once more.

He rested. He waited. He did not think at all.

After a time his repose was broken by that inner voice, the one that had been trying to question him during the wildest moments of his molting. It spoke without sound, from a point somewhere within the core of his torpid consciousness.

—*Are you awake?*

—*I am now,* McCulloch answered irritably.

—I need definitions. You are a mystery to me. What is a McCulloch?

—A man.

—That does not help.

—A male human being.

—That also has no meaning.

—Look, I'm tired. Can we discuss these things some other time?

—This is a good time. While we rest, while we replenish ourself.

—Ourselves, McCulloch corrected.

—Ourself is more accurate.

—But there are two of us.

—Are there? Where is the other?

McCulloch faltered. He had no perspective on his situation, none that made any sense.—*One inside the other, I think. Two of us in the same body. But definitely two of us. McCulloch and not-McCulloch.*

—I concede the point. There are two of us. You are within me. Who are you?

—McCulloch.

—So you have said. But what does that mean?

—I don't know.

The voice left him alone again. He felt its presence nearby, as a kind of warm node somewhere along his spine, or whatever was the equivalent of his spine, since did not think invertebrates had spines. And it was fairly clear to him that he was an invertebrate.

He had become, it seemed, a lobster, or, at any rate, something lobsterlike. Implied in that was transition: *he had become*. He had once been something else. Blurred, tantalizing memories of the something else that he once had been danced in his consciousness. He remembered hair, fingers, fingernails, flesh. Clothing: a kind of removable exoskeleton. Eyelids, ears, lips: shadowy concepts all, names without substance, but there was a certain elusive reality to them, a volatile, tricky plausibility. Each time he tried to apply one of those concepts to himself—"fingers," "hair," "man," "McCulloch"—it slid away, it would not stick. Yet all the same, those terms had some sort of relevance to him.

The harder he pushed to isolate that relevance, though, the harder it was to maintain his focus on any part of that soup of half-glimpsed notions in which his mind seemed to be swimming. The thing to do,

McCulloch decided, was to go slow, try not to force understanding, wait for comprehension to seep back into his mind. Obviously he had had a bad shock, some major trauma, a total disorientation. It might be days before he achieved any sort of useful integration.

A gentle voice from outside his cave said, "I hope that your Growing has gone well."

Not a voice. He remembered voice: vibration of the air against the eardrums. No air here, maybe no eardrums. This was a stream of minute chemical messengers spurting through the mouth of the little cave and rebounding off the thousands of sensory filaments on his legs, tentacles, antennae, carapace, and tail. But the effect was one of words having been spoken. And it was distinctly different from that other voice, the internal one, that had been questioning him so assiduously a little while ago.

"It goes extremely well," McCulloch replied: or was it the other inhabitant of his body that had framed the answer? "I grow. I heal. I stiffen. Soon I will come forth."

"We feared for you." The presence outside the cave emanated concern, warmth, intelligence. Kinship. "In the first moments of your Growing, a strangeness came from you."

"Strangeness is within me. I am invaded."

"Invaded? By what?"

"A McCulloch. It is a man, which is a human being."

"Ah. A great strangeness indeed. Do you need help?"

McCulloch answered, "No. I will accommodate to it."

And he knew that it was the other within himself who was making these answers, though the boundary between their identities was so indistinct that he had a definite sense of being the one who shaped these words. But how could that be? He had no idea how one shaped words by sending squirts of body fluid into the all-surrounding ocean fluid. That was not his language. His language was—

—words—

—English words—

He trembled in sudden understanding. His antennae thrashed wildly, his many legs jerked and quivered. Images churned in his suddenly boiling mind: bright lights, elaborate equipment, faces, walls, ceilings. People moving about him, speaking in low tones, occasionally addressing words to him, English words—

—*Is English what all McCullochs speak?*

—*Yes.*

—So English is human-language?

—Yes. But not the only one, said McCulloch. I speak English, and also German and a little—French. But other humans speak other languages.

—Very interesting. Why do you have so many languages?

—Because—because—we are different from one another, we live in different countries, we have different cultures—

—This is without meaning again. There are many creatures, but only one language, which all speak with greater or lesser skill, according to their destinies.

McCulloch pondered that. After a time he replied:

—Lobster is what you are. Long body, claws and antennae in front, many legs, flat tail in back. Different from, say, a clam. Clams have shell on top, shell on bottom, soft flesh in between, hinge connecting. You are not like that. You have lobster body. So you are lobster.

Now there was silence from the other.

Then—after a long pause—

—Very well. I accept the term. I am lobster. You are human. They are clams.

—What do you call yourselves in your own language?

Silence.

—What's your own name for yourself? Your individual self, the way my individual name is McCulloch and my species name is human being?

Silence.

—Where am I, anyway?

Silence, still, so prolonged and utter that McCulloch wondered if the other being had withdrawn itself from his consciousness entirely. Perhaps days went by in this unending silence, perhaps weeks: he had no way of measuring the passing of time. He realized that such units as days or weeks were without meaning now. One moment succeeded the next, but they did not aggregate into anything continuous.

At last came a reply.

—You are in the world, human McCulloch.

Silence came again, intense, clinging, a dark warm garment. McCulloch made no attempt to reach the other mind. He lay motionless, feeling his carapace thicken. From outside the cave came a flow of impressions of passing beings, now differentiating themselves very sharply: he felt the thick fleshy pulses of two anemones, the sharp stabbing presence of the squid, the slow ponderous broadcast of something dark and winged, and, again and again, the bright, comforting, unmistakable output of other lobster creatures. It was a busy, complex world out there. The McCulloch part of him longed to leave the cave and explore it. The lobster part of him rested, content within its tight shelter.

He formed hypotheses. He had journeyed from his own place to this place, damaging his mind in the process, though now his mind seemed to be reconstructing itself steadily, if erratically. What sort of voyage? To another world? No: that seemed wrong. He did not believe that conditions so much like the ocean floor of Earth would be found on another—

Earth.

All right: significant datum. He was human, he came from Earth. And he was still on Earth. In the ocean. He was—what?—a land-dweller, an airbreather, a biped, a flesh-creature, a human. And now he was within the body of a lobster. Was that it? The entire human race, he thought, has migrated into the bodies of lobsters, and here we are on the ocean floor, scuttling about, waving our claws and feelers, going through difficult and dangerous moltings—

Or maybe I'm the only one. A scientific experiment, with me as the subject: man into lobster. That brightly lit room that he remembered, the intricate gleaming equipment all about him—that was the laboratory, that was where they had prepared him for his transmigration, and then they had thrown the switch and hurled him into the body of—

No. No. Makes no sense. Lobsters, McCulloch reflected, are low-phylum creatures with simple nervous systems, limited intelligence. Plainly the mind he had entered was a complex one. It asked thoughtful questions. It carried on civilized conversations with its friends, who came calling like ceremonious Japanese gentlemen, offering expressions of solicitude and goodwill.

New hypothesis: that lobsters and other low-phylum animals are actually quite intelligent, with minds roomy enough to accept the sudden insertion of a human being's entire neural structure, but we in our foolish anthropocentric way have up till now been too blind to perceive—

No. Too facile. You could postulate the secretly lofty intelligence of the world's humble creatures, all right: you could postulate anything you wanted. But that didn't make it so. Lobsters did not ask questions. Lobsters did not come calling like ceremonious Japanese gentlemen. At least, not the lobsters of the world he remembered.

Improved lobsters? Evolved lobsters? Superlobsters of the future?

—*When am I?*

Into his dizzied broodings came the quiet disembodied internal voice of not-McCulloch, his companion:

—*Is your displacement, then, one of time rather than space?*

—*I don't know. Probably both. I'm a land creature.*

—*That has no meaning.*

—*I don't live in the ocean. I breathe air.*

From the other consciousness came an expression of deep astonishment tinged with skepticism.

—*Truly? That is very hard to believe. When you are in your own body you breathe no water at all?*

—*None. Not for long, or I would die.*

—*But there is so little land! And no creatures live upon it. Some make short visits there. But nothing can dwell there very long. So it has always been. And so will it be, until the time of the Molting of the World.*

McCulloch considered that. Once again he found himself doubting that he was still on Earth. A world of water? Well, that could fit into his hypothesis of having journeyed forward in time, though it seemed to add a layer of implausibility upon implausibility. How many millions of years, he wondered, would it take for nearly all the Earth to have become covered with water? And he answered himself: In about as many as it would take to evolve a species of intelligent invertebrates.

Suddenly, terribly, it all fit together. Things crystallized and clarified in his mind, and he found access to another segment of his injured and redistributed memory; and he began to comprehend what had befallen him, or, rather, what he had willingly allowed himself to undergo. With that comprehension came a swift stinging sense of total displacement and utter loss, as though he were drowning and desperately tugging at strands of seaweed in a futile attempt to pull himself back to the surface. All that was real to him, all that he was part of, everything that made sense—gone, gone, perhaps irretrievably gone, buried under the weight of uncountable millennia, vanished, drowned, forgotten, reduced to mere geology. It was unthinkable, it was unacceptable, it was impossible, and as the truth of it bore in on him he found himself choking on the frightful vastness of time past.

But that bleak sensation lasted only a moment and was gone. In its place came excitement, delight, confusion, and a feverish throbbing curiosity about this place he had entered. He was here. That miraculous thing that they had strived so fiercely to achieve had been achieved—rather too well, perhaps, but it had been achieved, and he was launched on the greatest adventure he would ever have, that anyone would ever have. This was not the moment for submitting to grief and confusion. Out of that world, lost and all but forgotten to him, came a scrap of verse that gleamed and blazed in his soul: *Only through time time is conquered.*

McCulloch reached toward the mind that was so close to his within this strange body.

—*When will it be safe for us to leave this cave?* he asked.

—*It is safe any time, now. Do you wish to go outside?*

—*Yes. Please.*

The creature stirred, flexed its front claws, slapped its flat tail against the floor of the cave, and in a slow ungraceful way began to clamber through the narrow opening, pausing more than once to search the waters outside for lurking enemies. McCulloch felt a quick hot burst of terror, as though he were about to enter some important meeting and had discovered too late that he was naked. Was the shell truly ready? Was he safely armored against the unknown foes outside, or would they fall upon him and tear him apart like furious shrikes? But his host did not seem to share those fears. It went plodding on and out, and in a moment more it emerged on an algae-encrusted tongue of the reef wall, a short distance below the two anemones. From each of those twin masses of rippling flesh came the same sullen pouting hungry murmurs: "Ah, come closer, why don't you come closer?"

"Another time," said the lobster, sounding almost playful, and turned away from them.

McCulloch looked outward over the landscape. Earlier, in the turmoil of his bewildering arrival and the pain and chaos of the molting prodrome, he had not had time to assemble any clear and coherent view of it. But now—despite the handicap of seeing everything with the alien perspective of the lobster's many-faceted eyes—he was able to put together an image of the terrain.

His view was a shortened one, because the sky was like a dark lid, through which came only enough light to create a cone-shaped arena spreading just a little way. Behind him was the face of the huge cliff, occupied by plant and animal life over virtually every square inch, and stretching upward until its higher reaches were lost in the dimness far overhead. Just a short way down from the ledge where he rested was the ocean floor, a broad expanse of gentle, undulating white sand streaked here and there with long widening gores of some darker material. Here and there bottom-growing plants arose in elegant billowy clumps, and McCulloch spotted occasional creatures moving among them over the sand that were much like lobsters and crabs, though with some differences. He saw also some starfish and snails and sea urchins that did not look at all unfamiliar. At higher levels he could make out a few swimming creatures: a couple of the squidlike animals—they were hulking-looking ropy-armed things, and he disliked them instinctively— and what seemed to be large jellyfish. But something was missing, and after a moment McCulloch realized what it was: fishes. There was a rich population of invertebrate life wherever he looked, but no fishes as far as he could see.

Not that he could see very far. The darkness clamped down like a curtain perhaps two or three hundred yards away. But even so, it was odd that not one fish had entered his field of vision in all this time. He wished he knew more about marine biology. Were there zones on Earth where no sea animals more complex than lobsters and crabs existed? Perhaps, but he doubted it.

Two disturbing new hypotheses blossomed in his mind. One was that he had landed in some remote future era where nothing out of his own time survived except low-phylum sea creatures. The other was that he had not traveled to the future at all, but had arrived by mischance in some primordial geological epoch in which vertebrate life had not yet evolved. That seemed unlikely to him, though. This place did not have a prehistoric feel to him. He saw no trilobites; surely there ought to be trilobites everywhere about, and not these oversize lobsters, which he did not remember at all from his childhood visits to the natural history museum's prehistory displays.

But if this was truly the future—and the future belonged to the lobsters and squids—

That was hard to accept. Only invertebrates? What could invertebrates accomplish, what kind of civilization could lobsters build, with their hard unsupple bodies and great clumsy claws? Concepts, half remembered or less than that, rushed through his mind: the Taj Mahal, the Gutenberg Bible, the Sistine Chapel, the Madonna of the Rocks, the great window at Chartres. Could lobsters create those? Could squids? What a poor place this world must be, McCulloch thought sadly, how gray, how narrow, how tightly bounded by the ocean above and the endless sandy floor.

—*Tell me,* he said to his host. *Are there any fishes in this sea?*

The response was what he was coming to recognize as a sigh.

—*Fishes? That is another word without meaning.*

—*A form of marine life, with an internal bony structure—*

—*With its shell inside?*

—*That's one way of putting it,* said McCulloch.

—*There are no such creatures. Such creatures have never existed. There is no room for the shell within the soft parts of the body. I can barely comprehend such an arrangement: surely there is no need for it!*

—*It can be useful, I assure you. In the former world it was quite common.*

—*The world of human beings?*

—*Yes. My world,* McCulloch said.

—*Anything might have been possible in a former world, human McCulloch. Perhaps indeed before the world's last Molting shells were worn inside. And perhaps after the next one they will be worn there again. But in the world I know, human McCulloch, it is not the practice.*

—*Ah,* McCulloch said. *Then I am even farther from home than I thought.*

—*Yes,* said his host. *I think you are very far from home indeed. Does that cause you sorrow?*

—*Among other things.*

—*If it causes you sorrow, I grieve for your grief, because we are companions now.*

—*You are very kind,* said McCulloch to his host.

The lobster asked McCulloch if he was ready to begin their journey; and when McCulloch indicated that he was, his host serenely kicked itself free of the ledge with a single powerful stroke of its tail. For an instant it hung suspended; then it glided toward the sandy bottom as gracefully as though it were floating through air. When it landed, it was with all its many legs poised delicately *en pointe,* and it stood that way, motionless, a long moment.

Then it suddenly set out with great haste over the ocean floor, running so light-footedly that it scarcely raised a puff of sand wherever it touched down. More than once it ran right across some bottom-grubbing creature, some slug or scallop, without appearing to disturb it at all. McCulloch thought the lobster was capering in sheer exuberance, after its long internment in the cave; but some growing sense of awareness of his companion's mind told him after a time that this was no casual frolic, that the lobster was not in fact dancing but fleeing.

—*Is there an enemy?* McCulloch asked.

—*Yes. Above.*

The lobster's antennae stabbed upward at a sharp angle, and McCulloch, seeing through the other's eyes, perceived now a large looming cylindrical shape swimming in slow circles near the upper border of their range of vision. It might have been a shark, or even a whale. McCulloch felt deceived and betrayed; for the lobster had told this was an invertebrate world, and surely that creature above him—

—*No,* said the lobster, without slowing its manic sprint. *That animal has no shell of the sort you described within its body. It is only a bag of flesh. But it is very dangerous.*

—*How will we escape it?*

—*We will not escape it.*

The lobster sounded calm, but whether it was the calm of fatalism or mere expressionlessness, McCulloch could not say: the lobster had been calm even in the first moments of McCulloch's arrival in its mind, which must surely have been alarming and even terrifying to it.

It had begun to move now in ever-widening circles. This seemed not so much an evasive tactic as a ritualistic one, now, a dance indeed. A farewell to life? The swimming creature had descended until it was only a few lobster lengths above them, and McCulloch had a clear view of it. No, not a fish or a shark or any type of vertebrate at all, he realized, but an animal of a kind wholly unfamiliar to him, a kind of enormous wormlike thing whose meaty yellow body was reinforced externally by some sort of chitinous struts running its entire length. Fleshy vanelike fins rippled along its sides, but their purpose seemed to be more one of guidance than propulsion, for it appeared to move by guzzling in great quantities of water and expelling them through an anal siphon. Its mouth was vast, with a row of dim little green eyes ringing the scarlet lips. When the creature yawned, it revealed itself to be toothless, but capable of swallowing the lobster easily at a gulp.

Looking upward into that yawning mouth, McCulloch had a sudden image of himself elsewhere, spread-eagled under an inverted pyramid of shining machinery as the countdown reached its final moments, as the technicians made ready to—

—to hurl him—

—to hurl him forward in time—

Yes. An experiment. Definitely an experiment. He could remember it now. Bleier, Caldwell, Rodrigues, Mortenson. And all the others. Gathered around him, faces tight, forced smiles. The lights. The colors. The bizarre coils of equipment. And the volunteer. The volunteer. First human subject to be sent forward in time. The various rabbits and mice of the previous experiments, though they had apparently survived the round trip unharmed, had not been capable of delivering much of a report on their adventures. "I'm smarter than any rabbit," McCulloch had said. "Send me. I'll tell you what it's like up there." The volunteer. All that was coming back to him in great swatches now, as he crouched here within the mind of something much like a lobster, waiting for a vast yawning predator to pounce. The project, the controversies, his coworkers, the debate over risking a human mind under the machine, the drawing of lots. McCulloch had not been the only volunteer. He was just the lucky one. "Here you go, Jim-boy. A hundred years down the time line."

Or fifty, or eighty, or a hundred and twenty. They didn't have really precise trajectory control. They thought he might go as much as a hundred twenty years. But beyond much doubt they had overshot by a few hundred million. Was that within the permissible parameters of error?

He wondered what would happen to him if his host here were to perish. Would he die also? Would he find himself instantly transferred to some other being of this epoch? Or would he simply be hurled back instead to his own time? He was not ready to go back. He had just begun to observe, to understand, to explore—

McCulloch's host had halted its running now, and stood quite still in what was obviously a defensive mode, body cocked and upreared, claws extended, with the huge crusher claw erect and the long narrow cutting claw opening and closing in a steady rhythm. It was a threatening pose, but the swimming thing did not appear to be greatly troubled by it. Did the lobster mean to let itself be swallowed, and then to carve an exit for itself with those awesome weapons, before the alimentary juices could go to work on its armor?

"You choose your prey foolishly," said McCulloch's host to its enemy.

The swimming creature made a reply that was unintelligible to McCulloch: vague blurry words, the clotted outspew of a feeble intelligence. It continued its unhurried downward spiral.

"You are warned," said the lobster. "You are not selecting your victim wisely."

Again came a muddled response, sluggish and incoherent, the speech of an entity for whom verbal communication was a heavy, all-but-impossible effort.

Its enormous mouth gaped. Its fins rippled fiercely as it siphoned itself downward the last few yards to engulf the lobster. McCulloch prepared himself for transition to some new and even more unimaginable state when his host met its death. But suddenly the ocean floor was swarming with lobsters. They must have been arriving from all sides—summoned by his host's frantic dance, McCulloch wondered?—while McCulloch, intent on the descent of the swimmer, had not noticed. Ten, twenty, possibly fifty of them arrayed themselves now beside McCulloch's host, and as the swimmer, tail on high, mouth wide, lowered itself like some gigantic suction hose toward them, the lobsters coolly and implacably seized its lips in their claws. Caught and helpless, it began at once to thrash, and from the pores through which it spoke came bleating incoherent cries of dismay and torment.

There was no mercy for it. It had been warned. It dangled tail upward while the pack of lobsters methodically devoured it from below, pausing occasionally to strip away and discard the rigid rods of chitin that formed its superstructure. Swiftly they reduced it to a faintly visible cloud of shreds oscillating in the water, and then small scavenging creatures came to fall upon those, and there was nothing at all left but the scattered rods of chitin on the sand.

The entire episode had taken only a few moments: the coming of the predator, the dance of McCulloch's host, the arrival of the other lobsters, the destruction of the enemy. Now the lobsters were gathered in a sort of convocation about McCulloch's host, wordlessly manifesting a commonality of spirit, a warmth of fellowship after feasting, that seemed quite comprehensible to McCulloch. For a short while they had been uninhibited savage carnivores consuming convenient meat; now once again they were courteous, refined, cultured—Japanese gentlemen, Oxford dons, gentle Benedictine monks.

McCulloch studied them closely. They were definitely more like lobsters than like any other creature he had ever seen, very much like lobsters, and yet there were differences. They were larger. How much larger, he could not tell, for he had no real way of judging distance and size in this undersea world; but he supposed they must be at least three feet long, and he doubted that lobsters of his time, even the biggest, were anything like that in length. Their bodies were wider than those of lobsters, and their heads were larger. The two largest claws looked like those of the lobsters he remembered, but the ones just behind them seemed more elaborate, as if adapted for more delicate procedures than mere rending of food and stuffing it into the mouth. There was an odd little hump, almost a dome, midway down the lobster's back—the center of the expanded nervous system, perhaps.

The lobsters clustered solemnly about McCulloch's host, and each lightly tapped its claws against those of the adjoining lobster in a sort of handshake, a process that seemed to take quite some time. McCulloch became aware also that a conversation was under way. What they were talking about, he realized, was him.

"It is not painful to have a McCulloch within one," his host was explaining. "It came upon me at molting time, and that gave me a moment of difficulty, molting being what it is. But it was only a moment. After that my only concern was for the McCulloch's comfort."

"And it is comfortable now?"

"It is becoming more comfortable."

"When will you show it to us?"

"Ah, that cannot be done. It has no real existence, and therefore I cannot bring it forth."

"What is it, then? A wanderer? A revenant?"

"A revenant, yes. So I think. And a wanderer. It says it is a human being."

"And what is that? Is a human being a kind of McCulloch?"

"I think a McCulloch is a kind of human being."

"Which is a revenant."

"Yes, I think so."

"This is an Omen!"

"Where is its world?"

"Its world is lost to it."

"Yes, definitely an Omen."

"It lived on dry land."

"It breathed air."

"It wore its shell within its body."

"What a strange revenant!"

"What a strange world its world must have been."

"It is the former world, would you not say?"

"So I surely believe. And therefore this is an Omen."

"Ah, we shall Molt. We shall Molt."

McCulloch was altogether lost. He was not even sure when his own host was the speaker.

"Is it the time?"

"We have an Omen, do we not?"

"The McCulloch surely was sent as a herald."

"There is no precedent."

"Each Molting, though, is without precedent. We cannot conceive what came before. We cannot imagine what comes after. We learn by learning. The McCulloch is the herald. The McCulloch is the Omen."

"I think not. I think it is unreal and unimportant."

"Unreal, yes. But not unimportant."

"The Time is not at hand. The Molting of the World is not yet due. The human is a wanderer and a revenant, but not a herald and certainly not an Omen."

"It comes from the former world."

"It says it does. Can we believe that?"

"It breathed air. In the former world, perhaps there were creatures that breathed air."

"It says it breathed air. I think it is neither herald nor Omen, neither wanderer nor revenant. I think it is a myth and a fugue. I think it betokens nothing. It is an accident. It is an interruption."

"That is an uncivil attitude. We have much to learn from the McCulloch. And if it is an Omen, we have immediate responsibilities that must be fulfilled."

"But how can we be certain of what it is?"

—*May I speak?* said McCulloch to his host.

—*Of course.*

—*How can I make myself heard?*

—*Speak through me.*

"The McCulloch wishes to be heard!"

"Hear it! Hear it!"

"Let it speak!"

McCulloch said, and the host spoke the words aloud for him, "I am a stranger here, and your guest, and so I ask you to forgive me if I give offense, for I have little understanding of your ways. Nor do I know if I am a herald or an Omen. But I tell you in all truth that I am a wanderer, and that I am sent from the former world, where there are many creatures of my kind, who breathe air and live upon the land and carry their—shells—inside their body."

"An Omen, certainly," said several of the lobsters at once. "A herald, beyond doubt."

McCulloch continued, "It was our hope to discover something of the worlds that are to come after ours. And therefore I was sent forward—"

"A herald—certainly a herald!"

"—to come to you, to go among you, to learn to know you, and then to return to my own people, the air people, the human people, and bring the word of what is to come. But I think that I am not the herald you expect. I carry no message for you. We could not have known that you were here. Out of the former world I bring you the blessing of those that have gone before, however, and when I go back to that world I will bear tidings of your life, of your thought, of your ways—"

"Then our kind is unknown to your world?"

McCulloch hesitated. "Creatures somewhat like you do exist in the seas of the former world. But they are smaller and simpler than you, and I think their civilization, if they have one, is not a great one."

"You have no discourse with them, then?" one of the lobsters asked.

"Very little," he said. A miserable evasion, cowardly, vile.

McCulloch shivered. He imagined himself crying out, "We eat them!" and the water turning black with their shocked outbursts and saw them instantly falling upon him, swiftly and efficiently slicing him to scraps with their claws. Through his mind ran monstrous images of lobsters in tanks, lobsters boiling alive, lobsters smothered in rich sauces, lobsters shelled, lobsters minced, lobsters rendered into bisques—he could not halt the torrent of dreadful visions. Such was our discourse with your ancestors. Such was our mode of interspecies communication. He felt himself drowning in guilt and shame and fear.

The spasm passed. The lobsters had not stirred. They continued to regard him with patience: impassive, unmoving, remote. McCulloch wondered if all that had passed through his mind just then had been transmitted to his host. Very likely; the host earlier had seemed to have access to all of his thoughts, though McCulloch did not have the same entrée to the host's. And if the host knew, did all the others? What then, what then?

Perhaps they did not even care. Lobsters, he recalled, were said to be callous cannibals, who might attack one another in the very tanks where they were awaiting their turns in the chef's pot. It was hard to view these detached and aloof beings, these dons, these monks, as having that sort of ferocity: but yet he had seen them go to work on that swimming mouth-creature without any show of embarrassment, and perhaps some atavistic echo of their ancestors' appetites lingered in them, so that they would think it only natural that McCullochs and other humans had fed on such things as lobsters. Why should they be shocked? Perhaps they thought that humans fed on humans, too. It was all in the former world, was it not? And in any event it was foolish to fear that they would exact some revenge on him for Lobster Thermidor, no matter how appalled they might be. He wasn't here. He was nothing more than a figment, a revenant, a wanderer, a set of intrusive neural networks within their companion's brain. The worst they could do to him, he supposed, was to exorcise him, and send him back to the former world.

Even so, he could not entirely shake the guilt and the shame. Or the fear.

Bleier said, "Of course, you aren't the only one who's going to be in jeopardy when we throw the switch. There's your host to consider. One entire human ego slamming into his mind out of nowhere like a brick falling off a building—what's it going to do to him?"

"Flip him out, is my guess," said Jake Ybarra. "You'll land on him and he'll announce he's Napoleon, or Joan of Arc, and they'll hustle him off to the nearest asylum. Are you prepared for the possibility, Jim, that you're going to spend your entire time in the future sitting in a loony bin undergoing therapy?"

"Or exorcism," Mortenson suggested. "If there's been some kind of reversion to barbarism. Christ, you might even get your host burned at the stake!"

"I don't think so," McCulloch said quietly. "I'm a lot more optimistic than you guys. I don't expect to land in a world of witch doctors and mumbo jumbo, and I don't expect to find myself in a place that locks people up in Bedlam because they suddenly start acting a little strange. The chances are that I *am* going to unsettle my host when I enter him, but that he'll simply get two sanity-stabilizer pills from his medicine chest and take them with a glass of water and feel better in five minutes. And then I'll explain what's happening to him."

"More than likely, no explanations will be necessary," said Maggie Caldwell. "By the time you arrive, time travel will have been a going proposition for three or four generations, after all. Having a traveler from the past turn up in your head will be old stuff to them. Your host will probably know exactly what's going on from the moment you hit him."

"Let's hope so," Bleier said. He looked across the laboratory to Rodrigues. "What's the count, Bob?"

"T minus eighteen minutes."

"I'm not worried about a thing," McCulloch said.

Caldwell took his hand in hers. "Neither am I, Jim."

"Then why is your hand so cold?" he asked.

"So I'm a *little* worried," she said.

McCulloch grinned. "So am I. A little. Only a little."

"You're human, Jim. No one's ever done this before."

"It'll be a can of corn!" Ybarra said.

Bleier looked at him blankly. "What the hell does that mean, Jake?"

Ybarra said, "Archaic twentieth-century slang. It means it's going to be a lot easier than we think."

"I told you," said McCulloch, "I'm not worried."

"I'm still worried about the impact on the host," said Bleier.

"All those Napoleons and Joans of Arc that have been cluttering the asylums for the last few hundred years," Maggie Caldwell said. "Could it be that they're really hosts for time travelers going backward in time?"

"You can't go backward," said Mortenson. "You know that. The round trip has to begin with a forward leap."

"Under present theory," Caldwell said. "But present theory's only five years old. It may turn out to be incomplete. We may have had all sorts of travelers out of the future jumping through history, and never even knew it. All the nuts, lunatics, inexplicable geniuses, idiots savants—"

"Save it, Maggie," Bleier said. "Let's stick to what we understand right now. "

"Oh? Do we understand anything?" McCulloch asked.

Bleier gave him a sour look. "I thought you said you weren't worried."

"I'm not. Not much. But I'd be a fool if I thought we really had a firm handle on what we're doing. We're shooting in the dark, and let's never kid ourselves about it."

"T minus fifteen," Rodrigues called.

"Try to make the landing easy on your host, Jim," Bleier said.

"I've got no reason not to want to," said McCulloch.

He realized that he had been wandering. Bleier, Maggie, Mortenson, Ybarra—for a moment they had been more real to him than the congregation of lobsters. He had heard their voices, he had seen their faces, Bleier plump and perspiring and serious, Ybarra dark and lean, Maggie with her crown of short upswept red hair blazing in the laboratory light—and yet they were all dead, a hundred million years dead, two hundred million, back there with the triceratops and the trilobite in the drowned former world, and here he was among the lobster people. How futile all those discussions of what the world of the early twenty-second century was going to be like! Those speculations on population density, religious belief, attitudes toward science, level of technological achievement, all those late-night sessions in the final months of the project, designed to prepare him for any eventuality he might encounter while he was visiting the future—what a waste, what a needless exercise. As was all that fretting about upsetting the mental stability of the person who would receive his transtemporalized consciousness. Such qualms, such moral delicacy—all unnecessary, McCulloch knew now.

But of course they had not anticipated sending him so eerily far across the dark abysm of time, into a world in which humankind and all its works were not even legendary memories, and the host who would receive him was a calm and thoughtful crustacean capable of taking him in with only the most mild and brief disruption of its serenity.

The lobsters, he noticed now, had reconfigured themselves while his mind had been drifting. They had broken up their circle and were arrayed in a long line stretching over the ocean floor, with his host at the end of the procession. The queue was a close one, each lobster so close to the one before it that it could touch it with the tips of its antennae, which from time to time they seemed to be doing; and they all were moving in a weird kind of quasimilitary lockstep, every lobster swinging the same set of walking-legs forward at the same time.

—Where are we going? McCulloch asked his host.

—The pilgrimage has begun.

—What pilgrimage is that?

—To the dry place, said the host. *To the place of no water. To the land.*

—Why?

—It is the custom. We have decided that the time of the Molting of the World is soon to come; and therefore we must make the pilgrimage. It is the end of all things. It is the coming of a newer world. You are the herald: so we have agreed.

—Will you explain? I have a thousand questions. I need to know more about all this, McCulloch said.

—Soon. Soon. This is not a time for explanations.

McCulloch felt a firm and unequivocal closing of contact, an emphatic withdrawal. He sensed a hard ringing silence that was almost an absence of the host, and knew it would be inappropriate to transgress against it. That was painful, for he brimmed now with an overwhelming rush of curiosity. The Molting of the World? The end of all things? A pilgrimage to the land? What land? Where? But he did not ask. He could not ask. The host seemed to have vanished from him, disappearing utterly into this pilgrimage, this migration, moving in its lockstep way with total concentration and a kind of mystic intensity. McCulloch did not intrude. He felt as though he had been left alone in the body they shared.

As they marched, he concentrated on observing, since he could not interrogate. And there was much to see; for the longer he dwelled within his host, the more accustomed he grew to the lobster's sensory mechanisms. The compound eyes, for instance. Enough of his former life had returned to him now so that he remembered human eyes clearly, those two large gleaming ovals, so keen, so subtle of focus, set beneath protecting ridges of bone. His host's eyes were nothing like that: they were two clusters of tiny lenses rising on jointed, movable stalks, and what they showed was an intricately dissected view, a mosaic of isolated points of light. But he was learning somehow to translate those complex and baffling images into a single clear one, just as, no doubt, a creature accustomed to compound-lens vision would sooner or later learn to see through human eyes, if need be. And McCulloch found now that he could not only make more sense out of the views he received through his host's eyes, but that he was seeing farther, into quite distant dim recesses of this sunless undersea realm.

Not that the stalked eyes seemed to be a very important part of the lobster's perceptive apparatus. They provided nothing more than a certain crude awareness of the immediate terrain. But apparently the real work of perceiving was done mainly by the thousands of fine bristles, so minute that they were all but invisible, that sprouted on every surface of his host's body. These seemed to send a constant stream of messages to the lobster's brain: information on the texture and topography of the ocean floor, on tiny shifts in the flow and temperature of the water, of the proximity of obstacles, and much else. Some of the small hairlike filaments were sensitive to touch, and others, it appeared, to chemicals; for whenever the lobster approached some other life-form, it received data on its scent—or the underwater equivalent—long before the creature itself was within visual range. The quantity and richness of these inputs astonished McCulloch. At every moment came a torrent of data corresponding to the landslide senses he remembered, smell, taste, touch; and some central processing unit within the lobster's brain handled everything in the most effortless fashion.

But there was no sound. The ocean world appeared to be wholly silent. McCulloch knew that that was untrue, that sound waves propagated through water as persistently as through air, if somewhat more rapidly. Yet the lobster seemed neither to possess nor to need any sort of auditory equipment. The sensory bristles brought in all the data it required. The "speech" of these creatures, McCulloch had long ago realized, was effected not by voice but by means of spurts of chemicals released into the water, hormones, perhaps, or amino acids, something of a distinct and readily recognizable identity, emitted in some high-redundancy pattern that permitted easy recognition and decoding despite the difficulties caused by currents and eddies. It was, McCulloch thought, like trying to communicate by printing individual letters on scraps of paper and hurling them into the wind. But it did somehow seem to work, however clumsy a concept it might be, because of the extreme sensitivity of the lobster's myriad chemoreceptors.

The antennae played some significant role also. There were two sets of them, a pair of three-branched ones just behind the eyes and a much longer single-branched pair behind those. The long ones restlessly twitched and probed inquisitively, and most likely, he suspected, served as simple balancing and coordination devices much like the whiskers of a cat. The purpose of the smaller antennae eluded him, but it was his guess that they were involved in the process of communication between one lobster and another, either by some semaphore system or in a deeper communion beyond his still awkward comprehension.

McCulloch regretted not knowing more about the lobsters of his own era. But he had only a broad general knowledge of natural history, extensive, fairly deep, yet not good enough to tell him whether these elaborate sensory functions were characteristic of all lobsters or had evolved during the millions of years it had taken to create the water world. Probably some of each, he decided. Very likely even the lobsters of the former world had had much of this scanning equipment, enough to allow them to locate their prey, to find their way around in the dark suboceanic depths, to undertake their long and unerring migrations. But he found it hard to believe that they could have had much "speech" capacity, that they gathered in solemn sessions to discuss abstruse questions of theology and mythology, to argue gently about omens and heralds and the end of all things. That was something that the patient and ceaseless unfoldings of time must have wrought.

The lobsters marched without show of fatigue: not scampering in that dancelike way that his host had adopted while summoning its comrades to save it from the swimming creature, but moving nevertheless in an elegant and graceful fashion, barely touching the ground with the tips of their legs, going onward step by step by step steadily and fairly swiftly.

McCulloch noticed that new lobsters frequently joined the procession, cutting in from left or right just ahead of his host, who always remained at the rear of the line; that line now was so long, hundreds of lobsters long, that it was impossible to see its beginning. Now and again one would reach out with its bigger claw to seize some passing animal, a starfish or urchin or small crab, and without missing a step would shred and devour it, tossing the unwanted husk to the cloud of planktonic scavengers that always hovered nearby. This foraging on the march was done with utter lack of self-consciousness; it was almost by reflex that these creatures snatched and gobbled as they journeyed.

And yet all the same they did not seem like mere marauding mouths. From this long line of crustaceans there emanated, McCulloch realized, a mysterious sense of community, a wholeness of society, that he did not understand but quite sharply sensed. This was plainly not a mere migration but a true pilgrimage. He thought ruefully of his earlier condescending view of these people, incapable of achieving the Taj Mahal or the Sistine Chapel, and felt abashed: for he was beginning to see that they had other accomplishments of a less tangible sort that were only barely apparent to his displaced and struggling mind.

※

"When you come back," Maggie said, "you'll be someone else. There's no escaping that. It's the one thing I'm frightened of. Not that you'll die making the hop, or that you'll get into some sort of terrible trouble in the future, or that we won't be able to bring you back at all, or anything like that. But that you'll have become someone else."

"I feel pretty secure in my identity," McCulloch told her.

"I know you do. God knows, you're the most stable person in the group, and that's why you're going. But even so. Nobody's ever done anything like this before. It can't help but change you. When you return, you're going to be unique among the human race."

"That sounds very awesome. But I'm not sure it'll matter that much, Mag. I'm just taking a little trip. If I were going to Paris, or Istanbul, or even Antarctica, would I come back totally transformed? I'd have had some new experiences, but—"

"It isn't the same," she said. "It isn't even remotely the same." She came across the room to him and put her hands on his shoulders, and stared deep into his eyes, which sent a little chill through him, as it always did; for when she looked at him that way there was a sudden flow of energy between them, a powerful warm rapport rushing from her to him and from him to her as though through a huge conduit, that delighted and frightened him both at once. He could lose himself in her. He had never let himself feel that way about anyone before. And this was not the moment to begin. There was no room in him for such feelings, not now, not when he was within a couple of hours of leaping off into the most unknown of unknowns. When he returned—if he returned—he might risk allowing something at last to develop with Maggie. But not on the eve of departure, when everything in his universe was tentative and conditional. "Can I tell you a little story, Jim?" she asked.

"Sure."

"When my father was on the faculty at Cal, he was invited to a reception to meet a couple of the early astronauts, two of the Apollo men—I don't remember which ones, but they were from the second or third voyage to the Moon. When he showed up at the faculty club, there were two or three hundred people there, milling around having cocktails, and most of them were people he didn't know. He walked in and looked around and within ten seconds he had found the astronauts. He didn't have to be told. He just *knew*. And this is my father, remember, who doesn't believe in ESP or anything like that. But he said they were impossible to miss, even in that crowd. You could see it on their faces, you could feel the radiance coming from them, there was an aura, there was something about their eyes. Something that said, *I have walked on the Moon, I have been to that place which is not of our world and I have come back, and now I am someone else. I am who I was before, but I am someone else also.*"

"But they went to the *Moon*, Mag!"

"And you're going to the *future*, Jim. That's even weirder. You're going to a place that doesn't exist. And you may meet yourself there—ninety-nine years old, and waiting to shake hands with you—or you might meet me, or your grandson, or find out that everyone on Earth is dead, or that everyone has turned into a disembodied spirit, or that they're all immortal super-beings, or—or—Christ, I don't know. You'll see a world that nobody alive today is supposed to see. And when you come back, you'll have that aura. You'll be transformed."

"Is that so frightening?"

"To me it is," she said.

"Why is that?"

"Dummy," she said. "Dope. How explicit do I have to be, anyway? I thought I was being obvious enough."

He could not meet her eyes. "This isn't the best moment to talk about—"

"I know. I'm sorry, Jim. But you're important to me, and you're going somewhere and you're going to become someone else, and I'm scared. Selfish and scared."

"Are you telling me not to go?"

"Don't be absurd. You'd go no matter what I told you, and I'd despise you if you didn't. There's no turning back now."

"No."

"I shouldn't have dumped any of this on you today. You don't need it right this moment."

"It's okay," he said softly. He turned until he was looking straight at her, and for a long moment he simply stared into her eyes and did not speak, and then at last he said, "Listen, I'm going to take a big fantastic improbably insane voyage, and I'm going to be a witness to God knows what, and then I'm going to come back, and yes, I'll be changed—only an ox wouldn't be changed, or maybe only a block of stone—but I'll still be me, whoever *me* is. Don't worry, okay? I'll still be me. And we'll still be us."

"Whoever *us* is."

"Whoever. Jesus, I wish you were going with me, Mag!"

"That's the silliest schoolboy thing I've ever heard you say."

"True, though."

"Well, I can't go. Only one at a time can go, and it's you. I'm not even sure I'd want to go. I'm not as crazy as you are, I suspect. You go, Jim, and come back and tell me all about it."

"Yes."

"And then we'll see what there is to see about you and me."

"Yes," he said.

She smiled. "Let me show you a poem, okay? You must know it, because it's Eliot, and you know all the Eliot there is. But I was reading him last night—thinking of you, reading him—and I found this, and it seemed to be the right words, and I wrote them down. From one of the *Quartets*."

"I think I know," he said:

> *"Time past and time future*
> *Allow but a little consciousness—"*

"That's a good one, too," Maggie said. "But it's not the one I had in mind." She unfolded a piece of paper. "It's this:

> *"We shall not cease from exploration*
> *And the end of all our exploring*
> *Will be to arrive where we started—"*

"*And know the place for the first time*," he completed. "Yes. Exactly. To arrive where we started. And know the place for the first time."

The lobsters were singing as they marched. That was the only word, McCulloch thought, that seemed to apply. The line of pilgrims now was immensely long—there must have been thousands in the procession by this time, and more were joining constantly—and from them arose an outpouring of chemical signals, within the narrowest of tonal ranges, that mingled in a close harmony and amounted to a kind of sustained chant on a few notes, swelling, filling all the ocean with its powerful and intense presence. Once again he had an image of them as monks, but not Benedictines now: these were Buddhist, rather, an endless line of yellow-robed holy men singing a great *om* as they made their way up some Tibetan slope. He was awed and humbled by it—by the intensity, and by the wholeheartedness of the devotion. It was getting hard for him to remember that these were crustaceans, no more than ragged claws scuttling across the floors of silent seas; he sensed minds all about him, whole and elaborate minds arising out of some rich cultural matrix, and it was coming to seem quite natural to him that these people should have armored exoskeletons and jointed eyestalks and a dozen busy legs.

His host had still not broken its silence, which must have extended now over a considerable period. Just how long a period, McCulloch had no idea, for there were no significant alternations of light and dark down here to indicate the passing of time, nor did the marchers ever seem to sleep, and they took their food, as he had seen, in a casual and random way without breaking step. But it seemed to McCulloch that he had been effectively alone in the host's body for many days.

He was not minded to try to reenter contact with the other just yet—not until he received some sort of signal from it. Plainly the host had withdrawn into some inner sanctuary to undertake a profound meditation; and McCulloch, now that the early bewilderment and anguish of his journey through time had begun to wear off, did not feel so dependent upon the host that he needed to blurt his queries constantly into his companion's consciousness. He would watch, and wait, and attempt to fathom the mysteries of this place unaided.

The landscape had undergone a great many changes since the beginning of the march. That gentle bottom of fine white sand had yielded to a terrain of rough dark gravel, and that to one of a pale sedimentary stuff made up of tiny shells, the mortal remains, no doubt, of vast hordes of diatoms and foraminifera, which rose like clouds of snowflakes at the lobsters' lightest steps. Then came a zone where a stratum of thick red clay spread in all directions. The clay held embedded in it an odd assortment of rounded rocks and clamshells and bits of chitin, so that it had the look of some complex paving material from a fashionable terrace. And after that they entered a region where slender spires of a sharp black stone, faceted like worked flint, sprouted stalagmite-fashion at their feet. Through all of this the lobster-pilgrims marched unperturbed, never halting, never breaking their file, moving in a straight line whenever possible and making only the slightest of deviations when compelled to it by the harshness of the topography.

Now they were in a district of coarse yellow sandy globules, out of which two types of coral grew: thin angular strands of deep jet, and supple, almost mobile fingers of a rich lovely salmon hue. McCulloch wondered where on Earth such stuff might be found, and chided himself at once for the foolishness of the thought: the seas he knew had been swallowed long ago in the great all-encompassing ocean that swathed the world, and the familiar continents, he supposed, had broken from their moorings and slipped to strange parts of the globe well before the rising of the waters. He had no landmarks. There was an equator somewhere, and there were two poles, but down here beyond the reach of direct sunlight, in this warm changeless uterine sea neither north nor south nor east held any meaning. He remembered other lines:

> Sand-strewn caverns, cool and deep
> Where the winds are all asleep;
> Where the spent lights quiver and gleam;
> Where the salt weed sways in the stream;
> Where the sea-beasts rang'd all round
> Feed in the ooze of their pasture-ground...

What was the next line? Something about great whales coming sailing by, sail and sail with unshut eye, round the world for ever and aye. Yes, but there were no great whales here, if he understood his host correctly, no dolphins, no sharks, no minnows; there were only these swarming lower creatures, mysteriously raised on high, lords of the world. And mankind? Birds and bats, horses and bears? Gone. Gone. And the valleys and meadows? The lakes and streams? Taken by the sea. The world lay before him like a land of dreams, transformed. But was it, as the poet had said, a place which hath really neither joy, nor love, nor light, nor certitude, nor peace, nor help for pain? It did not seem that way. For light there was merely that diffuse faint glow, so obscure it was close to nonexistent, that filtered down through unknown fathoms. But what was that lobster song, that ever-swelling crescendo, if not some hymn to love and certitude and peace, and help for pain? He was overwhelmed by peace, surprised by joy, and he did not understand what was happening to him. He was part of the march, that was all. He was a member of the pilgrimage.

He had wanted to know if there was any way he could signal to be pulled back home: a panic button, so to speak. Bleier was the one he asked, and the question seemed to drive the man into an agony of uneasiness. He scowled, he tugged at his jowls, he ran his hands through his sparse strands of hair.

"No," he said finally. "We weren't able to solve that one, Jim. There's simply no way of propagating a signal backward in time."

"I didn't think so," McCulloch said. "I just wondered."

"Since we're not actually sending your physical body, you shouldn't find yourself in any real trouble. Psychic discomfort, at the worst—disorientation, emotional upheaval, at the worst a sort of terminal homesickness. But I think you're strong enough to pull your way through any of that. And you'll always know that we're going to be yanking you back to us at the end of the experiment."

"How long am I going to be gone?"

"Elapsed time will be virtually nil. We'll throw the switch, off you'll go, you'll do your jaunt, we'll grab you back, and it'll seem like no time at all, perhaps a thousandth of a second. We aren't going to believe that you went anywhere at all, until you start telling us about it."

McCulloch sensed that Bleier was being deliberately evasive, not for the first time since McCulloch had been selected as the time traveler. "It'll seem like no time at all to the people watching in the lab," he said. "But what about for me?"

"Well, of course for you it'll be a little different, because you'll have had a subjective experience in another time frame."

"That's what I'm getting at. How long are you planning to leave me in the future? An hour? A week?"

"That's really hard to determine, Jim."

"What does that mean?"

"You know, we've sent only rabbits and stuff. They've come back okay, beyond much doubt—"

"Sure. They still munch on lettuce when they're hungry and they don't tie their ears together in knots before they hop. So I suppose they're none the worse for wear."

"Obviously we can't get much of a report from a rabbit."

"Obviously."

"You're sounding awfully goddamned hostile today, Jim. Are you sure you don't want us to scrub the mission and start training another volunteer?" Bleier asked.

"I'm just trying to elicit a little hard info," McCulloch said. "I'm not trying to back out. And if I sound hostile, it's only because you're dancing all around my questions, which is becoming a considerable pain in the ass."

Bleier looked squarely at him and glowered. "All right. I'll tell you anything you want to know that I'm capable of answering. Which is what I think I've been doing all along. When the rabbits come back, we test them and we observe no physiological changes, no trace of ill effects as a result of having separated the psyche from the body for the duration of a time jaunt. Christ, we can't even tell the rabbits *have* been on a time jaunt, except that our instruments indicate the right sort of thermodynamic drain and entropic reversal, and for all we know we're kidding ourselves about that, which is why we're risking our reputations and your neck to send a human being who can tell us what the fuck happens when we throw the switch. But you've seen the rabbits jaunting. You know as well as I do that they come back okay."

Patiently McCulloch said, "Yes. As okay as a rabbit ever is, I guess. But what I'm trying to find out from you, and what you seem unwilling to tell me, is how long I'm going to be up there in subjective time."

"We don't know, Jim," Bleier said.

"You don't *know?* What if it's ten years? What if it's a thousand? What if I'm going to live out an entire life span, or whatever is considered a life span a hundred years from now, and grow old and wise and wither away and die and then wake up a thousandth of a second later on your lab table?"

"We don't know. That's why we have to send a human subject."

"There's no way to measure subjective jaunt-time?"

"Our instruments are here. They aren't *there.* You're the only instrument we'll have there. For all we know, we're sending you off for a million years, and when you come back here you'll have turned into something out of H.G. Wells. Is that straightforward enough for you,

Jim? But I don't think it's going to happen that way, and Mortenson doesn't think so either, or Ybarra for that matter. What we think is that you'll spend something between a day and a couple of months in the future, with the outside possibility of a year. And when we give you the hook, you'll be back here with virtually nil elapsed time. But to answer your first question again, there's no way you can instruct us to yank you back. You'll just have to sweat it out, however long it may be. I thought you knew that. The book, when it comes, will be virtually automatic, a function of the thermodynamic homeostasis, like the recoil of a gun. An equal and opposite reaction: or maybe more like the snapping back of a rubber band. Pick whatever metaphor you want. But if you don't like the way any of this sounds, it's not too late for you to back out, and nobody will say a word against you. It's never too late to back out. Remember that, Jim."

McCulloch shrugged. "Thanks for leveling with me. I appreciate that. And no, I don't want to drop out. The only thing I wonder about is whether my stay in the future is going to seem too long or too goddamned short. But I won't know that until I get there, will I? And then the time I have to wait before coming home is going to be entirely out of my hands. And out of yours, too, is how it seems. But that's all right. I'll take my chances. I just wondered what I'd do if I got there and found that I didn't much like it there."

"My bet is that you'll have the opposite problem," said Bleier. "You'll like it so much you won't want to come back."

Again and again, while the pilgrims traveled onward, McCulloch detected bright flares of intelligence gleaming like brilliant pinpoints of light in the darkness of the sea. Each creature seemed to have a characteristic emanation, a glow of neural energy. The simple ones—worms, urchins, starfish, sponges—emitted dim gentle signals; but there were others as dazzling as beacons. The lobster-folk were not the only sentient life-forms down here.

Occasionally he saw, as he had in the early muddled moments of the jaunt, isolated colonies of the giant sea anemones: great flowery-looking things, rising on thick pedestals. From them came a soft alluring lustful purr, a siren crooning calculated to bring unwary animals within reach of their swaying tentacles and the eager mouths hidden within the fleshy petals. Cemented to the floor on their swaying stalks, they seemed like somber philosophers, lost in the intervals between meals in deep reflections on the purpose of the cosmos. McCulloch longed to pause and try to speak with them, for their powerful emanation appeared plainly to indicate that they possessed a strong intelligence, but the lobsters moved past the anemones without halting.

The squidlike beings that frequently passed in flotillas overhead seemed even keener of mind: large animals, sleek and arrogant of motion, with long turquoise bodies that terminated in hawserlike arms, and enormous bulging eyes of a startling scarlet color. He found them ugly and repugnant, and did not quite know why. Perhaps it was some attitude of his host's that carried over subliminally to him; for there was an unmistakable chill among the lobsters whenever the squids appeared, and the chanting of the marchers grew more vehement, as though betokening a warning.

That some kind of frosty detente existed between the two kinds of lifeforms was apparent from the regard they showed one another and from the distances they maintained. Never did the squids descend into the ocean-floor zone that was the chief domain of the lobsters, but for long spans of time they would soar above, in a kind of patient aerial surveillance, while the lobsters, striving ostentatiously to ignore them, betrayed discomfort by quickened movements of their antennae.

Still other kinds of high-order intelligence manifested themselves as the pilgrimage proceeded. In a zone of hard and rocky terrain McCulloch felt a new and distinctive mental pulsation, coming from some creature that he must not have encountered before. But he saw nothing unusual: merely a rough grayish landscape pockmarked by dense clumps of oysters and barnacles, some shaggy outcroppings of sponges and yellow seaweeds, a couple of torpid anemones. Yet out of the midst of all that unremarkable clutter came clear strong signals, produced by minds of considerable force. Whose? Not the oysters and barnacles, surely. The mystery intensified as the lobsters, without pausing in their march, interrupted their chant to utter words of greeting, and had greetings in return, drifting toward them from that tangle of marine underbrush.

"Why do you march?" the unseen speakers asked, in a voice that rose in the water like a deep slow groaning.

"We have had an Omen," answered the lobsters.

"Ah, is it the Time?"

"The Time will surely be here," the lobsters replied.

"Where is the herald, then?"

"The herald is within me," said McCulloch's host, breaking its long silence at last.

—*To whom do you speak?* McCulloch asked.

—*Can you not see? There. Before us.*

McCulloch saw only algae, barnacles, sponges, oysters.

—*Where?*

—*In a moment you will see,* said the host.

The column of pilgrims had continued all the while to move forward, until now it was within the thick groves of seaweed. And now McCulloch saw who the other speakers were. Huge crabs were crouched at the bases of many of the larger rock formations, creatures far greater in size than the largest of the lobsters, but they were camouflaged so we'll that they were virtually invisible except at the closest range. On their broad arching backs whole gardens grew: brilliantly colored sponges, algae in somber reds and browns, fluffy many-branched crimson things, odd complex feathery growths, even a small anemone or two, all jammed together in such profusion that nothing of the underlying crab showed except beady long-stalked eyes and glinting claws. Why beings that signaled their presence with potent telepathic outputs should choose to cloak themselves in such elaborate concealments, McCulloch could not guess: perhaps it was to deceive a prey so simple that it was unable to detect the emanations of these crabs' minds.

As the lobsters approached, the crabs heaved themselves up a little way from the rocky bottom, and shifted themselves ponderously from side to side, causing the intricate streamers and filaments and branches of the creatures growing on them to stir and wave about. It was like a forest agitated by a sudden hard gust wind from the north.

"Why do you march, why do you march?" called the crabs. "Surely it is not yet the time. Surely!"

"Surely it is," the lobsters replied. "So we all agree. Will you march with us?"

"Show us your herald!" the crabs cried. "Let us see the Omen!"

—*Speak to them,* said McCulloch's host.

—*But what am I to say?*

—*The truth. What else can you say?*

—*I know nothing. Everything here is a mystery to me.*

—*I will explain all things afterward. Speak to them now.*

—*Without understanding?*

—*Tell them what you told us.*

Baffled, McCulloch said, speaking through the host, "I have come from the former world as an emissary. Whether I am a herald, whether I bring an Omen, is not for me to say. In my own world I breathed air and carried my shell within my body."

"Unmistakably a herald," said the lobsters.

To which the crabs replied, "That is not so unmistakable to us. We sense a wanderer and a revenant among you. But what does that mean? The Molting of the World is not a small thing, good friends. Shall we march, just because this strangeness is come upon you? It is not enough evidence. And to march is not a small thing either, at least for us."

"We have chosen to march," the lobsters said, and indeed they had not halted at all throughout this colloquy; the vanguard of their procession was far out of sight in a black-walled canyon, and McCulloch's host, still at the end of the line, was passing now through the last few crouching places of the great crabs. "If you mean to join us, come now."

From the crabs came a heavy outpouring of regret. "Alas, alas, we are large, we are slow, the way is long, the path is dangerous."

"Then we will leave you."

"If it is the Time, we know that you will perform the offices on our behalf. If it is not the Time, it is just as well that we do not make the pilgrimage. We are—not—certain. We—cannot—be—sure—it—is—an—Omen—"

McCulloch's host was far beyond the last of the crabs. Their words were faint and indistinct, and the final few were lost in the gentle surgings of the water.

—*They make a great error,* said McCulloch's host to him. *If it is truly the Time, and they do not join the march, it might happen that their souls will be lost. That is a severe risk: but they are a lazy folk. Well, we will perform the offices on their behalf.*

And to the crabs the host called, "We will do all that is required, have no fear!" But it was impossible, McCulloch thought, that the words could have reached the crabs across such a distance.

He and the host now were entering the mouth of the black canyon. With the host awake and talkative once again, McCulloch meant to seize the moment at last to have some answers to his questions.

—*Tell me now*—he began.

But before he could complete the thought, he felt the sea roil and surge about him as though he had been swept up in a monstrous wave. That could not be, not at this depth; but yet that irresistible force, booming toward him out of the dark canyon and catching him up, hurled him into a chaos as desperate as that of his moment of arrival. He sought to cling, to grasp, but there was no purchase; he was loose of his moorings; he was tossed and flung like a bubble on the winds.

—*Help me!* he called. *What's happening to us?*

—*To you, friend human McCulloch. To you alone. Can I aid you?*

What was that? Happening only to him? But certainly he and the lobster both were caught in this undersea tempest, both being thrown about, both whirled in the same maelstrom—

Faces danced around him. Charlie Bleier, pudgy, earnest-looking. Maggie, tender-eyed, troubled. Bleier had his hand on McCulloch's right wrist, Maggie on the other, and they were tugging, tugging—

But he had no wrists. He was a lobster.

"Come, Jim—"

"No! Not yet!"

"Jim—Jim—"

'Stop—pulling—you're hurting—"

"Jim—"

McCulloch struggled to free himself from their grasp. As he swung his arms in wild circles, Maggie and Bleier, still clinging to them, went whipping about like tethered balloons. "Let go," he shouted. "You aren't here! There's nothing for you to hold on to! You're just hallucinations! Let—go—!"

And then, as suddenly as they had come, they were gone.

The sea was calm. He was in his accustomed place, seated somewhere deep within his host's consciousness. The lobster was moving forward, steady as ever, into the black canyon, following the long line of its companions.

McCulloch was too stunned and dazed to attempt contact for along while. Finally, when he felt some measure of composure return, he reached his mind into his host's:

—*What happened?*

—*I cannot say. What did it seem like to you?*

—The water grew wild and stormy. I saw faces out of the former world. Friends of mine. They were pulling at my arms. You felt nothing?

—Nothing, said the host, *except a sense of your own turmoil. We are deep here: beyond the reach of storms.*

—Evidently I'm not.

—Perhaps your homefaring time is coming. Your world is summoning you.

Of course! The faces, the pulling at his arms—the plausibility of the host's suggestion left McCulloch trembling with dismay. Homefaring time! Back there in the lost and inconceivable past, they had begun angling for him, casting their line into the vast gulf of time—

—I'm not ready, he protested. *I've only just arrived here! I know nothing yet! How can they call me so soon?*

—Resist them, if you would remain.

—Will you help me?

—How would that be possible?

—I'm not sure, McCulloch said. *But it's too early for me to go back. If they pull on me again, hold me! Can you?*

—I can try, friend human McCulloch.

—And you have to keep your promise to me now.

—What promise is that?

—You said you would explain things to me. Why you've undertaken this pilgrimage. What it is I'm supposed to be the Omen of. What happens when the Time comes. The Molting of the World.

—Ah, said the host.

But that was all it said. In silence it scrabbled with busy legs over a sharply creviced terrain. McCulloch felt a fierce impatience growing in him. What if they yanked him again, now, and this time they succeeded? There was so much yet to learn! But he hesitated to prod the host again, feeling abashed. Long moments passed. Two more squids appeared: the radiance of their probing minds was like twin searchlights overhead. The ocean floor sloped downward gradually but perceptibly here. The squids vanished, and another of the predatory big-mouthed swimming-things, looking as immense as a whale and, McCulloch supposed, filling the same ecological niche, came cruising down into the level where the lobsters marched, considered their numbers in what appeared to be some surprise, and swam slowly upward again and out of sight. Something else of great size, flapping enormous wings somewhat like those of a stingray but clearly just a boneless mass of chitin-strutted flesh, appeared next, surveyed the pilgrims with equally bland curiosity, and flew to the front of the line of lobsters, where McCulloch lost it in the darkness. While all of this was happening the host was quiet and inaccessible, and McCulloch did not dare attempt to penetrate its privacy. But then, as the pilgrims were moving through a region where huge, dim-witted scallops with great bright eyes nestled everywhere, waving gaudy pink and blue mantles, the host unexpectedly resumed the conversation as though there had been no interruption, saying:

—*What we call the Time of the Molting of the World is the time when the world undergoes a change of nature, and is purified and reborn. At such a time, we journey to the place of dry land, and perform certain holy rites.*

—*And these rites bring about the Molting of the World?* McCulloch asked.

—*Not at all. The Molting is an event wholly beyond our control. The rites are performed for our own sakes, not for the world's.*

—*I'm not sure I understand.*

—*We wish to survive the Molting, to travel onward into the world to come. For this reason, at a Time of Molting, we must make our observances, we must demonstrate our worth. It is the responsibility of my people. We bear the duty for all the peoples of the world.*

—*A priestly caste, is that it?* McCulloch said. *When this cataclysm comes, the lobsters go forth to say the prayers for everyone, so that everyone's soul will survive?*

The host was silent again: pondering McCulloch's terms, perhaps, translating them into more appropriate equivalents. Eventually it replied:

—*That is essentially correct.*

—*But other peoples can join the pilgrimage if they want. Those crabs. The anemones. The squids, even?*

—*We invite all to come. But we do not expect anyone but ourselves actually to do it.*

—*How often has there been such a ceremony?* McCulloch asked.

—*I cannot say. Never, perhaps.*

—*Never?*

—*The Molting of the World is not a common event. We think it has happened only twice since the beginning of time.*

In amazement McCulloch said:

—*Twice since the world began, and you think it's going to happen again in your own lifetimes?*

—*Of course we cannot be sure of that. But we have had an Omen, or so we think, and we must abide by that. It was foretold that when the end* is near, an emissary from the former world would come among us. And so it has come to pass. Is that not so?

—Indeed.

—Then we must make the pilgrimage, for if you have not brought the Omen we have merely wasted some effort, but if you are the true herald we will have forfeited all of eternity if we let your message go unheeded.

It sounded eerily familiar to McCulloch: a messianic prophecy, a cult of the millennium, an apocalyptic transfiguration. He felt for a moment as though he had landed in the tenth century instead of in some impossibly remote future epoch. And yet the host's tone was so calm and rational, the sense of spiritual obligation that the lobster conveyed was so profound, that McCulloch found nothing absurd in these beliefs. Perhaps the world *did* end from time to time, and the performing of certain rituals did in fact permit its inhabitants to transfer their souls onward into whatever unimaginable environment was to succeed the present one. Perhaps.

—Tell me, said McCulloch. *What were the former worlds like, and what will the next one be?*

—You should know more about the former worlds than I, friend human McCulloch. And as for the world to come, we may only speculate.

—But what are your traditions about those worlds?

—The first world, the lobster said, was a world of fire.

—You can understand fire, living in the sea?

—We have heard tales of it from those who have been to the dry place. Above the water there is air, and in the air there hangs a ball of fire, which gives the world warmth. Is this not the case?

McCulloch, hearing a creature of the ocean floor speak of things so far beyond its scope and comprehension, felt a warm burst of delight and admiration.

—Yes! We call that ball of fire the sun.

—Ah, so that is what you mean, when you think of the sun! The word was a mystery to me, when first you used it. But I understand you much better now, do you not agree?

—You amaze me, McCulloch said.

—The first world, so we think, was fire: it was like the sun. And when we dwelled upon that world, we were fire also. It is the fire that we carry within us to this day, that glow, that brightness, which is our life, and which goes from us when we die. After a span of time so long that we could never describe its length, the Time of the Molting came upon the fire world and it *grew hard, and gathered a cloak of air about itself, and creatures lived upon the land and breathed the air. I find that harder to comprehend, in truth, than I do the fire world. But that was the first Molting, when the air world emerged: that world from which you have come to us. I hope you will tell me of your world, friend human McCulloch, when there is time.*

—So I will, said McCulloch. *But there is so much more I need to hear from you first!*

—Ask it.

—The second Molting—the disappearance of my world, the coming of yours—

—The tradition is that the sea existed, even in the former world, and that it was not small. At the Time of the Molting it rose and devoured the land and all that was upon it, except for one place that was not devoured, which is sacred. And then all the world was covered by water, and that was the second Molting, which brought forth the third world.

—How long ago was that?

—How can I speak of the passing of time? There is no way to speak of that. Time passes, and lives end, and worlds are transformed. But we have no words for that. If every grain of sand in the sea were one lifetime, then it would be as many lifetimes ago as there are grains of sand in the sea. But does that help you? Does that tell you anything? It happened. It was very long ago. And now our world's turn has come, or so we think.

—And the next world? What will that be like? McCulloch asked.

—There are those who claim to know such things, but I am not one of them. We will know the next world when we have entered it, and I am content to wait until then for the knowledge.

McCulloch had a sense then that the host had wearied of this sustained contact, and was withdrawing once again from it; and, though his own thirst for knowledge was far from sated, he chose once again not to attempt to resist that withdrawal.

All this while the pilgrims had continued down a gentle incline into the great bowl of a sunken valley. Once again now the ocean floor was level, but the water was notably deeper here, and the diffused light from above was so dim that only the most rugged of algae could grow, making the landscape bleak and sparse. There were no sponges here, and little coral, and the anemones were pale and small, giving little sign of the potent intelligence that infused their larger cousins in the shallower zones of the sea.

But there were other creatures at this level that McCulloch had not seen before. Platoons of alert, mobile oysters skipped over the bottom, leaping in agile bounds on columns of water that they squirted like jets from tubes in their dark green mantles: now and again they paused in midleap and their shells quickly opened and closed, snapping shut, no doubt, on some hapless larval thing of the plankton too small for McCulloch, via the lobster's imperfect vision, to detect. From these oysters came bright darting blurts of mental activity, sharp and probing: they must be as intelligent, he thought, as cats or dogs. Yet from time to time a lobster, swooping with an astonishingly swift claw, would seize one of these oysters and deftly, almost instantaneously, shuck and devour it. Appetite was no respecter of intelligence in this world of needful carnivores, McCulloch realized.

Intelligent, too, in their way, were the hordes of nearly invisible little crustaceans—shrimp of some sort, he imagined—that danced in shining clouds just above the line of march. They were ghostly things perhaps an inch long, virtually transparent, colorless, lovely, graceful. Their heads bore two huge glistening black eyes; their intestines, glowing coils running the length of their bodies, were tinged with green; the tips of their tails were an elegant crimson. They swam with the aid of a horde of busy finlike legs, and seemed almost to be mocking their stolid, plodding cousins as they marched; but these sparkling little creatures also occasionally fell victim to the lobsters' inexorable claws, and each time it was like the extinguishing of a tiny brilliant candle.

An emanation of intelligence of a different sort came from bulky animals that McCulloch noticed roaming through the gravelly foothills flanking the line of march. These seemed at first glance to be another sort of lobster, larger even than McCulloch's companions: heavily armored things with many-segmented abdomens and thick paddle-shaped arms. But then, as one of them drew nearer, McCulloch saw the curved tapering tail with its sinister spike, and realized he was in the presence of the scorpions of the sea.

They gave off a deep, almost somnolent mental wave: slow thinkers but not light ones, Teutonic ponderers, grapplers with the abstruse. There were perhaps two dozen of them, who advanced upon the pilgrims and in quick one-sided struggles pounced, stung, slew.

McCulloch watched in amazement as each of the scorpions dragged away a victim and, no more than a dozen feet from the line of march, began to gouge into its armor to draw forth tender chunks of pale flesh, without drawing the slightest response from the impassive, steadily marching column of lobsters.

They had not been so complacent when the great-mouthed swimming-thing had menaced McCulloch's host; then, the lobsters had come in hordes to tear the attacker apart. And whenever one of the big squids came by, the edgy hostility of the lobsters, their willingness to do battle if necessary, was manifest. But they seemed indifferent to the scorpions. The lobsters accepted their onslaught as placidly as though it were merely a toll they must pay in order to pass through this district. Perhaps it was. McCulloch was only beginning to perceive how dense and intricate a fabric of ritual bound this submarine world together.

The lobsters marched onward, chanting in unfailing rhythm as though nothing untoward had happened. The scorpions, their hungers evidently gratified, withdrew and congregated a short distance off, watching without much show of interest as the procession went by them. By the time McCulloch's host, bringing up the rear, had gone past the scorpions, they were fighting among themselves in a lazy, half-hearted way, like playful lions after a successful hunt. Their mental emanation, sluggishly booming through the water, grew steadily more blurred, more vague, more toneless.

And then it was overlaid and entirely masked by the pulsation of some new and awesome kind of mind ahead: one of enormous power, whose output beat upon the water with what was almost a physical force, like some massive metal chain being lashed against the surface of the ocean. Apparently the source of this gigantic output still lay at a considerable distance, for, strong as it was, it grew stronger still as the lobsters advanced toward it, until at last it was an overwhelming clangor, terrifying, bewildering. McCulloch could no longer remain quiescent under the impact of that monstrous sound. Breaking through to the sanctuary of his host, he cried:

—*What is it?*

—*We are approaching a god,* the lobster replied.

—*A god, did you say?*

—*A divine presence, yes. Did you think we were the rulers of this world?*

In fact McCulloch had, assuming automatically that his time jaunt had deposited him within the consciousness of some member of this world's highest species, just as he would have expected to have landed had he reached the twenty-second century as intended, in the consciousness of a human rather than in a frog or a horse. But obviously the division between humanity and all subsentient species in his own world did not have an exact parallel here; many races, perhaps all of them, had some sort of intelligence, and it was becoming clear that the lobsters, though a high life-form, were not the highest. He found that dismaying and even humbling; for the lobsters seemed quite adequately intelligent to him, quite the equals—for all his early condescension to them—of mankind itself. And now he was to meet one of their gods? How great a mind was a god likely to have?

The booming of that mind grew unbearably intense, nor was there any way to hide from it. McCulloch visualized himself doubled over in pain, pressing his hands to his ears, an image that drew a quizzical shaft of thought from his host. Still the lobsters pressed forward, but even they were responding now to the waves of mental energy that rippled outward from that unimaginable source. They had at last broken ranks, and were fanning out horizontally on the broad dark plain of the ocean floor, as though deploying themselves before a place of worship. Where was the god? McCulloch, striving with difficulty to see in this nearly lightless place, thought he made out some vast shape ahead, some dark entity, swollen and fearsome, that rose like a colossal boulder in the midst of the suddenly diminutive-looking lobsters. He saw eyes like bright yellow platters, gleaming furiously; he saw a huge frightful beak; he saw what he thought at first to be a nest of writhing serpents, and then realized to be tentacles, dozens of them, coiling and uncoiling with a terrible restless energy. To the host he said:

—*Is that your god?*

But he could not hear the reply, for an agonizing new force suddenly buffeted him, one even more powerful than that which was emanating from the giant creature that sat before him. It ripped upward through his soul like a spike. It cast him forth, and he tumbled over and over, helpless in some incomprehensible limbo, where nevertheless he could still hear the faint distant voice of his lobster host:

—*Friend human McCulloch? Friend human McCulloch?*

He was drowning. He had waded incautiously into the surf, deceived by the beauty of the transparent tropical water and the shimmering white sand below, and a wave had caught him and knocked him to his knees, and the next wave had come before he could rise, pulling him under. And now he tossed like a discarded doll in the suddenly turbulent sea, struggling to get his head above water and failing, failing, failing.

Maggie was standing on the shore, calling in panic to him, and somehow he could hear her words even through the tumult of the crashing waves: "This way, Jim, swim toward me! Oh, please, Jim, this way, this way!"

Bleier was there, too, Mortenson, Bob Rodrigues, the whole group, ten or fifteen people, running about worriedly, beckoning to him, calling his name. It was odd that he could see them, if he was under water. And he could hear them so clearly, too, Bleier telling him to stand up and walk ashore, the water wasn't deep at all, and Rodrigues saying to come in on hands and knees if he couldn't manage to get up, and Ybarra yelling that it was getting late, that they couldn't wait all the goddamned afternoon, that he had been swimming long enough. McCulloch wondered why they didn't come after him, if they were so eager to get him to shore. Obviously he was in trouble. Obviously he was unable to help himself.

"Look," he said, "I'm drowning, can't you see? Throw me a line, for Christ's sake!" Water rushed into his mouth as he spoke. It filled his lungs, it pressed against his brain.

"We can't hear you, Jim!"

"Throw me a line!" he cried again, and felt the torrents pouring through his body. "I'm drowning—drowning—"

And then he realized that he did not at all want them to rescue him, that it was worse to be rescued than to drown. He did not understand why he felt that way, but he made no attempt to question the feeling. All that concerned him now was preventing those people on the shore, those humans, from seizing him and taking him from the water. They were rushing about, assembling some kind of machine to pull him in, an arm at the end of a great boom. McCulloch signaled to them to leave him alone.

"I'm okay," he called. "I'm not drowning after all! I'm fine right where I am!"

But now they had their machine in operation, and its long metal arm was reaching out over the water toward him. He turned and dived, and swam as hard as he could away from the shore, but it was no use: the boom seemed to extend over an infinite distance, and no matter how fast he swam the boom moved faster, so that it hovered just above him now, and from its tip some sort of hook was descending—

"No—no—let me be! I don't want to go ashore!"

Then he felt a hand on his wrist: firm, reassuring, taking control. All right, he thought. They've caught me after all, they're going to pull me in. There's nothing I can do about it. They have me, and that's all there is to it. But he realized, after a moment, that he was heading not toward shore but out to sea, beyond the waves, into the calm warm depths. And the hand that was on his wrist was not a hand; it was a tentacle, thick as heavy cable, a strong sturdy tentacle lined on one side by rounded section cups that held him in an unbreakable grip.

That was all right. Anything to be away from that wild crashing surf. It was much more peaceful out here. He could rest, catch his breath, get his equilibrium. And all the while that powerful tentacle towed him steadily seaward. He could still hear the voices of his friends onshore, but they were as faint as the cries of distant seabirds now, and when he looked back he saw only tiny dots, like excited ants, moving along the beach. McCulloch waved at them. "See you some other time," he called. "I didn't want to come out of the water yet anyway." Better here. Much much better. Peaceful. Warm. Like the womb. And that tentacle around his wrist: so reassuring, so steady.

—*Friend human McCulloch? Friend human McCulloch?*

—*This is where I belong. Isn't it?*

—*Yes. This is where you belong. You are one of us, friend human McCulloch. You are one of us.*

Gradually the turbulence subsided, and he found himself regaining his balance. He was still within the lobster; the whole horde of lobsters was gathered around him, thousands upon thousands of them, a gentle solicitous community, and right in front of him was the largest octopus imaginable, a creature that must have been fifteen or twenty feet in diameter, with tentacles that extended an implausible distance on all sides. Somehow he did not find the sight frightening.

"He is recovered now," his host announced.

—*What happened to me?* McCulloch asked.

—Your people called you again. But you did not want to make your homefaring, and you resisted them. And when we understood that you wanted to remain, the god aided you, and you broke free of their pull.

—The god?

His host indicated the great octopus.

—There.

It did not seem at all improbable to McCulloch now. The infinite fullness of time brings about everything, he thought: even intelligent lobsters, even a divine octopus. He still could feel the mighty telepathic output of the vast creature, but though it had lost none of its power it no longer caused him discomfort; it was like the roaring thunder of some great waterfall, to which one becomes accustomed, and which, in time, one begins to love. The octopus sat motionless, its immense yellow eyes trained on McCulloch, its scarlet mantle rippling gently, its tentacles weaving in intricate patterns. McCulloch thought of an octopus he had once seen when he was diving in the West Indies: a small shy scuttling thing, hurrying to slither behind a gnarled coral head. He felt chastened and awed by this evidence of the magnifications wrought by the eons. A hundred million years? Half a billion? The numbers were without meaning. But that span of years had produced this creature. He sensed a serene intelligence of incomprehensible depth, benign, tranquil, all-penetrating: a god indeed. Yes. Truly a god. Why not?

The great cephalopod was partly sheltered by an overhanging wall of rock. Clustered about it were dozens of the scorpion-things, motionless, poised: plainly a guard force. Overhead swam a whole army of the big squids, doubtless guardians also, and for once the presence of those creatures did not trigger any emotion in the lobsters, as if they regarded squids in the service of the god as acceptable ones. The scene left McCulloch dazed with awe. He had never felt farther from home.

—The god would speak with you, said his host.

—What shall I say?

—Listen, first.

McCulloch's lobster moved forward until it stood virtually beneath the octopus's huge beak. From the octopus, then, came an outpouring of words that McCulloch did not immediately comprehend, but which, after a moment, he understood to be some kind of benediction that enfolded his soul like a warm blanket. And gradually he perceived that he was being spoken to.

"Can you tell us why you have come all this way, human McCulloch?"

"It was an error. They didn't mean to send me so far—only a hundred years or less, that was all we were trying to cross. But it was our first attempt. We didn't really know what we were doing. And I suppose I wound up halfway across time—a hundred million years, two hundred, maybe a billion—who knows?"

"It is a great distance. Do you feel no fear?"

"At the beginning I did. But not any longer. This world is alien to me, but not frightening."

"Do you prefer it to your own?"

"I don't understand," McCulloch said.

"Your people summoned you. You refused to go. You appealed to us for aid, and we aided you in resisting your homecalling, because it was what you seemed to require from us."

"I'm—not ready to go home yet," he said. "There's so much I haven't seen yet, and that I want to see. I want to see everything. I'll never have an opportunity like this again. Perhaps no one ever will. Besides, I have services to perform here. I'm the herald; I bring the Omen; I'm part of this pilgrimage. I think I ought to stay until the rites have been performed. I want to stay until then."

"Those rites will not be performed," said the octopus quietly.

"Not performed?"

"You are not the herald. You carry no Omen. The Time is not at hand."

McCulloch did not know what to reply. Confusion swirled within him. No Omen? Not the Time?

—It is so, said the host. *We were in error. The god has shown us that we came to our conclusion too quickly. The Time of the Molting may be near, but it is not yet upon us. You have many of the outer signs of a herald, but there is no Omen upon you. You are merely a visitor. An accident.*

McCulloch was assailed by a startlingly keen pang of disappointment. It was absurd; but for a time he had been the central figure in some apocalyptic ritual of immense significance, or at least had been thought to be, and all that suddenly was gone from him, and he felt strangely diminished, irrelevant, bereft of his bewildering grandeur. A visitor. An accident.

—In that case I feel great shame and sorrow, he said. *To have caused so much trouble for you. To have sent you off on this pointless pilgrimage.*

—No blame attaches to you, said the host. *We acted of our free choice, after considering the evidence.*

"Nor was the pilgrimage pointless," the octopus declared. "There are no pointless pilgrimages. And this one will continue."

"But if there's no Omen—if this is not the Time—"

"There are other needs to consider," replied the octopus, "and other observances to carry out. We must visit the dry place ourselves, from time to time, so that we may prepare ourselves for the world that is to succeed ours, for it will be very different from ours. It is time now for such a visit, and well past time. And also we must bring you to the dry place, for only there can we properly make you one of us."

"I don't understand," said McCulloch.

"You have asked to stay among us; and if you stay, you must become one of us, for your sake, and for ours. And that can best be done at the dry place. It is not necessary that you understand that now, human McCulloch."

—*Make no further reply*, said McCulloch's host. *The god has spoken. We must proceed.*

Shortly the lobsters resumed their march, chanting as before, though in a more subdued way, and, so it seemed to McCulloch, singing a different melody. From the context of his conversation with it, McCulloch had supposed that the octopus now would accompany them, which puzzled him, for the huge unwieldy creature did not seem capable of any extensive journey. That proved to be the case: the octopus did not go along, though the vast booming resonances of its mental output followed the procession for what must have been hundreds of miles.

Once more the line was a single one, with McCulloch's host at the end of the file. A short while after departure it said:

—*I am glad, friend human McCulloch, that you chose to continue with us. I would be sorry to lose you now.*

—*Do you mean that? Isn't it an inconvenience for you, to carry me around inside your mind?*

—*I have grown quite accustomed to it. You are part of me, friend human McCulloch. We are part of one another. At the place of the dry land we will celebrate our sharing of this body.*

—*I was lucky*, said McCulloch, *to have landed like this in a mind that would make me welcome.*

—*Any of us would have made you welcome*, responded the host.

McCulloch pondered that. Was it merely a courteous turn of phrase, or did the lobster mean him to take the answer literally? Most likely the latter: the host's words seemed always to have only a single level of meaning, a straightforwardly literal one. So any of the lobsters would have taken him in uncomplainingly? Perhaps so. They appeared to be virtually interchangeable beings, without distinctive individual personalities, without names, even. The host had remained silent when McCulloch had asked him its name, and had not seemed to understand what kind of a label McCulloch's own name was. So powerful was their sense of community, then, that they must have little sense of private identity. He had never cared much for that sort of hive mentality, where he had observed it in human society. But here it seemed not only appropriate but admirable.

—*How much longer will it be,* McCulloch asked, *before we reach the place of dry land?*

—*Long.*

—*Can you tell me where it is?*

—*It is in the place where the world grows narrower,* said the host.

McCulloch had realized, the moment he asked the question, that it was meaningless: what useful answer could the lobster possibly give? The old continents were gone and their names long forgotten. But the answer he had received was meaningless, too: where, on a round planet, is the place where the world grows narrower? He wondered what sort of geography the lobsters understood. If I live among them a hundred years, he thought, I will probably just begin to comprehend what their perceptions are like.

Where the world grows narrower. All right. Possibly the place of the dry land was some surviving outcropping of the former world, the summit of Mount Everest, perhaps, Kilimanjaro, whatever. Or perhaps not: perhaps even those peaks had been ground down by time, and new ones had arisen—one of them, at least, tall enough to rise above the universal expanse of sea. It was folly to suppose that any shred at all of his world remained accessible: it was all down there beneath tons of water and millions of years of sediments, the old continents buried, hidden, rearranged by time like pieces scattered about a board.

The pulsations of the octopus's mind could no longer be felt. As the lobsters went tirelessly onward, moving always in that lithe skipping stride of theirs and never halting to rest or to feed, the terrain rose for a time and then began to dip again, slightly at first and then more than slightly. They entered into waters that were deeper and significantly darker, and somewhat cooler as well. In this somber zone, where vision seemed all but useless, the pilgrims grew silent for long spells for the first time, neither chanting nor speaking to one another, and McCulloch's host, who had become increasingly quiet, disappeared once more into its impenetrable inner domain and rarely emerged.

In the gloom and darkness there began to appear a strange red glow off to the left, as though someone had left a lantern hanging midway between the ocean floor and the surface of the sea. The lobsters, when that mysterious light came into view, at once changed the direction of their line of march to go veering off to the right; but at the same time they resumed their chanting, and kept one eye trained on the glowing place as they walked.

The water felt warmer here. A zone of unusual heat was spreading outward from the glow. And the taste of the water, and what McCulloch persisted in thinking of as its smell, were peculiar, with a harsh choking salty flavor. Brimstone? Ashes?

McCulloch realized that what he was seeing was an undersea volcano, belching forth a stream of red-hot lava that was turning the sea into a boiling bubbling caldron. The sight stirred him oddly. He felt that he was looking into the pulsing ancient care of the world, the primordial flame, the geological link that bound the otherwise vanished former worlds to this one. There awakened in him a powerful tide of awe, and a baffling unfocused yearning that he might have termed homesickness, except that it was not, for he was no longer sure where his true home lay.

—*Yes,* said the host. *It is a mountain on fire. We think it is a part of the older of the two former worlds that has endured both of the Moltings. It is a very sacred place.*

—*An object of pilgrimage?* McCulloch asked.

—*Only to those who wish to end their lives. The fire devours all who approach it.*

—*In my world we had many such fiery mountains,* McCulloch said. *They often did great destruction.*

—*How strange your world must have been!*

—*It was very beautiful,* said McCulloch.

—*Surely. But strange. The dry land, the fire in the air—the sun, I mean—the air-breathing creatures—yes, strange, very strange. I can scarcely believe it really existed.*

HOMEFARING

—There are times, now, when I begin to feel the same way, McCulloch said.

The volcano receded in the distance; its warmth could no longer be felt; the water was dark again, and cold, and growing colder, and McCulloch could no longer detect any trace of that sulphurous aroma. It seemed to him that they were moving now down an endless incline, where scarcely any creatures dwelled.

And then he realized that the marchers ahead had halted, and were drawn up in a long row as they had been when they came to the place where the octopus held its court. Another god? No. There was only blackness ahead.

—*Where are we?* he asked.

—*It is the shore of the great abyss.*

Indeed what lay before them looked like the Pit itself: lightless, without landmark, an empty landscape. McCulloch understood now that they had been marching all this while across some sunken continent's coastal plain, and at last they had come to—what?—the graveyard where one of Earth's lost oceans lay buried in ocean?

—*Is it possible to continue?* he asked.

—*Of course,* said the host. *But now we must swim.*

Already the lobsters before them were kicking off from shore with vigorous strokes of their tails and vanishing into the open sea beyond. A moment later McCulloch's host joined them. Almost at once there was no sense of a bottom beneath them—only a dark and infinitely deep void. Swimming across this, McCulloch thought, is like falling through time—an endless descent and no safety net.

The lobsters, he knew, were not true swimming creatures: like the lobsters of his own era they were bottom-dwellers, who walked to get where they needed to go. But they could never cross this abyss that way, and so they were swimming now, moving steadily by flexing their huge abdominal muscles and their tails. Was it terrifying to them to be setting forth into a place without landmarks like this? His host remained utterly calm, as though this were no more than an afternoon stroll.

McCulloch lost what little perception of the passage of time that he had had. Heave, stroke, forward, heave, stroke, forward, that was all, endless repetition. Out of the depths there occasionally came an upwelling of cold water, like a dull, heavy river miraculously flowing upward through

471

air, and in that strange surging from below rose a fountain of nourishment, tiny transparent struggling creatures and even smaller flecks of some substance that must have been edible, for the lobsters, without missing a stroke, sucked in all they could hold. And swam on and on. McCulloch had a sense of being involved in a trek of epic magnitude, a once-in-many-generations thing that would be legendary long after.

Enemies roved this open sea: the free-swimming creatures that had evolved out of God only knew which kinds of worms or slugs to become the contemporary equivalents of sharks and whales. Now and again one of these huge beasts dived through the horde of lobsters, harvesting it at will. But they could eat only so much; and the survivors kept going onward.

Until at last—months, years later?—the far shore came into view; the ocean floor, long invisible, reared up beneath them and afforded support; the swimmers at last put their legs down on the solid bottom, and with something that sounded much like gratitude in their voices began once again to chant in unison as they ascended the rising flank of a new continent.

The first rays of the sun, when they came into view an unknown span of time later, struck McCulloch with an astonishing, overwhelming impact. He perceived them first as a pale-greenish glow resting in the upper levels of the sea just ahead, striking downward like illuminated wands; he did not then know what he was seeing, but the sight engendered wonder in him all the same, and later, when that radiance diminished and was gone and in a short while returned, he understood that the pilgrims were coming up out of the sea. So they had reached their goal: the still point of the turning world, the one remaining unsubmerged scrap of the former Earth.

—*Yes,* said the host. *This is it.*

In that same instant McCulloch felt another tug from the past: a summons dizzying in its inoperative impact. He thought he could hear Maggie Caldwell's voice crying across the time winds: "Jim, Jim, come back to us!" And Bleier, grouchy, angered, muttering, "For Christ's sake, McCulloch, stop holding on up there! This is getting expensive!" Was it all his imagination, that fantasy of hands on his wrists, familiar faces hovering before his eyes?

"Leave me alone," he said. "I'm still not ready."

"Will you ever he?" That was Maggie. "Jim, you'll be marooned. You'll be stranded there if you don't let us pull you back now."

"I may be marooned already," he said, and brushed the voices out of his mind with surprising ease.

He returned his attention to his companions and saw that they had halted their trek a little way short of that zone of light that now was but a quick scramble ahead of them. Their linear formation was broken once again. Some of the lobsters, marching blindly forward, were piling up in confused-looking heaps in the shallows, forming mounds fifteen or twenty lobsters deep. Many of the others had begun a bizarre convulsive dance: a wild twitchy cavorting, rearing up on their back legs, waving their claws about, flicking their antennae in frantic circles.

—*What's happening?* McCulloch asked his host. *Is this the beginning of a rite?*

But the host did not reply. The host did not appear to be within their shared body at all. McCulloch felt a silence far deeper than the host's earlier withdrawals; this seemed not a withdrawal but an evacuation, leaving McCulloch in sole possession. That new solitude came rolling in upon him with a crushing force. He sent forth a tentative probe, found nothing, found less than nothing. Perhaps it's meant to be this way, he thought. Perhaps it was necessary for him to face his climactic initiation unaided, unaccompanied.

Then he noticed that what he had taken to be a weird jerky dance was actually the onset of a mass molting prodrome. Hundreds of the lobsters had been stricken simultaneously, he realized, with that strange painful sense of inner expansion, of volcanic upheaval and stress: that heaving and rearing about was the first stage of the splitting of the shell.

And all of the molters were females.

Until that instant McCulloch had not been aware of any division into sexes among the lobsters. He had barely been able to tell one from the next; they had no individual character, no shred of uniqueness. Now, suddenly, strangely, he knew without being told that half of his companions were females, and that they were molting now because they were fertile only when they had shed their old armor, and that the pilgrimage to the place of the dry land was the appropriate time to engender the young. He had asked no questions of anyone to learn that; the knowledge was simply within him; and, reflecting on that, he saw that the host was absent from him because the host was wholly fused with him; he was the host, the host was Jim McCulloch.

He approached a female, knowing precisely which one was the appropriate one, and sang to her, and she acknowledged his song with a song of her own, and raised her third pair of legs to him, and let him plant his gametes beside her oviducts. There was no apparent pleasure in it, as he remembered pleasure from his days as a human. Yet it brought him a subtle but unmistakable sense of fulfillment, of the completion of biological destiny, that had a kind of orgasmic finality about it, and left him calm and anchored at the absolute dead center of his soul: yes, truly the still point of the turning world, he thought.

His mate moved away to begin her new Growing and the awaiting of her motherhood. And McCulloch, unbidden, began to ascend the slope that led to the land.

The bottom was fine sand here, soft, elegant. He barely touched it with his legs as he raced shoreward. Before him lay a world of light, radiant, heavenly, a bright irresistible beacon. He went on until the water, pearly pink and transparent, was only a foot or two deep, and the domed upper curve of his back was reaching into the air. He felt no fear. There was no danger in this. Serenely he went forward—the leader, now, of the trek—and climbed out into the hot sunlight.

It was an island, low and sandy, so small that he imagined he could cross it in a day. The sky was intensely blue, and the sun, hanging close to a noon position, looked swollen and fiery. A little grove of palm trees clustered a few hundred yards inland, but he saw nothing else, no birds, no insects, no animal life of any sort. Walking was difficult here—his breath was short, his shell seemed to be too tight, his stalked eyes were stinging in the air—but he pulled himself forward, almost to the trees. Other male lobsters, hundreds of them, thousands of them, were following. He felt himself linked to each of them: his people, his nation, his community, his brothers.

Now, at that moment of completion and communion, came one more call from the past.

There was no turbulence in it this time. No one was yanking at his wrists, no surf boiled and heaved in his mind and threatened to dash him on the reefs of the soul. The call was simple and clear: *This is the moment of coming back, Jim.*

Was it? Had he no choice? He belonged here. These were his people. This was where his loyalties lay.

And yet, and yet: he knew that he had been sent on a mission unique in human history, that he had been granted a vision beyond all dreams, that it was his duty to return and report on it. There was no ambiguity about that. He owed it to Bleier and Maggie and Ybarra and the rest to return, to tell them everything.

How clear it all was! He belonged *here,* and he belonged *there,* and an unbreakable net of loyalties and responsibilities held him to both places. It was a perfect equilibrium; and therefore he was tranquil and of ease. The pull was on him; he resisted nothing, for he was at last beyond all resistance to anything. The immense sun was a drumbeat in the heavens; the fiery warmth was a benediction; he had never known such peace.

"I must make my homefaring now," he said, and released himself, and let himself drift upward, light as a bubble, toward the sun.

Strange figures surrounded him, tall and narrow-bodied, with odd fleshy faces and huge moist mouths and bulging staring eyes, and their kind of speech was a crude hubbub of sound waves that bashed and battered against his sensibilities with painful intensity. "We were afraid the signal wasn't reaching you, Jim," they said. "We tried again and again, but there was no contact, nothing. And then just as we were giving up, suddenly your eyes were opening, you were stirring, you stretched your arms—"

He felt air pouring into his body, and dryness all about him. It was a struggle to understand the speech of these creatures who were bending over him, and he hated the reek that came from their flesh and the booming vibrations that they made with their mouths. But gradually he found himself returning to himself, like one who has been lost in a dream so profound that it eclipses reality for the first few moments of wakefulness.

"How long was I gone?" he asked.

"Four minutes and eighteen seconds," Ybarra said.

McCulloch shook his head. "Four minutes? Eighteen seconds? It was more like forty months, to me. Longer. I don't know how long."

"Where did you go, Jim? What was it like?"

"Wait," someone else said. "He's not ready for debriefing yet. Can't you see he's about to collapse?"

McCulloch shrugged. "You sent me too far."

"How far? Five hundred years?" Maggie asked.

"Millions," he said.

Someone gasped.

"He's dazed," a voice said at his left ear.

"Millions of years," McCulloch said in a slow, steady, determinedly articulate voice. *"Millions.* The whole earth was covered by the sea, except for one little island. The people are lobsters. They have a society, a culture. They worship a giant octopus."

Maggie was crying. "Jim, oh, Jim—"

"No. It's true. I went on migration with them. Intelligent lobsters is what they are. And I wanted to stay with them forever. I felt you pulling at me, but I—didn't—want—to—go—"

"Give him a sedative, Doc," Bleier said.

"You think I'm crazy? You think I'm deranged? They were lobsters, fellows. *Lobsters.*"

After he had slept and showered and changed his clothes they came to see him again, and by that time he realized that he must have been behaving like a lunatic in the first moments of his return, blurting out his words, weeping, carrying on, crying out what surely had sounded like gibberish to them. Now he was rested, he was calm, he was at home in his own body once again.

He told them all that had befallen him, and from their faces he saw at first that they still thought he had gone around the bend: but as he kept speaking, quietly, straightforwardly, in rich detail, they began to acknowledge his report in subtle little ways, asking questions about the geography, about the ecological balance, in a manner that showed him they were not simply humoring him. And after that, as it sank in upon them that he really had dwelled for a period of many months at the far end of time, beyond the span of the present world, they came to look upon him—it was unmistakable—as someone who was now wholly unlike them. In particular he saw the cold, glassy stare in Maggie Caldwell's eyes.

Then they left him, for he was tiring again; and later Maggie came to see him alone, and took his hand and held it between hers, which were cold.

She said, "What do you want to do now, Jim?"

"To go back there."

"I thought you did."

"It's impossible, isn't it?" he said.

"We could try. But it couldn't ever work. We don't know what we're doing, yet, with that machine. We don't know where we'd send you. We might miss by a million years. By a billion."

"That's what I figured, too."

"But you want to go back?"

He nodded. "I can't explain it. It was like being a member of some Buddhist monastery, do you see? Feeling *absolutely sure* that this is where you belong, that everything fits together perfectly, that you're an integral part of it. I've never felt anything like that before. I never will again."

"I'll talk to Bleier, Jim, about sending you back."

"No. Don't. I can't possibly get there. And I don't want to land anywhere else. Let Ybarra take the next trip. I'll stay here."

"Will you be happy?"

He smiled. "I'll do my best," he said.

When the others understood what the problem was, they saw to it that he went into reentry therapy—Bleier had already foreseen something like that, and made preparations for it—and after a while the pain went from him, that sense of having undergone a violent separation, of having been ripped untimely from the womb. He resumed his work in the group and gradually recovered his mental balance and took an active part in the second transmission, which sent a young anthropologist named Ludwig off for two minutes and eight seconds. Ludwig did not see lobsters, to McCulloch's intense disappointment. He went sixty years into the future and came back glowing with wondrous tales of atomic-fusion plants.

That was too bad, McCulloch thought. But soon he decided that it was just as well, that he preferred being the only one who had encountered the world beyond this world, probably the only human being who ever would.

He thought of that world with love, wondering about his mate and her millions of larvae, about the journey of his friends back across the great abyss, about the legends that were being spun about his visit in that unimaginably distant epoch. Sometimes the pain of separation returned, and Maggie found him crying in the night, and held him until he was whole again. And eventually the pain did not return. But still he did not forget, and in some part of his soul he longed to make his home-faring back to his true kind, and he rarely passed a day when he did not think he could hear the inaudible sound of delicate claws, scurrying over the sands of silent seas.